Dear

Welcome to the w
and thank you for choosing ...
edition.

If you love a great twisty murder mystery, check out all the books in the series and better still, why not join the Maggie Bainbridge Fan Club for exclusive special offers, freebies and previews?

Go to www.robwyllie.com for details.

A Rob Wyllie paperback
First published in Great Britain in 2020 by Rob Wyllie
Books, Derbyshire, United Kingdom

Copyright @ Rob Wyllie 2020
The right of Rob Wyllie to be identified as the author of this work has been asserted by him in accordance with the Copyright, Design and Patents Act 1988
All rights reserved. No part of this publication may be reproduced, stored in a retrieval system, or transmitted. in any form or by any means, electronic, mechanical, photocopying, recording or otherwise, without the prior permission of the copyright owner.
All the characters in this book are fictitious and any resemblance to actual persons, living or dead, is purely coincidental.
RobWyllie.com

A Matter of Disclosure

Rob Wyllie

PROLOGUE

It was parked opposite the main entrance of the building, taking no notice of the fading school safety zone markings painted on the street. For several months now, the school had run a largely ineffective campaign to stop their cadre of entitled, high net worth parents parking their Range-Rovers, BMWs and Mercedes in the zone at drop-off and collection time. But today, the prime spot was taken by an unremarkable white van sporting the anonymous logo of one of dozens of parcel delivery firms that have sprouted like crazy in this Amazon age.

3.15pm on a sunny September afternoon and a shrieking multi-cultural mass of Year Ones and Twos streamed into the playground in their neat white polo-shirts and grey trousers and skirts. Outside the gate, a troupe of expensively-dressed yummy-mummies, many with toddlers in arms, talked of designer brands, reality TV stars, property prices, hopeless husbands and fantasy lovers, as was their daily routine. The fathers, fewer in number, talked Fulham, Arsenal, Chelsea and made politically-incorrect observations under their breath about the attractiveness or otherwise of the mothers assembled at the gate. Then gradually the Lucys, Milos, Nikitas and Aarons began to emerge on to the pavement, some scanning the street for their mothers or child-minders, others reluctant to leave behind their playmates. Before long the throng had spilled into the street, in a scene that was repeated here every day as in countless primary schools up and down the land. Such an easy target.

No-one noticed as the driver of the white van started her engine and gently slipped the gear selector into Drive. It sat idling for a few moments as she gave thanks to her god for choosing her for this important work, and then there was a roar from the engine as she jammed the wooden stake against the accelerator pedal and a screech of tyres as the brake was released, sending two and a half tonnes of metal careering across the road at a frightening speed. There were no screams at first, the ghastly horror being played out in silent slow motion, young bodies tossed into the air like skittles, pushchairs transformed into unrecognisable masses of twisted plastic and aluminium, a dozen or more lives crushed out of existence in an instant under the wheels of the van or against the sturdy stone wall of the school. It was all over in a heartbeat.

Except it wasn't over. As a stunned crowd began to gather around the scene, unable to even begin to comprehend the enormity of what had just happened, the electronic timer crudely taped to the dashboard counted down the last few seconds of its life. Five...four...three...two...one...zero.

Across the street, a safe distance away, the hooded driver gave a smile of satisfaction before slinking away un-noticed into the leafy backwaters of Notting Hill.

Chapter 1

She had awoken a full hour before dawn, bounding out of bed bursting with excitement about what lay ahead. *The most important day of her career, ever*. Not for the first time in recent months, she left behind an empty bed, for that day Philip was to be show-boating for the international media in the Lebanon, pretty much a normal day for this rock-star of the human-rights industry. Checking her phone, she saw he had sent her a text. *'Big day! Best of luck, tough case but hope it all goes well p.s. in Jerusalem tomorrow, back Friday.'*

No kisses, and not exactly an optimistic tone, but defending a child-murdering terrorist bomber was never going to be easy. And tough case, that was the understatement of the decade. Pulling on her dressing gown, she crept quietly into Ollie's bedroom, kissing him lightly on the cheek without disturbing him. There was just time for a quick shower before getting dressed. But at least this morning there was no need for Maggie to do what she had done almost every morning for the last two or three months. Opening the doors on her husband's side of their fitted wardrobe, slowly and methodically, working from left to right, searching through the pockets of Philip's suits. Because yesterday, after over one hundred days of drawing a blank, she had found what she was looking for. *Evidence*. A payment receipt from The Ship, which she vaguely knew to be a trendy gastropub in Shoreditch, just round the corner from Philip's office. Two hundred and sixty-nine pounds - about the going rate for dinner for two at that over-rated establishment. And the date on the slip - two weeks ago on Thursday, recent enough for her to remember that evening he came in after midnight, trailed by a faint but discernible scent of perfume. Expensive perfume, because Philip wouldn't be cheating with some cheap tart. He said he had been in a client meeting all evening. He was always in client meetings, according to him. *Liar*.

She sank down on the edge of her bed, briefly covering her face with her hands. Glancing up, she caught sight of her reflection in the wardrobe mirror. Forty-two years old, the shimmery bloom of youth now gone. Was she still attractive? On a good day perhaps she was, but she had to face it. If she wasn't quite in the autumn of her years, it was definitely late summer. But she wasn't going to cry, not on this day of all days, a day she hoped would turn out to be special. *The breakthrough*. She had to shut everything else out of her mind. Keep calm and carry on.

Running downstairs to fix a quick coffee, she was momentarily surprised to find Daisy already up and about. Most days her niece - more accurately, Philip's niece, the only daughter of his twin brother Hugo and currently employed as their temporary nanny - would not surface until well past 7.30am and then there would be a frenzied explosion of activity compressed into ten minutes or less as Ollie was dragged from his bed then dressed, breakfasted and ushered into the old Fiesta for the frantic three-mile drive to school.

'Morning,' Daisy mumbled, distractedly stirring a mug of instant coffee with one hand whilst scrolling her phone with the other. Maggie noted that her niece's usual sullen mood was present and correct, but that she was already dressed, looking uncharacteristically conventional in a pretty Boden print dress, her unruly mass of red hair neatly held back with a cheap faux tortoise-shell clasp. Then she remembered that for Daisy too, this was going to be a special day.

'Good morning Daisy dear, you look nice. Of course, you're going to visit your dad today, aren't you, I've just remembered. Will you be ok?'

'Of course, why shouldn't I be?' Daisy said. 'It's no big deal.'

Actually it is a big deal, thought Maggie, visiting your father in prison for the first time, but there was nothing to be gained from expressing that view right now. Daisy was angry, angry with the world. Angry because she had lost her addict mother when she was only ten, the wound still open and raw. Angry with her activist father for continually putting his pathetic causes ahead of the needs of his vulnerable young daughter. And especially angry with her aunt for failing to get him off the manslaughter charge. It hadn't been her finest hour, Maggie had to admit, but there was only so much a defence barrister could do in the face of overwhelming evidence, and a guilty verdict had been inevitable no matter what she had said. He was damn lucky not to have been charged with murder and damn lucky to get away with an eight-year sentence, considering the seriousness of the offence, that was Maggie's blunt view. Hugo Brooks had been -still was - an arse and fully deserved everything that he got, but no, you couldn't very well say that to your nineteen-year-old niece.

Instead she said, somewhat uncertainly, 'Well, as long as you are going to be alright. There's money in the drawer for a taxi, and of course you need to be there on time or else they won't let you in, so just allow plenty of leeway. But you know that already. And remember, you don't need to worry about collecting Ollie from school today, he's going back with Felicity Swift to play with his friend Tom.'

Daisy didn't look up from her phone, her thumbs tapping out a message to an unknown recipient. An angry message, if the ferocity with which she smashed down on the keypad was any guide. 'Yeah, as you say, I know all that already. I'll be fine'.

Maggie's Uber arrived at 6.15am as arranged, and was soon threading its way through the quiet streets of Hampstead on the wet and gloomy April morning. By 7.20 am she was at her desk. Yesterday, she had printed out the email and its attachment and was now reading it for what must have been the ninth or tenth time. Explosive, to say the least. With the trial set to resume at 1.00pm, she only had the morning to decide what to do. Five hours before what was almost certain to be the most important moment of her career, if she had anything to do with it.

Her mind drifted back to that weird day three months earlier, when, returning from yet another car-crash of a court hearing, she had found Nigel Redmond, the scheming Clerk of Drake Chambers, lurking by her desk.

'Nigel. This is an unexpected pleasure. To what do I owe

this great honour?'

'Eh bah gum lass, you look thoroughly hacked off.'

He did it every time they met. The crass mockery of her Yorkshire roots, evidently believing that it was amusing. But it wasn't.

'Another tough day on the coal-face of justice my dear, am I right?'

He had got that right at least.

'Stupid stupid police,' Maggie said. 'The two moronic cops on my case turn up all suited and booted and then suddenly one says to the other, *I thought **you** were bringing the evidence file?* Can you believe it? Of course, the judge goes ape-shit and re-schedules the trial way out to November. And now my slime-ball client goes free and I've just lost three days' work. Justice, don't make me laugh.'

Redmond was under no illusions as to why many of his learned colleagues had decided to practice law. For them, it was all about the remuneration, handsome and bountiful, and he liked to use that knowledge to his advantage.

'Well, don't worry young Maggie,' he had said in an obsequious tone, 'because I'll make sure you still get paid for today.'

And then, quite out of the blue, he had dropped the bombshell. 'And anyway, you're going to be in the money big-time because haven't I got a *beauty* of a brief for you. You're going to just *love* this.'

Then without a further word of explanation he had passed her *Crown verses Alzahrani*. Passed to Maggie Brooks, she of the exceptionally low-flying career, little miss distinctly average, not yet a QC despite nearly twenty years as a barrister. And if she was being honest, that wasn't just because she was a female working-class northerner swimming in a sea of white male public-school dickheads. That didn't help, but in occasional moments of honesty she forced herself to consider the possibility that maybe, just maybe, she really wasn't that good. But whether that was true or not was at this moment immaterial, because now, quite improbably, she was defending the notorious teenage terrorist. Finally she was in the spotlight, the big break she had always dreamed of but which until now had always eluded her. Later today she would be centre stage at the Old Bailey, and she was determined to do everything in her power to win. That was all that mattered, win at any cost, do or die, and then the big briefs would start to come in, when she could expect to clear at least one hundred and fifty grand a year, maybe more. Then she might be invited to apply to take silk. At last. Maggie Brooks QC. Or maybe it should be Maggie Bainbridge QC? Actually, she preferred her maiden name. It tripped off the tongue rather nicely, she thought.

But there was no time for idle daydreaming when she was due back in court at one o'clock sharp. Which meant she had only the morning in which to decide what to do about the Khan report. She perched her reading glasses on her nose and began to leaf through her scribbled notes, refreshing herself on his background, cobbled together from internet searches and a helpful article from the online edition of the Lancashire Evening Chronicle.

Dr Tariq Khan. British Pakistani, raised in Blackburn, Lancs. Grandfather arrived in the UK in the early fifties, worked as a bus driver, had four children including Khan's father Imran. Tariq born in 1970, eldest of four siblings. First member of his family to go to university, wins place at Cambridge to study physics. Graduated with first in 1993, then did PhD, subject unknown. Research scientist at Rutherford Appleton Laboratory in Oxfordshire for seven years. Father Imran active in community - Imam at local mosque.

He had done well, this Dr Khan, considering his modest background, and now it would appear he was occupying a very senior position at the Government Communications Headquarters up in Cheltenham. She turned to her laptop and clicked on the folder she had created just two days before, then opened an image file. The photograph was a typical end-of-conference group shot, showing Khan to be in his early-to-mid forties, bearded and smartly dressed in a three-piece suit but otherwise of unprepossessing appearance. It had been taken three or four years earlier in

Denver in the US, at something called the *Third International Symposium on Automatic Recognition Technologies*. A further internet search had turned up the conference agenda, which listed him as Dr Tariq Khan, Head of Recognition Technologies, GCHQ, England. The subject of his presentation had been *The Future of Automatic Facial Recognition in Civil Society*. It looked as if he knew his stuff all right.

So the big question had to be, why in hell had he decided to write this damn report? A report, if she had interpreted its densely-written technical arguments correctly, that could blow the prosecution case out of the water? The obvious answer was that as a Muslim, he sympathised with the terrorist Alzahrani and this was an effort to see her freed. With a start, Maggie pulled herself up, recognising the lazy racial stereotyping thinking that it was. Tariq Khan was as English as she was and probably as proud a Lancastrian as she was a proud Yorkshire lass. Besides which, he worked for GCHQ for goodness sake, and he wouldn't have got through that door without the most intense scrutiny of his background and politics. So no, it had to be something else, surely?

The email had come in just three days earlier from an organisation calling itself *British Solidarity for Palestine*. She had found a website, poorly-designed and amateurish in construction, the home page stridently condemning Israel, the US and Britain for what it called their war crimes. There were a smattering of celebrity endorsements, the usual suspects, including, they claimed, the present Prime Minister Julian Priest. No surprise there, given his long-standing support for the cause, although it seemed unlikely that he would be involved with such an unprofessional outfit. She had asked Philip if he knew anything about them and he said he had never heard of them, his verdict being they were probably a bunch of wanky virtue-signalling sixth-formers jumping on a bandwagon. This, from the king of wanky virtue-signalling himself.

But whoever they were and whatever their motivation, there was little doubt in her mind that the report was genuine, and she found it hard to suppress her excitement. This was going to be the giant coup, the big high-profile victory against impossible odds, the win that would make her reputation. Then the work would surely come flooding in and with it, the fat fees and everything you could do with it. Things like dumping a cheating pig of a husband. And then maybe in a year or two she could take silk. God, she wanted that so badly.

Of course, she knew exactly what was the right thing to do next. She should tell the judge about the report, get the police to track down Dr Khan, call him as a witness and let the estimable British justice system take its course.

But she wasn't going to do any of that, because she had a *much* better plan. Not entirely her own idea it was true, but brilliant nonetheless. For the final time, she checked that sentence in the email. No, she hadn't misread it. There it was, absolute dynamite, the phrase that she had carefully underlined in red pen.

We have evidence that the prosecution has had Khan's report since the start of the trial, perhaps earlier.

Perhaps earlier. She leaned back in her chair and smiled to herself. Just for a moment, she had forgotten about the crumpled credit card receipt in her pocket. And about her cheating husband, a man she was unsure if she had ever really loved. But sod him, she was on her way.

Chapter 2

The armoured Foxhound, still incongruously painted in its desert camouflage, was parked around sixty metres away, close enough to get a clear view of the suspect vehicle, a nondescript silver-grey Peugeot, but not too close to make them vulnerable should the car bomb choose to detonate. At least this time there had been a coded warning. It had taken the skeleton team of PSNI officers the good part of an hour to clear the immediate area. Even at four-thirty on a dank and misty April Saturday, the street had been busy with shoppers, each resolved to take full advantage of Easter weekend bargains by turning up in person rather than relying on the internet. The Explosives Ordnance Disposal team had arrived whilst the police were still on their loud-hailers repeating 'we have had a bomb warning, please clear the area. This is not a drill, this is not a drill' over and over again. Armed officers in flak jackets and cradling Heckler & Koch MP5SF semi-automatics were positioned every thirty metres or so, nervously scanning the horizon for an unseen enemy.

'Bloody hopeless sir, don't you think? Those PSNI lot I mean.'

Captain Jimmy Stewart took another draw on his cigarette before answering. 'Aye well Naomi, the problem is they've not yet come to terms with the fact that the troubles are back. They can't believe that Northern Ireland is going back to the seventies, who does? Nobody wants it, but the local politicians hope if they ignore it, it will just go away.'

Naomi Harris, his young sergeant, was just one month into her first deployment with 11 EOD&S Regiment, the army's bomb disposal outfit. An Essex girl, she had spent her first three years' of service over in Afghanistan, dismantling and packing up all the kit the Army had left behind when the fighting men and women had come home. When the opportunity to retrain as a technician in the Explosive Ordnance Disposal and Search Regiment came up, and with it promotion, she jumped at the chance and here she was, just one year later, alongside one of the army's most experienced bomb disposal officers - experience that was soon to be lost to the military, because Jimmy Stewart, at thirty-two years old and with ten years' service behind him, had little more than three more months in uniform before hitting civvy street.

'You were there at that terrible thing in London weren't you sir? That school in Notting Hill.'

'Aye, I was.'

It wasn't something you were likely to forget. Just like Helmand all over again, except the victims weren't young squaddies but innocent little kids. And just like so often out there, his disposal team had arrived too late to do anything about it. Not that it mattered whether it was a Taliban IED or a Palestinian nutter with a white van and two kilos of cheap IRA Semtex, the carnage was just the same. He hoped that girl who did it would be locked away for life. Pity they didn't have the death sentence still.

'There wasn't any warning, was there sir?'

Jimmy was beginning to get irritated by Harris's prattling, but he recognised it as an involuntary reaction to her fear. First time in action. He could remember how it felt.

'No there wasn't. So let's just concentrate on the job in hand, shall we?'

He hadn't meant for it to sound as harsh as it did. She fell silent for a moment before the nerves got the better of her again.

'So just remind me again sir, which one's Catholic and which one's Protestant, Rangers or Celtic? I don't really follow football.'

A broad smile spread across his face. 'Christ sake Harris, that could get you knee-capped over here. Rangers are the Protestants, Celtic the Catholics. The clue's in the colours. Celtic, green, shamrock in the badge and all that.'

Of course unlike him, Naomi hadn't grown up in a city where the curse of Protestant-Catholic sectarianism was everywhere. How could she be expected to know? And every Glasgow generation were taught the same old tired prejudices, the same stupid songs, *The Sash My Father Wore* and the Irish rebel songs celebrating an uprising that was nearly a century old. Now here on the streets of Belfast it was back, in its deadliest form. Brainless beyond belief.

The radio crackled into life. *'EOD 12, are you in position?'*

'Affirmative Control' Jimmy replied. 'How are we doing with the phone sweeps?'

'Just awaiting the information from Vodaphone. They're the last one. They have given us an ETA of 17.05. Just a few minutes to wait then we can put all the info together and see where we are.'

'Thanks Control, not too long to wait then. And they're all lined up to do the call blocking once we've had a look?'

'Affirmative EOD12. Should only take a few minutes to get that implemented, that's what they're telling us.'

'Ok thanks Control. So just keep us in the loop, will you? Over and out.'

Thirty years ago, the scene would have been swarming with soldiers, but now security was in the hands of the local police force, the Police Service of Northern Ireland. With still no devolved government sitting in Stormont, the province was once more under direct rule from Westminster and ministers were reluctant to provide any further provocation to dissidents on both sides of the divide by once more having troops on the streets, although looking at the cop's quasi-military garb, it was hard to tell what difference it would make.

At ten past five there was still no update from Control on the phone scanning. 'Just have to wait,' groaned Jimmy, taking another cigarette from the pack. 'We need to know if there's a phone in that car, 'cause if there is, it's ninety percent certain that's going to be the trigger mechanism, and also, it probably means we're being watched by the bad guys. They'll want to do more than just blow up an old motor, won't they?'

They only had to wait a few minutes for the report to come through.*'EOD12, four devices have been detected within the area in question.'*

'Four? Bloody hell! Probably means some of these half-wit

cops have left theirs switched on. Ok Control, we'll just have to assume that one of them is in the suspect vehicle. Let's just get on to the telecoms guys and get them to block all incoming calls to these cells. We can't risk some lowlife setting it off with a nicked Galaxy 10. Over and out.'

'More waiting sir?'

'Afraid so sergeant, nothing else for it.'

After a few minutes she broke the silence. 'Sir, our guys in Didcot are saying that the explosive used in that Notting Hill bomb was Semtex, and it was probably supplied from here. I thought all that stuff was supposed to have been turned in as one of the conditions of that Good Friday agreement?'

'Aye, and if you believe that you believe in the tooth fairy. They'll have kept a big stash somewhere, you can bet your backside on that. They've probably got a wee e-commerce site on the dark web too, and making a nice living out of it. And they'll still have all the old contacts in Libya and Iran in their wee books, so no problem finding customers.'

Still there was nothing from Control.

'So what are you going to do when you leave the army sir, if you don't mind me asking? Any ideas?'

'Well yeah, got a few ideas kicking around, but not really settled on anything yet,' he replied. 'Maybe have a nice wee holiday, and then I'll start looking around for something.'

In actual fact, Jimmy Stewart didn't have a clue what he was going to do when he left, but what he did know was that it couldn't come too soon. Then maybe the nightmares and flashbacks might fade or even go away for good. Because the truth was, it was screwing him up, big time. In Afghanistan, OED were always first on the scene after an Improvised Explosive Device had gone off. It was the Taliban's prime modus operandi, and in the early years, even the most amateur of bombs ripped the inadequately-armoured personnel carriers into pieces like coke cans. You never forgot the carnage, the stench of burning flesh, the scattered body parts, the pathetic moans from the mortally wounded and all the time you were thinking - is there another one waiting for me? And now, nearly four years after he had left

Helmand, it was starting all over again, right here in the UK. No, he couldn't wait to get out. And maybe he could concentrate on what he really wanted to do. Rebuilding his shattered marriage.

'OED12, we have confirmation from the telecoms guys. Incoming calls are now blocked.'

'Right Harris, we're good to go,' Jimmy shouted. 'Let's get the Dragon out the back and get cracking.'

He prodded a button on the dashboard and with a loud whirring sound, the bottom-hinged tailgate began slowly to descend, forming a steep ramp down to the roadway. A few moments later the Dragon Runner Remote Control Vehicle powered up and began to inch down the ramp under Naomi's remote guidance.

Her eyes were focused on the bright LCD screen of her control pad. 'The Dragon's on the road now sir. I'll just bring it round to the front, do a few checks and then we can start moving it up to the target.'

Manipulating the joystick, she spun the Dragon round one-hundred and eighty degrees on its tracks then piloted it forward until it sat directly in front of the Foxhound. With a click on the keypad, the articulated manipulator arm which gave the device its name began slowly to extend, the hydraulic control rams emitting a soft hiss as it achieved its full reach of nearly two metres. At the tip of the extended arm was the dragon's head, fitted with a powerful high-definition video camera with a three-hundred-and-sixty-degree field of vision.

'Good, everything seems to be working ok. So I'm going to prime the Small Explosive charge sir, do you think we'll need that today?'

'I don't know, we might. Let's just move her up to the target and have a wee nosey with the camera first. Although I doubt whether they would be so stupid to leave the bomb in full view, but you never know our luck. These New IRA lads haven't been doing this for long.'

It had begun to rain, spraying a fine mist on the pillar-box windscreen of the Foxhound, making visibility even more difficult than it already was. Jimmy narrowed his eyes and peered out along the wide street towards the Peugeot. He caught sight of a young police officer standing in the doorway of a department store, no more than thirty or forty metres away from the suspect car. 'Crikey, he's a bit close,' said Jimmy, shaking his head. 'Sixty metres we said. Bloody amateurs.'

The silence of the evening was broken suddenly by the shrill wail of a car alarm. It was the Peugeot, its bright hazard warning lights flashing in syncopation with the alarm.

'Oh-oh,' Jimmy said, 'what's this?'

After about a minute, the alarm stopped. 'Might be something interfering with the car's electronics sir?' Naomi said enquiringly. 'Like the signal from a radio transmitter?'

'Aye, might be. Let's get the Dragon up there sharpish.'

'Ok sir'. She pushed forward the joystick, setting the track-wheeled robot trundling along the roadway. It had only moved a few metres when the car's alarm went off again, and then suddenly a figure came into view on the remote's screen. Horrified, they watched as the young policeman stepped out of the doorway and began walking tentatively towards the car.

Naomi screamed out a warning. 'Stop! Hell, what is he doing? What is he doing?' Tossing the control pad onto Jimmy's lap, she shouldered open the heavy door and jumped down on to the pavement.

'Harris,' Jimmy screamed, 'what the hell are you thinking! Get back in the truck, get back into the truck! That's a bloody order!'

A second later, the still evening was disturbed by the crack of a high velocity rifle. A sound only too familiar to Jimmy Stewart from his service in Afghanistan. Then the bullet smashed into Naomi's face, her head exploding as if in slow-motion, splattering a torrent of blood, flesh and bone against the windscreen of the Foxhound.

He sat transfixed, paralysed with shock. *Please, not another one, please, not another one*. And then he started to weep, sobbing inconsolably, the cumulative pain and anguish of loss finally too much to bear. He was still weeping ten minutes later when the backup team finally arrived.

Chapter 3

Maggie re-read her summing-up for the fifth or sixth time, tweaking a word here and there, testing a theatrical pause or two at the critical points. This was just for backup, she reminded herself, because if the day panned out as she expected it to, there would be absolutely no need for a defence summary. But best to be prepared, just in case. It had briefly crossed her mind that if the Khan report was to be believed and the identification evidence was really flawed, then maybe Alzahrani was actually innocent as she had claimed, and that maybe her case wasn't so hopeless after all. But this wasn't the time for self-doubt. The plan was good and she was resolved to stick to it.

She had made the decision, rightly or wrongly, not to tell her client about the existence of Dr Tariq Khan's report. Well, to be honest, she knew it was wrong but she didn't want Alzahrani screwing everything up at the last minute. Ethically a bit suspect, to say the least, but Maggie was not interested in the opinions of a terrorist like Dena Alzahrani. All that mattered was the outcome of the trial. Hopefully, when they had their final meeting this morning she wouldn't do anything stupid like deciding to plead guilty. It was unlikely, because she hadn't said more than two words in any meeting they had had so far.

Finally satisfied with the summing-up, she gave a thumbs-up to her junior Ricardo Mancini and soon they had gathered up their documents before setting off down Giltspur Street. A few minutes later she was striding across the immense oak-panelled entrance hall of the Central Criminal Court in her wig and flowing robes, trailed by Mancini, who had charge of the several thick buff folders containing the case notes. The beautiful building, more commonly known as the Old Bailey after the street on which it stands, was erected in 1902 on the former site of Newgate gaol. In the early Victorian era the gaol was the scene of the public hangings that were a popular public entertainment. Today, there was to be no hanging, but the interest in this modern-day case was equally intense, the public gallery jam-packed and the press out in force for what was expected to be the final day of the Alzahrani trial.

On the way, Mancini had still been nagging on about the damn report. 'And you're sure we're good about this Maggie?' he had asked for the fifth or sixth time, as they threaded their way through the buzzing throng of morning commuters. It was evident he was not going to let it go without some resistance. 'This is our last chance, isn't it?'

'I've told you, just leave it please Ricardo,' she had replied, more than a hint of exasperation creeping into her voice. 'We're making this into more than it really is you know.' You are, was what she meant. Now she was glad she hadn't told him about it until the very last minute possible. He was a nice guy but not very imaginative, and actually, a bit of a prig too. She knew he wouldn't approve of what she had planned, of that she had been certain, and worse still, if he'd known about it from the start, he might well have turned whistleblower and that would really have buggered everything up. So it had definitely been the right decision to keep him in the dark.

'In the scope of things it's probably not that important,' her words the exact opposite of the truth. It was important, but not because of the actual content of the thing, since she had no idea whether the dramatic conclusions of Khan's report could be trusted or not. No, it was important simply by the fact that it existed at all.

Generally, she was nervous before the final day of a trial, no matter how weak the case against her or how unconvincing the evidence, but today she was calmness personified. Her opponent Adam Cameron QC was absolutely premier league when it came to advocacy, that was her opinion, with a string of high-profile victories to his credit. Hadn't he made her look stupid in the Hugo Brooks trial, a humiliation she wasn't going to forget in a hurry? If she hadn't considered herself strictly second division before that monumental failure, then she had no option but to face up to that fact in the aftermath. But now, like a minor league football club on an extended cup run, she was playing in the premier division. The only problem was, she was certain the jury had already bought Cameron's version of the case hook, line and sinker. It didn't matter that there was just one piece of evidence, some suspect and grainy video footage that when analysed with the fairy dust that was automatic facial recognition software, had claimed to identify Alzahrani. AFR, as the experts called it, was absolute catnip to judges and juries alike. Couldn't be argued with. Besides which they just didn't like her client, and who could blame them? But that was all going to be irrelevant now once she had enacted her master-plan. At least she hoped so.

She met Cameron in the entrance hall just as they were preparing to enter the courtroom, where he greeted her with a fake bonhomie that was entirely in keeping with his character. No doubt he had been waiting for her, lurking in the shadows, waiting his opportunity to unsettle his opponent, like a sledging cricketer at the start of an important test match. It was a tired old tactic, but perhaps it revealed he wasn't so confident about the outcome after all. Or maybe he had a secret to hide. *We have evidence that the prosecution has had Khan's report since the start of the trial. Perhaps earlier.*

'Maggie darling, I'm surprised you've even bothered to turn up today,' he purred. 'Nothing for you to work with of course, but really, I thought you might have put up at least a bit of a fight. In the interest of justice and all that. At least give the jury something to think about in return for giving up a month of their lives. Put on a bit of a show, eh?'

'Piss off Adam darling,' she answered, good-humouredly. The smug git wouldn't be laughing in an hour or two if she had anything to do with it.

'Ha ha, no-one likes a bad loser,' he said, but then, strangely, 'so, no last-minute cats waiting to be pulled out of bags, I hope?'

Was it her imagination or was there a hint of nervousness and uncertainty behind the confident veneer? Damn, that would ruin everything.

***

'I'm your barrister, and it is my job to advise you. And my advice is once again, please don't wear your headscarf in court.'

She didn't expect to get an answer, and she wasn't disappointed. All through her custody and right up to the moment she was charged, Dena Alzahrani had given a brusque 'no comment' to every question she had been asked, and she had been no more forthcoming with Maggie since she had taken on the case. In the witness box, she had simply denied everything, coldly and dispassionately, in a manner guaranteed to get up the noses of even the most liberal-minded juror. And that damn headscarf. Maggie fully respected her right to wear it of course, and she was equally sensitive to the possible accusations of racism that might be directed at her for trying to dissuaded her. But the jury, now that was another matter. To say that it lacked diversity was the understatement of the year, and she didn't want to play to its prejudices any more than she had to. But all of that was going to be immaterial because she'd realised early in the relationship that her client was going to be immune to any coaching or guidance as to how to behave in court. It was normal for some sort of relationship to be formed between barrister and client, because even the most obtuse defendant knew that their fate was in the hands of their lawyer, and they all wanted to get off -usually. But Alzahrani was different. For a start, they didn't even know her true identity. She'd entered the country on a fake Jordanian passport stamped with a fake student visa, but other than the fact that her accent marked her as Palestinian and that she looked around nineteen or twenty, they knew no more about her.

'Ok, well it's up to you.'

Suddenly Alzahrani asked,

'What do you think will happen to me?' For the first time, Maggie saw fear in her eyes, the mask of defiance finally slipping, albeit briefly. *So she is human after all. Ten minutes before we're due back in court. Don't tell me she's going to plead guilty at the last minute. Hell, that's all I need.*

'Well, we will be hoping for the best of course, but I think, honestly, it's highly likely that the jury will find you guilty. You will then be held in custody for several months and then we will come back to the court for sentencing.'

And they'll lock you up and throw away the key, was what she didn't say.

'Ok, as I said it's up to you. But my advice is lose the scarf, look like a scared and vulnerable young girl exploited by evil men, and you might just persuade one juror to give you the benefit of the doubt.'

In an instant, the default surly mask returned. She was as stubborn as she was stupid, this young woman. Maggie had known that much from the start. The only pity was if her plan worked, then her client, almost certainly guilty, would walk free. But that was simply collateral damage. What was important was the victory, the triumph of a case won against the odds.

Today, that was all that mattered.

***

'All rise.'

Judge Margo Henderson QC was presiding, peering up over her half-rimmed glasses at the public gallery as she walked into court. Aside from the spectacles, she was in many ways the antithesis of the stereotypical high court judge. Not grey-haired, not male, decidedly glamorous, and about the same age as Maggie. Their age was the only thing they had in common, Henderson's career trajectory having been as meteoric as her own had been mediocre. Although possessed of a needle-sharp sense of humour which was deployed frequently to deflate the more pompous of the QCs who stood in front of her, she was no soft touch. Today her mood was serious, the gravity of the crime dictating a sombre tone and the defendant if found guilty could expect a sentence as stiff as the law would allow. Dena Alzahrani had been taken to the dock a few minutes earlier, handcuffed, and then, as throughout the trial, she sat slouched in her chair with a defiant expression on her face. And wearing that bloody headscarf. The judge thanked the Clerk then prepared to explain to the jury how this, the final day, would pan out.

Maggie might not have regarded herself as much of a barrister, but she thought she knew how to read juries and always kept notes about the reaction of each of the twelve as a trial progressed. And almost to a man or woman, this lot had already made up its mind. Perhaps she had her doubts about the twenty-something crop-haired girl who, quite without evidence, she imagined to be central-casting's go-to left-wing activist. *She* wasn't going to be swayed by the charms of a smarmy toff like Adam Cameron, but she was the exception, and Maggie doubted if even Miss Crop-Hair could hold out in the jury room when under pressure from eleven fellow citizens pressing for a guilty verdict. No, this was already a done deal. But that didn't matter, not if her plan worked as she expected it to.

Now the judge was speaking.

'Members of the jury, I will give both prosecution and defence one final opportunity to present evidence or summon witnesses, although I think we heard yesterday that they had both concluded their respective cases. Then you will hear the summing up from both sides, and I urge you to listen carefully to the points that my learned friends will make before finally deciding on your verdict. It is important you do not allow your decision to be swayed by any judgement you make on the character of the defendant, nor by the undoubtedly serious nature of the crime.'

Some hope of that, Maggie thought. And in any case, other than Miss Crop-Hair, they had already decided.

'Instead you must base your verdict only on the strength of the evidence that has been laid before you,' the judge continued. 'I hope that is clear. So firstly Mr Cameron, do you have any final matters you wish to bring before the court?'

A long silence. Five seconds...ten seconds...fifteen seconds...thirty seconds. Hell, don't tell me he's going to bring it up *now*. Surely not, not at this late stage?

'Mr Cameron?'

Finally. 'No m'lady, the Crown is ready to sum up.' Relief.

'And you, Mrs Brooks?'

Maggie did have a matter to bring up, but she was going to hold back that little bombshell until Adam Cameron had done his summing-up. Maximise the humiliation, maximise the theatre. And then boom - light the blue touch-paper and take cover.

She gave the judge a prim smile. 'Nothing more m'lady, thank you.'

'Very well Mrs Brooks. Mr Cameron, please proceed.'

Getting to his feet, he slotted his reading glasses into his waistcoat pocket then strolled over towards the jury, smiling his trademark obsequious smile.

'Good morning ladies and gentlemen. Well, Judge Henderson has summed up admirably what are your duties today, and I know you will perform them to the very best of your ability. You have sat and listened diligently through the twenty-one days of this long and complex trial, and no doubt many of you will already have made up your mind about the guilt or otherwise of the defendant. My job today is simply to remind you of the case against Dena Alzahrani, which I believe to be overwhelming. I do not think you will need to be reminded of the dreadful crime itself...'

And then of course, he proceeded to remind them. The cold-blooded murder of eighteen innocent people, ten of them little children under the age of ten years old, their young lives cut short, blown to pieces by an indescribable act of violence by the young woman who now sat in the dock. If the jury hadn't been convinced before, they would be now, but Maggie wasn't in the least concerned. Because it wasn't going to make any difference to the outcome no matter what Cameron said.

She scanned the jury for signs of a reaction. It would have been nearly five weeks since the terrible details of the crime had been described to them and Cameron would not want to take the risk that its impact had diminished through the simple passage of time, although there was little likelihood of that, given the graphic horror of the attack. No doubt he was now going to spell out the evidence, and in as simple terms as possible. No fancy legal jargon and critically, no more than two or three facts for them to take in. But this case wasn't even as complicated as that. Automatic facial recognition had identified the perpetrator. AFR, the new DNA. That was all they needed to know.

First however, he was going to remind them of the character of the accused, lest any misguided juror should be harbouring even a morsel of sympathy for her. Perhaps he had sized up Miss Crop-Hair and didn't like what he was seeing.

'You will remember you saw a video where Alzahrani boasted of carrying out a *spectacular*, right here in London. For that, we must thank the clever men and women from our cyber warfare teams and of course their CIA counterparts, for their splendid work in breaking into what I believe is known as the Dark Web - and forgive me if my terminology isn't quite correct. In that video, she was very specific about the attack being here in our city, and very specific about the date on which it was to take place. It was of course the eleventh of September last year, the day of the terrible atrocity in Notting Hill. I do not need to remind you, ladies and gentlemen, of the significance of that particular date. *Nine-eleven*. The most infamous date in our recent history, and chosen quite cynically by the defendant to maximise the publicity that her atrocity would command. An atrocity, ladies and gentlemen, for which she herself was wholly responsible.'

Very good Adam, Maggie thought, but you've still got to prove that, haven't you? Judge Henderson evidently shared her view.

'Mr Cameron, that is your case to make, it should not be stated as if it is a fact.'

'My mistake m'lady, you are quite right,' he said, smiling, 'I apologise.'

Unperturbed, he continued. 'Now you will remember a chilling phrase from that video...' he took his reading glasses from a waistcoat pocket and read from his notes... *'I will make those infidel children burn in hell*. Appalling, horrifying and savage, undoubtedly. But what I would like you to focus on is the fact that the defendant had full knowledge of the act in advance, both its location here in London and the exact nature of the planned attack. *I will make those infidel children burn in hell* - her intention could not be more clear.'

He stole a quick glance at his watch. Yes thought Maggie, about three minutes so far. Keep it brief and to the point, that's what you're doing, don't want the jury falling asleep with boredom.

'But of course the fact of Dena Alzahrani boasting that she would carry out the act does not in itself constitute proof that she actually did it - although you might well conclude, ladies and gentlemen, that so specific was her threat that you might on the balance of probability find her guilty on that alone.'

Judge Henderson raised an eyebrow, but on this occasion decided against intervention. Maggie smiled to herself. She had to hand it to him, he was damn good, and now he could go in for the kill. It was just such a shame for him that it was all going to be in vain. So here it was. What he was describing as the concrete evidence.

'You will remember that we heard from the key witness Mr Wojciech Kowalczyk - I think I have pronounced that correctly...' - drawing a smile from several members of the jury, but not Miss Crop-Hair - '...who saw a hooded figure jumping out of the driver's door of the lorry and then running along Princedale Road towards his parked van. Mr Kowalczyk is a Polish plumber - a very rich man' - more smiles from the jury - 'and as you have heard, was sitting in the driver's seat talking on his phone having just completed a job in a nearby property. He had started his engine and as a result his dash-cam device had began to record. That dash-cam, ladies and gentlemen, caught in full view the escape of the defendant on video, and despite her being hooded and wearing sunglasses in an attempt to prevent identification, the police were able to use automatic facial recognition technology to identify the fleeing figure as Dena Alzahrani.'

That had been a pretty stupid mistake, not to know that the authorities kept a database of digitised facial images of all visitors from so-called 'countries of interest' and that Jordan was on the list. It was a school-girl error, but then Alzahrani wasn't much more than a school-girl herself. They had picked her up that same afternoon, blithely sitting at the back of her UCL classroom as if it was a quite normal day.

'Now as we heard from Professor Walker, the Crown's expert witness, there is no doubt at all about the identification of the accused. The new DNA, that's how Professor Walker described this clever technology. A memorable and apt phrase, I think you will agree.'

Maggie gave a wry smile. This case wasn't going to tax the mental powers of the jury very much, of that she was sure. The new DNA, they would remember that, and DNA evidence was full-proof, wasn't it? Except that Dr Tariq Khan, world-renowned expert at GCHQ, disagreed. Adam Cameron knew that and keeping it to himself was going to be the biggest mistake of his career. But then unexpectedly, a wave of uncertainty swept over her. Because there was absolutely no proof at all that the email she had received was genuine. And even if it was, all it had said was that the *prosecution* knew about Khan's report. That didn't mean that Cameron himself had seen it. She knew something of how these things worked and it wasn't beyond the bounds of possibility that it had gone direct to the Crown Prosecution Service where some public-spirited official had decided it would be better if their famous QC didn't get to know about this little inconvenience. If that was the case, then her carefully-conceived plan was about to go up in smoke.

Cameron was now standing motionless as if in an act of meditation, his eyes closed, breathing deeply, his hands clasped in front of him as if in prayer. Amateur dramatics it was true, but effective because the jury was giving him its full attention. Lady Justice Henderson was less impressed.

'Can I take it then that your summing up is complete Mr Cameron?' she said sharply. 'If so, we will have a short break before asking Mrs Brooks to take the floor.'

'Eh? - ah, no,' he blustered, 'eh - I was just gathering my thoughts.'

'Well, please gather them up quickly, and continue.'

'Yes, thank you m'lady.'

Maggie shot her an admiring smile as Cameron, momentarily deflated, pressed on.

'Now in a moment I expect you will hear the defence claim that Miss Alzahrani is no more than an immature fantasist who is not capable of planning and carrying out a sophisticated crime such as this. It is true that no evidence was found that showed her to be the bomb-maker, but that is irrelevant to this case. What is unarguable is that she was positively identified leaving the scene, not by a pair of fallible human eyes, but by infallible state-of-the-art automatic facial recognition technology. The new DNA. We may not like how it is creeping into our everyday lives. We may well be uneasy that it threatens our privacy, but today, we see how it can be a fantastic force for good. Ladies and gentlemen, Alzahrani is no fantasist. She is a calculated cold-blooded killer, driven by the pursuance of a distorted strain of Islam, a grotesque agenda that bears no resemblance whatsoever to the true meaning of this peace-loving religion. She was clearly identified on camera leaving the scene of the crime, leaving no doubt whatsoever that she was the perpetrator.'

Several jurors were now nodding their heads in involuntary agreement, including Miss Crop-Head, outwardly at least giving the impression of a late conversion to the prosecution camp. That was it as far as he was concerned. Job done.

'I said at the start that our duty, yours and mine, is to see that the victims and their families get justice.' A few more affirming nods from the jury. 'I think you will agree that only a verdict of guilty will deliver that justice... a justice they so richly deserve. Thank you, ladies and gentlemen. Thank you m'lady.'

A good performance thought Maggie, but watching as he returned to his seat, she was taken by the complete absence of emotion on his face, not even the slightest smile of satisfaction. He wasn't a modest man by any means, and she was expecting to see the usual self-satisfied expression, rather like the one she had to suffer three months ago when she had lost the Hugo Brooks trial. But today he looked distracted, relieved, furtive even. Rather odd. *He knows*. She was sure of it now.

Judge Henderson was now speaking.

'Thank you Mr Cameron. Mrs Brooks, given that the Crown's summing up was commendably short and to the point, are you ready to present the defence summary without a recess?'

'Thank you m'lady, but I'm afraid a matter has arisen which I need urgently to bring to your attention.'

The judge peered at her over her spectacles, an expression of mild irritation on her face. She did not like it when a barrister disrupted the smooth running of one of her trials.

'Very well Mrs Brooks, let's hear it.'

'If you would, m'lady, I think this is matter which I need to discuss with you in private.'

Another sigh of irritation and a glance at her watch.

'Is this absolutely necessary Mrs Brooks?'

'Absolutely necessary I'm afraid m'lady. It's a matter of disclosure.'

Maggie caught sight of Cameron out of the corner of her eye. He sat motionless, the colour visibly draining from his face.

He knows.

'Very well. Ten-minute recess.' The judge turned to the Clerk, 'John, can we get some tea in my chambers, thank you. Come with me, both of you.'

Chapter 4

'A matter of disclosure you said Mrs Brooks?' Judge Henderson peered over her glasses as she stood up to pour tea from the elaborately-decorated china pot. 'Sugar Mr Cameron?'

The judges' chamber, a large room not far off half the size of the courtroom itself, was elaborately panelled in oak, carpeted in a luxurious thick patterned Wilton, expensive when new no doubt, but now rather threadbare in patches. Around the room hung portraits of former Lord Chancellors, going back all the way to Sir Thomas More who had held the post more than five hundred years earlier. Maggie and Adam Cameron sat on opposite ends of a large mahogany desk, perched on the edge of their chairs like naughty pupils up in front of the head teacher

'No thank you m'lady'. As he leant forward to pick up the saucer, his shaking hand causing the cup to rattle loudly. It wasn't just the teacup that was rattled.

'Well, tell all please Mrs Brooks, tell all.'

'M'lady, the defence has reason to believe that the Crown has in its possession a technical report from the government's own leading authority on automatic facial recognition that states quite unarguably that the reliance on such technology for the identification of my client is in this case unreliable. And I'm sure I don't need to tell you m'lady the significance...'

'Mrs Brooks, please forgive me,' interrupted the judge, 'but that was quite a sentence, so let me be clear on what you are saying...'

'Sorry m'lady, put simply, the government's leading expert, a Dr Tariq Khan, is saying that is not possible to be certain that it was Alzahrani in that dashcam video. His report says there is an eighty-six percent chance that she was identified in error.'

'I thought we were led to believe that this technology was the new DNA and therefore infallible. Am I given to understand that this is not the case?'

'In this instance m'lady, it does seem that way, yes.'

Henderson stroked her chin in contemplation and took a sip of her tea. 'And you say this was known to the prosecution when?'

'We believe that the Crown has had the report in its possession since before the start of the trial m'lady,' Maggie replied. 'A few days before, is my information.'

And then the bombshell. 'And so I'm concluding that they chose not to disclose it to the defence because they knew it would weaken if not destroy their case.'

'Quite so Mrs Brooks, quite so. And you had it when?'

'Just three days ago m'lady.'

'And how did it come into your possession may I ask?'

'It was emailed to my chambers by an organisation that claimed sympathy to the Palestinian cause, m'lady.'

'And you did not think you had a duty to immediately bring this before the court?'

Maggie had been expecting this one. 'I don't think it was a defence responsibility, no m'lady. It was a leaked document, of uncertain provenance supposedly sent to us by a group about which little is known. My junior has carried out some cursory investigation work in the short time we had available and we believe it may be genuine, but of course we do not know how it came into being. For that you must ask Mr Cameron.'

Through all this Adam Cameron had sat in silence, staring at his shoes, his discomfort manifest, with the look of a man about to mount the scaffold. And now the executioner was speaking.

'Mr Cameron, what do you say to all of this?' Henderson leaned forward as if to hear the explanation more clearly.

'Eh, well we discussed the matter...' He sounded nervous.

'We? Who is we?'

'We? Yes, the CPS m'lady. When the report was passed to us, obviously we discussed it in some depth but in the end decided it was not material to the case.'

'Really,' she said, 'and pray tell me, when exactly was this report passed to you, as you put it.'

He was clearly fumbling for an answer. 'Eh... when?... eh, I'm not exactly sure.'

'Well let me simplify the question Mr Cameron. Was it passed to you before or after the start of the trial?'

This will be good, thought Maggie.

'It eh... I think it was around the start of the trial, but I'm not sure, I would need to check.' It was not convincing.

'Let me repeat my question. Before or after, Mr Cameron?'

He crumbled. 'Before m'lady. We had it before. Just a few days before it started.'

The judge paused to make some notes in the ring-bound pad that she had taken earlier from a desk drawer.

'So let me get this clear. The trial is just about to start after several months of careful preparation, then along comes an inconvenient piece of late-breaking evidence and you decide to dismiss it there and then. Tell me, did you even bother to try and speak with this Dr Khan?'

'M'lady, it wasn't like that...'

Henderson's irritation was obvious. 'Mr Cameron, did- you- try- to- speak- to- Dr- Khan?'

'Not personally, no m'lady. I believe he was interviewed by some of my senior Crown Prosecution colleagues, but no, I did not speak to him myself at any point.'

'And so you, as the Queen's Counsel for the Crown, did not think it important that you should meet with this individual and judge for yourself whether his evidence was indeed material? A key witness, with the potential of undermining the whole case, and you did not seek to speak with him yourself?'

Cameron looked as if the noose had been placed around his neck and Margo Henderson was about to pull the lever that opened the trap door.

'No m'lady, as I said, I believe he was interviewed by CPS lawyers and it was felt that it was not relevant to the case. But perhaps on reflection, yes, I probably should have spoken to him myself.'

'Perhaps you should have reflected a bit sooner, Mr

Cameron,' she replied.

'M'lady, may I raise a point?' Maggie said, and without waiting for an answer, 'It would be good to know how the report came into the hands of the CPS in the first place.'

Henderson did not seem offended by the interjection. 'Yes, a good point Mrs Brooks. Mr Cameron, I assume you can help us with this?'

Still he did not look up, instead mumbling something inaudible under his breath.

'What? Speak up Mr Cameron.'

'I believe it came via a government department m'lady.'

Maggie could not hide her astonishment.

'Government? What do you mean government?' Henderson asked. 'Who in the government? The Home Office, the Department of Justice, MI6, who?'

'I don't know. It just came to me via the CPS.' If he had access to the lever, he would have opened the trapdoor himself.

'You know, I am finding this rather hard to understand. I say it again - you Mr Cameron, as the QC for the Crown, did not think it important to understand the source of this report? Frankly I'm astonished, I cannot think of any other way to put it.'

She glanced down at her notebook, nodding slowly, her lips pursed.

'So, I have to say this is a grave matter, very grave indeed. Frankly it's not the first time in recent years that I have had to deal with the police and the CPS failing to disclose material evidence...'

'M'lady, honestly, it wasn't like that...'

'Mr Cameron, I'm not finished. Please do not interrupt again. As I was saying, this is not the first occurrence of this reprehensible behaviour, and I'm getting very fed up with it, very fed up indeed. I would go so far as to say that I fear it is becoming somewhat of a trend. And in this case, it seems we may have government interference too. That is something I thought I would never see in this country in my lifetime. This is very serious, you must know that Mr Cameron.'

She did not wait for his answer.

'Look, I need to consider this very carefully before deciding what I'm going to do. For now, I'm going to suspend the trial so I can take advice and consider the next steps. I will see you two back in this room, let's see, in three days' from now. Clerk, could you please inform the court room and ensure the jury are reminded again of their obligation not to discuss the case with anyone whilst they have been stood down.'

With that, she picked up her notebook and swept out of the room followed by the Clerk, leaving Maggie and Cameron alone. Now he was angry. Very angry.

'You bastard.' He was visibly shaking and looked close to tears. 'This will ruin me, you know that. You bastard.'

'You ruined yourself Adam,' Maggie replied, getting up to leave. 'Both sides have an obligation to disclose all material evidence. That's law school one-oh-one, as our American friends would say. You should know that, you've been at it long enough. See you on Friday.'

As she left, she gave a quiet smile of satisfaction. *This was it. At last, the career breakthrough.* Just a couple of days to wait, and then, welcome to the big time. Maggie Bainbridge QC. It sounded rather good.

***

Three days later, they were in the anonymous Victoria Street building that housed the Office of the Attorney General, a measure perhaps of how serious the judge was taking the disturbing news that had been revealed on the last day of the trial. Lady Justice Henderson kept them waiting for over forty minutes, a receptionist shepherding them on arrival into a stark waiting-room furnished with cheap plastic chairs most of which had seen better days. Maggie and Adam Cameron sat in opposite corners of the room, having exchanged nothing but a cursory 'good morning.' She, relaxed and confident, he still wearing the demeanour of a condemned murderer.

Finally a smartly-dressed young woman appeared and announced 'Lady Justice Henderson will see you now'. Today

Maggie had chosen a slim tailored skirt and crisp white blouse, since this wasn't a courtroom appearance and therefore there was no need for the stuffy wig and robes. Margo Henderson too was dressed informally in navy trousers and a lavender cashmere cardigan over a white tee-shirt. Cameron by contrast had decided to play it safe, opting for a standard barrister-issue three-piece navy pinstripe suit.

'Good morning Mrs Brooks and Mr Cameron.'

They answered in unison. 'Good morning m'lady.'

She sighed as if to underline the seriousness of what was about to be discussed. 'You both know very well why you are here. As I said on Tuesday, it's a grave matter, a very grave matter indeed.'

'Yes it is,' Maggie said.

'Grave,' Cameron agreed.

'So, as you might expect, I have consulted widely with learned colleagues and with the Attorney General herself. I have also been able to find out more about Dr Khan from his bosses in Cheltenham. Coming to that first, it may interest you both to know that I spoke at length with the Director of his division, a Dr Jane Robertson, on Wednesday afternoon. Firstly, it should be said that Dr Robertson was not aware that Dr Khan had written his report, and she stressed that it had not been commissioned by any legitimate authority that she knew of, certainly not within GCHQ or any of the security services.'

'So who did commission it?' Maggie asked, her tone sounding more blunt than she intended. A flicker of annoyance crossed Henderson's face.

'I was coming to that Mrs Brooks. Dr Robertson interrogated Dr Khan on Wednesday morning on that subject. It seems quite simply that he had been following the case in the media and was uneasy when he heard that Professor Walker was to be the Crown's expert witness. Dr Robertson promulgated the view that Dr Khan may have been driven by professional rivalry. He apparently does not recognise Professor Walker as an expert in the field, and says that they have crossed swords in the past on what she calls the conference circuit.'

'So that's all it is?' Maggie said, surprised. 'Just some geek's ego trip?'

'Apparently so Mrs Brooks,' Henderson said, 'but Dr Robertson did yesterday discuss Dr Khan's report with other senior scientists in his department and there was a unanimous view that if Dr Khan questioned the Walker testimony, then it must be flawed. They have great faith in his technical expertise, and if he believes the identification of the defendant is not reliable, then it must be so. I don't have to remind you Mr Cameron, that it is upon that evidence which your entire case rests.'

He was evidently not sure if he was expected to comment on this so remained silent.

'But do we know m'lady how the report got to the prosecution?' Maggie asked. 'Mr Cameron thought it may have come via a government department or agency.'

'I said I thought the CPS got it that way,' Cameron said. 'I personally had no direct interaction with any government agencies or officials.'

'Well I think I can answer that,' the judge said. 'It seems Dr Khan simply searched for the email address of the Head of the Crown Prosecution Service, and then sent a copy through to Lady Rooke's office. Elizabeth Rooke claims that her officials passed it on to the case director without looking at it, a claim I am inclined to believe. I have also spoken to the Attorney General and to the Home Secretary...'

'You spoke to Lucinda Black and Gerrard Saddleworth?' Maggie said, surprised.

'Naturally. In a trial of this importance, I would expect both to be constantly kept up to date with developments, but it seems in this case, the CPS team did not deem to share the information with them. Neither the Head of the CPS, the Attorney General nor the Home Secretary were aware of the existence of this report. I cannot help but think this will be highly damaging when it reaches the public domain, to both the CPS and the government.'

Great, thought Maggie, but what are you going to do about the case itself? She did not have to wait long for an answer.

'So, this has really been a shambles from start to finish,' Henderson said. 'I cannot really put it any other way. But what is absolutely clear to me is that the Crown does not have a case without reliance on what is now seen to be the highly unreliable facial recognition evidence obtained from the tradesman's dashcam. Had the Khan report been properly considered I have little doubt that the case would not, indeed could not, have been brought before this court. In mitigation, I do accept the fact that the report was not available when the case was being prepared, but only surfaced after the pre-trial and plea submission. That is an explanation but not an excuse. I am given to conclude that this, and not for the first time in recent years I must add, is a serious attack on our justice system. I cannot and will not allow this reprehensible trend to continue.'

This is it. This is it.

Henderson peered over her half-rimmed reading glasses, her gaze fixing first on Maggie and then on Adam Cameron. Now, it seemed, it was time for her verdict.

'So I have consulted with Ms Black, Lady Rooke and Mr Saddleworth and have informed them that I will have no option but to declare a mistrial.'

A mistrial. Maggie had hoped against hope for that outcome, but for it to come true was beyond her wildest dreams.

'They are understandably dismayed, but agree with me that the integrity of our justice system is bigger than any individual case. I will return to the court at two o'clock this afternoon where the jury will be dismissed and the defendant will be free to go.'

Now Maggie was struggling to conceal her elation. It was the result she had longed for more than any other. Her client was to be freed despite impossible odds, and she now had the big win she had hoped and prayed for, but never really believed could happen.

Adam Cameron bowed his head, stunned into silence. Maggie, misjudging the mood, said with a smile. 'Thank you m'lady,' and stood up as if to leave.

'Sit down please Mrs Brooks,' Henderson said sternly. 'I'm not finished with you two yet.'

And then slowly and forensically, Maggie's whole world, her very future, was crushed into extinction by Lady Justice Margo Henderson QC.

***

She did not remember anything about the journey home that evening, so deep was her distress, and was relieved that Daisy had already put Ollie to bed by the time she got back. All she wanted to do was sleep, sleep for a week, sleep for a month or a year until it all just went away. She filled her wine glass to the brim and drank it in two gulps, then, shaking, she stumbled over to the fridge and filled it once again. *Sleep, please, please let me sleep.*

But she could not sleep that night and as she lay tossing and turning, question after question filled her mind, gnawing away, hour after hour. *Why oh why did I think I could get away with it? So bloody stupid.* Adam Cameron, the smooth Old Etonian, gets off with a light wrap on the knuckles, whilst inept but anonymous CPS lawyers take the bulk of the flak. *A serious collective error of judgement, but with no deliberate intention to pervert justice.* That's what the judge had said. Not great from Cameron's point of view, but hardly ruinous.

And then, like a bolt from the blue, Henderson casually dropped her bombshell, leaving Maggie stunned, disorientated and broken. Information from an authoritative source, identity not disclosed, proving that the defence team, and by implication Mrs Maggie Brooks, had in fact received the Khan report more than six weeks ago, not just in the last few days as they claimed.

It was a damn lie, of course it was a lie. It had been scarcely more than a week since she had seen the damn report for the first time. What authoritative source, and what information? Henderson wouldn't say, no matter how much Maggie pleaded with her. This was turning into a complete nightmare.

And now she was to be referred to the Bar Standards Board, accused of, what was it, *conduct likely to diminish public confidence in the legal profession or the administration of justice*. A stunt, Henderson had called it, a blatant attempt to circumvent the jury system. Worse, she stood accused of lying to the court about the timeline of the report. Lying to the court, about the worst offence a barrister could be accused of. Now she faced a fine or perhaps more likely a long suspension. That was bad enough, but what it really meant was that her career in all practical senses was now over.

She sat up and peered groggily at the clock by her bedside, having finally accepted that sleep would not come. It was 4.30 am. She picked up the TV remote and pressed the standby button bringing the set to life. The BBC was broadcasting its interminable rolling news, leading with the murder of a young woman soldier in Belfast who had been shot through the head whilst attending a suspected bomb incident.

Following closely in the running order was the freeing of Alzahrani and the sensational collapse of the trial. Lady Justice Henderson was not scheduled to release her report until 10.00am the next morning, but already it was leaking like a chocolate teapot. The BBC's legal correspondent was talking about 'another failure to disclose evidence by the CPS,' and that the judge's report 'is expected to be particularly critical about the role of inexperienced defence barrister Mrs Maggie Brooks.'

This was not how it was meant to be. Now the anchor was saying 'Now let's take a look at tomorrow's papers'. There was Alzahrani, pictured on the front page of the *Chronicle* under the headline 'Notting Hill Bomber to be Freed'.

Then, eventually, they cut to other news. In a dusty refugee camp a few miles from the Syrian border their Middle East correspondent was interviewing the famous human rights lawyer Philip Brooks. Alongside him, looking like bloody Lara Croft in combat trousers and a tight-fitting

Action for Palestine tee-shirt, was the dark Mediterranean beauty Angelique Perez, one of his firm's up-and-coming Associates. He had told Maggie he was travelling alone.

Chapter 5

A mistrial. The celebrations were muted of course as they had to be, since they knew that it wasn't seemly to be exultant over the release of a child-murdering terrorist onto the streets of the capital. But family is family and that's what always comes first for anyone, no matter who you are, no matter how important your position in life. It's family first and everything else is secondary. The plan had been crazy and audacious, and none of the group had given it a hope in hell of success - except its conceiver, who through sheer force of conviction persuaded them to go with it. Trust me, that's what the conceiver had said, and in the end, but not without considerable reservations, that's what they had done. And without knowing, little Maggie Brooks had played her part to perfection. Naive, vain, stupid. She had been the perfect choice.

Now they sat in the quiet committee room just off the Central Lobby, sipping on stiff gin and tonics and reflecting quietly on a job well done. All neat and tidy and consigned to history, and it would stay that way as long as everyone kept their mouths shut. And even if they didn't, there was always Plan B.

Chapter 6

Penelope White didn't much like coming into the office these days. Admittedly there was seldom the need, given that all her copy could be submitted electronically, but the less she saw of Rod Clark, her editor at the *Chronicle*, the better. For she was the award winner, the controversialist, the bona-fide journalistic superstar. It was her opinion that poxy editors didn't have the right to mess about with her copy, but Clark still liked to try. He seemed to have difficulty in understanding that it was her who sold the damn papers, not him.

But even she could see that today was different, which is why she had set the alarm for the god-awful hour of 6.30am and braved the tube to get to the Kensington offices for 8.30am. Too bloody early.

'Morning Penelope, this is indeed a rare pleasure.' She knew Clark would have already been in for hours, if indeed he'd actually gone home the previous evening. He lived and breathed the paper, to the detriment of every other relationship in his life. As did she.

'Morning Rod. I hope you've got the coffee on.'

He smiled. 'All ready to go, and brewed just the way you like it. Nice and strong.' He resented the amount of arse-licking that White demanded, but was prepared to put up with it in return for her genius. For now at least.

She was holding a copy of the first edition. 'So, this was your work then was it Rod? The best we could come up with was *Bomber Disappears after New Evidence Emerges*?'

'You weren't around for the website deadline. I got Yash Patel to knock it up. He's a bright lad, great future.'

Her expression suggested she didn't agree with his assessment. 'I suppose it qualifies as accurate reporting, if nothing else.'

He ignored her sarcasm. 'That's why I asked you to come in. There's a lot of angles on this story and I wanted to ask your advice on how to play it. Any thoughts?'

Of course she had thoughts, she had scarcely thought of

anything else since Henderson had declared the mistrial. She would have to be careful of course, after attending that dinner with Gerrard and Philip and Dr Kahn, but that shouldn't be too difficult.

'As you say Rod, lots of angles. But you know my mantra, it's got to be about the players. Readers are only interested in the human side.'

'Got that, yep. Brilliant.' As if he didn't know, having clocked up thirty years in the industry.

'So there's a lot of people with shit on their shoes after what's happened. Adam Cameron, that smoothie QC, he's been made to look like a complete tit for a start.'

Clark pursed his lips. 'Well, I suppose so, but he's one of ours, don't forget.' What he meant was Eton and Oxford, solid establishment. 'Might not get the universal approval of our loyal readership if we make him look stupid.'

She rolled her eyes. 'Not that it would be difficult, but I agree.'

'There's Margo Henderson too,' Clark said. 'The judge. It was her that actually let Alzahrani walk after all, even though the police wanted her held in remand. We could run a nice line about the out-of-touch judiciary.'

'No. Apart from the minor problem that the police didn't have any evidence to support their demand, we've run the judge-as-enemy-of-the-people story more times than I've forgotten.'

He knew she wasn't going to accept any of his suggestions, and he didn't mind. Unlike her, he didn't run on ego. This was just a ritual mating dance, the display of brightly-coloured feathers before they got it on. It was only a matter of how much foreplay she would tolerate before they settled on the idea she had had from the start.

It seemed as if the foreplay might be running on a bit longer. 'So, my first thought was to do something on the CPS and the disclosure cock-up, but make it personal. *Really* personal. Elizabeth Rooke - *Lady* Rooke - she's the boss, as I'm sure you know...'

White's tone suggested that she knew he didn't. She was right.

'...and the general consensus is that she has been way over-promoted. I talked to a few people and found out that she's been married three times and, listen to this, she's recently invested in some top-of-the-range cosmetic surgery. Tits, face, arse, the whole package.'

His eyes narrowed. 'That sounds interesting Penelope. Though I'm sensing a but.'

'Yeah Rod. It's a good story alright, but I think it's got limited shelf-life.'

'So maybe I'll give it to Yash to run as a side story. Page seven or eight, something like that, he'll make a good fist of it. And I can tie it into my editorial.' He knew how to wind her up, and he liked doing it. Very much.

For once, she didn't take the bait. 'Whatever, you're the boss. So I also thought about the government's role in all of this. What I mean is the Home Office and the Justice Department have sat on their backsides for years whilst the CPS and the police treated the rules of disclosure as a minor inconvenience.' She knew that would tick Clark's boxes and ring all his bells at the same time. Because he couldn't afford to miss a chance to put the boot into the administration. Not because he was a supporter of HM's opposition himself, although she assumed he was, but because those were his instructions from the paper's owner.

But for the story to be any good, it had to be personal, and that meant attacking the Home Secretary. The Right Hon. Gerrard Saddleworth MP. Dear Gerrard. Her current lover. No, that wasn't going to happen.

Clark was sensing another but. 'Perhaps we can slip that one into the online edition for the subscribers if you don't want to front-page it.'

She shrugged. 'Yeah, give it to Yash. Anyway...'

He relaxed his shoulders and gently rapped on the table. It was time. 'So Penelope, let's have it.'

'Maggie Brooks and Dena Alzahrani. That's the angle.'

She picked up her phone and showed him the photograph she had got from Philip. One that showed Maggie at her very best, but with perhaps just a hint of smugness and entitlement in her expression. At least, that's how White intended to describe it.

Clark raised an eyebrow. 'She's quite an attractive woman. I didn't know that.'

'Exactly,' White replied. 'Attractive but useless. So, it's quite simple. We cast her in the part of the villain. Smart-arsed lawyer, completely out of touch with the public mood, pulls a stunt and a vile killer walks free.'

'Some might say she was only doing her job,' Clark said. 'Everybody is entitled to a fair trial.'

'Sod that Rod, this has got nothing to do with justice, you know that. This is about selling papers and that's what you want, isn't it?' She knew he would have no answer to that, and she didn't wait for one.

'So right on the top corner of the front page, we put a huge big counter. That shows the number of days that Alzahrani has been walking free on our streets, and we print it every day until she is caught. Centre stage we put a big picture of Maggie Brooks and day after day we pile on the pressure. Drip, drip, drip, drip. We write about the previous cases that she lost. We talk to grieving parents of the victims who tell us they are disgusted with what she had done. We question her marriage, suggest that all is not well in that department. We even go back to her school and find out that she was a horrible little creep that nobody liked. In summary, we pile on the shit. Standard stuff really.'

Clark nodded. He'd known from the start that he would have to agree with whatever she came up with, but he always tried to retain some semblance of dignity. 'Ok Penelope, but just make sure you check anything contentious with legal first, alright?'

'Of course I will Rod,' she lied. 'By the way, I've got tomorrow's headline.'

She picked up her pen and scribbled a few words on her notepad, and then spun it round so Clark could read it.

Maggie Brooks - the Most Hated Woman in Britain?

It looked good alongside Brooks' photograph. And this was only the first day of Alzahrani being on the loose. Give it a couple of weeks when they still hadn't tracked her down and there would be no need for the question mark. Penelope White would see to that.

Chapter 7

Jimmy Stewart lounged back in the battered armchair, idly flicking through the day-old newspaper. The Chronicle's garish banner headline declared it their 'One Hundred Day edition'. One hundred days since the Palestinian Dena Alzahrani, to the deep embarrassment of the security services, had disappeared into thin air. After having been whisked away from her trial in a black limo. The infamous black limo. That had really pissed off the papers, qualities and tabloids alike. Especially when just four days later, the anti-terrorist boys had come up with some new evidence. On a whim, some junior forensic geek had decided to have another look at what was left of the van. And had found some DNA. Dena Alzahrani's DNA, only it was nine months too late. Embarrassing for the Met, since the teenage terrorist had disappeared into thin air, causing an almighty stink. Since then there had been nothing. No leads, no sightings, nothing. He saw too that the paper was still sticking it into the hapless barrister who had engineered her release. Maggie Brooks, the most hated woman in Britain. The label had stuck, and there she was again on the front page. Very pretty, but goodness, what must it be like to live with all that crap being thrown at you.

Tucked away in the inside pages, they were breaking the news of the discovery of a huge stash of bomb-making materials in an anonymous warehouse in Pinner. Nearly one hundred thousand disposable ice-packs, containing enough ammonium nitrate to blow up Wembley Stadium. A forty-six-year-old Iranian with suspected links to Hizbollah had been arrested. Why he had been allowed to roam the streets of London unchecked in the first place was the subject of much outrage in the article, a viewpoint with which Jimmy agreed.

He was in the mess room of RAF Northolt, his EOD team having been permanently transferred to London a fortnight ago after the discovery of the Pinner bomb factory. Nearly three months to the day after the Belfast attack. He dreamt about it every night, a recurring nightmare on top of all the other recurring nightmares, this the worst of all. The pretty face of Sergeant Naomi Harris smiling at him, earnest and eager, eyes sparkling with love for life. 'So what are you going to do when you leave the army?' she asks, over and over again. And then the crack of the bullet from the gunman's rifle, smashing her head into little pieces.

'Penny for them sir.'

Private Alex Marley, straight out of training, fresh-faced, brimming with enthusiasm. Jimmy groaned inwardly. *Bloody hell, not another one*. Why did they keep sending him these bloody novices, he wasn't a bloody babysitter. And after what had happened in Belfast, for Christ's sake. For once it would be nice to get some grizzled old hand, someone who had been round the block a bit, with a bit of street smarts. Problem was, not many of the EOD&S guys made it to veteran status. The 'killed on duty' stats weren't good, and if you survived that then the PTSD got you. Only mugs like himself tried to carry on, and where had that got him?

'Just daydreaming Marley. My Euro millions numbers have come up and Scotland have won the World Cup.'

'Woman or men sir?'

'Sorry?'

'The woman's football team or the men's. Your woman's team is actually pretty good sir.'

'And the men's is pretty rubbish,' Jimmy laughed. 'Yes, I know, that's why it's only a dream. You're interested in footie then?'

'I am sir. I play a bit too. I'm hoping to make the joint services team this year.'

'Well good luck with that, hope you make it. No Scottish blood in your background?'

'Not as far as I'm aware sir. Jamaica and Catford I'm afraid. Although I'm told I did visit Carlisle once with my grandmother, when I was three.'

'Marley, I think you'll find that's in England actually, but it's probably close enough for you to qualify.'

Out of the blue, his personal radio cracked into life.

'Captain Stewart, I think we have a live incident'. A glance at the wall-mounted television, permanently tuned to Sky News, confirmed his worst fears. Their breaking news was of a suspected terror attack at a Hampstead primary school. Grainy pictures of the scene, evidently captured on the phone of an eye-witness, showed a large white van jammed against the gates of the school. The flashing blue and green lights of the police cars and paramedics were eerily reflected by the film of autumn rain that had fallen earlier that day.

'Shit,' Jimmy said, 'c'mon Marley, we need to get down there quick.' He had been briefed on the earlier Notting Hill attack, and this already had all the hallmarks of a copy-cat operation. That time there had been a bomb, and it was surely odds-on that there would be one again today. The technicians had already got the Foxhound's engine running when they reached the garage, the postcode remotely programmed into the vehicles military-grade sat-nav system.

'Control, what's the status?' he barked. Marley swung the heavy vehicle in behind the police escort waiting on West End Road. It set off at pace, its sirens wailing, clearing a path through the busy traffic.

'Reports of an on-board IED. Incident Commander has ordered police, fire and ambulance personnel to clear the area. There are multiple impact casualties at the scene, and a woman trapped under the front wheels of the van.'

All these kids and mothers, seriously injured and no way for the paramedics to help them until his bomb squad gave the all-clear. He shuddered at the thought, the agony they were suffering, lying alone and terrified. Here they were in London and the nightmare was starting all over again.

It took nearly eighteen minutes for them to arrive at the school. He knew that would be too late for some victims who would already have died as a result of their injuries, victims who might have been saved if the paramedics could have got to them sooner. Commander John Rufford was waiting for them as they approached the crime scene barriers. Jimmy jumped down from the cab and shook his hand warmly.

'Captain Jimmy Stewart, EOD&S. I can see where the van

has ended up. We'll get started right away but please make sure you keep everyone at least a hundred metres back.'

'Roger and good luck Captain,' replied the Commander. 'We won't get in your way, but at the risk of stating the bleeding obvious, the quicker the better'.

'I know sir, we'll do everything we can.'

Jimmy had now been joined by Private Marley, looking pale and frightened. It was her first live incident and it was slowly dawning on her that this job was going to have to be done without the help of the Dragon or any of the other high-tech machinery in their extensive armoury.

'What are we going to do sir?'

He heard the fear in his colleague's voice, and he liked that. Bravery and over-confidence got you killed in this job, and with just two weeks' service left, he was not about to have the loss of another young life spinning round his brain in the small hours.

'You Marley, are going to stay right here by the Foxhound and keep in touch with Control. Do not move from the vehicle unless I specifically tell you to, understand? I want you to watch all the video that I send back from the helmet camera and let me know if you spot anything, anything at all. I need you as my second pair of eyes. Got that?'

'Yes sir, but...'

'No ifs or buts, that's procedure and we're playing this one by the rule book'.

Except it wasn't quite going to be played by the rule book. The rule book would dictate working down a long check list before putting any EOD lives in danger. The rule book would mean first sending in the Dragon to do a thorough video survey, and then waiting until Control had reviewed the footage and made its recommendations. The rule book would mean more people would die. Jimmy was going to rip up the rule book.

He slung the heavy toolkit onto his back and sprinted down the road to where the van lay, its windscreen smashed and bonnet crumpled where it had crashed into the heavy stone gatepost. As he approached, he began to hear the moans and cries of the injured. A little girl, her neat uniform ripped and splattered with blood, lay on her side, crying for her mummy. Beside her, a boy of about the same age. Already it looked too late for him. The young woman trapped under the wheels of the van looked in a bad way, but was still clinging to consciousness. She saw Jimmy approach and let out a faint 'help me,' but he couldn't help her, not at this moment. This was like Afghanistan all over again, except the wounded weren't professional soldiers who were paid to put their lives in danger day in day out. These were innocent civilians, woman and children caught up in a conflict they knew little about and about which they cared even less.

You had to steel yourself, tell yourself that the only way to help these people was to do your job and disarm this bomb, but it was damn hard and today Jimmy knew that he'd come to the end of the road. Just this one more operation, that was all he had in him. He just had to get out while he still could.

Come on man, think. The chances were that the bomb's trigger mechanism would be in the van itself, rather than being detonated remotely. Probably a motion or vibration sensor or just a simple electronic timer. If this was another Palestinian attack by the same group responsible for the Notting Hill incident, then it was logical to think they would use the same tried and tested method as before. Besides that, it was not easy to prime a motion sensor without blowing yourself up in the process, and this lot did not seem intent on joining the ranks of the suicide bombers. And then he noticed that the driver's door was closed. *Yes*. That meant that the attacker must have shut it behind him when he fled the scene, most probably an unthinking automatic reaction. So that almost certainly ruled out motion or vibration sensors. Good- then it had to be a timer. Only problem being that it might be programmed to go off in the next two seconds. Not so good.

He clicked on his two-way communicator and pulled down the helmet-mounted microphone.

'Ok Marley, I'm going in now, ok, just keep your eyes fixed on that video.'

'Ok sir, I'm on it.'

The timer was easy to detect, being stuck to the front of the dashboard in full view and attached by double-sided tape. It was nothing more sophisticated than a simple electronic stopwatch, costing no more than two quid on Amazon - cheap and deadly. He looked at the rapidly-changing display, calibrated to the millisecond. Only six minutes before it went off. *Oh-oh*. Examining it, he saw that eight or nine coloured wires sprouted from below the device, leading to an open storage cubby-hole on the passenger side. There it was, slotted into a large manila envelope - half a kilo of prime IRA Semtex, packing enough stored explosive energy to blow a twenty-metre-wide crater in the roadway below. He examined the package closely, counting the number of wires going in - eight of them, and just one that, when snipped, would disarm the detonator. It was like Russian roulette, but with the odds stacked eight to one against you.

'Shit, shit, shit.'

'Sorry sir?'

'I think we're buggered here Marley. There's just so much decoy wiring, there's no way I can risk mucking about with it.'

'I can see that sir. Could you not try and dismantle the timer, see if you can figure out how it's wired?'

'I thought of that, but I'd bet my arse that it will have some sort of anti-tamper mechanism. Remove the cover and boom, up it will all go. That's not going to work I'm afraid.'

The sweat was now pouring down his brow as he began to comprehend the sheer hopeless of his situation. *C'mon, think man, think*. But there was nothing, absolutely nothing they could do. And procedure, the book, dictated that he now withdrew to safety. Right away. No room for sentiment or mindless valour in the army. Nothing could be done for the wounded, so get out whilst you can, saving a valuable human asset to fight again. Leaving the gravely injured to their fate, waiting until the timer ran down and the bomb wreaked its terrible carnage. That's what he had to do.

Suddenly the radio crackled into life.

'Sir, I think I might have an idea. I'm not sure if you will like it though.'

'Go on.'

'We think it might be IRA technology in the bomb sir, don't we, same as that Notting Hill one? So that probably means that it was delivered to the terrorists as a complete package. All wired up and ready to go. And probably fairly stable, no motion detectors or suchlike in the bomb itself.'

'So?'

'So maybe you could take it out of the van as a whole package too.'

Clever. Why hadn't he thought of that? It was because it was a stupid plan and still way way out of procedure. There was only five minutes or so left, and it might take him as long to disentangle the bomb from the van. One slip, a wire gets broken and it goes off, meaning certain death for him, and probably not even saving the victims either. And let's face it, he didn't want to die, and no-one would condemn him if he got out there and then. It was definitely a dumb stupid plan. If it went wrong, they would probably court-martial him. Posthumously. For thirty seconds he sat rooted to the spot, his mind in turmoil, a morass of indecision. The bloody army, they could only expect so much of a man, and hadn't he done more than his fair share over the years? Surely this was a step too far. Get out man, whilst you still can.

'Sir? Sir, we don't have much time.'

'I'm just thinking Marley, give me a minute.' But they didn't have a minute.

'Oh screw it, look, I'm going to give it a try. Can you get on to the Commander and make sure they clear everyone at least another sixty metres outside the cordoned zone. Oh, and just one more thing Marley.'

'Yes sir?'

'Does your plan say what we should do with the bloody thing once we get it out?'

'No sir. Sorry sir.'

'Thought not. Over and out.'

He set to work, taking off his backpack, placing it on the

passenger seat and opening the top flap. Good, there was plenty of room in there beside his tools for the device. Next, he carefully prised the little timer off the dashboard, taking great care not to put any tension on the wiring. Fortunately, there was enough play in the wires to allow him to put the timer straight into the backpack. So far so good, now for the bomb itself. Fairly stable was what Private Marley had said, but he wasn't taking any chances. He managed with some difficulty to slide the package part-way out of the cubby-hole, but then for no obvious reason, it refused to go any further. *Shit*. He tried to squeeze his fingers into the narrow gap between the bomb and its receptacle, probing to see if he could find out what was jamming it, but it was just too tight for him. *Come on, come on, come on*. He stole a glance at his watch. Only about four minutes to go. *Shit, shit, shit*. His heart was pounding in his chest, his head throbbing with pain. Feverishly he began rooting around his backpack, looking for the long yellow-handled screwdriver that he always carried with him. Where the hell was it? But finally he located it, deftly pulling it out of the bag then carefully inserting it between the bomb and the side of the cubby-hole. It seemed to reach all the way to the bottom, but no matter how much he wriggled or probed, he just couldn't budge it.

'Sir, we're running out of time.'

'Do you think I don't know that Marley, for Christ's sake.'

He tried again one more time to free the package, tightening his fingers around the protruding edge and tugging with as much force as he dared, but still it refused to move. Shit, this was all going tits-up.

And now he had just a few agonising seconds to make the decision. Live to fight another day, that was official policy. Get the hell out of there whilst you still could. Leave the wounded, you can't do anything more for them, that's what they drummed into you in all these Sandhurst courses. Easy enough to say when you were sitting in a warm classroom.

'Sir...' Marley's voice was anxious. *'What's happening sir?'*

There wasn't time to answer, but then what was he going

to say? Then he had a sudden thought, the surging adrenalin clearing his mind. *Ninety seconds, that's all I'll give it, and then I'm out of here.* He grabbed a pair of wire-cutters from his toolbag and dived under the steering column, searching for the wiring leading to the ignition switch. Red... green... blue, yep there they were. Snip the red one, snip the green one, then strip the coating away to expose the bare wire. Done. Now twist them together, see what happens. He looked up to see the dashboard ablaze with warning lights. Yes, we have ignition. Jumping into the driving seat, he stabbed the start button. The big diesel began to turn over. *Rah-rah-rah-rah*. Come on, fire will you! He let the starter motor spin a few more times but still the engine would not start. But just as he was slamming his fists on the dashboard in frustration, the comms channel crackled into life.

'Maybe you could move it on the starter motor sir?'

'Private Marley, you're a blooming genius.' He rammed down the clutch pedal, crashed the gearbox into reverse and pushed the start button once more. As soon as the starter motor began to churn, he released the pedal, causing the van to shoot backwards a few metres. *Keep it going, keep it going.* He managed to reverse it about ten metres before the battery finally gave up the ghost, but at least that was something. He pushed open the door of the van and jumped down onto the road, and as he did so, his eyes met with those of the young woman who had been trapped under the wheels, still conscious and surely in unimaginable pain. To the left of him lay the little schoolgirl, no more than five or six years old, covered in blood and still crying for her mother. *Leave the wounded, you can't do anything more for them.* With just seconds left before the timer ticked down to zero, there was no time to save them, of course there wasn't. *Leave the wounded, you can't do anything more for them, that's procedure.* Live to fight another day, preserve the asset.

In a split second he had made the decision. He scooped up the little girl in his arms then, without a backward glance, ran for his life to the shelter of the school's sturdy stone wall.

Chapter 8

So it had been a hundred days? That's what the headline in the *Chronicle* was saying and she had no reason to doubt its accuracy, although to Maggie, it felt more like a hundred years. She still came into the office every day, but that was just through force of habit, the inexplicable human desire to cling to routine in times of difficulty. There was no work for her of course and their Clerk Nigel Redmond had barely spoken to her since the trial let alone brought her any briefs, not even the crappy ones she was used to. Colleagues avoided her in the corridor and it went strangely silent around the water-cooler whenever she came into view. The most hated woman in Britain was evidently no more popular in Drake Chambers, as if mere association with her was enough to taint their own precious reputations. And she thought they had been her friends.

As she sipped her lukewarm coffee, the same question went round and round in her head. *Who could have done this to me?* But done what? She had checked her inbox a dozen times, and it was absolutely the case that Khan's report had arrived just three days before the last day of the trial. She was no IT expert and she wondered if perhaps it had been *sent* weeks earlier and had somehow got lost somewhere in cyberspace, but a thorough Google investigation had ruled that out. The sender's timestamp was just a few seconds before she had received it. This was no mix-up, and so whoever had told the judge that she had it earlier was lying. But the question remained unanswered. *Who and why?* It didn't make any sense. To make matters worse, the organisation that had purportedly sent her the report had vanished into thin air. The website of *British Solidarity for Palestine* had disappeared and their email address returned a *mailbox unavailable* error. There was nothing to show that they had ever existed.

In twenty-three days' time she would be in front of the Bar Standards Board when her only defence would be -what? It would be her word against Lady Justice Henderson, and that verdict was only going to go one way. She hoped they would finally tell her who it was who had made the assertion that she had that report more than six weeks earlier than she had actually received it. Because otherwise, how could she be expected to get a fair hearing? But deep down, she knew that wasn't going to happen. They would all close ranks against her because who really cared about the fate of a second-rate barrister who had been too much in the public eye for their liking?

Not her husband Philip, for a start. Their marriage had been in trouble before all of this had happened, she knew that, but now he was spending the whole working week away, and at weekends if he did come home, he was cold and distant. It was only Ollie, her sweet precious Ollie, that kept her sane. He was only six and she wondered if he could feel the tension between his mummy and daddy, both of whom he loved unconditionally. For his sake if nothing else she thought she should keep the marriage together, but with each passing day that seemed to become less and less likely. Now she was spending more and more time working out how she would adjust to life as a single mum. There would be enough money for her to buy a small place, obviously nowhere as grand as their Hampstead home, but it would be more than fine for the two of them. She would not be able to practice at the Bar, but she could easily go back to the more mundane side of her profession. Wills and probate, property conveyancing, it was hardly thrilling but it would pay the mortgage. They would be ok, she was sure of that.

She looked up to see Redmond standing in front of her desk. From his expression, she could tell that there was something badly wrong.

'Maggie, there's been an attack on Ollie's school. A van. It's been driven at the school gates. The BBC is saying there are casualties. I think you'd better get there. I'm sorry.'

Instantly, her heart was crashing, her stomach churning as she tried to process what he had said. *Please, please, please let him be ok*. Through the fog of confusion she realised that Redmond was still speaking.

'Look, I can order a taxi, it will be the quickest way. Do you want anyone to come with you?'

'What? No, no I brought my car in today. I'll be ok.'

She grabbed her coat and rushed through the door leading to the stairwell. It had been a spur of the moment decision to drive in that day, but now she was glad she had, as she ran through the dark underground car-park to where her Golf was waiting. At least she would be in control, because she just had to get there, as fast as she could. She fumbled around in her handbag, searching for her gate pass. Hell, why was that barrier always so slow? She screeched out into the narrow street, attracting a barrage of horns as she recklessly threaded her way through the late afternoon traffic. These damn traffic lights, why were they never at green?

As she drove her head was swimming with emotion, her mouth dry, her eyes moistening. If anything happened to Ollie, she would die, she knew she would. Then suddenly, she thought about Daisy, her niece. She would have been standing at the gates waiting to collect Ollie. This was all too hard to bear.

As she battled along City Road the phone rang. It was her mother calling from home in Yorkshire. She could tell from her wavering voice that she was already beside herself with worry.

'Maggie, I've just seen the news. Is Ollie safe?'

'I don't know mum, I don't know, I'm just trying to get to the school now.'

Without warning, a pensioner in a Honda Jazz pulled out of a side street then proceeded to dawdle along at twenty miles an hour, neck craned forward peering through his windscreen.

'Get out of the way!' Instinctively, Maggie jammed her foot hard on the accelerator to overtake, narrowly missing an oncoming delivery van. The driver gesticulated wildly, mouthing an obscenity and blaring his horn.

'Maggie, are you ok?'

'London traffic mum. Look, I need to go, I'll call you as

soon as I hear anything. I'm sure Ollie will be ok.' How she hoped against hope that this would be true.

Soon she was on the Holloway Road, where the traffic was moving at a snail's pace as the tail end of the school run clashed with early commuters on their homeward journey. Then the phone rang again. This time it was Philip. His voice was frantic, desperate, close to breaking down.

'I've just heard. I've been trying to call the school but it's constantly engaged. Can you get up there right away and see if he's all right?'

'I'm on my way Philip. I've not heard anything more than they're saying on the news.'

'Look, I'm going to catch the earliest flight back I can. Angelique has been looking and we can get the 5.30, should get us through Heathrow by 7.00. I'll get there as fast as I can. And call me as soon as you have news.'

Angelique. What the hell was she doing there? He was supposedly there for an important two-day meeting with the Scottish First Minister and her Justice Minister. Why would you take a junior associate to that? But there was no time to think about that now, she had to get to Ollie's school. *Come on, come on!* A long queue of vehicles was backed up at the junction with the Seven Sisters Road, seemingly grid-locked. She blasted her horn at the driver in front who was texting on her mobile, oblivious that the car in front of her was now moving. Then she saw the red sign that had been placed at the road side. Shit, it was road-works, and of course the temporary traffic lights which controlled them were at red. They always were. She banged the steering wheel in frustration, then jabbed the phone icon on the Golf's touchscreen. Scrolling down the phonebook, she chose Felicity Swift, mother of Ollie's friend Tom, but it went straight through to answerphone. Hardly surprising in the circumstances. And then a cold shiver passed through her as she remembered that Felicity was one of the many rich stay-at-home mothers who were able to collect their children from school each day. She would have been outside the gate, laughing and joking with the other mums and nannies. Like

Daisy. *Please no.*

The lights had finally changed and she accelerated through the junction, moving to the outside lane and, ignoring the speed cameras, driving as fast as she dared. Then up Highgate Hill and onto Hampstead Lane. At last, nearly there.

She arrived at the school to a scene of frantic activity. Dozens of armed police and soldiers were on patrol, guarding the formal crime scene which had been established around a two or three hundred metres radius from the school gates. Tents had been erected and a string of ambulances were parked along the roadside, blue lights flashing through the gloom of the damp autumn afternoon, waiting to take the injured to the nearby Royal Free Hospital. Maggie abandoned her car in the middle of the road and ran to where two police officers, one male, one female, guarded a gap in the red-striped perimeter tape.

'Stop there madam please,' the male officer said sharply.

'I'm a parent,' Maggie cried. 'I need to see if my little boy is all right.'

'I'm afraid we will need to search you first,' the other said, more kindly, adding unnecessarily, 'This is a terrorist incident.'

'Please, as quickly as you can,' Maggie pleaded, almost in tears. 'Please.'

But the policewoman was not to be rushed. With painful precision she checked each arm in turn then filleted inside Maggie's coat with her hands, progressing down her back and over her bottom.

'Can you remove your boots please madam,' she ordered.

The policewoman stood impassively as Maggie removed her boots, leaving her stocking-footed on the cold tarmac. But at last the search was completed and she was directed to a tent to the left of the gates where teachers were trying to help the dozens of parents that had rushed to the school when they heard the news. Immediately she saw Miss Roberts, Ollie's young class teacher, armed with a clipboard and talking animatedly with a number of agitated parents.

'Look, it's really hard to get information, we can't get in the way of the emergency services and keep asking them for updates. I have a list of my class here and thankfully most of them have been accounted for.' *Most of them.* 'Please, please, that's all the information I have at the moment. Your children have all been taken to the school hall where they are being looked after by members of staff.'

In the crowd, Maggie spotted Felicity Swift and she could tell immediately that something was terribly amiss. She went over to her and gently took her arm.

'What's wrong Felicity?'

'It's Tom. He's not on Miss Roberts' list, and I've been to the hall and he's not there either. She thinks he may be one of the injured, I'm just waiting for my Jules to arrive and then we can go to the hospital.' Her voice was frantic with worry.

'I'm so sorry Felicity,' Maggie said quietly. 'I don't know what to say, but I'm sure he will be ok, little boys are so tough.' She wrapped her arms around her friend and squeezed her gently. 'It will be alright, it will be alright.'

'I saw Ollie in the hall,' said Felicity through her tears. 'He's ok. You should go and see him. I'll be fine, honestly.'

Thank god. Maggie took her phone from her pocket and texted 'Safe' to Philip and her mum. Now she must go to Ollie, hold him in her arms and never let him go.

She became aware of Miss Roberts approaching her.

'Mrs Brooks. Look, I'm afraid I've got some bad news. It's your niece, Daisy isn't it? She was... well, it seems she was hit by the van and was trapped beneath the front wheels for some time.'

She could see the young teacher was struggling to hold her emotions in check.

'They've taken her to the Royal Free. I think it's quite serious. I'm so sorry.'

***

They sat in the cold corridor alongside the trauma unit, not speaking. From time to time they stood up to look through the window where Daisy was lying unconscious, wearing an oxygen mask and connected to a barrage of high-tech monitoring equipment. It was nearly a week since the attack, during which time the highly-skilled medical team had fought tenaciously to save her life. She had multiple broken bones and serious internal injuries, and already she had endured three major operations, with more to come. The doctors were cautiously optimistic. She was young and the young possessed remarkable powers of recovery. That was the message of hope they were giving the family. She was going to be ok, that's what they were saying.

Along the corridor, holding hands, sat Felicity and Jules Swift, their faces pale and drawn, eyes bloodshot from the crying. Their son had been in a coma for five days now, and privately, the doctors had given up hope, but the parents had been given the same assurances as the Brooks. *Tom was a child and children possessed remarkable powers of recovery.* It was not convincing but whilst he clung onto life, there was hope, and hope was all they had to sustain them.

The surly guard who had escorted Hugo Brooks from Belmarsh prison had sloped off for a coffee and a cigarette. A bit of a risk and he shouldn't be doing it but he considered it unlikely that his charge would try an escape in the circumstances.

'You don't have to stay Maggie,' Hugo said. 'I'll be fine, honestly. And Philip is coming back later, you should go and get some sleep if you can.'

She could really do with some sleep, that was for sure. She was dog-tired, but she didn't want to leave him. Although they had never got on, even before his trial, she did feel terribly sorry for him, as you would for anyone in his dreadful situation. In appearance, he was exactly like Philip but he possessed none of the magnetism that had so attracted Maggie to his brother. Whereas Philip was smooth, urbane and driven, Hugo had been content to potter around in his comfortable little world of progressive activism, getting by on his English teacher's salary and spending his weekends with his placards and banners on the demo frontline. And all the better if there was to be a bit of ruckus with the police, the chance to call them fascist pigs and hopefully get filmed by the BBC as you were dragged away struggling. Until it had all gone wrong when that young policewoman had died.

'No honestly Hugo, I'm fine. I'll stay for the next couple of hours then go and collect Ollie from school.'

It was the children's first day back, only five days after the attack, it being the view of the psychologists that it was best for kids to get back to normality as quickly as possible. Maggie's mum had been staying with them to look after Ollie whilst he was off school, but this morning she had returned to Leeds to look after Maggie's ailing father.

She looked at her watch - just coming up to half-past-twelve. Her mum should be home by now. Time for a quick call.

'Mum, how was the journey?'

'Fine darling.' She sounded strained, hesitant, not like herself at all.

'Mum, what's wrong?' asked Maggie, alarmed. 'Is it dad?'

'Maggie, have you seen the news?'

'No mum, what is it?'

'I've just seen it on the BBC News website. You should look at it now. It's bad news I'm afraid.'

Maggie pulled up the news app and read the headline. It hit her like a sledgehammer, her spirit crushed in an instant as she processed what it meant. The first reaction to a shock as big as this was usually denial, but this couldn't be denied, because there it was in bold type, unmissable and unequivocal.

Freed Alzahrani set to be named as Hampstead Bomber.

Suddenly a loud piercing alarm came from the heart monitor, and almost instantaneously, an amber beacon started flashing and a deafening siren shattered the quiet calm of the trauma wing. Within seconds, Daisy's bed was surrounded by a scrum of doctors and nurses, pulses racing, working in frantic unison to try and save the young woman's life. There was no time to pull down the blinds that screened the trauma room from the corridor, and Maggie watched in a daze as the electrodes of the theatre defibrillator were attached to Daisy's chest, her body involuntarily convulsing as the high-voltage charge was fired. Again and again they tried, but the heart monitor did not respond. A powerful injection of adrenaline was prepared and plunged into her chest, but still no response, and now there was a change in the atmosphere, something in the demeanour of the medics that told her that it was already too late.

Hugo was wailing uncontrollably, alternatively calling out his daughter's name, then clasping his hands in prayer, repeating 'Please god please god' over and over again.

'I'm sorry Mr Brooks, we did everything we could'. The consultant placed his hand on Hugo's shoulder, his voice steady, exuding warmth and professional compassion. *Multiple organ failure caused by the trauma of the accident. Difficult to diagnose or treat. We did everything we could.* Of course, what else would they say, could they say?

Along the corridor, six-year old Tom Swift's life-support machine was finally switched off. He died peacefully with his mummy and daddy and his favourite teddy bear by his bedside. *We did everything we could.* Dena Alzahrani had claimed two more victims.

And it was Maggie Brooks that had set her free.

***

Only one thought had occupied her mind. She had to get home, as fast as she could, to bury her head in her pillow, to drink until she could remember nothing, to just make it all go away, even if for only a moment. She would call Philip, make him leave his damn office early and go and collect Ollie for once. She had raced down a busy corridor towards where she thought the exit was, only to end up instead in the packed waiting room of the Blood Test clinic. Damn, these hospitals were like a maze. Eventually, she had spotted an ill-placed exit sign suspended from the ceiling which pointed her in the opposite direction from where she had come. Weaving through a crush of medical staff, porters, patients and visitors, she had eventually reached the heavy revolving doors of the entrance. Outside, she had breathed in a gulp of cool air then joined the long queue waiting at the parking machines to authorise their tickets. *Come on.*

The traffic around the hospital had been its usual nightmare but at last she had reached her quiet Hampstead street, where she had been surprised to see Philip's navy blue Range Rover parked outside.

In the kitchen, she had found Angelique Perez, dressed in one of her husband's striped shirts, her hair wrapped in a towel. A few seconds later, there was Philip in the white dressing gown she had bought him for his birthday. She would never ever forget his words on that day. *It's over Maggie, I should have told you before*. That was all he could find to say, on that day when her world was collapsing, where she desperately needed someone to help and comfort her, when she thought she would die. All he could say was *it's over,* whilst Angelique Perez looked on. So young, so beautiful, so bloody triumphant.

It had taken her just five minutes to get to the school, and only a few minutes more to reach Ollie's classroom. 'Mrs Brooks, you can't just march in here during class,' Miss Roberts had tried to protest, but sod that, Ollie was her son and she could do what she wanted. 'Where are we going mummy?' he had asked again and again, but she hadn't answered, because she didn't know. She just had to drive, anywhere, just keep driving, for hour upon hour - north, south, east, west, it didn't matter where.

She had not really been conscious of driving onto the level crossing or stopping the car so that it straddled one of the railway tracks. She vaguely remembered the sound of bells, which later she supposed had been the signal that the barriers were closing because of an approaching train. From the back seat, she thought that she may have heard Ollie crying but it was distant, detached and it did not disturb the feeling of peace and calm which had now blissfully enveloped her. At last, it would be over, the pain would be gone and everything would be okay. And then a dull thud as the articulated lorry rammed the back of the Golf, pushing it to safety. Seconds later, an altogether more violent crash as the Brighton express, travelling at ninety miles per hour, smashed through the lorry's trailer, sending debris flying in all directions.

PART TWO
One Year Later

Chapter 9

She watched him from across the room, transfixed, as he mooched around the neat exhibition stands, picking up a brochure here and exchanging a few words there with eager recruiting officers from the big names of the profession. What's he doing here, she thought, surely he's not hoping to get a training contract dressed like that? Perhaps just looking for an internship, but he's too old for that, isn't he? At least late twenties, no, older, early thirties at least. Scruffy and unshaven, with unkempt dark hair touching his shoulders, dressed in skinny black jeans and a crumpled black T-shirt bearing a washed-out AC/DC logo - and was that really cowboy boots he was wearing? But tall, ripped and good looking. *Very* good looking, a fact that had not gone unnoticed by her rival recruiters, both female and, it should be said, male too. A pretty young redhead from Addison Redburn, the distinguished City firm where Maggie's own career had started, glided up to him as he wandered past, gently placing a hand on his arm to arrest his progress, whilst drawing his attention to the contents of a glossy flyer that she held in the other. She was clearly intent in luring him to the confines of Addison's elegantly-furnished stand, where a high-pressure hit squad would take over, tasked with selling the ethereal prize of a glittering career at the bar to naive recently-minted graduates. Modern slavery more like, thought Maggie, although a bit better paid. But he was seemingly not to be ensnared, smiling ruefully and raising his hand to decline the young woman's offer, but accepting the leaflet as if in way of apology, even feigning to read it as he continued along the gangway before disappearing out of sight behind another stand.

In her peripheral vision, she became aware of a figure heading towards her, and in a split second she was drowning once again in the horrible emotional mash-up of hopelessness, fear and anger that had been her constant companion in the dark months since her perfect life had been turned upside down. The man, grey-haired, late forties, be-suited, marched onto her stand, brandishing a letter in his hand, demonstrably agitated. Trailing a few steps behind was a striking woman of around thirty, immaculately dressed in Armani and tottering uncertainly on a pair of expensive red stilettos.

'What the hell is this Maggie? What the hell is this? A custody hearing? You know, you are a seriously deluded bitch if you think a judge is going to let a nut-job like you anywhere near my son. That's not going to happen. Never. Not on my watch.'

Maggie had been expecting a reaction but not so soon, not here and not with *her* in attendance.

'Our son Philip, Ollie is our son. And you know very well I'm getting my life back together. I've got a job and a home...'

'You call this a job? What the hell do you know about investigations? And a home? Yeah, some seedy little bedsitter in Clapham is what I'm hearing. But what I'm really interested in is what the hell you are going to say to the judge? *Oh of course m'lud, I know I tried to murder my son last year, but honestly, I promise not to do it again, honest I do*. That's going to be an entertaining day out, that's all I can say.'

'I need to see him Philip. I need to see Ollie.'

She knew she should remain in control of her emotions, but her voice cracked as she struggled to get the words out. She stretched out her arm to steady herself against the pillar of the exhibition stand, waves of nausea threatening to overwhelm her. Pathetic, broken, she hated herself for what she had become. But she wasn't about to start begging to *him*.

'I know I won't get full custody, not after...not after what happened. But a child needs his mother, and you can't cut him off from me completely, it's so cruel. So I'm going to fight for this with every bone in my body. I'll never give up, no matter how long it takes.'

He moved slowly and deliberately, so that his face was almost touching hers. And then, speaking as if spelling out each word. 'This is the most stupid thing you've ever done, and that's saying something for a stupid bitch like you. So you can try what you like, but you won't be seeing *my* son, not now, not...'

'Hey, what's going on here pal?'

The voice was West of Scotland, working-class. Surprised, Philip Brooks swung round to confront his interlocutor.

'Sorry, are you talking to me?'

'Oh my, are you from Glasgow or something? I've not heard anyone say that for years. Mind you, by the look of you I don't think you would last five minutes on Sauchiehall Street.'

He extended a massive hand towards Brooks. 'Stewart. James Stewart. My pals call me Jimmy'. It was ignored.

'I was just having a private conversation with my wife,' Brooks said, his composure partially regained. 'Really, I don't think it's any of your business.'

Jimmy gave a disarming smile. 'Well in my neck of the woods pal, men don't go around threatening women. So I'm making it my business, ok?'

And then, recognition.

'Hang on pal, I know you. That *Question Time* program on the telly, *that's* where I've seen you before. The human rights guy. And Julian Priest's pal. Yeah, I remember you now.'

'What of it?'

'Well I don't see much human rights going on here,' Jimmy said. 'Happy to talk the talk but not walk the walk, is that what it is? So my suggestion is you take your human rights and get the hell out of here before I shove them up your backside. And believe me, if you don't take my advice, it will be the most stupid thing *you'll* have ever done. And I also guarantee it.'

It was evident from Brooks' expression that he wasn't used to being spoken to like this. He stood motionless as if weighing up his options. But finally he turned to his companion.

'Ok Angelique, I think we're done here.' His tone suggested he was anything but finished, but the intervention of Captain Jimmy Stewart had clearly prompted a change of plan. But as they walked away, he suddenly spun round and making no effort to hide the bitterness in his voice, shouted, 'You've not heard the last of this Maggie, believe me. I said it before, and I'll say it again. You are not getting within a million miles of my son. Understand that.'

Maggie was vaguely aware of an arm being gently wrapped around her shoulder and of her being led to a wickerwork armchair at the back of the stand. She sat down, head bowed, whilst her rescuer struggled to rip the cellophane off a pack of paper tissues.

'Bugger, why do they make these things bloody impossible to open?'

'Th..thank you,' she said, her voice barely audible, and then to her surprise, came a quite unexpected sliver of a smile 'Yes, they are impossible to open aren't they? But thank you so much for helping me.'

Finally he had managed to rip open the pack but with such force that the tissues sprang out and spilled across the carpeted floor of the stand.

He laughed. 'That always happens, doesn't it? Bugger it. Come on, let's wipe away these tears and see if we can clean up some of that scary mascara, shall we? Would that be ok?'

Without waiting for her reply, he kneeled down in front of her and started to dab the tears from under her eyes. His touch was kind, gentle, caring, considerate and for Maggie, simply overwhelming. She threw her arms around him and buried her head in his shoulder. Then started to cry.

'There, there, let it all out, just let it all out.'

And for nearly ten minutes she did let it all out, the former wannabe hotshot barrister and soon-to-be former wife of the UK's highest-profile human-rights brief crying her eyes out on the shoulder of the man the papers had christened the Hampstead Hero.

***

Jimmy placed two polystyrene cups of tepid milky coffee on the table. 'Do you take sugar? I hope not, since I forgot to get any.' They had repaired to the scruffy little cafe that sat adjacent to the entrance hall of the exhibition centre. Maggie had made an effort to pull herself together, and now the tears had gone but she could not stop shivering, although she knew the room wasn't cold. She had draped her coat over her shoulders and pulled down the sleeves of her grey cardigan to warm her hands. She thought she must look like a refugee on one of these black-and-white Second-World War newsreels.

'No, just milk please. And thank you so much for helping me. Jimmy, isn't it?'

'Aye, it's Jimmy and that's about the tenth time you've thanked me in the last ten minutes. No more required now please, I get the picture fine. You're grateful for my intervention.' This accompanied by a broad disarming smile that she would come to love.

'No, I mean yes but... well I don't know what would have happened if you hadn't come along when you did. So thank you...' she smiled, realising what she had done '...sorry, sorry, I can't help it.'

'Not surprising, after all you've been through. Your husband seems like a right pig, if you don't mind me saying. Mind you, I'm not surprised, because he always comes across as a pompous idiot on the telly.'

'You must know who I am then, I suppose?

'Well, you don't exactly need to be Sherlock Holmes to work it out. I've seen your picture in the papers. *'Is this the most hated woman in Britain?'* I think that's how the *Chronicle* described you. Of course I know who you are - you're the infamous Maggie Brooks.'

She laughed. Hell, she had actually *laughed*, despite the fact that she knew, without doubt, that she did not deserve to laugh ever again in her life after everything she had done and everything that had happened.

'Yes, I'm afraid that is me. The most hated woman in Britain.' It was true, more than a year on, and no easier to come to terms with despite the time that had passed.

'So what are you doing here?' Jimmy said.

'I was going to ask you the same thing. I was watching you earlier, you know, before Philip turned up.'

'Ooh, a stalker too are you? Only joking. Actually, I'm looking for a job Maggie, same as everybody here.'

'Dressed like a half-stoned rock singer? That's a novel approach, I must say. You certainly stand out from the crowd.'

'I wasn't expecting to be interviewed today. I was just doing a bit of a high-level survey of the market, collecting a few brochures, looking at what's on offer, etcetera etcetera.'

'If you don't mind me saying so, aren't you a bit old for a graduate recruitment fair?'

'And if you don't mind me saying so, I'd guess I'm still quite a bit younger than you.' Again, delivered with the same devastating smile that instantly defused any potential offence. 'No, after Uni, my future as a lawyer was all talked about and planned, but I gave it up for music and the Free Electric Band.'

'Excuse me?'

'It's a line from an old song from the seventies by Albert Hammond. The Free Electric Band. Sorry, lame joke. My old man really wanted me to become a lawyer but I didn't fancy it so I joined the army instead. Did twelve years, Iraq, Afghanistan, Belfast, the lot. Got demobbed about twelve months ago and been bumming around ever since trying to figure out what to do next. Well, to be honest, I did have a few wee problems to sort out but nothing that I couldn't deal with. It was a wee bit tough, but I'm good now.'

She was half-expecting him to elaborate, but he didn't, so for a while they sat without exchanging a word, toying with their coffee cups, immersed in private thoughts of pain, loss and despair. It was Jimmy who finally broke the silence.

'Goodness, what have I been going on about? We've only just met and I'm banging on about my pathetic little troubles. And after all you've been through. I feel a right idiot. Look, I'll shut up right now.' Once more, the captivating smile.

She took a sip from her coffee. 'No no, please don't worry about it. Everybody's pain is real to them, it's not a competition.'

'You say that, but I've no idea how you've coped with

everything.'

The truth was she hadn't coped at all.

'You just well -*cope*, you have no choice.' That, also, was not true. You can decide not to cope, not to carry on with your wrecked life, to put an end to the agony for good, like she had so nearly done not much more than a year ago. It was this memory more than any other that made sleep so difficult to attain, and it was this nightmare that shook her awake on the rare nights when she did manage to drop off.

'But look, I mustn't keep you any longer. The fair closes soon, you'd better carry on with your job hunting. Thank you again for helping me.'

He groaned. 'Aye, and welcome to the end of Jimmy Stewart's short but sweet hippy dream. Time to put on the suit, get a haircut and knuckle down to the nine to five. Time to get a proper job like my big brother.'

'Is he a lawyer?' Maggie asked.

'No, a copper. Detective Inspector actually, here in London somewhere. I don't know exactly what he does, except he works in some dodgy department or other. Detective without portfolio he always calls himself. To be honest, I think there might have been some incident a year or two back, but I'm not surprised because he's a complete nutcase and a piss-head into the bargain'. The tone was affectionate.

'He sounds interesting, but talking of proper jobs, they probably won't start handing out offers until early in the new year at the earliest, so you've still got a bit of time left as a rebel without a cause.'

And then from nowhere, she had a crazy idea.

'Jimmy, now honestly please tell me right away if I'm being an idiot, but well, the reason I'm here is... I'm looking for an associate for my new business. I can't pay very much, not much more than minimum wage to be honest, but well, maybe it might tide you over for a few months and you could still apply to the big firms at the same time. And it might help you, you know, put some experience on your CV...'

He laughed. 'That would be very beneficial. 'Experience: I

spent six months working for the most hated woman in Britain'. No but seriously, that actually might not be such a bad idea. What exactly will the work entail, if you don't mind me asking?'

She rummaged in her handbag for a few seconds, eventually emerging with a business card that she placed on the table. It read *Bainbridge Associates - Investigation Services to the Legal Profession* with a contact phone number and e-mail address.

'In case you're wondering, Bainbridge is my maiden name. You see, I had no option but to start my own firm after...well, after everything that has happened. Nobody's going to employ me as a lawyer now, are they, let's be honest, and my friend Asvina says I need a job and an income and be able to show some stability in my life if... if I'm ever going to convince the courts to let me see Ollie again.' Once more she struggled to hold back the tears. 'I'm sorry Jimmy, look, just forget I ever raised this, it was a stupid idea...'

He evidently did not agree.

'No, not at all Maggie. You know, this might not be such a bad plan. For a start, I could certainly do with earning a few quid whilst I'm trying to figure out what to do in the long term. Go on, tell me more, I'm interested, honestly.'

'Well, it's very dull work. We're not like the private detectives on telly, in fact we're not private detectives at all. We just do all the boring leg-work that needs doing in every big case but that the law firms can't justify charging their clients five hundred pounds an hour to do. So we check bank statements, verify the value of assets, do some basic internet searches on the other parties, that sort of thing. Mainly in the family law sphere, divorces, probate, property disputes...'

Maggie knew all about the work of legal investigators, having used them plenty of times in the past, but at this moment her own firm could best be described as embryonic, a fact she did not try to conceal.

'... I've made it all sound rather grand, but we've... I've only just started up and I don't actually have any paid work as of yet. But Asvina wants me to help her on a big divorce case she's about to kick off. In fact, I'm supposed to meet the client tomorrow for the first time. You could come along if you want, no obligation or anything, just to see if maybe it's something you would like.'

'I'll do it,' he grinned, 'but do I need to get a haircut?'

She smiled. 'No, but lose the AC/DC T-shirt if you don't mind.'

'No worries, I washed my Zeppelin one yesterday. I'll wear that. No, don't worry I'll find something. Just text me the address and I'll see you tomorrow.'

And so they shook hands on the deal, a strangely formal act considering the remarkable intimacy of what had gone before. An announcement over the tannoy signalled that the fair was scheduled to close in ten minutes. Maggie closed down her laptop, slipped it into its leather case and prepared to return to her cold lonely flat. But tonight, if only imperceptibly, something felt different, better. For the first time in over a year there had been ten minutes of her life when she wasn't thinking about Ollie and she wasn't thinking about the van crushing the life from her beautiful niece. It wouldn't last, she knew that, that would be too much to expect, but tomorrow after the client meeting she would at last sign off on the divorce - she knew she must, despite all the pain that it brought. Sign the damn form and wipe the slate clean. Encase the past eight years in concrete and try to forget.

Then Asvina Rani would explain her plan for the custody hearing. Her one true friend Asvina, the most brilliant family law solicitor in all of London, and the person who had single-handedly kept her sane -just - throughout her trauma. Asvina would have a plan, a brilliant plan and soon, Maggie and Ollie would be reunited.

Chapter 10

Jimmy spotted her a few feet away in the crowd as he emerged into the street from the concourse. 'Morning Maggie, blooming nightmare this, isn't it?'

True to his word, he had made an effort to smarten up. His hair looked freshly-washed and was tied back in a neat pony-tail. He wore a crisp light blue shirt with button-down colour and smart black jeans. The cowboy boots were still extant, but had been cleaned and polished and were relatively discreet, tucked under his trouser-leg.

'Yes, it's this Palestinian peace thing, what a laugh that is. Philip and all his mates will be there of course, virtue signalling like mad. Arseholes.'

They had agreed to meet up at the DLR station in Canary Wharf, five minutes' walk from the swish glass palace that housed the distinguished international law firm of Addison Redburn. It was approaching nine o'clock and the station was still packed with commuters, but today they were joined by the unsettling presence of heavily-armed police officers. This time it was just an exercise, in preparation for the conference that was due to take place in a few weeks' time, but it was still unnerving for the worker-ants as they scurried about their business. Critics considered the conference a complete waste of time, nothing more than a vanity project by a dying administration, given that the US, the United Nations and, most conspicuously, Israel were not to be officially represented. This had not seemed to discourage Prime Minister Julian Priest, who was rolling out the red carpet for his old friend Miss Fadwa Ziadeh, the glamorous and charismatic new leader of Hamas.

The law firm occupied all thirty-two floors of the waterside tower block and as befitted her status, Asvina Rani had been allocated an impressive south-west facing suite on the second-highest floor, commanding a view in one direction over the river to the picturesque Royal Borough of Greenwich, and towards St Pauls and the City in the other. Her personal office had all the trappings of corporate success, some might say excess; upmarket furniture, tasteful wall hangings and on two sides, wall-to-ceiling windows. Outside her door, a small army of junior lawyers, paralegals and personal assistants beavered away to keep the whole lucrative show on the road. The need to keep this army fed was one reason why the services of Ms. Rani did not come cheap, but her results were often spectacular and few clients complained.

A young PA had been sent to meet Maggie and Jimmy from reception and the high-speed elevator had taken less than a minute to deliver them up to Asvina's suite.

'Miss Bainbridge and Mr Stewart,' she announced in broad Cockney, pushing open the door.

'Thanks Mary.' Asvina got up from her desk and walked across the office to greet them. 'Using your maiden name again Maggie I see. That's a big step forward.' The friends hugged warmly.

'And you must be Jimmy,' she said, extending a hand.

'That's me,' he agreed, giving her the opportunity to witness his heart-melting smile for the first time.

Mary returned with coffee and they took their seats around a large glass-topped conference table.

'Asvina, I can't thank you enough for giving me this opportunity to get my firm up and running,' Maggie said. 'You know how important it is to me, with the situation with Ollie and all that.'

'You don't need to thank me, I'm just pleased I can help.'

Jimmy laughed. 'I've known her less than twenty-four hours and she's thanked me fifty times already. That's what she does.'

Asvina nodded. 'I know, she's lovely, isn't she? Anyway, let me tell you both about the case.'

She pushed a brown A4 folder across the table, spinning it round so that they could read the label on the front.

Maggie looked surprised. 'Saddleworth verses Saddleworth? Not *Gerrard* Saddleworth surely?'

'The same,' Asvina said. 'The Right Honourable Gerrard Saddleworth, HM Government's esteemed Home Secretary.

But actually it's his wife Olivia who's my client, not her husband. You'll get to meet her in ten minutes or so once I've given you some background. That's assuming you haven't met her before?'

'I've been to one or two events the Saddleworths have also been at, I'm pretty sure of that,' Maggie said, wrinkling her brow, 'but I don't think I've actually spoken to her or been introduced. It's Philip and his brother Hugo who are old friends of Saddleworth and Priest, not me. From their university days.'

'They move in high circles don't they?' Asvina said, smiling. 'But I assume you've read the tittle-tattle in the papers about Mr Saddleworth's affair with a journalist?'

Jimmy nodded. 'Aye, with Penelope White of the *Chronicle*, I remember seeing the story somewhere. But hang on, wasn't it her who went for you big-time Maggie? The most hated woman in Britain crap, that was her doing.'

'Yes it was,' Maggie said. And perhaps it was no more than she deserved, because there was no denying the fact that she and she alone had been responsible for the freeing of Dena Alzahrani. Setting the notorious Notting Hill bomber free to repeat her heinous crime, just one hundred days later. Setting her free to murder her beautiful niece Daisy. Setting her free to condemn Jules and Felicity Swift to a life of unimaginable pain. Set free by the stupid selfishness of Maggie Bainbridge.

Jimmy was the first to notice her eyes moistening.

'Look, I'm sorry. I didn't mean to bring back the bad memories.'

'Come on, let's get to work,' Asvina said, sensing the mood. She removed a sheaf of papers from the folder and spread them across the table.

'This is what I have on the couple so far. So just for the record, they have one daughter, Patience, nineteen, and currently studying modern languages at Cambridge. Naturally, her future welfare is Olivia's priority. And this,' she said, pointing to a densely-printed spreadsheet, 'is the financial disclosure that we've got from her husband. Just one current account with Nat West, in joint names, that gets his parliamentary salary and a few thousand a year from his occasional guest appearances on an Andrew Neil TV show. About eighty grand in savings, mainly in bog-standard high street ISAs and NSI bonds, and a few thousand pounds' worth of Footsie shares. And of course there's the future value of his minister's pension, at about forty grand a year for life, guaranteed against inflation. No other significant income declared on the register of member's interests, other than acting as trustee for a couple of charities, for which he received only expenses. The house in the constituency is in joint names, worth about £450k but with over £100k mortgage still on it. His London flat, allegedly the regular venue for carnal activity with one Penelope White, journalist, is rented. He's from a modest background, so no big fat inheritance to look forward to and no other significant assets to speak of. As I said, bog-standard and squeaky-clean. He's comfortable, but not a rich man by any stretch.'

'So that all seems quite straightforward,' Maggie said, who had been listening intently, 'but there must be something else, otherwise why would you need us?'

Asvina nodded. 'You're right. But I'll let Olivia tell you about that herself. I can see she's just arrived.'

There was a knock on the door, Mary opening it just enough for them to make out her disembodied voice.

'Mrs Saddleworth's here Asvina. Shall I bring 'er in?'

Olivia Saddleworth was tall and slim but of rather plain appearance, although dressed head-to-toe with the expensive good taste of the prosperous country lady. Maggie estimated her to be in her early to mid-fifties, registering the Harris Tweed skirt, Barbour checked shirt and gilet, a pair of brown Duberry riding boots and the Mulberry handbag that she knew must have cost a thousand pounds or more. It seemed a bit out of place in central London and probably no less so in her husband's working-class South Yorkshire constituency.

Asvina quickly dispensed with the introductions then said, 'Olivia, I've just been bringing Maggie and Jimmy up to speed with your situation. They're going to help us with the investigations into your husband's financial status. As I told you on the phone, their job is to find evidence of undisclosed financial assets but I don't want to hold up too much hope because it is a very difficult task. You know we can't force banks and other financial institutions to disclose their clients' private affairs, only the courts can do that. And we have to be as certain as we can be before asking the court to intervene, because if we're wrong they'll award costs against us, and it'll negatively prejudice any future applications.'

'I understand Asvina,' Olivia said. 'I'll need to take that risk.'

Asvina raised an eyebrow in Maggie's direction.

'Olivia, I'm not sure you understand the level of costs we could be talking about here. I'm afraid you don't have the level of assets to survive a negative award. We are totally dependent on Maggie and Jimmy uncovering strong evidence if we are to make a court challenge.'

Jimmy directed his smile at Mrs Saddleworth. 'No pressure then.'

'So Olivia, perhaps you could tell Maggie and Jimmy why you are suspicious,' Asvina said. 'Specifically, the matter of the deposit box.'

Olivia Saddleworth settled back in her chair, her expression suggesting she had been looking forward to this opportunity for some time.

'I expect you all know about his... his affair with Penelope White. I'd confronted him about her, but of course at first he denied everything, so I started opening all his mail,' she said, matter-of-factly. 'It was quite easy, with him being in London all week. I wasn't sure what I was looking for, I don't suppose she was writing him love-letters or anything, but well... I just needed to do something.'

'I can understand that,' Maggie said. She knew all about powerful men who had decided to trade in their wives for a younger model. She also knew that tampering with mail was illegal and therefore whatever Olivia was going to tell them might not be able to be used in court.

'So, a week ago I found this.' From her leather attaché case she withdrew a glossy estate agent's brochure, the kind they only produce for their top-end properties, and placed it on the table. 'Hampstead Heath. And do you see the price? Three and a quarter million pounds. He can't afford that on his salary.'

'We can assume he is buying it jointly with White though, can't we?' Jimmy asked. 'She must be earning a good whack, national newspaper journalist and all that.'

'Yes she will be,' Asvina agreed, 'but low six-figures at best I would guess, still not enough to buy that sort of place, I wouldn't have thought.'

'That's true,' Maggie said, 'but I suppose just because he has asked for a brochure, it doesn't mean he is planning to buy it. Do you have anything else Olivia?'

'Yes, well...I know... I know it sounds terrible but I've been going through all his pockets and some of his private files and well, I did find some things...'

Maggie smiled. 'Been there, done that.'

Mrs Saddleworth rummaged again in her attaché case and brought out two brown A4 envelopes. She shook out the contents of one of them onto the table.

'Receipts for the type of hotels and restaurants that he never took me to. I assumed he was there with that bitch.'

'Do you mind if I take a look?' asked Maggie softly. She knew from her own experience how hard this must be for her. Sifting through them, she saw there were more than a dozen large bills from some of the most fashionable, and in her opinion, most over-priced establishments in the country, mostly in London but some in the provinces too. Over five grand in total.

'I don't suppose these could have been incurred on government business?' Jimmy asked.

Asvina laughed. 'I don't think so, there'd be a taxpayers' revolt if this got out.'

'And there is this too.' Olivia removed a crumpled letter from a second envelope and passed it to Maggie, who took it and began to read aloud.

'Dear Mr Saddleworth, Thank you for continuing to choose Geneva Swiss Bank for your private banking needs. May we respectively bring to your attention that the annual fee for your secure deposit box service is now overdue. If you have already paid, please ignore this letter, and thank you once again for choosing Geneva Swiss.'

She noticed the date printed on the top left hand side of the letter. 'But this was nearly eight years ago, is that right?'

'Yes, that's right.'

'And I assume your husband had some explanation for it?' Maggie said. 'Otherwise it would have turned up in the disclosures that Asvina showed us earlier.'

'He played it down,' Olivia said. 'He claimed it had been set up on the advice of a financial adviser he was using at the time, who said there would be tax advantages in taking some of his fees for public speaking engagements in cash.'

'Tax avoidance more like,' Jimmy said.

'Exactly. And so he says he had second thoughts about how wise that was for an MP and didn't go through with it.'

'Did you believe him?' Maggie asked.

'No, but the bank won't reveal any information so of course there's no way to check it.'

Clutching at straws, thought Maggie. 'Olivia, is there anything else you can think of that might help us?'

'I don't really know. I suppose maybe he is facing up to the fact that his party is going to lose the election, and at his age, he's never going to become Prime Minister.'

'So you think this is some kind of late mid-life crisis?' Jimmy said. 'That might explain the relationship with Penelope White?' Not surprisingly, he had struck a raw nerve.

'White is a bitch,' Olivia said in an indignant tone. 'All that female empowerment crap she spouts when she's just a cheap tart like all the rest.'

'Gerrard has a history of this then?' Maggie asked softly. 'Affairs, I mean.'

'Oh yes. I'm pretty sure he has had several liaisons over the years, but I've stupidly just put up with it, because I've never thought he would ever leave me, especially not for a woman like her. You know how black and white the Labour party can be. There are large sections of the party that would never forgive him for running off with a Tory.'

A woman like her. The right-wing warrior Penelope White, attractive and at least ten years younger than Olivia Saddleworth. The outspoken scourge of the political-correctness movement, a climate-change denier and the woman who had ran a year-long campaign to destroy Maggie Brooks' reputation. *The most hated woman in Britain*. That was Penelope White's work, and she despised her for it. But perhaps thanks to this case, she might finally get the chance to meet her, where she would tell her to her face what she felt about her. But as far as Gerald Saddleworth was concerned, it seemed obvious that he was at a turning point in his life, and had decided quite clinically to dispose of his old life and start afresh with a new one. New life, new wife. Maggie knew all about that.

'I've no idea what he sees in her, or her in him, and I don't really care,' Olivia was saying, 'but I expect he'll tire of her soon enough, like he seems to have tired of me.' Maggie felt it was said in hope rather than expectation.

'I expect you're right,' she lied. 'But let's see if we can put you in the very best possible position for the future. Our focus is to uncover as much as we can about your husband's finances, and I think we have enough to get started on. Jimmy and I will review it first thing tomorrow and come up with a plan of attack. Rest assured we'll leave no stone uncovered, and we'll be in touch as soon as we have anything.'

It sounded convincing, but with very little to go on, the truth was Maggie had not the faintest idea at all where to start. It wasn't surprising considering she had never done anything like this before.

***

'What do you think to that then Jimmy?' Maggie said, when the meeting was over. 'It didn't seem to take you long to get into the swing of it. Anybody would have thought you'd been doing it for years.'

'Aye, it was great. I really enjoyed it actually. Looking forward to getting stuck into the case and nailing that swine.'

'What about innocent until proven guilty?'

Jimmy shrugged. 'He sounds about as innocent as Stalin in my opinion, but fair enough, I suppose we do need to find some evidence.'

'Ok, well if you're absolutely sure you can cope with working with me, then we'll start tomorrow at 9am sharp, in my offices.'

He looked surprised. 'You've got an office?'

'I do. It's one of these serviced places down near Fleet Street. I rent one tiny room with two desks and it costs three times a month what I pay for my flat. It's called Riverside House, although it's nowhere near the river - you can Google it for the address. Turn up tomorrow - I'll arrange for Elsa to give you a pass card and a user code and password for one of the desktop computers. She's the receptionist for the facility, a very nice Czech girl - you'll like her.'

And she will like you, thought Maggie, what woman wouldn't? She couldn't really afford the office, but Asvina had argued that without it, it would be harder to convince a court that the business was respectable and therefore capable of providing a stable income. One that could pay for a decent home in which to bring up a child. Because that was the ultimate goal. Start off with a modest aim, one afternoon a month, then maybe even go for one or two days a month of supervised access and then take it from there. Of course, any access would be infinitely better than the current agony of legally-enforced estrangement, but a child belonged with his mother, and her life could not resume any semblance of normality until Ollie was again living with her.

'Ready for five minutes on the hearing?' Asvina had returned to the conference room, having momentarily left to escort Olivia Saddleworth to the elevator.

'So, we're on in about six weeks from now - just to remind you, it's Wednesday 19th at 2.00pm, so for goodness sake, make sure that's etched in stone in your calendar. As we agreed, we're going to ask for Ollie to spend just an afternoon with you each month, and also to allow moderate contact via phone, e-mail and text during the month. We've talked about the basics before. You're going to have to show that your life is back on track after your breakdown, that you have a decent place to live and a steady job etc etc. Social services will also talk to Ollie to see how he feels about the situation. I know it seems crazy when he is only six but it's very likely that he is missing his mummy and that will have a great bearing on the case. Remember, the court's only concern is for the welfare of the child, they don't care at all about your feelings or your husband's either for that matter. Got all that so far? I mean, I know you're a lawyer Maggie, but family law is very different to criminal cases in the High Court.'

'Yes,' replied Maggie meekly. 'I understand.'

'Social services will also want to interview you before the hearing of course. They like to do it at home, and they also like to turn up unannounced to get the real picture of what home is like. So I need to ask you this Maggie so please don't take offence - but are you still drinking?'

What she meant was 'are you still drinking yourself into oblivion every night?' She thought about the last few months, where only the comfort of cheap Chardonnay had stopped her going insane. Eight, ten bottles a week, more if she was being honest with herself, but frankly, that's where you end up when you've screwed up big time. You have to drink to blot out the awful cost of that one stupid error of judgement, you wander around your dirty flat talking to yourself, crying, and hoping against hope that today is the day it will all turn out to have been a ghastly dream. But it isn't a dream, it's real, and no matter what you do, you can't erase the horror. *Who could?* All that pain, terror, loss. And all because of you and your stupid ego.

She realised that Asvina had repeated the question.

'No..., I mean yes,... well, I have been drinking too much, I know I have, but I've started to get a grip on it. I know how important it is that I do, really.'

And it was sort-of true, if only in the last forty-eight hours where at last there had been a tiny chink of light at the end of a dark, dark tunnel.

'Ok, Maggie, I believe you, but I can't say this other than bluntly. If social services find you drunk or hung over at home, or if they find your bins full of empty bottles -and believe me, they will look before they even knock on your door- then it's over - maybe for years. So I can't stress enough how important it is that you keep your nose clean in the next six weeks. Understand?'

'I understand.'

Asvina smiled. 'Good. Now, I've had a letter from Miranda Padgett your husband's solicitor, informing us that they intend to contest the case.'

'I knew that,' replied Maggie, remembering the events of the previous day.

'So just to set your mind at ease, there's no need for us to worry about that unduly. It's a pretty routine tactic where access is disputed and there's no likelihood of an amicable settlement. As I said before, the court is only interested in the welfare of the child, not the wishes or needs of either parent. Miranda knows that of course, so their approach will be to try and provide evidence that you are an unsuitable person to be responsible for the care of a six-year-old child. So please Maggie, don't give them any material to work with.' It was said with a smile but her tone was serious.

'I won't Asvina, and I can't thank you enough for all you've done for me.'

They hugged warmly before agreeing that they must meet for lunch in the near future. 'A dry one,' added Maggie with a wry smile.

But now there was just one more thing she had to do that afternoon. It would have been a similar scene on that terrible September day in Notting Hill, approaching two years ago. Specifically, the eleventh day of that month. *Nine-eleven*. Not a co-incidence either, but the date specifically chosen by Alzahrani for her first atrocity because of its symbolism amongst supporters of radical Islam. The greatest day in their history, according to their warped credo. And then almost one year later, and exactly one hundred days after Maggie had conspired to have her freed, she had repeated her ghastly crime at Ollie's school.

Today, just like then, at 3.15pm on a cool early spring day, mothers were beginning to gather around the school gates waiting for their children to come out. Three sturdy concrete bollards had now been erected in front of the school gates, and parents in the main were respecting the one hundred metre no-parking zone that had been established following the bombing, but in every other respect the scene was unchanged. Maggie had arrived a good half an hour earlier so that she could park her anonymous Golf at the first unrestricted spot just where the School Zone hatching began, the location being slightly elevated affording a clear view of the gate. In an attempt at disguise, she had thrown on a grey hooded sweatshirt and wore large designer sunglasses to conceal her features. It was a risk, but on previous occasions the swarms of mothers and child-minders streaming past on the pavement had paid her no attention, and today was no different.

Soon the children began to emerge from the school, at first a trickle and then a steady flow. She scanned the pavement looking for the comfortably rotund figure of Marta, Philip's new au pair - but she was nowhere to be seen. This was not in itself unusual, since Marta's time-keeping was not of the first order, and Maggie pictured her at that moment sprinting down North Street, terrified that she would miss the ten-minute deadline that the school imposed on pick-up time.

But then at last, there he was. Maggie's wonderful, beautiful, precious Ollie. He stopped at the gate, looking right, left and then right again, and then with a broad smile of recognition, ran excitedly to where Angelique Perez was waiting, throwing his arms round her in a loving embrace, before slipping his little hand into hers.

Chapter 11

It was well past eleven when Maggie finally made it into the office, after yet another sleepless night and another futile stupid attempt to drink herself into a pain-numbing stupor. For the first few hours, her brain had played over and over and over again the heartbreaking scene she had witnessed outside the school, only this time their hugs were more intense, their hands gripped tighter, their laughter louder. Later in the night, she became a fly on the wall of a dark depressing interview room, where Ollie was telling a nice social worker that he had a really nice new mummy now and he didn't want his old one back.

'No offence, but you look rough,' Jimmy said, raising an eyebrow. 'Big night, was it? Let me get you a coffee, you look like you could do with one. Elsa showed me how to work the machine, it was the first thing she did when I got here this morning.'

'Thanks Jimmy, I really could do with one.'

'And you can tell me what's wrong if you want to. After all, we've only known each other three days and already we know all of our deepest emotional traumas, so a few more won't hurt. And on that subject, take a look at this.' He passed her his phone.

It was the Facebook page of Astrid Sorenson. *Astrid Sorenson*. The beautiful star of country music, the genre-busting singer who was now famous all over the world. She had uploaded a photograph of herself striking a lascivious pose with her lips pressed against the sculpted cheek of an unidentified man who could easily be mistaken for a male supermodel. They looked like they were in an advert for an upmarket aftershave. The caption below read *New Man, New Band, New Life,* followed by ten smiley emojis.

'I didn't think you were a country music fan,' Maggie said, puzzled as to why he was showing it to her.

'So you've heard of her then? Astrid Sorenson is the woman who ruined my marriage. Correction, the woman who caused me to ruin my own bloody marriage.'

'What, *the* Astrid Sorenson? I'm sorry, I didn't even know you were married,' Maggie said, even more confused.

Jimmy shrugged. 'Aye, I was. Until Astrid bloody Sorenson came into my life. Maybe one day I'll tell you the story.'

That was going to be quite a story, she could tell that already. Captain Jimmy Stewart and the Swedish queen of country music. But she sensed now wasn't the time.

'Don't take this the wrong way,' she said gently, 'but if it hurts so much, why don't you just unfriend her?'

'Aye you're probably right.' It didn't sound as if he meant it. 'So, what about you, do you want to talk about what's eating you? No worries if you don't.'

She hesitated. 'No, not at the moment.' In fact there was nothing she wanted more than to share her agony with this strangely comforting man, a man she had known barely seventy-two hours, but instead she forced a smile. 'No, business first. Let's see if we can make anything of the Saddleworth case, shall we?'

She saw he had spread the meagre pile of documents that Asvina had given them across Maggie's desk. 'So where do we start?' she asked.

'Good question. I've been working on that for the last couple of hours, whilst you were having a lie-in.' He shot her a warm smile. 'Ha-ha, and to be honest we've got bugger all to go on. A fancy estate agent's brochure, a few receipts, an old letter from a Swiss bank. As I said, bugger all...'

'I thought as much.' She tried not to sound too despondent.

'...but,' Jimmy continued, 'so, I went on a cyber warfare course at Sandhurst a few years ago, and they taught me that data only comes alive when you draw a picture of it and attach it to a timeline. It was the only thing I remember from it actually, but it stuck in my mind. And I know it sounds like bullshit, but it actually works. Data visualisation, that's what they call it. Helps you see patterns and connections that you might not otherwise see. So that's what I've been doing. Here, take a look.'

On a sheet of A4 copier paper, he had drawn a table with four columns, headed *'Work'*, *'Relationships'*, *'Associates'* and *'Other Information'*. There was a row for each year going back about thirty years.

'So you see Maggie, although we don't have much hard data at the moment, we already can see some interesting connections. If for example we go back eight years or so to when that private deposit box letter was written, we can see under *'Work'* that he was at that time MP for Sheffield South. And in opposition, not in government. We go back twenty years, and he was an official with the miner's union, and a local government councillor.'

'That's interesting,' Maggie said. 'And I see you've not got anything much earlier than that, but we know he was at Oxford with Philip and Hugo, and with Julian Priest too. A right little gang of pound-shop revolutionaries they were by all accounts. That's when Philip and his brother started up their *Action for Palestine* pressure group, with our much-loved Prime Minister Julian Priest.'

Jimmy smiled. 'I didn't know that, I'll stick that on the chart right now. And your husband is still heavily involved with the group, isn't he?'

'That's right,' Maggie said. 'He is. His brother Hugo too, at least he was before he got sent down. But Gerrard Saddleworth was never really into it all, as far as I know. He likes to cultivate the image of being solid working-class, warm beer and pigeon racing and all that. So he's always tried to distance himself from metropolitan liberals like Priest and his mates.'

'Mates like your Philip.'

'Exactly. Pretentious arseholes like my ex.'

Jimmy evidently decided against making a comment. Instead he said, 'Well, the web's stuffed with info about guys in the public eye like Saddleworth so it should be a doddle to get this chart fattened out.'

Maggie laughed. 'I'm not so sure about that, but at least it gives us something to go at. Anything else you've been doing this morning, or have you spent all the time chatting up Elsa?'

'Being chatted up more like. She's...'

They were interrupted by Elsa herself poking her head around the door.

'Do you want coffee Jimmy? I put fresh brew in machine just one minute ago. Just for you.'

Maggie was amused to see his face reddening. 'What?' he said distractedly. 'Oh, yes that would be great.'

'I go get it now. Oh, and your face, it is very strange colour,' she said, closing the door behind her.

'She's in love with you already,' Maggie teased, 'and such a pretty girl too.'

'I don't think so. I mean, the love bit, not that she's not pretty.'

Elsa returned a few minutes later with the coffee. Maggie was pleased to see she had brought her one too. 'Believe me, I need this Jimmy. My brain hurts.'

'Mine's ok actually. I suppose it's because it's so much younger than yours.'

'Cheek. I'm only thirty-nine I'll have you know.'

He raised an eyebrow but made no comment.

'Aye, well I'm going to do a bit of rooting around the net,' he said. 'See what I can dig out on Gerrard Saddleworth, then maybe we could have a wee bit of a brainstorm, see what else we can come up with.'

She gave him a thumbs-up. 'That's sounds like a plan, but if you don't mind, I'm going to have to pop out for ten minutes to get several packs of ibuprofen, because my brain is storming but not in a good way. So you carry on and I expect an answer when I get back. And no flirting with Elsa, ok?'

He snapped his heels together and made a smart salute. 'Yes ma'am.'

**

The problem was, where to start? You couldn't just Google *'Gerrard Saddleworth bank accounts'*, could you? Well actually, you could, and he did, with predictable results. Plenty of results about what Saddleworth's party politics would mean for your life savings, and on the administration's plans to create a national business investment bank, and a report about an obscure question he had asked in the House of Commons about foreign ownership of UK-registered financial institutions. But nothing about his personal financial affairs. That was no more than Jimmy expected.

So where to next? Maybe it would be worth looking to see if he could find out anything related to these fancy restaurant bills. At least they were something tangible. Some place called *The Bull* in Southwark, and another place up in Gloucester, they seemed to be amongst his favourites. Searches for *'Gerrard Saddleworth The Bull Southwark '*and *'Gerrard Saddleworth Seven Cathedral Close Gloucester'* failed at first glance to bring up anything of significance, but as he scrolled further down the Google results, an item buried away on page eight caught his eye. The *Gloucester Journal* reported that the government minister Gerrard Saddleworth had visited GCHQ in nearby Cheltenham, meeting with the Director and several members of staff. The purpose of the visit was not disclosed. Jimmy checked the date - 14th October. Quickly, he looked down the list of receipts he had created earlier and yes, Saddleworth had dined at Seven Cathedral Close that evening. So that perhaps explained why he was in Gloucester, but would you really then entertain your colleagues - Jimmy was working on the initial presumption that the dinner was work-related- in such lavish fashion? Normal protocol would surely dictate a more modest venue, especially since it would be the Home Office expense budget that would be footing the bill.

Not bad for a first go, he thought, but it didn't help to identify who Saddleworth had dined with that evening. So he ran the searches again, but this time selected 'Images' instead of 'All' and included '14th October' in the search string. A micro second later, the screen was filled with a mosaic of photographs of the town's cathedral and its surroundings. Damn - too specific, maybe just try *'Gerrard Saddleworth Gloucester'*. Better - this time the mosaic was made up mainly of faces, pleasingly, some of the current Home Secretary, although surprisingly it appeared the world was not short of men with that name. Jimmy scrolled down, as the search engine relentlessly filled the screen with images, outpacing his gentle movement of the mouse, but there were none that captured that visit to the expensive restaurant on that evening.

It had been a long shot of course and he was disappointed but not really surprised by the outcome. But then something struck him, something he should have thought about from the start. The receipts showed that he had dined at the restaurant on four occasions. He obviously loved it, that was clear. But why should it be assumed that *he* always paid the bill?

Jimmy punched in *'Seven Cathedral Close October Saddleworth'*. No specific day this time, just the month.

Once again, the screen filled with images, but this time dominated by exterior and interior shots of the upmarket restaurant, many featuring diners appearing to enjoy themselves despite the extravagantly-priced menu.

And then, astonishingly, unexpectedly, there it was. Gerrard Saddleworth, looking serious with a glass of red wine raised to his lips. Beside him, a good-looking man of about fifty, formally dressed in an expensive-looking shirt and matching tie, holding up his glass for a young waiter to fill. Next to him, a younger man, south Asian, also well-dressed. From his expression it appeared that it was he who was leading the conversation at that moment. Opposite them, recognised from the photograph that accompanied her by-line, sat Penelope White of the *Chronicle*, engrossed in her mobile phone. Next to Penelope, a man with his back to the camera who Jimmy thought he vaguely recognised. He clicked on the image, revealing it had originally been uploaded to Facebook by someone called Amber Smith; the powerful Google web-crawlers linked to Facebook's clever automatic facial recognition technology had had no trouble linking Saddleworth's features to Jimmy's search. One more click, and he was on Amber's Facebook page and looking at her timeline. It always amazed him why people were so naive when it came to their social media privacy, but in this case he gave thanks. She was evidently a party girl, her timeline dominated by selfies of her having a good time. A pissed Amber with a gaggle of equally-pissed friends. A skimpily-dressed Amber snogging some man or other. A sunburnt Amber lifting her top to show off her small white breasts. Pure class.

It didn't take him long to find the picture he was looking for. Sure enough, it had been uploaded on 20th October, which turned out to be Amber's thirtieth birthday, explaining why she was at the upmarket establishment. The text with the picture read *'Out with ALL the girls for my 30th at this FAB place. A bit pissed, of course :-). This guy from the government is here, Samantha thinks he's called Julian Saddleworth and he's the chancellor or something, who knows xxxxxxxxx.'*

'Oh yes!' he bellowed to the empty office, 'oh yes, oh yes, oh yes!'

***

'So I've managed to make a wee bit of progress. Don't know how you're feeling but maybe you could come and take a look?'

Maggie had returned nursing a large Americano which she had strengthened with a double espresso shot. Simultaneously the ibuprofens were beginning to take effect and she was already thinking more clearly.

'Yes sure Jimmy. What have you got?'

'Well whilst you were out- for ages by the way, where did you get to?'

She raised her coffee cup and gave a sheepish grin. 'Got waylaid by Starbucks I'm afraid.'

'Aye right, well as I said, whilst you were out, I came up with what I can modestly describe as a mind-blowingly brilliant thought.'

He folded his arms, leaned back in his chair and said nothing.

She smiled. 'Well alright then, tell me.'

'Ok, so I took a look at a couple of these restaurant bills that Olivia discovered. So there were a couple of eight hundred quid- plus bills at Seven Cathedral Close - that's Paul Waterson's Michelin-starred joint in Gloucester, of all places. Then there's seven hundred quid at The Bull in Southwark - that's one of these pretentious bistros, claim they serve plain hearty food but it's fifteen quid for the soup and forty quid for a main course.'

'How do you know about these places? You move in these circles, do you?'

'Interweb. But the thing is, we're living in the social media age, worst luck, and no-one goes to a hundred-quid a head restaurant without posting at least a dozen photographs on their Facebook or Instagram. Not my generation at least,' he said, smiling.

'Shut up. I told you I'm only thirty-nine.'

'I thought you said thirty-eight. Anyway I rest my case, m'lady. But seriously, if you see someone in the public eye, like Saddleworth, it's ninety-nine percent certain you're going to try to get a selfie or at least a photo so you can say 'guess who's also here at the *very* expensive Seven Cathedral Close tonight'. So I reckoned with an hour or so online, there was a reasonable chance I might be able to find out who he was dining with at these restaurants.'

'And...?'

He pointed at the screen.

'And I found this. Look, these are some folks who were sharing a fancy dinner with Saddleworth in Gloucester. And the interesting thing was, it was the second night in a row he had eaten there, although it looks like someone else picked up the tab on this occasion. That looks like Penelope White on her phone, and if I'm not mistaken Maggie, that's your husband, isn't it, with his back to us? But I don't recognize any of the others, do you?'

Maggie stared at the photograph on the screen, struggling to make sense of it. For if Jimmy didn't recognise the other diners, Maggie did. *All of them.*

Adam Cameron, Queen's Counsel and superstar prosecutor. Penelope White of the *Chronicle* and next to her, Philip Brooks.

But taking centre stage, clearly the star attraction judging by the way the others were apparently hanging on his every word, was Dr Tariq Khan, world expert in automatic facial recognition technology. The question was, why were they meeting only a few weeks before the start of the Alzahrani trial. Indeed, why were they meeting at all?

Chapter 12

For a moment she sat in stunned silence, rendered speechless by what Jimmy had just uncovered. Then finally she spoke.

'Cameron said he had never met Tariq Khan. He said he'd never met him. Christ, he lied to the judge. I was there, in that anti-room, and he lied. And Saddleworth and my husband, what the hell were they doing there? This is crazy, I just don't understand it.'

Jimmy voiced what she was already thinking. 'Do you think it might have something to do with your trial? '

'Khan, Cameron and Saddleworth in the same room? For goodness sake, what else could it be?'

She grabbed for her phone and swiped to her husband's number. It rang a few times before going through to voicemail. That didn't surprise her because now he never took her calls or answered her messages. It was as if for him she no longer existed.

'Philip, it's Maggie. You need to call me now'. Frustrated, she slammed the phone down on the desk.

'He's a pig. Look, I'm going to send him that photograph and ask for an explanation, that should make him call me back.' She could feel the anger rising up inside her like an erupting volcano.

Jimmy struck a cautious note. 'Perhaps we should just take a rain check on that. Don't you think we need to think this through a bit, try and figure out what it all means? Then we can decide what we should do. Cool heads and all that.'

Her brain was swirling as she tried desperately to make some sense of it all. What the hell was Philip doing there and why was Gerrard Saddleworth there, what did it all mean? It had to be something to do with the trial, didn't it? Perhaps Khan had made his concerns known to his GCHQ bosses and it had been escalated all the way up to the Home Secretary. Maybe they were trying to persuade him to just let it go, buttering him up with fancy meals and flattering him with a meeting with a top government minister. But that still didn't explain why Philip was there. None of it made sense.

'What?... sorry Jimmy, I was just thinking about the whole crazy thing. Yes, I suppose you're right, we should take a rain check. To be honest, I've no idea what...'

They were interrupted by the opening riff of Nirvana's *Smells Like Teen Spirit* blasting from his phone.

'Sorry, need to take this Maggie. It's my brother Frank.'

He didn't have to switch to speakerphone for Maggie to follow the conversation.

'Well hello wee brother, how's it going?' boomed the voice at the other end of the line. *'Long time no see. I hear you're not seeing the Swedish princess any more. Not surprised at that really, she was a right piece of work, best out of that one pal, if you want my opinion. Oh, and I heard about you getting a job, can't believe it. You, back on civvy street. Actually, I googled your new boss this morning. Now that Maggie Brooks, she looks one fit bird. Bit old for you maybe, but still in good nick, by the looks of it...'*

'Frank, Frank,' he shouted, desperately trying to stem the flow, his face turning crimson. 'Maggie is with me right now actually. And it's Miss Bainbridge now. Maggie Bainbridge.'

'Aw great,' replied the voice, seemingly unperturbed. *'Single is she? That's brilliant, I'm really looking forward to meeting her. So anyway I'm fine for tonight - about half-five in my Southwark office, and you're buying, right? See you later.'*

'That was my brother Frank,' Jimmy said, somewhat unnecessarily. 'Detective Inspector Frank Stewart. I'm really sorry about all that, he's a bugger.'

'Don't worry about it. Actually, he seems quite funny.' *One fit bird.* Less than poetic perhaps, but right now she would take that.

'A complete nutcase. But yeah, a good copper, so he tells me himself. Actually Maggie, that's why I texted him earlier. I hope you don't mind but I thought we might try and pick his brains about how you go about doing an investigation, you know, given that we... '

She finished his sentence for him.

'...given that we don't really know what we're doing?'

'We don't, do we? It's just that you... we, we are pretty new to this game...' He stopped abruptly, as if conscious of how easily he could cause offence. But he needn't have worried.

'No, to tell you the truth Jimmy, I *haven't* got any idea what I'm doing. I just kind of hoped if we followed our noses something would turn up. But it would be great if your brother was able to steer us in the right direction. And especially now that that photograph has turned up. So where is the meeting? His Southwark office did he say?'

'His little joke. He means the Old King's Head. It's a pub, just round the corner from The Bull actually. He's in there more than he's in the office. All strictly in the line of duty of course, that's what he'll tell you. I'm sure he'll be able to help us. I mean this thing with Cameron and Khan and the rest, it looks serious. It should be police business.'

***

It was only just past six o'clock, but the Old King's Head was packed to capacity, Thursday evidently being a popular night for after-office booze-ups. Jimmy had to shout to make himself heard above a cacophony of conversation and laughter as they threaded their way towards the bar.

'He'll be sitting on a bar stool and onto his second or third one now if it goes to form.'

'What?'

'Never mind,' he mouthed, shaking his head and taking her hand to drag her the last few steps to the bar.

She recognised him immediately, Jimmy's description of him as an older, shorter and fatter version of himself being broadly accurate, although he wasn't much shorter, she thought, five foot-ten at least, and she would have said strong and powerful rather than fat. Good looking too, like his brother, and probably around her own age. His pint stood on the bar, temporarily parked whilst he finished off a jumbo-sized sausage roll. Flakes of pastry were strewn on the floor beneath him and several surrounded his mouth. He wiped his face with his shirt sleeve as he saw them approach, then extended his hand. 'Hello wee brother. Looking good pal.'

'Wish I could say the same for you Frank. I see you've not gone vegan yet. This is Maggie Bainbridge, my new boss.'

'Good to meet you Maggie,' he roared, 'but c'mon, let's wander off to the pool room so we can hear ourselves think. There's a wee bar in there so we'll be fine.'

He swilled the last of his beer and indicated a door in the far corner of the bar. 'Be with you in a minute, just need a quick wee-wee. Get us another pint of Doom Bar Jimmy, there's a good boy.'

They settled in at a corner table in the dimly-lit room. 'He's a model of sophistication, my brother,' Jimmy said, then evidently remembering that morning's overheard conversation, 'but of course you know that already.'

'He's nice, I can tell that already.' More than nice, she thought. Just like you.

'My mate Pete Burnside from Paddington Green ran your attempted murder investigation,' Frank said on his return. 'Just as well for you it never went to trial because it would have been a damn lynch mob with all the publicity surrounding the case at the time. And for what it's worth, I never thought for a minute that you tried to kill your boy, and neither did DI Burnside for that matter. It was just our lily-livered arse-licking bosses bowing to the hysteria of the press, a bloody modern day witch-hunt.'

More than a year later, every second of that terrible terrible day was imprinted in her mind in vivid technicolor, as if it had only happened yesterday. And yet still she was unable to answer the critical question - had she or had she not, in her hopelessness and desolation, in her utter despair and in her blind hatred of Philip, really tried to kill herself and Ollie? Eventually the CPS had decided the evidence was inconclusive; they could not say for certain -and nor could she. But Camden Council Social Services did not need conclusive evidence. They could work on the balance of probability, and on the balance of probability they had concluded that Maggie Brooks was a danger to her son.

'Thank you,' she said quietly. 'It was a very difficult time.'

'Aye, sorry, I didn't mean to bring back bad memories. Shouldn't have said anything. Anyway, what was it you two wanted to talk to me about?'

'So Frank,' Jimmy began, 'what it is, is that Maggie and me need your help and advice on something that's come up on the big divorce case we're working on. The husband is Gerrard Saddleworth...'

'What, the Home Secretary?'

'The same. His wife Olivia is convinced that he hasn't been exactly truthful about his finances. She thinks he's got a wad of cash salted away somewhere, and we've been tasked by her solicitor Asvina Rani to see what we can find out.'

'Well this wife must be bloody sure about that wad of cash if she's using Rani, 'cos she doesn't come cheap, at least that's what I've read about her.'

Maggie laughed. 'You're right there, but she gets results.'

'Well I'm sure she does,' Frank said, 'but you know folks, I don't want to burst your bubble or anything, but the Met doesn't really do divorce cases, no matter who it is. But you might as well tell me what you've got, you know, like evidence and that.'

'We've not really got much bruv. A letter from about eight years ago suggesting he might have had a secret bank deposit box, a few mega bills from top restaurants, and an estate agent's brochure for a fancy pad in Wimbledon.'

'That's all?'

'I know it's not much, but it's all we've got. But actually, that's not really what we want to talk to you about. There's something else, not connected to our divorce case. Something we think might be a whole lot bigger than that.'

He passed his phone over to his brother. 'We came across this photograph on the net and we're not really sure where to go next.'

Frank took a moment to scrutinise it.

'I recognise Gerrard Saddleworth of course, the others I don't. Who are they?'

'The woman is Penelope White,' Maggie said. 'She's a columnist with the *Chronicle*...'

'Ah, well I'm strictly a *Sun* man myself, so I wouldn't know her,' Frank said.

'... and she also happens to be the woman Saddleworth is leaving his wife for. That man there is Adam Cameron. He's a barrister. He was my opponent in the Alzahrani trial. And the man with his back to the camera is my husband. He's quite well known as a human rights lawyer.'

Frank frowned. 'No, sorry, never heard of him.'

She laughed. 'That would really piss him off.'

'I don't like lawyers.' Too late, he remembered Maggie's profession. '...well, as a general rule, that is.'

He groped for a quick change of subject. 'Anyway, who's that other guy, the Asian bloke?'

'That's Dr Tariq Khan,' Maggie said. 'He's a government technology expert, and it was his unofficial intervention that caused the trial to collapse.'

Frank's eyes narrowed. 'Oh aye, I remember reading about that. In the Sun, as it happens. He wrote some report that said the facial recognition evidence was a pile of poo, didn't he? But forgive me for saying, but I don't really know where you're going with this.'

'Adam Cameron told the judge at the Alzahrani trial that he had never met this Dr Khan. This picture proves he was lying.'

He gave a low whistle. 'What, and you smell a conspiracy? This does sound a bit out of the ordinary, I must admit. So when exactly was this picture taken?'

'Just a couple of weeks before the start of the trial,' Maggie said.

'Whoa! And answer me this, what's your husband got to do with all of this?'

'We don't know yet, but he does know Saddleworth and Julian Priest from way back. They were all at Oxford together, involved in every fashionable cause. It was all typical student politics except some of them never grew out of it. But as for the reason for this dinner, I've asked him to explain, but we're not exactly on speaking terms at the moment. We're getting divorced you see.'

'Aye, well I'm sorry to hear that,' Frank said sympathetically. 'But you know, there's probably nothing in it. For a start, if you were going to be whipping up a big nasty plot of some kind, would you do it in full view of the public at some fancy restaurant? No, I don't think so. What makes you think this one is suspicious?'

Jimmy was the first to answer. 'As Maggie said, Adam Cameron told the judge at the trial that he had never met Dr Khan. This picture proves he was lying.'

'Aye, but come on. The prosecution getting together, getting their ducks all lined up, that's not so unusual, is it?'

'Cameron lied to the judge,' Jimmy said, spelling it out. 'In a terrorist trial. Or are you saying that's not unusual either? And what the hell is a bloody journalist doing there?'

'That's a fair point wee Jimmy. Well, we've probably kicked off investigations on a lot less, but this is the Home Secretary. That's potential dynamite, and we'd need a lot more than you've got to persuade my gaffers to take this one up, if that's what you are asking me to do.'

'We didn't really have a plan,' Maggie said uncertainly. 'We were really only looking for some advice. So have you any suggestions what else we could do?'

'Just let me get another round in first and I'll think about it on the way to the bar. Large Chardonnay again Maggie and another Doom Bar for you, wee brother? And three sausage rolls?'

'I shouldn't,' she replied, then, 'oh why not, yes to both please Frank. I'm actually starving.'

'He's buying you dinner already,' Jimmy said, grinning. 'I think you're in there.'

'Shut up, will you.' But just for a moment she thought how nice it would be to go out on a proper dinner date again. She was still thinking about it when Frank returned with a tray and set the drinks and napkin-wrapped sausage rolls on the table.

'Right, where were we.' He picked up the nearest sausage

roll and took a large bite. 'Excuse me talking with my mouth full. Yeah, so it's stating the bleeding obvious that the meeting was either innocent or it wasn't.'

Jimmy laughed. 'Aye, bleeding obvious.'

Frank spoke through a mouthful of pastry. 'So what you will find in my experience is that if it was innocent, if you talk to any of the participants, they're ninety percent certain to tell you quite straightforwardly what it was about. Nothing to hide so might as well tell the truth.'

'Makes sense,' Maggie agreed.

'But if there was something dodgy going on, then it's very different. Generally they won't answer or they'll tell you some crap, but it's what happens afterwards that's often the most interesting. Because no matter how cool they think they are, they always get spooked when people start questioning what it was all about. There'll be panic phone calls, attempts to get stories straight, you might find that someone breaks ranks and won't go along with the collective plan, all sorts of shit hitting the fan. That's when all the good stuff starts to come out. Then when you get the mobile phone records it all starts to unravel.'

Maggie nodded. 'Yes, I get that.'

'So, of course you guys could do this in your role, as what is it...?

'Investigation services,' Jimmy said. 'Investigation services to the legal profession.'

'Aye, whatever. However, no offence, but it would be a lot more effective if they got a wee call from the police.'

'What, are you saying you could help us with this Frank?' Maggie asked, surprised.

'It would be a lot more successful if you did,' Jimmy said. 'I know you can be very scary when you want to be.'

'Thanks, I'll take that as a compliment, but we can't have coppers harassing innocent citizens willy-nilly, especially if they are government ministers, *Chronicle* journalists and big-time QCs. But look, I'm intrigued with all of this so I'll have a word with my gaffer, see what she thinks. I'm not promising anything mind you, but she's not that keen on lawyers and politicians and things are a bit quiet at the moment, so you never know.'

Frank picked up his pint and drained the last dregs.

'Oh, and one other thing I just thought about. Have you got a copy of that report you were talking about, you know, the Khan one?'

'Yes, I've got one,' Maggie replied.

'Well you see, one of the wee jobs I'm working on at the moment is connected to AFR, you know the facial recognition stuff. It's a big thing at the moment, with all the worries about civil liberties and everything, and I've got a wee lassie working with me who's a bit of an expert on the subject. Obviously not to the level of your Dr Khan, but I think she does know her business. Actually, she's a bit of an expert on just about everything technical.'

Jimmy looked puzzled. 'Where are you going with this Frank?'

'Not sure at the moment Jimmy, not sure. There's just a wee thought going around in the back of my head and well, I'd just like the lassie Eleanor to take a look, that's all.'

'We'd be so grateful for your help Frank,' Maggie said. 'You know, anything you can do would be fantastic.'

'Aye, no bother. Anyway, must get on now, loads of bad guys to catch. I just hope I was some help to you. Oh, and Maggie, I better have your phone number, in case anything comes up.'

It was an innocent request, but she was still surprised by the unexpected flutter in her stomach. But then it had been a long time since anyone had asked for it.

Chapter 13

Department 12B of the Metropolitan Police occupied a dank and musty room stuck at the end of a dank and musty corridor of Atlee House, a scruffy sixties office block that had started life as an outpost of the Department of Health and Social Security. Eventually deemed too decrepit for even the careworn job-centre automatons, it had passed through a succession of ever more obscure government departments before being reluctantly adopted by the Met. This was the office that DI Frank Stewart now called home.

'Morning ma'am.' He slouched in, crumbs from a recently-despatched cheese croissant still visible on his chin, 'big day ahead, eh?'

This was his habitual greeting to his boss. Generally speaking, there were no big days to look forward to in Department 12B, although today, to be fair, was looking a bit more promising than most.

'Morning Frank,' she said brightly, 'Yes, big day ahead indeed. Get yourself a coffee and we'll go through what you've got on at the moment. Joy of joys, I've got my monthly meeting with the Chief Super to look forward to this afternoon and I need to get up to speed with what's occurring.'

DCI Jill Smart just about managed to suppress the groan. It had never been on her career plan to end up in this godforsaken department, in fact it would never be on anyone's career plan, but for Jill, it had been a convenient fast-track to the DCI rank that she had long coveted and deserved, and so she had gritted her teeth and accepted the post when Chief Superintendant Wilkes had offered it. Not that she had much choice, but she was determined to make the best of it. Give it a year or so, make a reasonable fist of it, move swiftly on, that was the master plan.

The role of the department was fuzzy at best, but in essence it was the dumping ground for cases that couldn't quite find a home with more conventional investigating teams - cold cases, internal corruption enquiries, the early stages of suspected fraud and suchlike. It was also the dumping ground for detectives who had been chucked out of more conventional investigating teams, which is why Frank Stewart had ended up on the team.

He returned to her desk clutching a tepid white coffee from the ancient vending machine and a Mars Bar from the same source.

She grinned at him. 'Breakfast?'

'No, done that one already. Call this elevenses. I love a Mars Bar, you know that, can't beat them. You should try one sometime yourself. You're too skinny ma'am, no offence.'

'None taken.' He was always teasing her about her fanatical dedication to her daily gym sessions, she responding with interest about his terrible diet. She liked Frank, considering him one of the only jewels amongst the motley collection of losers, loners and has-beens that she had inherited with Department 12B. 'And by the way, it's nowhere near eleven o'clock by my watch. Anyway, can you just give me an update on what you've been working on.'

'Aye, well it's only really been that corruption enquiry down in Brixton, but it's going well, 'cos I'm pretty sure now that DS is on the take. You remember I said that I got some CCTV footage of him associating with known drug-dealers on his patch? So that caused me to mount a wee one-man surveillance operation, and a couple of days ago I got him on my iPhone just as a wee brown envelope was being handed over. He was wearing a hoodie and shades but my new best pal Eleanor says that's not going to be a problem because some new facial recognition software she's got a hold of will still nail him. A good capture, that's what she said my photograph is. Better than DNA, that's what wee Eleanor says.'

'Sorry Frank, who is this Eleanor of whom you speak so highly?'

'Haven't I mentioned her before ma'am?' He knew he hadn't. Frank had learnt to keep these things quiet, otherwise the other disreputable rejects who clogged up Department 12B would be muscling in, getting her to take a look at their half-arsed cases too. He wanted to keep this highly-valuable resource all to himself.

'Eleanor Campbell, she's fairly new to the Forensic lot. An automatic facial recognition specialist amongst other things. She's telling me that the technology around automatic facial recognition is just advancing so quickly, and soon every force in the country will need to have an expert on their team. The Met were one of the first to get one.'

'That's great Frank, and great timing for my meeting with the Chief Super.'

'Aye, well boss, I'm glad it's all worked out quite well. We can probably hand it over to the regular anti-corruption squad next week.' Since that had gone quite well, he decided to strike whilst the iron was hot.

'So boss, there's a new one come to my attention that might be worth a look. I need to declare an interest, it's come to me from my wee brother Jimmy, but nonetheless I think it might be our sort of case. And before you say anything, I know our investigations are supposed to come by referral from other departments, but well, this one's a wee bit different... anyway, see what you think.'

He showed her the photograph on his phone and explained who was present at the dinner. Jill seemed intrigued.

'And you think this might be connected to the Alzahrani case? But that's still a live enquiry, isn't it? The suspect is still at large.'

'Aye, more than a year now and still not a sniff of her ma'am. I expect she's fled the country by now. But this is actually to do with the trial itself, because that picture was taken just before it started and of course it might be nothing except *that* guy...' He pointed at the photograph. '...Adam Cameron, said in front of the judge, that he'd never met *that* guy, Dr Tariq Khan.'

Smart furled her brow. 'Ok I can see what you're getting at, but shouldn't this go straight to our Alzahrani team?'

He adopted his favoured sarcastic tone. 'What, you mean to the fat-arsed detecting genius that is DCI Colin Barker? Oh aye, I think that would work.'

She laughed. 'Oh yes, I'd forgotten, he was the DCI that you punched, wasn't he?'

'All in the line of duty ma'am. He was and still is a complete moron and had it coming to him. The way I look at it, it was sorely needed to raise the morale of the rank-and-file. I took one for the team, that's all.'

And there was quite a few of his peers and senior officers too that rejoiced in the obnoxious Barker getting his face smashed in. In actual fact, it was only that unspoken support amongst the senior ranks that had prevented Frank Stewart being sacked on the spot. Instead, he was ordered to take three months' sick leave due to 'stress', his HR file was quietly marked as 'unsuitable for a leadership role', and then he was shunted off to Atlee House.

'And he got his reward by being given the Hampstead bombing investigation. Completely typical of the Met, promoted to your level of incompetence. Present company excepted ma'am,' he added hurriedly. 'So I know it obviously will have to go to Barker eventually, but I'd like to do a few hours on it first, follow up a couple of hunches, and see where they lead. I think this might be a good one for the department ma'am.' *And for you and your career too, might even hasten your escape.* He knew how to push her buttons.

She smiled. 'Well ok Frank, you can give it a few hours but I don't want to open up a new case at this point.'

'Too much paperwork, eh ma'am?'

'Exactly Frank, the bane of my life. So just try and lose the hours somewhere, will you?'

'Yes ma'am, will do.'

He found Eleanor Campbell skulking in the semi-dark just behind the coffee machine, her phone wedged between ear and shoulder, a flimsy plastic cup of indeterminate pale brown liquid in each hand.

'Lloyd, frig's sake Lloyd...Lloyd, look I've told you about a thousand times...No Lloyd, you must be frigging joking...Look Lloyd, you know I can't discuss this now...'? The conversation had evidently ended abruptly, as she let out a loud four-letter explicative before placing the cups on the ground to enable her to retrieve her phone.

'Problems?' He hoped he had succeeded in making it sound diplomatic.

She held up her hands in an apologetic gesture.

'That was Lloyd. He's my sort-of boyfriend.'

Frank decided to take the matter no further, although there was a tinge of disappointment about the discovery of this sort-of man in her life. He didn't know why that should be, other than the fact that he had of late developed a soft spot for the kooky forensic scientist. Not in any sort of romantic way, definitely not, but then to his dismay he realised what it was. *Fatherly concern.* Not good, since he doubted if he was much more than ten years her elder.

'Lloyd eh? Aye well, I hope it all works out,' was the best he could come up with. 'Anyway Eleanor, I've got this report that's come into my possession which is right in your field. Guy called Dr Tariq Khan wrote it, you might have heard of him?'

'Yes, I have. He like spoke at a symposium I was at a few months ago. Smart dude.'

'Oh good. So I was wondering, could you take a look at the report, and let me know what you think about it? Just a general opinion will do, I don't need too much detail at this stage. I'll email it to you when I get back to my desk.'

'Sure Frank. Do you have a case number I can book my time to?'

He laughed. 'Bloody bureaucracy. I forgot you guys can't even wipe your backsides without a case number.'

'Not allowed Frank, the boss goes like mental.'

'All right I'll get you it, it's on my phone. It shouldn't need more than a few hours of your time I wouldn't think.'

Lose the hours somewhere, that's what Jill Smart had said. That wasn't going to be a problem.

'Here it is Eleanor, M-P-4-7-3-9-4'. He figured the Alzahrani case could absorb a few more hours, after all they had already spent over a million quid and still not a sniff of her since she vanished into thin air. Not that it was a great surprise with an idiot like Colin Barker in charge.

'Ok thanks Frank, I should be able to take a look at it later today,' she replied, as they wandered back to the office.

It wasn't just the back room teams who were under the thumb of the bureaucrats and bean-counters. It had extended to the front-line officers too, under the catch-all banner of 'safeguarding.' So as he booted up the ancient mainframe user interface of the Police National Computer system, Frank too was obliged to enter a case number before beginning his search. No problem, it would be a pleasure to stick a few more hours on Barker's budget. This was one thing Maggie and Jimmy couldn't do, looking into citizens' criminal records. And there was another thing they couldn't do either. More recently, and unbeknown to most of the population, the police had gained access to certain MI5 databases, so that intelligence on 'persons of interest' could be shared between the police and the spooks. Most of the persons on these databases had committed no crime, and their very existence occupied a murky legal no-man's-land between protecting the public from harm and protecting their civil liberties. Especially now since version two-point-naught of that software included facial recognition search. It wasn't just the *Guardian* that would go mental if that ever got out into the open.

But unfortunately, Frank couldn't get access either, not at this point in time at least. It was good that Britain still paid some regard to civil liberties and human rights and all that stuff, of course he agreed that, but it could really slow things down when you were working on an investigation. To get access to the MI5 databases, you needed the say-so of a senior officer, DCI rank as a minimum, and they had to get an official form signed by their boss too. Fair enough, but it really was a pain in the bum. Especially in this case, since it was public knowledge that Gerrard Saddleworth had a history of student activism. It was odds-on therefore that he would have come to the attention of MI5 at some point in the past, so that would be worth looking at. And senior GCHQ staff like Khan were given an MI5 file as a matter of routine, even if there was nothing of interest to put in it. But no matter, he would ask Jill later and maybe she would take a quick look for him, off the record.

The PNC was a reasonable place to start in the meantime. After eighteen years in the force, Frank knew that success in a case came from putting in the hours, slogging through reams of forensic data, trying to make sense of conflicting witness statements, looking for that little overlooked nugget of information that tied it all together. That was his experience, and he had no reason to expect this one to be any different. Which is why it was all the more surprising that just twenty minutes after he had sat down in front of his computer, he was feeling like he'd just bagged a hole-in-one at St Andrews in the Open.

He had started with Gerrard Saddleworth and Penelope White, but had drawn a blank. Squeaky-clean records as far as the police were concerned. He wasn't too worried about that, because the juicy stuff on Saddleworth, if there was any, would most likely turn up on the wee MI5 database.

But then five minutes into his search came the remarkable discovery that Dr Tariq Khan had a criminal record, and one serious enough that he would surely go to extraordinary lengths to keep it buried deep in the past. This was a hell of a lot more serious than a parking ticket. No, it was absolute dynamite.

Then just a few minutes later, bang, another one. Unbelievably, Adam Cameron had a drugs bust. Thirty-odd years ago, when he was up at Oxford. Just a caution for possession, but he had been damn lucky it hadn't derailed his career. Not something to boast about in his profession.

And then he had got the call from Eleanor, with her initial verdict on the Khan report. She sounded hesitant.

'Frank, I've had like a couple of read-throughs and I have to admit I don't quite know what to make of it.'

'What do you mean?'

'Well, I need to qualify this you'll understand, because he's one experienced dude and I've not got half the knowledge that he's got, but well, it's like a bit weird. What I mean is the

conclusion and summary is black and white, he says that there's an eighty-six percent chance that the identification by that dashcam is wrong. That's as close to a hundred percent certain as you can be in scientific terms.'

'So what's the problem?'

'It's the workings. I mean the scientific evidence he uses earlier in the report to reach his conclusion. You see, to me, and as I said, I'm nowheres-ville compared to him, but to me, it doesn't stack up. Without getting technical or anything...'

'Aye, please don't,' he grimaced, 'or I'll get lost.'

'Don't worry, I'll keep it simple - well simple-ish. So facial recognition systems work by recording the geometry of the face, how far apart your eyes are, the distance between the tip of your nose and your mouth, that sort of thing. These are called facial landmarks, and the technology uses around seventy of them. These are unique to each face and once you have them it's actually simples-ville to do matching searches on a database. Too simple, some might say, but that's another story. The other thing is, and this is either like really scary or really powerful depending on which way you look at it, you don't need all the seventy landmarks to be able to do an accurate match. And Frank, it's this feature that your case depends on, isn't it? The terrorist's face was partially covered by sunglasses and a headscarf, but the photograph captured enough of these landmarks to allow a match. That's how she was caught, I think.'

'Ok.' He spoke slowly. 'I think I understand this. Carry on.'

'Right, so what the Khan dude is saying in simple terms is that the plumber's dashcam photograph didn't capture enough facial landmarks to allow a reliable match. He dresses it up in some highly technical words that I don't understand, but that's the essence of it.'

'But I'm getting the sense that you don't agree.'

'Correct, I don't. I haven't seen the actual photograph, but I would have thought that there would definitely have been enough landmarks recorded for a positive identification. In fact I'm sure of it.'

'So you're saying that Dr Khan's conclusions might not be

correct?'

'Just my opinion as I say, but yes. And remember, he's probably forgotten more about the subject than I'll ever learn, so you know, I might be like way off the mark here.'

'Yeah point taken Eleanor,' Frank said, 'and I'm obviously not going to hold you to it or anything, don't you worry about that. But it's very interesting, although I'm not sure if I have a clue right now what it means. But yes, thanks again for your efforts.'

'Any time Frank, and I hope it helps.'

So not a bad morning's work, all in all. Two of the persons of interest with something to hide, and a technical report that might not be all it seemed. What it all meant, he had no idea at the moment, but this was the way you worked the early stages of an investigation like this. Dig out some interesting facts and gradually start piecing them all together until a pattern emerges. Do the leg work, put in the hard graft and you'll get results. Time now to smooth-talk Jill Smart in to opening up that MI5 database.

Chapter 14

It was over twelve hours since Maggie had received the irritating phone call from Frank. Some extremely interesting facts had emerged that warranted further investigation, that was the tantalising message. *Extremely* interesting, he had said, not *quite* interesting or just merely interesting. She had pressed him for more, but he said it was too complicated to discuss on the phone. So for further details, she would have to wait until she and Jimmy met up with him later that evening. The truth was, she had been in turmoil since that photograph had turned up, and the wait was only going to add to the agony. Because now there was something tangible, something that might help her answer the question that had haunted her every moment, waking or sleeping, since the end of the trial. Who was it that had lied about the point in time when she had received Khan's report?

Further contemplation of the situation would have to wait however, because today was an important day. The most important in her life for over a year. Because today was Ollie's seventh birthday, and Philip had grudgingly agreed that she could see him for one hour. Just one hour. It wasn't nearly enough, nothing like it, but right now her ex-husband held all the cards and she had no option but to go along with it. Her mum was coming too, and would soon be arriving at King's Cross. *Damn*. She glanced at her watch and realised that she was already too late to meet her at the station. The news from Frank and the gut-wrenching anticipation of the day ahead had knocked her for six and she had already lost all sense of time. But maybe Jimmy could help. Was it a bit cheeky to ask?

He answered his phone after just one ring.

'Hi Jimmy, it's me.'

'Aye, I know, it says 'mad woman' on my phone.' He seemed to have detected the agitation in her voice. *'Are you ok?'*

'Where are you at the moment?'

'I'm just walking down from St Pancras now. About half

way down Judd Street.'

'Jimmy, I don't really like to ask, but I've really screwed up my timings this morning. Would you mind awfully going back to King's Cross and meeting my mum off the Leeds train and directing her to the Victoria Line? We're seeing Ollie at the McDonalds in Oxford Circus at twelve and there's no way I can get to the station to pick up mum without making us all horrendously late. What if I tell her to stand outside WH Smiths and wait for you to call her? I'll tell her to look out for a tall dark stranger that some people might call handsome.'

He laughed. '*Ha ha, visually challenged people do you mean? Consider it done.*'

'I can't thank you enough Jimmy, you've saved my life.' *Again*, she thought. She changed the subject. 'So what do you think about all that stuff that Frank found out yesterday? I assume he called you too?'

'*Aye, I spoke to him last night. It is crazy, right enough, I don't really know what to make of it. We're meeting up at his pub tonight aren't we? Anyway, I'll drop you a message once I've chucked your mother onto the tube.*'

Maggie reached Oxford Circus with fifteen minutes to spare and made her way to McDonalds where she was pleased to see her mother was already waiting. They hugged warmly, drawing strength for the momentous hour that lay ahead.

'Mum, I'm so sorry I didn't make it to the station,' Maggie said. 'I just lost all track of time.'

'Darling, I'm only sixty-six years old and perfectly capable of navigating my way across London. But it was very nice to meet your Jimmy, he's lovely and ridiculously good-looking, I must say. Yes, I'm not too old to notice.'

'He's not my Jimmy mum,' Maggie laughed.

'Well, he should be, if I'm any judge.'

'And how's dad?'

'About the same. He gets very confused still but he is perfectly happy as far as I can tell. And he asked me to take plenty of pictures of Ollie, so he does remember some things, thank goodness.'

'That's nice.'

They fell into silence, nerves jangling with excitement but some apprehension too. It was over two months since Maggie had last been with her son. Social services had quite rationally ruled that she couldn't be trusted, so it was entirely down to Philip when she could see him if at all. He used it like a nuclear weapon, inflicting unimaginable agony that with every second of separation burned a searing pain into her heart. Her recurring nightmare was that Ollie had already forgotten her, warm and secure in the care of the dazzling Angelique Perez. She knew that her mum was suffering too, the grandparents as so often being the forgotten collateral damage in a marriage breakdown. It was completely understandable therefore that despite Asvina's strict advice to the contrary, she was still driving to Ollie's school once or twice a week to catch a fleeting glimpse of her son, however brief, but that only succeeded in making the pain so much harder to bear. Today she just wanted to hold him in her arms and never let him go, ever, but she knew that could not be. But it wasn't long now until the custody hearing, when surely no court would decide that a child should be separated from his mother. That was the only thing that mattered and she had to stay strong.

At ten past one they still had not arrived, her mum fussing that they had got the arrangements wrong and should have been at another restaurant. But Maggie knew differently. This was just another of Philip's little power games, designed to cause maximum suffering. Right from the start, she knew that she had made a mistake in marrying him, but she had been nearly thirty-five and single and obsessively conscious of her biological clock ticking ever faster. Like a fool, she had gone ahead with the marriage, believing that she could grow to love him, like some ill-fated heroine of a Victorian novel. But she had grown to hate him instead. And now she found herself inextricably linked to him through her adored son.

Her mum was pointing to the door. 'Here they are at last.' There was Philip, with Ollie. And with them, unexpected and uninvited, Angelique Perez, holding Ollie's hand. They were laughing, sharing some private joke, a scene no doubt orchestrated by her ex-husband to maximise the pain. *Pig.* And now Maggie was struggling to hold it together.

Her eyes welled up. 'What is she doing here mum? What the hell is she doing here?'

Her mother gripped her arm. 'Let it go dear, just go to Ollie.' He had caught sight of her and was snatching his hand free from Angelique's and running towards her.

'Mummy, mummy. My mummy.'

Maggie scooped him up in her arms and hugged him tight to her breast, as tight as she dared. It was going to be alright.

'My darling, my darling.'

A muffled voice came from the folds of her arms. 'Ugh, you're squeezing me mummy.'

She released him, planting a gentle kiss on his head. They started to laugh, quietly at first, then a bit louder, and soon so uproariously that everyone in the restaurant suspended their refuelling to look. It was going to be alright.

'You've got one hour,' Philip said coldly. 'We'll be back then and don't try anything stupid. Come on Angelique.'

It was awkward at first, of course, because so much of the easy babble of family conversation depends on the quiet routine of normal life, a life which cruelly they no longer shared. But the laughter had helped, and there was 'happy birthday' to be sung, candles to be blown out and piles of presents to be opened, brought in four garishly-decorated gift bags. 'Star Wars Lego!' Ollie shouted as he tore the wrapper off a particularly large package, 'and a new football! Thank you mummy, thank you nana!'

They laughed when he squeezed his Big Mac too tightly and a jet of ketchup shot out and splattered down his new clean t-shirt, they laughed when he let out a huge burp, and of course they laughed at his terrible seven-year old's jokes, fresh to him but fondly remembered from Maggie's own schooldays. For an hour, it was as if the last eighteen months had been a sick dream from which they had now thankfully awoken, but then all too soon it was over. Philip was back, alone this time, tapping his watch theatrically. Just fifty-four minutes had elapsed, exactly what Maggie had expected.

'Right, that's it, time's up. Ollie, come to me please.'

Ollie began to cry. 'No, I don't want to. I want to stay with my mummy.'

Maggie cuddled him close. 'Darling, we've had a lovely time but you know what we said. You need to go with daddy just now. It won't be long until I see you again and we will have another lovely time, won't we? Now go and give your nana a big kiss and a hug. I love you darling.'

He struggled to dry his eyes on the sleeve of his sweatshirt. 'I love you too mummy.'

He kissed his grandmother on the cheek then shuffled over to where his father stood. However, it seemed that Philip was not yet ready to leave. 'Ollie, go back and sit over there with your nana and play with your new toys,' he said sharply. 'I need to talk to mummy for a few minutes.'

Maggie noticed he was carrying a buff A4 envelope.

'You need to see these I think.'

He extracted a sheaf of large photographs and spread them across the table. The scene they depicted was unmistakeable.

'You pig, you complete pig.' And then, comprehension. 'You've had someone following me. I can't believe that.'

'Your own fault Maggie, nobody else's. Skulking around outside a primary school with a camera and binoculars, that's just pathetic. Anyway, I just want you to know that this morning I've raised an injunction at the High Court to prevent you going anywhere near Ollie's school again, or anywhere else where Ollie might go. I've taken advice, not that I need it, and I fully expect it to be granted tomorrow. Of course, that's you up shit creek as far as access is concerned. I mean you can still go ahead with the hearing if you want, but you've got two-thirds of bugger-all chance of it being granted now.'

She struggled to make sense of what he was telling her. 'You can't do that Philip. It's too cruel, even for you.'

He looked at her with contempt.

'I can do what the hell I like and you can't do anything to

stop it.'

A fierce anger swelled up inside her, fired by the utter injustice of her situation. It wasn't fair that he could keep her from seeing her own son, and she wasn't going to just lie down and let him walk all over her. Not now that she knew all about that Cathedral Close dinner. She didn't know what that was all about but she was bloody well going to get to the bottom of it if it was the last thing she did. Red-faced, she walked over and violently pushed him in the chest with her outstretched palms. Taken by surprise, he was toppled over by the force of it, ending up prostrate on the floor, face upwards. An instant later, she was straddling him, her face inches away from his, her forearm locked across his throat.

'You listen to me you pig. Don't you ever threaten me again, do you understand?' Reaching in her back pocket, she took out her phone and pushed the photograph into his face.

'You see Philip, I know all about your scheming. I don't know what it's all about but believe me I'm going to find out and when I do, you'll be sorry. I'll make damn sure of it.'

An excited crowd had gathered round, led by the manager of the restaurant in his striped green shirt and *'here to help'* badge. Maggie bounded to her feet, running her hands through her hair and smoothing down her t-shirt.

'Nothing to get worried about here.' She shot a sweet smile in the direction of the manager. 'My husband and I were just having a bit of a domestic. We do this all the time. Very therapeutic. Come on darling, get up.'

The manager looked at her uncertainly. The last thing he wanted was to have to call the police, with all the hassle and disruption that would bring. 'Well, if you are sure...'

'Yes, we're quite sure, aren't we darling? Come on, up you get.'

It took several seconds for him to struggle back to his feet, like a boxer trying to beat the count. He looked rattled but his voice spat defiance.

'I don't know where you got that photograph, but you really are a stupid woman Maggie, imagining all sorts of drama and conspiracy when there's really nothing there at all. It was just an innocent dinner between friends and colleagues, nothing more.'

'I don't believe you.'

'Well that's up to you. But what really puzzles me is the obvious thing that you and your genius Scotsman haven't worked out yet.'

She looked him straight in the eye. 'What thing?'

'You mean you don't know?'

'What thing?'

She could feel the anger and loathing burning her up. How could she have ever loved this man? All through their relationship he had revelled in his ability to wound her, exploiting her weak spots like a mediaeval swordsman finding gaps in the armour, and now she could spot the signs of another attack.

'How a useless barrister like you got to defend Alzahrani in the first place. Forty-two years old, still not a Queens Counsel, and a variable record at trial to put it mildly. Just saying.'

He snatched his son's hand and with a terse 'Come on Ollie, we're going now,' swept out of the restaurant.

What did he mean by that? Nigel Redmond, the Clerk at Drake Chambers, had been straight with her when the brief came her way. Normally one for a QC, this one, that was what he said. She remembered how her initial reaction was utter astonishment and disbelief, that it must be a mistake and that he had meant it to go to one of the more illustrious members of their chambers. But no, he had confirmed that the CPS were happy for her to defend the case. He offered no further explanation and she did not ask for any, accepting it as a gift of fate, a wonderful gift that she meant to take full advantage of. But now the nagging doubts she had at the time began to resurface. Did Philip know something that she didn't? But forget all of that for now. Because there was no doubt about the look on his face when she had showed him the photograph. He had been scared shitless, not to put too fine a point on it.

She shouldn't have shown him it, she knew that the

second she had done it, but it was done now and shortly, she assumed, a huge dollop of dung was going to hit a bloody great spinning fan.

Chapter 15

The phone calls and messages started within seconds of him leaving the fast-food restaurant, setting off a wave of panic, anger, recrimination and fear. For the first time for many of them came the stomach-churning realisation that because of that damn dinner, careers might be ruined and lives trashed. But who would succumb meekly to the inevitability of being unmasked, and who was prepared to fight to the death, that was the question. And who could be trusted to keep their mouth shut?

Meanwhile, in an exclusive gentlemen's club on Pall Mall, the distinguished member relaxed in a comfortable leather armchair, sipping on a fine malt and coolly contemplating how to react to this interesting news. There had always been a risk of it getting out and it was as well he had made plans to deal with the eventuality. A bit of a shame of course, much better if they could have kept it under wraps, but he had no doubt his associates would do a tidy job and nothing would connect it back to him.

It needed only a simple encrypted text and the operation was up and running. *Plan B*. Signalling the waiter to fetch him another whisky, he gave a wry smile and returned to his copy of the Guardian.

Chapter 16

'What are you drinking Maggie?' They were back in Frank's surrogate office at the Old King's Head, quieter on an early Wednesday evening than on their last visit but still buzzing.

'I'll just have a lime and soda please,' Maggie shouted over the hubbub, 'it's my new regime, I mean, have you seen the size of my bum right now?'

Just in time, Frank remembered the two-day 'ethics at work' training course he had been recently forced to attend. Generally, he had thought it was a load of bollocks, but even he could see that the first response that had come into his head - 'actually Maggie, you've got a lovely arse' - was probably inappropriate, if unarguably true. This evening he was in high spirits because the sainted DCI Jill Smart had quietly and efficiently worked the system to gain permission to access the precious MI5 database, and what she had discovered from no more than a cursory search was absolute pure gold.

'And I'm going to start running again. Jimmy said he would be my personal trainer. He said I should start with just half a mile but I'm aiming to do a 5k.'

'Aye, well rather you than me.'

'You should try it,' Jimmy said. 'You look like you're carrying a bit of timber at the moment.'

'Bugger off.'

'Boys, boys,' Maggie said, smiling. 'Anyway, I bet your days weren't as interesting as mine. Wait to you hear this.' And then she launched into a colourful dramatisation of the earlier events in the fast-food restaurant.

'...so in the end I just lost it you see. Went completely mental. You should have seen his face afterwards though. It was priceless.'

'Interesting day right enough,' Frank said, draining his pint.

'Good for you,' Jimmy laughed. 'That arse had it coming to him. I wish I'd been there.'

'Aye, but I wish you hadn't shown him the photo,' Frank said, more seriously. 'I did say not to, didn't I?'

'Yes, I know Frank, I'm sorry, but I was just so bloody angry.'

'Aye, well I can understand that. It's done now.'

'Yes, look I knew you might not be too pleased, but it just sort of happened.'

'I'm not really angry Maggie, it just makes things a bit more difficult, that's all. Anyway, let me bring you up to speed with what I found out yesterday. You're going to love this, believe you me. But before that, I think another drink is called for. You still on the orange juice?'

Her resolve to go easy on the alcohol had lasted all of five minutes.

'Chardonnay please Frank. Large one if you don't mind.'

'Aye, no bother. Jimmy, your round I think.'

'What a cheek,' Jimmy protested, but he set off in the direction of the crowded bar nonetheless. It was nearly ten minutes before he returned.

Frank took his drink and raised the glass in silent appreciation. 'So, here's what happened. It's about three years ago, Cheltenham Spa railway station. It's about eight o' clock in the evening and one of the ticket office staff is just about to knock off for the night. Then he realises he's pretty desperate for a crap so heads along to the gents at the end of platform one. Pushes open the door of the first stall, which he assumes to be empty, and is surprised to find a bloke sitting on the bog with his pants around his ankles whilst a young lad kneels in front of him giving him a nice wee blow job. Taken by surprise, the lad jumps up, barges past the railway guy and disappears off into the night. The ticket officer is of upstanding morals and so calls the police, who arrive five minutes later and arrest Dr Tariq Khan under the Sexual Offence Act 2003, which has a lot to say specifically about acts of indecency in a public convenience. Under questioning the ticket guy, who's a racist bastard, says he's pretty sure that the lad pleasuring the good doctor couldn't have been more than thirteen or fourteen. Suddenly it's all got a lot more serious, and Khan is in deep shit. Sex with a minor, I mean, that's a life sentence potentially. Not to mention the shame in his community.'

'Bloody hell,' Maggie said.

'Aye, exactly, bloody hell. But it turns out that Dr Khan is working on some very important stuff for the government, top security, very hush-hush and it's not really the kind of work he could do from a cell in Belmarsh Prison. Furthermore, the police aren't able to find the youth, and the station's CCTV footage which caught both his arrival and his escape, is inconclusive with regard to his age. Naturally he's wearing a hoodie, so he could be fourteen, he could be twenty-four, it's impossible to tell. What's more, Khan says it had been purely a commercial transaction, arranged over some dodgy gay encounters website. Cost him fifty quid apparently.'

'Rent boys in leafy Cheltenham?' Maggie smiled. 'Who would have thought it?'

'Yes I know. But anyway, it's not long until there are a few discreet phone calls, quiet words in the ears of some of the CPS bigwigs, a rubber-stamp from the Home Office and suddenly it's all conveniently swept under the carpet. Khan gets away with a caution and two weeks later he's back at work as if nothing's happened.'

'He must be pretty good at his job then,' Jimmy said.

'Yeah, I think we can assume that's the case. He manages to avoid an entry on the Sex Offenders Register too. Of course, he's now got an MI5 file as thick as a telephone directory but only a wee caution on the criminal records system.'

He took a large swig of his pint then emitted a loud burp.

'Ah, that's better.'

'Pure class,' laughed his brother.

'Anyway, this brings us neatly on to that report of his. I think I might have told you about Eleanor Campbell, that wee girl that's been helping us with my bent copper enquiry? She knows a bit about facial recognition herself and not surprisingly, she also knows all about Dr Khan and his reputation too. I ask her to take a look at the report, and about an hour later she's on the phone, bamboozling me with techno-speak about how this AFR works - that's what we experts call it, by the way, automatic facial recognition to you lesser mortals. You probably don't know this, but it's all about facial landmarks and geometry and stuff like that.'

'Stuff like that,' Jimmy said, grinning. 'Stuff like what, exactly?'

'Eh, how big your eyes are, the size of your nose, that kind of stuff.'

'Oh yes, that's very clear.'

'Shut up will you? Anyroads the thing is, whilst the report undoubtedly dishes the dirt on the evidence that Professor Walker produced in court, Eleanor thinks the actual science behind Khan's conclusion is a bit suspect. As if he was trying to make the facts fit the conclusion that he wanted. Which is damned annoying, because it's all the wrong way round if it's going to fit in with a half-arsed theory I've got spinning around my head.'

Jimmy frowned. 'So?...I don't think I get this at all.'

'I don't get it either,' Maggie said. 'It's just.. well, weird.'

'No I didn't at first either,' Frank said, 'but just an hour ago I learned something from my boss Jill Smart that perhaps made some sense of it. Well I think so at least. Or maybe not, I'm not sure.'

'Come on then, tell us,' Jimmy said.

'Patience Jimmy, patience. Before we start, I sense we are in need of further refreshment. Toddle off to the bar will you, and refresh our glasses, there's a good lad.'

'I got the last one, you cheeky bugger.'

Frank looked at him deadpan. 'Aye but this information I'm about to share with you is worth it. At least two drinks' worth, if not three.'

Maggie laughed. 'Now then boys, don't make me tell you again. Actually, I think it's my shout. Same again?' They nodded in unison as she left for the bar.

Frank glanced over his shoulder to make sure she was out of earshot. 'She's nice Jimmy, is she not?'

'What, fancy her do you?'

'Who wouldn't brother, who wouldn't? But do you fancy her, that's what I want to know'

'Think I'd tell you if I did pal? No chance. But what's this all about then? You suddenly fallen in love or something?'

Before he could answer, Maggie returned with the tray of drinks. They fell into an awkward silence.

'What's going on here?' She laid the tray down on the table.

'Nothing, nothing.' It wasn't exactly convincing.

Frank raised his glass. 'Cheers Maggie. So, let me tell you what I found out from my boss just a wee while ago. She's brilliant Jill Smart, so she is.'

'Fancy her too, do you?' Jimmy said.

Frank glared at him. Jill was nice but he wasn't going to give his bloody brother any more ammunition to work with. 'No, being serious for once. As I said, Jill's brilliant and it only took her about an hour to get the green light from her boss to look at the MI5 database...'

'Which database is that?' Jimmy said.

'You don't want to know brother, believe me. You don't even want to know that it exists at all. Which in fact it doesn't, officially, if you know what I'm saying. Anyway, if you don't mind me continuing...'

'Please do.'

'So Jill's rooting around the database looking for anything on our persons of interest. Naturally, she starts with our excellent Home Secretary, the Right Honourable Gerrard Saddleworth MP, and low and behold comes across a heavily-redacted MI5 file marked 'Top Secret'...'

Jimmy was unable to help himself. 'Ooh, top secret, so that means she couldn't look at it. That's a shame.'

'Will you shut the bleep up please, if you'll pardon my bleeping French. So it turns out that just six weeks before the start of the Alzahrani trial, Gerrard Saddleworth is in Moscow in a seemingly unofficial capacity, purpose unknown. Naturally, an MI6 agent on the ground over there is given a surveillance brief, that's standard procedure for something like this apparently.'

Maggie raised an eyebrow. 'You mean our security services are spying on our own government? And that's standard procedure?'

'As Frank said, standard procedure,' Jimmy said, 'I know this from my army days. These MI5 and MI6 guys are still mainly public school, Eton and Oxbridge all that, and they're still expecting to uncover reds under the beds, even thirty years after the fall of the iron curtain.'

'Exactly as Jimmy says. Anyway, for the first day or two, there's nothing much of interest, just a few meetings with some low-level government officials and the like. But then on the day that Saddleworth's due to return to London, he's whisked off early doors in a government limo to a dacha about thirty miles from the city. Naturally, he's tailed by our agent who on reaching the dacha, parks his car out of sight and settles himself down behind a convenient tree with a pair of high-powered binoculars and a camera fitted with a telescopic lens. Fifteen minutes later another black Mercedes turns up, and who should emerge but Miss Fadwa Ziadeh, who had not long before been anointed as leader of Hamas following the retirement or resignation, call it what you want, of her father Yasser.'

'Ziadeh?' Jimmy said. 'She's the woman who's coming here soon for that peace conference, isn't she?'

'Exactly. So Saddleworth and Ziadeh are in there for about an hour or so, topic of conversation unknown, then our agent snaps them leaving, exchanging a polite handshake on the porch. Saddleworth is then whisked off straight to the airport and returns to London that evening, where he attends the House of Commons to support some big three-line whip.'

'The thing I don't get is that Saddleworth's never been a big supporter of the Palestinian cause,' Maggie said. 'In fact, he's been pretty scathing about the Party's fixation on it over the years. Says it doesn't play well on the doorsteps in his constituency. So how come he suddenly becomes all matey-matey with Miss Ziadeh?'

'Well I don't know,' Jimmy said. 'Maybe it's not such big

news that he's meeting with her. I guess it could be something to do with the peace conference that's coming up.'

'Well yes possibly, but why a secret meeting in Moscow? No, I don't think so. You see, I've got a theory - a crazy theory - which I think might explain why they were meeting and also might explain what was going on at that Cathedral Close dinner.'

Frank knew his idea was a bit left-field, but no matter how hard he tried, he just couldn't think what else it could be. With a bit more time and a bit more information, he might be able to come up with something better, but for now, this was the best he could do. But probably better to run it pass Maggie and Jimmy before making himself look a pure idiot in front of the professional cynic that was DCI Jill Smart. There was only one problem, a big problem that he would have to face up to in the next minute or so. It was absolutely certain that Maggie Bainbridge was not going to like what he had to say.

'All right then, tell us,' Jimmy asked for the second time that evening.

Frank inhaled deeply. 'Ok, what I think is... and I emphasize, it's only a half-cocked idea at this moment ...what I think is that this was all about making sure Dena Alzahrani definitely was found guilty. An insurance policy if you will.'

'Explain,' Maggie said, looking puzzled. 'I'm struggling a bit at the moment.'

'So, we've read a lot about how Fadwa Ziadeh seems to be wanting to take Hamas in a new direction. No more rockets being fired into the West Bank, no more suicide bombers on Jerusalem buses. She seems to be offering an olive branch to the Israelis in return for financial investment and greater self-determination for her people. But after decades of murder, or freedom fighting, depending on your viewpoint, the organisation is not trusted in the West and certainly not in Israel. Given this background, the last thing she needs is a notorious terrorist like Alzahrani getting off. No, she wants her found guilty and locked away for life so she can condemn her barbarous act publicly in the world's media and give full support for the punishment that's been dished out.'

'I think I see where you're going with this,' Jimmy said.

'Yeah, so what if Ziadeh arranges to meet with her old friend Saddleworth, and says Gerrard, what can you do to make sure the case is as tight as it can be? Saddleworth's not a fanatic but he's broadly sympathetic to the cause, so he agrees to help. When he gets back, he talks to Lady Rooke, big boss at the CPS, he talks to his old mate Philip Brooks. He says, guys, have you any ideas what we could do to make this happen?'

And now it was time to bring the elephant into the room.

'So perhaps somebody asks, who's in line to prosecute, and Rooke tells them that Adam Cameron's the favourite for the job. Who, by the way, also has a wee secret that he might want to keep well-buried. But anyway, he's a top man they say, with a brilliant track-record, never loses a case and everyone's happy with that. Thank god he's not defending then, someone laughs. And that puts an idea into their head.'

Frank paused for a moment, conscious that he had better choose his words carefully. But there was no way to sweeten the pill.

'It would be better, someone says, if we can steer the defence to someone well, a bit more plodding, a bit more average...'

He looked at her, seeing the anger in her expression as she began to understand.

'So they picked me. Because they thought I was rubbish.'

'Sorry Maggie, but I think that's maybe what happened.' His tone was sympathetic.

'It's not your fault Frank,' Maggie said. 'I've been a bit of a fool, haven't I?'

Jimmy placed his arm around her shoulders and held her close. 'No you haven't been a fool, not at all. And anyway, it didn't exactly work out well for them, did it? Backfired big time.'

Frank, unsure if he had done the right thing, swilled down his beer and stared into the distance, lost in thought. His theory made sense of course, except for two glaring facts that shot it out of the skies. Firstly, why would a government minister go all the way to Moscow just to say 'we're doing what we can to get her put away.' Why not just send a bloody text? And secondly, surely the smart thing would have been to get the world-renowned Dr Khan to shore up the facial recognition evidence, to make it absolutely bullet-proof in the eyes of the court. With his little past indiscretion he's not in any position to say no, so you would think he would write anything he was damn well told. But instead, his report blasted the expert witness's testimony out of the water. Why?

Yes, it was all the wrong way round, but he consoled himself by reflecting that you often found that in the early stages of a case. Two persons of interest with something to hide, government ministers attending secret meetings in Moscow and an expert's report that wasn't quite what it seemed. That was a decent haul so far. And not to forget a nice-but-average barrister cynically parachuted into a high-profile trial.

A barrister who shouldn't have shown her ex-husband that bloody photograph.

Chapter 17

Penelope skimmed through the opening paragraph one more time then gave a faint smile of satisfaction. Yep, that read just right, powerful but succinct and to the point. It had to be of course otherwise Clark would ask for a rewrite or even do it himself and she hated when he did that, not that he dared do it very often.

It was a relief to be able to bury herself in work after the unsettling events of the last couple of days. She had never trusted Philip Brooks, a slimy snake of a guy if there ever was one. God, she couldn't stand the man. She had only gone to the bloody dinner because Gerrard had arranged for them to have a yummy overnight stay in a nice Cotswolds country house hotel nearby. A little bit of business, and then it's all pleasure, that's how he had described it. She was happy to go along with it on that basis, and it couldn't be denied that it had been an interesting evening. It was meant to be a celebration of some deal or other that Brooks and Gerrard had concocted, although that guy Khan hadn't seemed in a joyful mood. Which wasn't a surprise once she found out what it had been all about.

Now Brooks was in a funk, on the phone about a dozen times urging her to keep quiet about everything that was said, wittering that if it got out it would ruin everything and there would be what he called 'consequences'. Ruin everything? What was there to ruin? Stupid little man.

Forget that, it was time to get on with her work. The first few lines read pretty well, she thought. *Barely eighteen months ago, on a cold and wet night in Belfast, Captain James Stewart sent twenty-two-year-old Sergeant Naomi Harris to her certain death. Despite an army cover-up, this paper exposed the truth, and now her parents are demanding justice. They deserve no less.*

She uploaded the document to her email and clicked 'send'. Now the paper's lawyers would review the article and if it passed muster, Clark would concoct a suitably lurid headline and they would be ready to go. Barring the emergence of any particularly big stories in the next day or two, it would make the front page of Saturday's edition, with a two or three-page spread across the inner pages too. Just how she liked it.

It was her high public profile that had caused the grieving Dawn and Peter Harris to contact the paper in the first place, and she had met with them a few times over the last few weeks as she pieced together the story. Nice enough couple she thought, but a bit stupid. It was tragic what had happened to their daughter of course, but what had they expected when she had decided to join the bloody army? That was besides the point because White knew a blockbuster story when she saw it. Dawn Harris was good-looking like her daughter, sexy even, appearing much younger than her forty-four years, and her husband Peter was dark, brooding and rugged like the hero of a Victorian novel. The photogenic couple were sure to capture the public's imagination, and leaving nothing to chance, the paper had already spent a small fortune on stylists and photographers to help them look their best. The Chronicle just loved a big campaign and what a campaign this was going to be. Rod Clark had already composed the launch headline and for once it met with Penelope's approval. Simple but powerful.

Today, the Chronicle calls for Captain James Stewart to face court-martial.

It had everything, this story. The beautiful victim, the distraught relatives, the flawed hero and his link to Maggie Brooks. Then there was Stewart's wronged wife Flora, a classically pretty Scottish redhead, and the stunning temptress Astrid Sorenson, the woman he had left her for. Sorenson's image alone on the front page was enough to sell another fifty thousand copies. Of course, she knew the army wasn't going to court-martial Captain Jimmy Stewart, not in a month of Sundays, but that didn't matter to Penelope. What was important was the story. This was one that would run and run, with endless angles and viewpoints. First, there would be the strident calls for the court martial. *Justice must be done and be seen to be done.* After a few weeks when it was clear that was not going to happen, there would be the attacks on the government and military establishment, with accusations of cover-ups and of ministers and the military brass closing ranks. Then, when the public was losing interest in all of that, they could focus back on the tragic but attractive parents, crestfallen, defeated and crushed. Yes, this was going to be some story, no doubt about it.

She heard the faint click of the key in the front door and then the quiet thud as it was closed.

'Gerrard? I wasn't expecting you this evening my darling.'

Darling Gerrard. Yes, he was her darling, but strictly in a part-time basis for her, if not for him. He was fun, good company and she very much enjoyed their love-making, but that was it. In truth, relations had been strained since she made it clear she had no intention of marrying him, for it was then he told her he was breaking it off and going back to his dull wife. Such a drama queen. But she didn't believe him, he didn't have the balls, and anyway he knew he couldn't resist her. And just to prove it here he was again, slinking back to her like a love-sick puppy.

'Gerrard?'

Still there was no answer from the hallway. Strange that.

'Gerrard darling, stop mucking about and come through. I want a kiss.'

Turning round, she caught only a passing glimpse of her assailant framed in the doorway. The figure, wearing the white protective suit, mask and gloves normally reserved for scene-of-crime officers, wordlessly raised the silencer-equipped handgun and with deadly efficiency despatched three rounds from close range. Blowing her head apart and splattering a torrent of blood all over the designer wallpaper of the stylish flat. Satisfied with his work, he retraced his steps back into the hallway and called the elevator. On the way in he had disabled the CCTV system through the simple expedient of taping over the lens, so was able to remove his protective garments unobserved, placing them in the small backpack which he had conveniently left just outside her door. A few seconds later, a subtle 'ping' announced the arrival of the lift, descending from an upper floor. He had factored into his thinking the possibility that the lift might be occupied, which would present an irritating but easily-resolved complication, but fortunately it was empty. Soon the lift glided to a halt on the ground floor and the assassin slipped out into the dark evening.

Back in Pall Mall, the distinguished member relaxed in his armchair with the Guardian, insouciantly awaiting the encrypted text that would confirm that the first task had been completed satisfactorily. Plan B, up and running.

Chapter 18

It hadn't been Maggie's overt intention to pry into Jimmy's private life, but once again she had been unable to sleep, consumed with anger about what Philip had done to her. She couldn't be sure, but it now seemed pretty likely that he was involved in some way in her getting the Alzahrani defence brief. We need a crap barrister, that's what they had said, and bloody Philip had suggested her. Such love and loyalty.

Giving up the struggle, she had risen at 5.30am, arriving in the office well before seven. As she sat at her desk drinking the customary mega-strong first coffee of the day, she found herself idly googling 'Astrid Sorenson'.

She was beautiful, there was no doubt about it. Tall and slim with a huge mane of blonde curls, piercing blue eyes and a look that radiated an intoxicating sexuality. She was older than Maggie had imagined she would be, going on thirty-five, which might be considered ancient for an up-and-coming pop star, but Astrid's genre was modern country, where a predominately adult audience lapped up syrupy tales of kids and family and home. It was a massive business, and though she had had some hits in Scandinavia before moving to London, it was only since relocating to Nashville that her career had gone stratospheric.

What's more, Frank Stewart's description of her as the Swedish princess, rather than being the mild insult she imagined it to be, actually turned out to be true. A minor royal admittedly, but nonetheless she seemed to be a favourite of the Swedish tabloids, her every move arousing intense interest and documented in graphic detail. And yes, there she was about four or five years ago dressed in army desert fatigues, in Iraq or Afghanistan on a morale-boosting visit to Swedish troops attached to the UN force. Was it then she had met up with the rugged and handsome Captain James Stewart, kicking off an unlikely and doomed relationship, a relationship that he seemed to now bitterly regret?

And then Maggie noticed the photograph. It was from The

Sun showbiz pages about a year ago and had caught Astrid with Jimmy at some minor awards ceremony, she dazzling in a minimal gold lamé mini-dress and six-inch stilettos, he looking uncomfortable and self-conscious stuffed into formal evening wear. But it was the headline that stopped her in her tracks.

Astrid boyfriend is Hampstead Hero.

He had managed to keep that quiet. The army had never revealed the identity of the bomb squad officer involved in the incident for obvious reasons of security, but here it was for all to see in the Sun of all places. *Brave Captain saves six-year old Amelia.* The veracity of the revelation had neither been confirmed or denied by the army, who stuck to the usual bland statement that they did not publicly comment on operational matters for reasons of security. Whatever the truth of it, there must have been some intense hush-up activity behind the scenes, because as far as she could tell the paper nor any other media outlet for that matter hadn't mentioned it again.

She was interrupted by the soft vibration of her phone on the desk. Glancing at the screen, she saw it was Asvina again, calling for the fourth or fifth time since yesterday evening, no doubt to talk about Philip's injunction. She had a good idea what her friend was going to say, that it was really serious, and that Maggie would blow even the slim chance she had of having Ollie back in her life if she broke its terms. She knew all that, but really, what could they do to her that was worse than what she had already suffered? Better answer it this time, she thought.

'Hi Asvina,' she said, sighing, 'yes, I know, it's very serious and I promise to be a good girl.'

'What? Oh, yes the injunction. Well I'm very glad to hear you're intending to behave for once, but that's not why I called.'

'Oh? I'm sorry Asvina, I just assumed...'

'No, what it was is there's been a development in the Saddleworth case. A big one, in fact. Olivia has just phoned to tell me.'

'And...?'

'According to her, Gerrard and Penelope White have split.'

'What?'

'Yes. Apparently it's all over and he wants to go back to Olivia and try again.'

Maggie was shocked. 'So does that mean she's calling off the divorce?' Putting her and Jimmy out of work at the same time.

Asvina had read her mind. *'Don't worry, she's not having him back under any circumstances. She actually sounded quite upbeat when she told me about it. Gerrard told her he was in big trouble and was almost pleading for her help. She said it had been a great pleasure to tell him to sod off. Her words, not mine.'*

Big trouble. So the pressure was getting to them, just as Frank said it would.

'Well this is unexpected Asvina, but as far as Saddleworth verses Saddleworth is concerned, I guess we still need to track down that money. We'll keep trying as hard as we can, obviously.'

'Glad to hear it,' she laughed. *'Well best of luck with your investigations, and above all, please, please, please, don't break that injunction. I mean it, I really do. Bye now.'*

It was nearly nine before Jimmy arrived at the office. It had become his routine to enjoy several minutes of flirtation with Elsa in the reception area before settling in behind his desk, but today he walked straight past her without a word, and his mood seemed sombre and downbeat.

'Morning Maggie, you ok?'

She was bursting to tell him the news. 'Yes, not bad. Well actually, I'm pretty good in fact. But you'll never guess what Asvina has just told me. Gerrard Saddleworth has chucked Penelope White.'

'What? You're kidding.'

'No, it's true.'

'That's bloody interesting, isn't it? You don't think this could this have anything to do with the Cathedral Close dinner?'

'More likely the Cathedral Close photograph. I'm thinking Saddleworth must be really spooked by it. But look, I've been awful, I didn't ask how you are.'

'Aye, well to be honest, I've been better. Actually, I wanted to talk to you about something, you being a proper lawyer and all that. I got this letter yesterday morning. From the bloody *Chronicle* of all people.'

He took the sheet from his pocket and handed it to her. 'Here, take a look.'

She unfolded it and began to read, growing more uneasy with each word. The letter, phrased in formal legalise, was forewarning him that the newspaper was about to run a story questioning his role in the Belfast bombing, that the paper was satisfied that everything it was about to publish was truthful and factual, but suggested that nonetheless he might wish to appoint a legal adviser to 'protect his interests,' as they put it.

'Jimmy, this is awful, it's nothing more than a witch-hunt. Obviously I can help with the legal side but... I don't think it will be possible to stop them printing this. It's ridiculous that they can do this, it really is. And I see this is one of Penelope White's. She really is a bitch.'

'I know it's not going to be good, Maggie. You know, I understand the pain that Naomi's parents must be feeling. And it was my fault, I should have stopped her.'

'It wasn't Jimmy,' she said. 'I'm sure it wasn't.'

'She was scared. It was her first operation, and I played down the danger when I should have scared her shitless. But she just opened the bloody door before I had a chance to stop her. I've asked myself a million times if I could have done anything different but I couldn't. She just opened that bloody door and stepped out.'

'She was young and inexperienced,' Maggie said. 'It was her mistake, not yours. You can't keep blaming yourself, it won't do anyone any good and it won't bring her back.'

He gave her a look steeped in regret. 'Aye maybe, but it doesn't make it any better.'

'You never told me it was you who was there on that

awful day, at Ollie's school,' Maggie said, anxious to change the subject. 'When I read about what you did, it was just so unbelievably brave. You saved that little girl's life, it was incredible.'

He shook his head, a tight-lipped expression on his face. 'You found that bloody Sun story I suppose. It's not something I like to talk about, to be honest, not good memories. Because if you want to know the truth Maggie, I screwed up that day, good and proper, but it was an impossible situation... I mean, you always try for the best possible outcome, work out probabilities, but sometimes...' His voice tailed off, aware of how inadequate it all sounded.

'I don't expect you know this,' said Maggie quietly, 'but it was my niece that was trapped under that van.'

'I didn't know that. I'm really sorry. I heard she died...'

'She did, but what you did gave her a chance. Her father was with her when she passed, and that wouldn't have been possible if it hadn't been for you. It was important. For all of us.'

To her surprise she saw his eyes moistening. 'I'm sorry. I'm so sorry...'

In a moment she was standing behind his chair, wrapping her arms around him, her head nestling on his shoulder. Now it was her turn to be the comforter.

'Just let it all out,' she whispered, 'remember, that's what you told me. Just let it all out.' And there they remained, locked together in silent grief, united by tragedy and a deep pain that now seemed impossible to bear. Until unexpectedly, he turned and kissed her, softly, gently, his lips barely touching hers.

'Thank you. Thank you Maggie.'

And then the moment had passed, evaporating into the atmosphere as if it had never happened. But it had happened, and could not be easily undone.

Chapter 19

'I'm just going to go and talk to him, that's all. I've got to do something or I'll go crazy.'

It was early afternoon and Maggie and Jimmy had been forced to repair to the local Starbucks, the office's in-house machine having suffered a catastrophic failure on account of Elsa omitting to re-order sufficient, or indeed any, coffee beans. The incident of the previous afternoon had not been mentioned, but it was there, evidenced by an uncharacteristic awkwardness between them.

'Mad woman, that's what comes up on my phone when you call me.' Jimmy Stewart was smiling but his tone was serious, 'and believe me Maggie, that would be bloody mad, total madness. That's just my opinion of course.'

'But the pig set me up. Have you any idea how that feels, to be set up to be so humiliated by your own husband?'

She was beginning to realise that it wasn't the action itself that hurt the most, but the fact that his professional opinion of her advocacy skills had been so low. *We need a rubbish barrister so we thought of you.* That hurt.

'Ok Jimmy, so you think it's mad, and I'm sorry, but I'm going round there to have it out with him. The damn injunction only applies to Ollie, not to him, doesn't it?'

He gave a wry smile. 'I don't suppose anything I can say will make you change your mind?'

'No.'

He sighed. 'Ok then Maggie, if we must.'

'We? What's this we?'

'Aye well, there's no way I'm letting you do this on your own. Goodness knows what you might do. I seem to remember you punched him last time you met, if I'm not mistaken. In bloody McDonalds of all places.'

She smiled broadly. 'Pushed, not punched I think you'll find. I might smash his face in this time though.'

He shook his head. 'Yeah exactly, that's why I'm coming with you. But I still don't know what you are hoping to achieve.'

The offices of Philip Brooks LLP were located halfway up Gray's Inn Road, just ten minutes' walk from Starbucks' Fleet Street branch. Until the breakdown of her marriage she was a frequent visitor to the chambers, and she was pleased if a little surprised to see that Samantha Foster was still on reception duties. Philip was not the easiest man to work with and so his admin staff rarely stayed long, but Samantha was the exception. Maybe that was because until two years ago Samantha had been Samuel, and it wouldn't be a good look for the human rights champions to be on the end of a trans discrimination suit.

'Mrs Brooks, it's nice to see you again.' The greeting was spontaneous and genuine, although Maggie couldn't help notice the hint of surprise in her voice.

'Nice to see you too Samantha. This is my colleague Mr Stewart. We're here to see Philip. Is he in?'

'Yes, he is in, but you don't seem to have an appointment.' She narrowed her eyes as she scrutinising her computer screen, her manner suddenly guarded and suspicious, the initial bonhomie evaporating.

'We don't need one, we're family,' Jimmy said bluntly. 'C'mon Maggie.' He walked over to the glass-panelled double doors that led through to the main office, and pushed. They were locked.

'You need a pass for our access control system.' The tone was officious. 'You won't be able to get in without one.'

Jimmy walked slowly back to the reception area, placing his hands on the desk and leaning forwarded until his face was just six inches from Samantha's. It was meant to be intimidating and it succeeded in being so. 'So you'd better give us one then, hadn't you, my love?'

'I don't know, I'll need to check...'

'Give us one.' Now his voice was gangster-movie menacing, causing Maggie to let out an involuntary giggle.

Samantha's voice dropped an octave, betraying her provenance. 'All right, just give me a second.' She took a credit-card sized pass from a drawer and slotted it into the reader on her desk. 'There you go. All set.'

Maggie smiled sweetly. 'Thank you ever so much Samantha.' She touched the card against the proximity sensor mounted on the door frame, triggering a loud click as the lock was released and then a quiet whirring as the automatic doors slowly opened inwards. 'Follow me Jimmy, I know where I'm going.' Behind them, the receptionist was already on the phone, ringing ahead a warning.

'His office is just here on the left.' They entered a generously-proportioned wood-panelled office furnished somewhat incongruously with upscale chrome and glass furniture. It was empty, but only temporarily vacated if the piles of papers and half-empty coffee-cups, two of them, were any guide.

'Looking for me darling?' Philip's voice was cold and menacing as he stood in the doorway, 'and I see you've brought your trained gorilla with you. How quaint.'

Jimmy smirked and stared him straight in the eyes. 'Aye, and you best not forget that either. Gorillas can be dangerous.'

He gave a dismissive look. 'My god, you are the complete neanderthal, aren't you? Anyway, what do you want Maggie? I'm a busy man.'

'Philip, is that us finished...' Brooks had been joined at the door by a smartly dressed man of about his own age.

Maggie's eyes widened with surprise. 'Well well, if it's not Adam Cameron. Now fancy meeting you here.'

'Hello Maggie.' His expression was cold and suspicious.

'You look well Adam.' He didn't actually, but it was the kind of thing you said to someone you hadn't met in a while. His hair was greasy and unkempt and his nose red and bulbous from over-indulgence on the fine Merlot she knew was his penchant. 'Everything ok with you?'

'As if you would care, after what you did to me.' Evidently it was still irking him after nearly two years.

'What I did to you? I didn't do anything. And to be honest, I think you got off rather lightly. No deliberate attempt to mislead? Don't make me laugh.' She couldn't contain her bitterness.

'Look, can we cut the psychodrama,' Philip said coldly. 'What is it you want Maggie, I haven't got time for all of this.'

Cameron interrupted before she could reply, struggling to conceal his obvious anger. But it wasn't with her he was angry. It was with Philip.

'I'm going now, and you heard what I said. I need you to fix this, do you understand? It's frigging important. Fix it.' He picked up his coat and swept out without another word.

'Shitting himself about the photograph is he?' Jimmy said. 'I would be if I was in his position right enough.'

Brooks shook his head slowly, disdain written all over his face. 'Really, you are so out of your depth. Both of you.'

'Aye, you've said that before. Quaking in my boots mate.'

Brooks ignored him. 'Come on Maggie, I'm waiting. What is it you want?'

It was a perfectly reasonable question. But as she stood here in front of this man, her nemesis, the truth was plain to see. Because she didn't know what she wanted other than for some stupid fairy godmother to suddenly appear and wipe away the last two years with a swish of her magic wand. And that wasn't going to happen, was it? But she had to say something.

'Did you set me up for the Alzahrani trial? You did, didn't you?'

'I don't know what you're talking about.'

'The government. They wanted to make sure Alzahrani was convicted, so they thought they would get a rubbish barrister to defend her. It was all your idea, wasn't it? Push the brief out to Drake Chambers and let Nigel Redmond do the rest. That's what you meant that time in McDonald's.'

He gave a withering look. 'I've said it before, but you really are a stupid bitch, aren't you? I mean, what makes you think I've got that sort of influence? It was perfectly natural that the case should go to Drake. They have an excellent reputation, which makes it all the more puzzling that they would give it to a second-rate barrister like you. Why the hell that weasel Redmond did that is simply inexplicable. I assumed you must have been sleeping with him.'

Maggie struggled to keep her cool. 'I don't believe you for one minute. I know you were involved and I'm going to find out how. And then I'm going to make you pay for it. I don't know how and I don't know when, but I will.' It sounded like a bad line from a bad movie, she knew that, but it was all she could think of. Pitiable.

'Heard all of that before Maggie.' She could almost reach out and touch the malevolence in his voice. 'You really are so pathetic. Now if you're quite finished, I suggest you both leave.'

With a sudden lunge, Jimmy grabbed Brooks by the lapels and pushed him against the wall, his voice spitting anger. 'Oh no pal, we're not finished, far from it.' Brooks staggered back, stunned, before steadying himself against the tall book case. The look of fear on his face was unmistakeable, any thought of retaliation rapidly extinguished by the realisation that he stood no chance against the six-foot-two former soldier.

'What are you doing Jimmy?' Maggie's voice betrayed alarm.

'I came here to stop you doing anything stupid to this bastard. I didn't say I wasn't going to do something myself.'

Now he turned his attention to her cowering ex-husband. 'You think you are so bloody smart, don't you mate, but you don't frighten us, not one bit. We're on your case, and it's you that had better feel the fear. We're going to make sure all of this comes crashing down around you. And don't you bloody forget it. Come on Maggie, we're done with this arse.'

***

'That was bloody amazing, but bloody stupid too. You realise you could get me struck off.'

They were making their way back down Gray's Inn Road towards the office, Maggie a few paces behind, straining to keep up with Jimmy's adrenalin-fuelled stride.

'I thought you were already struck off?'

'Black-balled, actually, it's not quite the same thing.'

'Got it. But anyway, do you really think he's going to report us to the police? I don't think so. I looked him right in the eye in there, and behind all that bravado he looks scared out of his wits. No, he's not going to call the police.'

Maggie reached out and grabbed his arm, struggling to catch her breath. 'Will you slow down please? I've got something to show you.'

She began rummaging in her handbag. 'Here we go, take a look at this.'

He looked at her with an amused expression.

'You stole Philip's phone?'

'Just borrowed. It fell out of his pocket when you and him were having that little heated discussion. Anyway, what's so funny?'

Jimmy plunged his hand into his jacket pocket. 'Great minds think alike. Sneaked Cameron's out his coat when he was having that wee conversation with you.'

Chapter 20

The delegation had landed at Stanstead just after midnight aboard an elderly British Airways 757, generously paid for by the British taxpayer, although whether they would have approved of this use of their hard-earned money had they been asked was open to question. The Essex airport had been chosen because it was felt to be marginally easier to secure compared with Heathrow or Gatwick, but it still required a huge operation from the army and the police, involving more than three hundred personnel. The terminal had been cleared of all passengers at 6pm, operations being diverted to Luton, not exactly convenient for the thousands of travellers affected. The flight itself had been escorted all the way from Beirut-Rafic Hariri International Airport by a brace of RAF Typhoons, causing further outrage in the press about the considerable expense of the operation.

Now the fleet of armoured limousines was speeding through the deserted early morning streets, the flashing blue lights of the police escorts reflecting back from darkened bedroom windows, their occupants' sleep disturbed by the howls of the sirens as the motorcade raced past. Fadwa Ziadeh shared an affectionate smile with her teenage son who sat opposite, momentarily distracted from his game of *Call of Duty*. After all was said and done, it was all about family, and at last her family, her poor oppressed Palestinian people, ignored and marginalised for seventy years or more, despised even in the Arab world, were to be given a voice. A new era dawned, more outward-looking, more conciliatory, more civilised. What did she care about the hard-liners in her party who were trying their best to undermine her every move? They had tried it their way for the last seventy years, and where had it got them? Nowhere. Now it was time for a new approach. Not before time.

In two days' time, the peace conference would begin. Sure, Israel had declined to officially attend, but they too were under pressure in their own country from a new younger generation, tired of the old conflicts and eager for a different future. So they had sent an observer instead, unofficial maybe, but an important step in the long and winding road to reconciliation. *The peace conference*. The British Prime Minister Julian Priest, her old dear darling friend Julian, had made all of this possible and she meant to take every advantage of the opportunity in front of the world's press. This was the new Hamas under her dynamic leadership, terrorism and violence to be replaced by diplomacy, exploiting the glamour and sexual power she knew she still possessed, captivating the dull grey men who still by and large held the power in western democracies. Fools, all of them.

In the car behind travelled her personal security detail, shadowy assassins armed to the teeth and trained by her Iranian allies. Hopefully they wouldn't be needed, especially since it seemed the team on the ground were already doing a good job, but it was always wise to have insurance just in case the diplomacy failed. Now it would be like an old eighties band getting back together. Julian and Philip and herself, the classic line-up. No Hugo of course, but he was always the crazy hothead, didn't every band need one? All these sweet entitled upper middle-class boys, Oxbridge-educated and safely wrapped in the comfort blanket of mummy and daddy's money, furiously trying to deny their privileged upbringing through their devotion to the cause. The smart ones grew out of it, becoming barristers or something big in the city, embracing their privilege, every one of them. Luckily, there were enough like Julian and Hugo and Philip, useful idiots keeping the conflict in the public eye, recruiting febrile support from young left-leaning idealists. And most importantly, keeping the cash rolling in. It had been her life for nearly thirty years now and it had been a good life. Excitement, international travel, lovers - everybody in the band had been her lover at some time - recognition, she had it all and she wanted it to continue forever. She feared that Julian's well-meaning conference was doomed before it started, that was a pity, but it was a significant step in the process, and it did give her another chance to get on CNN and deliver her message of conciliation to America and Israel and the West.

But more importantly, there was the other matter to be dealt with. Julian had said he would fix it, and so far he had been true to his word. She had never liked Gerrard Saddleworth, a pathetic little man with an inflated opinion of himself, but the British Prime Minister could hardly have come to Moscow himself, and to be fair, it looked like for once Julian's poodle had actually delivered. Now there was just a few minor details to be sorted out, that's what he had said, and then her living nightmare would finally be over.

They were on the last leg of their journey, the sirens and lights switched off as they glided silently down Pall Mall. Had she chanced to look out the window of the Mercedes, Fadwa might have caught a glance of the elegantly dressed middle-aged man slumped in the doorway of the Oxford & Cambridge club, his expensive navy wool overcoat already stained with blood seeping through from the deep stab wound which was draining the life from him.

Eight miles away in Hounslow, Olga Svoboda rubbed her eyes then stretched out an arm to put her phone alarm on snooze. Four forty-five, too damn early for most people, but she was used to it now. Thank god her sex-mad boyfriend was still asleep, and she had a chance of getting out the door on time. Not that she minded too much of course, it was rather lovely and it was nice to be desired, but work was work and the agency had made it plain that they would sack her if she turned up late at a client's again. Five more minutes and she would need to be up and about and then just ten more to get showered and dressed then hurry down to the station for the journey to St Katherine's Dock. As she prepared to leave, she double-checked that she had Miss White's key, slung the back-pack containing her cleaning materials over her shoulder and closed the door behind her.

Chapter 21

Journalist Penelope White murdered at home.

The news was of course all over the papers, not least the *Chronicle*, where she had been the undoubted star attraction. She wouldn't have liked that headline, so dull and unimaginative, but she had been much too young to have already written her own obituary. Alongside the rather too-fulsome eulogies, the paper was furiously speculating on the motive. The police had already admitted to being puzzled, given the obvious professional nature of the killing. Campaigning journalists like White made plenty of enemies, but they didn't usually get murdered, not in this country at least. So who could have wanted her dead?

The same thought was occupying Maggie's mind as she hurried along Clapham High Street towards what she now was forced to call home, her collar turned up against the biting April wind. But unlike the police, she knew that White had been at that Cathedral Close dinner.

Flat 4A, number 98 was beautifully situated above Kalib's Kebabs, a bargain at fourteen hundred and fifty pounds a month. The takeaway was destined never to receive a Michelin star, but was popular with its loyal and frequently inebriated client base and this evening was no exception, with ten or more customers packed into the tiny shop and one or two more waiting outside, puffing cigarettes and slurping from cans of strong lager. She wasn't a food snob, but the smell from Kalib's turned her stomach, and so she was glad she had managed to grab a Pret A Manger at Waterloo.

Access to the flat was through a narrow passageway on the left side of the takeaway and then up a rickety staircase. She pushed open the rot-infested wooden gate and made her way down the unlit path.

'Maggie.' The man's voice came out of the darkness, literally making her jump. She recognised it immediately.

'Christ Adam, you scared the shit out of me. What the hell

are you doing here?'

'I need to speak to you. About everything. Everything that's going on.' He sounded frightened.

'Sure, come on up. And watch these steps, they're lethal in the wet.' As she fumbled in her handbag for her key, she remembered the mobile phones. Two days since she and Jimmy had stupidly stolen them, but yet they had heard nothing from either of them about it. Neither Philip nor Adam. Not a word.

'Would you like a drink? I've got tea and coffee, just instant I'm afraid, and I might have some Chardonnay in the fridge if you would prefer.' No might about it, she always had some Chardonnay in the fridge.

'A glass of wine would be nice. Thank you.'

They sat at either ends of the cheap but comfortable flat-pack-store sofa, glasses resting on the cheap flat-pack coffee table. They weren't stylish by any means, but Maggie was inordinately proud of her achievement in assembling them single-handedly. For nearly two months after moving in, she had sat on an uncarpeted floor in the echoey room, paralysed by the trauma of her breakdown. Buying and building the sofa and table had been a critical step in her slow rehabilitation into something like a normal life, and now she would not part with them for anything.

Cameron took a large gulp from his glass then cradled it in his hands. Maggie saw that they were shaking.

'We took your phones. Yours and Philip's. It was a mistake. The police have them at the moment, but you and I both know that nothing that is found on them can be used in evidence, given the circumstances in which they were acquired.'

It was a little white lie, because the police didn't have them yet, but they would pretty soon. When she plucked up enough courage to tell Frank what they had done.

'The police have them?' His eyes betrayed his anxiety.

'Well, *a* policeman, to be accurate. He's attached to a special department of the Met and he is trying to figure out at the moment what to do with them. They're a bit of a hot potato to be honest.'

He did not appear to be listening.

'What do you know? I mean, about that meeting. The dinner. I know you have the photograph of it. What do you know?'

Maggie's eyes narrowed. 'We don't know anything. We weren't there, were we? I was hoping you would tell me what it was all about.'

He didn't answer.

'Come on Adam, you can tell me. What was it all about?'

'It was just an innocent get-together. Just a dinner with friends and colleagues.'

Maggie recognised these words immediately. So that was why he was here, sent by her ex-husband to find out what they knew. Too cowardly to do his own dirty work, that was just *so* Philip.

'One of the people at your cosy little dinner has just been murdered Adam, for god's sake. And in case you've forgotten, you told Judge Henderson that you had never met Tariq Khan, who I don't think you could describe as either a friend or a colleague. So it wasn't a bloody innocent little dinner, was it?' Maggie's voice was steady, her manner crisp. Just like the old days in the courtroom, cross-examining the witness, exposing the inconsistencies in the testimony. As if she had ever been any good at that.

Cameron hesitated before answering. Maggie could see he had prepared like a witness in the dock, pre-programmed with pat answers to the questions that were expected to be thrown at him. The difference was hardened criminals were good liars, distinguished QCs less so.

'The murder is awful of course, quite awful, but it doesn't have anything to do with the dinner. Penelope White had made many enemies in her career. She was always getting death threats.' It wasn't convincing.

'So why are you here then Adam, behaving like a frightened little rabbit?'

'I'm not frightened.'

'Of course you're not. Why would you be when all you've

done is attend a dinner where the topic of conversation was so innocent that someone got murdered to keep it quiet? Believe me Adam, I would be frightened if I had been there. So don't give me that crap.'

'It was an innocent dinner. I don't know why Penelope has been killed.' That was his story and he was going to stick with it.

'Well that's good for you,' Maggie said, 'so it's safe to assume the police won't find anything interesting on your phones when they examine them.' She knew from the other's reaction that she had struck a raw nerve.

'Ok you're right,' Cameron said. 'There was a reason why we held that dinner. The truth is, we had lost some confidence in the authority of our expert witness Professor Walker. We heard about Dr Khan's reputation and wondered if he might not be a better bet. That was all.'

'So why meet in such a public place?' Maggie said. 'And why did it have to be kept so secret that you were prepared to lie to the judge about meeting him at all?' This evidently was a question he had not rehearsed.

'He...well, it was simply the fact he worked in GCHQ in Cheltenham and it made sense to meet locally. We thought if we entertained him and made him feel important, then it might persuade him to help us.'

'What, so you and a cabinet minister and a journalist and my shitface ex-husband traipsed up the M5 to a one-hundred quid a head eating place just to smooth-talk some geeky boffin? A geeky boffin, by the way, who works for the government and could just have been ordered to co-operate. And then, someone dies. Coincidence? No, I don't think so, you'll have to do better than that.'

'Well that's what happened. If you don't believe me, that's your prerogative.' He had regained some of his composure, buoyed no doubt by Maggie's admission of how little they knew.

Without asking, she topped up his wine glass.

'I do know something, as it happens. I know there was a move to make sure someone rubbish was appointed to defend Alzahrani. Whose idea was it to get me appointed as defence barrister? Oh yes, you don't need to look so surprised, because that's one thing we have worked out. The crap barrister plot, let's call it that.'

To Maggie's surprise, Cameron gave an audible sigh of relief, the words blurting out before he could stop himself.

'So that's all you think it was?'

So that's all you think it was. Condemned by the words from his own mouth. Of course, it had to be much much more than that, something big enough to cause someone to be assassinated and to scare the life out of Adam Cameron QC. Something very big indeed. But she was pretty certain he wasn't going to tell her what it was.

She picked up his almost-full glass and stood up.

'I think you'd better go now Adam. Tell Philip whatever you like, but believe me, we will get to the bottom of all this. Oh, and I'll get you your phone back as soon as I can.'

He gave her a distracted look, his mind obviously on more important matters. 'What, that? You can keep it, I've already got a new one.'

Afterwards, Maggie reflected that perhaps she hadn't played the meeting as well as she could have. Perhaps she shouldn't had given away how little they knew. That was a mistake, but still, a lesson learned. Cameron had come to find out what they had, and had gone away with the knowledge that they had nothing. Mission accomplished as far as she was concerned. So far.

***

Pall Mall was all but deserted when Cameron's taxi dropped him off at his club. Hell, how he deserved a drink this evening. In fact maybe he would spend the night there, get a good sleep, with a nice cooked breakfast to look forward to. Right now, there was plenty of time for a shower and to enjoy some of the excellent steak and ale pie, washed down with a nice bottle of Merlot.

The evening passed pleasantly enough and he was feeling much better as bed-time approached. He checked his watch. A quarter past twelve, he hadn't realised how late it was. Just time to slip out for a quick smoke and then he would retire.

The entrance was well-lit and covered by a barrage of close-circuit cameras, although they hadn't really helped the police in the subsequent investigation of his killing. The best they could say was it was a slim tall figure, almost certainly young and male based on his lithe movements, face indistinguishable behind the balaclava and dark glasses. They had got a capture, but unfortunately nothing for the facial recognition software to work with. A single stab wound, driven upwards with force into his heart.

A neat professional job.

Chapter 22

It took nearly four days for the second victim's identity to be released to the press, but only one day for the Met to put DCI Colin Barker in charge of the investigations.

'What's the bloody place coming to ma'am?' Frank was on the phone to his boss as he drove through the morning traffic towards Paddington Green police station, where the incident rooms had been established. 'Crappy Colin running a double murder. I mean, come on.'

'Are you hands-free?'

'Yes boss,' he lied.

'Good. Well if you look on the bright side, it's a big boost for the Alzahrani investigation now they've taken him off it. Maxine Wood has taken that one over, and she's a good cop. Now listen Frank, just tell him what we know and then leave and please, don't get into any more trouble. That's an order.'

'Me ma'am, trouble? When do I ever cause trouble? Not getting into trouble in any way whatsoever is my middle name.'

'Very funny. You know what I mean. Just do your job in a nice professional manner.'

'I promise ma'am, I'll be a very good boy indeed. All I'm going to do is see what the knobhead has to say and then I'll report straight back to you. See you later.'

It turned out the police station car park was full, but then he spotted a gleaming silver BMW bearing the registration number 'CB 3' in a reserved slot next to the main entrance. It said everything about the tiny-dick syndrome of the man that he had gone to all the trouble of getting a private plate on his police motor. It would have taken hours of form-filling and a tower of bureaucracy to get that one signed off. Crazy. And what did the '3' signify? Probably the number of cases he had ever solved. Or the length of his dick. In centimetres. He pulled his battered Mondeo up behind the BMW, blocking him in, and blocking up the rest of the car park too. Not to worry, this was only going to take five minutes at the most.

There were mutters of surprise and anticipation from the

investigation team as Frank wandered insouciantly through the huge open-plan office towards Barker's glass-walled enclave. He had worked with many of them in the past, and was pleased to see that his old mate Pete Burnside, veteran DI and witness to that punch that had sent cheers reverberating across the Met, occupied one of the untidy paper-strewn desks. He gave a friendly 'Hey Frank, good to see you mate,' which was acknowledged with a thumbs-up.

A pretty uniformed WPC sat at a desk alongside the door to Barker's office. Down the pub, he probably called her his personal assistant. What an arse.

'Morning constable,' said Frank cheerily, flashing his badge, 'I need a wee word with the DCI. Important stuff about these murder cases. I'll just go in now, ok?'

The WPC looked up in alarm. 'Well sir, I think he's in a meeting...'

Frank spread his arms, gesticulating through the glass at the empty office.

'What, a meeting with himself? You know what they call guys who play with themselves.'

She blushed faintly and tried to suppress a smile.

'What I mean sir, is I think one's about to start...'

'Aye, well, I'll tell you what constable, I'll have a wee meeting with him now. I'll only be five minutes, won't take up much of his time.' Smiling, he strolled past her into Barker's office.

The DCI was on the phone, pacing the office with his back to the door and from the obsequious tone, Frank gathered that he was speaking to his boss.

'Yes sir, we'll have them wrapped up pretty quickly I hope. The reason I called actually was to let you know we've already got someone in custody for the Cameron stabbing... yes, that's right...we're pretty confident we'll be charging him before the end of the day...yes sir, it is quick work on my part...thank you sir... yes, you know we always get results when I'm in charge...yes... ok sir, I'll give you an update later today.'

He was evidently surprised and not terribly pleased to see

Frank in his office.

'What the hell do you want Stewart? I thought they'd made you a traffic warden, or was it a lavatory attendant, I can't remember.'

'Morning sir. No, not been promoted to those jobs yet, I think they're still keeping them open for you. Oh, and did I really just hear you say we always get results when I'm in charge? You mean like the Alzahrani job they've just had to take you off to save further public embarrassment? Aye, you always get results right enough.'

Too late, he remembered his promise to Jill Smart. *Don't get into any trouble.* But this time it seemed he had got away with it, as Barker either ignored or was oblivious to the insults. He shouted out to the young WPC.

'Ellie, will you get DI Burnside in here right away. So what is it you want Stewart, I'm a busy man.'

'I've got some information on the Cameron and White murders from another case I've been working on sir. My boss DCI Smart felt it was our duty to share it with your investigation and sent me over. It's up to you what you do with it'.

DI Pete Burnside entered the office, winking at Frank and ignoring his superior officer.

'Great to see you Frank mate. How's tricks?'

'Good Pete, really good. It's a laugh a minute down in Department 12B, I can tell you. You should apply for a transfer, DCI Smart's always looking for smart guys like you, ha ha.'

'I might just do that mate.'

'Aye, it's good. We don't get the free coffee to be fair, but there's a well-stocked vending machine. Twixes and Mars Bars usually.'

'Look, can we just get on with this,' said Barker impatiently. 'So what crap is it you've got for me?'

'Aye, all right then sir. So we've just started on something in the Department, it's connected to the Alzahrani case as a matter of fact.'

He took his phone from his pocket and scrolled to the

Seven Cathedral Close photograph.

'Look, you can see here. That's Adam Cameron and that's Penelope White, your murder victims. This was taken about two years ago, just before the Alzahrani trial kicked off. Doesn't mean their murders are connected of course, but it is something of interest I think. The reason I'm saying that is because, you see this other guy in the picture? That's Dr Tariq Kahn, you know he was the guy who wrote that report that the CPS suppressed, causing the mistrial and all that.'

He wasn't surprised by Barker's reaction. It was no more than he had expected from the useless halfwit.

'So you've wasted my time with a picture of some guys having dinner together? What does that prove? Bugger all Stewart, bugger all. I've already established that there's no connection between these two murders. One was a shooting and the other one was a knifing for a start, or maybe you didn't figure that out.'

'But sir,' Frank said, persisting, 'the other thing is, Adam Cameron said to the judge that he had never met Khan. This picture proves that for a reason we don't yet know, he was lying. Do you see what I'm saying? Why would he lie if he didn't have something to hide? And if he had something to hide, maybe that's would be a motive to shut him up permanently.'

'Frank, do these guys know of the existence of this picture?' Burnside asked.

'You're a very clever guy Pete,' Frank said with pointed admiration. 'Aye, I think there's every chance that they do. One of them does certainly, that's this guy Philip Brooks, and I would bet my pension that he's gone and told everyone else by now. That was the other thing I came here for. We need to bring Brooks in for questioning pronto, see what he knows.'

'Brooks, who the hell's he?' Barker said. 'Not on my radar'.

Not surprising thought Frank bitterly, you wouldn't recognise a suspect if he was wearing a t-shirt with 'suspect' printed on the back in capital letters.

'Sir, don't you think Frank might have something here?' asked Burnside cautiously. 'What I mean is, if someone wanted to keep the purpose of this meeting a secret, as he says, that might be a motive for the murders. And if this guy Brooks knows that the meeting is all out in the open now, maybe we should bring him in, find out what he knows...'

'That's total bollocks,' Barker replied shortly. 'What, you start murdering people just because of a dinner conversation? Complete shite. No, I told you, there's nothing connecting these murders in my very expert opinion, and I'm a man who knows what he's talking about. And anyway we've already got someone bang to rights for the Cameron stabbing.'

'Aye, I heard you saying that to your boss,' Frank said suspiciously. 'There's no way that can be true.'

'Well, we have and it is true,' smirked Barker. 'The result of superior police work, but of course you wouldn't know anything about that, would you?'

'Superior police work from you? Yes, I must bow to your superiority, no doubt about that sir.'

Petulance was evidently Barker's default mode. 'You just remember Stewart that you are talking to a senior officer and it's none of your business frankly, but we just happened to stop and search a youth the next day and low and behold, wasn't he found in possession of Mr Cameron's phone.'

This was a turn of events that hadn't occurred to Frank. It was beyond bad luck that some opportunist thief had taken Cameron's phone as he lay dying.

Barker gave a sickly smile. 'Stop and search. I've always believed in it. Gets results you see. And now we've got it all wrapped up. Neat and tidy, just the way we like it.'

'Aye, fitted up more like,' said Frank bitterly, 'and don't tell me, you've not been able to find any DNA or fingerprint evidence connecting this poor lad to the murder, but you're working on it. And that's because you haven't found the knife yet but you're working on that too.'

'We don't need to worry about these little technicalities, do we Burnside? They're all the same, dangerous thieving little toe-rags, every one of them. But this one wasn't so smart, was he? He was found with the phone in his possession, he hasn't got an alibi for his whereabouts at the time of the murder, and it turns out he's got a string of previous convictions as long as his arm. CPS lawyers are happy with it, they agree it's all we need to charge him, all neat and tidy. Nice speedy clear-up, just the way the Super likes it. DCI Colin Barker strikes again. Yes!'

He pumped his fists in a grotesque gesture of triumph. Frank could feel the anger swelling up to bursting point.

'You're an arse-licking bent bastard,' he said quietly, 'and a bloody disgrace to this force and every other. Well, I'm going to see you get exposed for the lying fuckwit you are if it's the last thing I do.'

Burnside looked alarmed. 'Calm down Frank, just calm down mate. Don't do anything stupid.'

Now Barker was hitting his stride, arrogant and confident in equal measure. He evidently knew how easy it was to wind up Frank Stewart.

'Well, you'll no doubt be pleased to know that we've got a suspect for the Penelope White case too. We found out from her paper that she was working on a big story to expose the army officer that was responsible for the death of that young soldier in Belfast. A right bloody coward, letting that young girl die while he sat all safe and sound in the armoured vehicle. And now that's she's dead, that coward is off the hook. Very convenient, don't you think Frank? You see, that's what I call a real motive for murder, not some stupid dinner party.'

Burnside tried to stop him, but he wasn't quick enough. Frank leaped forward, grabbing Barker by the lapels and smashing him against the wall.

'You go near my brother, and you're dead Barker, understand that? I mean it.'

Taken by surprise, Barker struggled for breath as Frank wrestled him to the floor. Burnside tried again to restrain him, grabbing him by both arms and pulling him back.

'C'mon Frank, he's not worth it. Just leave it. Please mate, leave it.'

Frank shrugged him off, directing a final withering glance

at Barker as he lay prone and dazed.

'Aye, you're probably right mate. But make no mistake Barker, I'm coming for you. There's nothing worse than a bent copper, so you'd better start browsing the job sites. Because you're finished here.'

With that, Frank turned on his heels and with a pleasant, 'it was nice to meet you' in the direction of the young WPC, strode purposefully through the incident room towards the exit. To his delight he was accompanied by a discreet ripple of applause, causing him to smile and tip an imaginary cap in the manner of a major-winning golfer striding towards the eighteenth green.

Driving back to the office, he reflected that maybe he could have handled it a tad better, but what was certain was that the case was going be a bloody disaster under that fool Barker. The black lad had been stupid to nick Cameron's phone as he lay dying, but there was no way he could have carried out what was an obviously professional killing. And now valuable police time was to be wasted on a stupid investigation of his brother Jimmy, whilst the real killers were still on the loose.

Because if as he strongly suspected the murders were as a direct result of the Seven Cathedral Close dinner, then there were people clearly anxious to make sure nobody talked, meaning there was every chance they would strike again. Now he desperately needed to get Jill Smart's backing to make the investigation official. Department 12B wasn't supposed to run parallel cases, but he felt confident that when he gave Jill the feedback from his meeting with Barker, she would be supportive. They needed access to phone records, they needed to be able to bring the participants in for interview, and they needed clearance from the spooks to talk to the elusive Dr Khan, and for all that to happen, the investigation had to be official.

Above all, they needed to find out what the hell was going on before the killer or killers struck again.

Chapter 23

'Means, motive, opportunity, that's what we have to think about isn't it? For every suspect.'

Maggie and Jimmy had been joined at their Fleet Street Starbucks by Frank, who was in dire need of a caffeine infusion after a gruelling and uncomfortable morning with his boss. He shook his head in mock disgust. 'The good Lord save us from the amateur detective. Anyway, is this your new office or something? You're always here.'

'No, it's just that Elsa's ran out of beans again and we were desperate. But don't you change the subject Frank Stewart. I am right, aren't I? About means motive and opportunity? I've seen it on that whiteboard on Midsummer Murders.'

He struggled to suppress a smile. 'Aye, so it must be true Maggie, that's an authoritative source, so it is.'

She could sense they were all trying hard to remain upbeat, but the truth was that for different reasons it was all getting a bit difficult. She had suffered a rapid crash in her mood when she realised that it might have been her impetuous decision to show Philip that photograph which had triggered the murders of Penelope White and Adam Cameron. Frank had expressly told her not to, but in the heat of the moment, she had lost control, with terrible consequences. It was increasingly her opinion that everything she touched turned to disaster, an opinion strongly backed up by facts that could not easily be ignored. And if that wasn't bad enough, she was now beginning to realise the practical implications of Philip's court injunction. Not being able to see Ollie, even at a distance, was unbearable agony, made even worse by the loveliness of the fleeting hour she had spent with her son on his birthday. But she knew that her chances at the upcoming custody hearing were already slim, and that incident at his office the other day had hardly helped matters. Any further transgressions would surely ruin them for good. Now her determination to get revenge on Philip was dissipating as she faced up to the hopelessness of her situation.

Jimmy smiled, judging the mood. 'We're a right bunch of miseries, aren't we? Anybody would think the end of the world was nigh. C'mon, it's not that bad, is it?'

Frank did not seem to share the sentiment. 'Speak for yourself pal.'

'I'm sure I would feel a lot better if we could actually do something,' Maggie said. 'I don't mind admitting I'm really struggling at the moment. Look at this.'

She showed them a Facebook post with a photo of a laughing Ollie playing catch with Angelique Perez on Hampstead Heath.

'Maggie, why are you following Angelique's social media, for goodness sake?' Jimmy said. 'Do you really think that's going to help?'

Frank gave him a withering look. 'Says the man who checks out the Swedish princess ten times an hour.'

Jimmy ignored him. 'Take it from me, it doesn't help at all.'

'But you still look, don't you?' Maggie said kindly.

'No, not now. Never.' She could tell he was lying.

'Social media, I've always said it's a curse.' This from Frank, the man who did not even own a smartphone.

'Aye, and you know all about Facegram, being mister techno man and all that,' Jimmy said, 'You've still got a flip-up phone for god's sake.'

'My star trek communicator, do you mean? It works fine for me. And yes, I do have a Facegram account. I get lots of likes, me.'

Jimmy caught Maggie's eye. She was trying very hard not to laugh.

'Ah well Frank, we'll look forward to looking up your Facegram page later,' she said, 'although I can't say I've heard of that app before. Anyway, how did you get on this morning with your boss? Did you manage to get the case up and running?'

'Well, the answer is yes and no. To tell the truth, Jill and I had a wee bit of argy-bargy when I told her about my run-in with DCI Barker...'

Jimmy eyed him with suspicion. 'What run-in?'

'Nothing for you to worry about son, we just had a little disagreement, that's all. So as I said, yes and no. Jill thought there wasn't enough solid evidence of conspiracy at this point for her to open up a full enquiry and devote all the resources that would demand, which is fair enough. But the good news is she's cleared the decks so that I can work on it full time for the next two or three weeks. Then, if *I* - I mean *we* - uncover anything of significance, she'll look at it again. Can't really complain about her decision, it's what I kind of expected to be honest.'

Maggie suspected the decision suited Frank very well. She guessed he preferred to work on his own whenever possible. From his point of view, it probably saved a lot of tedious cocking-about time which could be used more profitably on the case.

'That sounds good,' she said, 'so what's the plan?'

'Well, I know I laughed at you earlier, but we do actually need to look at means, motive and opportunity for each suspect.'

'See, told you.'

'No, this is serious. For a start, we have got to face the possibility - no, stronger than that, the likelihood - that one or more of that dining group could actually be responsible for the murders. Looking at motive, then it's got to be that someone or some group did not want the subject of that meeting to get out. That would be my initial thought.'

Jimmy nodded his assent. 'Yep, agreed, but it would be good if we actually knew what was said at that dinner, wouldn't it?'

'I think we can probably make a guess at that, can't we?' Maggie said. 'If it's all about how to make the case watertight, maybe they are trying to put pressure on Khan to write a report that does that, or maybe even trying to get him to appear as an expert witness.'

'It might be that, right enough,' Jimmy agreed, 'but what we don't know is, what were the dynamics around that table? What I mean is, who was driving the agenda? For example, was it the Government as represented by Saddleworth putting pressure on the CPS and their barrister.'

Maggie had been thinking about that. 'That's all plausible, but what's been puzzling me is why they held that meeting in a public place.'

'You can't kick up a fuss in a public place, can you?' Jimmy said. 'I'd imagine that was the main reason.'

'Yes. I hadn't thought of that,' Maggie said, unconvinced. 'That's probably what it was. But what was Penelope White doing there? Perhaps it was to put more pressure on Khan. He must have this constant terror that he is going to be exposed, so whoever is behind all this brings a journalist along so that he is reminded what will happen if he suddenly decides not to cooperate with whatever plan they have cooked up.'

Frank broke his silence. 'Aye, but it's all wrong, this case. I've said it before but it's all the wrong way round.'

Jimmy looked puzzled. 'I don't understand what you're saying brother.'

'Look, is it credible to think that this wee dinner can lead to two murders if all they were trying to do was beef up the case against Alzahrani? No, it isn't, there must be more to it than that. Remember, our mastermind DCI Barker hasn't figured this out yet, but these killings were professional jobs. Penelope White was shot cleanly through the head three times, and not a single neighbour heard a thing, which points to a silencer being used. And I've been told by my mate Pete Burnside that the SOCOs have not found any DNA or fingerprints in her flat that shouldn't be there. Not a trace. And then we have Adam Cameron, killed by a single upward stab through the heart, clean and accurate. That wasn't done by some scumbag mugger, I can assure you of that. No, as I said, this whole thing has got to be about something way more serious. Something deadly serious.'

Maggie was mulling over whether this was now maybe a good time to bring up what was likely to be a slightly delicate subject. Uncertainly, she decided to go for it.

'Frank, is it right that you said it was normal procedure after something like this to check the phone records of the suspects? You said there would be panic calls and attempts to get stories straight and stuff like that. I'm sure that's what you said.'

Frank looked at her suspiciously. 'Aye, I did, but Jill Smart hasn't given me the go-ahead to do that yet.'

'Well maybe we could help you with that. It's rather unofficial, but well...'

She rummaged in her bag, emerging with the two smartphones and laying them on the table. 'These are Philip Brooks' and Adam Cameron's. We thought they might come in handy.'

Frank's expression registered utter disbelief. 'You stole their bloody phones? And one of them a murder victim? This is crazy, I shouldn't even be looking at these, never mind being anywhere near them. I should arrest you two, so I should.'

Maggie shot him a weak smile and pointed at Jimmy. 'Arrest him you mean, nothing to do with me. I'm just a lawyer.'

'You lying toad,' Jimmy laughed, and then wished he hadn't.

She could tell that Frank was struggling to suppress his anger. 'This isn't something to joke about guys. Christ, if Jill finds out about this, I'm a dead man.'

'I don't know about that,' Maggie said, raising a quizzical eyebrow, 'but I'll tell you what's strange about this. Neither Philip or Adam Cameron ever tried to contact us to get them back.'

Frank was shaking his head with obvious disgust.

'Bloody amateurs, that's what you are. And bloody dangerous amateurs at that. Of course they haven't asked for their phones back. Because when they realised they were gone, then their panic and fear would have been off the scale. The bloody dial was always going to be jacked up to eleven. God knows what you two have set off. It doesn't bear thinking about, it really doesn't.'

He picked up Brooks' iPhone and punched the home button. It was locked of course, as he expected, but a notification box showed it had received more than thirty missed calls in the last twenty-four hours. Adam Cameron's, the same.

'You'll have seen that I expect, he said, shoving the phone in her face. 'The shit's really hit the fan.'

Maggie looked sheepish. 'Yes, we know. We thought it would be good if we could find out what these calls were about.' Her tone was contrite. She knew they had screwed up and was anxious to get back on the right side of Frank.

But only because she knew he had access to Eleanor Campbell. And she would know how to crack a phone password.

Chapter 24

Naturally the distinguished member had made contingency plans, but now it seemed there was a definite risk of this matter spiralling out of control. Careless and stupid in equal measure. So now they had to assume the police would be all over the phone records, and goodness knows where that would lead. And it's not as if they hadn't been warned. *Careless talk cost lives*. Keep your bloody mouths shut, whatever happens. That's what they had been told.

So be it. Now the decision had been made for them. Regrettable of course, it would have been better if this little messiness could have been avoided, but now there was no other option. Plan B, robust thus far, would need to be seen through to its logical conclusion. There were a few new obstacles to be overcome, but that was to be expected, and it was built into the programme.

He placed his empty glass on the walnut coffee table and signalled for the attendant to bring his coat. Another one would have been nice, but he was expected back at the House for another tedious division bell. Plan B. The Ayes have it.

Chapter 25

Frank stood outside Atlee House puffing on a cigarette and reflecting on the day's events. When he got back to the office, Jill had reminded him that the evidence pack for the pre-hearing on his drugs corruption case needed to be with the CPS the next day. Being forced to work late, he was not in the best of humours. On top of that, the stolen phones had been handed over to Eleanor but that hadn't gone as smoothly as he had hoped. It was his own fault really for letting slip how he had come by them, and she was insistent that she would not touch them with a bargepole. He'd forgotten her fondness for form-filling, and it was only when he promised, lying, that he would get her an authorising e-mail from DCI Smart did she take them off his hands, and that was with great reluctance. 'Don't you trust me Eleanor?' he had asked guilelessly. 'No,' she had answered bluntly. So not a great day overall and he still had the big issue weighing on his mind. He knew there was something very wrong in their analysis of the Cathedral Close case.

Maggie had been set up, that was *probably* true. Dr Tariq Khan had been coerced into writing that report, that was *definitely* true. But whilst he could understand why the Home Secretary wanted Alzahrani locked up -after all, keeping the country safe was in his job-spec and he was no friend of Palestine - why the secret trip to Moscow to meet Ziadeh?

He was just about to head back inside when his phone rang. It was DI Burnside, sounding ebullient as ever.

'Hey Frank, how's things mate?'

'Aye, good Pete, good.' It was always nice to catch up with his pal and he cheered up a little.

'Well that's funny, 'cos a little bird told me there was some trouble about a couple of nicked phones, top of the range ones from what I hear. You running a little business on the side or something? I'm looking for a new Galaxy myself.'

'How the hell did you find out about that Burnside?'

The man was incredible, with an uncanny knack of finding out just about everything that was going on in the Met.

Except it wasn't really a knack, more the result of running a small army of inside informants across the organisation.

'Ear to the ground pal, ear to the ground. And on that topic, you will definitely want to hear what a little bird told me the other day.' When you heard his signature phrase 'a little bird told me', you knew you were in for a gem.

'This is a different little bird, I assume? Well, all right then, lay it on me.'

'Yeah, well you know we're working on the Penelope White murder?'

'The one that Barker thinks has got nothing to do with the Cameron case.'

'I think even he's now beginning to acknowledge that there might be a connection. Anyway, getting back to the White case, as part of our investigation we talked to her paper to find out what else she had been working on. Routine and all that.'

'You know she was doing something about my wee brother Jimmy, don't you? Bloody outrageous.' And it had been White too who had christened Maggie the most hated woman in Britain. If that wasn't a motive for murder, what was? Luckily Barker was too stupid to ever work out *that* connection.

'Yeah, we know that but I was able to get it into the gaffer's thick head that your brother didn't know about the Chronicle's campaign at the time of her murder. He's off the hook.'

'Cheers for that mate, he'll be bloody relieved.'

'No problem, all part of the service. What we did find out though, was that she was investigating something else, what was it called...wait a minute, I've got it written down somewhere...oh yeah, the Miner's Emphysema Trust. It was some big scandal a long time ago, nearly fifteen years ago in fact. 2004. This trust thing was meant to look after sick miners, but it turned out the chairman was running a massive scam and creaming off some of the cash for himself. When it all came out, the guy killed himself. Len Pringle, that was his name. He was an ex-miner.'

'I don't remember anything about that.'

'Well as I said, it was a long time ago. Pre-internet era and also I think the government of the time tried very hard to hush it all up. Point is, there was a lot of money went missing that was never accounted for. Two million quid in fact. That was the story that Penelope White was working on. Where did the money go, and who took it, all that sort of stuff.'

'That's a big story right enough. But Pete, why are you telling me all this?'

'Patience boy, patience. The reason I'm telling you this is because amongst the trustees at the time was one Gerrard Saddleworth MP.'

'Christ, that *is* interesting. You know that they're lovers, don't you? Gerrard and White. I mean, they *were* lovers, before she died.'

'Of course I knew that mate. That's the whole point. It seemed she was quite prepared to shaft her lover in pursuit of a story, if you'll pardon the expression. Nice girl.'

'Yeah exactly. So did White think that it was Saddleworth who took the money then?'

'I don't know, she was obviously just at the early stages of her investigation. But she had been in touch with the accountants that were brought in afterwards to clear up the mess. Reed Prentice & Partners they're called. They're still going, quite a big firm based up in Leeds. Anyway, her editor thought that that was the angle she was most excited about. I've got a contact name, Lily Hart, she's a partner or something. No idea what it's all about but it could be one for Department 12B to follow up on whilst us grown-ups work on the proper crimes.'

'Frig off Pete. But thanks, I'm grateful for this.'

'No problem mate. I'll text you what I have, and by the way, you owe me a pint. And let me know how it goes. Over and out.'

One for Department 12B? Frank wasn't so sure that Jill would sanction him swanning round the country on what might turn out to be a wild goose chase. But there was nothing to stop his hopeless amateur assistants filling the gap, and he figured their Saddleworth divorce case could easily stand the cost of a return rail ticket to Leeds. He picked up his phone and dialled his brother.

'Hey Jimmy, how do you fancy a wee trip to Yorkshire?'

Chapter 26

To say that events began to move fast following the brutal murder of nineteen-year-old Jack Wyatt would be the understatement of the millennium. Within hours, the new case had been wrestled from the grasp of the Gloucestershire Constabulary and allocated to the dead hand that was DCI Colin Barker. Not much later, DCI Jill Smart had learned from Eleanor Campbell that Frank Stewart was in possession of two stolen mobile phones, one belonging to a recent murder victim, and thus had no option but to grass him up, as he might have expressed it. All of this being why Barker and Smart and Frank and Maggie Brooks *nee* Bainbridge had been gathered together in the faceless Number Two conference room at Paddington Green police station on the orders of an apoplectic Chief Superintendant Brian Wilkes. Just down the corridor in two separate interview rooms languished the hot-shot international lawyer Philip Brooks and, sensationally, Her Majesty's Secretary of State for the Home Department, The Right Honourable Gerrard Saddleworth. Over in Cheltenham, the same Gloucestershire force was trying to track down Dr Tariq Khan, who seemed to have gone AWOL. It was all kicking off big time.

'I really don't know where to begin.'

Wilkes paced up and down at the front of the room, the sleeves of his crisp white shirt rolled up above the elbows. The atmosphere was tense. With only a year or two until retirement he didn't want his pristine reputation sullied by a momentous screw-up on a high-profile murder case like this.

'I'm grateful to you Jill for bringing it to my attention.' DCI Smart smiled back sweetly, ignoring Barker's drawn daggers. 'So who's going to bring me up to speed with where the hell we are with this bloody car crash of a case?'

'I will sir.'

Jill Smart did the introductions. 'DI Frank Stewart sir. He's one of the best DIs in my 12B team.'

Wilkes peered down his nose at him. 'One of the best, eh?' He knew the competition wasn't exactly stiff in that department. 'I know all about you Stewart. You've got history, haven't you?' Barker shuffled uncomfortably and stared at the floor.

'Yes sir.' The answer shot out like an arrow from a crossbow. 'Proud of it sir.'

'Well proceed DI Stewart, and keep it short and to the point.'

'I will do that sir. So you know the sort of stuff we do in the department, early investigations of things that might turn out interesting and that...'

'I know what you do in 12B,' Wilkes said impatiently, 'please get on with it.'

'Aye, sorry sir. So the latest victim is Jack Wyatt. He's only nineteen and he worked as a waiter at the Seven Cathedral Close restaurant in Gloucester. The lad was killed last Friday evening whilst on a night out with some mates in Cheltenham. A single stab wound through the heart.'

'So what's this got to do with the other two murders then?' Wilkes asked.

Maggie stood up. 'He was in our photograph.'

'Who are you again?' Wilkes barked.

'Maggie Bainbridge. I was the defence barrister on the Alzahrani case and now I'm an investigator working on a divorce case. Saddleworth verses Saddleworth. That's the Home Secretary and his wife Olivia.'

'I've heard of you. You're the most hated woman in Britain, are you not?' She wasn't sure, but it sounded like a compliment.

'Not any more I hope,' Maggie grinned. 'So I'll spare you the details, but as part of the investigation into Mr Saddleworth's financial status, we came across this photograph.' She had loaded the picture onto her phone earlier, in anticipation of the direction the meeting would take.

Wilkes took the phone and peered at it closely. 'So, what am I looking at here?'

'We were interested in this because in the trial -the Alzahrani trial I mean -Adam Cameron - he was the prosecuting barrister - told the judge that he had never met this guy - Dr Tariq Khan. The photograph proves he was lying and we wanted to know why. And then two of the diners were murdered and it all got serious and scary. And now poor Jack Wyatt is dead too. That's him pouring the wine.'

'More than a coincidence, eh sir?' Frank said. 'One dinner, three murders. And wee Jack could only have been killed for one thing, and that was to make sure he couldn't tell anything he might have overheard. '

'That's why I took the initiative and brought Mr Brooks and Mr Saddleworth in for questioning.' Jill Smart knew that she had acted way outside of her brief, trampling all over Barker's investigation, but she was ready with a semi-plausible justification. 'As you heard, there was suspicion of conspiracy in our case sir, and therefore we had plans to interview all the diners. That was before Jack Wyatt was murdered, of course.'

'Sir, what she did was completely out of order.' Barker face was slowly turning purple. 'She could have ruined my investigation.'

Frank stepped in.

'You knew as much as we did Colin and could have acted. After the first two murders, I told you all about the photograph and the big lie we'd uncovered, but you're obviously so much cleverer than me and you decided that my theory was bollocks. Total bollocks in fact, I think was your exact words. Am I right sir?'

To Frank, it looked as if DSI Wilkes was ruing his decision to move Barker off the Alzahrani case onto this one. The guy was a liability and he of all people should have known that. Now he slammed the table in frustration.

'Barker, is what the DI says true? You were aware of this possible connection and you decided to ignore it?'

'Yes, but we had other promising lines of enquiry...'

And now Frank went in for the kill.

'What DSI Barker is trying to say is that he already had someone in the frame for the Cameron murder sir. For what it's worth, I thought his evidence looked a bit flimsy but of course I'm just a lowly DI.'

Wilkes shook his head in disbelief.

'Christ's sake. And now we have a third murder. An innocent boy, barely more than a child. This really is a total arse-in-the-air shit-fest.' Frank knew Wilkes would be thinking how the press would play it when it got out that Jack Wyatt's murder was linked to a case they were already working on. Already there was revulsion across the nation about the death of the kid and it wasn't going to look good for the force.

'We're running the operation on very tight resources sir. It's easy to miss things when you're several heads light.'

Wilkes gave Barker a look of contempt. 'I don't want to hear any more from you DCI Barker.'

'But sir...'

'Shut up Colin.' The brutality of the put-down momentarily silenced the room. He turned to Jill Smart.

'You did good work bringing in those other two Jill. How did you manage to get Mr Saddleworth here, that couldn't have been easy?'

She hesitated for a moment. 'That photograph... we believe the group of diners had got to know of its existence. I emailed his office telling them that we wanted to talk about a dinner that he had attended several months ago. When we told him we had a photograph, he didn't even ask which dinner. Just agreed to come in.'

'So he had seen it.' Maggie said. 'Philip must have shown it to him, or at least told him about it.'

'Aye, well hopefully Pete Burnside is asking them just that question as we speak,' Frank said.

'So you've got DI Burnside on your team?' Wilkes mood seemed to lighten a notch. 'He's a very sound officer in my experience. A good man. Thank god we still have some of them on the force.' It was obvious to whom the last remark was directed.

'Aye, he's a top guy right enough. Just a pity guys like that have to put up with piss-poor leadership.' Frank was enjoying Barker's discomfort. 'Not in my case, of course sir.' He aimed an exaggerated smile at Jill Smart.

There was a quiet knock on the door. A few seconds later, it was pushed open and the head of Burnside peered round.

'Come in Burnside,' Wilkes said warmly. 'Come and tell us all you know.'

'Thank you sir.' He sat down at the head of the table and nervously flicked to the top page of his notebook.

'So obviously we went through the routine stuff you would do on a murder enquiry. Principally, establishing where they each were at the times of the murders. The funny thing was, their reactions were quite different but also a bit odd. So Mr Saddleworth, he seemed relieved when I told him my questions were about the three murders.' Burnside paused to check his notes. 'That was so strange, considering that he had allegedly been in a relationship with one of the victims, and so would obviously be a prime suspect. But what he said was 'so it's not about the money then' and when I asked him what he meant by that, he clammed up. I found that interesting, particularly in the light of another line of enquiry that is proceeding at the moment.' He gave Maggie a knowing glance, hoping he could brush over the unofficial nature of that investigation. Wilkes' eyes narrowed.

'What money?' he asked sharply.

'We don't know right now sir,' Burnside replied, 'but as I said, we have a lead on that one.'

'Who's working that?' It was getting a bit awkward and Maggie decided to help out.

'My colleague James Stewart is following up something on that one. Saddleworth's estranged wife believes he has hidden some money away, cash that he has not declared in the divorce financial statement.'

'Your colleague? So we've got some bloody amateur working on a triple murder case? God save me.' It wasn't clear to whom the remark was directed, but Jill stepped in to smooth the waters.

'Sir, I think it's just a coincidence that this came up on Miss Bainbridge's divorce case. That's a civil case, but I will of course get an officer allocated to it right away now that it's clear it's a police matter.'

That seemed to satisfy him. 'Well, just make sure you do Jill. Carry on Burnside.'

'Ok sir. Well anyway, as far as Mr Saddleworth goes, we will be following up his alibis of course, but with his reaction I'd say it's odds-on that they will stack up. I mean, it seems highly unlikely that a cabinet minister can sneak out of parliament unnoticed to shoot his lover then dive out again to expertly stab a QC. Every hour of his life is arranged by his advisers and civil servants, isn't it? Not to mention the fact that he's shadowed by security officers twenty-four-by-seven.'

'There's sense in that,' Wilkes said. 'So, tell us what this Brooks guy had to say for himself.'

'He's a smart-arsed bastard sir, that's one thing I can tell you. I had to restrain myself from shoving his teeth down his throat.'

'You're not allowed to do that nowadays,' Frank said, 'more's the pity.'

Burnside laughed. 'Yeah, exactly Frank. Anyway, I think he's another one with alibis that are going to stack up. When I said I was questioning him in connection with the murders, he just lounged back in his chair and laughed at me. Arrogant little shit. Then I asked him about the dinner, what it was all about and everything. He said it was just an innocent dinner with a few colleagues.'

'That's the party line,' Maggie said. 'We've heard that one before.'

'Sure, but anyway I told him I didn't believe that for a minute, and that I was quite happy to let him stew until he came up with something better. So finally, he spins a line that they were just trying to shore up the case against Alzahrani. He said that he had been invited along to give advice because they were worried she might try and pull some human rights stunt, and he's an expert in that field. Khan was there to offer his opinion on the recognition evidence, to see if it would stack up.'

'Did he say anything about me?' Maggie asked quietly.

'That the CPS had steered the case towards a less experience barrister?'

'No, he didn't. Neither of them did.'

'And did you believe their accounts?' Wilkes asked.

'Well, I don't know sir. It's all a bit irregular perhaps, but I can't see anything illegal about it at first glance. Although it's probably not something they would want to widely advertise, you know, trying to manipulate the outcome of a trial and all that.'

'The CPS are doing that every other day of the week,' Wilkes said bitterly. 'You know what, this is all nonsense. The whole thing.' His outburst was as unexpected as it was definitive. 'Pure unadulterated nonsense.'

'Sir?' Jill Smart could not hide her surprise.

'I've been a copper thirty years and believe me, I recognise a heap of dung when I see it. Whatever was being plotted at that dinner was serious enough for three people to be killed. Three people, for god's sake. This story that Brooks and Saddleworth are spinning just doesn't stack up. No way. There's something massive buried in here, I can feel it.'

He drummed his fingers on the table, his lips pursed in thought. Finally he spoke.

'Look, this is in danger of getting out of control and making us look mugs. Jill, I want you to take charge of the case with immediate effect. I assume you'll want DI Stewart and DI Burnside on the team, and you've got a free hand to draft in any officers you need. I want a result on this and I want it fast, do you understand?'

Maggie could see Jill struggling to conceal her pleasure at this turn of events. 'Yes sir, I'll get on to it right away.' DCI Colin Barker didn't look quite so delighted. He tried to mount a rearguard action.

'Sir, I assuming that DCI Smart will be under my command?'

The response was brutal. 'You assume incorrectly Colin. Come and see me at my office tomorrow and we'll have a chat about your future.' Code for *you're finished*.

Frank didn't try to hide his triumph. 'You'd better learn

how to use that parking ticket machine Colin. Nice wee steady job that, gets you out in the fresh air. Good for the complexion.'

Maggie sat quietly at the far end of the table, her body surging with adrenalin, her mind racing. It was the words that DCI Wilkes had used that had triggered the thought. He was right, the story didn't stack up. Whatever was being plotted at that dinner was serious enough for three people to be killed. *Three people*. And as the fog blew away, she could see it all too clearly. She didn't know why and she didn't know how, but she had never been more certain about anything in her life.

Because that dinner hadn't been about making sure Dena Alzahrani got convicted. *No way*. It was about making sure she got freed. And *that* was a secret you would kill for.

Chapter 27

It had taken all Jimmy's considerable powers of persuasion to set up the meeting with Reed Prentice. Whilst it was relatively straightforward to sweet-talk the receptionist into putting him through to the senior partner, using a combination of charm and what he imagined was his commanding voice, Lily Hart proved a tougher nut to crack. The mention of the Miner's Emphysema Trust caused an instant transformation in her demeanour, and she became at once both guarded and taciturn. Only when Jimmy mentioned, in desperation, that he was working as an agent of the Metropolitan Police did her mood soften and after some hesitation she agreed to a meeting - 'but only twenty minutes, and I can't fit you in until four-thirty.' That was good enough.

The journey to Leeds passed without incident, and two hours later Jimmy was leaving behind the bustling and impressively restored art-deco station. On the phone, she had assured him that their office was only ten minutes from the station, but Lily Hart's estimate had been optimistic to say the least, and it took nearly half an hour at a brisk pace to reach the offices of the accountants. Reed Prentice & Partners occupied a tastefully converted former rectory located on a leafy street on the edge of the university campus. On arrival, an efficient elderly receptionist ushered him through to a small meeting room, took his order for coffee, and with a brisk 'Mrs Hart will be with you in a few minutes,' retreated.

Hart was not at all what he had imagined. From her voice, he had pictured her as short, plump and dowdy, dressed in an old-fashioned knitted two-piece. In fact she was tall, slim and rather attractive. She looked around forty, wearing a crisp white tailored blouse and navy pencil skirt which accentuated a nice figure. Her hair was blond, probably natural he thought, with just a hint of grey beginning to show through. She exuded the cool and confident aura of a woman at the top of her game.

'Look I'm sorry Mr Stewart...' she began.

'Jimmy, please...'

'Jimmy, and I'm Lily... yes, so I'm really short of time so I hope you don't think I'm rude but I can only spare twenty minutes or so.'

Jimmy gave her his maximum-charm smile. 'I totally understand and it's great that you could see me and so quickly. As I mentioned on the phone, we're interested in what Penelope White was investigating around the Miners Trust affair. We wanted to ask you what you know. I believe you've found out something about it.'

She looked at him warily. 'You said on the phone you were with the Metropolitan Police.' This could be awkward, he thought.

'So Lily, I'm not exactly with the Met, but we - that's my firm, Bainbridge Associates - are working on a divorce case that's kind of transformed itself into a murder case, which is how the police got involved. Saddleworth verses Saddleworth, that's the divorce case. Gerrard Saddleworth, the Home Secretary. It's the wife Olivia who's seeking the divorce.'

'But you're not from the police then?' To his surprise, she sounded relieved.

'No, but they are aware of my visit. You can check with them if you'd feel more comfortable about it. I have the name and phone number of the Detective Inspector who's in charge of the case, I'm sure he would be happy to reassure you.'

'No no, it's just that.. well, what has come to light, I've thought about it, and to be honest, I don't really know whether I should go to the police or not.'

'Well without knowing, I'm not really in a position to advise you. Why not just start at the beginning, if that would be ok?'

His answer appeared to mollify her. 'Ok Jimmy, thank you. So how much do you know about the Trust?'

'Assume nothing.' That was pretty much the truth.

'It was reported in the media at the time so it's no secret, but it was more than fifteen years ago. Emphysema has always been a massive health problem in the mining industry. It's a terrible disease. It badly damages the lungs through breathing in all that coal dust.'

Jimmy nodded. 'Yeah, I sort of knew that much.'

'So, it had been known about for over a hundred years but it was just seen as collateral damage. But after the industry contracted in the eighties, the government had a sudden outbreak of guilt and decided to do something about it. They established a compensation scheme, and the sums involved were very substantial. More than fifty thousand pounds for each living miner. The initial fund from the government was nearly four hundred million pounds of taxpayer's money.'

'Bloody hell, that *is* huge,' Jimmy said.

'Exactly. A massive sum. Of course it was all very politically charged, and that's why they agreed to put a chap from the miner's union in charge of the organisation.'

'That was Len Pringle?'

'That's right. There was a lot of scepticism amongst ordinary miners at the time as to whether the trust was a government stitch-up, and so it seemed a good idea to put one of their own in charge. Pringle was the perfect candidate. He'd been a big hero during the miners' strike and so they trusted him.'

'And how did that work out?'

'Not good,' she replied. 'He scammed the fund out of millions in the end.'

Jimmy gave a low whistle. 'Goodness, nice work if you can get it. So how did the scam work?'

'It was ridiculously simple really. The trust was a rather shoestring operation. They only had about thirty staff administering the whole thing from a scruffy office in Barnsley. They kept a database of miners on a spreadsheet, running to about thirty thousand names, and twice a year they sent out an information pack which explained what a former miner had to do to claim their compensation. They just had to fill in a simple form accompanied by a doctor's letter confirming they were suffering from the disease and that was it. Nothing else. Then all it needed was Pringle's signature on the form and the cash was paid out.'

'And no other authorisation was needed?' Jimmy asked. 'That sounds like a gift to a fraudster.'

Lily nodded. 'It was. So of course in the natural way of things the list was being reduced by deaths, nearly a thousand a year. These guys didn't exactly have a great life expectancy, and in its wisdom, the rules of the trust were that eligibility for compensation ceased on death, which was cruel on the families who hadn't yet had the benefit of a payout.'

'So how did they get to find out when a miner had died?'

'Again, that was quite straightforward,' she replied. 'They got a note through from the miners' pension scheme and then they updated their spreadsheet accordingly. And that's the loophole that Pringle spotted and exploited. Not long after the trust was set up, he began to take personal responsibility for updating the records when a miner died. Or not, as was actually the case. It was then a simple job for him to fill in a benefits form in the name of a deceased miner, forge a doctor's certificate and divert the funds to a bank account he had set up for that specific purpose.'

'Goodness, was it as simple as that?' Jimmy said. 'But surely there was at least some scrutiny, an annual audit or something like that, with all that public money washing about?'

'Yes, of course. That was in the hands of Morton Waterside the London firm, but frankly they did a rather poor job. But you have to remember that the political pressure was to show that the former miners were getting their compensation, and frankly no one cared too much if a few rogue claims slipped through the net. Success was judged by how much was paid out, not how much was saved.'

She stole a glance at her watch. 'Look, I'm sorry Jimmy, I've only got ten minutes or so...' She sounded genuinely apologetic.

'No no, that's fine Lily, I really appreciate the time you've given me already. So how much did he get away with?'

'A lot. Nearly seven million pounds was siphoned off over four years.'

'As much as that? Crikey.'

'Yes, but remember that Pringle only had to make around a hundred false claims out of about five thousand legitimate ones that were processed each year. So you can see why it was so easy for him to conceal what he was doing.'

'Very clever,' he agreed. 'So how did he get found out in the end?'

Lisa smiled. 'There was a keen new girl joined the trust's admin team, Carrie Jackson I think her name was. She had a customer services background, worked in a big car dealership before, and she thought it would be a great idea to do a satisfaction survey. You know, to find out what the miners thought about how they had been dealt with throughout the application process. So one day, completely off her own bat, she sent a little survey form out to everyone who had been awarded compensation that year.'

'I see,' Jimmy said, smiling. 'I guess some letters would have gone to miners that were actually dead, causing their relatives to kick up a stink.'

'Exactly. Within days Miss Jackson had received seven or eight replies from indignant loved ones castigating the trust for its insensitivity. Naturally she was somewhat surprised by this, and decided to do a bit of digging and was shocked to discover that all the money supposedly awarded to these miners had in fact been paid into a single bank account. A smart girl, she went straight to the police and that's when it all started to unravel for Pringle.'

'And that's when you guys got involved?'

'That's right. I wasn't a partner at that time, just one of the young associates doing the legwork. To be honest it wasn't that difficult to uncover the money trail. It wasn't a sophisticated operation by any stretch of the imagination.'

'What do you mean?' Jimmy asked.

'Well, Pringle had set up a company selling garden sheds...'

'Garden sheds?' He couldn't explain why he found that so

funny.

'I thought that would make you laugh,' she replied, smiling. A very nice smile, he noticed. 'Yes, garden sheds. Expensive ones costing a few grand each, and all sold online so he never had to hold much stock. He laundered all the embezzled money through the shed company and again its auditors never once smelled a rat.'

He was conscious that time was running short, but Lily Hart now seemed happy to ignore her own deadline.

'Carry on please,' he said, 'only if you have time of course. This is fascinating.'

'Sure, no worries, I can spare a few more minutes. So anyway we uncovered that over four years he had processed one hundred and thirty-seven fraudulent claims, worth a total of six-point-eight million pounds.'

'That's unbelievable. And what did he do with it all?'

'Well, not very much at all, that's the odd thing. He took his wife on a couple of exotic cruises and that was about it. No fancy cars or big houses or anything like that. In fact we found nearly four and a half million sitting in the deposit account of the shed company earning a miserable one point five percent.'

'But wait a minute,' Jimmy said, 'by my rough calculation he still managed to get through nearly two million quid, or am I missing something?

'Yes, very perceptive Jimmy. In fact when we checked his bank statements, we found he had been withdrawing large amounts of cash, which we assumed he then squirreled away in a safety deposit box somewhere as a kind of rainy day fund. A sort of under-the-mattress stash if you like.'

'But I'm guessing you never managed to track that down?'

'Well, at the time, that was true,' Lisa said. *'He* obviously knew where it was going, but even when questioned by the police he wouldn't say anything. In the end, the authorities were happy to be able to recover a fair chunk of the money and sweep the whole thing under the carpet.'

'And then Penelope White got involved. How did that happen, do you know?'

'Well, yes I do. Did you know that Len Pringle committed suicide soon after the affair was exposed?'

'Yes, I did know that,' Jimmy said. 'The police told me.'

She smiled and for a second, their eyes met, exchanging a look that suggested the meeting might not end at five o'clock sharp as scheduled. Or was he just imagining that? He was too out of practice to be sure.

'So, he was found dead in his office, slumped over his desk with his wrist slashed. A knife was found lying on the floor beside him. The obvious conclusion was that he'd killed himself because of the shame of it all. It made perfect sense of course. But then a few weeks later, allegations appear in the press that the police had fouled up the crime-scene investigations. A police whistleblower told the Yorkshire Post that some idiot Detective Sergeant had picked up the knife, meaning that any chance of getting fingerprint evidence was lost. At the inquest, the coroner was highly critical of the officer in charge, but the political pressure was to tidy the whole thing up and so a suicide verdict was returned.'

'But from how you describe it, I'm guessing there were doubts,' said Jimmy.

'Oh yes. The family never accepted the verdict but they couldn't get anyone in authority to pay attention.'

'What, they think he was murdered?'

'They always have maintained he was, even after all these years. But earlier this year, they decide to take a different approach. They contacted Penelope White at the Chronicle and she started to take an interest in the story.'

'She's a damn terrier that woman. Was, I should say.'

'I met her you know. She came here just a few weeks ago. I quite liked her, she was funny. I couldn't believe it when I heard she had been murdered.' Lily gave a frown as if the consequences of that visit had entered her mind for the first time. 'You don't think her death could be connected to this, do you?'

Suddenly she looked frightened.

Jimmy did his best to reassure her. 'The police are still trying to establish a motive. She made a lot of enemies in her line of work. But no, I don't think they are suggesting it was connected to this.' For now at least.

'You see the thing was Jimmy, at the time I always thought our firm was anxious to wrap the whole thing up as quickly as possible. Too quickly I thought. There was a lot more digging that myself and the team wanted to do, but Neville Prentice wouldn't approve the work.'

'Neville Prentice?'

'He was the managing partner here and took personal charge of the project. The only grandson of one of the founders, you know, the guy with his name above the door. He was the last of the line.'

'Is he still around?' Jimmy asked.

'Physically yes, mentally no. He's in his eighties and now stuck in a retirement home in Harrogate with dementia. He was already pushing seventy at the time of the affair and retired soon afterwards.'

'So did you take over from him?'

'Goodness no, I was only twenty-eight at the time. We've gone through three managing partners before I took over earlier this year.'

Jimmy laughed. 'Yeah sorry, dumb of me.'

'No,' she smiled, 'it's very flattering.' She reached across her desk and picked up a buff folder. 'But remember I told you that something had come to light? Partly as a result of the Penelope White investigation? It's very delicate.'

'I'm intrigued,' Jimmy said.' Please tell me more.'

'Well, a couple of months ago we were having a clear-out of our archives. We pay a lot of money to store them securely off-site and it doesn't take long to fill up our allocated space. So we operate a fifteen-year rule, anything older we review and then dispose of. It's a lot of work as you can imagine, but unfortunately rather necessary.'

'Glad I don't have to do it,' Jimmy smiled.

'It *is* a pain, and particularly for me, because I have to make the final decision as to whether a file can be shredded or not. Not surprisingly, the staff err on the side of caution, so much of it gets dumped on me. Which is why this particular file ended up on my desk.'

The front of the folder bore a printed label with the legend *MET- Private & Confidential*. She opened it and took out a letter bearing the Reed Prentice letterhead.

'Obviously I was interested in this in the light of Penelope White's visit. Needless to say I was badly shocked by what I found.' Jimmy took it from her and began to read.

'As advised, I have set up a security deposit account with Geneva Swiss Bank, Lombard Street, London EC3. A welcome pack with full instructions will be sent to you within the next working week. Naturally, privacy is assured since as you will know under Swiss law the bank is prevented from divulging the identities of its account holders.

As agreed, my fee for this service is one hundred and fifty thousand pounds, payable please in cash. I enclose the signed non-disclosure agreement as drawn up by your legal advisors, and assure you of my utmost discretion on this matter at all times.

Yours faithfully,
Neville Prentice

Jimmy gave her a look of astonishment. 'Lily, this is unbelievable. Who was this addressed to?' Of course, he already knew the answer.

'There were two copies. One was sent to Gerrard Saddleworth. As you know, he was a trustee at the time. The other was to the solicitor who drew up the non-disclosure agreement.'

So Olivia Saddleworth was right all along. Sneaky little Gerrard did have a mountain of cash stashed away. A bloody humongous pile in fact. Asvina Rani was going to be very pleased indeed.

'And your senior partner was in on it too? I can't believe that. A hundred and fifty grand quid to keep his mouth shut. And he covered his arse with an NDA. A very smart guy.'

'Yes, it seems bizarre there should be an NDA involved in what is a very shady affair, but in fact when I thought about it, old Neville probably didn't actually do anything illegal himself. He may have known how Saddleworth came by the cash, but he wasn't involved in procuring it in any way so he could turn a blind eye. As you said, a smart guy.'

'And how *did* he come by the cash, do you think?'

'I don't know for certain, but I'd speculate blackmail. It's my guess that Saddleworth found out what Pringle was up to, and made him pay up to keep quiet.'

Jimmy nodded. 'Yeah, that stacks up. And as long as he kept the cash hidden out of sight then even if Pringle grassed him up to the authorities, there would be no evidence. He could just deny everything.'

Lily gave him a wry smile. 'Exactly. So you can see my dilemma Jimmy. This looks bad for the firm, but I don't think I can keep this under wraps. I need to tell the police.' It was half-question, half-statement of fact.

Suddenly a chilling thought came to him. 'Do you think Saddleworth might have murdered Pringle? Perhaps he'd decided to confess what he had done, and take Saddleworth down with him. So he was killed to shut him up.'

She looked surprised. 'That I think is a step too far, isn't it? Government ministers don't go around murdering people.'

'Except he wasn't a minister back then. But you know Lily,' Jimmy said, his mind racing, 'what if that's what Penelope White had found out? It would be the story of her life, wouldn't it? *I was in love with killer minister.*'

And then perhaps her lover had decided that she had to be killed too. Because Jimmy knew from his brother's long experience that the crime-novel cliché was actually true. That when you had killed once, it was much easier to do it again.

'Look, I'll make sure the police are informed about all of this,' Jimmy said, 'and of course let them know that it wasn't your fault in any way. That you didn't know anything about Neville's NDA.'

He noticed her stealing another glance at her watch.

'I'm sorry Lily, I know I've overstayed my welcome, I'm really grateful for your time...'

'No no Jimmy, I was just checking if it was five o'clock yet.

I wonder, are you rushing back to London this evening? I could really do with a drink and something to eat.'

The offer was tempting. *Very tempting*. A drink, a quick dinner and then back to London on a late train. He looked again at her lovely face. A face that said there wasn't much chance that the evening would simply end with coffee. And for just a moment he wavered. Until he thought of Flora. If he wanted his wife back, and he did, and desperately, then sleeping with beautiful accountants would not help the cause.

'I need to get back to London.' He could see the disappointment in her eyes. 'It would be lovely, but really, I have to get back.' He wasn't sure who he was trying to convince.

As he walked back to the station he was able to console himself by reflecting on the success of the mission. Now they had proof that Saddleworth had squirreled away two million pounds in a safety deposit box, the transaction conveniently arranged by his financial advisor. A financial advisor who had covered his own backside with a non-disclosure agreement, drawn up by a lawyer mate of Saddleworth's. And though it was only a guess, he'd put money on that mate being Philip Brooks. A web of deceit, and a web he was convinced had its sticky silk wrapped all around that Cathedral Course dinner.

He was just about to go through the ticket barrier when he felt his phone vibrate in his pocket. It was a text. From Lily Hart.

Still time to change your mind xx.

Chapter 28

It was nearly two o'clock before Jimmy made it back to Kings Cross. Maggie had no idea what had made it necessary for him to stay overnight in Leeds, but no doubt he would tell them when they met up in a few minutes' time. A few days earlier he had added her to his *Find a Friend* list, which meant she was now able to track him as he crawled down Grays Inns Road at a pace normally reserved for old ladies pushing wheeled walking frames. Normal duration, twelve minutes. Time expended so far, twenty-three minutes. He was obviously in no hurry to get back to the office, which wasn't at all like him. She jabbed the call button and flicked it on to speakerphone.

'Hi Jimmy, are you anywhere near our Starbucks?' She knew he was, and he would know that she would know too. 'Elsa's run out of bloody beans again and I was desperate. I think Frank's going to pop round in a bit too.'

'Funnily enough, I'm just a couple of minutes away,' he said, his voice feigning surprise. *'Quite a coincidence that you should call when I'm only a skip and a jump from the front door.'*

'So, how did you get on?' Maggie asked as he pulled up a stool alongside her. 'Must have been a worthwhile visit given how long it took.'

'Yeah sorry about that. I took the opportunity to look up an old army pal afterwards. From the Helmand days. Had a few beers and grabbed something to eat and then crashed out on his sofa.'

She didn't like to tell him that she already knew some of that, having tracked his about-turn at the station and all his movements thereafter. Except of course, she didn't know who he had been with. Although she'd found it interesting that he had walked back to Lily Hart's office just twenty minutes after he'd left.

'That's nice.'

'Yeah, it was,' he said hesitantly. 'It was a great evening. He's a good lad, old Lawrence. One of the best.'

Maggie gave him a wry smile. 'And Lily Hart? What was she like?'

He shrugged. 'Lily? Yeah, good, very helpful. And smart. She reminded me a bit of you actually.'

She assumed it was meant as a compliment, but if he had spent the night with her, she wasn't sure she welcomed the comparison. And she didn't really want to find out either, so she steered the conversation onto business.

'But did you find out anything interesting from her?'

He too seemed keen to move on. 'You could say that,' he said, grinning. 'Aye, you could say that.'

And then he told her. About the Trust, and the safety deposit box stuffed with two million in cash, and the non-disclosure agreement. The non-disclosure agreement that had been drawn up and witnessed by Philip Brooks.

She wasn't at all surprised by the revelation. Philip hadn't told her anything during their marriage, let alone what he'd done before they met, and this would be just one more in a long list of skeletons in his cupboard.

'Did you know he was involved?' Jimmy asked. 'I guess it was quite a few years before you married him.'

She shrugged. 'No. One of many things he kept from me.'

'But don't you think the whole thing is bloody unbelievable?'

'What's unbelievable?' Frank had strolled in, taking a final drag on his cigarette before extinguishing it between his fingertips, ignoring the reprimanding stare of a tattooed barista.

'All of it.' Her mind was racing, trying to process this new information that Jimmy had mined up in Yorkshire. Even with a cursory review, she could see that it supported her crazy theory. One hundred percent. She *had* to be right, there was no doubt about it now, and it couldn't be kept to herself any longer. The words rushed out in a torrent.

'Guys, I want to run something past you. Something that came into my head yesterday when we were with Chief Superintendent Wilkes. Something mental.'

'Aye ok,' Frank said calmly. 'We're all ears.'

'I like mental,' Jimmy said.

And then she told them. *It was all about freeing Alzahrani.* Yes, they hadn't misheard her, that's what she had said. There had been a conspiracy to ensure that Alzahrani walked free. She didn't know why, and she had no idea who was behind it all, but she couldn't be more sure she was right. There was a long silence as each of them tested the sense of Maggie's premise, trying to force the facts of the case into place, like pieces in a particularly complex jigsaw. Frank was the first to speak.

'There's a lot of stuff going on in this case, stuff that's way, way out of the ordinary. Five people have dinner and now two of them have been murdered, along with the waiter who served them. Professionally murdered too, don't forget. And now we know that at least three of them have big secrets that they really wouldn't want to come out into the open. Dr Khan with his fondness for rent-boys, and now we find out Brooks and Saddleworth are all implicated in a multi-million fraud. That's all serious shit.'

'And what about Saddleworth's visit to Moscow?' Jimmy said, 'and Cameron's drugs bust and the fact we think there's something suspicious about Maggie getting the defence brief.'

'Yes, there's all of that,' Frank agreed. 'As I said, a lot of stuff going on.'

'It's got to be Saddleworth, hasn't it?' Jimmy said. 'Behind all of this, I mean. He's got the most to lose.'

'Or Philip,' Maggie said. 'Remember, he's a long-time supporter of the cause.'

But then she thought about it again. Yes, he was a supporter, but not a believer. Philip wouldn't give a sod whether Alzahrani got freed or not, because Philip didn't believe in anything other than himself. The rights of the Palestinian people were no more than a lucrative market niche, a niche that paid big bucks. Money, that was all that Philip believed in.

Frank did not answer directly. 'You know, it's not exactly rocket science but people with big secrets are vulnerable to coercion. And I think that's what is in play here. Maybe all of these guys are being forced to do something they really don't want to do.'

'*Were* being forced,' Maggie corrected. 'Penelope White and Adam Cameron are both dead.'

'Aye, and that's the next step when coercion stops working,' Frank said, looking serious. 'I laughed at you two when you brought up the means, motive, opportunity thing, but guys, I'm not laughing now. We're still struggling with the motive, but it's the other two I'm worried about right now.'

'What do you mean?' Maggie asked.

'What I mean is we've got professional killers on the loose here and they've always got multiple options when it comes to both. We've had a clinical shooting and two expertly-executed stabbings. So as I said, professionals.'

'So where does that get us?' Maggie asked.

'Nowhere,' Frank said flatly, 'because until we know why someone wanted Alzahrani freed, we're buggered. Totally buggered.'

***

It was Yash Patel at the Chronicle who had originally broken the 'Saddleworth and his murdered lover' story. Poignant too, given that the lover in question was his former boss Penelope White. Not that he had shed many tears for her himself. She was a bitch, and a racist bitch too, although she had tried hard to keep that under the radar. Keen too to take all the credit for everything, when often as not it was him who had put in all the legwork. But what the hell, now he was the columnist with the photoshopped mug-shot alongside his by-line, so you could say that whoever had murdered her had done him a big favour. That's the way he saw it and the paper was secretly pleased with the outcome too, having previously been a bit light on diversity amongst its columnists. He wasn't too modest to admit it had been a stonking article, with just enough innuendo for the readers to go away thinking, you know what, maybe he did kill her. Perhaps he had, Yash wasn't ruling it out. What a story that would be.

And now Gerrard Saddleworth was doing what all politicians did after being caught with their pants down. Round up the wife, children and pets, stick them on a platform in a nice conference room in a nice hotel convenient for the media and turn on the tears. Except Saddleworth's estranged wife Olivia had told him to bugger off, so he was left only with his beautiful nineteen-year-old daughter Patience by his side, and judging by her expression, she didn't look too pleased to be there either. The room was packed with hacks and TV crews from all around the world, so much so that it was standing room only. Yash had anticipated this and had arrived nice and early, being rewarded for his diligence by a seat in the front row, close enough for a bit of subtle upskirting, and Patience had unintentionally obliged by wearing a micro-skirt and no tights. An innocent pastime in his eyes and ridiculous that it had been made illegal, but on balance, probably not the subject for one of his campaigning articles.

The party's press officer stood up, cleared her throat, gave a weak smile then began reading from a prompt card. 'Ladies and gentlemen, thank you for coming. May I introduce Gerrard Saddleworth, Minister of State for the Home Department. Gerrard.' She hadn't had to bust a gut to come up with that introduction, but maybe he was being a bit harsh on her. It was odds-on she had written what was to follow too, but even that wouldn't have been too difficult given the number of times she'd had to do it. A simple cut and paste job, no more than that.

Saddleworth was wearing the standard man-of-the-people uniform of navy suit with blue open-necked shirt. On the outside at least he appeared relaxed. Having stood in for PM's questions on many occasions, he was hardly going to be fazed by this lot. He smiled fondly at his daughter and she scowled back at him with a look that so clearly said 'wanker.' Yash assumed it was only the threat of her allowance being withdrawn that had brought her here.

'Ladies and gentlemen, thank you for coming,' he parroted. 'I've come here to apologise publicly to my constituents, my party and above all to my wonderful family for letting them all down...'

Yep, pretty much the same words that his colleague the Right Honourable James Haggerty had used just over six months ago when his pregnant Russian lover had spilled the beans to the *Sun*. Now there would be some crap about the pressures of office and no man being immune to temptation, and how much he deeply regretted his actions blah, blah, blah. The assembled press guys were listening politely and some were even taking notes, but this was only the starter for the main course to come. Because as soon as Saddleworth had finished, a hundred hacks were going to blurt out the only question everyone in the room wanted answered. 'Minister, did you kill Penelope White?' Already, the TV correspondents were making sure their camera crews and sound guys were properly lined up to make sure that it was nicely captured for the millions back home.

The risk assessment for the event had come back as only a Level 2, so they had decided to keep the security pretty-low key. They would go with just his regular undercover team, stationing one at the door and the other to the side of the stage. Adequate, and besides, he didn't want the press bitching about the cost of policing what was essentially a private matter. Both of them would be armed of course, but with no guns on display. More than enough to deal with anything that might arise that afternoon. Except that it wasn't.

The policeman watched on warily as the smiling young woman approached the closed doors of the meeting room. There was something familiar about her, he thought, but he couldn't quite put a finger on where he'd seen her before. She was holding out a press pass in front of her for inspection. He took the pass from her and smiled back.

'You're a bit late love. I think he's already started.' These would be the last words he would ever say, as she plunged the stiletto blade into his chest, thrusting upwards to pierce the heart. Death would be instant, not that she cared about that. She pulled on the clown facemask, took the silencer-equipped pistol from her coat pocket and then, pushing the door ajar a fraction, she slipped through, locking it behind her. No-one in the room realised she was there, nor the mortal danger they were in, until they heard the dying gasp of the second policemen as two bullets thudded into his chest.

Adopting a combat position with the pistol thrust out in front of her, she swivelled on her heels and swept the room, looking for heroes. Out the corner of his eye, Yash could see that a cameraman from a US network was still filming. Bloody idiot. The assailant took him out from twenty meters with a shot that smashed straight through his skull, drenching a dozen journalists in a satanic mess of blood and warm brain tissue. Ignoring the screams of horror, she advanced slowly down the aisle towards the platform, still holding the gun out in front of her.

Patience Saddleworth was screaming hysterically. 'Please don't, please don't, please don't.' Beside her sat her father, rooted to the spot, his face a mask of confusion. And now the young woman was raising the pistol, pointing it at Saddleworth's forehead, standing close enough to taste his breath.

'What do you want? Who are you? Why are you doing this?' The woman stayed silent, remaining perfectly motionless with the gun inches from his head. Waiting, just waiting until the shit ran down his leg. And then she turned slightly, no more than four degrees, and blew Patience Saddleworth's brains out.

'This wasn't supposed to happen'. Yash was sure that's what Saddleworth had whispered. His last words before the assassin shot him between the eyes, then disappeared through the fire exit at the back of the room.

This wasn't supposed to happen. What had he meant by that?

***

Within minutes, naturally, it was all over the news. The brutal murder of the Home Secretary and his daughter was bound to shock the country and it did. Since the press was not aware of the existence of the Cathedral Close photograph, early speculation was that this was a planned terrorist outrage aimed at the heart of our democracy, almost certainly Islamic in origin. Outrageous in planning and audacious in execution, it had clearly been arranged so that it was played out live in front of the worlds' media. There was condemnation about the lack of security at the event, which many said was another symptom of the general incompetence of the security services.

In the barrage of comment and analysis which followed, the words of a little-known Chronicle columnist went largely unnoticed. *'This wasn't supposed to happen'*. But Maggie Bainbridge read them with horror, instantly recognising what they signified. Everyone at that dinner was going to die. Meaning Philip Brooks and Dr Tariq Khan were in mortal danger. And their families too.

Now she had only one thought in her head. She had to get to Ollie and make him safe.

Chapter 29

'Shit, that was close.' Jimmy had the pedal nailed to the floor as he accelerated away from the junction, the engine screaming up to maximum revs. He had barged through the crossover at nearly sixty miles an hour, smacking into the rear flank of a big Lexus and narrowly missing being T-boned by the refuse truck proceeding lawfully at ninety degrees with the green light. The wing of the Golf was now hanging on by a thread, throwing up a kaleidoscope of sparks as they powered along, headlights on full beam and horn blaring.

'Sorry about the no-claims Maggie.' He knew it wasn't the time for jokes, but she looked as if she was close to passing out. 'We'll be there in ten minutes, but please when it's time for a change, can you trade this wreck in for something quicker.'

She responded with a weak smile. He could tell the tension would be gnawing at her stomach like a bad curry. *We just have to get there, we just have to get there.* There was a loud bang as the trailing wing smashed against a lamppost and detached itself, flying through the air and taking out the plate-glass window of a charity store.

'Whoa, lost a bit of weight there,' Jimmy exclaimed. 'All helps.' He reached across and took her hand, giving it a squeeze. 'It will be alright.' God, how he hoped that would turn out to be true.

They reached her Hampstead home - he knew she still thought of it as hers, even after all this time - without further incident, as he brought the Golf to a screeching stop with two wheels on the pavement. They threw open the doors and sprinted up the path. Suddenly Jimmy shot out an arm and shouted. 'Wait Maggie!' The front door was ajar, creaking quietly in the gentle breeze. This didn't look right. Helmand all over again, the old instincts kicking in.

'Maggie, you just stay here.'

'But Jimmy...'

'For god's sake Maggie, do as I tell you. Get back on to the police and find out where the hell they've got to.' No time for niceties, he didn't want another dead rooky on his conscience. Gingerly, he edged open the door and went in to the hallway. *Shit*. He could smell it. Cordite, and recently fired too. The smell of death.

'Philip!' he shouted. 'Philip Brooks!' No response. Every door in the hallway was closed tight, making the sweep doubly difficult and doubly dangerous. A professional job, no doubt about that.

'Philip!' He kicked open the nearest door, allowing it to slam against its brass doorstop before entering. A comfortable living room furnished with two soft leather sofas and a huge wall-mounted television. Fresh flowers in a crystal vase. Tasteful reproductions on the wall. *Nothing here.* Two more rooms yielded similar results. Three more to go. But wait a minute, what was that? The faintest of cries. He stood stock-still and listened hard. A child's voice. *My mummy, I want my mummy.* Please god, no! He dashed to the end of the hall and kicked open the door. Christ, he had seen some shit over in Afghanistan, but nothing like this. Spread-eagled on the terracotta tiled floor in a pool of blood lay Angelique Perez, two bullets holes drilled neatly through her forehead. Her white silk blouse, now blood-splattered, had been ripped away, exposing her breasts above her black silk bra. Her flower-patterned skirt had been pulled down to her ankles, and a pair of knickers lay discarded beside her. Whether she had been raped before or after her murder was impossible to tell.

Philip Brooks' body was slumped face down across the kitchen table, an exit wound clearly visible on the back of his head. Jimmy had seen this so many times before. A pistol rammed into the mouth, and then the killer would wait and wait, wait until the shit literally ran down the victim's leg before blowing his head off. Was Perez forced to watch her lover's execution, or was Brooks forced to watch her being raped? It turned his stomach just thinking about it.

But where was Ollie? Surely it was his voice he had heard, it must have been, but where the hell was he? Rapidly, he surveyed the big kitchen. What was that in the corner? A door, maybe a pantry or something. He leapt over and flung it open. There, tied to a wooden chair was little Ollie Brooks. A bloody swelling had almost closed his right eye and his cheek showed the weal marks where he had been struck with force. The bastards, the evil bastards.

And then, to his horror, Jimmy saw the package. Attached to one leg of the chair with cable ties. A package that he instantly recognised. Eight or more coloured wires emerging from the top, most likely leading to a trigger or timer. His eyes traced along the line of the wires as they snaked around the chair-leg and up the backrest. From there, they had been fed down the neck and along the arm of Ollie's jumper. Yes, it was a trigger all right. A trigger that little Ollie Brooks now held in his tiny hand.

The boy had been staring at him, paralysed with fear. And no wonder, because what the boy had witnessed didn't bear thinking about. Jimmy kneeled down in front of him. 'It's Ollie isn't it? I'm Jimmy, I'm a friend of your mummy's and I'm here to help you. Is that ok?'

The little boy nodded slowly then mumbled, 'I want my mummy.'

'She'll be here soon, I promise.' He wrapped his fist around his hand and squeezed gently. At least it was a trigger, not a timer. And then, the ghastly thought. What if it was both, he wouldn't put it past these bastards. Hopefully the police would be here in a minute and then they could get his old mates from the bomb squad on the case. But what if it was also a timer? Of course it will be, that's exactly what they would do. Shit.

Hearing footsteps behind him, he spun round, but it was too late to stop her entering the kitchen, as if he could do anything about it in his current situation. She stood frozen to the spot, unable to take in the scene of utter carnage that filled her field of vision. She staggered towards the wall before throwing up.

'Maggie, just close your eyes and get the hell out of here. Now!' She turned round in the direction of his voice, bringing her son into view. 'Ollie, Ollie, my Ollie!'

'It's a bloody booby-trap Maggie. A bomb. Please don't come any closer.'

'I'm not leaving Ollie. I need to be with him, whatever happens.' Of course she was never going to leave her son to his fate, what mother would? But maybe, just maybe, her presence offered a tiny glimmer of hope.

'Look Maggie, Ollie's holding a trigger in his hand. If he opens his fist, then that's it, the bomb goes off.'

She gasped and covered her mouth with her hand.

'I know, it's a shock,' Jimmy said, 'but I need you to help me. It's the only chance we've got, ok?'

She nodded but her eyes radiated fear.

'His little hand must be hurting so I need you to take over from me so I can take a closer look at the device. I need you to speak to him and tell him how important it is not to open his hand. Just for a second. Just when we're doing the switch. Is that ok?'

She sobbed but was able to wipe the tears from her eyes with her sleeve. 'Of course.'

Kneeling down, she planted a soft kiss on her son's forehead. 'Darling, I need you to be a big brave boy. You're very good at counting aren't you?'

'Yes, mummy I am.'

'And what's the biggest number you can count to my darling?'

He gave a weak smile. 'To infinity and beyond.'

'Infinity and beyond. That's amazing my love. So when I say go, start counting and don't stop squeezing your hand until you reach infinity. Can you do that for me?'

'Yes mummy.'

Jimmy gave her a silent thumbs-up. 'Just move your hand over mine. Once Ollie starts counting I'll slip mine out of the way and you can take over.'

She nodded. 'Ok, Ollie, are you ready? To infinity and beyond. One-two-three- go.'

Deftly, Jimmy slipped his hand away to be replaced in an instant by Maggie's. *Mission accomplished.* He kissed her gently on the cheek and whispered 'It's going to be all right.'

He kept telling her that. He just wished he believed it. Now all he needed was a pair of scissors and a massive dose of luck.

And then he remembered that he had the number of Private Alex Marley tucked away in his phone book. Thank god, she answered on the first ring. *'Sir, long time no speak. It's great to hear from you again. What are you up to, enjoying civvy street?'* As upbeat as ever.

'Well actually you might be interested to know I'm standing in a hundred-grand Hampstead kitchen trying to figure out how to disarm another bloody IED. I need your help.'

Instantly the cool professional soldier kicked in, her voice taking on an urgent tone. *'Roger sir, can I have a summary of the situation?'*

'Looks like a standard IRA Semtex package, eight-wire device with a trigger and probably some sort of internal timer wired up as a booby trap. Seen anything like it before?'

'Yes, I think we have sir. Eight wire, did you say?

'Yeah, that's right.' He shot an encouraging glance at Maggie.

'That's fairly good news then sir.'

'It is?' He had to admit that he wasn't seeing much upside at that moment.

'Yeah, so they would have used two wires for the timer circuit and two for the trigger. That means there are only four decoys.'

'Hang on a minute. Does that mean...'

'...fifty-fifty chance sir. Much better than the two out of eight that we normally get.'

'And that's supposed to be good news?'

'Yes sir. I'd best let you get on. Over and out.'

So that was what it now came down to. The lives of Maggie, her son and his own resting on a fifty-fifty throw of the dice, or more accurately, a fifty-fifty snip with a pair of scissors. But as Marley had said, nothing to do but get on with it.

'Scissors!' he barked. 'Where are they kept?'

'I used to keep them in the top drawer. Just left of the

hob,' Maggie shouted.

He'd forgotten this was no longer her home. He just hoped Angelique hadn't had a reorganisation. Yanking open the drawer, he rummaged around in the untidy pile of utensils. There they were, thank heavens for that. Two steps and he was back in the pantry, where Ollie was still counting in a lilting rhythm '...sixty-five, sixty-six, sixty-seven...' He hoped to hell he would reach one hundred.

He dropped to the ground, laying on his stomach so that he was eye-level to the device. Eight wires, colour-coded, but the problem was only the bomb makers had the key to the code. He shuffled up close, squinting hard to focus on the gap where the wires emerged from the buff-coloured padded envelope. It was hard to be sure, but was there the tiniest of gaps between the first two wires and the remaining six? He looked again. Yes, it was only a fraction of a millimetre but there was a definite gap. He spun onto his back, pulled out his phone and called Marley again, spitting out the question.

'Would we expect the wires to the battery to be next to one another?'

Her reply was instant. *'Yes sir, it's the only way they could route them. Problem is, you usually can't tell which two by looking.'*

But maybe today, they had got a lucky break. Trouble was they wouldn't get to know if he was wrong. And now it was the moment of truth.

'Maggie, I'm going to cut the wire. You know what that means. You should say your goodbyes to Ollie. Just in case.'

But there was nothing to say. He knew she loved him more deeply than any love in the history of the universe, and saying it wouldn't make it any truer. Besides, it was all going to be fine. Fifty-fifty. Given the shit she had been through in the last eighteen months, surely this time the fates would take pity on her.

'We're good. Cut it Jimmy.' She closed her eyes and rested her cheek against Ollie's.

This was it. Decision time. He had no idea where it came from, but bizarrely he began to hum a familiar lilting tune.

Que sera sera, whatever will be will be. Red and green, it had to be these two. Cut either, or both, and you cut the power to the detonator. Bomb disarmed, job done. He positioned the blades over the two wires, being careful to move the others well out of the way. *Come on man, just do it.* Unless you want the timer to do it for you anyway. He tightened his fingers on the grip and squeezed hard, looking away, as if that was going to make any difference. *Snip.* And then nothing. Glorious, sweet, life-affirming nothing.

He ripped the package off the leg of the chair and slid it along the floor until it rested against the back wall of the pantry. Wrapping his arms around the chair, he picked it up with Ollie still tied to it. The boy was still counting '... ninety-eight, ninety- nine, one hundred.'

Jimmy beamed a huge smile at him. 'A hundred. That's amazing mate, you can stop now. Come on Maggie, time to get out of here.' As if she needed to be told. They struggled down the hallway, reaching the front door just as the shriek of sirens announced the arrival of the Met, led by Jill Smart and Frank Stewart.

'Christ what's happened here?' Frank asked. 'C'mon, let me help you with the boy.' Gently, they laid the chair down on the driveway.

'Wouldn't rush in there if I was you,' Jimmy cautioned. 'Bit of a mess. And you need to call the bomb squad fast.'

Maggie was feverishly trying to free her son from his bonds, but not making much progress. From the depth of a trouser pocket, Frank retrieved an old-school flick knife.

'Allow me madam.' With a couple of expert slashes, Ollie was free.

There were of course hugs and kisses and tears and thank-yous, and chilling cold sweats when they each contemplated what might have been. For Jimmy, there was overwhelming relief that he hadn't lost another one. For Maggie, the weird realisation that the murder of her husband of eight years had triggered no emotion whatsoever. For now at least. Perhaps the eighteen months of sheer hell had shredded her capacity to feel anything, but whatever it was, right now she was glad he was dead, and Angelique too. Meanwhile, little Ollie was still counting. To infinity and beyond.

The ambulances had arrived to take them to the Royal Free. For Maggie and Jimmy, the injuries were merely psychological, as if that wasn't bad enough. Ollie would need a couple of stitches above his eye and an x-ray of that cheek to make sure there were no broken bones. As to the impact on his little mind of the unspeakable horrors he had witnessed, that would have to wait until the hoards of councillors and psychologists were sent in to do their work. Tonight, for the first time in over eighteen months, he would sleep under the same roof and in the same room as his mummy, and for both of them, it was a heavenly bliss that could not be described in words.

For the professionals of law-enforcement, late on the scene but relieved that events had turned out well, there was now only one priority, as voiced poetically by Detective Inspector Frank Stewart.

Where the fuck was Dr Tariq Khan?

Chapter 30

You could do a lot of things in Department 12B that you couldn't do over at Paddington Green nick. Things like giving two amateur investigators a fake pass to Atlee House and a quiet desk in the corner.

'Does Jill know about this?' Maggie asked as Frank led them down the warren of corridors to the depressing open-plan space they had newly-christened the Operations Room. DCI Smart had decamped to Paddington to head up the case leaving Frank behind, 'nominally in charge of the office' as she had described it.

'Yes, of course,' he lied. 'Tough case like this, we need all the resources that we can lay our hands on.' That much at least was true.

'Did you see her on the news last night? Did a good job I thought. A telly natural.' After the horrifying murder of Saddleworth and his daughter, no stone was being left unturned in the search for the missing Dr Khan, and DCI Smart had decided that a direct appeal to the public was called for. As well as the televised police press conference, photographs of the missing scientist would be plastered on every vacant wall from Lands End to John O' Groats, although logic suggested that he would be holed up somewhere in the North West, close to where he grew up, it being an established fact that fugitives from justice were generally picked up close to their own manor. Not that Khan was exactly fleeing justice, but broadly speaking the same rules applied.

Now Frank was revealing that he had that morning spoken with a detective constable with the Gloucestershire force who had been sent to interview Khan's wife. Contrary to his expectations, Mrs Khan had not denied knowledge of her husband's whereabouts, but was adamant that she would never reveal the location where he was hiding. When asked, politely according to the officer's account, to hand over her phone, she had consented, adding something along the lines of did they think she would be so stupid as to make that sort of school-girl error. Subsequent review of her phone logs, both mobile and landline, had revealed no calls to or from his phone since he had disappeared. Similar scrutiny of those of his three teenage daughters had also drawn a blank. Social media, the same. This was one disciplined operation.

'Take her in to a quiet interview room and water-board her' had been Frank's helpful advice, the slow-witted yokel DC responding in all seriousness that they didn't do things that way in their neck of the woods.

'Doesn't she realise the danger they are all in?' Jimmy said. 'I'd be shitting myself if I was them given what has been happening.'

'The local plod says she's in complete denial about all of it. But they're posting twenty-four-hour surveillance at the house and also keeping tabs on the kids' school. Don't worry, they are taking this very seriously.' He sounded more convincing than he actually felt.

Eleanor Campbell swung by their desks, noisily sucking up the dregs from a *grande* strawberry milkshake. She pointed to the new occupants of the corner desks.

'Who are these two?' Frank might have known that little miss I'm-not-doing-anything-until-I've-got-the-form-signed-in-triplicate would sniff out anything irregular.

'Work experience students.'

'Does Jill know about this?'

The lie was much easier the second time around. 'Of course she does Eleanor. Naturally.'

'I can like easily check.'

Maggie stood up and reached out her hand. 'Maggie Bainbridge. You must be Eleanor Campbell. Frank has told me so much about you. All good, I hasten to add.'

'Oh has he?' Her expression visibly softened.

'Technical genius he says you are.' With a twinkle in his eye, Jimmy looked at her and smiled his devastating smile. 'I'm Jimmy Stewart, it's great to meet you. A real pleasure.' That was the clincher. Eleanor was in, no matter what roguery Frank was planning. She perched herself on the edge of his desk and expertly propelled the empty cup into the waste bin.

'I assume you guys are looking for that Khan dude right?'

'You assume correctly,' Frank said, 'along with the whole of the Met, MI5, MI6 and every other police force in the land. Don't tell me you've started watching the news?'

She looked horrified. 'No way. But Khan is one real sick dude. I've got his three-point-four and it rocks.'

'I think sick is a term of approval Frank,' Jimmy said. Eleanor looked at him suspiciously, unsure if he was taking the piss or not.

'Three-point-four? What's that?' Maggie asked.

'It's his new version. Just beta and so it's pretty buggy but it's got some awesome features.'

'Ah right,' said Jimmy, beginning to cotton on, 'this is some software of Dr Khan's, is that it?'

'That's it. He put it up on the dot-gov secure download site so that we hackers could try and break it. It like takes face rec to a whole new level. It's now got enhanced landmark processing, family recognition search, cell synchronisation and public CCTV integration right out of the box. It's like, wicked.'

Frank furled his brow. 'Has anybody got a bloody clue what she's talking about? Can you run that past us again Campbell, this time in English.'

She threw him a pitying glance. 'There's a limit to how simple you can make it mate, and I think you're way below that limit. But I'll try and give you the idiot's version.'

Frank ignored the insult. 'Can't we just see this magical three-point-four? Like, on a screen?'

'No chance. It's classified. And these two certainly can't.'

Jimmy spoke softly. 'I understand totally Eleanor...' He lingered on her name, '... but it would really help us to understand what it's all about. We won't tell anybody, honest.' Frank smiled as he saw her resistance start to crumble.

'Well ok then. Come over to my lair.'

Her desk was surrounded by a wall of wide-screen

monitors, four wide and two deep, like she was running a NASA mission control franchise. Frank guessed that she was interpreting their amazed expressions as envy.

'Great for gaming. Not that I'm into that. As if.' She rattled a few instructions into the remote keyboard and a left-hand screen filled with a face shot of a bearded man of South Asian appearance. 'Dr Tariq Khan in person. Well, not in person, but you know what I mean.' Alongside the image, a table revealed his personal details, date of birth, address, occupation, passport number, bank accounts and much more besides. 'I think he's hacked GCHQ's HR database to harvest some test data. All his colleagues are on there. Bad man.' It was a compliment.

'So, nice and secure then?' Maggie said. The irony was wasted on Eleanor. She clicked a button and immediately Khan's face was painted with an intricate array of dots and gridlines. 'That's three-point-four's new landmark algorithms. Twice the resolution of three-point-three and nearly up to Chinese standards. And it's got an ethnicity differentiation processor now too. We don't think Beijing can do that yet.'

'Duh?' Frank said.

'Ethnicity differentiation. The old version only worked reliably on white faces.'

'This is awesome,' Jimmy said. 'And what about all that other stuff you talked about, are you able to show us any of that?'

She threw him a glance that said for you, anything. 'Sure. Where did you say this guy was from again?'

'Blackburn. That's in Lancashire.' Frank was pretty certain that Eleanor would never have heard of it.'

'Lancashire. That's in England, right?' A couple of clicks and she was scrolling down a selector box headed *CCTV Integration*. 'There it is, Blackpool'.

'Black-burn.'

'Whatever.' Another click, and a video feed from what looked like a shopping mall appeared on one of the monitors.

'Is this live?' Maggie asked.

'Pseudo live. There's about a ten-second delay for the

servers to process the images and make it available to the network.'

'Good to know,' Frank said.

'So just remember this is a beta version, so it might not work, but we'll have a go anyway.'

She clicked a button labelled 'Match' and then leaned back in her chair. A few seconds later red-bordered boxes started to appear above the head of each of the shoppers captured in the video. Inside each box were two numbers, one labelled *Mobile* and the other *Match %.*

'We're running both family recognition and cell synchronisation here. What you see is the number of any mobile device they're carrying, and if they are likely to be related to our reference subject. Red border and a low percentage says they are not. That will be most of the subjects here of course.'

Maggie's eyes widened with astonishment. 'So Eleanor, are you saying that this can pick out whether any of these people are related to Khan? That's mental.'

'Yeah, exactly, like why not? Family members usually share some likeness, don't they? Three-point-four just turns their facial characteristics into data to make a digital match possible.'

'Bloody hell, look at this one.' Jimmy was pointing at a woman who had just entered the scene. 'She's got a green box above her head.'

'Green, yeah, that's a match. Awesome. That's a score of twenty-seven percent. Could be a cousin, looking at the age of her.'

'Christ's sake, this is scary and incredible at the same time,' Frank said. 'It's like bloody big brother, and I don't mean the TV show.'

'This is big brother two-point-zero,' Eleanor said. 'Awesome, isn't it? Like I said, your Dr Khan is one clever dude.'

At that moment, an older man wearing traditional Pakistani dress wandered into view. Suddenly Maggie blurted out 'The mosque. The mosque.'

'What?' Frank said.

Maggie's voice was crackling with excitement. 'Eleanor, can we see the location of any mosques in the area?'

'Yeah, 'course.' She punched an instruction in to the keyboard and a large-scale map of Blackburn town centre appeared. 'There we go, Blackburn Central Mosque on Mary Street.'

'Can we see it on CCTV?'

'Sure. These green dots, they're cameras hooked up to the national online CCTV network. Red ones are stand-alone. We can still get the footage but we need to ask for the DVD.' She clicked on the green dot nearest the mosque and instantly the building came into view.

'Live?' Maggie asked. 'I mean, pseudo live?'

'Yep. Look, trees swaying in the breeze.'

Frank could see Maggie's mind was working overtime.

'What are you thinking?' he asked.

Her eyes were blazing with excitement as the words tumbled out in a torrent. 'Listen to this guys, see what you think. So tomorrow's Friday. That's when the males of the local Muslim community will gather in the mosque for prayers. I'm right, aren't I?'

'Friday prayers, that's right,' Jimmy said.

'So what if we run three-point-four tomorrow on that camera before and after Friday prayers? I guess it's a long shot, but we might be able to find at least one or two of Dr Khan's relatives, maybe more if we are lucky. Because I think if he's hiding in the area, it's pretty likely that someone in his family will be helping him. We get their phone numbers, give them a call out of the blue, and one of them might panic and spill the beans. What do you think?'

'You know what,' Jimmy said, speaking slowly. 'I think this might just work. Definitely worth a shot.'

Frank anticipated that Eleanor might object to the scheme if the proper procedures weren't followed. Deadpan he said, 'Aye, it's a great idea, but I'll need to run it passed DCI Smart first. She'll probably have to get a warrant or something from a judge. But I'll sort it before tomorrow.'

It seemed to satisfy her.

'Yeah, awesome, I'll set it up. Sweet.'

Now they had a plan.

***

Up until now Plan B had been executed flawlessly, but this situation had now become very concerning. Khan had always been at the epicentre of the whole affair, so it was obvious in hindsight that he should have been taken out right at the start. Instead, they had waited to see how events unfolded, and now he had gone into hiding. Inconvenient, to say the least. He was proving to be a very clever guy, and for three and a half weeks he had outsmarted them. But no matter, they were playing the long game. Mrs Khan loved her husband and he loved her, and eventually they would be able to bear the agony of separation no longer. Chances are they had equipped themselves with burner phones, and sooner or later Mrs Khan would be compelled to switch hers on so that she could hear her husband's sweet voice once more. Or maybe drive to a remote pay-phone and call him from there.

An asset had been stationed such that movements into and out of the Khan's modest semi could be monitored. It was a bonus that the police seemed to be taking the threat to Mrs Khan less seriously than they perhaps should. This kind of thing didn't normally happen in Gloucestershire, and they didn't like the fact that it was disturbing their routine. So it was that whilst their chief constable had promised the Met twenty-four-hour surveillance, in reality there was a half-hour gap in the schedule around five-thirty when the afternoon shift knocked off. The asset had observed that most times, the evening shift didn't turn up to about six o'clock, sometimes more like six-thirty. Sloppy.

Naturally the distinguished member had been both pleased and relieved to get the message that finally the target was on the move. One afternoon, Mrs Khan had waited until the surveillance officer had been gone a few minutes before slipping into the family Corsa and racing off. Soon she had joined the Tewkesbury Road heading north-east, the asset, name of Kareem, following undetected three or four cars behind. After four miles, she had swung left onto a minor road that headed towards the Coombe Hill canal and in a few hundred yards pulled up onto a grass verge. With his powerful binoculars Kareem had maintained observation from a safe distance, simultaneously booting up the portable Scanner-Pro cell phone detector to ensure he was ready. He hadn't had long to wait.

Blackburn, Lancashire. That was going to be a nice day out.

Chapter 31

The operation was scheduled to launch around eleven thirty that day. Not only had Jill Smart given her approval, but she had signed off the requisition to allow Frank to drive to Blackburn the previous evening and check into a faceless business hotel on the ring-road. Jimmy and Maggie were there too and in separate rooms, but not on the public purse, although they had suffered the four-hour drive north with him in the Mondeo. Back at Atlee House, Eleanor Campbell was all geared up to run three-point-four's awesome search capabilities.

A team from Lancashire Constabulary's anti-terrorist response squad had been rounded up into a brightly-lit conference room, where they were now listening to the incident commander giving his briefing. Maggie and Jimmy sat quietly at the back, being introduced by Frank as psychological profilers seconded to the case. The commander had accepted the explanation without comment. He probably thought every cop in the Met travelled with at least one of them.

'Guys, this is DI Frank Stewart from the Met. Department 12B isn't that right Frank? Best not to ask what goes on in that unit, I'd imagine,' he joked. If only he knew.

Frank got to his feet and smiled at the room. 'Thanks Commander. So, to cut to the chase, our profilers here think there's a good chance that our Dr Khan could be hiding in perfect sight right here in Blackburn. But as you guys know, conventional enquiries have got us nowhere. We've talked to his wife, we've talked to his father, we've talked to his known associates and got nowhere. Everybody's doing a good job of keeping schtum, but we still think it's likely that he's being helped by a family member, maybe a cousin or someone who's not on our radar. So this is where this stuff comes in.' He pointed to the large screen behind him which was displaying the video feed from the mosque. 'Back in the smoke, we're running some new real-time surveillance technology which hopefully can tell us if any of the attendees at Friday prayers are related to him in any way. We will also get their mobile numbers if they are carrying a device, which of course is highly likely.'

The expressionless faces around the room betrayed their scepticism, but up on the screen a few early worshippers had wandered into shot, their heads trailed by a red box filled with numbers. 'You see, red says these guys aren't related to Khan, but for most of them, we are getting a mobile number. So what do you think to that, eh? Awesome.' It was fast becoming his favourite word. On screen, they saw a member of the public stop, take out his mobile and stare at it, in the way you did when you did not recognise the incoming number. Tentatively, he raised it to his ear. 'He-llo?' The distorted voice echoed around the conference room. A young detective shook his phone in the air and laughed. 'Whoa, this stuff really works.'

'Told you,' Frank said. 'So, we just sit, watch and take notes. Can't say I'm confident, but you never know.' As twelve o'clock neared, the street in front of the mosque became increasingly busy. Many worshippers were dropped off directly outside, their faces invisible to the CCTV, and many more came from the direction of town such that their backs were to the camera. Soon the last few stragglers were making their way up to the front door, but still they had registered no positives.

'Let's not get too despondent folks,' Frank said. 'We'll have a much better chance to clock them on the way out.' An hour or so later, members of the flock began to emerge. *Red, red, red, red, red*. Every box was red. 'Doesn't mean it's not working, just hasn't registered a match yet.' They all hoped to god it was true.

A grizzled DC who looked at least ten years past retirement age piped up. 'This is a friggin' waste of time. I don't know why we don't just send a team up there and question everyone as they're leaving.' The younger woman DC sitting beside him voiced what everyone was thinking. 'Genius John. That would be brilliant for community relations. A squad of coppers swarming all over the mosque.'

'Let's just be patient,' said another, 'not even half of them have left yet.' More than three-quarters of an hour later, there were still no matches. You could almost taste the mood of despondency that seeped through the room, tinged with no little schadenfreude. 'Load of shite, I knew it was,' DC Grizzle said, not quite under his breath. 'Met wankers, they're all the same.' Frank decided to let it pass. This time. The commander was more diplomatic, but it was obvious he shared the opinion of his outspoken colleague. His manner was condescending.

'A bit of a waste of time I'm afraid Frank. We rely too much on new technology these days in my opinion.'

'What, like DNA profiling and CCTV and mobile call records sir? Aye, bring back old-fashioned policing, magnifying glasses, bobbies on the beat, all that stuff.' His bitterness was driven by disappointment, but even he recognised he might have gone too far. 'Sorry sir, I didn't mean to be disrespectful.' Although he did.

'Ok, I think we're done here,' the commander said sharply. 'Now if you don't mind, could you take your... your profilers or whatever they are and let us have our conference room back. You should be able to find a couple of desks in the general office if you have more work to do.'

'Thank you sir.' He beckoned to Jimmy and Maggie to follow him. No way was he going to face the scorn that would be heaped upon them in that cauldron of naysayers. Technology? They'd only just got colour telly up here.

'Starbucks is it?' Maggie said.

'Pub more like. Come on guys.' Jimmy gave a thumbs up and followed them to the front door.

The pub was dull and depressing, and deserted too, a function as much of local financial deprivation as to it being three-fifteen in the afternoon. In the corner, a large TV blared out Sky Sports News. Jimmy had just got to the bar when his phone rang.

'Hi Eleanor, nice to hear from you.'

Frank pulled a face. 'Eleanor? Why's she calling you?'

Jimmy shrugged and covered an ear with his cupped palm.

It was apparent he was having difficulty hearing her above the din of the television. 'Sorry Eleanor, you need to say that again. Frank, can you get them to turn that bloody thing down.' There was no-one serving. Frank banged his fists on the bar and bellowed 'Service!' Eventually a bored-looking barmaid appeared, chewing gum.

'What can I get you?'

'Maybe you could turn that thing down.'

'The customers like it,' she said, unsmiling.

'Sorry love but we're the customers and we don't.' Reluctantly the barmaid picked up the remote and pointed it at the set.

'Thank you.'

'You're welcome.' She didn't sound it.

'That's better,' Jimmy said, returning to his phone-call. 'Eleanor, I'm going to put you on speaker phone. Don't go away.'

They found a table by the window and sat down. 'Ok, go ahead.'

'Hi guys.' She sounded excited.

'Hi Eleanor,' they replied in unison.

'So the reason I'm calling you guys, did you know that mosque thing had a back door? Like, you know, a fire escape or something.'

'No, we didn't...' Frank's heart began to race.

'Yeah, so there's a camera covering the back of the place. We missed the live feed, but I found a hack that let me download a recording. It's like awesome how quick it gets onto the servers. They must have a shit-load of tin in that datacentre.'

'Awesome,' Frank said, being rewarded by a scolding look from Maggie.

'So I ran three-point-four against the recording and holy shit, within minutes the alerts were going like mental. I saw seven hits just as a bunch of these guys in nightshirts were all coming out together.'

'Wow!' Maggie was now struggling to contain her excitement. 'And did you get all their phone numbers?'

'Shit to that. So, like in the middle of this group is a guy wearing a funny little hat and dark glasses and a scarf over his mouth and nose. Thinks he's in some sort of disguise or something but three-point-four only needs eleven reference points for a hit. Bang, a big dialogue box fills my screen, bang, bells ringing everywhere, and bang, a message tells me we've got a one-hundred-percent match.'

'Holy shit!' Jimmy exclaimed. 'Did you get his...'

'Number? 'course. 07835 098871. And then we triangulated him to 78 Granville Street. He's there right now. Oh, and I've messaged you the directions.'

***

'That's just three minutes away,' Jimmy shouted. 'Come on, let's get our arses round there now.'

'What, without back up?' Frank said. 'Not a good plan.'

'Well why don't you head back to the station to pick up the car and phone in on the way,' Maggie said. 'Jimmy and I will go and hang around outside the house until the teams arrive. We can't risk missing him, not when we're this close.'

'Aye all right then, but please don't try anything stupid. Wait for us to arrive, is that understood?'

Without answering they tore out of the pub, Jimmy's eyes fixed on his phone, Maggie blowing heavily but determined to keep up.

'It's just at the top of this street,' he shouted back. 'We'd better go carefully when we get there in case we're spotted. I'll wait for you up there.'

She gave a breathless thumbs-up, gritting her teeth and trying in vain to ignore her burning thighs. Granville Street turned out to be a classic northern industrial-era thoroughfare, the narrow street lined on both sides by well-kept two-up two-downs terraced properties which once would have been the crowded homes of mill workers and their families. The mills were long gone, and the homes were now almost exclusively occupied by members of the town's long-established Muslim community. They may have been here since the sixties, but that didn't mean that community relations were always good, so much so that the local council found it necessary to run a large team of 'community integration officers' to maintain an uneasy truce.

Maggie finally caught up with him, panting as she placed her hands on her hips, head bowed. 'I need to get fitter Jimmy, I really do.'

He gave her a sympathetic smile.

'The house is just along there on the left, according to my google maps. Should have a blue door if this Streetview shot is reasonably recent.'

She was beginning to catch her breath. 'So are we going to wait for Frank and the cavalry to arrive or what?'

'Don't see any reason to, do you? It's not as if Khan's going to be surrounded by armed guards or anything. I say we just wander up and knock on the door, see if he's in.'

Cautiously they crossed the deserted street and edged towards number seventy-eight, located about two hundred yards ahead. The street was lined on both sides by residents' parking bays, the majority unoccupied on this work-day afternoon, save for the occasional white van belonging to a visiting tradesman. Suddenly there was screech as a black Mercedes S-class powered out of a side road, clipping the wing of a parked van in the process.

'Bloody hell, he's in a hurry,' Jimmy said. Their eyes followed the car as it sped past them, then with another screech of brakes, pulled up right outside the blue door. Jimmy sensed the threat immediately.

'Maggie, you wait here and don't bloody move ok? Get on to Frank and tell him we've got a situation developing. We need an armed response team fast.'

Two men had emerged from the Mercedes and were now standing at the front door, a finger jamming on the doorbell. Even from a distance, Jimmy recognised the deadly outline of the weapons they were carrying. *AK-47s.* These guys meant business. They waited a few seconds for a response and then with practised synchronization, applied their boots to the door, bursting it open with little resistance. A few seconds later came a gunshot, causing Jimmy's heart to sink. *Damn, we're too late. The last man standing has now been silenced.*

But then unexpectedly, the two gunmen emerged through the door dragging a third man by the scruff of his neck, an automatic shoved into his face in case he had any thought of escaping. As they reached the end of the short path, one of the men stopped and then with a sickening thud, smashed the butt of his assault rifle into the face of their captive. Satisfied that he was subdued, they bundled him into the back of the car, leapt into the front seats, and with a roar of the big vee-eight, accelerated violently away from the kerb.

Jimmy sprinted after them without a thought of what to do if he caught up. He'd figure that out when he got there, just playing it by ear as he had done so many times in the army. Except this time he wasn't in an armoured personnel carrier and there wasn't a comforting helicopter gunship hovering overhead.

But then suddenly and without appearing to look, a vehicle pulled out of another side road immediately in front of the escaping Mercedes. It was a white parcel delivery van, the driver proceeding at a snail's pace as he peered at the house numbers, straining to locate the address for his next delivery. The assailants blared their horn to no effect, white-van-man continuing to dawdle along, blocking their path, oblivious to their presence. That was going to prove to be a mistake. Without warning, the passenger door of the car flew open and a gunman leapt out and ran towards the driver's side of the van. He yanked opened the door and gestured for the driver to get down from the cab. Maybe he hadn't seen the gun, but evidently the driver was not in any hurry to comply with the request. That was his second mistake, as a bullet shattered his ribcage and smashed out through the roof of the van. The gunman dragged him from his seat and threw him to the ground, not caring whether he was dead or alive.

That gave Jimmy his chance. He put on an extra spurt and a second later was within touching distance of the Mercedes, gambling on the fact that the driver would be too occupied by events playing out in front of him to glance in the rear-view mirror. Dropping to the ground he crawled along the pavement on his stomach, being careful to keep below the line of sight of the wing mirror, until he was alongside the rear kerbside door. And now everything depended on what the driver had done with his AK-47, because there would be only one chance to get this right. The odds must be at least fifty-fifty that it was just lying there on the passenger's seat. That was the obvious place to leave it. Time to find out if he was right. He started counting down to steady his nerves. *Five-four-three-two-one*. Reaching up, he grabbed the handle with his left hand, simultaneously pulling open the door as he slipped his right hand in to feel for the automatic. Too late, the driver realised what was happening, just as Jimmy snatched the butt-end of the weapon and wrenched it out of his grasp. In a microsecond he was on his feet, thrusting the barrel of the gun through the open door just as the driver tried to escape. In Helmand, he would have simply taken him out, leaving the awkward questions for later, but that was a long time ago. A different life, thank god. The terrorist was looking him straight in the eye, perfectly calm even though he must have supposed he was about to die. Jimmy had seen that so many times in Afghanistan, a faith so certain that death was not something to be feared. He waved his gun to indicate he should raise his hands.

'You'll need to wait a bit longer for your fifty virgins pal. Today's your lucky day, or maybe not.'

Ahead, the second gunman was just beginning to absorb what was happening. He stood motionless beside the delivery van, straddling the dead driver with his AK-47 held tightly across his chest, seemingly weighing up the options. *Fight or flight, what was it to be?* And then without a word, he climbed into the cab and raced off. Thank heavens for that. The last thing Jimmy wanted was a fire-fight on a sleepy suburban street.

Then he remembered Khan, slumped semi-conscious in the back seat after his brutal beating. 'Dr Khan, are you all right sir?' he shouted, not daring to take his eyes off his captive for a single second. 'My cousin, my cousin,' Khan moaned, 'they killed her.' Christ, he'd forgotten the shot.

Who were these bastards and who was running them? Now at least they'd got one of them, and soon surely everything would fall into place. He tried to comfort him the best he could.

'Sir, the police will be here soon, and then everything will be ok.' And on that subject, where the hell were they? Because he was stuck here with his captive until they arrived.

'Dr Khan I presume?'

He heard Maggie's voice, a breath of wind brushing his cheek as the rear door was opened. 'I thought I told you to keep away.' But he was bloody pleased to see her.

'You looked like you needed some help mate,' she said wryly. 'You're not the man you used to be.'

'Yeah, thanks. Anyway how does Dr Khan look?'

'He looks like he's about to pass out. His face is a right mess too.'

At last the police squad had arrived, tumbling out of their vehicles and barking out terse instructions. Frank spotted Maggie at the Mercedes and ran over, giving a rueful shake of the head.

'Sorry we're a bit late. That commander needed to do his damned risk assessment before he would send in any of his precious officers. Anyway, there'll be an ambulance here in a minute I think.' Glancing at Khan he said, 'He looks in a bit of a bad way.'

'Excuse me Frank,' Jimmy said, forcing a smile, 'but never mind chatting up young Maggie here, could you slap some cuffs on this guy? Only if you can fit it into your busy schedule.'

'Any idea who he is?' Frank pulled the gunman's arms behind him and snapped the cuffs closed.

'No idea. He hasn't opened his mouth once. Looks middle-eastern but I can't tell.'

Frank beckoned to two armed officers. 'Over here boys, take this guy off my hands.' They led him away to the detention van, sullen and silent.

'Maybe they'll run three-point-four on him, that should tell us who he is.' Two female paramedics were now tending to Khan's wounds, offering soothing words as he winced with the pain of the stinging antiseptic. 'Soon have you in hospital sir, it's only five minutes away.'

'My cousin. What's happened to my cousin...'

'Shit,' said Jimmy, suddenly remembering. He took one of the paramedics to one side, speaking quietly. 'There was a shot. Inside. It might be pretty messy, I should warn you.'

'We've seen everything in this job sir,' she answered, taking no offence. 'But thanks.' She tapped her colleague on the arm and nodded towards the front door.

***

Khan had been kept in the Royal Blackburn hospital overnight under heightened security and then flown by RAF helicopter down to Northolt air base, where he was questioned at length by DCI Jill Smart and a nameless officer from MI5. Later on Saturday, Khan's family had been driven up from Gloucester under police escort for an emotional reunion. Afterwards, it had been decided to keep them all on the base for a few days until the authorities could assure their immediate safety.

Now it was Monday morning, and Smart was making a rare visit back to Atlee House to brief the team. Not that she had found out much.

'He wouldn't say anything. He's absolutely beside himself with fear, mainly for his family it should be said. But also, despite everything that's happened he's still terrified that his secret will get out.'

'His family still don't know about the Cheltenham Spa incident then?' Maggie asked.

'Apparently not. And he wants to keep it that way.'

'What about the cousin?'

'She's going to be ok, thank goodness. She's got a pretty bad shoulder wound, but it's not life-threatening. That was a huge relief for Dr Kahn and his family as you can imagine. But he's very grateful for the part that you lot played in his rescue.'

'He kind of rescued himself,' Jimmy said. 'It was all down to his own three-point-four software, wasn't it?'

'There is something else,' Smart said. 'He wants to talk to you Maggie. Says he has some information that's for your ears only. They're all travelling back to Gloucester this afternoon but maybe you can get over there later this morning.'

Despite its use as a convenient arrival and departure point for royals and government ministers, the base was no oil-painting. Spread around the site were a hotchpotch of ancient buildings in various state of disrepair, most with the corrugated roofs and ugly metal-framed windows that dated them to the fifties or even earlier. An RAF policeman had driven Maggie from the entrance gatehouse to a block out near the perimeter, ushering her into a small meeting room then standing guard outside the door. The room was provided with a small formica-topped desk and two wooden chairs. Dr Tariq Khan sat at the desk tapping into a slim notebook computer, his head heavily bandaged and an extravagant purple-black bruise spreading from his left cheekbone to the eye-socket. He stood up to greet her.

'Mrs Brooks, we meet again. But my apologies, I'm told you are now Ms. Bainbridge.'

She smiled at him. 'Call me Maggie, please. How are you feeling after your ordeal?'

'I'm ok actually. It frightened my wife and kids when they saw my face but it looks a lot worse than it feels. Please sit down here beside me. I've got something to tell you. And to show you.'

He took a sip of water from a plastic cup. 'They never fully told me what it was all about you know. I knew they wanted to get her freed, but I never knew why. They just used my...my little indiscretion to force me into it. I had no choice, really I hadn't.' She wasn't sure if he was expecting forgiveness from her or not.

'Who were *they* Dr Khan? Who is it you are talking about?'

'Both of them. Saddleworth. And Brooks, who was your husband I believe.'

'And all of them now dead.'

'Exactly. So you can understand why I was so frightened.'

'I understand, totally. But you said you had something to tell me.'

'Yes. You see, they did talk of you many times. Your role was clearly important, although I did not know how or why. I was hoping you might be able to tell me. All I knew was it was something to do with disclosure, they used that term a lot.'

Have you thought about disclosure? She remembered that phrase, casually dropped into conversation by Philip. So innocuous but setting off a chain of events that had devastated her life and taken that of her beautiful niece Daisy. And little Tom Swift and all the other tragic innocents. Christ, how she had been played. *Totally played.*

'I... I wasn't part of it. Not knowingly at least. We've both been used, haven't we? And yet we still don't know why.'

'That's what I wanted to show you Maggie,' he said quietly. 'I think I might have worked it out. In fact I know I have.'

She recognised the distinctive light-blue launch screen as soon as he started it up.

'We all love your three-point-four,' she said brightly. He gave her a faintly scornful look.

'Three-point-four was ok I suppose, but this is three-point-five. My latest version. A hundred times better. This takes family recognition technology to a whole new level. As you will see.'

'Awesome,' she said, without irony.

***

It had been a complete foul-up, no-one could argue with that. That's why the distinguished member had insisted that they go to all the trouble and expense of using professionals, exactly to avoid this sort of occurrence. They should have killed Khan on the spot rather than dragging him off for a pointless interrogation. Now he would be guarded twenty-four-by-seven and they would never be able to get to him.

But on the other hand, think about it rationally. Even if Khan had told everything he knew, it wouldn't have mattered. Because really he knew nothing. He didn't know why he'd had to write that report or who was really behind it either. No, on reflection, they were still quite safe and he could concentrate on cementing his legacy. It was stupid really, because by the time they came to write the history books, you were long dead, too late for you to give a damn about what they said about you. But you did it anyway. They all did, all his predecessors. It was your legacy and it was important. And quite definitely, he was safe.

Except what he didn't know was that Maggie Bainbridge had worked it all out. Why it was done and how it was done and who did it. *Everything*. From start to finish. And now she was coming for him.

Chapter 32

It took them just eight minutes to make the journey from Atlee House to the Savoy, the path through the drizzly evening rush-hour eased by the flashing blue lights and penetrating siren of Frank's commandeered patrol car. As they screeched into the hotel's canopied drop-off zone, two armed officers bounded over, nervously pointing their automatics at the windscreen. Frank brandished his credit card-sized ID pass through his open window.

'Steady on pal, we're police.' One of the officers gestured with his gun. 'Ok sir could you just get out of the car, nice and slowly, and make sure I can see your hands at all times.'

'God's sake man.' It was frustrating, but he knew he would be doing exactly the same thing if he was in their position. Slowly, he opened the door of the BMW and slid out as gracefully as a man of his physique could manage.

'Look, here's my ID. DI Frank Stewart, Department 12B of the Met.'

The officer took the pass and examined it carefully, then looked up at Frank, still covering him with his automatic. Evidently he was satisfied that the photo was an adequate likeness.

'That looks in order sir, and are you able to vouch for the others in the motor car?'

'Aye, aye, they're pukka, no worries on that score. Now you guys need to come with me right now.'

The PC was uncertain whether to comply. 'But sir, we're under strict orders not to let anyone in.'

'We're not worried about people getting in now lads,' Frank replied. 'It's people getting out we need to worry about. Come on, move it!'

Now Jimmy and Maggie were by his side, and a moment later they were sprinting down a long plush-carpeted corridor towards the ballroom which was hosting the peace conference.

'You don't think they'll really try and make a break for it do you?' Maggie gasped.

'Not all of them, but we're only interested in one person, aren't we?'

As they expected, there was further armed presence outside the ballroom, two female officers stationed either side of the elaborately-panelled oak doors of the room. From inside they could just make out the muted tones of Prime Minister Julian Priest delivering his closing speech to the assembled media. 'A significant breakthrough'...'the dream of a Palestinian state within our grasp'. He could have written it before the conference was even arranged. He probably did.

Frank flashed his ID at the officers. 'Has anyone entered or left here since this session started?'

'No sir, not this way. There are four fire exits as well but they're all alarmed and guarded too. But Chief Super Clarke is in charge sir, she's inside at the moment, I can get her on the radio if you like.'

'No, I think we'll keep it low-key for now. We're just going to slip in at the back of the room, nice and quietly.' He gestured to Jimmy, Maggie and the police officers to follow, opening a door just wide enough for them to squeeze through. The room was packed to capacity with reporters, the TV journalists accompanied by camera and sound crews, all anxious to get a hearing when the session was opened up for questions. A few turned round to see what was happening at the back of the room, momentarily disconcerted by the arrival of yet more armed police. Julian Priest though was unmoved, continuing to deliver his speech from behind the official HM Government-crested podium which had been placed in the middle of the long table. Behind the table sat the key figures of the government's hopeful peace initiative. Maggie did a quick mental roll-call. Philomena Forbes-Brown, over-promoted to the Home Office after the murder of Gerrard Saddleworth, looking bored and disengaged, struggling to stifle a yawn. Robert Francis, the new Attorney General, appointed to sweep up the mess left over from the Alzahrani foul-up.

Then there was Lillian Cortes, the twenty-nine-year-old firebrand Democrat congresswoman and darling of America's emerging radical left, sitting alongside Otaga Mombassa, an obscure and very junior UN official from Nigeria. Both had been parachuted in in a desperate attempt to lend the conference a semblance of international credibility. To the left of Julian Priest, the beautiful Fadwa Ziadeh, and to his right, her son Mohammed.

And at that moment Maggie could see it, in crystal-clear high-definition, just as if she had been looking at a finely-realised family portrait painted by an old master. It didn't need the help of Dr Khan's super-sophisticated three-point-five software, because in the flesh, the resemblance was as striking as it was startling. Mohammed Ziadeh shared the delicate cheek bones and wide mouth and full lips of his mother, but there was no mistaking from whom he had inherited the piercing green eyes, close-set under a fine Roman forehead. It was from the man who a few seconds earlier had finished his speech and now sat alongside him. *His father, Julian Priest*. Now too, Maggie recognised what Khan's sophisticated algorithms, developed to be as reliable as DNA matching, had already unveiled. The sibling likeness was obvious and undeniable. Dena Alzahrani, the Hampstead bomber, the woman who had ruined her life and that of so many other innocents, was Mohammed Ziadeh's twin. Now the motive behind the whole ghastly conspiracy could be and would be revealed.

Slowly and purposefully, Maggie began walking towards the platform. 'Where is she Priest? Where is she? We know she's your daughter. So where have you hidden Dena?'

An audible gasp reverberated around the room as stunned media hacks struggled to process the accusation. There were murmurs of surprise as some recognised the interlocutor to be the notorious defence barrister from the Alzahrani trial. The BBC's sharp young political correspondent was the first to react, struggling to believe she was actually about to ask this crazy question.

'Is it true what Mrs Brooks says, Mr Priest. Is it true? Are you Dena Alzahrani's father?'

But it could not be denied, for now everyone in the room

could see it with their own eyes, and in the outside-broadcast control trucks, sharp-reacting producers were zooming in on the faces of Priest, Fadwa and Mohammed Ziadeh and piecing together collages that added the notorious image of Dena Alzahrani for the benefit of their millions of viewers. And he did not try to deny it. With a sudden surge of rage, he upended the table, sending water jugs, glasses, mobile phones and laptops flying in all directions, unleashing a maelstrom of confusion. Lillian Cortes was now in tears as her much-anticipated grandstanding event turned into a PR disaster. Otaga Mombassa had been joined by his burly private security detail and was remonstrating furiously with a stunned Forbes-Brown, sitting with her head in her hands. And there, centre-stage was the Right Honourable Julian Peregrine Priest, eighty-seventh Prime Minister of Great Britain and Northern Ireland, with his hands tightening around the throat of Maggie Brooks.

'You interfering bitch. I told Philip he should have dealt with you but he wouldn't because of that damned brat of yours. Well now I'm going to do the job for him.' She gripped his wrists in an effort to free herself but he was too powerful. The room began to spin and she realised that she was beginning to lose consciousness.

It took Jimmy only a fraction of a second to react. He bounded onto the stage and placed a crushing arm-lock around the throat of Priest, tightening it until he slumped back into his chair.

'It's all over for you now pal. Frank, get over here and take this bastard out of my sight.'

He gave him a thumbs-up, 'I'll take it from here bruv.' He grabbed Priest by the arm. 'We can make this as easy or as difficult as you want sir, it's up to you, but it would be best to avoid handcuffs, don't you think? Not a good look for the cameras.' Broken, Priest could only nod his silent consent.

They had been joined by Chief Superintendent Jennifer Clarke who had emerged from undercover deployment amongst the journalists.

'Who are you exactly?' she asked, looking puzzled.

'DI Frank Stewart ma'am. I'm working the Cathedral Close murders.'

'And is all of this true? Is Priest really that terrorist's father?'

'We think so ma'am, almost certainly. That's what it was all about. He was desperate for her to be freed.'

'And all these murders? Was he responsible for them too?'

'Aye, we're pretty sure he was. He didn't carry out the killings himself of course, but we're certain he ordered them. Iranians, we think, revolutionary guards. We caught one of them up in Blackburn and he should help us track the rest of them down. But we can work out the exact charges when we get him to the station.'

'Understood Inspector, and very good work here.' She barked an order to a uniformed officer. 'Get the media out of here and lock down this room. This is now a crime scene.'

Now only Fadwa Ziadeh and her son remained in the room, sharing some private joke, calm and unmoved despite the turmoil of the last few minutes. Safe in the knowledge that they were immune from prosecution because of their diplomatic status, and probably smart enough not have taken any active role in the crime. Conspirators undoubtedly, but participants probably not. Clever bastards.

'So you're Maggie Brooks?' she said, her voice laden with venom. 'I was so hoping to get to meet you. Philip told me so much about you during his little trips to my country. Pillow talk, that's what they call it, don't they? He was a very good lover. So caring and considerate. You were very lucky to have had him for a few years. Although in the end I think he found you, well, just a little dull.'

Maggie found it easy to ignore the provocation.

'Where is Dena?'

'My beautiful but stupid daughter? Her name is Hasema and I assume she is still in Cairo at the moment, or perhaps she is already on her way back to Gaza. She flew out yesterday on her brother's passport you see, on your excellent British Airways, business class naturally. An easy disguise. My children, they look so alike, of course.' Maggie knew from Dr Tariq Khan that the border force scanners would have been unable to tell the difference between the twins. They were still running three-point-one.

'Do you really care about Palestine, that's what I want to know. Because to me, it looks just a big game to you, a bloody lifestyle choice. So where is it next for you Fadwa? Gstaad, Davoz, Rio, after we have you deported of course.'

She smiled. 'Stockholm actually. So nice in midsummer, don't you think? But you're wrong Maggie, I do care, I care very much. And one day we will achieve our destiny and have our homeland returned to us, but it won't be through killings and hatred. That way is the fool's way.' It was said with such passion and conviction that Maggie could not help but believe it.

'So you must be so disappointed in Hasema. All that hate and anger in such a beautiful young woman.'

'I'm afraid Hasema is young and foolish, and was so easily led astray by her stupid grandfather and his cynical Iranian supporters. She has her father's blood you see, and we all know what a fool he is. But I love her of course, and Julian loves her too and so she had to be rescued. And dear Philip, he arranged it all so beautifully. He played you Maggie, just like he said he would.'

She was conscious of Jimmy's presence, his arm around her shoulders, hugging her close to him. He kissed her gently on her forehead. Perhaps it was only a platonic brotherly kiss, but she didn't care. It was still nice.

'Don't rise to it Maggie, she's not worth it. You have only good things to look forward to now.'

And it was true, there could be no doubt. Perhaps her reputation could be restored and she might be able to go back to the Bar - but did she still want all of that now? Because the truth was, she had enjoyed the last few weeks more than she could have ever imagined, and the thought of not having Jimmy and Frank Stewart in her life already seemed impossible. And Asvina was already talking about another case, some famous soap-star who had tired of her husband. But now it was too soon, too raw to make these kind of decisions. Now she must concentrate on the one thing that mattered above all others. Soon she would have Ollie back with her and everything would be wonderful again.

***

'Eighty-eight quid for a steak, and it doesn't even come with chips? Ridiculous.'

This time they had rejected Frank's favourite Shoreditch pub in favour of a lunchtime table for three at the rather more upmarket Ship just around the corner. A few minutes earlier, a good-looking waiter had reeled off a list of complicated-sounding specials before presenting each with the eye-wateringly expensive menu.

'It's chateaubriand,' laughed Maggie, 'and it's for two. And besides, I'm paying, so you don't need to worry about the price.'

Jimmy adopted a tone of mock concern. 'Oh dear, I've had a look, and they don't seem to have sausage rolls on the menu today mate. Do you want me to choose something for you?'

'Oh aye, and you're mister sophistication, are you?'

'Boys, boys, we're here to have a lovely time and to celebrate our great success. Let's not behave like little school boys in the dinner-hall.'

'Sorry miss,' Jimmy smiled.

'Aye sorry miss,' Frank said.

After much discussion, food and wine was finally ordered, accompanied by three very large gin and tonics procured at the insistence of Maggie. Frank dealt with his in just two swigs.

'All right then, you two smart-arse private dicks. I want to know the full story from the beginning, sparing no detail.' He raised his hand to draw the attention of a white-shirted waiter who was just passing. 'Pint of Doom Bar please mate. Right Maggie, sorry, where were we?'

'I hadn't actually started yet. But I think it all goes back nearly twenty-five years ago to Palestinian Solidarity. That was the pressure group founded by Philip's brother Hugo. It was a deeply fashionable cause back then for any left-leaning politician...'

'Still is,' Jimmy said.

'Indeed, and as it is now, it was a great thing to have on your CV when you were trying to make the candidate short-list in one of these fashionable metropolitan seats. That's what attracted the likes of Saddleworth and Priest, and a host of others too who didn't manage to climb the greasy pole and have now slipped into obscurity.'

'Slipped into obscurity down the greasy pole. Very good Maggie,' Jimmy smiled.

'Purely accidental, honest.'

'And that's when Priest and Fadwa hooked up I assume,' Frank said. 'She looks pretty amazing now, so god knows what she looked like in her twenties.'

'Irresistible by all accounts, and as the daughter of Yasser Ziadeh she was also at the centre of the fight for Palestinian self-determination. Intoxicating for these young idealists.'

'Or opportunists,' Jimmy said.

'Exactly. So before long, Fadwa finds herself pregnant and gives birth to twins. She was always headstrong and so she refused to name the father, but there was a lot of speculation at the time that it was Julian Priest. We don't know of course what the subsequent relationship between Priest and Fadwa was like, but we can imagine the likely difficulties just taking into account the geography. And it's hard to think of either of them settling down to cosy domesticity.'

'So just a shag, not a big love affair then.'

Maggie gave an amused look. 'Yes, I suppose that's one way of describing it Frank.'

'But Priest must have kept some contact with his children over the years?' he asked.

'Yes, he was still quite heavily involved with Palestinian Solidarity, and was a regular visitor to Gaza. So yes, he did keep in touch. But I don't think he was going to birthday parties and school sports days or anything like that.'

'So why the hell did he risk everything to get involved in

getting Dena freed?' Frank said. 'That seems really dumb to me if he didn't really give a shit about her.'

'Pretty simple,' Jimmy answered. 'We think that Fadwa threatened to expose him as Dena's father if he didn't cooperate. Can you imagine the storm that would be stirred up if the Prime Minister is exposed as the father of the notorious terrorist?'

Frank nodded. 'Aye, and so Priest ropes in his old mates to help him out. But why did they agree to help him, that's what I don't quite understand? I would have just told him to bugger off.'

'We know now from Fadwa that Philip was Priest's fixer. He was given the job of working the whole thing out,' Maggie said. 'That was typical Philip. He would have weighed up that helping Priest would give him some bargaining chips which he could cash in at some unspecified time in the future. And although it's hard to stomach, I was the first piece in the jigsaw. It made sense to have someone he thought he could influence defending the case.'

'You see Frank, I talked to that Clerk at Maggie's Chambers,' Jimmy said. 'He admitted he'd been paid by Philip to pass the brief to her. Didn't see anything wrong with doing that, he just thought Brooks was trying to help his wife's career.'

'Yes, at that stage I don't think Philip had any particular plan worked out,' Maggie said. 'But in the back of his mind he knew he could use the Miner's Trust situation to get Saddleworth to do anything he wanted.'

'So it was blackmail then,' Frank said. 'Or coercion to be exact.'

'Indeed,' Maggie agreed. 'Gerrard almost certainly knew that Priest was Dena's father, and probably the last thing on earth he wanted was to be caught up in this conspiracy. But Brooks played the Trust scandal card and so he had no choice but to cooperate.'

Frank shook his head in disbelief. 'So now I suppose the big question was how to get the jury to deliver a not-guilty verdict. The bloody government trying to get a murdering terrorist freed, I mean you couldn't make it up.'

'Yep Frank, but that's what happened. And then my shit-face husband Philip has the brainwave that engineering a mistrial might be a whole lot easier than trying to convince a jury of Alzahrani's innocence. There had been so much focus on all these failure-to-disclose-evidence scandals that he knew every judge in the land would be hypersensitive to even a hint that it was happening in one of their trials.'

'That was it,' said Jimmy. 'Now Brooks and Saddleworth had to come up with some scheme to engineer a mistrial and that was not as easy as it looks. I think at first they were hoping for some technicality around Alzahrani's human rights, you know given Philip's background, but I don't think they were getting far.'

'And then Saddleworth the blackmailer remembered the Khan affair,' said Frank. 'That was a gift right enough.'

'It was,' agreed Maggie, 'and in fact you uncovered it yourself Frank. The devout Muslim family man cautioned for using rent boys, the affair swept under the carpet because of his importance to national security. Of course, as Home Secretary, the file would have passed through Saddleworth's office. And naturally, Khan is going to do anything to stop his family knowing about his little indiscretions.'

'So,' said Jimmy, 'Khan looks at the official report and says there's nothing wrong with it, only eighteen percent chance it could have identified the wrong person, what do you expect me to do? Saddleworth says, what we expect you to do is rubbish it, that's what we expect you to do, unless of course you want your sick habit of putting your hands down the pants of young boys splashed all over the papers. Oh, and as it happens, we've been talking to Penelope White of the Chronicle about your story. She would absolutely love to put your photograph on her front page.'

'That's why she was at the dinner you see,' Maggie added, 'just in case he has a last-minute change of heart. Although I'm not sure Gerrard had told her the full background.'

'That's right. So of course Khan has no choice. He writes a counter-report that says there's a high percentage chance that the identification was wrong. Scientifically, it's a heap of crap, but it delivers exactly what Saddleworth wants. Because now he is able to go to the CPS and bring up this rather inconvenient difficulty that has emerged just before the start of the trial.'

'So the CPS were involved in it too?' Frank asked.

'Yes, but they didn't know about the conspiracy. Elizabeth Rooke their boss is guilty through negligence, that's all. I expect the way it was raised was that Saddleworth says to her something's come up, some mad scientist guy who works for the Home Office has written a report, probably not that serious, but I thought we'd better run it past Cameron, see what he thinks. He knows that the last thing Rooke wants is to delay the trial, which would be a PR nightmare for her department, and so she says, go ahead, not really knowing what she's agreeing to.'

'So they arrange the dinner,' Frank said.

Maggie nodded. 'So they arrange the dinner. Right from the start, there's already pressure on Cameron from the CPS to sweep the whole thing under the carpet. Five minutes in, he realises that the geeky Dr Khan will be hopeless if he tries to put him in the witness box.'

'Yeah, we think that's probably what happened,' Jimmy said. 'So there's a discussion, Khan gives a complicated and confusing pitch, Cameron asks some questions but still can't make head or tail of it. He knows that Rooke just wants it to go away, and so after two or three bottles of rather nice Beaujolais and a call or two, they collectively decide that on balance it's best to leave things as they are.'

'Aye, I see it,' Frank said. 'Cameron has fallen into a bloody great bear-trap without even knowing it, because now that he's seen the report, the non-disclosure scam is in play. He knows it exists but now he's in on the decision not to use it. That's bloody clever, I've got to say.'

'Exactly,' Jimmy agreed. 'The trap is set, and the only person left to snare is Maggie.'

She gave a rueful smile. 'And how easy was that? By some ridiculous coincidence, a report turns up right at the end of the trial that could change everything for me. Too improbable for words of course, and I should have smelt a rat, but I was so bound up in my own dreams of glory. What a stupid idiot I was. And I remember now so clearly how interested Philip suddenly becomes about how the trial is going. Of course, I tell him about the report and surprise-surprise, he casually says, have you thought about using a disclosure angle? *Have you thought about disclosure.* That's all it took. And I fell for it one hundred percent.'

'But the judge was told you had got the report much earlier than you actually had it, wasn't she?' Frank said. 'That's why you got reported to the Bar Council. So how did that happen?'

'That was Philip's doing too. He spoke to Lady Rooke at the CPS. He said that I had told him I'd got it, you know, just as part of casual husband and wife conversation.'

'Weeks before you *actually* got it?'

'Exactly,' she said. 'What a hero he was, don't you think?'

Frank nodded. 'Aye he was, and bloody evil too. But there's something else I don't get. Why did Cameron have to be killed if he didn't know about the conspiracy?'

Maggie held up her hands and sighed. 'I'm afraid that was my fault again. Dr Khan told me that Philip panicked when he found out we had that photograph. Within minutes, he'd called everyone up and told them to keep quiet. Of course, Khan and Cameron who are all in the dark say, keep quiet about what?'

'And that's what signed his death warrant,' Frank said. 'A real tragedy. Priest decided it was too risky for any of them to stay alive and told the Iranian hoods to take care of all of them.'

'And they murdered that poor young waiter too,' Jimmy said ruefully. 'Presumably they were worried he had overheard something.'

Maggie nodded. 'Yeah, I know, in some ways that one was the most shocking of all. All Priest's doing, and he was our sodding Prime Minister.'

Jimmy laughed. 'Aye, but I don't think he'll be running for

re-election any time soon.'

Frank let out an exaggerated yawn.

'Well it's all as clear as mud to me. But you know what guys, I say we've had enough talk. I'm already bored stiff with all this Cathedral Close stuff. So how's about another round of these G-and-Ts before our puddings come?'

'Did someone say something about G-and-Ts? Yes please.'

Surprised, they spun round to greet the tall willowy figure of Asvina Rani. It was the first time Jimmy had seen her both out from behind a desk and not wearing her glasses, and he could not hide his appreciation of her loveliness. Frank meanwhile was looking at him with a non-too-subtle expression that said 'who the hell is this and how do you know her?'

'This is Asvina,' Jimmy said, reading his thoughts. 'Our patron. The lady who brought us Saddleworth verses Saddleworth.'

Maggie had leapt to her feet to envelop her friend in a warm hug. 'Asvina! I didn't expect to see you here. How did you find us?'

'A very nice girl at your office told me where you were. Elsa I believe her name is.' They noticed she was carrying a crisp white foolscap envelope. Gently, she freed herself from Maggie's embrace and began to wave the envelope above her head. There was an unmistakable air of triumph about her.

'So then Miss Bainbridge, I happened to be in front of a family court this morning, with magistrate Mrs Evelyn Black presiding. We were there to hear a petition, which I raised on your behalf, that Oliver Jonathon Brooks, aged seven, should be removed from the care of Camden Council Social Services to the care of his mother Mrs Magdalene Jane Brooks. I did not ask you to attend Maggie because quite frankly, and I say this as your best friend, I could not trust you not to get aggressive and not to get emotional and not to say a four-letter swear word, even under your breath, if an official made a statement you did not agree with.'

Maggie had collapsed back in her seat and now tears

streamed uncontrollably down her face. Jimmy tilted his head and gave her a thumbs up. 'She knows you, that's all I can say.'

Asvina smiled. 'As it happens, a stern and rather overweight woman who called herself the Assistant Deputy Director of Children's Services did make many statements that I did not agree with, and she made them with considerable force and at considerable length. However, you will be pleased to hear that I did not get aggressive, I did not get emotional and above all, I did not say a four-letter swear word, not even once.'

She handed the letter to Maggie, her voice the faintest whisper. 'Why don't you open it?'

Ollie was coming home.

The Leonardo Murders

Rob Wyllie

Chapter 1

Two-thirty pm on a late June afternoon, and for once the forecast had proved accurate, the sun splitting an azure-blue sky, its elevation perfect and its alignment about one hundred and ninety degrees off north. Eddie Taylor checked his little light meter, which only confirmed what he could see plainly with his own eyes. Ninety thousand lux. Couldn't be more perfect.

Carefully he removed his kit from the padded leather holdall. High-end digital SLR, super-steady tripod and the ultra-long zoom. Over two grand's worth in the lens alone, but it was his firm belief that a good workman needed the best tools, so it was money well spent. Particularly since he was having to set up nearly five hundred metres away, a distance that the big Canon lens would make short work of. He liked these little catalogue shoots, as he called them. Twelve hundred quid in his back pocket for half an hour's work, and no ghastly bridezillas to deal with like on his routine wedding work. He'd done two or three in the last couple of years, including the nice all-expenses jaunts to Europe. There was that trip down to the Dordogne and then a couple of months ago the Amsterdam job. And they'd sent him business class and put him up in a quality hotel. What was there not to like?

Today's assignment wasn't without risk of course, because understandably the authorities weren't too keen on primary schools being photographed, but he was far enough away not to arouse immediate suspicion, and for back-up Eddie always carried that estate agent's business card. Up here in Hampstead you couldn't move for the parasites, the district being one area of the capital that was immune to property-price wobbles. Knock up a fake e-mail with their letterhead arranging a fake appointment to survey the property, and that would be enough to fend off any local busybodies.

This was stage one in the surveillance operation. The idea was to get some decent identification shots of the target and to make sure you understood the pick-up routine. Then a bit of discreet tailing, figuring out the route they took home and sussing out one or two places where the snatch could take place with minimal risk of interruption.

It only took a few minutes to get set up, mounting the camera and lens securely on the stand and connecting the cable that operated the remote shutter release. A couple of adjustments and the school gates were sharply in focus. All set, giving him time to reflect that this assignment was a bit of an odd one. The last two or three, it was obvious why those kids had been targeted. With parents in the public eye and the prospect of a big fat juicy ransom, it made perfect sense. But as far as he knew, this kid was a nobody. Still, such musings were above his pay grade. Just do the job and take the money, thank you very much.

Now it was approaching three o'clock, and a gaggle of mums and carers were beginning to mill around the gate. Sometimes they got in the way and made it difficult to get a clear shot, but the problem wasn't insurmountable. The key was to shoot as soon as the subject was in sight and not worry too much about the finer points of composition. He stole another glance at the photograph they had sent him, then scanned the scene, eyes struggling to focus in the bright sunlight. He'd had his first brief look at the boy yesterday, but the trouble was, they all looked pretty much the same to him in their neat school uniforms, and the boss wouldn't be happy if he got the wrong one. So it was important to be sure. But *there*, no doubt about it in his mind, that kid was the one. Skinny, tall for his age, smooth pink skin, thick glossy shoulder-length hair and a mischievous smile. He watched as the boy scanned along the pavement, looking for the fat girl who he assumed was his nanny or au pair. Yesterday she'd been nearly five minutes late and he wondered if maybe she made a habit of it. But today she was on time, the boy giving a broad smile of recognition before running over and throwing his arms around her. A quick peek at the viewfinder, a squeeze on the shutter release and the shot was in the can. *Result*.

He tossed the camera bag into the back of his hatchback, blipped the lock and casually began to stroll down towards the school. The nanny had got into conversation with a couple of the mums whilst the boy wrestled with a robustly-built younger girl, ending up with him spread-eagled on the pavement as she easily overpowered him. But soon they were on the move, heading south-east down Christchurch Hill at a brisk pace. He kept about fifty metres behind them, close enough to maintain visual contact without causing any suspicion, not that they ever looked back. Besides, the pavement was full of pedestrians at this busy school pickup time. No chance of him arousing alarm even if they did glance round.

After about half a mile the pair swung right onto Pilgrims Lane then left into one of the quiet upmarket residential streets, lined both sides by neat million-pound-plus terraced properties. This was more promising, with nobody about even at this busy period in the day and plenty of access to get a fast motor in and out in an instant. He removed his smartphone from his pocket, noted down the street name then took a few snaps of the general layout. Great, that was probably enough for today. He'd do one more trial sweep tomorrow and then they would be all set.

About half way back to where he had parked his car, he heard the ping of a message coming through on his phone. Mechanically, he removed it from his pocket and gave it a fleeting look. Another wedding enquiry, checking his availability for October and requesting a mates-rate price. He thought it was a bit of a cheek given the bride-to-be was absolutely minted, but then the enquiry was from an old school pal from his East End days. Good old Roxy Kemp.

She being the actress now known as Melody Montague.

Chapter 2

DI Frank Stewart launched one final kick at the ancient vending machine before issuing a heart-felt *bollocks*. Despondently, he shuffled back down the dank corridor of Atlee House to his ancient battered desk. Boy, how he had been looking forward to that mid-morning Mars Bar, but now he was to be disappointed - again. He resolved that this was the last time he was going to risk a two-pound coin in that frigging machine. No frigging Mars Bar and no frigging change either.

That was the problem with working in poverty-spec Department 12B. It had the crappiest building, the crappiest equipment and the crappiest detectives, who quite naturally were assigned the crappiest cases. Present company excepted of course. Frank had been banished to this god-forsaken outpost of the Metropolitan Police not for being crap but because of an unfortunate incident involving his then commanding officer. An incident that involved a push, a punch, a torrent of colourful Glaswegian invective and resulted in six stitches above the eye for the huge pile of twatness that was DCI Colin Barker. Only the general agreement at the most senior levels of the force that Barker fully deserved it had saved Frank from instant dismissal from the job he loved. Instead, he was sent into semi-permanent exile amongst the has-beens and never-had-beens that occupied Atlee House.

Nonetheless, Department 12B did perform a useful function, being the dumping ground for cases that couldn't find a natural home elsewhere in the Met. Or cases that the brass would rather see swept under the carpet. Cases like the Jamie Grant abduction. Almost two years to the day since the wee toddler had been snatched in broad daylight as he was being wheeled home from playgroup by his child-minder. The fact that he was the son of the soap actor Charles Grant guaranteed maximum publicity for the case, but it hindered rather than helped the investigation, generating a ton of false sightings that swamped his mate DI Pete Burnside's stretched team. The case had been a disaster from start to finish, and when it was clear that there wasn't going to be a happy ending, the Assistant Commissioner quietly shut it down and shunted it off to Atlee House, telling the press it had been put in the hands of a specialist team. That had made Frank smile. Specialist team? It was obvious that the AC had never met any of the fuckwits and losers who called themselves his colleagues.

Before heading to the vending facilities, he'd given the empty buff folder sitting in the middle of his desk an appraising look. So far, all he'd managed to do was stick a white label on the front of the folder and scribble the name of the case on it. *Operation Shark.* He wasn't sure why, but he liked to give all his investigations a code name. This one hadn't taken long to come up with and he didn't really know why he picked it, it just sounded sort-of, well, *solid.* He had a hunch that this investigation was going to turn into something big and he didn't want it saddled with a rubbish name.

On his return, he was pleased to see Eleanor Campbell waiting at his desk. He liked the quirky government forensic officer, and he thought she liked him too. Not romantically of course, in either direction, absolutely not, and that wasn't just because of the age gap - he was forty-two but looked about fifty on a good day, and she, he wasn't quite sure, probably thirty-two or thirty-three, but looked about sixteen. No, the gap in years might have been no more than ten, but culturally it was wider that the Grand Canyon. Beside which, there was the spectre of Maggie Bainbridge hovering over him. Very definitely out of his league, that was what he believed, but at least she was about his age. He was seeing her in a couple of days with his brother Jimmy, and was very much looking forward to it.

'Well hello wee Eleanor,' he said brightly. 'Ready to go then?'

She nodded enthusiastically, which was very much unlike her. 'Yeah, can't wait.'

He looked at her suspiciously before remembering. Eleanor had a new toy and this was the first time she would have a chance to test it in the field. The woman was a sucker for new technology, especially the shady stuff she seemed to have no trouble procuring from her mates at the Government Communications labs up in Cheltenham. She wouldn't tell him what this one was all about, except she was helping the GCHQ geeks with something called a beta testing programme. She'd explained it once, but he still had no idea what it meant.

'Are we like walking then?' she asked.

'No way,' Frank replied, grimacing. 'It must be nearly four miles. No, we'll take a squad car and stick the blue lights on.' He could tell from her expression that she wasn't sure if he was joking or not. He wasn't.

'I've googled it,' she said in a serious tone. 'It's only two point four miles.'

'Exactly. Too far to walk. Come on, we better get our arses in gear or we'll miss the start.'

He grabbed the keys of an Astra from the board and they headed out to the car park behind the building. Atlee House was located just off the Uxbridge Road and ordinarily it wouldn't take much more than five or ten minutes to get to Speakers' Corner, especially on a Saturday. But today was different. The calendar was approaching midsummer, and with the sun blazing down from a crystal blue sky it was the perfect day to get the crowds out for the biggest protest rally of the season so far. *Stars Against Fascism.* Frank laughed to himself at the colossal self-regard of some of those so-called celebs. But maybe they believed in it all, who was he to say?

The traffic was nose-to-tail along the Bayswater Road, which confirmed he'd made the right decision with regard to mode of transport. Flicking on the blue flashing lights, he pulled out from behind a bus and cruised down the wrong side of the road, giving an occasional burst on the siren to warn oncoming vehicles. Glancing over into the park, he could see his mates in the riot squad were already there in force, a dozen or more lightly-armoured minibuses parked up and ready for any argy-bargy, should it arise. Which as far as Frank was concerned, was a one-hundred-percent certainty.

As he had expected, the entrance to West Carriage Drive was closed, guarded by a pair of sour-faced constables who were unarmed but in riot gear.

'What do you want?' one of them barked as he pulled the Astra up in front of a temporary barrier that had been erected.

He flashed his warrant card. 'DI Stewart. Department 12B.'

The constable gave his mate an uncertain look, not sure if he should have heard of it or not. Frank kept schtum, hoping to avoid long and tedious explanations as to why he was here. It seemed to work.

'Yeah, all right sir,' the constable said, his voice betraying doubt as to whether he was doing the right thing, 'on you go.'

Frank gave him a nod of acknowledgement and threaded the car through the narrow gap that had been opened up for them. He drove on for two or three hundred yards then pulled over onto the grass verge.

'We'll just dump it here Eleanor,' he said, 'and then take a wee stroll over towards the stage, so we can get a good view.'

She muttered something under her breath, her attention fully given to her smart phone. Looking at her, he saw she was wearing a perplexed expression.

'What did you say?'

'Their stuff is always pretty buggy but I can't get it to boot up. I might have to check the release notes.'

He shrugged, uncomprehending. 'Aye, well I'm sure you'll figure it out. Come on, let's go.'

They got out of the car and began walking towards the large stage, she still head-down and swiping a finger furiously across her screen. Taking in the scene, he struggled to estimate the size of the crowd that had assembled. Six, maybe seven thousand at the most, still decent but nothing like the half a million the organisers had claimed were going to turn up. That figure had made Frank chuckle. *Bow Road* was a popular soap, he knew that, and some of the actors were household names, but it wasn't as if they had the draw of an Angelina Jolie or a Beyoncé.

There was quite a broad demographic from the age perspective, but much less so from a socio-economic viewpoint. Alongside the placards and banners, the protestors had come armed with tartan travel rugs, wicker picnic baskets and a seemingly inexhaustible supply of prosecco. For this was almost without exception a nice middle-class day out, attendance seen almost as a duty by the comfortably-off and comfortably-smug Islington set. But they weren't the only group driven to attend by a sense of duty, which explained the heavy presence of the riot squad boys. Because whenever the virtue-signalling left came out to play, the right-wing bully boys came out too. Right now, there was definitely a bit of a party atmosphere, but he didn't expect that to last. As they snaked their way through the crowds, he looked again at Eleanor. This time she was smiling.

'Sorted?' he asked, feigning interest.

'Yeah, think so.' She held the phone out in front of her at arm's length and began to scan the horizon. 'Yeah, sorted. Look.' She thrust the phone into his face.

'What am I looking at?'

'Facial rec linked to the PNC. It's awesome.'

'And it's also illegal.' He'd got to know more than he really needed or wanted to know about facial recognition technology as a result of his last case, and he hoped he'd heard the last of it. But apparently not.

'You can like tell in an instant if someone's got a criminal record. It does real-time interrogation of the Police National Computer. With sixty-four-bit encryption.'

'Good to know,' Frank said, 'but just be careful who you point it at around here, will you? Every second one of them is a human-rights lawyer and they would go ape-shit if they got a sniff of what you're doing.'

'It's only like a test,' she said defensively.

'Whatever.' It was one of her favourite expressions, and he liked to use it whenever he could just to wind her up. This time, she scowled but said nothing.

A moderately well-known indie rock band were just closing their set with their sole hit, the lead singer having peppered the six-song performance with obligatory anti-Tory rants. Frank, something of a music buff, knew the guy's background. Public school, Durham Uni, old money. But he didn't hold it against him.

'Great song this,' he shouted to no-one in particular. He saw that Eleanor had her phone focussed on the vocalist.

'He's got a drugs bust,' she said, her tone smug, 'back in twenty-twelve.'

'Put the bloody thing away,' he said. 'You've proved it works, so that's a tick in the box. Let's just enjoy the speeches.'

The speeches. Because that's why they were here, and to hear one speech in particular. Operation Shark's Charles Grant, the left-wing activist nicknamed the Pound-Shop Martin Luther King by his enemies in the press. He'd need to do some research to find out how he'd come by the name, but he knew that they hadn't meant it as a compliment. But before Grant, it seemed there was to be a warm-up act.

'Ladies and Gentlemen, thank *you* for coming. Stars against fascism!' Frank recognised the compère as Paul somebody-or other, a comedian familiar to millions from his appearances on TV panel shows, and known for his left-of-centre politics. Then again, everyone on these shows had left-of-centre politics. It was mandatory, and more important than actually being funny.

'Ladies and gentlemen, may I introduce to the stage, Mr Benjamin Fox and Miss Allegra Ross.' As the two soap actors walked on from the wings, the crowd, seemingly reluctant to divert attention from their picnics, gave a ripple of polite applause. Frank didn't follow the soaps, but he vaguely knew of Fox. Played the randy doctor, the one lucky not to be struck off when caught with his trousers down. The woman, he was pretty sure he hadn't seen before but there was no doubting she was easy on the eye.

'Thanks Paul,' Fox said, waving to the crowd. 'Are you all right!' This time, the response from the audience was more enthusiastic, a loud *yes* followed by laughter. Alongside him, Allegra Ross beamed a smile and raised her hands in salute. It seemed in fact that it was she who would be the first to speak.

'We're here today, united in our great cause. The fight against fascism, the fight against the rise of global right-wing extremism.'

'Fuck off.'

Frank heard the shout, and knew instinctively that it was all about to kick off. To the left of the stage, a group of young men had gathered, slurping from bottles of lager and directing single-finger gestures towards the platform.

'Commie wankers.'

'As I said, we're gathered here today, united in the fight against fascism.' Allegra had evidently decided not only to ignore the hecklers, but to confront them too. That was going to prove to be a mistake. She pointed at the group. 'And if we ever needed evidence as to how important it is for us to win this fight, you can see it here. Right here in front of you. Fascist scum.'

Frank guessed she'd used these words plenty of times on her Twitter feed, but she was about to find out it was a whole order of magnitude more dangerous to use them in the real world. There was a horrified gasp from the crowd as a bottle smashed onto the stage just in front of the actress. But this bottle wasn't filled with beer.

'Christ, bloody molotovs,' Frank barked, as a sheet of flame shot up from the stage. Where the bloody hell were the riot boys when they needed them? Especially when he could guess what was coming next. He ran to the front of the stage and gestured to the actors.

'Get off the bloody stage now,' he screamed, then howled in pain as something hard struck him on the back of the head. In front of him, he saw that Benjamin Fox had been hit too, a stream of blood flowing down his face from where the sharpened coin had sliced into his forehead. Spinning round, he saw that Eleanor had her phone focussed on the ring-leader, and was shouting out a name to him.

But Frank didn't need the help of GCHQ's fancy beta software to recognise who stood just thirty feet from him, his face contorted with hatred. *Darren Venables*. The man known as D-V to his devoted following, and the self-proclaimed leader of the White British League.

Shit. The WBL was a proscribed organisation and here was their leader blatantly committing common assault in Hyde Park and not giving a shit who witnessed it. So much for Frank's hope of a quiet day out. He knew he should wait for the riot boys to get here, but they didn't seem to be in any hurry. And the thing was, he didn't want the scumbag getting away with it. He checked in his back pocket for his handcuffs, then made the decision.

In for a penny, in for a pound.

Chapter 3

The dress code on the invitation had been a bit enigmatic. *Dress to Impress*. What the hell did that mean in these luvvie circles? It wouldn't have mattered what Jimmy had chosen of course, because he always looked amazing straight out of the box. For Maggie, the process had been more stressful, but in the end she had decided you couldn't go too far wrong with a little black dress. Even if it was about three inches too short and half a size too small. A pair of shoes three inches higher than her normal wear had completed the transformation. Too tarty? You couldn't be too tarty in this company. And besides, a couple of complimentary proseccos into the evening, she no longer gave a monkey's what anybody thought of her appearance. Scanning the packed room, she spotted her colleague about to stuff a *vol-au-vent* into his mouth with the palm of his hand. She shook her glass in the air to draw his attention, drizzling herself with sticky warm fizz in the process. *Bugger*.

Jimmy Stewart had interpreted the code as black tie, and was looking sensational in his elegant dinner suit and spotted bow-tie. So sensational in fact that Melody Montague, the *raison d'être* for their attendance at the not-quite A-listed awards event, already had him pinned against the wall. *Fading soap star*, that was how the red-tops generally described the serially-married actress. Serially married as in three times in real life and about the same in her role as Patty West in *Bow Road*. But fading? She might be a bit past her prime, but she still radiated effortless sexuality. One seriously fit bird, that's how Jimmy's brother Frank had described her when he heard they were going to meet her. Age indeterminate, anywhere between late forties and mid-fifties according to her frequently-updated Wikipedia entry. It had to be frequently updated because there was always something going on in Melody's chaotic life. Maggie made her way over to them.

'Evening Jimmy, hope I'm not interrupting anything.'

He smiled. 'No boss, nothing at all. This is Melody Montague by the way. Melody, meet my boss Maggie Bainbridge.'

The actress shot Maggie a sideways glance, as if to say does this woman *really* not know who I am? Surely *everyone* knows Melody Montague. But she didn't seem too offended.

'My new friend Jimmy here was telling me that you're going to help me with my divorce settlement.'

'That's right,' Maggie answered, 'that's why we're here.' What she didn't say was that they were there on a bloody mission impossible, having received the legal equivalent of a hospital pass from her best friend Miss Asvina Rani, London's go-to divorce lawyer for the rich and famous. Asvina charged three hundred pounds an hour and there were no discounts, no matter how celebrated a celebrity you were. So that gave a good marker as to how loaded Melody Montague must be.

'But it's actually your ex-husband we need to see of course. I assume he's here?'

Melody shrugged. 'Yeah, he'll be here somewhere. Why don't you ask around for Allegra Ross? I would imagine you would find him with his little tin-pot revolutionary, tagging along like a pathetic poodle.'

Jimmy looked at her, unsure if she was serious or not. 'Did Asvina talk to you about the plan?' he asked.

Maggie gave a silent laugh. Actually, there wasn't a plan. How could you make a plan out of such a stupid objective? She guessed he'd have been on the end of some dumb orders in his army days, but this one was off the scale. Dumber than a dumb thing that had lost its voice.

Melody nodded. 'She did say something about it but I didn't really take it in. You see, all I want is to make sure my pathetic ex doesn't get his hands on my assets.'

Maggie was taken aback by the coldness in her manner. This was a man she had married hardly more than three years earlier, telling everyone who would listen that she had found her soul-mate at last and they couldn't wait to start a family. Some soul mate. The marriage had lasted barely eighteen months, but at least there hadn't been any children, who were always the innocent victims of any split. That's when it could get really bitter. And now, three months after the *degree nisi* and the ending of their dream, they were still haggling over the spoils.

'Hang on,' said Jimmy, interrupting her thoughts, 'isn't that him over there?'

He pointed across the room to a conspicuously good-looking man of about fifty who was leaning against a wall, drink in hand. But contrary to Melody's prediction, he wasn't with Allegra Ross, but with a man they didn't recognise. And as they made their way towards them, they couldn't help but recognise the corrosive atmosphere.

'You can't do this Benjamin,' the other man was saying, his voice plaintive. 'You'll ruin my career and that's just not fair.'

'You should have thought of that before you came up with all that *shite*,' Fox replied. From his faintly slurred tones, it wasn't too hard for Maggie to work out he'd been taking full advantage of the free bar.

'You see, they're all the same,' Fox said, playing to his new audience. 'They get a third-class honours in creative writing from some ghastly provincial college and they think they're Earnest Hemmingway. But I won't have it, you see?'

Now the other man's eyes were bulging, his face turning noticeably crimson. 'You won't get away with this you know,' he said, spitting out the words. 'This won't be the last you hear of this, believe me.'

Fox gave a contemptuous laugh. 'Oh yes I think it will be Jack. You see, you think *way* too much of your meagre talents. Boys like you are simply expendable. I shall watch with great pleasure as you sink into obscurity.'

His words seemed to tip the other man over the edge.

'You're an evil bastard,' he sneered, jabbing his finger an inch from Fox's face, then raised his fist as if to swing a punch.

Jimmy reacted in an instant. 'Probably not a good idea sir,' he said, taking hold of his arm and tightening his grip. 'Always best to talk these things through calmly.' The man tried to shake himself free but Jimmy was too strong for him.

'Let's just leave it at that sir, shall we?' Jimmy said calmly but firmly. The man shot him a defiant look but that was the limit to his reaction. Finally he mumbled,

'Yeah, ok,' straightening his shirt as Jimmy released his grip.

He walked away slowly, turning to direct a scowl at Benjamin Fox as he left.

'Well thank you,' Fox said to them, struggling to regain his composure, 'I didn't really want another eye to match this one.'

Maggie smiled. 'Yes, that eye looks painful.'

'It's bloody sore,' he said ruefully. 'Four stitches too. They say it shouldn't leave much of a scar. But I guess I shouldn't worry at my age. Adds a bit of character, I suppose you could say. But I don't think we've met, have we?'

'No, I'm Maggie Bainbridge and this is my colleague Jimmy Stewart. We were hoping to have a word with you about your pre-nuptial agreement with your ex-wife. But do you mind me asking what that was all about?'

He laughed. 'Not at all, but just a moment.' He signalled to a passing waitress who came over to him holding out a tray.

'Red's Shiraz, white's Pinot,' she said in a cockney accent worthy of Bow Road itself.

'Thanks, I'll have one of each,' Fox said, helping himself.

'Ah yes, the little scene. That was Jack Redmayne, one of the scriptwriters on the show, or story consultants as they like to call themselves. Frightful little weasel. So he came up with this idea that my Dr Manners character should be *murdered* by an aggrieved husband of one of my lovers. And it's not the first time he's come up with some crap like that. Well bollocks to that. I've just told him that I'm going straight to the producers to tell them if he continues working on the show I'm walking out. Him or me, a straightforward choice.'

Maggie wasn't sure what to say. 'I'm afraid I don't understand the world of entertainment. But if you don't mind Benjamin, I'd like to get straight to the point. It appears that there is a bit of a misunderstanding about the pre-nup and we want to try and sort it out as soon as we can. With your assistance of course.'

'A bit of a mix-up?' Fox said, laughing. 'That's what she's calling it, is she?'

'Well, as you know, her copy of the agreement has been mislaid. Or to be more exact, her solicitor Mr McCartney with whom she had entrusted it seems to have mislaid it. We think as a result of his recent business difficulties.'

'Business difficulties? Well that's one way you could describe it I suppose. What was it, five years he got?'

Maggie nodded. 'Yes, but embezzling the client account is rather frowned on in our profession as you can imagine.' *Our profession*. It was so easy to forget she was no longer a lawyer.

'Indeed, and so it should be. But getting back to the matter in question, what is this misunderstanding of which you speak?'

She gave him a stern look. 'I think you know exactly what I'm referring to. It concerns the page that lays out how the assets should be split in the event of their divorce. You see, it appears your copy records a settlement that is quite different to that which Melody recalls.'

In the background she could hear Jimmy humming quietly to himself. *Doo-doo-doodoo-doo-doo*. The opening bars of the *Mission Impossible* theme. She shot him an admonishing look before pressing on.

'Miss Montague was quite clear about the intention of the original agreement. In the event of your divorce, she was entitled to seventy-five percent of the assets, and she is quite adamant that the document which was entrusted to her solicitor states that.'

'Ah but that's where you're mistaken,' Fox replied, his tone betraying no concern, 'and it's quite extraordinary that she should think that was the split we agreed. Oh, you are correct about the proportions, but in fact it's the other way around. *I* get seventy-five percent and she gets twenty-five, I think you will find. That is of course simply reflecting the value of assets we each brought into the marriage.'

She gave him a bewildered look. 'But that's not what we were led to believe by Miss Montague. She was quite sure about it.'

There was an edge to his reply, the subject matter seemingly having the effect of sobering him up. 'You know, this is quite ridiculous. I've no idea what kind of stunt she is trying to pull here. But I can guess *why* she's doing it. She simply wants to prevent me getting what's legally mine. Please understand, I don't intend to let that happen.'

Maggie knew from personal experience the rancour that could be unleashed when a marriage fell apart, but though Fox's outburst was controlled, the underlying anger was obvious. Perhaps it wasn't surprising when, as she understood from Asvina, a couple of million pounds or more could be at stake.

'But anyway,' he continued, 'there's quite an easy solution to all of this.'

Maggie had a pretty good idea where the conversation was heading.

'You only have to speak to the witnesses, surely? That's what they were there for after all. And maybe you should pay a little visit to Pentonville prison too. After all, it was Blake McCartney who drew the thing up. I'm sure he can put you straight.'

'Yes, we'll do that,' Maggie said, her tone sharper than she would have liked. 'But as you suggest, we do intend speaking to the other witnesses. In fact we hope to have a word with Charles Grant this evening. He was a witness, wasn't he?'

He shrugged. 'He was, and I've no reason to doubt his recollection will be the same as my own.'

'Aye, but what about the other one?' Jimmy said enquiringly. 'Kylie Ward. What will her take be on the matter?'

Fox smiled. 'I'm afraid that may pose some difficulties. You see I'm sad to say that Kylie Ward died nine months ago.'

'What?' Maggie blurted it out, unable to conceal her dismay at this further complication to a matter that was already proving complex enough.

'Yes, she was killed in a road traffic accident near her home in Surbiton. A hit and run. It was a terrible tragedy. I was very upset by her death of course.'

'She was your friend?'

'Not exactly. More of a business acquaintance I suppose. She worked as a kind of gopher for my agent. But I did know her quite well.'

'Well enough to have her witness important documents like this one?'

'I wasn't aware witnesses required any particular connection to the parties,' he said sharply. 'It is enough that they are present at the signing. But all of this of course is quite irrelevant, since there is no doubt that I have the correct document. I don't know how I can make it any plainer than that.'

Maggie felt herself beginning to agree with Jimmy. There really wasn't anywhere this could go but downwards. *Mission Impossible*. But Asvina had dispatched them on this mission with clear orders, and they were honour-bound to go through with it as specified. So she went for it.

'Benjamin, this could all be settled quite straightforwardly if you were to accept that in fact Melody's version of the agreement is the correct one. Wouldn't it be great if it could be all done and dusted without any recourse to the courts?' Said out loud, it sounded even more desperate than when she was formulating it in her mind. And it got the exact response she was expecting. In fact, worse than she was expecting. Because now his manner had turned decidedly nasty.

'Look I don't know how to put this politely Maggie, so I won't even try. So let me just express it as plainly as I can. You can tell Melody that if she wants me to keep my side of our little arrangement, she had better give up this ridiculous charade and pay me what I'm due. Is that plain enough for you?'

It was plain enough for her to understand the words but that didn't mean she knew what he meant. But that would have to wait for later. She could always recognise when it was time to sound the retreat and live to fight another day. And this was such a time.

She gave him a half-smile. 'Well thank you Benjamin for speaking to us. I'm afraid the whole situation is very confusing and so I think we've probably taken it as far as we can today.'

'No hard feelings,' he said, his good humour returning. 'I'm sure you will be able to clear it all very nicely with Melody. But if you will excuse me now. The tabloid press is very keen to talk to Allegra and me about yesterday's events and we mustn't keep them waiting, must we? But first, I need another drink.'

***

'Our little arrangement? What do you think he meant by that?'

Maggie and Jimmy had retreated to the bar and now he was putting into words what she had been thinking. Yes, exactly what had he meant by that?

'I don't know Jimmy, but there was something odd about the whole conversation. I don't know what it was, but I don't think he was telling the truth.' She took a sip from her prosecco, cautioning herself that this should be her last.

'But we've seen his document and it definitely backs up his version of what was agreed.'

Maggie nodded. 'Yes, but documents can very easily be doctored.'

Which was why it was going to be so important to see what they witness had to say on the matter. Or the witness, to be exact, given that the other one had, rather inconveniently, died only nine months earlier. Idly, she wondered if that was a plotline that Jack Redmayne could use.

Chapter 4

He had a reputation for being difficult, Charles Grant, both on and off screen, but as an A-lister of the soap genre, if that wasn't an oxymoron, it was perhaps to be expected. That evening, he was also proving to be a difficult man to gain an audience with.

'I've been hanging around him for the last ten minutes,' Jimmy said, 'but he always seems to be with someone. You see, there he is over there.'

Maggie looked over to where he was pointing.

'Yes, and do you see who he's talking to now?'

'Aye, I see who it is. Come on, I think we can wander over and introduce ourselves.'

Grant was with Benjamin Fox and an actress who Maggie recognised as Sharon Trent, another member of the cast of Bow Road. Whatever it was they had been talking about, it looked like the subject was serious. Serious enough for them to immediately clam up when Maggie and Jimmy approached.

'Sorry if we're interrupting anything,' Maggie said brightly, 'but we wondered if we might arrange to have a word with you Mr Grant. Benjamin knows what it's about, I don't know if he's mentioned it to you at all. I'm Maggie Bainbridge by the way and this is my colleague Jimmy Stewart.'

She extended a hand in his direction, which he accepted, giving her an uncertain look. His eyes had a haunted appearance, impregnated with a sadness that seemed to come from deep inside. Hardly surprising after all he had been through, and didn't she know what that felt like. Although thank goodness her own son had survived his terrible trauma. Just about.

'And what do you two do?' he said suspiciously.

'Ah, so Benjamin hasn't told you,' Maggie said. 'We're working with Melody's divorce lawyer, Asvina Rani. There's a little issue we're trying to get to the bottom of.'

She saw Fox give a shake of the head as if to say *see what I mean,* then stand up and place a hand on Grant's shoulder.

'I'll leave you to it mate,' he said, wandering off. 'Catch you two later.'

'Yeah sure Benjamin,' Grant shouted after him, before turning his attention to Maggie and Jimmy.

'He did mention it. Some nonsense about a pre-nuptial agreement. So what's it all about?'

Maggie smiled sweetly. 'Yes, that's right Mr Grant. A simple question, we just wanted to know whether you remember witnessing it or not? It would have been in the offices of Melody's solicitor, Blake McCartney. About four years ago.'

'Yes, I remember.'

'And I wonder, do you remember any of the contents of the agreement or did Mr McCartney explain them to you?' She guessed it was unlikely that he would remember, because in her experience, witnesses were happy to sign anything that was stuck in front of them. But his answer took her by surprise.

'Well I don't remember the detail of course. But I did take the precaution of requesting a copy. I still have it somewhere I think. I can look it out if you'd like?'

So far the difficult Charles Grant was proving anything but difficult.

'Yes, that would be most helpful. But tell me, why did you request a copy?'

He shrugged. 'I don't know. I guessed it was an important document so I thought I'd better keep one, that's all.'

'Do you know that Melody is disputing Benjamin's version of the document?' Maggie asked him.

He shrugged again. 'I didn't. We have to work together of course, but we're not exactly friends. So she wouldn't discuss things like that with me.'

She remembered that his character Freddie Jack had once been married to Patty West, as played by Melody, so guessed they must have had a very close working relationship at one time. Maggie had always particularly liked his character. Freddie was one of life's losers, but the sort of guy the viewers felt sorry for, where every week they wished that just for once the poor guy would get a break. Rather like Charles himself, who had been dealt the cruellest of hands in real life. She just couldn't imagine how he had been able to carry on after what had happened to his little son. The agony of not knowing if he was dead or alive, his mind filled with images of what he might have gone through at the hands of his abductors. Then the rise of hope when the huge ransom was handed over, to be extinguished when the kidnappers failed to keep their side of the bargain. And now he would be longing each day that today there would finally be some news. But it had never come, and now deep inside he must know that all hope was probably gone. It had shattered his life and his marriage too, and now as far as she knew, he lived alone.

'Intriguing,' said Sharon Trent, who had been listening rapt to the sparse interchange. And who had been directing her full attention to Jimmy. 'So do tell Jimmy, what's this all about exactly? Has Melody made the whole thing up? It sounds rather like it to me.'

'I'm afraid it's confidential,' Maggie replied, butting in. 'We can't discuss the ins and outs of the case with you.'

'Very well,' she replied, unperturbed. 'I know when I'm surplus to requirements. Jimmy, hand please.'

She extracted a slim gold ballpoint from her clutch bag.

'Give me your *hand* please,' she repeated, reacting to Jimmy's puzzled look. She took his hand in hers and carefully wrote her number on the back of it, followed by her name, in a delicate and precise script. As if he was likely to forget who had written it.

'I know you'll want to call me. And darling, *please* don't wash it off by mistake. Now if you don't mind darling Charles, I'll leave you to your dull old document.'

Maggie watched with rising anger as she walked away. Poor poor Charles Grant. The man had lost his son and his marriage and now seemed to be investing his hopes of the future in this, this *brazen hussy*. She couldn't see the relationship turning out well, no matter how you looked at it. But that wasn't the only thing that was exercising her.

Because she couldn't help noticing that Jimmy Stewart already had a phone number scribbled on his *other* hand. Belonging to Melody Montague she had no doubt. Two women in the space of less than an hour. *Bloody* annoying.

She noticed that Grant was giving her a curious look. And then he spoke.

'I remember you of course, from the Alzahrani case. The most hated woman in Britain. Quite a label and quite a business that was. A terrible thing altogether.'

'Yes, that was me I'm afraid,' she said quietly. 'It seems a lifetime ago now, but it's only two years. The same time your little boy was taken. I remember it. I'm afraid it rather pushed your little Jamie's case off the front pages. I'm sorry about that. I can't even think how awful it must be for you, living with it every day. Not knowing what's happened to him.'

A terrible sadness returned to his eyes.

'You might have heard they've just closed the case. They don't say it in so many words of course, but they've taken the team off it so it amounts to the same thing.'

Jimmy gave a sympathetic nod. 'They never let these things go Mr Grant. The file always stays open.'

'It does,' Maggie said, but she knew the reality. Twice a year it would get a half-hearted look-over by some junior detective who wasn't trusted with anything more important.

'I'm not so sure Miss Bainbridge,' Grant said, 'but I appreciate your concern. Both of you.'

Suddenly Grant said, 'Would you take on the case?' Maggie thought she heard the words clearly enough, but was sure she must have been mistaken.

'I'm sorry?'

'You two are private investigators I'm given to believe? So I'd like you to take on the case. Find Jamie for me. I'll pay well.'

It was Jimmy who answered first, raising his hands apologetically as he tried to overcome his surprise at the request. 'Well, just a minute Mr Grant. We don't do that sort of stuff I'm afraid. I mean divorces and fraud and the like...

but we don't do criminal work. I'm not sure we're even allowed to. Don't you need a licence?'

Maggie shook her head. 'No, that's not necessary here in the UK, but really Mr Grant, we're not the right choice for this. There are plenty of firms who are way more qualified than us. Most of them ex-policemen with years of investigative work under their belts. You'd fare much better with one of them.'

He leaned across and placed his hand over hers. 'Look, I've been badly let down by the police. The man they had running it was a fool, and as soon as it started to look embarrassing on the statistics, they couldn't wait to push it into their cold-cases file. It's all very convenient for them because they get to close a live case and then it disappears into a black hole that no-one cares about.' There was a quiet desperation in his voice, the pain seeping out of him like blood from a deep wound. A wound that she knew would never heal until his son was found. Dead or alive.

'You see, I need someone I can trust, and already I feel I can trust you. I don't know why I feel that way, but I always go with my gut.'

She placed her free hand over his, clasping it tight. 'Mr Grant, we *can't* take this on in any formal capacity. As I've told you, we don't have any skills or experience in matters of this type. We'd be taking your money under false pretences if we were to accept.'

'The police were useless,' he said. 'Please, I really need this. Please.'

Maggie could feel her resolve wavering. No matter how you looked at it, he would effectively be placing his future happiness in their hands. Of course she couldn't take this on, no matter how sorry she felt for him. That would be crazy. But she remembered how at her absolute lowest moment Jimmy Stewart had come along, quite out of the blue, and literally saved her life. Without his intervention, delivered by the fates without any warning, she did not know how she could have carried on. And now she recognised a fellow human being in exactly the same position as she had been back then. Charles Grant needed her help and not just to find out what happened to his son. He needed help to simply carry on with life.

She leaned over, whispering so that Jimmy wouldn't hear. *'We'll do it.'*

'I can't thank you enough,' Grant said, his voice wavering. 'You're my only hope now.'

'We won't let you down Charles, trust me.'

Behind her, Jimmy had caught on to what was happening and was whistling that damn tune again.

***

In recognition of their nobody status, they had been allocated seats towards the rear of the auditorium, tucked away on the far left. Maggie couldn't quite explain it, but she was feeling more than a little jumpy. Maybe it was because the evening hadn't gone so well with regard to the pre-nup business but whatever the cause, she would have given much for another prosecco, or indeed something stronger. Unfortunately, that option was not available since the organisers had prohibited the consumption of alcohol during the ceremony itself. It wasn't a popular move, but it was prudent given the number of car-crash moments that had scarred or enlivened previous events, depending on which way you looked at it.

Had she been able to be honest with herself of course, she could have pinpointed at least one reason for her discomfort. It was Jimmy Stewart and his encounters with Allegra Ross and Sharon Trent and Miss Melody-bloody-Montague. Jealousy was such a destructive emotion, but it was easier to recognise than do something about. Actually it wasn't exactly jealousy, more a sense of possessiveness. In her mind he was *her* Jimmy, no-one else's, and at this point in her life, she didn't want any other woman taking him away from her. Not that it was likely of course, because right now Jimmy's only desire in life was making up again with his wife. So far, he'd got nowhere with that.

She looked at him, and it was clear from his dour expression he wasn't enjoying the evening at all. And then she remembered. Astrid Sorenson, the Swedish country singer. The woman who had destroyed his marriage. Of course, he would have been to quite a few of these events as a plus-one with the beautiful singer. A do like this one couldn't help but bring back painful memories. She knew he didn't like to talk about everything that had happened, and she didn't like to pry. One day perhaps she would ask him.

On entry they had been given a glossy programme laying out the running order for the evening. She groaned when she saw there were to be twenty-seven separate awards. And of course the big two, the only ones anybody was actually interested in, were scheduled right at the end. *Best Actress* and *Best Actor*, those were the ones that were most coveted. Before that, there was a pile of tedium to sit through. *Agony*.

The event was being broadcast as-live to the nation's soap fans, of which there were many millions. As-live meant that there was time to cut and re-shoot any cock-ups or beep out any profanities that crept into the acceptance speeches. The stage was flanked by two large video screens on which the proceedings were being displayed. Several cameras raked the audience, all the better to capture the obviously-faked reactions when an artist either received an award, or in a ratio of three to one, was overlooked.

Suddenly Jimmy nudged her with his elbow. Painfully. She let out an involuntary yelp.

'Sorry,' he whispered, pointing up at the screen, 'but do you see that?'

The cameras had picked out Benjamin Fox and Allegra Ross sitting together. It was clear from the scene being acted out that relations were strained. As he had reached across to take her hand, she had angrily pulled it away. He then leant across to try and kiss her cheek, prompting her to recoil and shoot a scowl in his direction. He tried again, to be met with the same angry reaction.

'So?' Maggie asked, a little too loudly.

A middle-age man sitting in front of them who Maggie recognised as the *Daily Chronicle's* entertainments editor turned round and gave a loud 'Shhh!'

Jimmy gave an apologetic smile. 'Sorry mate,' he mouthed. 'But they're not exactly lovebirds are they? Not like Melody was suggesting.'

She shrugged. 'He's an actor, she's an actress. It's what they do.'

Two hours into the proceedings, and she was rapidly losing the will to live. All throughout the evening, bored celebrities had been slipping out to the bar when they were sure the cameras weren't on them, like escaping prisoners of war trying to avoid the camp searchlights. But now one by one they were beginning to dribble back to their seats in anticipation of the main awards.

'It's best actress now,' said Jimmy, studying his programme whilst stifling a yawn, 'and I see that both Sharon Trent and our Melody are up for it.'

'And they'd both like to get their claws into you, you babe-magnet,' Maggie said, trying to lighten the atmosphere. 'I guess you'll pick whichever of them wins?' She wasn't sure whether her comment struck the right note but it was too late to take it back. Anyway, given how he felt about what he done to his ex-wife, she was fairly certain he wasn't likely to call either of them. At least she thought not.

The presenters were now announcing the nominees, the video screens running short excerpts from presumably what was regarded as their best work. Shakespeare it wasn't, but there was no shortage of entertaining if over-the-top drama on display. Mercifully, the director had kept it short.

'And to present the award, one of Britain's best-loved actors. From Bow Road, please welcome Mr Nice Guy himself, Charles Grant!' The young presenters turned to applaud as Grant bounded on stage left. He might have been Mr Nice Guy in Bow Road, but the less than tumultuous response he received from the audience tended to underline his real-life reputation as Mr Awkward. Not that he had been anything but nice to them.

'Thank you, thank you,' he mouthed, waving a hand above his head.

'Do you think they tell him in advance who's won it?' whispered Jimmy. 'He does look very pleased with himself.'

'What, does that mean it must be Sharon?' Maggie asked.

She didn't have to wait for his answer, as Grant tore open the envelope and without looking at the card, pointed triumphantly to where his girlfriend sat. 'And the winner is - of course - the delectable Miss... Sharon... Trent!'

The cameras caught her as she placed both hands over her mouth in fake astonishment. Maggie thought she might even have seen a tear. How did they do it, that crying to order? She supposed they must learn how at drama school. Naturally the director wanted reaction shots from the unlucky losers. Two out of the three managed the obligatory forced smiles and half-hearted applause, but not Melody Montague. Back in the control room, the director let out an expletive and screamed a panicky command. 'Cut, cut, stop the frigging broadcast! Christ, does she want to get me fired?' Simultaneously, the audience let out a sharp gasp followed by waves of laughter. That's what happens when a famous actress is caught giving the one-finger salute to camera.

The director was now on-stage, apologising for the delay and explaining that they would have to re-shoot the scene. The audience, experienced thesps who knew how these things worked, were already slinking out to the bar.

It was ten minutes before the director returned to the microphone and requested everyone took their seats for the retake. Out in the bar, production assistants ushered reluctant drinkers back into the auditorium. The retake passed without further incident, and soon it was time for best actor, the pinnacle award of the evening.

'Whoa, do you see this?' Jimmy said. 'It's only flipping Montague who's presenting this one.'

Melody, seemingly unfazed by the earlier excitement, had slipped in a costume change in preparation for her presenting duties. Now she wore a glittery gold mini-dress that was tighter, shorter and more revealing than her earlier outfit, an effect that Maggie would have believed impossible if she wasn't seeing it with her own eyes. Just as well Jimmy's brother Frank isn't here she thought, or he would have a flipping heart-attack. To her left, Jimmy was staring at the stage, open-mouthed. *Even him.* That was the general problem with men. They were so shallow.

As Melody glided onto the stage, the audience were on their feet, cheering wildly as she took a mock bow of acknowledgement. It was half a minute before the noise subdued sufficiently for the presentation to continue. Back at home, the viewers must have been wondering what all the fuss was about.

'Thank you all,' she said, smiling an obviously confected smile. 'Before announcing the award for best actor, I would like to extend my congratulations to Sharon...' She paused. One or two people clapped, uncertainly, then quickly stopped as they realised they were alone. 'I'd like to... but I'm not going to, the bitch.' There was an awkward silence, and then, deciding it must be a joke and that Sharon must be in on it, they began to laugh. Two rows back from the stage, Trent sat stony-faced, drawing daggers and swearing revenge under her breath. Backstage, the director took another large swig from his hip-flask and prayed that it would soon be over. Him, and most of the audience too.

Unfazed, Melody tore open the envelope and took out the card. 'Now ladies and gentlemen, the moment you have all been waiting for...' She screwed up her eyes to focus on the name, then scowled as she saw who it was. The producers must have known in advance that her ex-husband Fox was the winner when they picked her to present the award, but evidently decided to risk it.

With some effort, she managed to compose herself.

'And the winner is...my wonderful friend from Bow Road... Mr Benjamin Fox.'

As the audience burst into applause, the cameras scoured the room, looking for the winner. *In vain.* The reluctant hand-holder Allegra Ross was there, but beside her the seat Benjamin Fox had occupied was empty. On stage, the young female host was struggling to concentrate on the torrent of words the director was delivering into her earpiece. But presently her poise returned, along with her trademark beaming smile. *'So ladies and gentlemen, I'm afraid Benjamin is unable to join us tonight, but to accept the award on his behalf, please welcome back to the stage Mr Charles Grant.'*

What Fox might think about his activist colleague accepting the award on his behalf was destined never to be known. For at that very moment, he was in the emergency stairwell, lying in a pool of blood, his head battered in. Alongside lay his severed left hand. And on the back of that hand was scrawled a message that the police would find completely unfathomable.

Leonardo

Chapter 5

Frank tossed aside the day-old newspaper, nodding to no-one in particular as he drained his pint. The *Chronicle* wasn't his paper, but he had been drawn to the headline. *Society priorities questioned as missing soap star hits fifty thousand re-tweets.* He had only the vaguest familiarity with social media, but he knew enough to know that fifty thousand twitters or whatever they were called was big. The guy had only been missing a couple of days, for god's sake. In Frank's opinion, he just gone on one of his benders and they'd soon find him passed out in a gutter somewhere.

'Whoa, you're looking sharp tonight.' Frank spun round on his stool at the sound of his brother's voice.

'Cheeky swine,' he replied, as they clasped hands in greeting.

Jimmy's smile drained from his face as he got a better look at his brother.

'Bloody hell Frank, what happened to you? You look as if you've done twelve rounds with Tyson Fury.'

'Aye, and it feels like it. I was at that anti-fascist rally at the weekend and got mixed up in a bit of a punch-up. Hence my spectacular black eye.' He didn't mention the three stitches in the back of his head. Maybe he'd keep that one for Maggie.

'I read about that,' Jimmy said. 'They arrested that far-right guy didn't they? Darren Venables.'

Frank grimaced. 'Aye, *they* did. And don't I know it.'

Jimmy looked at him, wide-eyed. 'So that was *you*?'

'Can't deny it. Wish I hadn't though. He's pretty handy with his fists.'

'Well, much respect bruv. Top work. But what's with all the fancy clobber? It couldn't be anything to do with the fact that Asvina's coming tonight?'

'That's pure bollocks,' Frank replied, quite truthfully.

'Aye, right. So have you bought the stuff, or have you just hired it all from Moss Brothers?'

'Very funny. I needed to smarten myself up, that's all.'

'That's true at least,' Jimmy said, 'and to be fair, you only do clothes shopping about once every ten years. But I must say, I like it. Particularly the leather bomber jacket. Looks cool. I mean *it* does. *You* don't.'

'Sod off,' Frank said, the tone affectionate. 'Anyway, I was just reading about this missing actor guy Fox. It's true what they say you know. The country's going bananas because a frigging TV doctor's gone missing, whilst they've already forgotten about that wee toddler Jamie Grant, and he's been missing for nearly two years now. I mean, what's the world coming to?'

'Jamie Grant?' Jimmy said. 'Yeah, we met his father at that awards bash the other day. He's still completely broken by it as you would expect.'

'That's right. Just eighteen months old the kid was, it was bloody awful. Correction, it *is* bloody awful. My mate Pete Burnside was the lead DI and believe me it really did his head in. And now this Yash Patel guy in that paper is reminding everybody about it again. The last thing a good cop needs is to have the press on his back, but I think that's what's going to happen.'

Yes, and now that the case had moved into the orbit of Department 12B, it was his boss DCI Jill Smart who would now be getting the kicking, until another story pushed it once more out of the spotlight.

'You've met Burnside, haven't you?' Frank said.

'Yeah bruv, he's a good guy. But it was the same in the army. All the arse-licking shits got the big promotions. Thank god I'm not part of that world any more. Anyway, Maggie and Asvina should be here any minute. They've been to see our latest client and I'm really looking forward to finding out how they got on. Hey, look, here they are now.'

He gesticulated in the direction of the revolving doors from which first Maggie and then Asvina emerged. Catching sight of the brothers, they began to thread their way through the packed bar. As Frank had previously observed, crowds seemed to part in the presence of Asvina Rani. Tall, slim, beautiful and effortlessly elegant, with a cascade of shining black hair reaching almost to her waist, she looked like a supermodel and earned about five times as much. But contrary to his brother's jibes, it wasn't for this celestial apparition that Frank had invested nearly a month's beer money in the new designer jeans and leather blouson.

'Oh dear,' Maggie said, looking alarmed. 'What happened to your eye? And by the way, you're looking smart. Going on a date?'

His face reddened. 'Hi Maggie, and no, I'm not going on a date. As for the eye, it just took a wee bit of a bashing in the line of duty. It looks worse than it feels.' If only that was true.

Jimmy had already ordered for them and handed each a glass of wine.

'We had a very interesting time the other night at these soap awards,' he said. 'You'd have loved it Frank. That Melody Montague, she was looking absolutely sensational, and she's about your age.' He gave a chuckle at his own wit. Frank wasn't amused.

'Yeah Frank, your brother got all up close and personal with Miss Montague,' Maggie said, somewhat sourly. 'Our *client*.'

'Strictly business,' Jimmy said, grinning, 'but anyway, tell us, how did you two get on with her earlier?'

'Bizarre,' Asvina said. 'Obviously we were there to tell her what Fox had said to you two about the agreement. Not surprisingly she got really angry. She of course insists that hers is the correct one and that he is trying to pull some sort of scam. Slightly complicated of course by the fact her solicitor has managed to lose her copy.'

'And what about that other thing he said,' Jimmy asked, 'you know, *our little arrangement*. Did she say what that was all about?'

Maggie shrugged. 'She just said it was something private between them. She wouldn't give anything else away but she didn't seem too bothered about it.'

'But she must be worried about his disappearance?' Jimmy said.

Asvina laughed. 'You think so? There's not much love left in that relationship I'm afraid. She says he got too pissed on the night to accept his award, and so he's lying low somewhere until all the fuss has died down. The only person who seems to be worried about him according to the papers is Allegra Ross.'

'But wouldn't it be really convenient for Melody if something's actually happened to Benjy boy,' Jimmy said. 'Because his version of the pre-nup dies with him.'

Asvina shook her head. 'No, quite the contrary in fact. The agreement would still have legal force and his heirs would benefit from it. And since there would be little chance of reaching an amicable agreement about which of the two versions is the real one, then it's likely that a court would split the marital assets fifty-fifty. So I imagine Melody will be hoping very much that Benjamin turns up soon.'

Frank gave them a bewildered look.

'Excuse me but what's this all about, this agreement and stuff?'

Maggie laughed. 'Yes, sorry Frank, we should have explained. It's the pre-nuptial contract between Melody and Benjamin. There's a big argument about the details of the settlement. And there's a lot of money at stake.'

'Aye, but luckily there was a witness,' Jimmy said breezily. 'Our guy Charles Grant.'

'Hang on a minute,' Frank said, his eyes narrowing. 'Did I hear you right? What do you mean, our guy?'

He listened with growing anger as Maggie confessed to their arrangement with Charles Grant.

'What, you've promised him that you would find his son? I don't believe it! And after my mate Pete has been looking for two years and got nowhere you think you can just waltz in and fix it, just like that?'

His anger was directed at his brother, but he knew full well which of the two amateurs he should blame. Now he wondered whether the money he had spent on the new gear had been wasted.

'We said we would take a look at the case, that's all,' Maggie said defensively. 'No promises.'

'Well I'm so glad you haven't *promised* to find the boy,' Frank said. 'Of course you two don't know this, but it so happens the official case has been passed onto *me*. And all I've got to rely on is dull old-fashioned police work.'

Asvina laughed. 'Looks like we've got a bit of competition going now. But really Maggie, maybe you should think again about this. With Charles being a witness to the pre-nup, I can see a possibility that a conflict of interest might arise. So I say with a heavy heart that you probably need to choose which side you're on. Something to think about at least. But anyway, I need to go now.' She got up, shot Jimmy a brief smile and then glided towards the exit.

'I'm not surprised she feels that way,' Frank said, a hint of bitterness in his voice. 'You guys need to have a re-think about this, you really do.'

But he knew there was no chance of that happening. Maggie Bainbridge had been through a lot in her life and was lucky to have survived it, and he knew in Charles Grant she would have recognised a fellow casualty. She might have been rash, but she had promised the actor that she and Jimmy would help him, and he had little doubt that it was a promise she intended to keep. So be it, and hopefully with a little guidance from himself he'd stop the two of them doing too much damage. They might even be able to help, with a bit of luck on their side. God knows, the case had been a disaster from the start and it needed all the help it could get.

Tomorrow he would need to buckle down and sort out the tedious paperwork in connection with his arrest of Darren Venables. He was a real nasty bastard and Frank was glad he'd nailed him, even though he knew he'd get away with just a fine or a few hours' community service. But that would land him with a criminal record if he didn't already have one, and they'd take fingerprints, a high-resolution mug-shot for the facial recognition scans, and a DNA sample too. Going forward, the scumbag wouldn't be able to go for a crap without the authorities knowing about it.

And after that Frank would give some proper attention to the Jamie Grant kidnapping. Because out of the blue, a sliver of a half-remembered fact had leapt into his mind. He couldn't remember where or when he'd read about it but it was something that would require a phone call. To Lyon, France. It was a mad hunch and he didn't know how to make an international call on his recently-acquired smartphone but he was sure wee Eleanor would help him with that.

Chapter 6

It was four days before the body of Benjamin Fox was discovered. Frank guessed there wasn't much call to use the emergency stairwell when the conference centre was in normal use, and so his body could have lain silently decaying for many more days if a cleaner hadn't decided to slip down there for a sly smoke rather than trekking to the entrance, as was her normal habit.

The scene-of-crime team had worked swiftly and efficiently and within six hours the body had been cleared for release to the forensic pathology lab. According to the interim case report he had got his hands on, it hadn't taken much examination to determine the cause of death. A severe blow to the back of the head from a blunt instrument, provenance unknown. Establishing the time of death had been more imprecise, but since rigor mortis was no longer evident and the body had started to bloat with foam-speckled blood leaking from the mouth and nose, it could be assumed that death had occurred about three to five days earlier. The investigation team had done a cursory review of the footage from the show, which revealed that Fox had been absent from his place beside Allegra Ross on at least three occasions, once, according to Ross, to visit the loo and twice to fortify himself with a stiff whisky. On the second refreshment visit, he had been seen propping up the bar whilst in deep conversation with Charles Grant. He had not returned after his third visit and it was therefore assumed by the police that he must have been killed shortly afterwards, at about quarter-to-eleven.

Of course, with the victim being so well-known, identification was a mere formality, but it was a formality that had to be observed nonetheless. Ordinarily, it would be the responsibility of the next of kin, and his sister Edwina had been identified as the relative in question, but she was out of the country on business. As a result, the task fell to his activist friend and fellow Bow Road actor Charles Grant.

But the big question that Frank was wrestling with was why the hell the Met in its infinite wisdom had decided to allocate the case to the frigging walking disaster that was DCI Colin Barker. He wasn't even remotely half-competent and he was a total fuckwit and a complete shit to boot. Such were the views Frank was expressing to Frenchie as they waited in the stuffy press room at Paddington Green police station with the assembled media. DC Ronnie French, one of the most useless of the Department 12B cohort, an accolade which took some earning in that ocean of uselessness, was his normal reliably-cynical self. Meaning he agreed with ever word his gov'nor said on matters Barker-related. Generally speaking, Frank wouldn't have let Frenchie within a million miles of one of his cases, but he'd recently been on the end of a mild bollocking from Jill Smart about his aversion to working as a team. She was right, he bloody hated working with anybody, but such was his respect for his gaffer he was prepared to give it a try. *Reluctantly.*

'What I can't understand guv,' Frenchie was saying in his trademark laconic tones, 'is why he's still in a job after all his screw ups?'

'Said it before Frenchie, that's what always happens. Same as in every organisation. Guys like that get promoted to their level of incompetence. Peter's Principle, that's what they used to call it after some guy who wrote a book. Everyone knows they're crap, but no-one's got the balls to do anything about it. Seen it time and time again. But hold that thought, because here's a live appearance from the monumental arse in question.'

Barker waddled on to the platform, taking his place behind a wooden lectern. He was tall, but seriously overweight, with a prominent double chin and heavy jowls. In his younger days, he evidently had been quite good-looking. That, in Frank's jaundiced view, could have been the only reason for his inexplicable career trajectory. Behind him trailed Heather Green, a pretty black WPC whom Frank knew and rated, and who Barker introduced as his personal assistant. For him, she was there to look nice, tick the diversity box and operate the PowerPoint. That was the sort of guy Barker was.

'Personal assistant?' Frank said bitterly. 'It's a bloody assistance dog that he needs. Deaf dumb and blind doesn't even begin to describe it.'

The chatter in the room gradually died away as Barker cleared his throat in preparation to speak.

'Well, good morning ladies and gentlemen.' It was two-thirty in the afternoon. Genius.

Yash Patel of the *Chronicle* had sat through too many turgid Barker press-conferences and was evidently in no mood to suffer any more than was absolutely necessary. As was his way, he cut to the chase.

'D'you have any suspects, Chief Inspector? Do you have a motive? Are Melody Montague or Allegra Ross suspects? It's usually those closest to the victim, isn't that true? In ninety-three percent of the time it's a partner or former partner, that's what the statistics say, isn't that true?'

Barker studiously ignored the intervention and ploughed on in his droning voice whilst Frank provided a whispered running commentary. Yes, it was his intention to question everyone who had attended the awards ceremony and to trace everyone who had entered or left the building in the time window between Fox's last sighting and the discovery of the body ninety-six hours later. *'Aye, so that's narrowed it down to about ten thousand suspects.'* No, they did not yet have a motive but they were working on a number of lines of enquiry. *'They hadn't a damn clue and that's not going to improve with you in charge.'* Everyone was a suspect at this stage and nothing was being ruled out. *'That's not even a cliché.'* It was a complex case but he expected swiftly to bring the investigation to a successful conclusion. *'That'll be the first time.'*

This time he said it loud enough for everyone present to hear. Muted laughter rippled round the room, and up on the stage, WPC Green struggled to stifle a career-limiting giggle. Barker furrowed his brow and scanned the room, having recognised the voice of his nemesis, but decided against reacting. Because now he was about to move on to what he knew would be the big talking-point.

'But to conclude, we do have one very interesting piece of evidence that I would like to share with you. Heather, could you do the honours please.'

The WPC clicked her mouse, bringing up the next slide. There were gasps of surprise from the grizzled journalists as they began to make sense of the image.

'So is that the victim's hand?' asked one. 'Bloomin' hell.'

'Leonardo? Do you know what that means Chief Inspector? Is that who did it? It wasn't Di Caprio was it?' That drew a laugh, Patel giving a mock bow to the assembled hacks.

Frank was staring at the screen in disbelief. *God's sake, why the hell has he let that out? What a complete numpty.*

Barker gave a complacent smile. 'I don't think Mr Di Caprio is in town, but yes, we have a number of theories about its significance. However you will forgive me when I say we are not able to disclose these at this moment in time.'

Out of the blue, Frank got up and strode to the front of the platform. Ignoring the angry stare of Barker, he addressed the assembly.

'Look ladies and gents, I think we've had a wee bit of an IT malfunction here, we didn't mean to show you these pictures.' He gestured to the young WPC and immediately she understood, replacing the images with a blank screen. 'And folks, we don't want to read anything about this in your papers or see it on your telly reports. I know I can rely on your co-operation.' *As if,* he thought. Still, the fourth estate wasn't entirely without honour so he could hope for the best.

He shot Barker a serene smile. 'Sorry about that sir, just thought it was worth mentioning in passing. Back to you sir.' If looks could kill, Frank would already be dead, buried and probably cremated too.

Now Patel was on his feet. 'This must mean that the murder was pre-meditated, doesn't it? And that the killer was trying to leave someone a message or a warning of some kind. Are you following that line of enquiry Chief Inspector?'

Barker looked at him contemptuously. 'Yes, thank you Mr Patel, we had thought of that, funnily enough. So, if there are no more questions...' There were plenty of questions waiting to be asked, but evidently he did not intend to answer any of them. Instead he gathered up his papers, curtly thanked everyone for attending and made to leave. Less than six minutes from start to finish.

'What, is that all we're getting?' shouted an indignant Patel, a siren voice above the general mutterings of discontent. 'That's a total disgrace.'

'Come on guys,' Frank said, 'let's grab the fool before he leaves. I don't suppose he'll listen to us, but we can try at least.' They pushed their way through the throng of departing reporters to the podium.

'Excuse me sir, do you have a minute?'

It appeared Barker had not forgiven Frank's earlier intervention.

'What sort of frigging stunt was that Stewart? I thought they'd stuck you out to grass but here you still are, getting on everybody's tits as usual.'

'Just trying to be helpful sir, that's all. Many hands make light work and all of that. I thought it might be prudent to keep the details of the MO to ourselves for now, don't you agree?'

If he did, he wasn't going to admit it. 'If I needed any help Stewart, you're the last person I would ask. Now I don't know why you're here, but whatever it is, I haven't got time for it. In case you haven't noticed, I'm working on a very high-profile murder case.'

'High-profile? Of course sir. You wouldn't work on any other kind, would you sir? But this won't take a minute sir, I promise you. You might remember my private investigator pals Maggie Bainbridge and Jimmy Stewart? Bainbridge Associates, that's their firm. Well they dug up some information that may be important for your case sir. And of course they felt it was their public duty to share it with the police. So they told me.' He had tried his best to dial down the insolent tone, but he wasn't sure if he had succeeded. He wasn't bothered.

'Well come on, what is it?' Barker said,' I haven't got all day.'

Frank smiled sweetly. 'Detective Constable French wrote it all down in his wee notebook. Come on Frenchie, spill the beans.'

'Right then sir,' French began, furrowing his brow as he struggled to read his own handwriting. 'Those Bainbridge geezers seem to have been the last people to talk to the Fox guy before his death. It was in connection with a divorce case they was working on. Melody Montague, the soap actress. I'm sure you've heard of her. She's that sexy-looking old bird with the big tits. Very high-profile sir. Right up your street sir.'

Frank smiled to himself. Ronnie French might be fat, lazy and a complete waste of space, but he didn't give a shit about anybody, no matter what their rank. However it seemed that Barker had not tuned in to the not-very-veiled insult.

'So? What the hell has this got to do with my murder case?'

'Well as I understand it sir,' Frenchie drawled, 'there's a mega dispute about dosh in that matter. A shed load.'

'Aye, more than a million quid,' Frank said, 'and that sort of sum is normally enough to be a motive for murder, isn't it sir? Although to be fair, it appears that in this case the ex-wife actually loses out because of his death.'

Barker gave him a withering look. 'Stewart, do you think I give a shit about your half-arsed theories? You and your bunch of *cast-offs?*' He spat the word out, not bothering to hide his contempt.

It didn't seem to bother Ronnie either, self-awareness not being a concept familiar to him. He simply flicked over a page and carried on.

'This Miss Bainbridge states that she observed the victim in a heated argument with another man. By her account, that account corroborated by her *associate*, a Mr James Stewart, it got very nasty indeed. According to that Miss Bainbridge, the parties almost came to blows and threats were made against the life of the deceased.'

'And then not much later Mr Fox was observed having an argument with his new girlfriend,' Frank added. 'It was all caught on camera. On the BBC actually.'

'Look,' Barker said, forcing a condescending smile, 'we always welcome information from members of the public, and one of my officers will interview the Bainbridge woman in due course. But if you don't mind Stewart, I'm a very busy man.'

'I think that stuff that Miss Bainbridge reported is pukka,' Frenchie said, giving a shrug, 'but it's your shout sir. I would follow it up if I was you, that's all I'm saying.'

But Frank could see that Barker wasn't listening. Arrogant and stupid in equal measures, it was only a matter of time before this case slipped down the drain like all his others. Ok, if that's the way he wanted to play it, bugger him. The fat-arse would have to find out for himself about Fox's little run-in with the far-right and about the pre-nup dispute with his ex-wife and about his fall-out with Allegra Ross and about his punch-up with that scriptwriter. Motive? That wee list added up to four of them for starters, but Barker wouldn't recognise a motive if it was carved in stone and inserted up his back passage.

But that didn't matter. Because Department 12B had the remit to look at any case it damn well liked and when he got back to the office, he was going to get out another wee buff folder and stick a white label on the front. Then all he had to do was come up with a name.

Chapter 7

It wouldn't be wrong to say that the atmosphere in the office had been frosty since Maggie had agreed to take on the Grant case. Even Elsa, the sweet office administrator cum secretary they shared with the ten other businesses that occupied their Fleet Street premises, had projected an uncharacteristic coldness in her presence. Uncharacteristic because although she was deeply infatuated with Jimmy, she bore no grudge against her employer, whom she regarded as too old to be a rival for his affections. The infatuation was unrequited, Maggie had always assumed, although it occurred to her it had taken the pair of them rather a long time to fetch three skinny lattes from the nearby Starbucks.

Frosty atmosphere or not, she had made a promise to Charles Grant and she intended to fulfil it. So she had started where she assumed all investigations started nowadays. By typing 'Jamie Grant abduction' into her search engine. Gathering over half-a-million results. It wasn't difficult to gather together the bare facts of the case from the media reports of the time. Jamie Grant had been snatched in broad daylight as he was being taken home in his buggy from playgroup by his Australian nanny. It had happened on Merton Hall Road, about half a mile from the community hall that hosted the group. A typical residential street, although fairly busy with traffic in the daytime, running out onto the Kingston Road. According to Lydia Davis the nanny, a large blue SUV drew up - she thought it was a BMW but she wasn't sure - and two men got out. Obviously she was taken by surprise and had no idea what was happening. Next thing, one of the men ran over to her and started to attack her. She was coshed violently, suffering a fractured skull which kept her in hospital for nearly eight weeks afterwards. She passed out at the scene and remembered nothing more about it.

The police assumption was that the toddler was bundled into the vehicle and then driven off somewhere. An ANPR camera positioned at the junction recorded no sign of a car meeting the description, leading them to assume they probably dumped the snatch vehicle and transferred to another one before they got onto the Kingston Road.

A passer-by had witnessed the incident at a distance but was not able to provide any reliable information other than she thought the SUV was on a 62 plate but wouldn't swear to it, and that it was the younger man of the two who had been driving. There was only one other reported witness, a Mrs Molly Peters, who apparently was in her front garden about fifty yards away and saw it happening, but at eighty-four, her eyesight was poor and she was unable to provide a reliable description of the perpetrators or identify the car. However, she said she did overhear some of their shouted conversation. She was sure they were both Londoners from their accents, and that one of them might have called the other Henry.

And that was all they had. There was an appeal for any sightings of a BMW on a 62 plate, and a sketchy photo-fit from the nanny's brief sight of her assailant was splashed all over the media for a while, but no member of the public came forward with a credible identification of the man called Henry. From time to time the police had issued positive statements saying they were following up some encouraging line of enquiry or other, but everyone knew that it was the first few days that were critical in an abduction if the victim was to be saved. And during that crucial period that they had found nothing.

But then, unexpectedly, came the ransom demand. It was never revealed how much the kidnappers asked for, but the press speculation was that it was around one quarter of a million pounds, and that the money was put up by Brightside, the producers of Bow Road. What was known was that the money was handed over but the toddler wasn't. A disaster for the reputation of the Met and a tragedy for his parents.

As the months passed, the assumption grew that Jamie Grant had been murdered and in all probability his body would never be found. So almost two years to the day that he was taken, the case was shunted off to Frank Stewart's Department 12B.

Her thoughts were interrupted by the return of her colleagues, bursting back into the tiny office. It was obvious from their smirks that they had been sharing some private joke, a joke they did not seem keen to share with her. Elsa banged the coffee down on Maggie's desk with such force that warm liquid spilt out from under the plastic lid and down the side of the cup. Maggie smiled brightly at her and said 'Thanks Elsa,' deciding the best strategy was to ignore the elephant in the room. The secretary gave her a haughty look before walking out, slamming the door behind her.

Jimmy laughed. 'Don't worry, she'll soon get over it, and yes I know, I shouldn't have told her what I thought about us taking on the case. She's just a bit protective towards me, goodness knows why. I think I remind her of her dad.'

Maggie gave a wry smile. Jimmy Stewart, at thirty-two years of age, still either oblivious or indifferent to the stupid effect he had on women. Of all ages too, from school-girly Elsas to high-mileage man-eaters like Melody Montague. Goodness, even her mum fancied him. But she thought she had worked out the real reason for his reticence. Because the one time in his life he had succumbed, to the attractions of the beautiful temptress Astrid Sorenson, it had wrecked his marriage and his life with it. He never talked about it, but she knew. She knew his only goal in life was to get back together with his beloved Flora. But at least he seemed to have returned to the office in a sunnier mood than when he left, which was a relief.

He smiled at her as he sat down at his desk. 'Got anywhere yet? With our Charles Grant case I mean? Because I've been thinking about it when I was out.'

Our Charles Grant case. That was more like it.

She returned his smile. 'Only got the bare facts about the abduction and the investigation. There's not a huge amount to go on. Sadly.'

'Yeah, that's what I thought. But I guess we have to go back to basics, you know, the old motive, method and opportunity thing. I know it sounds like a cliché but I think it still holds true.'

She nodded. 'Yes, you're right, I did kind of think about that myself. I mean the method and opportunity bit is simple and straightforward, isn't it? Drive up in a fast motor, take them by surprise and whisk the kid away.'

'And the motive,' Jimmy said. 'Money. Simple as that, surely? A quarter a million a pop's not to be sniffed at. Find a rich celebrity, track their kid's daily routine, and then grab them. Not hard, is it?'

But then it struck her. Was the explanation really as simple as that?

'Jimmy, what if there was more to it? What if there was a deeper motive?'

'I'm sorry, I don't get where you're coming from.'

She wrinkled her nose. 'You see, the thing that's odd about this crime is that it's not repeatable. Organised criminals are no different from legitimate businesses in that they need a reliable business model that they can use again and again, one that always delivers results. But don't you see what the problem with this one is?'

He nodded. 'Aye, I do. If you take the cash, but don't deliver the goods, then that's it. The next time you do one, you're not going to get your ransom money.'

'Exactly Jimmy. So maybe we have to look at another angle. What if this was a one-off, and the primary motive was to hurt the Grants and the money was just an added bonus?'

'Could be,' Jimmy said. 'We know a bit about Charles but do we know anything about the wife?'

'Only that she's politically active like he is. I think she works as an editor for a publishing house but she was also a Labour councillor if I recall correctly.'

'It would be nice to speak to her,' Jimmy said, 'but maybe that would be one for Frank. Help him to feel involved in our investigation.'

She laughed. 'If he's still speaking to us, that is.'

'I've just had a thought,' Jimmy said. 'Charles was due to speak at that anti-fascist rally last week wasn't he?'

Maggie nodded. 'Yeah, that's his thing. He's very passionate about it.'

'So maybe that's an angle worth exploring?'

'Ok, let's give it a try.'

Punching in 'Charles Grant Activist' returned over a hundred thousand results. Photographs, videos, chat magazine gossip, fan sites, his Wikipedia profile, the sheer weight of information threatened to overwhelm them before they got started. But tucked away, three or four pages down the search, was a headline that simultaneously caught the interest of both.

Soap star and activist quits social media after Bow Road spat.

They looked at one another quizzically. 'Yeah, go for it,' Jimmy said in answer to her unspoken question.

Maggie clicked the link and screwed up her eyes to focus on the article. 'Ah, *that's* interesting. So maybe this goes some way to explaining his reputation as a difficult man.'

'Aye, it seems like it.'

Reading on, it seemed to have started with an inflammatory tweet from Grant postulating that many of his fellow celebrities were guilty of nothing more than virtue-signalling and publicity-seeking when it came to broadcasting their support for what he called *his* progressive causes. Surprisingly from Maggie's point of view, he had, without naming names, called out some of his Bow Road cast members as being guilty of this crime. Less surprisingly, it had generated a virulent response from some of those unnamed colleagues, who clearly knew whom he had been referring to. Including, most directly, Benjamin Fox.

'Do you see this?' Maggie said, wide-eyed. 'Somewhat blunt and to the point, don't you think?'

'Yeah, you could say that,' Jimmy laughed. *'Eff off you conceited twat. Power to the people*. Do you think Fox was being ironic with that last bit?'

'Yes maybe, but it soon gets pretty nasty. And it went on for days and days. It must have been fun on set after all of that.'

'Aye,' Jimmy nodded, 'so not surprisingly our boy Charlie decides to take a break from on-line life.'

Maggie laughed. 'Yes, but not for long.'

She pointed to another of the search results. 'Did you know he has a monthly opinion column in the Guardian? I didn't.'

'So he's just a normal lefty thesp then. Move along, nothing to see here. Ah, but wait a wee minute...' Another search result had evidently caught his eye. He clicked the link to explore it further.

'Look at this one, do you see the headline? *We ignore the rise of the far-right at our peril.* And look, here's another. *Far-right apologists pedalling fake news.* Jesus, he is the right little socialist warrior, isn't he? Not that there's anything wrong with that of course,' he added.

He needn't have bothered apologising on her account, since she didn't do politics. Her scumbag former husband had made her immune to all that. But then as she quickly scanned the first article, something struck her.

'You see, in this one, he talks about the dogs' abuse he gets from what he calls far-right trolls. He mentions one particular person, who apparently goes by the handle of da Vinci.'

'Da Vinci? Like in the Dan Brown book?'

'Yes, the same.'

'And we are assuming it is a guy?'

'What, with a username like da Vinci? Maggie said. 'Well, I suppose you're right, it doesn't have to be a guy.'

Jimmy had clicked on the Twitter link and was scrolling down through some of Grant's posting history.

'I tell you what, for such a quiet man, he's not scared to share his opinions, is he? Look, here he is, laying into the Catholic church. Half the responses have been moderated out, but I can imagine they wouldn't be very complimentary.'

Maggie read on. 'Yeah, and now he's accusing the Tories of being evil bastards - that's his actual words - only interested in enriching themselves by exploiting the poor and disadvantaged.'

Jimmy laughed. 'See what I mean? The socialist warrior right enough. And he doesn't seem to care who he upsets in the process. But you don't think this could have anything to do with the abduction, do you?'

'Yeah, I know it seems unlikely,' Maggie said, 'but as you say, he does seem to have upset a lot of people. Come on, let's keep looking.'

He nodded, punching in a few more search terms.

'So that's interesting,' Jimmy said, pointing at the screen. 'This is him just a few days before wee Jamie's abduction, calling out the far-right again.'

'Yeah, and look, here's da Vinci back too. It's really nasty, some of this stuff.'

'Too right,' Jimmy said. 'I don't understand why people do it. But our Charles seems to be addicted to it, doesn't he?'

Maggie nodded. 'Yeah, he does seem to be. But come on, let's see if there's anything else around that time.'

Jimmy modified the search to include the child's name and the month of the abduction. It took some time to find it, the single Twitter posting buried several pages down in the search. Under the hashtag *#GrantAbduction*, it had been posted two days after the event and was as brief as it was brutal.

Commie bastards always get what they deserve.

But this time, the troller wasn't hiding his identity behind a stupid handle. The author being the man known to his followers simply as D-V.

Chapter 8

Jimmy checked the map on his phone again to make sure he had got it right. Yep, 8 Harbledown Road, Parsons Green. It was another one of Maggie's hospital passes and so he wasn't exactly looking forward to this mission. But it had to be done. Go and talk to Allegra Ross and see if Benjamin ever spoke about the pre-nup. That was her orders, and Jimmy Stewart always obeyed orders.

Almost all of the properties in the street had been converted into flats, most configured with one dwelling on the ground floor and one above. The street exuded prosperity, every house smart and well-maintained, their elaborately-carved window surrounds pristine and whitewashed, front doors glossy with shiny brass letterboxes and handles. Not surprising when you wouldn't get any change from a million quid, even for the rare one-bedroom attic conversion.

Number 8 however turned out to be the exception, but in a good way, an end-of-terrace still in its original two-storey layout and with a two-car parking space alongside its end wall, currently occupied by a Range-Rover sporting a current-year plate. A hundred-grand car and a two-million-pound pad. Nice, but perhaps not so unexpected given the family background of Allegra Elizabeth Ross. New money, that's what they used to call it, the Ross family having built an industrial dynasty out of ships and armaments starting in the early nineteenth century. They might not be titled, but the family wealth ran to half a street in Mayfair and a couple of country estates. Compared to what she had grown up with, Allegra was slumming it in Parsons Green.

Jimmy had tried to call in advance to make an appointment, but Allegra it seemed wasn't taking calls. Hardly surprising after the murder of her lover, when even thicko DCI Colin Barker would know that the partner is the prime suspect in ninety percent of cases. And if he didn't before, Yash Patel of the *Chronicle* had brought him up to speed with that particular statistic. In all events, Allegra was probably already sick and tired of answering questions, and on top of that, it would surely only be a matter of time before the media ended their self-imposed and brief period of respect for the bereaved actress. Then it would be open season on her relationship and her life, and everything in between. Not something to be envied.

He closed the picket gate behind him on its clasp and pressed the bell. From somewhere inside, he could hear the faintest of rings. Good, at least it was working. He waited a few seconds and tried again. This time, he heard nothing. So what, probably the battery had taken its last dying breath, they didn't last long. Not a problem. He reached for the brass knocker and then stopped dead, puzzled. His action had caused the door to open a fraction, and a further light push revealed that it had been left on the latch. Odd.

'Miss Ross? Miss Ross?' Cautiously, he opened the door and went into the narrow hallway.

'Miss Ross?' A door on the left led to a small tastefully-decorated sitting room, where effort had obviously been made to retain as much period detail as possible, the centrepiece being a fine tiled fireplace and oak surround. Half a dozen sympathy cards were displayed on the mantelpiece, and several more were arranged haphazardly on a small coffee table. Jimmy could only imagine Allegra's present emotional state, trying to come to terms with the murder of her lover, although maybe the relationship hadn't been in the best shape given what he'd witnessed at the awards do. Suddenly it occurred to him that it wasn't outside the bounds of possibility that Ross had done it and that he could now be in the home of a killer. He hadn't thought of that before entering the house, and he realised with some annoyance how careless he had become since he left the army. You probably weren't going to fall foul of a booby-trap in SW6, but it was sloppy nonetheless.

He returned to the hallway and continued his search of the ground floor. A door was located directly opposite that of the lounge. He tried the handle but it appeared to be locked. It wasn't unusual for these old houses to have locks on the internal doors, and in any case he assumed it was only a cupboard. Something to look at a bit later.

As was the fashion, the original back parlour and kitchen had been knocked together and extended out into the garden, with full-width bi-fold glass doors drenching light into the room. Jimmy wasn't a student of interior design but he guessed that the stunning top-end kitchen would have cost as much as his own tiny Clapham pad. Of course there was twin Belfast sinks, an island unit the size of a football pitch and, naturally, an Aga. Further proof that Ross enjoyed a money-no-object lifestyle, and he was certain it wasn't paid for by her part in a crappy soap.

With no particular objective in mind other than nosiness, he started opening all the cupboards. On these Helmand house sweeps you always did a search, and on a good day you might find a stash of ammunition or some bomb-making chemicals, forlornly hidden just as the front door was kicked in. That wasn't going to happen here, but you never know. And half way around, his half-hunch proved accurate.

In the centre of the island unit was fitted an elaborate waste-bin system. He gave the handle a gentle tug and the unit slid open as in slow-motion. Two large-capacity nylon bins were suspended from a cradle, and the first, clearly designated by the actress for paper waste recycling, was stuffed to capacity with used kitchen-roll. Used, blood-stained kitchen roll.

'Miss Ross!' Now Jimmy's call was more urgent, worried. Looking down, he saw the faintest spots of blood on the white wood floor. Dropping to his knees to get a closer look, he noticed an effort had clearly been made to scrub off the spillage but the trail was still discernible. A trail that he, still on his knees, was able to follow back out in to the hallway and up to the locked door. He jumped up and pulled on the handle again but it wasn't going to move, and since it opened outwards, it couldn't be burst open by putting a shoulder to it. Rushing back to the kitchen, he grabbed a short broad-bladed knife and returned with it to the cupboard.

Examining the lock, Jimmy saw it was of a sturdy mortis design and his improvised tool was unlikely to be strong enough to prise it open. However the hinge-bearing edge of the door showed more promise. Those in contrast to the mortis were of flimsy construction and soon began to yield as he jammed the blade of the knife between the hinge plate and the door. Within a few seconds he had prised the top hinge free of the architrave and not much later the lower one was also freed. Carefully, he let the door topple out of its frame, and releasing it from the lock, rested it against the wall.

To his surprise, he saw that rather than concealing a cupboard, the door led to a steep stairway disappearing down into the darkness. He hadn't considered that these homes should have cellars, but this clearly was what it was. He felt along the wall for a light-switch, but in vain. He took his phone from the back pocket of his jeans and fired up the searchlight app, aiming the penetrating beam down the dank stairwell.

Jimmy edged his way downwards, one step at a time, in trepidation of what he might discover in the gloom. Before he had even made it half-way his fears were realised. Clearly visible at the bottom of the stairs, the body of Allegra Ross lay in a crumpled heap, congealing blood still creeping from a head-wound. He jumped down the last few steps and gently placed his fingers on the jugular, feeling for a pulse. It didn't bear thinking about, the number of times he'd had to do this, and you always knew when it was hopeless. Like in this case. Allegra's body was already cold and her beautiful face was betraying the first signs of rigor mortis. Jimmy guessed she had been dead four or five hours. Nothing could be done for her now.

The emergency services' operator was quite insistent. Polite but firm. An ambulance was on its way, but it was very important to be sure that the injured party was dead. She knew it was a difficult thing to ask, but could Jimmy please feel for a pulse once again? If there was even the slightest chance that the casualty was clinging to life, maybe some emergency first aid could be administered, winning precious minutes before the paramedics arrived. Jimmy didn't like to tell her that he'd seen dozens of dead bodies and he knew quite well what death looked like, thank you very much.

'Ok, hang on a minute please.' He was only going through the motions, but he understood why it had to be done. In Helmand of course, he had seen many separated body parts. Too many, the ghastly images still causing him regular nightmares, and he didn't expect them to fade away any time soon. But this was different. God, how had he missed it? He knew why. The understandable desire to nowadays keep as far away from death as was humanly possible.

At least he knew there was no point in taking Allegra's pulse now. He shone his phone torch on to the back of the severed hand to read the spidery message that was written on it.

Leonardo

Chapter 9

Frank had spotted them across the crowded lounge, and aware what his brother had just been through, waved to indicate that he was going to the bar before joining them. A few minutes later, he appeared with two pints and a large chardonnay for Maggie. And then noticed that Jimmy had already been hitting the single malts.

'Sorry bruv, didn't realise you were on the fire water, although I'm glad I didn't notice 'cos pints are a lot cheaper. But anyway, how are you feeling? I heard you've been in the wars. Aye, sorry, maybe not the best turn of phrase but you know what I mean. Hope you're ok.'

'Yeah, no bother, I'm fine,' Jimmy said. 'But it's not something you want to see every day, I can tell you that.'

'What, the hand? I'm with you there pal. A bit grizzly to say the least. Anyway, I heard you've been put through the wringer by my best mate big fat Colin. I suppose he thinks you did it, am I right?'

Jimmy smiled. 'Not exactly, but he did make it clear in his normal pompous manner, and I quote, that I would remain a suspect until my alibi was fully checked out and verified. He even asked me if I had a current passport and was planning to leave the country any time soon.'

'What?' Frank said, amused. 'He must have learned that line from the cop shows.'

'Yeah, it did make me smile. But obviously, his main interest was in finding out why I'd gone to Allegra's in the first place.'

'Oh aye? And why *did* you go there?'

Maggie intervened. 'We thought we would ask her if Benjamin had ever mentioned anything about the pre-nup. I mean, I know the timing might have been insensitive what with the death of her boyfriend and everything, but we do still have to do our jobs.'

'What Maggie meant to say was that *she* thought *I* should go and ask Allegra about the pre-nup,' he said, in a mock-bitter tone, 'but of course I never got the opportunity.'

Frank gave him a sympathetic look. 'Well I do feel sorry for what you've been through. It must have been awful.'

'It was, bloody awful. And I guess you heard about that thing scribbled on her hand?'

'Leonardo?' Frank said. 'Yeah, I heard. Look, I haven't told you this before, but this MO is exactly the same as the Benjamin Fox killing. Exactly the same. The right hand chopped off, the Leonardo thing, the lot.'

Jimmy frowned. 'Right hand, did you say? It wasn't Allegra's right hand, it was her left hand. I'm one hundred percent sure about that.'

'Well it probably doesn't mean anything,' Frank said, giving a shrug.

'So do you have any idea what it means?' Maggie asked. 'You know, Leonardo.'

'Absolutely no idea,' Frank said. 'But the good news is Pete Burnside and his wee team have been moved onto the case to boost the numbers so we might start to see sense emerging from Paddington Green for once.'

Maggie nodded. 'I know this will sound crazy, but it just came to Jimmy and me that there might be something linking Allegra's murder to the Jamie Grant abduction. And now you've told us that Benjamin Fox was killed in the same way, I think it's an even stronger possibility.'

Frank raised an eyebrow. 'How so?'

'Well, we found out that Charles Grant was very active on social media in the months leading up to little Jamie's abduction. Some of his postings were very provocative. He made a lot of enemies, virtual ones at least.'

'Is that right?' Frank said, interested.

'Yes it is. Anyway, Jimmy and I had this idea that if the abduction was some sort of a revenge attack, then maybe online would be a good place to look for suspects.'

'What, you think someone got upset just because he twittered or whatever you call it?'

Maggie nodded. 'Well, why not? Some of the stuff is really vicious and personal, you should see it. And as it happens, there was one name in particular who seemed to have it in for him in a big way.'

'Yeah,' Jimmy agreed, 'some weirdo going under the name of da Vinci. Don't you see? Leonardo is that odd message left behind by the murderer, and da Vinci is the handle of the person who's been harassing Charles Grant big-time. I mean, it's got to be more than a coincidence, hasn't it?'

'Leonardo da Vinci, eh?' Frank said, giving a half-smile. 'Aye, I've heard of the guy. And as you say, quite a coincidence.'

'There is something else too,' Maggie said. 'You know that Fox, Ross and Grant were friends who all shared the same politics? So we were thinking that maybe the abduction and murder of Jamie Grant wasn't about the money at all. That it was actually designed to *hurt* them, a kind of punishment for their political views. The Grants had their son murdered and Fox and Ross were killed themselves. So was it some sort of revenge, you know, someone trying to teach them a lesson?'

'We don't know for certain that the wee lad's been murdered,' Frank said, although he knew that he was clutching at straws with that one. 'And actually, we don't know that Fox, Grant and Ross were friends either. That's still to be established.' He hadn't meant it to sound condescending, but it did.

'And we thought it might be a good idea if you could talk to the boy's mother too,' Maggie said. 'Charles Grant's wife I mean. They're separated now, I guess the strain of the abduction and everything caused that.'

That had been job number one on the wee list that he had slipped into the *Shark* folder. But, anxious to avoid offending her, he decided on a diplomatic answer. That didn't mean that they weren't still bloody amateurs though.

'Aye, that might be a good idea Maggie,' he said, hoping the sarcasm he felt hadn't crept into his voice. 'I'll maybe get one of my guys to look her up.' It was good to remind them that he was the professional and he had the full resources of the Metropolitan Police at his beck and call. Or at least, he had that great pile of slovenliness known to his colleagues as DC Ronnie French. 'Yeah, I'll maybe get Ronnie to look at it.'

'Ronnie?' Jimmy asked.

Frank gave a grimace. 'You don't want to know. But I'll ask him to look her up, and in the meantime, I'll see what we can do about your da Vinci.'

He saw her eyes widen. 'That would be amazing if you could. I think it might be important to our enquiries.'

Frank gave a snort. 'Oh, so it's *our* enquiries now, is it?'

He thought about it for a moment. From his brief skim of the file, he knew that none of this social media stuff had come up in the official enquiry. In fact, pretty much nothing at all had come up in the official enquiry. He'd just need to be careful how he played it of course, because he didn't want his mate Pete Burnside implicated in the mess, but yes, this was definitely worth looking into.

'Aye, this might be another one for fat Ronnie to take a look at. Not promising anything mind you, but I'll see what I can do.'

'Good man,' Jimmy said, smiling, 'and if you've got any other cases you'd like us to help you solve, well, we've opened a new criminal investigations division. I'll give you a card.'

'Bugger off,' Frank said affectionately, but then his voice took on a serious tone. 'But just remember, we're dealing with a double killing here, and a missing wee boy who's probably been murdered too. There's dangerous people out there so please don't be doing anything stupid.'

'I understand Frank,' Maggie said soothingly.

He took her tone to mean she understood but that she wasn't going to pay any attention to him.

'Well be careful, ok?' Frank said. 'Anyway, I've got some bad guys to catch. Must dash.' He always said that, even though there wasn't much bad-guy catching going on in Department 12B. And with that, he was off.

***

It was always good to talk through the ins and outs of a case with colleagues and the meeting had proved useful, serving to clarify a few things in Frank's mind. Of course it was ninety-nine percent certain that Allegra Ross was killed by the same person who killed Benjamin Fox. Both had been bludgeoned to death with a blunt instrument, both had a hand severed and the same baffling message written on it. But in one case, it was the right hand that had been cut off, in the other it was the left. Was that significant? He had no idea, but he had managed to stop the media publishing any details of the MO, so few people knew that it was Fox's *right* hand that had been removed. It might be nothing, but it might prove to be something in the future.

But who did it and why? Were they killed to be silenced, or was it indeed revenge as Maggie and Jimmy thought? Or was it some other reason altogether? There were so many questions, and until he had some answers, they wouldn't get very far. He wasn't concerned about this state of affairs because he knew that cases like this always started slowly and messily. With a few promising lines of enquiry already in the bag, that was enough for him at this stage.

As for the link to the Jamie Grant affair, there was no denying that the Leonardo and da Vinci thing was rather bizarre. The problem was, there was more than a two-year gap between the wee kid's abduction and the Fox and Ross murders, which made him seriously question if there actually *was* a connection. He wasn't ruling it out, but for now he was going to work on the assumption that it was simply a coincidence.

Besides, tomorrow morning he had that conference call scheduled with the guys from Lyon, when he might find out if his crazy hunch with regard to the abduction had any substance to it. If it did, and in truth he had no expectations of the outcome, they would be looking at a whole different ball game. Then, Operation Shark would be up and running with a vengeance.

Chapter 10

It was going to be a good day. Frank's mood was sunny and optimistic as he carefully peeled back the wrapper of his Mars Bar and took a healthy bite. He wasn't generally in favour of early starts, but the call with Interpol was scheduled for seven-thirty and he would have gladly come in at two in the morning for that had it been necessary. The chocolate bar wouldn't last long but it didn't matter, because there smiling up at him from the meeting room table was a second one. Total calories, six hundred and forty, more than enough to power him through the rest of the morning, and what's more, he'd finally got his revenge on Atlee House's frigging vending machine. In had gone a two-pound coin and out had come *two* bars, even though he had only selected one. Then after a short symphony of whirrs and clunks, his two-pound coin had been returned to him. The tepid coffee still tasted like it had been dredged straight from the Thames, but that wasn't enough to dampen his spirits. Yes, it was going to be a good day. No doubt about it.

His thoughts were interrupted by the arrival of Eleanor Campbell. Her expression was thunderous, signalling that she had either just ended or was about to start a conversation with her sort-of boyfriend Lloyd. He gave what he hoped was a sympathetic smile.

'There's a wee breakfast Mars Bar here for you Eleanor if you're feeling peckish.' He knew she wouldn't want it. She was vegan, and from the militant wing.

'They're completely disgusting,' she replied. 'And I've told you about rennet a million times.'

This time he was prepared. Extremely well prepared. 'Oh aye, rennet. It comes from the stomach of wee calves, doesn't it? So any product containing it is not suitable for vegans or vegetarians.'

'Very good Frank. Have you been swallowing Wikipedia or something?'

'No, no,' he lied. 'I've known from birth that rennet is a chemical sourced from calves' stomachs used in the production of whey. One of the first things I was taught on my mammy's knee.'

She laughed. 'So like, how long did it take you to memorise that?'

The laugh was a good sign. Because he had something he needed to quickly bring up with her before the phone call, and he sensed it might be difficult.

'Eleanor, I've got a wee thing I'd like you to take a look at. To do with this Operation Shark thing. You know, if you can fit it in to your busy schedule.'

'Case number?'

Eleanor would do anything you asked, within reason, as long as you had a bloody case number. He assumed that even Lloyd had to produce one when he wanted to make love to her.

'Absolutely,' Frank lied, but in an authoritative tone. 'I have one. All signed and sealed by DCI Smart.'

'I'll check.'

'I know you will. Quite right to. I'd do the same,' he lied again.

'Ok, what is it you want?'

'I remember you told me about some cool new software you'd got from GCHQ?'

She gave him a guarded look.

'We get lots of cool new software from them. Like everything they send us is way cool. But I assume you're talking about the verbal style recognition processor that Zak was working with.'

'Who's Zak?'

'Well, he's Zak,' she replied, as if it needed no further explanation. 'I don't know his job title or anything but he's got admin rights to all GCHQ's beta software.' Clearly, that was all that mattered.

'Aye, well I think that would be it. Is that the one that uses that A-I stuff?'

What A-I was, he could not say, but he wasn't going to admit that to Eleanor. But he should have known that she wasn't going to let a golden opportunity like this slip by without comment.

'*That A-I stuff*? You've no idea what A-I is, do you Frank?'

'No,' he admitted, giving a wry grin, 'except that it's way cool.'

She gave him a derisive look. 'Well it's artificial intelligence, and trying to explain what *that* means would take like longer than we've got on this planet. Especially trying to explain it to you.'

He shrugged. 'You're not wrong there Eleanor. But Charles Grant, the boy's father, has been getting what you young people call trolled on his social media accounts. Obviously privacy laws mean the publishers don't reveal who is behind these postings, but I thought that maybe this...' He was about to say A-I stuff but checked himself. .'. this cool software might be able to reveal his or her identity.'

'And what's this got to do with Operation Shark?' she said suspiciously.

God, thought Frank, you'd think she was spending her own bloody money. Admirable in a public servant of course but a complete pain in the backside nonetheless. But this time he was able to tell the truth.

'His son you may remember was abducted two years ago. That *is* Operation Shark.'

Eleanor nodded, seemingly satisfied by the explanation. 'Well then I suppose I'll need to go over to Maida Vale and talk to Zak. I think it takes like ages to run these web-crawls but I'm not sure. As I said, I need to talk to Zak. '

He had no idea what a web-crawl was, and though vaguely interested, decided against asking her about it for now. Instead he said,

'Well that sounds great. So you'd better get over there after our call.'

She grimaced. 'But the traffic's a nightmare at this time in the morning.'

He shook his head in mock sympathy. 'I know, it's really awful. Look, I can get someone else to do it if you're too busy.' He expected that would do the trick, it always did. And he wasn't disappointed.

'No no, no,' she replied hastily. 'It's fine, I'll get over there as soon as we're done. Have you got any details you can give me?'

'Da Vinci.'

'What?'

'Da Vinci. That's the name of the troller or trollist. I don't know what you call them, but that's the name he uses.'

'His handle you mean. And that's all you've got?'

'More or less. But I thought this stuff used artificial intelligence? It should be able to work everything else out, shouldn't it?'

She shook her head in disgust. 'You owe me one mate. Big time.'

Frank smiled at her. 'I always do. Anyway, are we all set up for the conference call?'

He had asked her to join him for two reasons. Partly, it was because he was concerned that the Lyon guys might only speak French and he needed the polymath forensic officer to be his interpreter. But mainly it was because he didn't know how to operate the meeting room's speaker-phone.

'All set up?' she replied. 'You mean am I like all set up to press that big button labelled 'answer' when it rings? Yeah, I think I'm good for that. I've been on the training course.' She wasn't being sarcastic, she had been.

As he gave her a thumbs-up, the phone rang. Right on schedule. Eleanor lent over to answer. 'Good morning, this is the Metropolitan Police, Detective Inspector Frank Stewart and Forensic Officer Eleanor Campbell.'

'Bonjour. This is Inspector Marie Laurent from the Interpol international liaison section. I hope I find you both well this morning.'

She sounds lovely, thought Frank. It was the French accent of course, designed to seduce. A bit of a contrast with his rough Glaswegian. But you never know, maybe French women found Scottish accents equally enticing. He doubted it.

'We're both very well Inspector Laurent. All right if I call you Marie?' Quite a smooth chat-up line, considering that he didn't do chat-up lines, smooth or otherwise.

'Of course Frank. And hello Eleanor.'

'Sweet,' Eleanor replied.

'That's great,' Frank said, shooting an admonishing glance at his colleague. 'So, thank you for calling me back. I was wondering of course how you've got on with that enquiry I made? Is there any progress to report?' He was conscious that for some reason he had adopted his mother's telephone voice, speaking uncharacteristically slowly and taking extra care with the consonants. It was clearly unnecessary since Inspector Laurent spoke excellent English. With a beautiful accent too.

'Not a great deal at the moment Frank. You see, we don't really have a database that coordinates random individual crimes so I have had to send out special requests to my contacts across Europe. So far I have asked Holland, Belgium, Denmark, Germany and of course here in France. But I think it will take a few weeks to gather their responses. For most forces, it won't be a priority I'm afraid, but I have told everyone that it might be important, and I will call them weekly to remind them.' Her tone was apologetic, and he was grateful for that, for his previous dealings with the International Criminal Police Organisation had left him with a rather jaundiced view of its effectiveness. His optimism in this case was borne out of hope rather than experience.

'No, that's fine, I understand,' he said. 'I suppose I was unrealistic in expecting a breakthrough so soon. But no, I'm really chuffed that you've put so much effort into it already Marie. It's fantastic, it really is.'

'Chuffed did you say? I don't think that's a word I've heard before.'

Frank laughed. 'Yes sorry Marie, I'm not surprised. It means pleased or grateful. So when I say I'm really chuffed, I mean I'm really grateful.'

Out of the corner of his eye, he saw that Eleanor was clearly taking the piss out of him, her hand mimicking a phone handset with her little finger and thumb. He furrowed his brow and stared at her, which only succeeded in making her laugh out loud. With an expression that said I'm going to kill you later, he returned to his phone call, but this time, he dialled down the telephone voice.

'Yes, so Marie, maybe we can touch base every two weeks or so. I like to get a work in progress rather than wait until all the forces have made their reports, if that's all right. But as I said, I'm so grateful for your help.'

There was a pause before she replied.

'That's ok Frank. But I should tell you that I have the personal interest in this too, so I won't let it go, believe me.'

Her words made his pulse quicken. Quietly he said, 'What do you mean Marie?'

'It was about eighteen months ago, when I was a detective sergeant in the Gendarmerie. That's where I worked before I transferred to Interpol here in Lyon. At that time I was based in Bordeaux and we had a case that was very similar to the one that you described to me. I wasn't in charge of the case of course, I was just one of the team, but it was still very hard for me. For all of us.'

Frank indicated to Eleanor that she should take notes. She smiled and pointed to her phone, which was in *record* mode.

'I know how hard it can be, believe me. So what was the background on your case, if you don't mind me asking?' He was trying not to sound too excited.

'Well in our case, it was a little girl and she was just four years old. Her name was Kitty Lawrence, and of course it is easy for me to remember because her surname is very like mine. It was in May and she was at a kindergarten club where the boys and the girls too played outdoor games. Afterwards, her mother came to collect her at around four-thirty and then as they walked home, a car drew up and they were attacked by two men. The little girl was pushed into the car, leaving her mother very badly injured by the roadside.'

He could feel his heart beginning to pound. 'Marie, that is just *so* similar to our case here in London. But did you say her name was Kitty Lawrence? That sounds English.'

'New Zealand in fact. You see her father is a well known-figure. Harry Lawrence. He was a rugby player, but now he is a coach. You know the game is very popular in the South West region. He played for the local professional club and also for his country, before he took up his current position.'

'Marie, did you say he played for his country? So he was an All- Black?' He gave Eleanor a raised-eyebrows look, who returned it with a blank stare.

'Yes, I think that's what you call it. I don't know much about the game, but I know he was a very good player.'

'And did you think that was significant?' Frank asked. 'That he was in the public eye I mean.'

'Do you mean was he targeted? Yes we believe so. Because there was of course a ransom demand.'

'And don't tell me. It was paid, but the kid wasn't returned.'

There was silence on the line, before Marie finally answered.

'Yes. It was a mistake on our part. A big mistake.'

He nodded. 'Aye, we made the same mistake over here.' And his mate Pete was still struggling to come to terms with the consequences. 'But do you have any leads as to who might have done this.'

'No, not really,' she said. 'We could find no witnesses other than the girl's mother and her recollection was of course not so good because of her trauma. Little Kitty just vanished without the trace, as you would say. Every lead we followed led to the dead end. The case was our priority for over a year, but there was nothing. So then our commanders were so embarrassed by it that they pushed it into the cold-cases locker and disbanded the team. It was not for all of us a great thing for our careers. For me perhaps not so bad because I was only a sergeant, but it was very bad news for my chief inspector.'

Frank thought again of what the Jamie Grant case had done to poor Pete Burnside.

'Yes, I know how terrible it can be when a case goes like that. It hurts, it really does.'

'But there was one thing Frank. We did not get much from Mrs Lawrence but she thought she remembered her attackers speaking to each other.'

By the way she said it, he knew what was coming next. Intuition or experience, call it what you will, but please, please let it be true.

'And the interesting thing was, she was sure they were speaking in English.'

Frank was silent for a moment as his brain furiously processed what she had just told him. It was the same MO, exactly the same, and the father, like Charles Grant, was someone in the public eye. And now he'd learned that maybe the abductors were Brits. Surely it was just too much of a coincidence?

'Tell me Marie, do you know if this Harry Lawrence guy was especially active on social media?'

'On social media? I'm not sure if that came up in our enquiry. But I guess you must have a reason for asking?'

'Aye, in the case we're looking at in the UK, we think it might be a factor. Maybe if you don't mind, you can take another look at yours and let me know?'

'Of course Frank, I will get the Bordeaux police to look at it. And I'll e-mail a photograph of Kitty over to you.'

'To Eleanor please,' he said hurriedly.

He heard her laugh. *'Very well Frank and I will let you know if anything else comes up. Speak to you soon. Au Revoir.'*

Of course, it was only one incident. It might mean nothing, nothing at all. But Frank didn't believe that, not for a minute. As far as he was concerned, *Operation Shark* was now up and running, and he could allow himself a smile of satisfaction. Correction, a smile of *smug* satisfaction. Because when he thought about it, his two amateur pals just didn't have the advantages he had. They couldn't make phone calls to lovely French Interpol officers for a start, and they didn't have access to super-smart forensic scientists who would, more or less, do anything asked of them. Naturally it wasn't a competition, but if anyone was going to be first to find out what had happened to wee Jamie Grant, one thing was for sure.

It wasn't going to be them.

Chapter 11

Like Frank, Jimmy had been forced to make an unwelcome early start that morning. In the army, you were up at every ungodly hour under the sun or moon but it didn't matter how long you served, you never really got used to it. Especially since the things you had to get up for were usually unsavoury. He reckoned that's why so many squaddies found jobs in nightclub security after their demob. It wasn't because they were hard-men, it was because in that line of work they didn't have to get out of bed until noon.

As he left the tube station he glanced at his watch, squinting to focus through sleep-deprived eyes. Six-forty-five, the sun already beaming through wispy clouds on this early-summer morning. Luckily, the Met boys liked their lie-ins too and he didn't expect there to be anyone turning up for duty until eight at the earliest, even if it was the scene of a murder. As if he was ever going to forget that, having found the body. The mission briefing from Maggie was as detailed as many he had been given as a soldier. *'Pop round there and see what you can find.'* Since their little pre-nup project had hit a road-block with the unfortunate death of the headline star, it was all they could think of. Pop round there and see what you can find. Brilliant.

From the outside, it was impossible to tell that the house had been witness to such horrors only a few days earlier. The scene-of-crime mobile laboratories had gone from outside and even the 'do not cross' tapes had been taken down. Parsons Green was a genteel neighbourhood and he supposed that the residents had lobbied to ensure that disruption to their genteel lives, and to their rising house prices, had been kept to a minimum.

There were a lot of advantages to owning an end-of-terrace property, but enhanced security wasn't one of them. With a furtive glance behind him, Jimmy crept up the narrow gap formed between the end wall of the house and the couple's Range Rover. It was still only half-light and in his black jeans, black puffer jacket and black beanie hat he knew he would be difficult to pick out. He paused at the end of the wall to survey the outlook from the rear of the property, specifically weighing up if the house was overlooked or not by neighbouring properties. The garden was of a good length, probably thirty metres or more, and was bordered at the rear by a row of leylandii which did an excellent job of screening the house from the rear of the properties on the parallel road. Cautiously, he peered round the edge of the wall. Good, next door's property had also been extended and in fact their kitchen protruded a couple of metres further into their garden than this one. So that was one potential sight-line he didn't have to be concerned about. He could still just about be seen from one of the neighbour's upstairs windows but as long as he kept tight against the bi-fold doors that stretched the entire width of the Ross property, the angle would make observation difficult.

The doors were secured by an elaborate triple-deadlock system which the manufacturers claimed had repelled every attempt to break in to in the ten years they had been on the market. But that didn't worry Jimmy, because he had the keys, having on his last visit found a spare set hanging on a hook just inside the entrance to the basement. Now *that* had been a smart idea, pocketing them. He had had a vague hunch they might come in handy, and now here was the proof. He checked the handle but as expected it was locked. In normal circumstances, a burgling villain would have to worry about the alarm, but he was fairly certain that today it wouldn't be set. The police wouldn't have bothered because of all the hassle it would cause going in and out of the place, and in any case, with the death of both residents, there was a pretty good chance that the four-digit code had died with them.

He took the bunch of keys from his jacket and examined them. Helpfully, the manufacturers had stamped their distinctive logo on their key which averted a lot of tedious trial and error, and a second later he was in the luxurious kitchen. A sensor detected his entrance, bathing the room in cool blue mood lighting. Tasteful, and enough for what he wanted to do. But what exactly was he looking for? He only had the vaguest of plans. All the electronic stuff like laptops, computers and phones would have been taken away for examination by the scene of crime guys, and probably anything else of obvious interest too. But this was a house where a beautiful couple had lived, a beautiful couple who spent their lives in the public eye and who had been brutally murdered within days of one another. And a beautiful couple who were in a relationship that might have been falling apart just a few months after it had started. There had to be a motive for their killings and there had to be a reason why their relationship looked in trouble, and somewhere in this house, he might find something that would offer a clue.

He took out his phone and fired up the camera. It would take a lot longer, but it wouldn't be exactly smart to remove any items from what was still a crime scene, so they would have to make do with photographing anything of interest that turned up. Working methodically, he combed the room, opening every drawer to locate the one that every home had. The one where all the latest bills and correspondence were stuffed to keep the place tidy, and where bad news too could be buried out of sight and out of mind. It was the second-last one he tried. *Bingo*. He grabbed a handful of papers and spread them out across the worktop. The usual stuff, credit card and utility bills, old greeting cards shoved in and forgotten after the event they celebrated had passed, mail-shots for wine clubs and cruises and designer-label clothing, evidence of the high-end marketing demographic Ross and Fox had occupied. He dragged out a few bank statements and examined them more closely. Since it was early in their relationship, it wasn't a surprise that the couple managed their financial affairs independently. Each seemed to possess three or four credit cards but how they used them was starkly different. Allegra Ross's were a model of prudence, each with low or zero balances and the full amount outstanding paid off each month. Fox by contrast had run up high four-figure balances on all of his cards, and was paying off only the minimum permitted. Taken together, his credit card debt exceeded twenty grand and it was growing exponentially month on month. Jimmy arranged the statements neatly side-by-side and began to photograph them. As he did so, he uncovered a letter with the words DO NOT IGNORE printed in bold red type across the top. It was from a car finance company, recording that he had fallen three months behind with the thousand-quid a month repayment on the Range-Rover, and unless the full sum owed was paid in the next ten days, the company would with regret take steps to recover the vehicle. It was dated two months earlier.

So Fox was in financial difficulties. Problems around money were one of the major factors that caused relationships to go pear-shaped, and he could imagine how difficult it would be if one partner was a spendthrift and the other one was careful. That could cause tension, no doubt about it, but murder? That made less sense.

He finished taking photographs and stuffed the documents back in the drawer. Where to next? A quick survey of the front lounge and rear sitting room revealed nothing of obvious interest. He slipped back into the hall and bounded upstairs. The second floor contained two bedrooms and a large family bathroom. The first one he tried was little more than a box room, with a single bed squashed against a wall but otherwise empty. Next to it was what was obviously the master bedroom, furnished with a king-sized double, dressed with a vermillion duvet with colour-coordinated pillows and contrasting cushions. One wall was given over to fitted wardrobes, matching the bedside drawer units. They were divided as he expected into his and hers, Allegra's on the left, Benjamin's on the right.

Starting at her side, he pulled out each drawer in turn and rummaged through the contents. For some reason he felt a deep sense of embarrassment as he came across the one that contained her underwear. There was some very nice stuff in there, all satin and lace and expensive too. Suspender sets, seamed stockings, flimsy knickers, negligees. Benjamin Fox was a very lucky boy indeed if it was all for his benefit. But as far as he could see there was nothing of any interest with respect to the case.

He wandered round to Fox's side of the bed, and as he opened the top drawer, he let out an involuntary guffaw. Sitting on top of a pile of boxer shorts was a blister pack of the unmistakeable little blue pills, and a quick count confirmed just five remained out of a pack of twenty-eight. God, old Benjamin *was* a lucky boy. Mind you, he was fifty-ish and she was barely thirty so maybe it was no surprise that he needed some help in that department. But fair play to him, pulling a woman like that at his age. Maybe he had already seen the signs that the relationship wouldn't last, but Fox was clearly making the most of it whilst he could. Or at least he had been, until somebody murdered him.

But a cursory check of the other two drawers turned up nothing. That just left the wardrobes to deal with. Opening Fox's, his heart sank when he saw that it was stuffed to bursting, Jimmy estimating that the guy owned about fifty suits and not far off the same number of shirts and jumpers. With no real idea what he was looking for, he began to work his way along the row, checking each pocket in turn, inside and out. Ten minutes later, all he had harvested was a handful of coins, a few receipts, mainly from bars and restaurants, and a couple of cheap ballpoint pens. Mundane stuff in the main. Another ten minutes and a sweep of Allegra's wardrobe delivered the same result.

It was disappointing but it still left one obvious place to look. The pile of cash hidden under the mattress might be a hackneyed old cliché, but it had become a cliché precisely because sometimes it was true. He kneeled down at Fox's side and started at the top, slipping his hands between the divan base and the mattress, stretching his arms out to halfway across, then gradually working his way down to the foot of the bed. *Nothing*. Moving round to Allegra's side, he repeated the same routine except this time he started at the bottom and worked his way up. Then about three-quarters of the way up, he found it. As he felt his way around the object, there was no mistaking what it was. A book of some description, and from the texture, leather-bound. But having seen the contents of her underwear drawer, he was one hundred percent certain it wasn't a bible. *Allegra Ross kept a diary.*

Of course, it was the obvious place to keep it if you wanted to shield its contents from your new lover. A leather strap was wrapped around the cover, attached to a brass clasp secured by a tiny lock. But that was purely symbolic, signifying that that the contents were for the eyes of the author only. Jimmy removed his penknife from the pocket of his jeans, inserted a slim blade in the keyhole, and a second later the clasp sprung open. And as he opened it, something fluttered to the ground.

The photograph had been taken in a garden somewhere, the backdrop an elaborate trellis clad in a beautiful yellow climbing rose. The archetypal father and child picture, beloved the world over, although it wasn't easy to tell if the kid was a boy or a girl since the face was hidden behind an outsize pair of comic sunglasses. Whatever the gender, the child looked about four or five years old. The only problem was that as far as Jimmy knew, Benjamin Fox wasn't a father.

He checked his watch. Yes, pretty efficient. He had been in the property less than twenty-five minutes, and of course he still had the keys, so he could in theory come back any time he wanted. He would have liked to have had a quick read of the diary, but that would have to wait until later. So that was it. Not a bad morning's work, all in all. Some evidence suggesting that Fox might have been in financial difficulties in the months before he was murdered and this perplexing photograph. And of course the diary. Jimmy thought he might find more if he had more time, and he hadn't even looked at the basement yet, but this was enough for now.

As he slipped back out on to the landing, he thought he heard the faint sound of a key being inserted in a lock. Shit, was someone trying to get in? That was a surprise, since it was still only quarter-past-seven and the day shift coppers weren't supposed to be here until eight. If whoever it was decided to venture upstairs, then they couldn't help but see him standing there on the landing, and yet he didn't dare try to get back into the bedroom. On his way in he had noticed the creaky floorboards, a certain giveaway. All he could do now was stick it out and hope that their business was on the ground floor and that it was short in duration.

But then, shit, shit and triple shit. As he recognised only too plainly that distinctive beep-beep-beep-beep sound, he realised with a sinking feeling what was coming next. Someone had nipped round to set the bloody burglar alarm.

***

It was easy to deduce from her home's luxurious appointments that Allegra Ross didn't do anything on the cheap, and so it was no surprise to Jimmy that her alarm system too was state-of-the art. A barrage of motion sensors covered every cubic centimetre of the property, and the siren was loud enough to pin you to the wall. He'd had torture training in the army, but this was on a whole different level. Unable to think above the bedlam, he tumbled down the flight of stairs until with just a couple of steps he was at the front door. He flicked back the latch and yanked the handle but it wouldn't open. Bugger, the deadlock was on. Then he remembered that he hadn't locked the bi-folds behind him. Thank god for that. Feverishly, he sprinted through to the kitchen and swung them open, leaping out into the garden and into the waiting handcuffs of WPC Heather Green.

Chapter 12

It was around nine am when Maggie received the call that had every prospect of screwing up her day. She'd just got off the DLR at Canary Wharf when it came through. *'Oh hi boss, it's me. Look, I was just wondering if you could get over to Parsons Green, you know, to the Allegra Ross house. I think I've been sort of arrested.'*

'What do you mean, sort of arrested?' This wasn't in the script.

'It's a long story, I'll tell you when you get here. Anyway, I've tried to explain to the police officer that I did have permission from my boss to enter her house, and that I was just doing what I was told.'

'Brilliant Jimmy, that's excellent.' She knew he would appreciate her sarcasm.

'But the thing is, she won't let me go until she gets corroboration from you. And she says you need to turn up in the flesh so that she knows that it really is you. Sorry about this boss...'

'Yeah ok,' Maggie said, trying unsuccessfully to hide the exasperation in her voice. 'Look, I was just heading up to Asvina's office, so it might take me a while to get to you. But I'll get there.' She gave a chuckle, unable to help herself. 'And don't do anything stupid.'

Permission? They didn't have permission, of course they didn't, but she supposed he had to make *something* up to prevent him being instantly carted off to Paddington Green in a police van. Parsons Green was more than ten miles on the opposite side of the city from Canary Wharf so on impulse she grabbed a black cab. That was forty quid she wasn't going to see again.

The journey took about forty minutes, which was long enough for her to concoct a story. Although it wasn't much of a story. She paid the driver, made her way to the front door and rang the bell. A few moments later it was opened by a pretty WPC.

'I'm Maggie Bainbridge,' she said, smiling what she hoped was a disarming smile. 'Mr Stewart's boss.'

'Oh yes?' the WPC replied, giving her a suspicious look. 'Your...colleague is through here in the kitchen. Please follow me.' Maggie could sense that this was going to be difficult.

She found Jimmy sitting bolt upright in a kitchen chair, his arms behind him, and noting with a mixture of alarm and amusement that he was handcuffed. Heather Green was petite and pencil-thin, and the explanation of how her muscle-packed colleague came to be overpowered by this slip of a girl would be something to dine out on for years. Or at the very least, to share with Frank.

'Hi boss, thanks for coming.' He sounded suitably embarrassed. 'I've told WPC Green about our discussions with Allegra Ross. You know, how we were helping her out.'

Oh thanks very much Jimmy, she thought. That's just shot my crap story down in flames. But, on the other hand, maybe not.

'Ah, yes...yes, that's right. We were helping her out. You see, Benjamin Fox had asked Miss Ross to marry him.'

The policewoman's eyes narrowed. 'They were getting married?'

Suddenly she was interested, and Maggie saw the opportunity, pure naked ambition not being difficult to recognise. 'Yes, that's right, although I don't think they had set a date. But although Miss Ross was young, she was a very wealthy woman on account of her family background, and women like that have to be very careful when they marry.' It was nowhere near the truth, but it would do for now.

Visibly, Green began to soften.

'Well I didn't know about this. I don't think that has come up so far in our investigations.' No it wouldn't have, thought Maggie, since I only thought of it ten seconds ago.

'Yes,' Maggie continued, 'Miss Ross decided she needed a pre-nuptial agreement and asked us to help.' This was even further from the truth, but once you were in it, you had no option but to keep spinning.

'But you're not solicitors, are you?' Green said, looking puzzled. 'Why would she approach you?'

Jimmy picked up the thread. 'No we're not, but we happened to speak to Miss Ross in the course of our work on Melody Montague's divorce, and the subject came up. When she found out that we were private investigators, and we did mainly family law work, she also asked us to look into the affairs of her husband to be.'

Maggie smiled in silent admiration. It was so convincing, she almost believed it herself.

WPC Green was quiet for a moment as she appeared to inwardly debate her next move. Maggie could see what she was thinking. On the one hand, this good-looking guy had broken into a murder scene and ought to be arrested, there was no question about it. But on the other, these two seemed to have information that might prove of critical importance in both murder enquiries and if she was the one to uncover it and bring it to the attention of DCI Barker, then it couldn't help but be good for her career.

She got straight to the point. 'What else have you found out?'

Maggie was interested in that too. 'Obviously Jimmy hasn't had the chance to update me on the outcome of his visit yet. But since our involvement is strictly a civil matter, I wouldn't expect us to turn up much of relevance to the murder cases. Perhaps if you were to remove my colleague's handcuffs, we might be able to discuss this in a nice civilised manner.'

Green looked wary.

'All right then,' she said, with evident reluctance, 'but don't try anything.'

Jimmy looked as if he was struggling not to laugh at the cop-show cliché. 'No, no of course not, wouldn't dream of it. And I *have* found out some interesting stuff.'

Maggie smiled inwardly. Whatever he had found out, she was pretty sure he wasn't going to give the WPC even half of it.

'So, I rooted around a bit in the kitchen drawers... I assume you guys had already done that? But anyway as I said, I rooted around and found this stuff.' He took out his phone and scrolled through some pictures he had evidently taken earlier. 'It looks like Mr Fox might have had some financial difficulties. Could be nothing, but I thought it was quite interesting. But you guys will be able to do more with it than we can. I'll e-mail these to you of course, and see what you can make of them.'

Maggie could see the policewoman struggling to contain her excitement. *So Ross and Fox were planning to get married but it turns out one of them had financial problems. Important facts that were new to the investigation, important facts that she alone had discovered, more or less. She would need to come up with a story of how she had come by the information, but already an idea was half-forming in her mind. She'd been sent round to the property by DCI Barker to set the alarm after the security company that maintained it had given them the master code. On a hunch, she had decided to have a delve around the place to see if anything had been missed by the scene-of-crime team. Bank statements and letters from finance companies told the true picture of the state of their finances, and the fact they had maintained separate accounts suggested their relationship wasn't as close as they portrayed in public. Yes, that was all fairly plausible. Now she just had to make sure Mr Stewart and his gobby boss would keep their mouths shut if they had the misfortune to bump into DCI Barker.*

She took on an official air.

'So, this information could be very useful to our investigation. It's very important that it is kept confidential so that it does not jeopardise the case. If you give an undertaking to respect this, I might be able to let you off on this occasion with just a verbal warning.'

And no need to officially record the incident on the crime database either. They knew what she was suggesting, and she knew that they knew it too. It was an offer they couldn't refuse.

Jimmy took the house keys from his pocket and gave her one of his special smiles. 'I won't be needing these again. And thank you very much for your understanding.'

To her annoyance, Maggie could see the WPC starting to melt. *Flipping Jimmy Stewart and women*. She didn't want to prolong this encounter any longer than necessary.

'Come on, Jimmy I think we should go now.'

'Yep, no problem, just need to grab this.' With a deft move, he picked up the leather-bound book which had lain on the table unobserved and followed her out into the garden.

***

There would be time for a debrief later in the day, when Maggie could share her latest thinking on the Grant case and she would find out why Jimmy had taken that book. But overall, the morning which at one point had threatened to be a disaster had turned out all right. Ok, they had been less than truthful in a murder investigation, but it was all in a good cause, and at least they had something on WPC Heather Green that would ensure her silence in the future. And Jimmy had for once survived an encounter with an attractive woman without leaving with a bloody phone number on the back of his hand. Although as she sat alongside him on the tube train, she gave a quick sideways glance just to make sure.

Chapter 13

Their regular Fleet Street Starbucks was as packed as ever, but they managed to find three adjacent stools along a sidewall shelf. Naturally DI Frank Stewart would have preferred a pint but she knew if she offered him a grande Americano with a gratis blueberry muffin on the side he would turn up, and he did. Service for once being swift, they were soon mainlining copious oral injections of caffeine and ready to discuss developments.

'Thanks a lot for coming Frank,' Maggie said. 'I know you must be really busy with *our* Shark case.' She noticed he ignored the deliberate provocation.

He nodded. 'Well, that's not a problem, but actually it's what my wee brother mentioned on the phone that's really brought me here.'

Jimmy took the diary from his pocket and carefully removed the photograph, laying it on the shelf. 'This is it. I guess it might be a nephew or a niece or maybe even some fan's kid I suppose. But I think it looks a bit creepy.'

'Nice garden though,' Frank observed.

'Yeah, but it *is* a bit creepy,' Maggie said. 'So this is what you concealed from pushy WPC Green? Clever boy.'

'What's this about a WPC?' Frank sounded suspicious, but then Maggie knew that came naturally to detective inspectors.

'Nothing for you to worry about,' Jimmy said. It didn't sound too convincing. 'Anyway, how are *you* getting on with the case.' Maggie couldn't help but notice the hint of a challenge in his voice. And the mild deflation when Frank told him about his conversation with Interpol and the Kitty Lawrence abduction.

'So do you think these cases might be linked?' Jimmy asked.

'I don't know,' Frank said, 'but there are a ton of similarities. I just haven't figured out what the connection could be, but that will come. Anyway, tell me, how did you get a hold of this diary and that photograph?'

Maggie smiled uncertainly. 'You'll need to tell him.'

'Tell me what?'

So Jimmy told him, and as she had predicted, it didn't go down well.

'Christ's sake! Christ's sake! You broke into a *murder* scene? You used a set of keys that you had stolen on a previous visit. You traipsed all over the house no doubt leaving fingerprints and DNA behind which could screw up the evidence, and by the way, get you fitted up for the murder. You know, I really should arrest you myself.'

'I'm sorry Frank,' Maggie said, back-pedalling. 'It was my idea. Jimmy was just doing what I asked.'

'Well in that case I should bloody arrest you too. For god's sake Maggie, it was a really stupid thing to do. Damn stupid.'

'I was only in there for half an hour,' Jimmy said, evidently in an attempt at mitigation, 'and I don't think I disturbed anything. I don't know why you're getting so excited mate.'

The words 'red rag' and 'bull' sprang into Maggie's mind.

'You think this is funny, do you?' Frank spat out the words.

'But I thought that's what Department 12B did,' Jimmy said, not helping at all. 'The things that other cops can't touch? And anyway, we were only looking to see if Allegra knew anything about the pre-nuptial agreement.'

Frank grimaced. 'Yeah, well that's got sod-all to do with me. As for the murders, if the team need more evidence they'll get it through the proper procedures, not through some bloody amateur subterfuge. And you Maggie are a bloody lawyer so you should know what inadmissible as evidence means.'

She had never seen him this angry before, and now began to wonder if they had overplayed their hand. 'Look, I'm sorry Frank, it's just my enthusiasm getting the better of me. You're right, I know you are.'

He softened a bit as Maggie gave him what she hoped was a little-girl-lost smile. 'Aye, well no harm done yet I suppose. But we're going to have to hand that diary and the photograph over to Barker, and god knows how we're going to explain how we came by it.'

Maggie had a solution to that dilemma. Grinning, she said. 'Frank, cover your ears, but I think we may have somewhat compromised WPC Green....'

Frank shook his head and gave a sharp intake of breath.

'I've got nearly twenty years of unblemished service under my belt, then I have the bloody misfortune of running into bloody Maggie Bainbridge.'

And then he beamed a huge smile.

'But let's make sure we give that diary a thorough read-through first. And get a scan of that photo as well.'

Jimmy gave them a wry look. 'Well, actually folks, I've already had a good read. And it's *very* interesting to say the least.'

'We're all ears,' Frank said, through a mouthful of muffin, as Jimmy undid the clasp of the diary, opened it and began to read.

'Aye, so here we are about six months ago, and she's all loved up. *Benjamin Fox asked me to dinner. Bit awkward with Melody on-set. But he's v. nice.* And then a couple of weeks later it's all getting a bit x-rated.'

He'd told her about the underwear drawer and the Viagra, and she was amused to see the faint tint of crimson that now suffused his cheeks.

'I won't bother reading any of *those* ones out if you don't mind. Suffice to say there was a lot of action in the bedroom department. For the next month or two, it continues much in the same vein. There's a wee celebration when Fox's degree nisi comes through, and she begins to wonder if this might be the real thing. In one of the entries, she's speculating on her choice of bridesmaids.'

'All sounds a bit boring to me,' Frank said dismissively.

'Patience brother, patience, it gets better. So about three months ago, we get the first and only mention of the pre-nuptial agreement. *Benjy rather pleased with himself. Pre-nup sorted, problem solved he says.*'

'Nothing else?' Maggie asked.

'No, nothing. But there was obviously something going on there. No idea what.'

'Shame that's all there is,' Maggie said.

'Aye, it is,' Jimmy said, 'but it's what she wrote just three weeks ago that's the real dynamite I think. Listen to this. *Wednesday May 21st. Benjy told me something awful tonight. Everything is ruined. Distraught and broken.*'

'Everything is ruined?' Maggie repeated, open-mouthed. 'What does that mean. Isn't there anything else?'

Jimmy shook his head. 'Not that I can see. There was just one thing. The next day. *Need to see Edwina.* That was all she wrote.'

'Edwina?' Frank said. 'Who's that?'

'A friend I suppose,' Maggie said. 'Or maybe a sister?'

'Aye, a sister,' Jimmy said, his voice betraying excitement, 'but not *her* sister. *His* sister. I found a few greeting cards stuffed in a drawer when I was in his house and there was an old birthday card for Benjamin. *Dear Brother* it said and I took a quick look inside. Edwina, that was her name.'

Before he had finished speaking, Maggie was on Wikipedia. *Benjamin Fox, actor, born in London in 1968 to Peter and Mary Fox of Attringwell House, Devonshire. Married Melody Montague in 2014, no children.* And a sister Edwina, distinguished enough in her own right as a theatrical agent to merit her own separate entry.

***

It had only taken a couple of clicks to locate the website of The Talent Partnership, the agency for whom Edwina Fox worked. Her Wikipedia profile revealed her to be the older of the two children of Peter Fox and his first wife, and that she was married to a well-known actor, but like Maggie, preferred to use her maiden name for business. The agency was located on Warwick Street in the heart of theatreland, barely a ten-minute walk from their Fleet Street Starbucks.

'I can't believe she agreed to see us right away,' Maggie said. They were shown into a comfortable reception area, its walls plastered with portraits of famous clients old and new.

'My god, that's Lawrence Olivier, isn't it?' Jimmy said. 'With his wife Vivien Leigh. These guys must be really big-time to have had them as clients. And long-established.'

She hadn't heard of either but declined to admit it. 'Wonder if they represent Melody or Charles, what do you think?' she asked.

'Might do. I'd imagine they would have had Benjamin on their books at least.'

Edwina Fox was a woman of plain appearance, in stark contrast to the good looks of her younger brother. According to her Wikipedia profile, she had decided early on that her theatrical career was to be made out of the spotlight, and she had made rather a success of it. Beautifully dressed in a Prada pinafore subtly set off by an alarmingly expensive pearl necklace, she exuded the quiet confidence of someone at the top of her profession, but it wasn't hard to tell she had been through a lot in recent days. Her eyes were ringed with dark circles and her complexion had a dull pallor that a generous application of foundation had failed to disguise. 'Sit down please,' she said, as she ushered them into her tastefully-decorated office. More portraits lined the wall, Maggie assuming them to be some of Edwina's current roster. One face in particular she recognised.

'So you represent Sharon Trent do you?'

Edwina turned to look at the photograph. 'Her? I do, yes. Between you and me, she's not much of an actress, but as you probably know, sex sells in this profession. Always has and always will. Naturally it limits their shelf life, but she will find that out in due course.'

'And what about Melody Montague? Do you represent her too?' Maggie couldn't help reflecting that *she* was still selling sex, and she was well into her fifties. Or not so much selling it as giving it away for free to anyone who wanted it. Maybe that's what had extended her shelf-life.

'Not personally.' Her tone was cold. 'She is represented by one of my colleagues.' She didn't sound as if she approved.

'You don't like her then?' Jimmy asked.

'I don't. But that does not matter because as I said, I don't represent her, and in any case, it is not necessary to like one's clients.' Maggie took that as a reference to her relationship with Sharon Trent.

'Edwina,' she smiled, 'I know this must be difficult, but we wondered if Allegra Ross had been speaking to you in the days before Benjamin was killed. I don't mean about business, but about her relationship with your brother.'

Edwina gave her a sharp look. 'How did you know about that?'

There was no point in spinning a tale.

'We came across her diary,' Maggie said. 'In it she mentioned wanting to talk with you.'

'She came here, very upset. About something Benjamin had told her. But she wouldn't tell me what it was. All she would say was it concerned his marriage to Melody.'

'So what did she want from you?' Maggie asked, puzzled.

'I'm not sure. I think she was trying to find out if I knew anything too. But I didn't, so I think she went away disappointed. And uncertain what she should do about what she had discovered. But of course, had she told me her concerns, perhaps I could have helped her.'

'And Benjamin himself had never spoken to you about whatever it was?' Jimmy asked.

'Not in so many words. But there was *something*. I knew there was something not right. And then of course he was brutally murdered. My little brother, killed in cold blood.'

'I'm so sorry,' Maggie said. 'I really don't know what to say.' She knew there was nothing you could say that would be any good.

'Can we get someone to get you a cup of tea or something?' Jimmy said awkwardly. Maggie guessed he was wishing they hadn't come. But it seemed that Edwina was glad to have someone to talk to.

'You see, I've never really liked Melody Montague,' she began. 'So *common,* don't you think? But she and Benjamin seemed to be happy and there were great plans to start a family and build the perfect picture-book life that she so obviously craved. But it never came true, and I think that was what caused the marriage to fall apart.'

'Do you know what the problem in that department was?' Maggie said delicately. 'If you don't mind me asking.'

'Well she was so *old*,' Edwina said, sounding bitter. 'Too old to be a mother really, although they can do so much with medical science these days. But she was completely obsessed with playing happy families and it put such a lot of pressure on dear Benjamin. And then unfortunately the doctors found he was shooting blanks. I know it's such a vulgar expression, but that was the heart of the matter I'm afraid. Their great love seemed to evaporate at that point.'

Maggie nodded sympathetically. 'It's always so hard as an outsider to know what it's like inside a marriage, isn't it? You can hate someone and love them at the same time.'

'You sound as if you are speaking from experience,' Edwina replied.

She smiled. 'Yes, but I'm over it now.' That was nowhere near the truth, but she couldn't deny that since Jimmy Stewart had come into her life it had been getting better.

'I'm sorry to return to it,' Maggie said, 'but did you speculate about what Allegra might have found out from your brother?'

She shrugged. 'Really, I had no idea. I thought it might be something about the money. You know Benjamin and Melody were still arguing about it six months after the divorce, and I think he was rather dependent on it getting settled.'

'Yes, we know about that. Tell me, did he ever speak to you about a pre-nuptial agreement?'

She nodded. 'Well I can remember he was not exactly thrilled with it at the time it was drawn up. He never thought it fair, but it seemed that Melody insisted. Entirely typical of her of course. No *class*.'

Maggie shot Jimmy a look. So it seemed as if Melody's version of events was in fact the correct one. Contrary to what Fox had been claiming, and to what Charles Grant the witness was apparently corroborating. But then something else occurred to her.

'On the only occasion we met your brother, he mentioned something about a little arrangement he had with his former wife. Have you any idea what he might have been referring to?'

She shook her head. 'Sorry, it's not something he ever spoke to me about. Really, I've no idea.'

Maggie nodded, disappointed. 'So Edwina, is there *anything* else you can think of?'

She frowned 'Well I suppose there were her brothers.'

'What do you mean?' Maggie asked, interested.

'Her brothers,' she repeated. 'I guess you know she's a Kemp? Roxy Kemp, that's her real name, and she has two brothers, Terry and Harry I think that's their names. They're apparently well known in the East End as a pair of gangsters, if that's not an old-fashioned term, although I don't of course move in these circles myself. And they're a very unsavoury lot by all accounts, so it did occur to me that Benjamin might have got to know about some of their...well let's call it *activities*. And then perhaps he shared something he'd found out with Allegra. That's all I could think of.'

'But it must have been something incredibly serious,' Maggie said, furrowing her brow, 'because Allegra said that everything was ruined. That was her exact words. Everything is ruined. Have you any idea what she could have meant by that?'

'I really can't help you. I wish I could. Perhaps it would help me make sense of Benjamin's killing.'

Jimmy nodded. 'I'm sure the police will have asked you already, but do you have *any* ideas who might have wanted to do your brother harm?'

She shook her head. 'No I don't, really I don't. I think he was very popular on the show, and all his fans were very kind to him. He was of course involved with Charles Grant's little gang of revolutionaries, but I doubt if that had anything to do with it.'

'There was that attack the day before he disappeared,' Maggie said. 'By Darren Venables I mean.'

She gave a half-smile. 'Yes, but that was just a bunch of thugs lashing out because they hated his politics. I doubt if it was a reason for murder. Benjamin wasn't a fanatic, you see.

He did care about injustice but he wasn't an obsessive like Charles.'

'I take it you know Mr Grant then?' Maggie asked.

Edwina nodded. 'I've represented Charles for many years, and I would go as far as to say we are friends. He is the kind of client I like. Honest and hard-working, always turns up on time, and not too precious about the roles he takes on.'

'We know him too,' Maggie said. 'In fact we are helping him in the disappearance of his son.'

Edwina gave a weak smile. 'Really? Well I do hope you are successful because it was such a terrible business. That poor man needs closure so badly. He knows his son is dead of course, but without a body, well...' She tailed off, her eyes moistening.

'We will do everything we can,' Maggie said. 'And you have been a great help.' That wasn't exactly true, but it seemed the right thing to say. Getting up, she indicated to Jimmy that it was now time to leave.

'So thank you so much Edwina. And obviously if we uncover anything in regard to Benjamin or Allegra's murders, we will let you know immediately.'

***

She pushed open the door, the pair of them emerging into the busy hubbub of Warwick Street, already thronging with theatre-goers making their way to their pre-show suppers. As Maggie and Jimmy threaded their way through the crowd, they discussed how matters now stood. Had the meeting with Edwina Fox accelerated their understanding in any material way? Undoubtedly where the pre-nuptial was concerned. Benjamin Fox it seemed had lied about the terms of that agreement and why he had done it was quite obvious. Financial gain, pure and simple. But why he thought he could pull it off, that was a different matter altogether, and that would need to be the focus of their investigation for now.

But as for the plaintive entry in Allegra Ross's diary, they were no further forward. *Everything is ruined*. What had she been told by her lover that had left her, in her own words, distraught and broken? Was it the same thing that left her dead at the bottom of her basement steps just two weeks later? Whatever the reason, Maggie realised this was now much more than a simple marital dispute over money.

Now they were running a murder enquiry. Although it was probably best not to mention that to Frank.

***

After Maggie and Jimmy had left the coffee shop, Frank had sat quietly for a few minutes chewing over what Jimmy had discovered. Angry though he had been about the method, there was no arguing the importance of what his brother had uncovered. He had looked again at the photograph with its beautiful garden backdrop and air of innocence. And it *might* be innocent of course, as Jimmy had suggested, maybe Fox's nephew or a wee fan perhaps, or the offspring of friends. But after twenty years in the force, you learned to trust your gut, and his gut was saying something quite different. There was something odd going on here, and he meant to get to the bottom of it. The child wouldn't have a criminal record obviously, so Eleanor's jazzy wee app wouldn't be much use in identifying it. But he remembered they had used some other fancy facial-recognition software in the Alzahrani case a couple of years ago and wondered if it might be time to dust that down again. Time for another call to the wee forensic genius.

Chapter 14

Jimmy laughed to himself as he read the press release. Headed *exclusive* and rushed out by the actress's PR agency, it breathlessly announced that yes, the rumours were true. Melody Montague had been on a short break to a Caribbean island, was crazily madly in love, more than she had ever been before in her life, and she intended to marry her new *amour* Danny Black just as soon as a suitably lavish wedding could be arranged. The stress of her divorce had put her in grave danger of a breakdown, so the fairy-tale went, and for the duration of her island escape, she had taken a physical and digital detox, snubbing all social media and even going as far as not taking phone calls. Somehow however she had found time to fit in a couple of glossy photo-shoots and a tell-all interview with a tabloid journalist. In the blurb, headlined *Melody - My Marriage Hell*, she expressed hopes that she was going to be fourth time lucky in love.

Now she was home again and had decided it was time to properly celebrate her engagement with the hosting of a garden party. It was flung together at short notice, the guests given a mere five days to RSVP to the event which had been planned for the following Saturday, venue to be Melody's sumptuous Richmond home. The party would also celebrate the completion of the extravagant renovations to that home, the works rumoured to have cost over a million pounds. The showpiece was what she called the west wing, a huge oak-framed entertainment space with floor-to-ceiling panoramic glazing looking westwards across the beautiful garden. Beneath the house, a high-spec basement had been carved out, said to feature a swimming pool, gym, cinema room and servants' quarters. For over a year, the building work had been highly disruptive to the day to day life of the neighbourhood, but no-one dared to complain. Not because of the celebrity of the owner but rather due to the notoriety of her brothers. Terry and Harry Kemp were not a pair to be messed with, so nobody did.

Jimmy guessed that Melody herself was not responsible for any of the planning or the flinging together, the organisation of the event being sub-contracted out to a professional party-planning outfit, the likes of which could only exist in London. It was scheduled to start at three in the afternoon and the good news for young Ollie Bainbridge was that children were most welcome. Welcome too were divorce lawyers and their private-investigator side-kicks, which accounted for the presence on the guest list of Maggie and himself, and Asvina too, who was accompanied by her husband Dav and their two sons.

It was a perfect late spring afternoon, the sun splitting the sky and just a hint of a breeze cooling the air. They had arrived unfashionably early, the boys burning with excitement at the prospect of meeting Danny Black. Not because of his day job in *Bow Road*, but because he had recently taken over as one of the hosts of *Overdrive*, the hugely popular Sunday night motoring show.

'Mummy, mummy, will I get to meet Danny, will I get to meet Danny?' The seven-year old tugged at his mother's sleeve with his free hand, the other holding on tightly to the large white chocolate lollipop that had been handed to him on arrival by one of the hired-in hostesses.

Maggie bent over to kiss her son on the forehead.

'I don't know darling. He will probably be very busy with his grown-up guests but we'll see.'

Ollie had heard 'we'll see' many times before and had worked out what it really meant was 'probably not.' He tried a change of tact.

'Uncle Jimmy, Uncle Jimmy, will you help me meet him please. Honestly I'll be good.'

Jimmy laughed. 'Ollie, you're always good, but of course I'll see what I can do. I love *Overdrive* too, you know, it's my favourite show.' He wasn't lying either.

'And Danny's the fastest driver, he always wins all the challenges.'

That's because it's written into his contract, he thought with a hint of cynicism, but he wasn't going to burst little Ollie's bubble.

'Yeah, he is mate, isn't he? And some of the cars he gets to drive are just awesome. Did you see him doing doughnuts in that F40 last week?'

Ollie's eyes were sparkling with excitement. 'I'm going to drive a Ferrari too when I grow up.' Jimmy didn't have the heart to tell him that by the time he grew up Ferraris would almost certainly be driving themselves.

If the motoring hero Danny Black was the centre of attention for the kids, there was no doubt the topic that was way out in front with the adults.

'Asvina, have you any idea how much this place must have cost?' he heard Maggie whispering as she sipped on her champagne. 'I mean the garden must be about half an acre, in *Richmond*. And that house, Arts & Crafts, is that what they call it?'

'I don't know, but I remember Melody telling me what they were doing to it.'

'Worth a ton of money I'd guess,' Jimmy said.

'Five million, minimum.' He'd forgotten Dav Rani was in property. 'We sold one just up the road for that three months ago. And it didn't have the basement or the sun room, and it had a much smaller garden too.'

'So this one might be more than that Dav?' Asvina said, smiling at her husband. She stole a glance at Maggie and raised an eyebrow.

'Yeah, that's what I'm thinking too,' Maggie said. 'Where on earth does all this come from?'

They had been overheard by a pretty but stern-faced young woman who had been hovering nearby. She held out a hand and introduced herself as Lily.

'I'm a production assistant on the show,' she continued, unprompted. 'Bow Road. I look after Miss Montague mainly.' In what way the actress required looking after was not specified.

'We were just admiring Miss Montague's house,' Jimmy said, flashing her one of his smiles.

'Yes, it is beautiful, isn't it? I think it belonged originally to her third husband Mr Fox, but Miss Montague has been spending a fortune on it after they separated.'

Jimmy had forgotten that for nearly four years this had been Benjamin Fox's home too, so maybe it wasn't such a surprise that he was so exercised about the terms of his divorce settlement. No-one would want to give up a house like this without a fight.

Across the garden he noticed the actress Sharon Trent deep in conversation with two men. From a distance, it looked as if they were arguing.

'That's Jack Redmayne and our executive producer Robbie Wright,' Lily said, answering the question that was on their lips. 'Jack's a writer on the show. And Robbie's my boss. Well, he's everybody's boss I suppose.'

And then it came back to Jimmy. Redmayne was the guy they had seen arguing with Benjamin Fox at the awards do. And now it appeared that rather than being dismissed from the show as Fox had threatened, he had outlasted his adversary. Yet as far as he knew, the guy had never been identified as a suspect.

'Do you know what they're arguing about?' he asked Lily.

He found her reply both surprising and deliciously indiscreet. 'Sharon's a right diva, she's always bitching about something, complaining about the lines she's given and moaning if she doesn't have enough scenes. She's a total nightmare to work with.'

Jimmy smiled. 'So do you know what this one's about?'

Lily gave a conspiratorial look and dropped her voice to a whisper, evidently enjoying the actress's travails. 'Oh yes, I know all right.' Was she going to tell them more? It seemed like she was.

'You see, they're going to end the affair.' Jimmy assumed that 'they' were Bow Road's executive producers, who presumably dictated the direction of every storyline and the fate of every character on the show. 'You know, the affair between Tracy Short - that's her character - and Ronnie West.'

'He's played by Danny Black, isn't he?' Jimmy said, shooting Maggie a smug look. 'And his character is married to Patty, as played by Melody Montague.' He pumped his fist in triumph, causing Maggie to shake her head in mock disgust.

Lily gave a puzzled look. It evidently hadn't occurred to her that there was anyone in Britain who didn't know that most basic fact, so why was this amazingly good-looking guy celebrating it?

'Well yes, that's right,' she said. 'So they want to end the affair, which gives them a big-set piece scene to boost the autumn viewing figures, but that obviously means that going forward Sharon won't get anything like the screen time she used to get.'

'Does Tracy dump Ronnie, or does he dump her?' Maggie asked.

'So that's the other thing Sharon's not happy about. She has to dump Ronnie, which means he gets all the viewer sympathy and she's just the heartless bitch.'

'I can see why she wouldn't like that,' Jimmy said. 'Does that mean she's on the way out then?'

Lily shrugged. 'That's way above my pay grade, I'm afraid. But I think the direction of travel is towards Melody and Danny's characters over the next twelve months or so. It depends what the scriptwriters come up with I suppose, but I wouldn't be surprised if they write in some sort of a breakdown for Tracy and she's out of the show for a while.' Jimmy made a mental note to later ask Miss Montague what she made of these developments. For the moment, Lily had turned silent, perhaps worrying she had already said too much.

A marquee had been provided in the event of inclement conditions, and in their absence the sides had been rolled up, the shade providing welcome relief from the hot sun. Inside, a well-stocked bar in the charge of improbably good-looking staff of both sexes was doing brisk business, hardly surprising on account of it being free. Melody stood at the bar, in the process of ordering another glass of champagne. She was not alone. Her companion, a well-built man in his fifties stood alongside, puffing on a cigar, in defiance of the 'No Smoking' sign pinned to one of the supporting pillars. Anyone who thought for a moment of admonishing him would have soon thought again when they clocked his cropped hair, scarred cheek and general appearance of menace.

She saw them approach and smiled. 'I'll only be a second guys, just finishing up here.' On cue, her companion leaned over, kissed her lightly on the cheek, then moved as to leave. 'See you around doll.'

With the briefest nod of acknowledgment to Maggie and Jimmy he sauntered off, still smoking his cigar.

'That's Terry,' Melody said. 'He looks after some of my business interests.'

'Is he your agent then?' Jimmy asked.

She laughed. 'My agent? Good god, no, he's my big brother. I've got two but Harry couldn't be here today. Anyway, that's not why you're here is it?' she said, rising to greet them. They might have been long-lost friends such was the warmth of her embrace, Jimmy feeling his perhaps lasted rather longer than was strictly necessary.

'I'm still waiting for you to call me,' she said, lowering her voice to a sultry whisper. 'You haven't lost my number have you? Did I tell you it's my special burner phone? Nobody will know, so don't be scared.'

'Eh, no Melody, I haven't,' he mumbled. So much for her being crazily madly in love with Danny Black.

He saw Maggie giving him a sharp look which might have been of disapproval, or more like pity, but she made no direct comment. Instead she said, 'I hear congratulations are in order.'

Melody beamed. *'Thank* you, yes as you can imagine, I'm completely over the moon about it. What is it they say, third time lucky? Well this is my fourth, so that must be even better still.' Maggie and Jimmy exchanged a wry glance. 'Danny is my *absolute* soul-mate, and I'm so lucky to have found him at this point in my life, don't you think?' Lucky if it lasted more than six months Jimmy thought, but he didn't say it.

'And good for the show too, I'd imagine,' Maggie said. 'Lots of publicity and intrigue with you being married to him in the show as well.'

'Yes, isn't it just *fantastic*?' she said, making no attempt to hide her self-satisfaction. 'They've got Ronnie being dumped by that little bitch Tracy and running back to me. Now it's all going to be about the two of us, it's really going to be sensational viewing. They're even talking about having us adopt a child, a Syrian refugee or something, I don't think they've worked that out yet. I mean, how amazing will that be? Me, a mum at fifty.' Fifty-five more like, thought Jimmy sourly. But if that was the direction of travel, as Lily had described it, he could see why Sharon Trent would be upset.

'Anyway darling, you must come for the grand tour. I assume you two would like to see round the house?'

He guessed Maggie and Asvina wouldn't need a second invitation, so keen were they to see the inside of this palace. Jimmy, however, had other plans. He had spotted Danny Black in a quiet corner of the garden, surrounded by a scrum of excited boys, including Maggie's Ollie and Harjinder and Hammi Rani.

'I'll leave that to you Maggie, if you don't mind,' he said, grimacing.

'Got your autograph book with you?'

'Naw, I'm hoping for a selfie,' he responded. And he wasn't lying. He made his way over to them, where Black seemed to be in the process of organising some kids for a group photograph.

'Right, you, Ollie isn't it, could you stand up straight, I can't see your head. And Hammi, stand a bit closer to your brother, will you? And can we get this little girl over too please? What's your name darling?'

He looked like a harassed wedding photographer trying to round up the more inebriated guests for the final shot. He shouted across the garden.

'Eddie, where's Eddie?'

A man in his mid-forties appeared from behind a verdant azalea, adjusting his flies, holding a pint glass, a cigarette dangling from his mouth.

'Whoa, that's better,' he said to no-one in particular. 'Got it all sorted then boss?' His accent was more authentically East End than anyone in Bow Road could muster. 'Come on, hand over the phones and let's get on with it. Haven't got all day, have we?'

'Cheers mate,' Black replied. 'Where's Melody? Melody doll, get your arse over here pronto.'

Hearing her name being called, she broke off her conversation with Maggie and Asvina and skipped over.

'This is nice,' she said smiling, then addressing the photographer, 'Get me and Danny on either end then boy-girl-boy-girl. Here, can we have this nice little boy next to me.' She put her arm round Ollie and kissed him on the forehead. Jimmy could see his disappointment as his friend Hammi got to stand beside Danny Black.

'Right everybody say a big cheese,' she said. *'Cheeeeeeese!'*

This caused the children to collapse into a fit of giggles, requiring the scene to be re-composed and the shots to be re-taken. Next, Melody decided she wanted the same shot but with Jimmy in place of Danny, and so there was another five minutes of chaotic rearrangement until she was happy.

'Here, give us your phone mate,' Eddie the photographer said. 'Get you one for the family album.' Jimmy passed him his phone, setting off a third bout of messing about until finally Eddie deemed himself satisfied.

Now there was only one picture to be taken to complete the shoot. Jimmy took Danny to one side.

'Any chance of a picture with the boy?' he asked, nodding towards Ollie. 'He's a huge fan.'

'Yeah sure mate, no problem. Make sure you get my good side Eddie my son.' He placed his arm around Ollie's shoulders and gave him a wink. 'And make sure you get a good one of this lad too. What's your favourite car mate?'

Ollie smiled an adoring smile, and replied with painstaking precision, 'A Ferrari S-F-ninety **Stradale Hybrid. A red one. I saw you driving one last week.**'

'The old Stradale? That's right mate. That was a nice motor, and very good for the environment too. Hybrid you see, runs on its battery some of the time.' Yeah, for about two minutes Jimmy thought, wondering what the world's polar bears would think about it, but he said nothing. Danny Black noticed him looking at him and a quizzical expression crossed his face.

'By the way, I don't think I know you mate. You one of the dads?'

Jimmy extended a hand. 'Not exactly. I'm Jimmy Stewart. I'm a sort of private investigator, helping Miss Montague with her divorce. Working for Asvina Rani.'

He shook Jimmy's hand, nodding. 'Ah yeah, Melody told me about you guys. You're making sure that that bastard Fox doesn't get his hands on our money. Not wanting to speak ill of the dead of course.' *Our money*. That was an interesting way of putting it.

Black continued. 'That Asvina, she's one fit bird isn't she? You given her one yet mate?' Jimmy couldn't tell if he was joking or not, but it made him feel uncomfortable.

'Eh no,' he said, smiling. 'I don't think that would be very professional.' Changing the subject he said, 'I must say, it is very nice to meet you. *Overdrive* must be great to work on.'

'Yeah, it's harder than it looks though, with all that first-class travel to exotic locations and having to swan around in all those fast motors. No, I'm taking the piss mate. You're right, it's a dream job. Better than all the shite I have to do on the *Road*, that's for sure.'

Jimmy shrugged. 'I don't watch the show all that often I must confess, not like my partner Maggie. She's a huge fan. But what I've seen, I think you're really good, and I'm not just saying that.'

Danny gave a brief smile in response. 'Yeah, well cheers for that mate. And I suppose it pays the bills. Anyway, if you don't mind, I'll leave you to look after these lovely lads. I'd

better circulate as I'm supposed to be the host. Catch you later.'

***

Melody had kept up a running commentary as she led Maggie and Asvina through the house and up the stairs to her bedroom.

'The kitchen was a nightmare of course. We spent over a hundred grand and it took them three attempts to get the worktops to fit. Cost them a fortune of course and Danny was worried that they might go bust, but they got there in the end, and it is *lovely*, don't you think? And this staircase, pure marble and *so* heavy, it took three of their guys just to move each step. But well worth it I think.'

The bedroom was of impressive proportions and decorated in keeping with the opulence of the house, dominated by a super-king-sized bed with high-end fitted wardrobes around two sides.

As they entered, Melody was still in full flow. 'The decor in this room is *adorable*, don't you think? We found this simply excellent designer over in Twickenham who took care of everything. And it was her idea too that we should install a panic room. Apparently all of us celebs should have one, that's what she said. A wise precaution don't you think? The door leads off the en-suite and it's impregnable, I'm told. We've never had to use it of course, thankfully.'

A young woman in a pink apron holding a cleaning spray and cloth emerged from the en-suite. She smiled and greeted her employer in a thick East European accent.

'Good morning Miss Montague.'

'Good morning Bridget. This is Bridget, she's from Latvia or Lithuania, I always get them mixed up. She cooks and cleans for us. She lives in with her husband Gregor who looks after the house and the garden. I simply don't know *what* we would do without them.' Jesus, thought Maggie, domestic staff? Who can afford them nowadays? And a panic room, for god's sake. How the other half lives.

'I never had nothing like this, growing up of course,' Melody continued. 'My dad walked out when I was three years old and we never saw him again, me and my brothers. My mum took to the drink after that. Killed her in the end it did. And then we were taken into care.'

'I didn't know that,' Asvina said sympathetically. 'It must have been awful for you.'

'Yeah, it was. But I'm a survivor. We all were, me and my brothers.'

Maggie too didn't know about Melody's tough upbringing, but she could see how it perhaps explained her desire to build a little family with Benjamin Fox. And when that fell apart, to try again with Danny Black, hope triumphing once more over experience. As if she was anyone to talk, knowing now that it was only the ticking of her own biological clock that had persuaded her that marrying Philip would be a good idea. But at least she had Ollie, and for that reason and that reason alone it had been worth it. But she wasn't here to reflect on her own car-crash personal life. There was business to be attended to.

'Melody, I hope you don't mind me bringing this up, but you will be pleased to hear that Benjamin's sister seems to corroborate your version of events with regard to the intention of the original pre-nuptial agreement. It's not something that could be used in any court proceedings being only hearsay, but it suggests Benjamin may not have been entirely truthful with us.'

'Bridget, can you give us a moment.' She sat down on the edge of the bed, took a sip of her champagne and gave a cold smile. 'So he's been found out. I *am* pleased about that.'

'There is a complication though,' Maggie said. 'Although we haven't seen it yet, Charles Grant told us he has a copy of the agreement too. And that one apparently supports your ex-husband's story. And there is also your solicitor Mr McCartney, whose also I believe supports Benjamin's version.'

Melody spoke sharply. 'Then they must be lying too. Both of them.'

She took a cigarette from the pack that lay on the bedside table and rummaged through her bag looking for a lighter.

Her hand trembling, she finally managed to light the cigarette.

'I hate smoking in here,' she said distractedly.

Maggie frowned. 'I was thinking, and I accept he may not be the most credible witness, that we could perhaps speak to McCartney in prison. Do you think he might be prepared to do that?'

She shrugged. 'That bastard? How should I know.'

'But he is likely to remember drawing up the agreement and what it contained?'

'Suppose so,' Melody said. 'But if you want to try that, you'd be better to send Jimmy. Blake will think all his Christmases have come at once.'

'So he's gay?' Maggie asked. Not that it mattered, although she wasn't sure if Jimmy would feel the same way when she explained what she would like him to do.

'As they come,' Melody said. 'I'm sure he's very popular in that nick.'

Maggie gave her an uncertain look. 'Well I'm not sure about that. But yes, I think we will try and visit him and see if he is able to help us. But coming back to Mr Fox, there's just one more thing I'd like to ask you.'

'What?' She shot out the word, her growing irritation evident.

'Benjamin mentioned something about a little arrangement he had with you. Can you tell me what that might refer to?'

'I've no idea. There was no arrangement with Benjamin,' she replied coldly. 'Have you any idea what it was like for me, finding out that my husband was... was *sterile*. It ruined everything, all my dreams. I hated him for it. So no, there was no *arrangement*. I just wanted him out of my life as quickly as possible.'

'Look I'm sorry,' Maggie said, shocked by the coldness of this woman. Was that all the marriage had meant to her, simply a breeding arrangement? If so, perhaps it wasn't a surprise that Benjamin had bailed out when he met the beautiful Allegra Ross. 'I didn't mean to stir up bad memories. It must have been very painful for you.'

Melody gave her a disdainful look. 'Painful, is that what you call it? Finding out you'd wasted four precious years, years you can never get back? Oh yes, it was painful all right.'

She could tell the actress was growing tired of the conversation.

'Very well,' Maggie said. 'We will see what Mr McCartney and Mr Grant have to say and then maybe we might be able to tidy up this matter to your satisfaction.'

Melody fixed her stare on Asvina, ignoring Maggie. 'That's why I'm paying you your ridiculous fee Miss Rani,' she spat. 'You need to fix this. Just bloody fix it, understand? Or I'll fix it myself. Now if you will excuse me, I need to get back to my guests.'

***

Back in the garden, the band was tuning up whilst the pretty girl vocalist anxiously studied her lyric sheets in a final attempt to commit them to memory. The younger kids, boys and girls alike, had formed themselves into a human snake some twenty strong and were now doing a conga around the garden accompanied by loud shrieks.

'Met your hero then, did you?' Maggie asked Jimmy. 'What's he like?'

'Pretty normal guy, I suppose. Good with the kids too. Got some nice pictures.'

'They'll be talking about this for months,' laughed Asvina.

'Yeah, but our Melody's not too happy,' Maggie said. 'Suddenly went mental, saying she was paying Asvina to fix all this, and if she didn't, she would do it herself, whatever that means. A bit scary to be honest.'

Asvina seemed unconcerned. 'Well believe me, I've had scarier clients than her. It will all blow over I'm sure.'

Jimmy gave a wry look. 'I don't know, she's certainly a scary woman.'

'But vulnerable too, I think,' Maggie said. 'She told us about her tough upbringing. That kind of experience must shape you for life.'

And now here she was again, investing all her hopes and dreams in a new man. Maggie didn't like the woman, but she found herself praying that this time it would all work out.

It wouldn't.

Chapter 15

In Frank's world, events were moving slowly, but he wasn't bothered about that, because in his head, the flaky hypothesis that he hoped might form the bedrock of Operation Shark was beginning to look a bit less flaky. Now there was news of an abduction of startling similarity to the Jamie Grant incident, and that was progress, no doubt about it. It had been a hunch and he had learned if not to trust his hunches completely, then at least to give them a decent shot.

A fair result, but he knew it was just one more piece in the jigsaw. Admittedly, it was shaping up to be a thousand-piece puzzle but figuratively he felt that he had now completed the border, and as all jigsawists knew, things always started to accelerate once you had the border in place. Now he judged it was time to have a wee word with his boss DCI Jill Smart. Jill was the gate-keeper between half-arsed conspiracy-theory bollocks and a live grown-up investigation, with an official case number and all that went with it. With a case number, you could pull together a team, you could bring suspects in for questioning, you had access to a full range of technical support services far beyond what Eleanor Campbell alone could provide. You could even call in a press officer to spout nonsense at the media if you wanted to. The only problem was, Jill Smart guarded case numbers with her life. Because once an investigation got a case number, it had broken cover from the murky secretive world of Department 12B and was out in the open for all to see. Specifically, it got onto the spreadsheets of Chief Superintendents and Assistant Commissioners, target-driven automatons obsessed with clear-up rates who asked awkward questions like why so much money was being spent on a case and why hadn't it been solved yet even when it had only been running for a week. A case number caused Jill a whole heap of hassle and so generally, she didn't give one up without a fight. Even to Frank Stewart, who was the only detective in the department she trusted.

And making the mission a whole order of magnitude more difficult was the fact that he had already suffered a bit of a set-back, when Eleanor's facial-recognition sweep of the world wide web had drawn a complete blank. The kid in Fox's photograph hadn't shown up, the problem being, as she had explained in her customary teacher-to-six-year-old manner that she always adopted when speaking to Frank, was that all the commercial recognition capability like Google and Facebook purposely did not work for children, for obvious reasons. On top of that, the GCHQ citizens' database, which by the way did not officially exist, did not hold details of citizens under the age of eleven.

Nonetheless he was determined to persevere, this time deciding to make his pitch in person rather than on the phone, reasoning he needed to see the whites of her eyes to judge how well he was doing. And they had much better coffee over at Paddington Green, properly expensive barista stuff with a rich nutty aroma that pervaded the whole building. As ever, the car park had been rammed, but as he never bothered to find a space on his visits anyway, it had been no effort to dump the battered Mondeo as close to the door as possible and block in the sleek Beemers and Audis which were the public-purse provided rides of the most senior officers. He reasoned that since they were supposedly the smartest detectives on the force, it shouldn't tax them too much to find out whose motor it was if they wanted out.

DCI Smart occupied a cramped office on the third floor, overlooking the rear car park. Originally, she had been given a nice big one in the corner but DCI Colin Barker had objected, citing his longer service as a reason why it should be allocated to him. Cannily, Jill had acceded to the petty request. Everyone in the force thought Barker an arse, and this was just adding one more instance to the charge-sheet. God knows he'd been lucky to survive screwing up that Alzahrani terrorist case, and she figured he was now in the last-chance saloon. It was probably one more strike and he'd be out. And when that happened, she would move back into it before anyone else could grab it.

Today, however, nobody was in their offices, large or small. A desk in the middle of the vast open-plan space was piled with supermarket-bought cakes and savouries and all around the floor, officers were milling around, laughing and swigging bottled beer. Scanning the scene, Frank spotted his boss and made his way to her.

'Morning ma'am, so what's going on here? Somebody won the lottery?'

She laughed. 'Worse than that Frank. Barker's solved the Ross and Fox murders. They've been with the CPS team all morning and they've just given the go-ahead to prosecute.'

'What, he's solved the bloody thing in three weeks?' It was like hearing a supermodel saying she had brokered a Middle-East peace deal on a night out. 'No chance. Some poor innocent's been fitted up, more like.'

'Yes, well normally I would agree with you, but it seems on this occasion we may have to give him some credit. It does look like an open and shut case to me.'

Frank frowned and shook his head. 'Come on ma'am, you and I both know there's no such thing as an open and shut case where Colin Barker's involved. It never is, and it never will be.'

'Jealousy and bitterness aren't a good look you know.'

'I'm not jealous or bitter,' he lied. 'So come on, what's the story? And is it all right if I grab a beer?'

Jill smiled. 'Yes, of course, and I'll have one too. To commiserate of course, not to celebrate.'

Frank sauntered over to the desk, picked up a couple of beers and scooped a large chocolate brownie onto a paper plate. His super-skinny boss basically didn't eat so he knew she wouldn't think him selfish.

'So,' he said through a mouthful of dark crumbs, 'let's hear about how the genius detective did it. I'm all ears.'

She took a sip from her beer before continuing. 'It's that guy you had the run-in with at the Hyde Park demo.'

'What, Darren Venables? No way. Absolutely no way.'

'Way,' she said. 'Because Barker's team have worked out what Leonardo is all about, and that led them straight to him.'

'No way,' he repeated, conscious of the sinking feeling in his stomach. 'Come on ma'am, you know this can't be true.'

'I'm afraid it is,' she said. 'It looks that way to me.'

'Really ma'am? I know Venables is a piece of shit but I don't see him killing someone in the name of his poxy little party.'

But he knew in his heart that wasn't quite true. Venables and his White British League thugs were dangerous fanatics, and well capable of murder in pursuit of their deluded cause. It was just that he considered Venables, the history don turned champion of the neglected white working-class, to be too smart to do any of the dirty work himself.

'They had been looking at some of his published papers from his time in academia,' Jill said in way of explanation. 'You know he was a professor of history or something? At Oxford.'

'Well I'm not sure he was actually a professor. I think he was a reader, that's what they called it. That was until he got hounded out by the student body for not conforming to their narrow wee view of the world. Turned him a bit bitter after that.'

After arresting him, Frank had, out of interest, taken the trouble to read quite a few of the published papers of Mr Venables. The man's worldview was simple and unwavering. Socialist governments screw everything up and in particular, crush progress and innovation. Under socialism, according to D-V, there would have been no Einstein, no Henry Ford, no Crick and Watson. And, according to a particularly vituperative polemic he'd published a few years back, no Leonardo da Vinci either.

Jill laughed. 'Frank Stewart, I didn't see you as a foot soldier in the class war.'

'No no, don't get me wrong, he was an arse then, and he still is. But you've heard the old saying along the lines of I don't like what you're saying but I defend your right to say it?

I kind of believe in it, that's all. But anyway, let's hear what you've got.'

'Well I know it's not your thing Frank, but it all hinges around Venables' social media and something he posted in response to a Charles Grant twitter message. Something that was mirrored in some of his academic work.'

Frank's eyes narrowed. 'Ok....'

'So obviously Barker's team have been interviewing friends and associates of the victim. And when they interviewed Charles Grant, he told them about a post Venables had made just after his son was abducted. *Commie bastards always get what they deserve.* He also told them he had been a victim of a long-running campaign of harassment by someone using the name da Vinci.'

'Aye, I've heard all about that.' Although he hadn't mentioned to Jill that he was intending to find out for himself who was behind it. Now he wished he'd made more effort to chivvy Eleanor Campbell along with her investigations.

'Really?' she said, surprised. 'Well anyway, Grant said he had his suspicions and was now pretty sure that it was Venables. You know, D-V is his nickname, and so there's the link to da Vinci. And that of course gave the connection to Leonardo.'

Frank was getting that sinking feeling he always got when a precious theory crumbled to dust before his eyes. The theory that Venables hadn't even been a suspect for the murder, let alone the killer.

'But come on ma'am, that's totally circumstantial, if it can even be described as that. Even by Barker standards, it's a massive pile of crap. I mean, who's going to write their bloody name on a victim, even if it is just a bloody nickname?'

She nodded. 'Well this *is* a Colin case, so the case is always going to be flimsy, but the CPS have passed it so I guess it must be half-credible.'

'Half-credible?' Frank said bitterly. 'That's all they need nowadays is it?'

'Don't be so cynical until you've heard everything,' she replied. 'So firstly, it turns out that Venables was seen at the awards ceremony where Fox died. You know what that means don't you? That they can place him at the scene of the crime. And they've checked his alibi and he hasn't got one.'

Frank was struggling to process what he'd just heard. 'So come on, how did Venables explain that away?'

Jill gave a half-smile. 'He said he'd gone with the intention of apologising to Fox and Allegra Ross for what had happened at the Hyde Park rally. Complete rubbish of course, especially in light of the other things Barker's team found.'

'What other things?' Frank said despondently. 'What other things?'

'They found his fingerprints on Allegra Ross's front door. And there was a note. A threatening note, pushed through her door.'

'No way.'

'I wish you would stop saying that Frank,' Jill said irritably. 'Yes, it is the case. A note, printed on A4 paper and bearing the symbol of the White British League. It was addressed specifically to Allegra and bore the message *commie bastards always get what they deserve*. And for the record, Venables has been unable to produce a verifiable alibi to cover the time window of the Parsons Green killing either.'

'But if he *did* do it, and I'm not suggesting for a minute he did, I ask again. Why would he leave that message on the hands? Or any message at all?'

But as he said it, he could hear himself answering that question. Because Venables was an arrogant self-regarding little shit and it would be entirely in keeping with his character to leave some sort of calling card. If he'd done it, that was. Which of course he hadn't. *No way*.

But now could feel himself boiling up inside, and he recognised at least one of the reasons. He was angry at himself for his arrogance in assuming that only he could solve this case, and although he hated to admit *this*, there was anger and no little hint of envy that his nemesis had somehow outsmarted him.

The problem was, anger was never a good thing when he was within punching distance of DCI Barker. The last time he got so mad, bad things happened. But where was the fat arse? He must be here somewhere, it wasn't as if he was going to be absent for his big moment of glory. Yep, there he was, in the corner office, with a stupid grin on his face as he arse-licked a couple of the top brass. Two Assistant Commissioners, no less. No wonder he wasn't out on the floor sharing a spicy samosa with the *hoi polloi*. Glancing over, he caught sight of Frank and gave a barely-disguised look of disgust, before returning to his arse-licking.

'Don't do anything stupid Frank,' Jill said, clearly alarmed. She was smiling but the message was serious. 'It doesn't reflect well on the department, or me.'

'No, don't worry boss, I've learned my lesson,' he lied. 'Anyway, the real reason I came here was to talk to you about a case, you know, the one I mentioned on the phone. Operation Shark. The Jamie Grant abduction.'

But now his heart wasn't really in it.

***

So that was it then. No case number today, even though he'd told her about the Kitty Lawrence snatch and how it was almost identical to the Jamie Grant incident. *Ok, good work, but I need more than just some case that happens to have the same MO.* That's what Jill had said, and he couldn't really blame her.

And now against all odds Barker appeared to have solved the Ross/Fox case and the brass were going to make sure that it didn't get unsolved by some backwater has-been from Atlee House. The more he thought about it the more it became apparent that the evidence was shite, flimsier than a house of cards. *Leonardo leading to da Vinci, da Vinci leading to Darren Venables?* Even bloody Agatha Christie would have thought twice before coming up with that one. It was all wrong, Frank knew that, but there was zero chance of him influencing the course of events now.

So this morning had been a set-back, undoubtedly, but a few pints in the Kings Head and a good night's sleep would soon see off his temporary melancholy. Maybe Darren Venables was guilty, maybe he wasn't, but there was still plenty about the Fox and Ross murders that didn't add up. The mysterious little agreement Fox had with his ex-wife that had ended his relationship with his new girlfriend. *Everything is ruined*. That's what Allegra had said, so it must have been something bloody serious. And then there was that bust-up with the scriptwriter that Maggie and Jimmy had told him about. They might just be loose ends, but they would need to be followed up. But at least when he got back to Atlee House he would have something to write on that wee blank label stuck to the front of that new folder. And this was a code name, though obvious, he rather liked.

The Leonardo Murders.

Chapter 16

It was about a three and half mile walk from their Fleet Street office up to HMP Pentonville on the Caledonian Road, but Jimmy was glad of the exercise. He'd let himself go a bit since he left the army, there was no doubt of that, but whereas when you were out in Iraq or Afghanistan maintaining peak fitness could be a matter of life or death, it wasn't such a big deal in London EC4. As an interim private investigator, which is how he would describe the current stage of his career, it didn't really matter if you had the odd beer or two or mainlined on stuffed pizza. And he felt he could carry a bit of excess baggage, an advantage of being broadly-built and six foot two into the bargain. Nonetheless he recognised a slippery slope when he was sliding down it, and accordingly put on a bit of pace as he headed northwards up Farringdon Street.

He reflected that today's mission was likely to prove difficult to execute, if not impossible, a pattern in his employment with Miss Maggie Bainbridge he was beginning to recognise. Generally, her mission statements were terse to the point of non-existent. *Get a copy of the pre-nup from Benjamin Fox* or *break into a locked down crime-scene and see what you can find,* or this one, *ask the disgraced Blake McCartney to sign an affidavit saying he did actually draw up that bloody pre-nup in the way Melody said.* God, even in Helmand they sometimes gathered you in a room and gave you an hour's briefing in advance of sending you into action. Though to be fair, that would be the exception not the rule. But there was no arguing with the fact that Maggie Bainbridge would have made Major-General if she'd been in the army. Dish out the orders and let the poor bloody other ranks work out the details, that was the *modus operandi*. She was a natural.

Still, his mood remained upbeat as he approached the foreboding gates of the Victorian prison. Sure, the chances of success were two-thirds of not very much at all, but it would be fascinating in itself to see the inside of a jail, especially one that had opened as long ago as eighteen forty-eight, and McCartney sounded like an interesting character.

Signage directed visitors to a stark reception room where uniformed staff sat behind a glass panel, ignoring the assembling friends and family whilst they stared morosely at their computer screens. Every few minutes a name would be flashed up on a display screen and a guard would appear to lead the visitor into the search suite, where hi-tech scanning equipment was combined with a low-tech and highly invasive manual search by the assigned prison officer. It took nearly twenty minutes before the name 'Stewart, James' came up. A few seconds later, the automated door clicked and opened, and a hatchet-faced female officer emerged from the back office. At least, she was hatchet-faced until she caught sight of Jimmy.

'Nice day for a visit,' she said breezily, as she led him into a small windowless room, the walls painted a dull grey and harshly illuminated by a bank of fluorescent tubes. 'My name's Amanda Fletcher by the way. *Miss* Amanda Fletcher. I hope you don't mind being searched by a female officer today, but you see we're a bit short-staffed.' By her expression he gathered that whatever he thought about it, she herself was very much looking forward to it.

She handed him a large transparent plastic bag. 'Everything goes in there. Keys, coins, your wallet, your phone. Oh yes, and your trouser belt of course.' He was just waiting for her to offer to remove it for him.

He estimated her to be in her early forties, quite attractive but hard-looking, her hair bleach-blonde and eyes heavily-lined with black mascara. She looked as if she worked out too, her figure well-defined under the tight-fitting white shirt. A younger version of Melody Montague, that's who she reminded him of, and probably just as dangerous. Especially as it seemed they were to be on first-name terms.

And was it his imagination, but was the body search taking longer than strictly necessary? As she ran her hands methodically over his body - too methodically he thought, reaching places where he would have preferred her not to go

- she kept up a running commentary describing conditions past and present in the prison. To Jimmy's amusement, it sounded rather like the chat you got from your tour rep on the airport coach on the way to your summer-sun hotel.

'Drones is the big thing at the moment,' she was saying. 'They can fly in all sorts with them. Drugs, mobiles, knives, razors, you name it. They even got a gun in once, can you believe? Can't seem to stop them, no matter what we does. And violence, there's a lot of trouble in this prison, I can tell you. We're in the top five in the country for that. Stabbings, slashings, we get it all here.' She made it sound like a badge of honour.

'That's why our searches have to be so thorough of course,' she said, in belated apology.

'That's ok Amanda, I understand.'

'Course you probably don't need to worry so much in B Block. That's where your McCartney is. Mainly white collar, pimps, fraudsters and con-men and the like.'

'And bent solicitors,' Jimmy said.

'Yeah, exactly. We don't get no trouble with them because we just threaten them with a move to A Block.'

'A Block?'

'Yeah, that's right. That's where all the hard men are kept. Murderers and gangsters, every one of them. Mental cases. I wouldn't like to work there, although of course they don't allow no female staff.'

But now it seemed that the search was completed to her satisfaction. She smiled at him and said,

'Well, you're clean. So this is your first time, right?'

Jimmy nodded.

'Right, well you keep your hands on the table where the officers can see them and no touching, ok?' She gave him a lascivious wink. 'Although I think Mr McCartney is going to have his work cut out to keep his hands off *you*. Yeah, I can see you being his night-time fantasy for the next twelve months at least.'

Brilliant, so that was another thing that Maggie had failed to mention in the mission briefing.

***

Fletcher had escorted him to a set of double doors with a sign above that read 'Gymnasium.' Observing his puzzled look, she said, 'Yeah, it ain't been a gym for more than twenty years. The prisoners have got a fancy place now over in the new East Wing. State of the art of course, whilst us guards get a load of old shit stuff over in our welfare building.' The bitterness sounded well-rehearsed, a grievance that he expected was shared with anyone who would listen. 'So anyways, I'll just drop you off with Andy at the door and then I'll be back to fetch you when you're done. You only get twenty minutes because you're not family.' She gave him a cheeky smile. 'And remember, no holding hands.'

The room looked just as he imagined, with wooden parquet flooring and narrow windows that were set just below the high ceiling. It reminded him exactly of his old school assembly hall back in Glasgow. Three prison officers were hanging around just inside the doorway, chatting and laughing.

'I'm looking for Blake McCartney please,' Jimmy asked the one Amanda had identified as Andy.

'Sure, no problem mate,' he answered pleasantly, and led him to a table in the middle of the room occupied by a slightly-built man who looked well into his sixties although Jimmy knew he had barely turned fifty.

'Well well McCartney, here's a turn up for the books. Someone actually wants to see you.'

'Thank you Mr Smith,' he replied, without apparent rancour, then nodded at Jimmy. 'Sit down please, make yourself comfortable. I'd shake your hand, but it's not allowed. He's a decent screw that Andy Smith actually. Slips me the odd fag and gets my mobile topped up although he charges the earth for it. We're not supposed to have them of course.' From his lack of discretion, Jimmy assumed that the authorities must turn a blind eye to these activities. Probably preserving the peace was given higher priority and he didn't blame them for that.

He placed his hands in front of him as he had been instructed then said, 'I think you might have had a note from Melody, explaining what I wanted to talk to you about?'

'Oh it's Melody now is it?' he said bitterly. 'So now she's Miss La-De-Dah? But I suppose old Blake's not good enough for Roxy now. She was always Roxy to me, ever since we were kids. She's a Kemp you know. Roxy Kemp. Did you know that?'

'Yes I did,' Jimmy said, 'but I don't know much about the family.'

'Yeah well I do,' he said, reducing his voice to a whisper. 'If you knew what I done for them Kemps over the years. Got them out of all sorts of scrapes I did, and risking my reputation all the time.' Jimmy thought it unlikely that he had much of a reputation to risk, but he didn't say anything. In any case, McCartney was still in full flow.

'But do you think they supported me when I got into my little bit of difficulty? Did they hell. All I had was some cash flow problems which a few grand would have sorted out, but did they put their hands in their pockets, them Kemps? Did they hell. And so here I am, banged up for five years, and me an innocent man as well. It's a travesty of justice, that's all I can say. A travesty.'

Jimmy was conscious of the limited time he had to complete his mission and was already concerned that McCartney's venting of his grievances with the Kemps might easily take up the entire twenty minutes.

'Look Mr McCartney...'

'Blake, please.' He smiled what he no doubt imagined was a seductive smile, which caused Jimmy to mentally grimace, although he managed to hide it.

'Aye, so Blake, what I wanted to talk to you about is the pre-nuptial agreement you drew up for Melody - I mean Roxy - and her husband Benjamin Fox. About four years ago it would have been. I wondered if you remember it.'

He screwed up his face, stroking his chin. 'Let me think. A pre-nuptial did you say? I used to do a lot of them, make no mistake. A lot of my clients were minted you see, and well, you need to protect yourself if you're in that income bracket, don't you? But Roxy and that Fox guy? Yeah, course I remember that one. Sure I do. So what can I help you with in that regard?'

Jimmy gave him a sharp look. 'Well according to Roxy, it's gone missing. You told her you misplaced it during what you call your business difficulties. Is that right?'

He averted his eyes, staring down at the floor. 'Did I? Well you know, that time was all a bit of a blur I'm afraid. We had some stuff I thought we'd better get rid of quick, and, well to tell the truth I think it got mixed up with all that.'

'Brilliant,' Jimmy said wryly. 'So let me ask, do you remember the broad terms of that deal? I assume you do, given you had no trouble remembering drawing the thing up in the first place.'

He nodded. 'Yeah, I remember it no trouble. It was about a three quarters split in favour of Mr Fox. Or something along those lines. Yeah, that was it.'

'Are you sure?' Jimmy said, surprised. 'Because Roxy says otherwise. The exact opposite in fact.'

He shrugged. 'I can't help that, can I? She must have misremembered, that's all.'

'But she's quite clear about it. It was signed in your office, in the presence of two witnesses, and Benjamin himself of course.' He didn't tell him that Charles Grant had corroborated Fox's version of the bloody document, although they were still waiting to see the proof of that.

McCartney gave a short laugh. 'Yeah, but he's dead isn't he? Nasty sod. Good riddance to him, that's what I say.'

'So you knew him did you?'

Blake nodded. 'Yeah, a bit. As I said, me and Roxy go way back. I was at the wedding as it happened.'

'And I'm taking it you didn't like him?'

'Yeah, you could say that,' McCartney answered, his tone sardonic. 'Up himself and always on the piss too. I've no idea why she married him. In fact I thought he might be gay, 'cos you should have seen the way he used to look at me. And we always know, don't we?'

Having some knowledge of the kind of nights Fox had been having with Allegra Ross, Jimmy had to question the accuracy of McCartney's analysis. But irrespective of that, it was pretty clear that the conversation wasn't going anywhere. At least not in a direction that would please their client Miss Montague.

He smiled, adopting a conciliatory tone.

'Whether our boy Benjy preferred men or women is not really any concern of mine Blake. I just came here to try and sort out the pre-nup business and you've helped me do that, so thanks.' Not that he had helped at all, but there was nothing to be gained by saying it.

McCartney relaxed back in his seat, evidently glad that the subject of the conversation was about to change.

'Well, that's ok then. So, if we're done... I'm a busy man you know.' He gave a low cackle at his own joke.

'Just one more thing before I go,' Jimmy said pleasantly. 'Did you know Kylie Ward?'

His eyes narrowed. 'Who?'

'Kylie Ward. She was the young woman who was the other witness to the agreement.'

He gave Jimmy a wary look. 'She's dead too, isn't she? An accident, just a few months ago. I think I read about it.'

'So you remember her then?' Jimmy said quietly.

'Not really. I think we only met that once.'

And then something came to Jimmy, something he and Maggie should have thought of before.

'Blake, has it occurred to you how convenient it was for Fox that Kylie's not around to give her version of events?'

'What're you suggesting?' he blustered, his voice rising to a shout. 'I don't know nothing about that, and that's the truth.'

Out of the corner of his eye, Jimmy could see Andy the prison officer approaching them, alerted by McCartney's eruption.

'Right sir,' he said politely but firmly. 'Time to wrap up. Come with me please.'

As Jimmy got up to leave, McCartney, evidently regretting his outburst, said.

'Look I'm sorry you didn't get what you came for. It ain't my fault if the agreement got misplaced. But it was nice Jimmy. I don't get many visitors. You're welcome to come back any time you want.' His eyes were pleading, like a dog begging for walkies.

'Sure, that would be great,' Jimmy lied. 'So take care, see you again mate.'

Prison Officer Amanda Fletcher was waiting for him in the hallway as scheduled.

'This way,' she said, pointing to the large sign marked *exit*. 'Sad bastard isn't he? All we ever hear from him is how he's innocent and how the Kemps done him down. I expect you got some of that, did you?'

Jimmy laughed. 'Aye, big time. He would have gone on all day if I'd let him I think.'

'Yeah, he would have. But I bet that was a treat for him. The poor guy doesn't get many visitors. His old mum came down from Liverpool a few weeks ago, but that's about it. Although strange to say he did get a visit from that one from Bow Road a couple of months back. You know, the soap on telly? Said they were old mates.'

Jimmy raised an eyebrow. 'What, Melody Montague was here? She never told me that.'

She gave him a puzzled look. 'Nah, it wasn't her. It was that guy, the one whose son's missing. You know, Charles Grant.'

Charles Grant. What the hell had he been doing here? What with his social media spats and now this, Mr Grant had a few questions to answer, make no mistake. And then there was McCartney's surprising reaction when the death of Kylie Ward was brought up. Did he know something, something he wasn't telling? Perhaps if they figured out what that was, they might start to make some progress at last.

Still distracted by his musings, he became vaguely aware that Amanda was still speaking.

'Look, if you want to visit again, there's no need to go through the official channels,' she was saying. 'Just give me a call, I'll give you my mobile. Here, I'll write it on your hand.'

Chapter 17

It was only a couple of weeks since they had taken on the Charles Grant case, advisedly or otherwise, but regular progress meetings had been part of the arrangement and the first of them had now fallen due. And what a momentous period it had been with the brutal murders of Benjamin Fox and Allegra Ross still front page news in every paper. Maggie and Jimmy had learnt from Frank that Darren Venables of the White British League had been arrested for the crime, but all the media had been told at this stage was that a forty-six-year-old man was helping them with their enquiries. Reflecting the priorities of their readership, the entertainment correspondents seemed more concerned with the impact of the killings on Bow Road, speculating how the writers would deal with the loss of two of its leading characters. And now Maggie and Jimmy recognised they would need to watch what they said in front of Grant, knowing his link to Venables, however tenuous it might be.

They had offered to meet him for lunch, forgetting that eating in public could often be more pain than pleasure for those in the public eye, so instead agreed that he would come into their office at around eleven.

'And no selfies,' Jimmy had said to Elsa as he arrived earlier that morning, but he needn't have worried since she claimed never to have heard of Grant.

The actor arrived promptly, the young receptionist ushering him through to one of the office suite's shared meeting rooms.

'I've booked it for an hour,' Maggie said, smiling. 'Should be enough I would think.'

He nodded. 'I guess that means there's not been much progress?'

'To be fair, it's only been a couple of weeks,' Jimmy said, 'but actually we have got some ideas. Although it's early days it's not looking unpromising.'

Early days was one of his brother's favourite sayings, although Frank seemed to describe every case as being in its early days until five minutes before he solved it.

'Yes,' Maggie said, 'so I think I'm right in saying that from the start, the police always assumed it was about the ransom. You were targeted because you are a famous actor and they assumed therefore that you would be able to raise the kind of sum they were looking for '

Grant shrugged. 'Yes, well that's what the police thought. What else could it be?'

'And you definitely had no reason to think otherwise?' Jimmy asked.

He shook his head. 'No, why should I have?'

Maggie gave him an uncertain look.

'It's just that looking at your social media postings and your Guardian pieces, you're an advocate of what I think is described as progressive politics, is that right?'

The question did not seem to perturb Grant.

'Yes, that's correct. I've always been a strong supporter of the fight against inequality. It's in my DNA I think.' To Maggie's mind, there was more than a hint of superiority in the way he said it.

'But we can't help but notice that you seem to attract some pretty vitriolic trolling online,' Jimmy said. 'Doesn't it bother you?'

'On the contrary,' he replied, 'the far-right idiots hate to see their world view being challenged. I see it as my duty to do so. But I have to ask, why are you so interested in my political views?'

'I'm not sure how to put this diplomatically Charles,' Jimmy said, 'but you do seem to have made some quite vicious enemies.'

Grant sighed. 'Ah, I assume you must be talking about the cowardly da Vinci. Yes, he does seem to get particularly angry, which makes me assume he is some pathetic inadequate holed up in a ghastly bed-sit in Streatham or somewhere equally horrid.'

'And you're sure it's a he?' Jimmy asked.

'Oh yes, I'm quite sure it's a he. Women tend to be much more polite and usually choose an identifiable user name like JaneX or suchlike. But, tell me, where are we going with this?'

Maggie frowned. 'We're not sure. But it presents a possible motive that wasn't considered in the original case, so we think it is worth looking into.'

'What, some sort of far-right plot directed at little old me?' He sounded sceptical.

'Why not?' she said. 'There are people out there with extreme views and violence is in *their* DNA. So yes, it is something we at least want to explore.'

Including finding out who the hell da Vinci was, although that wasn't something she was going to promise her client right now. That would depend on Frank and his tame forensic officer. But of course, it wasn't difficult to have an intelligent guess of who it *might* be.

'You don't think it could be the work of Darren Venables, do you? He's known as D-V, isn't he? And we know that he made a particularly nasty comment on your social media just after Jamie was taken.'

Grant shook his head. 'Well, it did cross my mind, and in fact I did tell the police of my suspicions when they interviewed me in connection with Benjamin's killing. But afterwards I was not so sure. You see, I think Mr Venables is too full of himself to hide behind a *nom de plume.*'

The same thought had occurred to Maggie, but she was amused to hear this evidently self-regarding man attribute the same traits of vanity to someone whose views were opposed to his own in every way.

'I tend to agree with you,' she said, 'but da Vinci is very persistent isn't he? Because his activities have been going on for several years as I understand it.'

His tone was dismissive. 'Well, as I said, I'm sure he's just some inadequate holed up in a garret somewhere. I don't allow his activities as you call them to distract me from my very important work in the fight for equality.'

She shot Jimmy a raised eyebrow but made no comment. Instead she asked,

'And can I ask you about your relationship with Benjamin Fox? Were you friends, away from the show I mean?'

'Not really,' Grant said matter-of-factly. 'I presume you are asking because you have found out about our little quarrel last year. I admit I may have been rather sharp with him, but surely you can see how it might hurt our cause when we have rather minor celebrities jumping on the bandwagon simply for the publicity?'

'And how did Mr Fox feel about that?' Jimmy asked. 'Not too pleased I would imagine. And yet it didn't stop him turning up to speak at the Hyde Park rally last month, did it?'

'I don't wish to speak ill of the dead,' Grant said, 'but, really, I rest my case. Benjamin and Miss Ross were hardly likely to turn down such a prestigious opportunity to display their virtue in public, now were they?'

Maggie gave him a look that betrayed her surprise. 'They were *murdered* Mr Grant, and yet that doesn't seem to be causing you the least concern.' He was a client and she knew she ought not to speak to him in that manner, but it was hard not to, given the breathtaking narcissism of the man.

'It is a terrible tragedy of course. I'm sorry if I don't sound more regretful, but I didn't like either of them. They were very average actors in my opinion.'

'Yet you were a witness to Benjamin Fox's pre-nuptial agreement.'

He shrugged. 'That was a long time ago. Besides, that was purely business. And with regard to that matter, I've brought along my copy of the document.' He removed a slim booklet from the folder he was carrying and passed it across to them. 'You are welcome to keep it. It's of no use to me.'

Maggie picked up the document, and riffled through it until she came to the page that laid out the terms of the agreement. There was no doubt about it, none whatsoever. Benjamin Fox was due seventy-five percent of the marital assets, and in the absence of Melody Montague's copy, there was nothing to say otherwise. Except that Fox wasn't around to reap the benefit. Now she presumed the estate would pass to his sister Edwina. And one thing was certain. *She* hadn't murdered him, being five thousand miles away at the time of his death. But there would be plenty of opportunity to consider all of that later.

'Well, it does seem to support what Benjamin told us,' Maggie said. 'Now there's just one more thing maybe you can help us with. Blake McCartney. Why did you visit him in prison?'

Grant peered at her over his glasses. 'Who says I did?'

'I visited him myself,' Jimmy said. 'To see what he knew about the pre-nup. And when I was leaving, a prison officer told me you'd been to see him.'

'Ah well, I've been found out then,' he answered, quite calmly. 'Before his imprisonment, he had been helping me with a contractual matter with regard to some corporate work I was doing. But I fell out with the client and was anxious to understand if I had any redress under the contract. You see, in this case I had lodged the only copy of the agreement with him. That was a mistake which I will not repeat.'

It sounded half-plausible to Maggie, especially the bit about him falling out with his client.

'And was he able to help you?'

'No. He could not recall any of the detailed terms and conditions I'm afraid.'

'And yet, you visited him twice.'

Grant gave a rueful look. 'Yes, and what a waste of time that was. You see, on my first visit he promised he would have something for me next time, but he hadn't. I think he just said it so that I would come back. So that he could get out of his cell for an hour. He doesn't get many visitors you see.'

Jimmy gave a wry smile. 'Aye, he does seem to be Billy no-mates. But actually, there was one thing that struck me as odd. I asked him about Kylie Ward. He behaved very oddly when I mentioned her name. Why do you think that was?'

'I really can't help you with that,' Grant said impassively. 'As I said, I only met McCartney three times including when I witnessed the agreement, and her just once. But he is an untrustworthy little man in all respects so nothing would surprise me about him.'

Evidently he was now anxious to draw the meeting to a close. 'Look, I'd like to help you but really there's nothing I can add. Now, if there's nothing else, I've got a lunch appointment.'

'Yes, I think we're probably done for today,' Maggie said, reflecting that their client seemed to have quickly overcome his aversion for dining in public, 'and obviously if anything turns up before our next meeting I will let you know. So enjoy your lunch. Going anywhere special?'

Grant laughed. 'Oh goodness no, I'm not going to a *restaurant*. Sharon is cooking for me. At her flat. She's a very good cook, and I expect we will have a lovely lunch and then, well, what could be a better than a little spot of afternoon delight?' He dropped his voice to a conspiratorial whisper. 'We're in love you know, head over heels. In fact I've already bought the ring and I have high hopes she will accept me. You see, Sharon Trent is the best thing that's ever happened to me. I would do anything for her, she really is the most wonderful woman.'

That would be the same Sharon Trent who not more than three weeks ago had written her number on the back of Jimmy Stewart's hand.

Chapter 18

The call had come in at four twenty-two pm on that damp July afternoon. The fourteenth of the month to be precise and by coincidence, the national day of France. *La Fête nationale*, that was what they called it, but Frank Stewart knew nothing of French history. Bastille day? Up until that point in his life he'd never heard of it, but it was to be a day he was destined to remember for a very long time. In every investigation, there was a turning point, the sweetest of moments when all the hopeless hunches and futile going-nowhere speculations suddenly turned to gold, when the fog dispersed in front of your eyes and everything became crystal clear. That's how he felt after the phone call from Inspector Marie Laurent, still hard at work on her country's most important anniversary when most of her countrymen had buggered off to the beach.

He recognised immediately the three-three international dialling code, causing his heart to skip a beat. They had agreed to touch base once a month, but this call was barely a week since they had last spoken. Something must have turned up. Something big.

'Bonjour Marie, it's great to hear from you so soon.'

'Bonjour Frank, your French accent is improving, I must say.' And yours is lovelier than ever, he thought.

'I'm trying Marie, I'm trying, but us Glaswegians can't even speak English properly, never mind French.'

She laughed. *'Well I think it is very nice, and we French and Scots are great friends in history I think.'*

'That's right,' Frank said. 'We call it the Auld Alliance. Auld means old in proper old Scots.'

'Ah yes, I have heard of it. I think we had the common enemy in England, is that not true?'

'Aye, I think you're right Marie, but we're all big pals now. Us and the English I mean.'

'Well, I'm not so sure France and England will ever be lovers, but yes, I think we are quite good friends now.'

'Yes, I agree, I think. But I guess you're not calling me to give me a history lesson, are you?' Even though he clearly needed one.

'No, I'm not.' She hesitated before continuing. '*Frank, something has arisen that may be relevant to your enquiry. To our enquiry I should say.*'

He tried in vain to suppress his excitement. 'Goodness, that's fast work Marie. Tell me more, please.'

'*It's really just a very lucky break, but of course we are grateful for it. The big congratulations must go to our Dutch colleagues in the city of Leiden. To them it is very important to have the international cooperation especially within Europe and so they always consider Interpol in their investigations and communications. Frank, you remember I told you about the Kitty Lawrence case in Bordeaux?*'

How could he forget? That was the case that had transformed his crazy hunch into a reasonable each-way bet. Now he was longing for more, something that would turn it into an odds-on favourite.

'Sure Marie, I remember. Go on.'

'*Well I have been told of a new case in Leiden in Holland which is very interesting. It is a big university town, in fact it has the oldest university in the Netherlands and one of the biggest too, with over one thousand teaching and research staff. Which brings me to the name of Professor Henk van Duren.*'

'Should I have heard of him?'

'*If you are Scottish like you or French like me, no, you will probably not have heard of him. But if you are Dutch, yes. He is very famous in Holland, a popular historian who is always on television. And not just here in the Netherlands. He worked for many years in America at the famous Princeton University and is very well-known on the history channels over there too. You may have seen him too in England.*'

Frank laughed. 'I'm afraid history's not my specialist subject. Now if he was a rock guitarist, that would be a different thing all together. But I'm getting off the point, sorry. Tell me what's happened.'

'There has been another kidnapping. Exactly like our other two. Exactly like them.'

'Christ Marie, this is good news.' He knew the words were a clumsy choice but he was sure she would know what he meant. Another case with the same MO meant more information to get your teeth into and more chance that the perpetrators would make the stupid little mistake that gave them away. And they always did, no matter how clever they thought they were. So from the selfish point of view of the investigation, it *was* good news.

'This time it was a little boy, his name is Brandon and he is just six years old.'

'Hang on Marie. Brandon did you say? Is that name popular in Holland?'

'I don't know, but it seems Mrs Van Duren is American and Brandon was born there when his father was at Princeton so I think that is the reason. But Frank, I have to tell to you there is something terrible about this case which has caused a great public outcry in the Netherlands.'

'What was that?'

'Brandon had been left in the car outside a convenience store whilst his mother ran in to buy some milk.'

'Christ, don't tell me,' Frank said, feeling his heart sink. 'With the keys in the ignition and the engine running.'

'Yes, I am afraid that is the truth. The shop-owner told the police that this was the habit of Mrs van Duren almost every day.'

'And someone only had to jump in to the driver's seat and speed off with the boy in the back.'

'That is what happened, yes. That was three days ago. And now of course if the cases are connected, we must wait for the ransom call.'

***

This time the dialling code said three-one. Eight in the morning and barely ten hours since he had got the news from Interpol in Lyon, it seemed the Dutch *politie* already had something to share with him. This was all turning out too good to be true but he would take it any day of the week.

The voice at the other end of the line was loud, authoritative and over-familiar. That didn't bother Frank. He'd met a few Dutch cops in his time and recognised this as perfectly normal.

'Hi Frank,' boomed the voice, 'this is Marco from the Leiden police. Inspector Marco Boegenkamp. A good day to you.'

Instantly, Frank could tell he was going to like this guy. He didn't know why, it was just a gut feeling, and over the years, he had learned to trust his gut. He decided to reply with matching familiarity. 'Hi Marco, good to speak to you mate.'

'Ah, I hear from your voice Frank that you are Scottish. Kenny Dalgleish, Alan Hansen, Graeme Souness, I loved them all when I was a boy. They were great footballers and we Dutch know something about great footballers don't you think?'

Frank laughed. 'Aye, you're not wrong there, you've had a few in your time. Van Basten, Van Nistelroy, Bergkamp, and not forgetting Johann Cruyff the master. But I take it you're a Liverpool fan then Marco? You must be happy with how it's going at the moment.'

'Yes Frank, we're not normally great fans of Germans here in Holland but it is my opinion that Herr Klopp is a genius.'

'Yes, I think the fans would agree with you there Marco. Not the Manchester United ones though.'

A loud cackle blasted down the line. 'Ha ha, that's true. Anyway, I have an update for you on our van Duren investigation. It is a very big deal over here as you can imagine because the professor is quite famous here in the Netherlands.'

'Aye, so I've heard.'

'Yes, but now it is his wife who is the subject of all the attention. I think it is true to say that she is now the most famous woman in Holland. And not in a good way also.'

Frank knew someone else who had suffered that fate and he didn't envy Mrs van Duren one bit.

'So Marco, I guess you're expecting the ransom demand any time soon, am I right?'

'We have it already. That is just one reason why I'm calling you. And not only because the demand is in English. Because you see, we think the kidnappers might be from the United Kingdom also.'

'Why do you think that Marco?'

'There was CCTV footage from outside the convenience store. And we saw the driver at first went to the wrong side of the car.'

'Ah,' Frank nodded knowingly, 'we Brits do that automatically. But I guess you will have found the car by now?'

'Yes and as you would expect it has been burnt out to destroy any evidence. About twenty kilometres from where the boy was taken.'

Frank let out an audible sigh of disappointment. 'That's a shame Marco but I can't say I'm surprised. We didn't find anything in our Jamie Grant case either. The hoods running this thing are obviously very careful. But you say you've had a ransom demand?'

'Yes that's right Frank. It was sent to the family by post and arrived this morning. We have checked the note of course for DNA and fingerprints but we have nothing. They received also a text and of course we have been unable to trace the owner of that number.'

'And the note. Where was it posted?'

'Here in Holland, in Leiden.'

That wasn't a surprise to Frank. The kidnappers would have been holed up in the city for quite a few days, allowing them to observe Mrs van Duren's routine. A routine that include leaving her son in an unlocked car with the engine running.

'And how much are they looking for?'

'A million Euros Frank. A lot of money.'

Frank gave a sharp intake of breath. 'Aye, that is a lot. You know there were ransom demands in the Jamie Grant and the Kitty Lawrence cases?'

'Yes, I know that Frank. And I know the kidnappers did not return the children. It is a very worrying situation. Here the

van Duren family is very anxious for the ransom to be paid but we are advising them that they must not.'

Worrying situation? Marco was right, although Frank wasn't sure if his choice of words spoke for the difficulty the police faced. An impossible situation might describe it better, because no matter how you looked at it, there was no win-win scenario. If you didn't pay the ransom, you'd never see the kid again. If you did pay the ransom, you'd never see the kid again. Same difference. They only way there was going to be a happy outcome was if they caught the bastards who were doing this. And that wasn't going to be easy.

'Marco mate,' Frank said, more in hope than expectation, 'have you got *anything*? Anything at all?'

'Almost nothing Frank.'

Almost. So perhaps there was a sliver of hope after all.

'It is a very long shot I'm afraid, but we have a detective sergeant on our team who was born in the UK. And she said that the wording of the ransom note was slightly unusual. Of course we Dutch would not have noticed this because we are not native speakers of the language.'

Which made Frank laugh to himself because he'd yet to meet a Dutch person who didn't speak perfect English. Apart of course from that random *also* thing they peppered throughout their sentences. He'd need to watch he didn't start doing it himself. *Also.*

'What does it say?'

'I have it here Frank. It says "Make no mistake about it, I'm not joking you when I says it. A million Euros or the kid dies". Our sergeant says that is quite an unusual construction.'

'Is that all?' Frank said, failing to hide his disappointment. 'I assume you're talking about *I'm not joking you when I says it*? It is a *bit* unusual but I have heard it before. Plenty of times.'

Boegenkamp seemed unfazed. *'Well perhaps Frank, but you see here in the University of Leiden we have some of the greatest cyber-crime experts in Europe, maybe even the world. That's what they tell me and I have no reason to doubt them.'*

'That sounds great mate. But how does that help us?' He didn't mean it to sound as churlish as it came out, but if Boegenkamp was offended, he didn't reveal it. The more he got to know this guy, the more he was getting to like him.

'One of our team has worked in the past with a very clever young lady called Hanneke Jansen. I am told that Doctor Jansen has developed a web-crawler technology that can search the entire world-wide-web with next-generation phrase matching algorithmic processing.'

Frank could hear him convulse into laughter at the other end of the phone.

'I'm sorry Frank but I'm sure you can tell that I don't really know what I'm talking about.'

Frank didn't understand much of it either but he did catch on to one phrase. A phrase that he remembered from his chat with Eleanor Campbell just a few days earlier.

'Web-crawler did you say?

'Yes. You know of this technology?'

'Not got the faintest clue mate. But I know a woman who does.'

'Ah that is interesting,' Boegenkamp said. *'So maybe you have an expert in this technology also?'*

'Aye we do.' He didn't like to mention that Eleanor and her pal Zak-with-no-surname had been working on their wee da Vinci problem for nearly a fortnight, apparently without success.

'So perhaps we could get our two experts together to work on this case. I'm certain she would get on really well with our Doctor Jansen and we have a saying which I think you have also that two heads are better than one.'

There was no chance that Eleanor would get on with any woman she perceived as a rival, and in Eleanor's eyes, all women were rivals. Frank was not to know it, but Inspector Marco Boegenkamp was thinking exactly the same thing. But for both of them, the needs of the investigation trumped the fragile egos of any geeky forensic officer.

Frank tried not to sound too doubting. 'Well the thing is, our Eleanor isn't exactly a team player.'

Boegenkamp laughed. *'Well maybe Frank we will get some big fireworks when we put these two together, but I think it will be worth a try. When do you think your colleague can be here in Leiden?'*

That left a slight problem to overcome. True, he had failed with DCI Smart the last time he'd tried for the case number, but surely now with this new development, she couldn't refuse. A couple of hundred quid on a cheap flight and two or three nights in a budget hotel, that wasn't going to break the bank. Hell, if it came to it, he would pay for it himself.

'Marco, I think we can get her out to you in the next couple of days, depending on what she's working on at the moment.' Fingers crossed.

'Tomorrow would be better Frank. You know we do not have much time. I will of course arrange for one of my team to pick her up at Schipol and take her to her accommodation. Let's hope these two clever women can work their magic, eh?'

Frank grinned. 'Aye, if they don't kill each other first. I'll get it arranged as fast as I can and let you know. Anyway, it was nice to make your acquaintance Marco and maybe we can meet up in person sometime.'

'You too Frank. And now I have to go and see the parents, to tell them that they should not pay the ransom.'

Not that it would make any difference to the outcome.

***

As Frank had predicted, this time he had little trouble convincing Jill Smart to release a case number into his care. Although to be fair, she had raised an eyebrow when he told her the first task would involve the expense of sending Eleanor Campbell to the Netherlands for a few days and that he himself would need to fly over, with only one overnight stay involved, for a review with Inspector Boegenkamp. Sensibly, he had waited until the case number was in his possession before revealing this latter information.

Speaking of Miss Campbell, he had been unsure of the reaction he would get when he told her of her urgent overseas mission, but in the event, he needn't have worried. By good fortune she was in the midst of one of her semi-permanent relationship dramas with her sort-of boyfriend Lloyd, and so jumped at the chance of an enforced separation.

'It'll like show the pig what he would be missing if we ever broke up,' she had said, with, in Frank's opinion, greatly misplaced optimism. He liked Eleanor but he was under no illusions that she would be anything other than a nightmare to live with. There was every chance that Lloyd would indeed see what he was missing and, concluding that it wasn't very much at all, resolve to make the separation permanent. Nonetheless, he knew that blind encouragement was the way to secure the result he was looking for.

'That'll show him all right,' he had said, with fake but convincing sincerity. 'He'll be grovelling at your feet when you get back, mark my words.'

'Yes, I like that,' she had said. 'Pig.'

Having secured her assent to the mission, the problem still remained as to how to ensure the visit was productive. There was a lot in Eleanor that Frank recognised in himself, both of them sharing a preference to work alone, and both having a barely-suppressed inability to suffer fools gladly. The last thing he needed was for her to have a punch-up with the Hanneke woman over at Leiden Uni. So there would need to be a briefing. A brief one.

'I've heard that this Dr Jansen is pretty good,' he started. 'She's a cyber-crime specialist at the university so she should know her onions. Maybe not with your depth of hands-on experience of course, but she should be able to help you with some of the easier stuff.' He was pleased with how that sounded overall. Except for his stupid schoolboy error, which Eleanor immediately picked up on.

'*Dr* Jansen? So she's like a PhD or something?'

Frank shrugged. 'I think they dish them out like Smarties over there. Honestly, it's nothing to worry about, you'll get on great I'm sure. Anyway, are you clear on what we are trying to do out there?'

'Yeah, like it's a no-brainer. We're to phrase-match across cyberspace for that weird *joking you* phrase.'

'And does that involve web-crawlers?'

She gave him an amused look. 'Is that your new word of the day?'

'Two words actually. But I don't know what it means. Can you tell me?' And then wished he hadn't bothered.

'Like sure. So the tech giants have like catalogued the web into a giant cross-referenced multi-zillion terabyte database to support their search technologies but because of privacy *they say*, but really to protect their commercial interests, they won't share it with law-enforcement agencies. So governments have built this huge capability to roam all over the net and build their own ad-hoc search indexes using mega supercomputers that run at like mental speed.'

'Good to know,' Frank said. Normally he would have added a sarcastic quip, but he was painfully aware of the need to tread carefully given that she had already spent a frustrating fortnight trying to crack Charles Grant's da Vinci thing, without success.

'Aye, and it sounds as if they have some fancy tools over in Leiden that even your mate Zak hasn't got.'

Her eyes lit up with anticipation. 'Yeah, I've been on their website and they've got like two mega supercomputers. It's two Cray XC40s working in a cluster and they're like the size of a tennis court. And the cluster can generate twenty million database hits a second, which is beyond awesome.'

Beyond awesome? At last, Frank could relax, because if there was one thing he knew about Eleanor Campbell, it was that she was a sucker for big expensive kit and these Cray thingies sounded as if they were both big and expensive. Brilliant, the trip was going to be a success.

Then not more than five minutes after he had got back to his desk, Marco rang him again. And before they reached the end of their short conversation, it was arranged. Frank was going to be out there himself, sooner that he expected. Because the van Durens could not be persuaded that the ransom should not be paid, and now Boegenkamp wanted him in Leiden to see if he could do any better.

All things considered, that had every prospect of being a red-letter day. Or *een bijzondere dag*, as his new best pal Marco would say.

Chapter 19

At about the same time as Eleanor Campbell was meant to be flying out to Schipol, the highly-paid lawyers of the Crown Prosecution Service were filing the paperwork that would charge Darren Venables with the murders of Allegra Ross and Benjamin Fox, the task already having consumed an estimated thirteen hundred and thirty man hours at a cost to the public purse of three hundred and ninety thousand pounds. It was therefore inconvenient to say the least when on that very day another body turned up with the identical MO as the earlier victims.

It was an early-morning jogger who found it, slumped against the wall of a dark tunnel at the point where the north-bound lines out of St Pancras Station crossed the Regents Canal. At first she thought someone must have dropped a glove, pausing to pick it up with the intention of placing it for safe-keeping on the thin ledge that ran along the brick-lined wall of the tunnel. A second later, she was screaming uncontrollably as she realised with horror what she held. In her panic and shock, and quite understandably, she tossed the severed hand into the middle of the dirty canal, which was to cause the police diving team no little difficulty in the hours following the discovery of the dead man. But eventually it was recovered, and despite it having been submerged for some time, it was still just about possible to make out the message scrawled on the back. *Leonardo.*

Two hours later, in a darkened room somewhere on the top floor of Paddington Green police station, DCI Colin Barker was fighting a desperate rearguard action, pleading with anyone who would listen that nothing had changed, that Darren Venables was *clearly* responsible for the first two murders and so this one *must* have been the work of a copy-cat killer. The brass were in full damage-limitation mode, and had issued strict orders that under no circumstances should the MO of this new killing be released to the media, which resulted of course in it being leaked little more than five minutes later. Over at the *Chronicle*, the young award-winner Yash Patel was already salivating over the award-winning possibilities of a juicy miscarriage of justice story. One that would keep him on the front page for a week at least, with another month's worth of human-interest spin-offs. And that jogger who had found the severed hand, she looked so hot in her little running shorts and tight vest. Her picture alone was guaranteed box-office.

And for the second time in two years, DCI Jill Smart was being called in to clear up an almighty Barker-generated mess, and where Jill went, DI Frank Stewart went too. In charge of proceedings that morning once again was Chief Superintendent Brian Wilkes, a competent detective of the old school just weeks from retirement. You could tell he was old-school among other things by the way he addressed his charges as ladies and gentlemen and not guys.

'So ladies and gentlemen,' he began, 'who's going to give me the whole gory details of this monumental screw-up?'

No-one seemed keen to take the stage except Frank Stewart.

'Sir, I will do my best, although we're new to this case of course.' By we, he meant Department 12B, the rag-tag bunch of misfits headed up by Jill Smart of which he was part.

Wilkes smiled. He liked Frank, recognising solid competence when he saw it. 'Getting your excuses in early are you Stewart? Proceed, if you please.'

'The victim is one Daniel George Black. Forty-seven-year-old male of mixed race and an actor in that soap Bow Road. Don't know if you watch it at all sir?'

'I am aware of its existence Stewart. Carry on.'

'Very good sir. Well Mr Black was seemingly on his normal jogging route, which according to a neighbour we spoke to, he does pretty much every day, leaving around seven-thirty in the morning and returning around one hour later. We can only speculate at this stage, but it appears that his assailant was waiting for him under the railway bridge. He was killed by two severe blows to the back of the head, we assume on the towpath, and then the body was dragged to the piece of waste ground where it was found. Probably that's where the hand was severed and the message written on the back. *Leonardo.*'

Wilkes nodded. 'So exactly the same MO as the Ross and Fox killings?'

Frank shot a cruel smile in the direction of DCI Barker.

'Exactly sir. The same MO. No difference.'

The DSI shook his head in disgust. 'This is going to be totally embarrassing if it gets out. Just to reiterate, let's make sure we keep schtum on this, understood?'

Everybody nodded, although everyone knew it was already too late for that.

Wilkes sighed in exasperation. 'What a bloody foul-up. So where are we with this now? Any leads, suspects, witnesses?'

'Aye, sir, well we can assume it wasn't Darren Venables, unless DCI Barker let him out on compassionate leave.'

Jill Smart shot him an admonishing look.

'My little joke sir, sorry. No, we don't have any serious leads or suspects at the moment, and as far as we can see there's only one obvious connection.'

'Ok, so spit it out then.'

Frank smiled. 'It's that actress Melody Montague, she's also from Bow Road as you probably know. You see, our victim is her present fiancé, and she was also previously married to Benjamin Fox, victim number one.'

Wilkes was now pacing the room in an effort to focus his thoughts. 'So this Montague woman, did her name come up in the earlier enquiry? It must have, I assume. We always suspect partners and former partners. Ninety percent of the time it's one of them who has done it, isn't that the case?'

Jill Smart intervened. 'We weren't involved at that stage sir, but I'm sure Colin will be able to help you with that question.'

DCI Colin Barker's expression suggested that was the last question he would want to help anyone with.

'Eh...I don't think it *exactly* came up sir,' he squirmed. 'We did not think she had a motive or the opportunity, and she was able to produce convincing alibis for both murders. And also the team felt the case was so strong against Venables, we concentrated all our resources into that line of enquiry.'

Concentrated all your resources into fitting up the WBL's leader thought Frank, not that he felt sorry for him, not after that wee run-in they'd had at Hyde Park. The Chief Super contented himself with a shake of the head. There was a long and awkward silence, which no-one felt like breaking. Until finally Wilkes said quietly,

'So, anything else anyone wants to tell me?'

'Well DCI Barker dismissed it at the time,' Frank said guilelessly, 'but shortly before his death, Mr Fox had been involved in multiple incidents that could very well have provided a motive for his killing. Several of them were brought to my attention by a private investigations firm and we in turn brought them to the attention of the Fox enquiry.'

Barker was staring at the floor, no doubt dreading what was coming next. He wasn't to be disappointed.

'Bainbridge Associates is the firm in question,' Frank continued. 'As it happens, my brother Jimmy works for them too. I think you met Maggie and Jimmy in connection with the Alzahrani enquiry.'

Wilkes nodded. 'Ah yes, I remember them. Sound bunch, as I recall. Should work with them more often.'

'Yes, well I'm sure they would like that,' Frank said, storing it away for future use. 'So, as I said, the first victim had been involved in a number of incidents. First of all, there was a major dispute with his former wife over money which you've already heard about. But there were a couple of other things too.'

'Come on then, get on with it,' Wilkes barked.

'Ok sir. So there was an argument with a scriptwriter on the show, one Jack Redmayne, which was witnessed by Maggie and Jimmy. Strong words were used including a threat against Mr Fox's life, and also Redmayne had to be restrained when he tried to assault the victim.'

'And has this Redmayne been questioned in connection with the murder?'

'I believe not sir,' Franks said, deadpan.

'So what else?' Wilkes said, struggling to hide his exasperation.

'Well Mr Fox had also been involved in a political argument with Charles Grant sir, which became rather heated. He's another actor, the one whose son was abducted, you might remember. Another one of DCI Barker's cases if I'm not mistaken.'

'And was *he* ever questioned?'

'I believe not sir. At least not as a potential suspect.'

Frank heard him swear under his breath.

'And what about the other two killings? Do we have any theories about them?' Now he was ignoring Barker, directing his questions at Frank and Jill alone.

'Early days sir. In the case of Miss Ross, it's reasonable to suspect that she was killed for the same reason as her lover. As to Danny Black, I've no idea about that at the moment. But there must be a connection sir, mustn't there? Because it's the same killer. And so probably the same motive.'

'And so you've no idea what that motive may be?' Wilkes said.

'No idea at all sir. It needs work.'

Wilkes shook his head in disgust. 'Well, you and DCI Smart better get onto it right away then, hadn't you? And as for you, DCI Barker, I think you need to come with me.'

***

Of course, it needed work, a lot of work. There was something missing, something big, something that would tie the whole ragged mess together, but he just couldn't put his finger on it. At least now he could bring Redmayne and Grant and Montague in for questioning and make up his own mind if they were capable of murder.

But the truth was, knowing what he knew about them, he didn't much fancy any of them in the role of a serial killer. Because he was sure that was what this case had now become. It was a serial murder case, there was no doubt about it. Luckily Wilkes hadn't focussed too much on the *Leonardo* thing, because he didn't have a bloody clue what that was all about. Of course in Barker's simple view of the world, it led right back to Darren Venables and the White British League. But unless one of D-V's acolytes had picked up the baton, that theory was now dead in the water.

However, that didn't mean that the scrawled message wasn't important to the investigation. The exact opposite in fact, and he had a feeling that until he'd figured out where it fitted, the investigation would go nowhere.

And what of Miss Melody Montague, the one person with an obvious connection to all three victims? Could she have killed her fiancé Danny Black? Surely that was beyond unlikely, given her public displays of besottedness which gave every appearance of being genuine. And she couldn't have killed her third husband either, even if she wanted to, because her every move at that awards night had been caught on camera. Motive maybe, means debatable, but opportunity, definitely not.

So that was it then. Three identical murders, same MO, no credible suspects, no ideas. For the first time, he began to wonder what had possessed him to open that bloody file in the first place.

Chapter 20

Go safely, go dancing, go running home, into the wind's breath and the hands of the star maker. They had stood silently, heads bowed and immersed in their own thoughts as the celebrant committed the body of Danny Black to be incinerated to dust. They hadn't known him of course, not really, but it was Melody's wish that they should attend. Not many people liked a funeral, especially when the deceased had been taken before their time, but for Maggie and Jimmy it was the funerals they had missed that caused them almost unbearable pain.

She hadn't attended the ceremony for her husband Phillip. In fact no-one had attended the simple committal, such was the total ruin of his reputation, and she was glad of that because he deserved nothing better. And how could she go, after he had betrayed her in so many ways? His infidelity with that bitch from the office and the way he had cynically crafted the plot that had ruined her career. Worst of all, one day she would have to explain everything to her beloved son Ollie and she simply had no idea how she would ever be able to do that.

For Jimmy it was the agonising loss of the comrades-in-arms, the men and women under his command who had become his closest friends, great guys felled by an indiscriminate sniper or blown to bits by an IED when barely into their twenties. They gathered and tidied their mangled bodies as best they could before flying them home to Brize Norton or Northalt into the care of bewildered relatives, accompanied by a letter of condolence that he always took the trouble to write. Your son or brother or husband or daughter was a brave soldier, taken too young in the service of their country, that was always the gist of it, but he tried wherever he could to make it more personal by mentioning a small act of kindness or a humorous incident that he had shared with their loved one. He could never attend the funerals even if he had wanted to, and in truth he wasn't sure whether he did or not. But it didn't need him turning up at a freezing cold graveside in his dress uniform to show the respect he had for these men and women, for that was now fundamental to who he was, and he knew it would always be so.

A function room in a local golf club had been hired for the wake, and the small team of waiters and waitresses were now clearing away the remains of the buffet lunch. The mood was sombre because this was not a celebration of a long life well lived, but of a man in the prime of his life whose time on this earth had been cruelly and violently cut short. As well as family, the room was packed wall-to-wall with well-known faces from the world of entertainment. In particular, it seemed the entire cast of Bow Road had turned out to show their respects to their colleague, whom Maggie suspected had been just as popular with them as with his legion of fans. Although that hadn't prevented him being brutally murdered.

Melody Montague was sitting quietly in a corner, holding the hand of an elderly West Indian lady whom Maggie took to be Danny's mother. Throughout the ceremony itself the actress had been inconsolable, but now she simply looked sad and defeated. It was less than a month since she was telling the press how she was crazily madly in love, more than she had ever been before in her life, and now for the first time, Maggie felt sorry for her. She walked over and sat down beside her.

'I'm sorry for your loss Melody, I really don't know what else to say.'

The actress reached over and took her hand. 'Thank you Maggie. It's still not really sunk in yet. I look around this room and I expect to see him with a beer in his hand, laughing and joking like he always does. I mean, like he always did.' She struggled to stifle a sob.

'It will get better in time,' Maggie said. 'I know everybody tells you that, but it's true.' Yes, but what they didn't tell you was how *much* time it took. Sometimes it was months, sometimes it was years and sometimes it was never. But everything she knew about Melody suggested that she was a survivor, and that sooner rather than later she would bounce back from this terrible event in her life.

They had now been joined by Jimmy, who gave a nod of condolence and said that he too was sorry for her loss.

'Thank you Jimmy,' Melody said, forcing a half-smile, 'but who would want to kill Danny, that's what I don't understand? Everybody loved him.'

Presumably the same person who had wanted to kill Allegra Ross and Benjamin Fox, Maggie thought, and then had gone ahead and done so. But Melody wouldn't know that it had been the same killer who had had taken her lover, wouldn't know about *Leonardo* because this time with Jill Smart in charge of the investigation, the police had been very careful to keep that information to themselves. But tomorrow, they were going to have to release Darren Venables and then it would be all over the papers.

'I'm sure the police are covering every angle,' Maggie said. 'It takes time.'

'Yes, I'm sure you're right,' Melody answered distractedly. Maggie looked up to see she was staring at Charles Grant and Sharon Trent, who were standing alone in the middle of the room, he with his arm clasped tightly around her waist, she sipping on a glass of wine.

'Look at them,' she said, with some bitterness. 'It's not fair, is it?' Maggie assumed she was referring to Charles seemingly finding some consolation after the abduction of his son and the consequent breakup of his marriage. Although if she was writing a book about the happiness of the human condition, she wasn't sure she would select Charles Grant as Exhibit A. But at least there seemed to be some progress in the quest to figure out what had happened to his little boy, even if it was Frank who was making all the running.

'I suppose we all have to move on, don't we?' As soon as she said it, she recognised how stupid and badly chosen it sounded. Melody had just cremated her soul mate for goodness sake and here was she talking about moving on. But to her surprise, she seemed to agree with her.

'Yes, you're right Maggie. We do, no matter how hard it seems.' Maggie couldn't help noticing the look she shot in her colleague's direction, a quite involuntary response to the sheer force of manhood that was Jimmy Stewart. And it wasn't hard to deduce what Melody was thinking. With men like him around, there would always be something to live for.

She squeezed her hand. 'That's a brave thing to say Melody, and I hope we can help you a little. Let's try and get the pre-nup matter all tidied up so you can at least forget about that.' And if that sounded at first inappropriate, she remembered how grateful she had been to Asvina at the time of her greatest distress for helping her get her affairs in order.

'Yes that would be good,' Melody answered, without much conviction. But then out of the blue she asked, 'Jimmy, weren't you going to visit McCartney? How did that go?'

He shrugged. 'Not brilliant Melody I'm afraid. You see, his recollection of the terms of the agreement is the same as your late husband's. But please don't worry, we'll get it all sorted out, I promise.'

Maggie looked at him fondly. It was entirely in keeping with Jimmy's good nature that he wasn't going to burden their client with the uncomfortable truth in this most inappropriate of settings. The uncomfortable truth being that their client was going to lose seventy-five percent of her entire worldly assets.

***

Seeing Charles Grant had set Jimmy thinking about his encounter with McCartney, and the more he thought about it the more his reservations about the matter grew. That visit of Grant's to see McCartney in Pentonville for a start. His explanation about some minor matter with a corporate contract, well that wasn't convincing at all. But why should he lie to them unless he had something to hide? And the way McCartney had reacted when he'd mentioned Kylie Ward. That didn't stack up either. There was something not right about the whole thing and they needed to get to the bottom of it, and fast.

He became conscious of Melody tugging at his forearm. 'Please Jimmy, can you tell him to *stop* it, for god's sake. This is a funeral.'

He looked round to see that Charles had now drawn Sharon closer to him, his pelvis thrust hard against her thigh, his lips caressing her bare neck. She was struggling to push him away, her face contorted in anger. *'Not here please!'* she hissed, finally freeing herself before storming off in the direction of the bar. Grant made to follow her, but Jimmy had anticipated his move, gliding over and laying a gentle restraining hand on his shoulder. 'Not now Charles,' he said quietly. 'Not now.'

'She doesn't understand how much I love her,' Grant said, his tone plaintive, 'and after *everything* I've done for her.'

'I'm sure she does,' Jimmy lied, 'but you know, maybe this isn't the ideal time to tell her. She worked very closely with Danny on the show, didn't she, and I expect his murder must have hit her very hard.'

There was a wild look in his eyes as he answered. 'No, no, I have to tell her how I feel, I can't help it. It's important.'

Jimmy tried one more time to convince him. 'Look, I can see it means a lot to you mate, but wait till you get home, eh? Let's do the right thing, come on.' But Grant was not to be convinced, shaking himself free and striding off in the direction of his lover.

'What more can I do?' Jimmy said, grimacing at Melody. 'He's really lost it, the poor guy.' He'd seen it in the army, the descent into madness after life had crapped on you just once too often. *The straw that broke the camel's back.* He'd heard the shrinks trot out that old cliché so many times, but it was true. Of course, they'd had to tell him about the Kitty Lawrence case, and about the ransom being paid but the child not being returned. And at that moment, any faint hope he had of Jamie being found alive was surely finally extinguished.

Jimmy watched from a distance as he approached her, watching as she turned to face him, her face a mixture of disdain and apprehension, clearly worried that he was about to make another scene. But this time he appeared perfectly calm and respectful, purposely standing apart from her, almost motionless. And then he started to speak. Jimmy was too far away to make out what Grant was saying above the thrum of conversation in the room, but he focussed on his lips and thought he could make out his first words to her. *I love you.* Sharon gave an uncertain smile, tentatively stretching out a hand and caressing his cheek. He took her hand, squeezed it gently and then began to speak again. At first measured, and then the words began to spill out, like a torrent of white water crashing down a mountainside, his hands animated and his eyes blazing with a deranged passion. She stood transfixed, her hands covering her face, her expression transforming from incomprehension to revulsion. And then she let out a piercing scream that stunned the room into silence. As the mourners turned to see what was happening, her legs gave way and she collapsed to the floor.

A voice shouted from the back of the room, 'Let me through, I'm a paramedic,' and the crowd backed off as the medic pushed her way through and dropped to her knees beside the prostrate actress. She loosened the top buttons of Sharon's blouse, examined her eyes, felt her pulse, checked her breathing. Looking alarmed, she whipped out her phone and punched in *999*.

'Ambulance. Yes, it's an emergency. Ischaemic stroke. Yes, I'm sure, totally.'

Grant was inconsolable, sobbing hysterically, shuffling alongside the paramedics as they stretchered her to the ambulance. And over and over again he was saying to anyone who would listen, as if pleading for forgiveness. *'I asked her to marry me, that was all. The wedding and the honeymoon, they were all arranged. But I never got to hear her answer. I never got to hear.'*

Over in the corner Jimmy caught Maggie's eye, a silent acknowledgement that they were sharing the same thought. Why was it that fate seemed utterly determined to destroy this flawed but decent man?

***

'*Bow Road filming suspended after Sharon stroke*' read the headline, the quality *Chronicle* for once following the tabloids by putting the story on its front page. The photograph that accompanied the article did not feature the distraught actor Grant, instead showing Melody Montague with his lover Sharon Trent captured together on-set.

Frank tossed the paper across the desk. 'So drugs, was it? That's what they're saying here.'

Maggie nodded. 'Yes, apparently she has a cocaine habit. They're thinking it was a combination of that and shock that seems to have caused it. Poor woman, she's been completely wiped out and they can't say whether she'll make any kind of recovery.'

He shook his head. 'Aye, strokes are awful. And she's only forty-two, same age as me. Mind you, I think I might have one if anyone proposed to me.'

'Yes, very tasteful Frank,' she said, frowning. 'But you're right, she obviously wasn't expecting him to propose to her.'

Jimmy and Maggie had accompanied Grant to the hospital, following the ambulance in her car and sitting with him in the corridor for several hours whilst they waited for the initial assessment from the medical team. When it became clear that he was not going to be able to see her that evening, they organised a taxi to take him home to his Kingston flat.

Next morning they were holed up in Atlee House, Frank having persuaded Jill Smart that he found it easier to think when he was away from the stifling bureaucracy of Paddington Green. It wasn't a lie either, but it was also a lot easier to sneak Jimmy and Maggie into that decrepit cesspit, with its almost complete absence of any security measures. Irregular yes, but it wasn't as if what he was doing was without precedent. The Met often availed itself of the services of private eyes, and where would it be without its network of paid snouts, many of whom moonlighted in the murky waters of the investigation trade. And hadn't Chief Superintendent Wilkes himself opined that they should use them more often? So that was it then, it was all good. He was doing no more than following orders, although he had taken the precaution of making sure the two of them were tucked away out of sight in an obscure corner of the building. That wasn't difficult, Atlee House consisting of little more than obscure corners.

Jimmy was already at his adopted desk, pouring over an inch-thick document, addressed to his brother, that had landed earlier that day. Literally so, because although he could have had it delivered electronically, Frank liked to work with a hard copy, the ones that were professionally printed and bound at the government print works over in Elephant& Castle.

'Oh, hi guys,' Jimmy said brightly. 'Hope you don't mind Frank, it's the final forensic report on the Danny Black case. I've just given it a quick skim. It makes interesting reading, that's for sure.'

'No problem bruv, you just keep on reading.' He looked at the document with satisfaction. Yes, it had been the right decision ordering that hard copy. With a hard copy you could scribble notes, draw a ring round passages that interested you, turn down the corner of the pages you wanted to go back to again and again. And you could take it with you when you went to the bog, something you really didn't want to do with your police-issue laptop. He wouldn't have minded getting stuck into it himself, but in less than ninety minutes he was due to be sitting opposite Jill Smart over at Paddington Green for his monthly meeting. He was expected to have produced an advance briefing paper, centre stage of which would be the report on the proposed visit to Leiden, but with one thing or another, somehow he hadn't quite got round to it.

'Look, I've got to sort a few things out before I nip over to see Jill. Why don't you two do some work on the report, see if you find anything? And obviously, let me know if anything turns up. And then I'll see you back here at three-ish.'

Maggie winked at Jimmy. 'Don't worry Frank, we're not going to hide anything from you. So just leave us in peace and we'll get onto it. And yep, we'll see you at three or thereabouts.' Frank gave a distracted thumbs-up and scuttled towards the door.

'Ok then boss, where do we start?' Jimmy asked.

Maggie shrugged. 'From the beginning, I suppose.'

Scanning the frontispiece, they saw it was a Doctor Ashley Stone who had put this one together. Obviously neither of them had ever met this Dr Stone, didn't even know if it was a woman or a man, but a few pages in, it wasn't hard to recognise it as a great piece of work. Meticulous but concise, with summary tables laying out the facts of Black's murder and comparing them with those of the earlier killings. Clear photographs of the scene and of the body as it lay in the morgue, the impact point of the head trauma which had killed him clearly labelled, but without aimless speculation about the murder weapon, which had not yet been found. As they thumbed through it page-by-page, enthralled, their attention was drawn to a sidebar captioned *Issues and Concerns*. Half a dozen bullet points, some pretty trivial. But not the one at the top of the list, helpfully underlined and picked out in bold type.

Jimmy looked at Maggie with an amazed expression. 'Are you reading what I'm reading?'

She nodded. 'I think so. The top line of that table...'

'... where it says the method used to sever the hand in the Black case...'

'...in the balance of probability, was not the same as that of the earlier murders. Frank is going to have a complete heart attack when he hears this.'

'So if I understand this right,' Jimmy said, 'in the first two murders, the cut which removed the hand was neat and precise...'

'... probably done by an electric saw, I think I saw that earlier in the report,' Maggie agreed.

'Aye, that's right. Whereas in Black's case, it was much less precise. Dr Stone thinks it was probably done by hand using a large hacksaw, and would have taken at least ten minutes...'

'...as opposed to just a couple of minutes with the powered saw. This is dynamite, isn't it?' Looking up, she was surprised to see Jimmy trying hard to suppress a laugh. And failing.

'What? What's so funny?'

'I know, it's no laughing matter, but you know what this means, don't you? It means that Frank's best pal Colin Barker was right all along. It looks very much like this one *was* a copy-cat killing. You can't believe how much I'd love to be there when Frank has to tell him. He might even have to say sorry. I mean, can you imagine how hard that's going to be?'

Maggie giggled. 'Whatever happened to brotherly love, Mr Stewart?'

'No, you know I'm only kidding. It is a bit of a bitch for him. Seriously, we'll need to break it to him gently. And soon. Maybe you should call him, do you think?'

They caught him just as he was pulling into the car park, Maggie leading the call and Jimmy listening in on the speaker-phone. His reaction, as was predicted, was not positive.

'Aw for god's sake, that's all we need. Shit, shit shit.' They imagined him banging the steering wheel in frustration before reaching for the figurative hip-flask. *'Everyone in the force has been pissing themselves laughing at Barker's copy-cat thing, but unknown even to the twat himself, it turns out he's been right all along. Shit and double shit.'*

***

The news from Maggie and Jimmy had kicked Frank's brain into overdrive and now he struggled to process this fresh and vital information. So whoever had killed Danny Black, it now seemed if the evidence was to be believed it wasn't the same person who had killed Allegra Ross and Benjamin Fox. And more than that, there was something else that differentiated the killings, something obvious. The first and second ones spoke of preparation and knowledge, specifically a knowledge of how difficult it was to sever a limb and therefore how important it was to have the right tools for the job. A professional killing, carried out by someone with prior experience. The third one seemed quite the opposite, an amateur job, almost certainly. But amateur or not, it didn't make the case any easier. Having one killer on the loose was bad enough, but now that there were two, the complexity of the case had risen exponentially. *Bugger.*

He was still trying to figure it all out as he walked through the front door of Atlee House. And then another thought struck him. Apart from the media who had been at that shit-show of a press conference with Barker, nobody outside the immediate investigation team knew the detailed MO of the earlier killings, and certainly not the *Leonardo* bit which was the signature-mark of the earlier crimes.

Yeah, apart from the media. There had been nearly fifty journos at that Paddington Green do, and what was the chances that each of them had kept schtum as instructed? Precisely no chance at all, that was the answer to that question. Keeping their mouths shut just wasn't in their DNA and they only needed to tell a couple of mates, and then they in turn told a couple of theirs, and well, the maths was beyond him, but it was a lot. As the depression enveloped him like a Victorian pea-souper, there remained only one possible course of action. Once again, and breaking every rule in the book, he found himself fumbling in his jacket pocket for the hip-flask. And then one restorative swig later, it came to him. For there was *one* other individual who most assuredly knew the MO of the murders.

The individual who had formally confirmed the identity of Benjamin Fox.

Chapter 21

It had been quite a relaxing flight, all in all. The Met's travel team had done him a huge favour by booking him on British Airways from Heathrow rather than shunting him out to Luton or Stanstead on one of those ghastly low-cost jobs. The departure time was a civilised six-thirty in the evening and by good fortune he had been allocated an extra leg-room seat, and on the aisle too so he didn't have to clamber over a stranger to get to the loo. The food wasn't much to write home about, the main course being some sort of warmed up cheese and tomato croissant, but it filled a hole and importantly, there was a complimentary bar service, unusual in this day and age. The only thing that stopped the journey being perfect was that the traveller next to him was one of these guys who liked to talk, and the talk had continued without a break from the moment Frank had sat down beside him until the flight attendant was welcoming them to the Netherlands and reminding them to set their watches forward an hour. Not that he was by nature antisocial, far from it, but there was only so much interest you could squeeze from the subject of interlocking flooring systems, apparently the specialisation of his companion. Still, he had managed to anesthetise himself from the worst of it with a couple of double gin and tonics, and his spirits were un-dampened as he now scanned the small group of people milling around the arrivals area. At last he saw him, a tall figure of around forty years of age, crop-haired and wearing a vivid orange sports jacket, green open-necked shirt and blue chinos. Inspector Marco Boegenkamp was holding up a small whiteboard on which had been scribbled 'Mr Stewart,' sensible insurance in case they didn't recognise each other from their pictures.

Frank walked over to him and gave a broad smile. 'I'm guessing you must be Marco,' he said, extending his hand. 'I'm Frank. It's good to meet you at last.'

The greeting was returned with obvious warmth. 'Yes, and I'm Marco of course. Welcome to the Netherlands. Good flight?'

Frank laughed 'Yep, on time and smooth, what more can you ask for?' Well, not to be seated next to a crashing bore would have been nice, but he didn't share that thought with his new friend.

Twenty minutes later they were threading their way south in Boegenkamp's Audi, the busy motorway still thick with rush-hour congestion.

'It's always like this I'm afraid. I could put on the blue lights of course,' he laughed, 'but we are a very orderly society here in Holland and it wouldn't be right since we are only going to a little meeting in Leiden. But don't worry, the traffic usually thins out in a few kilometres and then we should be there in about an hour.'

Given the primary reason for his visit, Frank wasn't really in any hurry.

'What state are they in, the van Durens?' he asked. 'Pretty bad I'd imagine.'

'Yes very bad,' Boegenkamp agreed. 'Professor van Duren of course blames his wife for everything and he is finding it difficult to deal with his anger.'

'Not surprising. But they're still adamant they want to pay the ransom?'

'Yes, I'm afraid so. That's one of the main reasons I wanted them to meet you. So they can hear directly from you what happened in the other two cases.'

Leiden police headquarters was located in a nondescript low-rise office block located on a nondescript business park about three kilometres outside the old town. Boegenkamp led Frank through a warren of corridors to a small stuffy meeting room, windowless but ventilated by a noisy air conditioning unit. The room was sparsely furnished with a table and a half-a-dozen plastic chairs and seemed to have been purposely designed for maximum discomfort. The van Durens were already there, accompanied by a detective sergeant introduced as Johann.

'This is Inspector Frank Stewart from London,' Boegenkamp said, his tone serious. 'He is here to help us with our case.'

Professor van Duren was of medium height and slim with a shock of thick greying hair swept back from his forehead. His wife was small and petite and strikingly attractive, although the effect was diminished somewhat by the dark rings that circled her eyes, no surprise given what she had been through. From his opening remarks, it was evident the Professor was a man very much used to being in control.

'We've had the advice from the police here in Leiden,' he said briskly, 'but of course we do not intend to follow it. We must have our child back and therefore we have no option but to trust the abductors will return him as they have said they would. We wish to pay the ransom.'

'Well that would be a mistake sir,' Frank said, making no attempt to sugar-coat the message he was about to deliver. 'Look, I don't want to trash your faith in human nature, but criminals aren't wired the same as you and me. I don't know if you have the saying over here about no honour amongst thieves, well it's true. Professional criminals like these guys are driven by greed, pure and simple. They'll take your money all right, but they won't give you back your child.'

Mrs van Duren began to sob, drawing a look of cold disdain from her husband. The poor woman had been destroyed by one stupid mistake and it was clear he wasn't going to let her forget it. *Ever.*

'Shut up Rachel. This isn't doing anyone any good. So Inspector Stewart, what do you suggest we do?'

Frank knew the question was coming and he hadn't been looking forward to it one bit. Boegenkamp would have already told them about what had happened in the Grant and Lawrence cases, but it seemed they were in denial, so they would have to hear the unpalatable truth again from him. But luckily he had an idea, a stupid, crazy idea. An idea that might give them hope where there ought to be none.

'If you simply hand over the ransom money, then it's odds-on they won't return your child. I'm sorry to be blunt, but that's the fact of the matter. You see, from their point of view, doing a handover just introduces unnecessary risk and complication into the whole thing. So why bother if we still get the money, that's the way they look at it.'

'I'm sorry,' van Duren spat at Boegenkamp, 'but I don't see how *he's* helping the situation.'

And the guy was right of course, he wasn't helping much. Because nothing would help until they tracked down the scum responsible for this, and any prospect of that was a long way off right now. Which left only his crazy idea.

'Look, I said it was greed that drives these people. So there is *one* thing we could try.'

'What?' Rachel van Duren cried desperately, 'please tell us.'

'It's a risky play,' Frank said, catching Boegenkamp's eye, 'but if we make the reward worth their risk, there might just be a chance they'll go for it.'

And then he explained his crazy idea, and in the light of day it sounded even more stupid than when he had dreamt it up on the journey down from Schipol. But there was no denying Professor van Duren had an aura about him, an aura that radiated dignity and importance. *A man of honour.* On that, everything depended. Well, not quite everything.

'It depends on whether you can raise another half-million Euros,' Frank said.

'We can raise that on the Connecticut beach house?' his wife said, pleading to her husband. 'Can't we?'

And so it was arranged. Three-quarters of a million Euros would be paid in advance, with a further three-quarters of a million to be paid if the child was handed over unharmed. A deal that put the ball back in the court of the abductors. All they had to do was trust that Professor van Duren was a man of his word, a man who would keep his part of the bargain. In Frank's mind, the enticement of that three-quarters of a million gave it at least a fifty-fifty chance of success. And anyway, this was the only game in town.

The proposal was pinged off to the mobile number they had been given, obscured behind a wall of encryption somewhere on the dark web. Six minutes later they received the terse reply.

Deal.

***

It had always amused Frank that in the movies, ransom handovers were conducted in dark and dank abandoned warehouses in some moody and windswept riverside location. Of course it was great for creating the atmosphere of dangerous foreboding sought by the director, but it was hopelessly stupid in real life. No way of arriving un-observed for a start, and generally just one way out too. *Dumb.* Which is why he'd agreed with Boegenkamp the perfect location for this most high-risk of operations. Centraal Station Amsterdam, used by over a quarter of a million passengers every day, constantly teeming with arrivals and departures from all parts of the Netherlands and beyond.

Half an hour earlier, the money had been electronically transferred as instructed, to be laundered through a network of shadow servers hosted in a quiet Moscow suburb, the mafia-funded provider charging a flat ten percent fee for their expertise and discretion. And now all they had to do was wait for the appointed time. Eight minutes past eight o'clock, bang in the middle of the morning rush hour. *Send just the mother and no police.* That was a joke and both parties knew it. The place was already swarming with dozens of Boegenkamp's plain-clothes team, melting with ease into the background amongst the throng of commuters. Hard to spot, but then that worked both ways. Frank stood with his Dutch counterpart about fifty metres from where Rachel van Duren was waiting, her face etched with worry, at the entrance barrier to platform twelve. *Wait there, we'll bring him to you.* Neither spoke, but each knew what the other was thinking. *Fifty-fifty at best, but please for once let the odds fall in our favour.*

Out of the corner of his eye, he saw a man in a conspicuously-branded puffer jacket kneeling down, talking to a child, pointing in the direction of the barrier. Was it his imagination, or did the child look scared? Frank touched

Boegenkamp on the elbow, catching his attention and together they peered at his phone, studying Brandon van Duren's photograph. Was there a likeness? It was hard to tell from this distance. But then they saw Mrs van Duren had seen the pair too, and immediately they knew from her body language. *False alarm.*

They watched as the huge digital clock, mounted high above the travellers on a steel column, ticked over to the handover time. *Eight minute past eight.* Earlier, they'd speculating on how the handover might be effected. Would the boy have been pushed onto a train in some outlying suburb, eliminating the possibility of his abductors being caught in the act? Or would he be dropped off in person, his chaperone melting seamlessly into the crowd? Less likely, given that they would know the police would be observing the scene. But right now, that was all academic, because nothing was happening. Above them, the clock clicked over once more. Then another minute. And another. *Nothing.*

This was exactly what he feared the most, the raising of false hope only for it to be cruelly dashed. Never mind her marriage, he doubted if Rachel van Duren's sanity would survive this. But then a thought suddenly came to him. *God, I've been so dumb.* For the abductors, it was all about eliminating the risk of being caught, was it not? So why would they drop the kid exactly at the spot where every bloody cop in Amsterdam would be watching?

'Rachel,' he yelled, sprinting towards her, his tone urgent, 'Rachel, you need to come with me. Now.'

She spun round, her expression a mask of confusion. Without waiting for an answer, he grabbed her hand and began to run across the concourse, dragging her behind him, Boegenkamp following several steps behind.

'Where are we going Frank?' she shrieked, but not resisting. 'I need to stay at the barrier. Brandon will be here soon.'

'Trust me, he won't. But it will be ok. Come on.'

God, how he prayed his hunch was right. They were heading to the Western tunnel, which if he'd read the map correctly, burrowed below several of the platforms before emerging on the waterside. And according to the map, that was the side where the taxi rank stood. They barged their way down the escalator, Frank not bothering to apologise as they pushed aside an army of indignant commuters. Reaching the bottom, it seemed that the flow in the tunnel was in the opposite direction to theirs, and every second person had their head buried in their smartphone, making no attempt to get out of their way and thus slowing their progress. But at last they reached the up escalator, taking the steps two at a time, ignoring once again the protests of those who they had bundled past, until they reached street level once more. To his left, he saw the giant illuminated sign above a pair of automated sliding doors. *Taxi*.

'Come on, this way,' he shouted, dragging her in the direction of the doors. Boegenkamp had now caught them up and was on his radio, bringing his team up to speed on the change of plan. Not that they would be needed, the kidnappers being already over the Belgian border on their way to Calais. It had been, as far as could be arranged, a risk-free operation. Shove the kid in the back of the cab, slip the Leiden-based driver a hundred-Euro note and remind him it would be good for his health to forget who gave it to him. Now they just had to sit back and wait to see if the van Durens honoured their side of the bargain. If they did, then *result*. Three-quarters of a million in the bank, a tidy little job and no mistake, and plenty of other kids to go for to fill the vacancy. If they didn't, then they'd better not let the kid out of their sight ever again.

The boy was standing there, alone and bewildered, as the doors slid open. Boegenkamp was there first, bounding through the gap and gathering him up in his arms. Frank smiled at Rachel van Duren and gave her a thumbs-up, then watched as she ran towards her son. You didn't get many happy endings in this job, so you needed to savour them when they turned up. He might stay on another night, see if Marco fancied a wee pub-crawl around the city, maybe even check out the famous red-light district, although strictly as a social observer. They'd been bloody lucky, he knew that, because he was certain that the villains' original scheme hadn't included handing back the kid. But at least now he had a blueprint that he could use next time it happened, assuming of course the next victim's family had a cool million and a half going spare.

Because there would be a next time, he was sure of that.

Chapter 22

'Hi Amanda, nice to hear from you!'

Jimmy hadn't exactly been surprised when he glanced down and saw who was calling him. Whilst it was true that for most of his life he had been pretty hopeless at reading signs of attraction even when to an outside observer they were bloody obvious - at least that's what Maggie kept telling him - with Miss Amanda Fletcher of Her Majesty's Prison Service even he could tell there was an interest. An interest that was *definitely* not going to be reciprocated. For a moment Jimmy had debated whether he should take it or not, but eventually admitted to himself that he would like to know the reason for her call, and the easiest way to find that out was to answer it. She had seemed momentarily taken aback by the fact that he had actually picked up and by the effusiveness of his greeting.

'Yes, well thank you!' There was a pause during which he assumed she was catching her breath. *'It's lovely to talk to you too. I was beginning to think you'd lost my number.'*

'No no,' he said, quite truthfully, 'just been a bit busy, that's all.' He had been busy but that wasn't the reason he hadn't called her.

'All work and no play makes Jimmy a dull boy. You should come and play with me, we could have a lot of fun.' That wasn't the first time he'd heard someone say that, and he didn't doubt that it might be true, but it was how to escape afterwards that would be the problem. Especially given her profession.

'That would be nice,' he lied, 'but well, it would be a bit difficult, let's put it that way.'

'Don't tell me, you're with someone,' she sighed. *'All the nicest ones always are.'* By her tone he guessed that the revelation, untrue though it was, had neither surprised nor particularly upset her.

'Nicest ones? I don't know about that,' he laughed, 'but I guess you didn't call me just to tell me how amazing I am.'

'I did actually, but there was something else too,' she

answered. *'It's your friend Mr McCartney. He's in hospital.'*

Jimmy couldn't hide his surprise. 'What? What happened?'

'He fell over. In his cell. Smashed his face against the wall five or six times and broke his nose. He was unconscious when they got him to the Royal Free.'

'Fell over? Really?'

'That's what it will say in the official report. But no, of course not really.'

'So what did happen then?'

'Well the first thing is when I hears that our boy is getting moved to A Block.'

'What, where all the nutters are kept?'

'That's right, well remembered.' From her tone he could tell that she was enjoying the story, and that she was in no hurry to get to the end of it. *'I mean, that's highly unusual. Normally the only reason you get moved from our wing over to A is if you have done something really bad or upset someone very important, so I thinks, oh-oh, this doesn't look good for our Blake.'*

'So what did he do?' Jimmy asked. 'A bust up with one of the officers or something?' If he could have seen her expression, he would have realised how far from the mark he was with this supposition.

'Well, not exactly,' she said, sounding evasive. *'It was because he got on the wrong side of one of the organised crime crews. Not that I'm surprised because he's a right twat, isn't he?'*

'So, these guys can arrange for someone to be transferred to another part of the jail. As if they run the place?' Jimmy said incredulously.

She laughed. *'Well more or less. It's all about the give and take of prison life, ain't it? You do this little thing for us and we'll do something for you. Bob's your uncle then a couple of weeks later the governor is boasting to the Home Affairs Committee about a nice little drugs bust or about finding a stash of mobiles in the shower block.'*

'So who do you think beat him up then? Because I'm

assuming he didn't actually fall over six times.'

She laughed again. *'Oh, I know who did it all right. Everybody around here knows that. It was Johnny Watson and Pete Smart. A right couple of hard bastards they are. You wouldn't want to get on the wrong side of them, believe you me.'*

He was struggling to get his head around the fact that someone could order a beating inside a jail as easily as ringing for a takeaway. And that the authorities apparently knew who was responsible yet did nothing about it.

'This is an eye-opener for me Amanda, it really is. So what are these two guys in for? Murder or something I assume.'

She grinned. *'What are they in for? Watson and Smart aren't inmates, they're screws. Do you think we allow our guests to just wander into anyone's cell and do this sort of thing? What sort of establishment do you think we're running here?'*

'Jesus Amanda, there's a lot about the prison system I'm obviously ignorant of. But I'm guessing you must have some idea what it was all about?'

'Yeah, well sort of. My mate Andy Smith, remember the officer you met on your last visit, well he's kind of mates with the two of them and apparently it was all to do with some legal document or other.'

'You're kidding,' Jimmy said, unable to hide his surprise. 'It wasn't about a pre-nuptial agreement, was it?'

'I don't know the details, might have been mate. 'Course, that's why you came to see him, I remember now.'

'Aye, that's right.' Now his mind was racing as he skimmed through all the possible reasons he could think of why someone might want to beat up McCartney. With his history, there probably was no shortage of folks who might bear him a grudge, but surely the timing of this was too much of a coincidence just a few days after his own visit. And it was not as if that would have been kept a secret in that place. Someone had been doing some digging into McCartney's visitor log.

'So Amanda,' he asked her, 'do you or your mate Andy

have any idea who ordered this?'

'And do you think if I knew I would tell you?' she said disbelievingly. 'No way mate, I value my health too much for that. Some people are saying it was one of the Irish firms, but I don't think Andy knows and he doesn't want to know either. But you know Jimmy, you could always visit McCartney in hospital and ask him yourself, I'm sure he'd be *very* pleased to see you. We've got a rota for guard duties and as it happens it's my turn tomorrow afternoon. And then maybe we could go for a drink afterwards.'

Jimmy couldn't help but chuckle. 'Nice try Amanda, but some other time eh? But listen, thanks for letting me know all this.' And he *was* grateful to her, although at that moment he had no idea what it meant for the case, but he could figure that out a bit later. Satisfied he had all he needed, he was just about to bring the call to a close when she said,

'Now you just wait a minute Jimmy Stewart, because I've kept the best for last.'

'You're a right tease Miss Fletcher,' he said, grinning to himself. Aye, a tease in more ways than one. 'Come on, tell me.'

'So Andy says that the story going round is that McCartney was paid twenty grand by someone to make a document disappear and this seems to have displeased someone important. That's all Andy has heard.'

'Amanda, you're a wee darling!' And he meant that too. This was dynamite. Someone had been prepared to pay good money to make the Fox-Montague pre-nup evaporate, and there was only one person who stood to gain from that happening.

The only problem was, that person was now very much dead.

***

It was seven thirty in the evening, and for Maggie this was her sacred time, the blissful hour she got to spend with her son before bedtime, just the two of them, united in love as step by step they erased the trauma that had upended their lives just two years earlier. But the combined consequences of Jimmy's earlier call with Amanda Fletcher and the surprising text that Maggie had subsequently received was so startling that for once she had to make an exception. Which was why he was now sitting opposite her in her tiny kitchen hugging a mug of coffee and munching on a chocolate digestive. Ollie was naturally delighted about his visit, racing around in his P-Js and excitedly urging him to examine his latest Lego creation.

'It's a Buzz Lightyear, Uncle Jimmy. To infinity and beyond!' He picked up the spaceman and, holding it aloft, circled the room at speed, accompanied by a loud *whoosh*.

'Aye, I can see that mate. It's really good. I love Toy Story, it's one of my favourites.'

Maggie laughed. 'Now then Ollie, leave Uncle Jimmy alone, will you? I tell you what, if you're a good boy, you can watch it for ten minutes. Go through to the sitting room and I'll set it up for you.'

Ollie adopted a serious tone. 'But not the *original* film mummy, I like Toy Story Three best.'

'Already a wee film critic, eh?' Jimmy said, smiling. 'You know, I think that's my favourite too.'

'And then can we play football Uncle Jimmy? *Please*.'

'Of course mate. I'll go in goal and you can take penalties at me, how about that?'

Satisfied, Ollie followed his mum out of the room, leaving Buzz in the care of Jimmy. A few seconds later Maggie returned, grinning from ear to ear.

'I doubt whether he'll sit there for five minutes, but you never know, now that he's got a promise of a game a football with you.'

'He's a great kid Maggie, a real credit to you. After everything you've been through, I mean, it's just amazing.'

She nodded. 'Well maybe, but we just get through it day by day. And it's getting better, much better.' She didn't dare tell him how much of that was down to him. Jimmy Stewart had saved her life, in more ways than one, and one day she intended to tell him how much that had meant to her. But for now, they remained just colleagues, and maybe that's how they would stay.

'Well, as I said, he's a fine boy. But anyway, I suppose we'd better get down to work, don't you think? I don't want to waste your whole evening.' As if she could think of a better way to spend it.

'Yeah, so what about our Mr McCartney then?' Maggie said, shaking her head. 'Not the smartest sandwich in the picnic, is he?'

'Aye, you could say that. I bet he wished he hadn't taken that twenty grand now.'

'He's a troubled soul, let's put it that way.'

'And Charles? How did he get roped into it, because him and Benjamin Fox weren't exactly best mates, were they?'

Maggie shrugged. 'We can only assume Fox paid him to do it. That's all I can think of.'

'Aye, or maybe Benjy-boy had something on him,' Jimmy said uncertainly, 'because we know that our Charles is a very complicated man. So you never know what might be hidden away in his back-story.'

'The thing is,' Maggie said, thinking out loud, 'the poor man is completely broken, isn't he, so he wouldn't have been thinking straight whatever the reason. And then he decides to invest his whole future in Sharon Trent, and well, I think we knew that those feelings were all one way.'

'Aye, poor guy. Been there, done that.'

She gave him a surprised look. Surely it was impossible that there was a single woman on this earth who wouldn't fall for Jimmy Stewart? But then she remembered. Astrid Sorenson, beautiful, desirable and dangerous. The woman for whom he had left his adored Flora, only to find out when it was too late the terrible mistake he had made.

'Top-up?'

A mumbled sound which might have been 'Aye' emerged through a mouthful of digestive crumbs. He gave her a thumbs-up as a back-up.

Carefully, she filled his mug to the brim. 'But you know the thing with the pre-nup, that's really serious. Twenty grand to make Melody's copy disappear, I mean that's naughty.'

'So what will happen then?'

'Well if McCartney makes a full confession, then I think Asvina will put the matter in front of the family court and argue that Melody's recollection of the terms of the agreement, though not backed up by actual evidence, can be taken to be true.' Although if that text she had received was to be believed, then perhaps the picture wouldn't look quite so bleak.

'So Melody will get her seventy-five percent then?'

'Possibly. Except of course we have seen Charles Grant's copy of the agreement which says the exact opposite.'

Jimmy frowned. 'But that must be a forgery, surely?'

'Who knows. That's something that'll be very difficult to prove.'

'So it's still all a complete mess then?'

'Yes, just less of a complete mess than it was. But there might be a way through this if Charles can be persuaded to tell the truth about his copy.'

'You've been trying to get a hold of him, haven't you?' Jimmy asked. 'What were you going to say to him?'

'I don't know really. I was just going to tell him the police were looking into the da Vinci matter but hadn't made any progress yet. But I've left him a dozen messages and he hasn't got back to me. To be honest, I'm a bit worried he may do something stupid.'

'You don't mean ... what, kill himself?' Jimmy said. 'He wouldn't do that, surely not?'

They were interrupted by the reappearance of Ollie, hopping up and down on one leg and carrying a bright yellow indoor football. 'Can we play now Uncle Jimmy? Can we play now?'

He raised an enquiring eyebrow in his mum's direction. Smiling, she said, 'Ok darling, but just five minutes and then bed. Then Uncle Jimmy has to go out.'

Jimmy looked at her, mystified. 'Go out? No I don't.'

Now it was time to tell him about the text. The text from Miss Melody Montague.

'Look at this,' she said, shoving her phone into his face. 'See what it says?'

He gave a grimace as he read it out loud. '*Guess what!! Pre-nup has turned up! Send Jimmy. xx.* What the Jesus fuck is that all about?'

She'd seldom heard him swear and it sounded so out of place that she burst out laughing.

'Well just hang on a minute,' he continued, protesting. 'What, you want me to go *now*?'

'Why not?' she said, trying and failing to suppress her laugh. 'It's a lovely evening and it'll only take you twenty minutes to get there. I'll send her a text, tell her you'll be there by half-past eight. You only need to stay five minutes. In fact you don't even have to go in if you're a scaredy-cat.'

'I'm not scared,' he said, trying not to laugh himself. 'But why can't she just send us the bloody thing in the post?'

Maggie chuckled. 'Oh my goodness, what's the world coming to? Captain James Stewart of Her Majesty's Royal Ordinance Regiment refusing an order. I'll have to have you court-martialled or executed at dawn.'

'I'm not in the blooming army any more, thank god,' he railed, 'but I'd take the firing squad anytime over an evening with Melody Montague.'

'Don't be such a drama queen Jimmy, it needn't take more than a minute. Not unless she entices you in to her boudoir, that is.'

He ignored the jibe. 'I'm sorry, I'm not doing it. No way.' She could see he was doing his best to sound angry, but not really succeeding. A moment later, his face cracked into a smile.

'You're a bloody awful woman and a bloody awful boss, Maggie Bainbridge. But go on then, I'll do it.'

She tried not to sound triumphant. 'I knew you would. But thank you. I've already texted her to say you're on your way.'

***

The traffic had been quiet on the late July evening, the sun still warm but slowly sinking in a lovely pink-tinted sky. He'd been here a few weeks earlier when she staged her elaborate engagement celebration, but how everything had changed since then, Melody now the grieving widow, if that was the right description, given she had not actually been able to marry her great love.

He jabbed the button on the intercom that was mounted on one of the sturdy stone brick pillars of the entrance gates. The voice that answered was accented and unfamiliar. Of course, she had a maid. Bridget, that was her name, Latvian or Lithuanian. Maggie had told him that even Melody did not know which.

'Miss Montague is in the garden. She is expecting you sir.'

There was a click and then one of the automated gates began to swing inwards. He slipped through the narrow gap then looked around. She was seated in a shady corner, the table set for two and a bottle of something already on ice, the elegant silver wine-cooler alongside the table glistening in the fading sunshine. Champagne, if he knew anything about his client. The furniture was, as he expected, high-end, of a design that could be found in expensive Mediterranean hotels and on board private yachts, not that he had much experience of either. The garden was in full bloom, expertly-designed formal borders surrounding the luxuriant shaped lawn, clematis, honeysuckle and climbing roses clinging to ornamental trelliswork, the garden a secluded oasis walled on three sides by weathered dusky brickwork. A paradise, but a paradise that needed money to sustain. A ton of money.

He'd never seen Melody in anything but a dress but this evening she was informally attired in light blue jeans and a black loose-fitting T-shirt. She still looked nice, although he hated to admit it, and if anything even more attractive and alluring. But, no, nothing was going to happen, no way. This was strictly business. Grab the document, say thank you, exit stage left.

'I expect you're more of a beer man Jimmy,' Melody was saying, 'but I hope you can make an exception this evening. And this is a very good vintage.'

He smiled. 'I wouldn't know anything about that, but of course, I'd love some.'

Unnoticed, the maid had appeared beside them, filling both their glasses then slipping silently back through the patio doors and in to the kitchen.

'How are you coping Melody?' he said. 'It must be very difficult.'

'Yes, I'm still in shock. I can't believe it has actually happened. But life must go on, what else can you do?'

He wasn't quite sure how to react to this, because no matter what you said, they were just hopeless platitudes, of bugger-all use to anyone. *It'll get better in time, believe me. I'm so sorry for your loss. If there's anything I can do just ask.* So he didn't say anything, but hoped his look was warm and sympathetic. A look that must have been open to misinterpretation, because out of the blue, she leant across the table, straining to kiss him. 'I shouldn't really be doing this, should I? But, life is short as they say, and well, you know I've never been one for resisting temptation.' She extended a finger and gently ran it down his cheek. 'And you are *so* beautiful.' That explained it then. She just didn't do faithfulness. Even to the dead.

'Beautiful?' he replied, tensing up. 'I don't know about that. Melody, I can't believe I'm saying this but perhaps this isn't such a good idea. Look, you're incredibly attractive, but maybe you're aren't thinking so clearly at the moment...'

She drew away and gave him a surprised look. 'Well Jimmy boy, it will be your loss. No-one ever leaves my bed disappointed.' He didn't doubt that was true, but it was an extraordinary thing to say.

'I'm sorry Melody,' he lied. 'It's not you, it's just that I'm looking for something more at the moment.' It sounded like a cliché because that's what it was. But it was true.

She shrugged, evidently accepting his explanation. 'Yes, I know, my head is all over the place at the moment. It would have been nice, that's all. You see the loneliness and emptiness, it's quite unbearable. But whatever, I'll always be here when you change your mind.' He noted it was *when* not *if*.

She removed the bottle from the cooler and topped up both their glasses. There was an awkward silence and then she said,

'So, if it's just to be business, well, the pre-nup, I have it here. That's what you came for, isn't it?' She handed him a blue transparent plastic folder.

He gave it a brief glance. 'How did you come by it? Because when I spoke to McCartney he was quite sure he had lost it.' He had tried not to sound suspicious but it didn't come out that way.

'Yeah, that's what he said, but it was his paralegal guy, Len Green who managed to find it. He said he was having a sort-out and came across it, that was all. Hidden away in the bottom of my file, where it seemed to have been all along.'

Yes, he thought, Len just *happened* to come across it after McCartney had been beaten to within an inch of his life. After somehow finding out that an agent acting for her ex-husband had paid him twenty grand to make it disappear. What a coincidence that was. But of course maybe he was being unfair. Maybe she didn't know anything about it. So he decided to ask her, and wasn't surprised by her reply.

'Yes, I heard. It's a great shame. But the man's a slippery fool, so I can't say I was surprised.' She gave him a steady look, as if to say, *go on then, ask me. Did I have anything to do with it?* This time, he decided to let it pass, reasoning that had she or her brothers been involved as he suspected, she was unlikely to admit it. He had been there no more than ten minutes and had got what he came for. So time to call it a night.

'Melody, I think it's time I was off. It's been lovely, really it has.' He got up and walked round the table and placed his hand on her shoulder. Gently, she clasped it and stood up to face him, her lips almost touching his, her gaze steady as she looked into his eyes. Almost imperceptibly their lips came together and he felt the tip of her tongue in his mouth, gently probing. At the same time, he felt her free hand moving up his thigh, the physical reaction as inevitable as it was irresistible. Time to make his excuses before it all got out of hand.

**

Back in his flat, he picked up the plastic folder and carefully removed the agreement. Idly he flicked through the pages, vainly trying to make sense of the dense legalise, but after a few minutes, gave up the struggle. Sod it, it didn't actually matter what it said, the important thing was they had it back in their possession and so they could, however improbably, complete the mission they had undertaken for Asvina.

But then his attention was caught by the faint dark stain that had, unnoticed, spread across his fingers. Which struck him as odd, because you would think the ink would be dry by now on a five-year old document.

Chapter 23

They had been forced into a bloody huge change of plan and all because of an unexpected obstacle that had arisen in relation to that bane of his life, the case number. This particular one being the case number which had, belatedly, been allocated to his *Shark* investigation. The blame fell to some administrative assistant's assistant buried down in the basement of Paddington Green police station, or more accurately, to the stupid bureaucracy the Met had put in place to make everything three times more difficult than it needed to be. For it seemed an extra signature, rank of Chief Superintendent or above, was needed on the travel requisition form before a relatively junior employee like Eleanor Campbell could make an overseas trip, and since no officer of that rank could be arsed to sign it, there it sat in the stern and matronly clerk's virtual pending tray, ignored. From whence no amount of persuasion by Frank, subtle or otherwise, could release it. He'd even tried mild bribery, being rewarded with a stony stare and a threat to report him to his superior officer. As if Jill Smart would give a shit about that. *His* travel requisition had got signed without any such obstacle, and so at about the same time he was heading to the Netherlands to meet the van Durens, Dr Hanneke Jansen was heading the other way.

Now, back in London and four days after Jansen's arrival at Maida Vale labs, he was due to meet them for a progress report. But that was a couple of hours in the future, giving him time to catch up with his amateur colleagues in the Fleet Street Starbucks they seemed to call home. To tell the truth, he was in desperate need of a caffeine infusion on account of a crashing headache, induced by the extended drinking session he'd enjoyed with Marco last night. He had only been returning the favour extended by Boegenkamp when he'd stayed over in Amsterdam a couple of days earlier, but now he was paying the price. Still, there was no denying it was good for international relations and he looked forward to seeing what state his Dutch mate was in when they met up later that day.

Maggie and Jimmy were already there, sharing some private joke at the cramped little table they'd managed to secure. He was pleased to see they had already ordered for him, a steaming black Americano which he hoped benefitted from a double shot of Espresso. She smiled up at him, causing him to reflect again how simply lovely she looked. Not that he had yet plucked up the courage to do anything about it, and probably never would. But he didn't have time to think about all of that now.

'Hey guys, how's tricks? Solved the Jamie Grant case yet?'

'Sod off,' Jimmy replied, grinning, 'but we're following a number of promising lines of enquiry, that's all I can tell you.'

'Oh aye, is that right?'

'Not exactly,' Maggie said, 'but there have been developments.'

'Developments?' He was willing to bet they wouldn't be as interesting as what he'd recently found out from his useless mate DC Ronnie French.

'That's right,' she nodded. 'Jimmy will tell you all about them. But I heard about your big success with the van Duren boy. You must be incredibly relieved how it turned out.'

'Aye, I am,' Frank said, trying not to sound too pleased with himself. 'Gives us some hope if it happens again. But come on, let's hear these *developments*. What have you got?'

He listened intently whilst Jimmy told him about McCartney being beaten up in prison, and about the twenty grand payoff, and the unexpected re-emergence of Melody Montague's copy of the pre-nuptial agreement. And about the traces of ink on his hand. It was interesting enough, but how any of it had anything to do with either the Jamie Grant case or the Leonardo murders was beyond him.

'You see Frank, this all seems like some sort of scam engineered by the very late Benjamin Fox to cheat his ex-wife out of a couple of million quid. Gives her quite a motive, don't you think? I mean, if she found out about it.'

Frank shook his head. 'Except it doesn't. Because the terms of the pre-nup stand irrespective of whether Fox is dead or alive. I'm sure I heard Asvina telling me that.'

Maggie nodded. 'That's true. But maybe Melody was just angry with him.'

'Aye, maybe. But we've been through all of this before. Melody might have had the motive, and to be frank, even that's iffy, but she certainly didn't have the opportunity. Every single second of her time at that awards do was accounted for.'

'But it does point to the character of Fox, I suppose,' Maggie said, sounding uncertain.

'Aye, maybe. It does suggest he's careless with the truth if nothing else. But is it a reason for his murder? I don't know.'

The fact was, he'd already dismissed any connection between the pre-nuptial agreement and the murders or the abductions. It was just a wee spat over money, and nothing else, of that he was convinced. The only problem was, right now he didn't have a better theory about any of it, especially the Danny Black murder. And then he remembered Jimmy and Maggie saying they had met Black at that house-warming do over at Richmond.

'What was he like, this Danny Black?'

'Nice enough,' Jimmy said. 'A bit of a lad, perhaps. Eye for the ladies, definitely. He asked me if I was shagging Asvina, which I thought was a bit forward. But here, I've got a couple of photos from the do. Take a look.'

He took Jimmy's phone and peered at it.

'Good-looking guy. Him I mean, not you. A nice wee snap with the kids and Melody too. They must have been pleased, meeting their hero.'

'They were. And if you swipe through, you'll see wee Ollie got one with Danny too.'

Frank nodded. 'Nice picture. The wee lad would be thrilled I guess?'

'He was,' Maggie said, smiling. 'We've printed it out and he's got it stuck on his wall alongside the Ferraris. But getting back to the murders, I can tell you that Melody definitely didn't kill Danny.'

'Why do you say that?' Frank asked.

'She was desperate for it to work this time, to build the perfect little family. She told me all about her tough upbringing and about her previous failed marriages, and I really believed her. Danny was her last chance, that's the way she saw it.'

'But *somebody* must have wanted him dead,' Frank said. He knew it was stating the bleeding obvious and he wasn't really looking for a response, but he got one anyway.

'Well, what about Bow Road? That's how he was connected to Benjamin Fox and to Allegra Ross too,' Maggie said. 'Maybe that's something for us to look at.'

He laughed. 'What, you think it's the cast of a rival soap bumping them all off? That would be quite a plot-line.'

But there was no denying it was a connection. What's more, he realised it also provided a link back to Charles Grant and the abduction of his toddler. Which brought him back round to Frenchie and the meeting he'd had yesterday with Vivien Grant.

'My colleague Ronnie French finally got off his fat arse and went to interview Charles' wife. He said she was in a bit of a state and already hitting the vodka and oranges at ten in the morning. But the interesting thing was, she seems to blame wee Jamie's abduction on some photo-shoot the family had done for one of these glossy lifestyle magazines. It hit the newsagents just a month or so before the incident and she says it put her boy in the shop window. A funny way to describe it I know, but that's what she says.'

'God, that's interesting,' Maggie said. 'Did that come up in the original enquiry?'

'Nothing came up in the original enquiry. But it makes you think doesn't it? Some villain sees the article and thinks, yep, that boy will do nicely. Not that it takes us any further forward in terms of who did it.'

'Not really,' Maggie agreed. 'But you know, it might be interesting to know if the other two kids were involved in one of these photo-shoots too. Their parents were in the public eye after all.'

'Maybe that's one for you and Jimmy to look into,' he said, draining the dregs of his coffee, 'but I need to shoot. Got some hot-shot boffin over from Holland who might be able to nail this da Vinci bloke for us. I'll keep you informed.'

***

On the way over to Maida Vale, Frank reflected that he had to do some serious thinking about what the press was now calling the Bow Road murders. Danny Black's killing was definitely a copy-cat job, he now accepted that. And now Colin Barker was back in charge of the case, more smug and more stupid than ever, and with renewed determination to stitch up Darren Venables for the Ross and Fox killings. The far-right thug had barely been free for twenty-four hours when he was re-arrested, and all that da Vinci social media stuff was going to do for him. Frank would bet his pension that he was innocent, but he realised with some reluctance he would have to leave that for the jury to sort out. As for the Danny Black murder, where did you start? The only half-lead he had so far came from Jimmy, from that meeting at Melody Montague's place. He sounded like the sort of man who regarded infidelity as nothing more than an innocent hobby like fishing or golf. So was this the revenge of a wronged husband, a husband who somehow had got to learn the MO of the earlier killings and staged a neat if flawed re-make? He shook his head, swearing to himself under his breath. Of course it sounded ridiculous, because it *was* ridiculous. There had to be more to it than that.

***

Boegenkamp was waiting in reception when Frank arrived and, annoyingly, looked none the worse for his session the previous evening, where he had out-drunk Frank in a ratio approaching two to one.

'Good afternoon Frank. A little bird is telling me we have some good news to look forward to.'

Frank forced a smile despite his pounding head. 'A little bird called Hanneke is that?'

He nodded. 'Yes, she called me on my way over from my hotel.'

Frank collected their passes then led Boegenkamp up the stairs to the corner conference room where Eleanor and Dr Jansen had been installed for the duration. Eleanor smiled warmly in Frank's direction, a smile which he recognised as her pleased-with-herself one. Which was a surprise to him since she had been far from pleased when he told her she wasn't going to Leiden after all. However, the source of her good cheer was soon revealed by her first words to him.

'Hanneke got me access to her Cray. It's like beyond awesome.'

She looked as if she hadn't slept for a week, dark rings surrounding her eyes and her hair dull and matted, her favourite lavender t-shirt crushed to within an inch of its life, but then again, that wasn't much different from her normal look. Dr Hanneke Jansen by contrast was fresh-faced and smartly dressed in new-looking jeans and a crisp white tailored shirt. She was tall and slim, almost as tall as Boegenkamp in fact, and her general academic appearance was accentuated by a pair of circular wire-framed spectacles perched on the end of her nose. Despite the outward differences, it was clear that a bond had developed between the two women over the few days they had spent together, as they now shared a quiet joke which Frank suspected, correctly as it happened, featured himself in some way.

'Eleanor has told me so much about you,' Hanneke said in way of introduction. 'I have been very much looking forward to meeting you in person also.'

He gave her a suspicious look. 'Is that right? I can't imagine what she's said about me.'

Eleanor grinned. 'We were just trying to work out how to explain what we've found out, you know, in a simple way, as if you were like a five-year old.' The words may have been unkind, but the tone was affectionate.

He shrugged. 'Aye, well I'm sure you'll keep it dead easy, that's what I need.'

'And me also,' laughed Boegenkamp.

'So anyway,' Frank said, 'enough of this hilarity Campbell. Just tell us what you've found.'

'Can we wait for Zak?' she asked. 'He's just gone to the loo.'

He remembered her mentioning him before.

'Oh aye, he's the web-crawler guy.'

Dr Jansen let out an involuntary giggle.

'I'm sorry Frank,' she said, 'it sounded so funny.'

'I gather that,' he replied, without malice.

A few seconds later, they were joined by a smooth-skinned youth who looked as if he should still be at school. *Primary school*. He wore old-fashioned horn-rimmed spectacles with a mass of thick brown locks tidied into a ponytail. Frank knew the dress code in this building was shirt and smart trousers, and whilst Zak's attire just about obeyed the letter of that law, his light blue shirt though clean, was clearly antique and had not been ironed that morning or any other. The trousers were of a brown corduroy, and they too were un-pressed. The general effect was of a second-world war code-breaker, brilliant but so scruffy that he had to be hidden out of sight in some top-secret country manor house.

He raised a hand in greeting. 'I'm Zak. Zak Newton. Welcome to Maida Vale Forensic Labs. Eleanor probably told you, I've been trying to help with your da Vinci guy thing?'

Zak seemed already to be ending his sentences with that rising inflection thing that had become the norm for anyone under thirty-five, so Frank wasn't sure if he was expected to answer. But he did anyway.

'She told me.'

'Sweet. So I've been running the sweeps through GCHQ's Hitachi for the last couple of days. It's awesome capability but the beta version that we've got is fairly slow and a bit unstable.'

'Beta version?' Frank had heard Eleanor use the phrase many times in the past but didn't know what it meant.

'It's like untested software,' Zak explained. 'It's got lots of bugs and it falls over and some things don't work at all, but the developer guys get feedback from us so that they can fix it and make improvements and stuff. Once they've done that it goes alpha.'

Frank smiled. 'Sounds a bit like what my bank does to me every time they have an upgrade to their app.'

'Yeah, just like that,' Zak said, smiling. 'So this software is all about replacing manual analysis. It's state of the art and a lot more accurate. It can identify thousands of phrases and scan two hundred thousand documents an hour. Pretty awesome.'

Out the corner of his eye, Frank saw Boegenkamp giving a subtle tip of the head. Cottoning on, he looked over at Dr Jansen, who was wearing a face like thunder.

'Aye, nice one Zak,' hoping to steer proceedings in Jansen's direction. But he didn't need to intervene any further because Zak had picked up the atmosphere in the room. Not that you could miss it.

'But of course, it's nowhere compared with Hanneke's kit and well, her software is just off the scale, capability-wise. So I decided to hand over the problem to her and Eleanor. Always best to use the right tools and the right people for the job, don't you think?'

Frank chuckled to himself. This lad should dump his career in tech and join the diplomatic corps.

'Awesome,' he said, shooting a smile in Boegenkamp's direction. 'So Dr Jansen, perhaps you could take up the story from here?'

Returned to centre stage, her frown melted away. This was a woman who obviously craved the limelight. Something to remember for the future, although he wondered why Marco hadn't mentioned it to him. Maybe he hadn't noticed. Or maybe it was just her Dutchness.

'Of course Frank. So perhaps I can start with some history?'

'Please do.'

She smiled. 'We are the cyber security research group at the University of Leiden, and I of course am the leader of that group. For this project, we worked with the admissions administrators to recruit a control group of a thousand student volunteers. Each of them were asked to write one hundred posts on various social media platforms, under their usual handles. And then my A-I software, running on some high-powered computer hardware set up specifically for the purpose...'

'That's the Crays,' Frank said.

'...right. So the Crays analysed all the posts, looking for commonalities in the phraseology, comparing them with a control document prepared by each participant also.'

'Cool'.

'When they compared the identification data with the control document,' Jansen continued, 'there was about an eighty percent match. And the cool thing is, my A-I software learns from experience, so it gets better the more data it gets.'

'I get it so far,' Frank said, lying. 'What about you Marco?'

'Crystal clear also.'

Frank shot him a smile.

'So once we were happy with our matching technology, then I needed to develop a method to search across the internet.'

'Isn't that simply google?' Boegenkamp asked. Riskily, in Frank's opinion, and being rewarded with a withering look from Dr Jansen.

'Many people would think that,' she said in a smug tone, 'but of course we cannot use that facility because that is owned by the American corporation Alphabet Incorporated and they do not grant access to their databases or algorithms.'

'Aye, so *that's* why your team had to develop the web-crawler thingy.' Frank remembered Eleanor explaining this to him earlier and he was feeling pleased with himself for recalling the conversation.

'My team was involved, yes, but it was mainly me,' she replied, a hint of frostiness creeping into her voice. 'It is something I specialise in also.'

'Well that's all great Hanneke,' Frank said, trying to hide his impatience. 'So the big question is, how have you got on?'

It all went a bit quiet at that point. Meaning it didn't take long for him to realise that Dr Jansen might have oversold the good news bit when she'd spoken to Boegenkamp earlier.

'Frank, do you know the song, two out of three ain't bad?'

He nodded vaguely. 'Aye, Meatloaf, isn't it? But a bit before my time.' Jesus, did he look *that* old?

'Yes perhaps it was. But it is a very good old rock song in my opinion, one of my dad's favourites. Well this week, we change the song to be one out of two ain't bad. That's what we have achieved this week, so maybe we can call it a little success.'

And then came the excuses, which, showing great leadership, she left Eleanor to deliver.

'It's like a problem,' she said, frowning, 'if the person we are trying to detect doesn't have a big web presence. If they like don't have a Twitter or an Instagram for instance.'

'So, like if they're like over forty?' He hadn't meant to mock her way of speaking but it had just come out that way. 'It like, won't work? *Not* awesome.'

'It's not our fault,' she said defensively. 'If the data isn't there in the first place, we can't make a match, can we?'

There was no denying it, even he could see that. But then, totally out of the blue, an idea popped into his head. And if he made a fool of himself in front of these techie geeks, then so what?

'Listen, I get what you're saying. The guys we're looking for are villains, not bloody social-media stars. But I know one place where their words of wisdom are faithfully recorded for all time. You see the chances are we would have had them in for questioning at some stage in their pathetic little careers. And when we have them in for questioning, they have to make a statement, don't they?'

'And we record these statements in our computer systems,' Boegenkamp cried, catching on.

'Exactly Marco. So why can't we connect Dr Jansen's magic phrase-matching technology up to the Met's criminal records system?'

'It would be very difficult,' Jansen said, frowning. 'Several months work I would think.' He detected the sour tone. The tone that said it won't work because I didn't think of it.

'Our criminal records system has an API,' Zak said suddenly. 'An application program interface. You don't need to know what that means, but it like lets us connect to external systems very easily. I know some of the network services guys and I'm sure they could help set it up if it's too technically difficult for Eleanor or Dr Jansen. A day or two's work at the most.'

God, thought Frank, *I love this guy*. And evidently he wasn't yet finished.

'And of course Hanneke, I assume your software has an API too? It's pretty much mandatory these days, isn't it? You wouldn't write an app like yours without it.'

Ambushed. But to her credit, she seemed to get over it quickly, and five minutes later she and Eleanor were buzzing with excitement as they savoured the interesting technical challenge that lay ahead. One day, two days at the most, and they'd be able to do a sweep against the Met database, when maybe the abductor would be nailed on account of not paying attention in his English class.

That left just one question to be answered.

'One out of two ain't bad, that's what you said. So does that mean you've found out who da Vinci is?'

They had. And when they told him who it was, he couldn't help but laugh out loud. Now he couldn't wait to tell Maggie and Jimmy the news.

Because when it came down to it, professionals were going to beat amateurs every time.

Chapter 25

It was a rare treat indeed for Maggie to get the opportunity to collect her son from school. Theoretically since she worked for herself she could have arranged her workload around the school schedule, but in practice it seemed there was always things to do and people to see which inevitably got in the way. Today however it had been forced on her because her nanny Martha had to fly to Poland at short notice to tend to her sick mother. Inconvenient, but in truth it wasn't much of a problem. In the last day or two they had received a few enquiries for new work, and so Jimmy had been sent off to Kent to interview a local councillor who had contacted them directly about some irregularity or other in the accounts of the local leisure centre. It wasn't their normal line of work, but bills had to be paid whilst they were waiting for the next big assignment from Asvina. To his credit, Jimmy had assented to the mission without protest, citing the opportunity to look up an old army chum whilst he was down there. It seemed to Maggie that he had an old army chum in all four corners of the country and probably beyond too, and for a brief moment she mourned the loss of camaraderie she had suffered after her semi-successful barrister career had crashed and burned. But then when she thought about it again, they were all shits, so really, it was no loss.

They'd had a laugh on the phone after Frank had told them the crazy truth about da Vinci. That their client Charles Grant, right-on warrior for social justice, had, unbelievably, been trolling himself. She could just imagine the headlines in the *Mail* and the *Telegraph* if it ever got out. *Leftie actor invents fascist foe to reinforce victimhood narrative.* It hadn't been his smartest choice, that was for sure, but that seemed to be the pattern of his life. Evidenced by his bonkers decision to invest his whole future in Sharon Trent, when the feelings were all too clearly one way.

But then she thought about it again. If this ever got out, the poor guy would be totally humiliated, and knowing his strong self-regard, it would surely break him. So, what if Benjamin Fox or Allegra Ross or both had found out about it? With Grant's fragile state of mind, she could quite imagine him seeing murder as the only way out. This was something she would need to bring up with Frank as a matter of urgency. But that would have to wait until after she'd fetched Ollie.

The school stood at the head of a leafy cul-de-sac on the northern edges of Hampstead village. After the terrible events of the Alzahrani affair she had moved Ollie from his old private school to this state primary. It wasn't in any way a political statement on her part, the school having been chosen mainly for its convenient location to their home, and she knew it wasn't exactly an inner-city catchment area. The parents were no less middle-class than those of his old school, but tended to be of that group who liked to signal their virtue in all things, including and especially, the choice of education they had made for their kids.

The environment being the great concern of the age, the school encouraged parents if at all possible to leave outsized SUVs parked on driveways and to walk their children there instead. Encouragement was backed up by enforcement, the entire cul-de-sac a no-parking zone patrolled by a suitably officious female traffic warden in a conspicuous hi-viz jacket.

Maggie made sure she arrived outside the gates in good time, being unfamiliar with how long the walk would take. Group of mothers and childminders had already gathered, laughing and smiling as they enjoyed their familiar daily routine. She didn't know any of them, although she recognised a woman of about her own age who she recalled had recently moved in a few doors down the street from her and to whom she had spoken once or twice. Olivia, that was her name, easy to remember for someone with a son called Ollie. She stood a little detached from the others, her arms clasped protectively across her chest. From her City uniform of grey business suit, white silk blouse and heels, Maggie guessed an accountant or a banker, or heaven forbid, a lawyer like herself.

She smiled at her. 'Hi Olivia, I guess this isn't your normal afternoon. Me neither. But it's nice isn't it, to be able to fit it in occasionally?'

The other woman nodded. 'It's Maggie, isn't it, from number twenty-two? Yes, you're right, it is very nice. I don't generally get the chance. We've got a young French au pair who normally does it but we've only had her a couple of weeks and she's turned out to be hopelessly unreliable. Not because she's French or anything,' she added hastily.

Maggie gave a sympathetic laugh. 'No, I think it just comes as standard with these young girls, no matter where they are from.' Except for good old Martha, as solid and reliable as the day was long, and she was only twenty-four. 'It's Josh isn't it, your little boy? We must arrange to get together some time soon, I'm sure my Ollie would love to have a friend so close by. I bet they would get on very well.'

'Oh yes, that would be wonderful. Perhaps you could pop in for a coffee when we get back today and we can arrange something? Maybe this Saturday afternoon if you're both free.'

But now children were beginning to appear through the double doors of the school entrance, at first a trickle and then a steady stream, the noise level increasing exponentially as more and more emerged. Through the crowd she spotted her son, engaged in a mock-wrestle with another boy whom, as they got closer, she recognised as Olivia's Josh. She caught his mother's eye and smiled.

'Looks like our boys are ahead of us Olivia.'

'Mummy, what are you doing here?' Ollie shouted as he caught sight of her, immediately running over and throwing his arms around her waist, so forcibly that she was almost knocked off her feet.

'Wow, have you been doing rugby practice today darling? That was a great tackle.' She squeezed him tightly to her and kissed him gently on the forehead. 'Martha had to go and visit her own mummy in Poland so you've got me instead today.'

Momentarily he looked anxious. 'Can we still go to the shop for sweets on the way home mummy? Martha always lets me.' It was news to Maggie, and strictly against instructions too, but that was her good-hearted nanny all over.

'Well if you can show me the way, maybe we can do it as a special treat just for today. And perhaps Josh would like to come too if his mummy is ok with that?'

Olivia laughed. 'I don't think I could stop him even if I wanted to. Of course it's fine.'

They set off along the cul-de-sac, the boys hyper with excitement and the mums relaxed, chatting easily about work and houses and schools and husbands - dead husbands in Maggie's case. Time seemed to fly by as they trooped the half-mile along the busy main road to where they would turn off, disappearing into the warren of leafy suburban backwaters. Looking up, she saw that the two boys had sprinted ahead and then stopped at a junction which was unfamiliar to both the mothers.

'Do you know where you're going?' she shouted, struggling to make herself heard above the roar of the traffic.

'Of course mummy,' he shouted back. 'It's just along here a bit. Mr Aziz's shop is on the next corner.'

'Well don't go too far then,' she said, knowing they would ignore her. 'Wait for us!'

Across the street the occupants of a black BMW SUV sat quietly observing proceedings, as they had done for the last three days. If you were a politician or a celebrity or a prominent business person, you were likely to have had personal security training, which would have taught you the importance of avoiding regular routines in your day to day life. Change your times, change your route, change your mode of transport, that would make it more difficult for those that meant to do you harm. But kids going home from school, why would they know anything about that? Inside, the men had to make a decision. Same time, same place and there was the kid they were after, but today he wasn't with the fat girl, and today they weren't alone. It wasn't what they were expecting but a fraught phone call with the boss had left them in no doubt. It was to be done today, and so what if it was a bit more complicated, that was their job in the organisation. *Just get it sorted, understood?*

They left the engine running and clicked open the powered tailgate with the key-fob. It was quiet in this street, that's why they'd picked it, but it didn't pay to hang around any longer than was necessary. Just grab the kid, stick the bag over his head and cable-tie his hands, bundle him in the back, beat it. Didn't need to be more complicated than that.

To the mothers, now some eighty metres distant, the horror seemed to be unfolding in slow motion. There was two of them, a thick-set man in a leather bomber jacket, black jeans and trainers and a wiry youth in double denim. They looked around, hoping that they would be unobserved but not caring that much. In a second, they were on the other side of the street, the larger man grabbing Ollie by the hair and dragging him screaming over to the BMW. The boy, initially taken by surprise, now seem to realise what was happening and began to struggle, kicking his legs furiously and trying in vain to push himself away from his abductor. The second man, seeing what was happening, gave him a brutal slap across the cheek to subdue him, causing the other man to react furiously.

'Fuck's sake Vince, careful, we don't want no damaged goods.' He realised his mistake as soon as he said it, but Maggie and Olivia, who had now began running towards them, were still too far away to hear. With an expert motion he put two pre-prepared cable-ties around Ollie's wrist and jerked them tight, causing him to wince with pain. He yanked even more tightly on his hair, guiding him towards the open tailgate, and roughly pushed him into the luggage area. 'You fucking sit there and don't move, understand?' And then he remembered his slip of the tongue. 'Shit, we'd better take the other kid too, we don't want no witnesses. Come on, get him in the back of the motor.'

Throughout, Josh had stood stock-still on the pavement, open- mouthed with shock and fear, and it was a simple task for Vince to push him across the street and into the back of the SUV. At least it would have been, if at that moment Maggie and Olivia had not arrived on the scene.

Olivia flew at the youth, her arms flaying as she rained a barrage of weak punches in his direction. 'Leave him alone, leave him alone!' she screamed through her tears. 'Run, Josh, run. Get away!' but the boy was paralysed with fright, unable to comprehend what was happening to him and his mummy.

Simultaneously Maggie had rushed over to the BMW, where the older man stood guard, waiting to bundle Josh in the back. She tried to push past him to get to Ollie, but he grabbed her roughly by the shoulders and shoved her to the ground. As she fell, her forehead crashed against the pavement edge, driving a deep gash and drawing blood. Weakly, she got to her knees, her mind clear despite the pain. She had to free Ollie, she just had to, pleading with the gods to give her the strength, but as she tried to get to her feet, the hood smashed his fist into her face, shattering her nose and causing her to collapse into the road, ending up face down in a pool of her own blood.

Momentarily unconscious, she opened her eyes to see that across the street Olivia was still gripping desperately onto the younger man, who despite all his efforts, was unable to shake himself free. She could just about make out the words. *Fuck's sake dad, get the cow off me*. Then through her blurred vision, she caught the glint of steel in the sunshine as he ran across to his son and with a sickening movement, plunged the knife into Olivia's chest.

Chapter 26

Serious but not immediately life-threatening was how the young doctor had described Maggie's condition. Not *immediately* life-threatening, what the hell did that mean? That's what Jimmy was asking his brother, again and again, as they sat alongside her bed in a high dependency suite of the Royal Free Hospital. She looked for all the world as if she had come off second-best in a particularly one-sided boxing match. Her left eye was surrounded by a dark purple ring of puffy skin, causing it to be squeezed tightly and painfully shut. Her nose had fared even worse, the bone broken and the flesh swollen to twice its normal size, its colour a matching shade for her eye. Fortunately, the blow on her forehead, though causing a nasty bruise, had not broken the skin so no disfiguring stitches would be required. But along the corridor, Olivia Walton was fighting for her life, her distraught husband beside her, struggling to take in the shattering tsunami that had today, without warning, enveloped his family. He had been told not to hold out much hope, but he had not been listening. Olivia was just thirty-six years old and only yesterday they had received the news that she was pregnant with their second child. Thirty-six-year-old women didn't just *die,* of course they didn't, that was stupid, and seven-year old boys weren't abducted in broad daylight.

Jimmy and Frank had been joined by Asvina and DI Pete Burnside, who had been swiftly assigned to the case by DCI Smart. The stern male nurse had balked at having four visitors in the room, but Burnside had convinced him of the need for the police to be present when she awoke from her sedation, in case she had seen anything that would help them in the desperate search for the abductors of two young boys and the perpetrators of the vicious attacks on their mothers.

'What are we going to tell her about Ollie?' Jimmy whispered, his tone betraying his anxiety. 'I mean, it could send her over the edge, it really could.'

'What can we tell her? We know absolutely bugger-all at the moment,' replied Frank irritably. 'Look, I'm sorry mate, we just have to tell her the truth, she would want that.' It had only been a few hours, but already he knew the sense of helplessness that Burnside must have felt all through the Jamie Grant investigation.

'Maybe it's best if I speak to her,' Asvina said softly. 'I don't really know what to say, but well, as a mother, maybe it would be better...honestly, I don't know.'

Burnside was trying hard to be positive, without much conviction. 'This whole abduction thing didn't turn out at all as they planned it, I'm absolutely sure of that. The crime scene will be awash with evidence, believe you me. We'll get the bastards this time, we will. There's no doubt about it.'

Frank nodded, wishing he shared his colleague's confidence. Six hours on and no witnesses had come forward and there was nothing on the CCTV around the scene, not that they had a bloody clue what they were looking for. Burnside had a squad of uniforms conducting door-to-doors within a five-hundred metre radius, but so far they too had drawn a blank. A near-fatal stabbing and the snatching of two children had taken place on a sunny school-day afternoon and no-one had seen a thing. With Olivia Walton at death's door, the fact was that now they were totally dependent on Maggie to make any progress, and goodness knows what state she would be in when she came round.

Outside the door, another doctor had appeared and was immediately in deep conversation with the nurse. A moment later, she entered the room.

'Good evening, I'm Susan Blackford, Miss Bainbridge's consultant. Nurse Hamlyn has just been sharing the background of the case with me. It's a terrible thing altogether.'

'Is she going to be all right?' Jimmy asked.

'I think so. She has suffered quite a severe trauma to her forehead and that would have led to rather bad concussion, but luckily we don't think she has suffered an injury to the brain. These can take some time to develop of course so she will have to be kept here under observation for a few days, but the signs are good. And she has a broken nose too, which is going to be very painful.'

Frank nodded. 'Aye, she's been in the wars right enough.'

'Indeed,' Blackman replied, 'but my immediate concern is the effect any further emotional stress will have on her recovery. I've heard about what has happened to her son, and in my opinion, it may be sensible to keep her under light sedation when the news is broken to her. I'm genuinely worried about the effect any shock may have on her.'

'I understand that doctor,' Burnside said, nodding in sympathy but anxious to make his point, 'but you know we really need to speak to her as soon as you think it's safe. She's probably our only witness at the moment and so you see, everything depends on what she can tell us. To help us find the boys.'

The consultant shook her head. 'Yes, well I can see it's important, but I have to balance that with the needs of my patient. Look, I'm happy with one of you staying with her but not all of you. And please, when she wakes up, no questions until the nursing team and myself are here, is that clear?'

'That's absolutely fine,' Asvina agreed. 'Her mum is on the way from Yorkshire and should be here in a couple of hours. Who's going to stay with her until then?'

They looked at each other, uncertain. Finally Jimmy said, 'I will.'

He'd had plenty of experience dealing with trauma, too much if truth be told, but he'd never expected to have to face it in this job. Out in Helmand, telling an injured squaddie that some of their mates were dead was the worst thing he had to do, and now back here in London, he would somehow have to break it to Maggie about Ollie, and about Olivia and Josh too. He'd no idea how much she would have remembered about the attack but whatever the case she would be in deep shock. Of course, she'd been through a lot, about ten times more stuff in the last two years than most people saw in a lifetime, and seemed outwardly to have built up a resilience, but that too he had seen before, plenty of times. Sometimes, there was a tipping point, just one little thing, the straw that broke the camel's back. He prayed to Christ that this wouldn't be it.

Frank got up and patted him on the shoulder. 'Ok, we'll leave you to it mate. We'll be outside if you need a break, just give us a shout.'

Jimmy gave a thumbs-up as they left the room. For the moment there was nothing else to do but sit and wait, watching as she lay still and silent, her shallow breathing the faintest murmur above the background hum and rhythmic beep of the heart monitor. Hard to believe it was barely eighteen months since they had first met, both of them in different ways damaged goods, but to use the over-used phrase so beloved of celebs, they had since been on a journey together, and it was now quite impossible to imagine life without her. Yet it was difficult to put a finger on what exactly made the relationship so special. It wasn't romance, and it certainly wasn't sexual, he was never going there, attractive though she was, but it wasn't like brother and sister either. Actually, when he thought about it, they were like comrades in the army, brought together by life experiences that few had shared. Yes, the more he considered it, the more he saw it to be true. Captain James Stewart and Maggie Bainbridge, the not-quite-QC, were comrades-in-arms, and always would be, if he had anything to do with it.

It was nearly ten minutes before she stirred, first her head slowly tilting towards him and then with an obvious effort she opened her eyes. Her face wore a quizzical expression as she struggled to take in her surroundings, and then the faintest of smiles as she recognised Jimmy. For a few moments she lay silent, and then with no warning she sat bolt upright, wincing as a wave of pain shot through her.

'Ollie, Ollie! My Ollie!' Now her breathing was laboured, her face turning a deathly shade of white.

Jimmy leaped to the door and yanked it open. 'Get someone in here quick!' It was a few seconds before Dr Blackman arrived at her bedside, trailed by a young nurse.

Gently, she placed her hands on Maggie's shoulders and guided her down so that again she lay on her back.

'You're ok Maggie, you'll be fine. Just lie down and we'll get you comfortable. That's a good girl.' She glanced at the nurse. '1ml of Midazolam please,' and then to Jimmy, 'It's just a mild sedative, it's standard procedure.' The nurse bared Maggie's arm and then expertly administered the injection. 'It'll take a few minutes,' she said in way of explanation.

Now Maggie started to cry. 'Jimmy, Ollie, they took him, they took him... and Olivia...' She sobbed violently as the image came back to her. 'God, it was so awful. That man... I can't believe it, what he did.'

Jimmy was struggling to find the right words. 'Maggie... I know, it's just... so terrible. But listen, Pete Burnside's got more than a hundred officers out on the streets looking for him right now, and it's all over the news and in all the papers. They'll find him soon, I'm sure they will.'

But the sickening feeling in his gut said otherwise. Of course he wasn't sure, he wasn't sure at all. After all, it was more than two years since Jamie Grant had disappeared, and they still hadn't found him, not the slightest trace. Praying was useless, he'd found that out only too starkly in Afghanistan, but he still did it because it was human nature to cling to any comfort blanket, no matter how illogical. So he closed his eyes and made a silent plea. *Please God, if you're there, for once just show your hand. Prove me wrong, please please prove me wrong.*

The sedative was beginning to take effect and now she spoke more calmly. 'Jimmy, I need to get out of here. I need to go and look for him. I need to do *something* or I'll go mad. Please, where are my clothes, I need to go back there, I need to.'

'I know, I know,' he said, soothingly, 'but Maggie, you have to get well first. And you should take a look in the mirror. You'll scare the horses if you go out in that state.'

She forced a weak smile. 'Yeah, very funny. But I can't just lie here doing nothing. I just can't. Tell the doctor I want to go home, at least tomorrow.'

He stared at her, alarmed. 'Are you mad Maggie? Hell, you're in no fit state to go anywhere.' Turning to the doctor he said, 'Can you tell her please, she won't listen to me.'

Blackman tried her best professional voice. 'Maggie, as your doctor, I have to say it wouldn't be advisable...'

'Advisable? Look, I'm really ok and I'm not lying here whilst Ollie is...is.' She tailed off, unable to bring herself to say the words.

Jimmy took her hand and squeezed it gently. 'Maggie, we'll find him, we will.' It wasn't much use, but what else could he say? 'But look, maybe you'll be ok to answer a few questions. Are you up for that... I mean, will you be ok?'

She spat out her response. 'Ok? Of course I'll be bloody ok, what sort of a mother do you think I am?'

The doctor smiled. 'There's your answer I think. But please, not too long. I'll ask the policemen to come in, shall I?'

They had decided to leave the questioning to Pete Burnside, as the official lead investigating officer on the case, leaving Frank and Asvina sitting silently in the corridor. Burnside gave Blackman a quick glance as he entered the room and said quietly, 'Ok then?'

She nodded. 'Just five minutes though, that'll be enough.'

Jimmy stood up to vacate the bedside chair and gave a thumbs-up.

'Cheers mate,' Burnside said, taking his place. 'Now Maggie, I know this will be difficult, but can you tell me everything you remember. Even the tiniest detail can help us to find your boy.'

'I understand,' Maggie said, and then she went on to tell him everything she could remember. Of the utter horror when she realised what was happening, the pathetic sense of helplessness when she could not free Ollie from the car, and of course, the stabbing. It was all a terrible blur, the order of events all jumbled around, like waking up in the middle of a nightmare and not knowing what was real and what wasn't. But there was something else, something she sensed was important, but it just wouldn't come to her. What was it? *Come on.*

Doctor Blackman sensed her agitation and said quietly, 'Ok, I think that's enough for today Inspector.'

He nodded. 'Yes, thank you Maggie, you've been absolutely amazing. It's been really, really helpful.'

But it hadn't been, not really, she knew that. She hadn't got the make or number of the SUV, and that was likely to be fake in any case. She had got a look at both men, but she wasn't sure if she could identify them if she saw them again, certainly not the younger of the two. She guessed it wasn't much more than the police had already worked out for themselves, and that was probably two thirds of bugger-all.

But then quite suddenly she remembered what it was. *Dad.* The man who had taken Ollie and who had stabbed Olivia. The younger man had called him dad, she was quite sure of that. How that would help, she had no idea, but it was something. But then another thing came to her. That man he had called dad. She couldn't think where, but she was certain that she had seen him before.

***

Outside in the corridor, Frank felt his phone vibrate. Glancing down, he saw it was Jill Smart.

'Jill, hi. What's up?'

'Frank, I'm in the ops room over at Paddington Green. We've just had something come in, and it's really bad news I'm afraid. They found a body, on some waste ground near Putney Bridge. It's a real mess. SOCOs and the pathologist are there right now, I don't envy them. But it looks like shot wounds to the head.'

'Don't tell me Jill, please don't tell me that.' With every fibre of his being, he hoped that it wouldn't be true, but already he knew from Jill's tone that it was.

'It's a boy. A little boy, about six or seven.'

Of course, he had feared this might happen, although he hadn't dared to admit it to himself. Because he knew they didn't need little Josh Walton. He had just been an unexpected complication in an operation that had very nearly gone tits up. A complication that had to be tidied away.

Chapter 27

As soon as she awoke it started to come back to her through the fog of pain and confusion. Something had happened, something so dreadful that her body and her brain and her entire nervous system had shut down, like a computer placed in that semi-vegetative state known as sleep mode. She remembered someone saying that they would give her something, a nurse probably, and then there was only blackness. Glancing at the bedside clock, she struggled with the calculation. Five-sixteen and the light was beginning to creep through the ward blinds, so that meant it was morning. What was it, fourteen, fifteen hours that she had been asleep? And then as her operating system kicked back into life, she remembered what it was and instantly she was wide awake.

'Nurse! Nurse!' Now she was sitting up, struggling to throw off the bed-clothes as she swung her legs round, her feet recoiling as they brushed against the cold floor. Shakily, she pushed herself up, becoming conscious for the first time of the crashing pain in her head. Ignoring it, she flung open the door of the bedside cabinet and pulled everything out.

'My clothes! Where are my bloody clothes!'

Two nurses had heard her cries and rushed from their station. The first put her arm around her shoulder and gently tried to guide Maggie back to bed.

'Now then my love,' she said in a kindly tone. 'We're not in any fit state to be up and about, are we? Let's get you back to bed, there's a love.'

Maggie struggled to free herself, but the nurse's hold on her was firm.

'My clothes. I need them. Please. It's my son you see, he's been taken and I have to look for him.' She could feel herself starting to shake as the emotion threatened to overwhelm her. The other nurse had turned down the sheets and now took Maggie's arm and helped her sit down on the edge of the bed.

'I know love, I know, it's a terrible thing. Look, there's a policewoman waiting outside. Let's get you back into bed and I'll send her in so that she can give you an update. And your partner Mr Stewart is snoring away in our dayroom.' She grinned. 'He actually fell asleep at your bedside and nurse Short and I had a right job to wake him. Now we'll get you a nice cup of tea and send them through.'

It was Jimmy who was first to arrive, unshaven and dishevelled after a night of fitful sleep, but it didn't prevent a gaggle of nurses turning to stare as he strode down the ward. He bent over and kissed her on the cheek.

'How are you feeling?' he asked quietly.

She smiled weakly. 'Rather shit, if you must know. But you've got to get me out of here Jimmy. We've got to look for Ollie.'

'Aye, you said that last night. Over and over again, as I recall.'

The young uniformed WPC had been hovering discreetly in the background. Now she pulled out the chair next to Jimmy's and sat down.

'Miss Bainbridge, DI Peter Burnside has taken personal charge of the investigation. I think you know him. He's a very experienced detective and he will be pulling out all the stops to find your son. You're in good hands.' It sounded exactly like what it was. Classic platitudes from the victim support handbook.

'Is there any actual news?' Jimmy asked, looking at her.

She shook her head. 'They'll be doing more door to doors this morning and there's an update meeting at noon over at Paddington Green.' In other words, no.

Maggie tried to push herself up against her pillows, without success. 'Find me my clothes Jimmy, please I need to get out of here.'

He gave her a sceptical look. 'I don't think so Maggie. You're in no fit state...'

'They can't keep me here. I'll go crazy with worry. I've got to do something.'

***

He knew she was right, she would go crazy, but really, what could he do? Maybe they would give her something to help with the stress and anxiety, something to help her rest until she got strong again. That's what they had done with the worst cases out in Helmand. Pump them full of morphine so that they even forgot their own name. For their own good, that's what the medics said, and they had meant it too. And at that moment, that's what he wished for Maggie, more than anything in the world. He would squeeze her hand tightly as she drifted into a deep sleep, and only waken her when they had found Ollie safe and well. However long that took. But that was fantasy, not reality and he had to deal with the real world.

'Look Maggie, I need to talk to Dr Blackman. She'll know what's best for you.' But he already knew what she would tell him. There was no way she was going to agree to her discharge, you only had to look at her battered face to tell how stupid that would be. And he already knew what Maggie would say when he reported Blackman's advice back to her. Short of tying her to the bed, he wasn't going to be able to stop her. Which left him with one last option.

'Ok, promise me this. If the doctor says you will definitely die if you discharge yourself, you will agree to stay right here. If she says it would be incredibly dumb, foolish and stupid, and that you will need to sign fifty forms indemnifying the hospital from all responsibility in the matter, but you probably will not die, at least not right away, then you can leave with me.'

She did not reply but he took her silence as a yes.

***

Barely one hour later, they were outside in the cool air, a welcome relief after the stuffy hospital ward. Jimmy was pushing the wheelchair which the discharge team insisted must be used for the journey to the car-park, Maggie wrapped in a blanket and clutching an outsized paper bag containing her medication. She had protested, but Jimmy had told her it was at least a mile to where he'd left his old Vectra and he wasn't carrying her, no way. Especially since the car was up on the seventh floor of the multi-storey and he'd noticed when he arrived that to save energy they didn't switched the lift on until eight o'clock. He cursed inwardly as he propelled her up the steep accessibility ramp that wound its way up around the edge of the building. On another day he would have joked that she was putting on a bit of timber, but today wasn't that day. A few minutes later, and breathless, they were pushing open the double doors signed with a seven. The floor was now almost deserted of vehicles and so he had no trouble locating his own car. He blipped the remote and wheeled her up to the door.

'Right then, let's get you in,' he said, grimacing as he once again caught a glimpse of her bruised features, 'and if I were you, I wouldn't bother with the vanity mirror. I just need to go and pay for this ticket.'

She smiled weakly. 'I won't. Are we going straight to the scene? I hope that's the plan.'

'Straight there,' he shouted back to her, though what the hell they were going to do when they got there, he hadn't the faintest clue.

They slipped through the barrier out onto Pond Street and a minute later they were on Haverstock Hill, the road quiet as they headed northwards against the flow of the early-morning commuters.

'Heath Crescent, wasn't it?' Jimmy asked. 'I think I spotted that on the map. Shouldn't be more than ten minutes.'

Heath Crescent had a distinctly genteel appearance, leafy and lined with twenties semis like so many more in the capital, although the average house price here was close to double the city's average. Maggie screwed up her eyes and scanned left and right as Jimmy slowed the car to a crawl.

'I think it was on the left, just along here a bit. Yeah, right here. This is it.' Following her instruction, he pulled up and jerked on the handbrake.

'Ok then,' he said slowly, 'right. I guess we should get out and take a look, what do you think?'

Yes, but look at what? Twenty-four hours ago, the place would have been swarming with SOCOs, working round the clock under the harsh glare of their portable floodlights. The fact that they had been and gone meant that their work here was done, the scene presumably having yielded all the evidence it was likely to yield. What were they going to find that the team of highly-trained and professionally-equipped experts had missed? But they had to do something, he knew that, for Maggie's sake. They couldn't just sit around and wait. That would be a killer.

He helped her out, taking her arm to steady her, the hospital blanket still wrapped around her shoulders. Softly he said, 'Do you remember anything?'

She shook her head. 'No more than I told Burnside.'

They stood on the pavement for several minutes, brows furrowed in concentration, hoping for inspiration, but none came. How could it? It wasn't as if they were suddenly going to magic up the solution out of thin air.

'Look, maybe we could try going door to door, if you're up to it,' he said. 'There's always a chance that someone will give up some information to you as the mum that they wouldn't give to the police.'

She gave the slightest nod of assent, but already he could see the hope was being drained from her. And of course it was hopeless. He knew he had to keep going for her sake, but after two hours, all they heard was the same story. *It was so awful what happened, but I'm really sorry, I didn't see or hear anything.* He glanced at his watch.

'Maggie, it's nearly twelve o'clock and you need to take your medication. I think we'd better get you home, get you a coffee and a bite to eat.'

'Yes Jimmy, I'd like that,' she said, her reply barely audible. Her house was only a half a mile away, and a couple of minutes later he was pulling up the Vectra outside her front door.

He'd forgotten that Marta would be there. As soon as she heard the key in the door, the young nanny rushed to comfort Maggie.

'I'm so so sorry, I don't know what to say. Ollie will be ok, I know he will. I have prayed to God and I know it will be ok.'

He could see Maggie's eyes moisten as the young woman locked her in an embrace, desperate for anything that would provide a momentary relief from their agony.

'Marta, could you make us some coffee please?' Jimmy asked. 'And maybe a sandwich.' He took Maggie by the hand and led her through to the sitting room, settling her comfortably into the plump settee, tucking the blanket around her. Now all they could do was sit and wait. Wait for the phone call that said he'd been found, that he was perfectly safe and well and none the worse for his ordeal. Or wait for the phone call from the police liaison officer, the call that told her that her life would never be the same again. And he feared for her, if that was the outcome, after all she had been through. If anything happened to Ollie, he just couldn't see how she could carry on. He looked over at her, and to his relief, saw she was drifting off to sleep.

He slipped out of the room as quietly as he could and re-joined Marta in the kitchen. She had prepared a pile of cheese sandwiches that would have fed them for a week, but like her, his appetite had gone. She had been crying, her eyes black-ringed through lack of sleep and the tracks of her tears visible against her pale skin. 'Oh Jimmy, please tell me it will be all right,' she pleaded, but he couldn't comfort her, any more than he could Maggie.

'I hope so Marta. And I hope your prayer is answered, I really do.' He half-smiled and returned to the sitting-room, flopping down in the floral-patterned armchair that occupied the bay window recess. And soon he too was asleep.

He was awakened by a loud blast of *Feels Like Teen Spirit*, the strident opening of the Nirvana classic perfect as a ring tone but less than ideal as a wake-up call. It was Frank.

'Hey mate, how is she? Sorry I didn't call earlier but there's been some developments in the Danny Black case and that tied me up all day.'

'She's not good Frank. What time is it?'

'Nearly eleven o clock. At night.'

'Is it? We must have been out for hours.' He looked over to her, checking she was still asleep. Lowering his voice to a whisper he asked, 'Has Pete Burnside and his team made any progress?'

Frank sighed audibly. *'No, and there's bugger-all to work on. We know it's ninety-nine percent certain that it's the same gang that took those other kids but that's it. We've got Eleanor and her Dutch mate trying to do that phrase-matching thing and we've got old Mrs what's-her-name with her Henry, and Maggie with her dad guy and thinking she might have seen him somewhere before. That's the sum total of concrete facts and it's two thirds of bugger-all.'*

'That's not what I wanted to hear bruv,' Jimmy said.

'Aye, you're right but at least it's something. Oh by the way, Jill Smart's given me the ok to work on Ollie's case, not that I wouldn't have irrespective of what she said. I'm just going over to Paddington Green now to do some digging on father and son operations.'

'What, at this time of night?'

'Aye, I know. It's a long shot, but the fact is, I need to do something to take my mind off it. Anyway, must push on, just wanted to know how she was. Over and out.'

Maggie was now beginning to wake, yawning as she stretched an arm in the air. She saw Jimmy and smiled. 'What time is it?'

'Eleven. You've had a great sleep, you must have needed it. Fancy a cup of tea?'

'I'd rather have a whisky if it's that time. A large one please. There's a bottle of Glenfiddich in the cupboard over there. And some glasses.'

He fetched the bottle and glasses and placed them on the coffee table.

'Two inches?'

'Yes please. Has there been any news?'

'Frank's moved himself onto the case,' Jimmy said. 'He's over at the station right now following up some leads on your dad thing. Looking at father and son teams as he called them. It sounds quite hopeful.' It hadn't sounded the least bit hopeful, more like clutching at straws, but he had to say something.

She picked up her glass and gulped a large measure and then another. The combination of sleep and the single malt seemed to have stiffened her resolve, because now she closed her eyes and laid her head back on the thick cushion. 'I need to think, I need to think! She spat out the words, directed as much at herself as Jimmy. 'Where did I see that face before? Where! Come on, think!'

He could see that she did not need a response from him, did not want him to break her fierce concentration. But if she could force herself into the zone, why the hell couldn't he? Because for some reason, he was thinking about photographs. That photograph of Fox and the kid that he'd found in the diary that Allegra Ross kept hidden under her mattress, set in those picture-perfect gardens, gardens he was sure he had seen before. And of the celebrity magazine shots that Maggie had shown him of the Grants and the Lawrences and the van Durens, the glossy airbrushed images capturing the perfect family life.

And at that instant, he had worked it all out.

***

Over at Paddington Green, Frank too was fortifying himself with a whisky, his a smoky Islay malt that he swigged straight from his hip-flask. Normally he turned to it when things were going badly, but tonight it was the exact opposite. Tonight things couldn't be going better. This was a celebration, albeit perhaps a premature one. What the hell.

It was the call from Eleanor and Dr Jansen that had done it. *We've found a match.* A suspect's statement from three years ago, a routine investigation into a robbery at a warehouse just off the Bath Road, an investigation that had gone nowhere because they couldn't place the accused at the scene of the crime.

I'm not joking you when I says it, I've never been near the place in my whole life.

He punched a few keys on his laptop and pulled up that interview report from the Jamie Grant case. Old Mrs what's-her-name was eighty-four, half-blind and a bit hard of hearing. Yes, he *thought* he had read it correctly before. 'He called out a name,' she had told the interviewing officer. 'What was it again? Began with an 'H' I think. 'enry, that's what it was.'

'But it wasn't Henry, was it my love?' Frank said, smiling to himself. 'It was Harry, wasn't it?' The same Harry who'd never been near the place in his whole life. He took his ruler and carefully underlined a name on his list. 'And we know who you are, don't we Harry mate? You and Vince, that son of yours.'

Back in Hampstead their individual moments of epiphany had emerged at the exact same moment, as if by some weird celestial decree. Simultaneously they had leapt to their feet, even Maggie in her condition, and screamed and shouted at the top of their voices, and when they shared their revelations and they turned out to be identical, they hugged joyously, as if they would never let go. Three minutes later they were back in the Vectra preparing to head south-west.

Chapter 28

He pretty much knew the way, but just to be sure he punched the address into Google maps, steering with his knees as they raced along the Dunston Road. Glancing at the phone, he saw the sat-nav was directing him up on to the North Circular rather than the shorter route across town. Good, he would be able to put his foot down along there, with three lanes to play with and hopefully not much traffic at this time of night. Plenty of traffic lights and speed cameras of course, but that would be a discussion he could have with the police after the fact. As long as they didn't get stopped on the way that is.

Thirteen-point-six miles and thirty-five minutes, that's what it was saying, but he reckoned he could half that. He kept it in third, the engine screaming from the strain of operating right up at its rev limit. Ten minutes later, they were across Kew Bridge and skirting the high wall of the famous horticultural gardens, and only three red lights jumped on the way, his indiscretions no doubt caught on the traffic cameras. Nine points, three hundred quid fine, maybe a ban. But worth it.

On the way he had got Maggie to message Frank with their destination postcode and a terse note. *Get here fast and bring an armed response team.* He knew that they shouldn't be doing this, that they should wait for the professionals, but this wasn't any ordinary situation. Ollie's life depended on them getting there fast and he wasn't going to wait for anyone.

Now his mission head had kicked in and he was barking out instructions. 'Look Maggie, in your state you shouldn't be on this jamboree in the first place, but since against my better judgement you are, then it's role-reversal time for us. I'm in charge, I'm the officer, and you obey orders, understand? You do everything I say, without questions or arguments, and you *don't* do anything unless I tell you, ok?'

She nodded silently.

'So, I've got a bit of a half-arsed plan worked out. There's some stuff in my old hold-all in the back seat there. Could you drag it over and see if you can find the masks? We'll need them at some point so best to have them to hand.'

'Masks?'

'Aye, look, I'll explain later. Just dig them out and then put one round your neck so you've got it handy if we need it. And there's a wee back-pack in there too. Pull that out if you can.'

She spun round, straining against the tension of her seat-belt to reach the old canvas bag and drag it onto her lap. Pulling open the zip, she started to search inside, struggling to focus under the inadequate glow of the street lights shining through the windscreen. With both hands in the bag, he knew she was relying on feel rather than sight to find what she was looking for. And then he heard her gasp as she felt it. Cold, hard, metallic, the shape unmistakeable.

'Jimmy, a gun? Is that a gun?'

'Aye, it's a wee souvenir from my time in the army. Most of the boys kept one when they went back to civvy street.'

'I'm scared Jimmy. If you think we need guns.'

'I don't know if we do. But we've had four murders and Jamie and Kitty still haven't been found, dead or alive. These are dangerous people we are dealing with.' Which is why of course they should wait for the professionals. Except that the last thing they wanted here was some big Hollywood-style shit-storm. With these armed response guys, it was all battering rams and shouting and teams of trigger-happy hard men with automatics rampaging around the crime scene. He'd seen plenty of these operations in Helmand and the problem was, they had a nasty propensity to go arse over tit. Collateral damage, that's what they called it, but they couldn't afford collateral damage on this mission. No, what he had in mind was altogether more subtle. Employing stealth not strength. Well, sort-of, if you didn't count the smoke grenade.

'The gun's just a precaution,' he soothed. 'We won't be shooting anyone, don't worry.' As long as nobody shoots at us first, he thought.

He turned off the engine as they approached the house, coasting to a halt just alongside its perimeter wall. No more than six feet high, he estimated, not hard to get over and an easy drop on the other side. There would be security cameras of course, but he guessed they would be mainly focussed around the gates and driveway. There might be one mounted on a high mast or something, doing a sweep across the garden on a two or three-minute cycle, but they could time their entry to avoid that with little difficulty.

He reached over and took her hand. 'You can wait here if you want. Until Frank and his mates arrive. I'd prefer it if you did.' He knew before he said it what her answer would be.

'Ok, so you've got your mask, good.' Rummaging in the holdall, he took out the Glock-17, slid back the safety catch and slipped it into his pocket. 'Right, just need to get the ladder and we're good to go. Ready?'

She hesitated for a second, took a deep breath and then nodded. 'Ready.'

He slung on the back-pack and pulled a jumble of orange-coloured nylon cord out of the holdall. 'Rope ladder,' he explained. 'Ever climbed one before? It's easy.'

The short ladder was equipped with two sturdy grappling hooks. A deft throw and they were attached to the top of the wall. He gave the ladder a firm tug to confirm that it was securely attached. 'First time,' he said, smiling at Maggie. 'Not lost my touch, eh?'

'Right, so I'm going up first. Just going to check the lie of the land with regard to any cameras, and then I'll jump down into the garden. Then it's your turn. So you don't do anything until I shout the all clear, and then you've got to move as fast as you can. Got that?'

'Got it,' she replied, without hesitation.

With one final pull to check it was secure, he began to climb. On the journey, he had been mentally assessing the risks, as you did on every mission of this type. Security lights and cameras, they were a given, but what if they had dogs, or even guards patrolling the grounds? Hopefully it wouldn't be needed, but the Glock provided an element of reassurance, the only problem being you couldn't just order a dog to stop or you would shoot it. You just had to shoot first and say sorry afterwards. But then again, maybe he could just pat it on the head and say 'good boy'.

He paused on the fourth rung, gingerly bobbing his head just far enough above the wall to allow him a clear view, scanning left and right to assess the situation. Yes, as he had predicted, there was one CCTV camera, mounted on a swivel bracket on the wall of the house, conducting a leisurely one hundred and eighty-degree sweep of the perimeter wall. But that would allow plenty of time for them to get up and over undetected. He waited until it had reached the furthest extremity of its cycle, climbed the last couple of rungs of the ladder then swung his legs over the wall and jumped down. With a swift glance in each direction, he sprinted the few steps across a short section of lawn until he stood with his back up against the wall of the house and directly under the camera. In its blind-spot.

'Maggie, can you hear me?' He had to shout louder than he would have liked since the garden wall formed an effective sound barrier, but he didn't think anyone in the house would hear.

Her voice was faint but clear. 'Yes.'

'Ok, start climbing now, but don't stick your head above the wall until I say go. Then swing yourself over and then run to where I'm standing. Fast as you can. You'll be fine.'

The wait seemed interminable as she stood on the fourth rung, awaiting his signal. But finally it came. Mimicking Jimmy's actions, she managed to pull one leg over the wall until she was straddling it. A second later she was picking herself off the ground and dashing over to where he stood.

'Nice work,' he said, squeezing her hand, 'ok?'

'Yeah, apart from the crashing headache and only being able to see out of one eye. Oh, and I think I've just sprained my ankle. Both ankles in fact.'

'So you're fine then,' he grinned. 'Well at least you got here in more or less one piece. So here's the plan. We're just going to edge our way around this wall and then round that corner. We should if I remember rightly then come to a set of patio doors that open outwards. That's how we are going to effect our entry, if you'll pardon the military jargon.'

'Yeah, ok.'

The doors were of traditional style in keeping with the beautiful Arts & Crafts house, multi-paned and constructed in white-painted hardwood, opening out from the kitchen onto the block-paved patio area.

'Right,' Jimmy said, 'you need to be ready to pull your mask on in case I have to use this,' waving the object he had taken out of the backpack. He doubted if she could make it out clearly in the dark, the cylinder about the size of a baked bean can, attached to what looked rather like a skipping rope handle. 'Oh aye, and I nearly forgot, you'd better stick these in,' handing her a pack of tiny foam ear defenders. 'It can be a wee bit noisy when these things go off.'

'Hell Jimmy, how long have you been planning this?' Maggie said disbelievingly. 'What else have you got in that bag?'

He smiled. 'Fail to prepare, prepare to fail, that's what I was taught in the army. I always knew this op was a possibility so I started tucking things away in my hold-all a couple of weeks ago. Now, will you just shut up for a minute and stand back a bit whilst I get this door unlocked.'

He took the Glock from his pocket, stepped back a metre or so and aimed the pistol at the keyhole.

'Just a minute,' Maggie said, reaching over to the door handle. It yielded to her gentle pull. She smiled apologetically. 'I'm always forgetting to lock mine too.'

'Ah, right,' he said, momentarily nonplussed. 'Saves a bullet at least.'

'Pleased to be of assistance,' she grinned. 'So I assume we are going in? Because won't they have an alarm?'

'Yes, and yes. But let me qualify that. I'm going in, you're staying here. And yes they will definitely have an alarm. And that's what we want. Right, here we go.'

Taking a deep breath, he opened the left-hand door and took a step in. A second later he heard from somewhere in the house the faint beep-beep-beep as the alarm system prepared to unleash its full repertoire. And when it kicked off, it was everything he hoped for and more. The siren was deafening, even more so than the one at Allegra Ross's place, and the kitchen was instantly flooded with blinding white light from the ceiling-mounted floodlights, causing him to screw up his eyes so that he could barely see. *Excellent, that's job number one done.* He stepped back out into the garden.

There shouldn't be long to wait now, because no-one was sleeping through that. He assumed she would have some on-site security, but the really heavy squad would be on standby but off-site, at that very moment mobilising their forces in response to the automated alert triggered by his intrusion. He just hoped that Frank's wee army would get here before them. They bloody ought to, considering they had at least a ten-minute start. But that assumed Frank had a proper case number and had filled in the right forms. Terry and Harry Kemp wouldn't be bothering with any of that.

A moment later, the door from the hall was flung open and a figure charged into the kitchen. Gregor, the shaven-headed Latvian gardener, carrying a semi-automatic assault weapon.

Jimmy whispered to Maggie. 'Right, so get the mask and earplugs on and wait here with your back tight against this wall until I tell you otherwise.'

She nodded, pulling it up over her face, the built-in goggles clamped tightly against her cheeks and forehead, the lower mask causing her to gasp for breath as she adjusted to the restricted airflow. He gave her a quick look over to make sure she was prepared, and then removing the firing pin, tossed the grenade into the middle of the room. There was a muffled *doof* as the charge went off, the powerful shock wave blowing Gregor off his feet. Seconds later the room was filled with an acrid smoke that burned the eyes and made breathing impossible. With a barked 'Stay here,' Jimmy leapt back into the kitchen and sprinted across to the Latvian, who was still on his knees, retching loudly and rubbing his eyes furiously. And quite oblivious to Jimmy's approach. 'Sorry pal,' he mouthed to himself as he administered a savage blow to the side of his head with the butt of his pistol. As the guard crumpled to the ground, Jimmy snatched his assault gun and ran back to the door, thrusting the Glock into Maggie's hand, shouting above the deafening noise of the alarm.

'Look, I need you to cover this guy for a while, ok? Just stand here by the patio doors and keep the gun pointed at him. Don't get any closer, we don't want him making a grab for you. And if he wakes up, make sure he sees the gun is on him. Then shout for me as loud as you can. But whatever you do, don't pull that trigger.' Not the most helpful advice, he knew that, but he didn't want Maggie Bainbridge up on another murder charge. With a brief backward glance, he charged back into the kitchen. Hell, it was impossible to think straight above that bloody din. Smoke was still swirling around the room, and although sporadically infiltrated by shafts of light from the ceiling lamps, it was difficult to make out any distinguishing features. Now whereabouts was that door into the hall? Suddenly, his question was answered, as the door was flung open and silhouetted in the doorway stood Gregor's wife Bridget. With a gun. And she looked as if she was about to use it.

'Get out now Maggie!' he screamed at the top of his voice, gesticulating wildly towards the patio doors. 'Now!' He reached her in a second and bundled her towards the exit, both of them making it to the garden just as the first shot rang out. And then another and another and another, the crack of Bridget's automatic echoing around the room.

'Christ sake, she's just firing off at random! There's no way she can see a thing in that damn smoke.'

Then suddenly the shooting stopped and they heard it, so loud that it penetrated the air even above the satanic noise of the alarm. A scream of utter horror and anguish, the likes of which they had never in their lives heard before. And now lying prostrate on the kitchen floor was Gregor, a torrent of blood spurting from the three bullet wounds in his chest. It took Jimmy a few seconds to work out what had happened and a second more to make his decision. He threw down the automatic then took his pistol from Maggie, checking again that the safety was off. Cautiously he peered into the room. Through the smoke he could just about make out the kneeling figure of the maid, her hands pressed against her husband's chest in a futile attempt to arrest the flow from the bullet wounds that she had caused. Which meant she wasn't holding her gun now.

He ran across to them, scanning the tiled floor for the discarded weapon. There it was, tight against the kick board of one of the kitchen units. He stretched out a foot and dragged it towards him, then with a firm kick sent it spinning across the floor. 'Grab that!' he shouted to Maggie.

Bridget was now sobbing, pleading. 'Help me, help me, please.' There had been quite a few of the lads out in Afghanistan who would have helped her by putting a bullet in her skull, and sod the Geneva convention. He'd witnessed a few of those incidents, and it left bitter memories that never quite faded. It was one for all, all for one in time if war and you had to turn a blind eye and just make sure everyone stuck to the same story. But this wasn't war. He knelt down beside her and placed a hand on her shoulder.

'The police will be here in a moment and they'll call an ambulance. Keep the pressure on his chest. He'll pull through.' There was no chance of that, but it didn't cost anything to give her a little hope.

He ran back to the patio doors, and grabbing Maggie by the hand, dragged her across the kitchen and out into the hall. Slamming the door behind them, he helped her pull off her mask before removing his own, both grateful for the ability to breath properly again. Now they could do what they had come here to do.

First though, he needed to do something about that bloody alarm. He ran towards the front entrance, on the assumption that she would have a cloakroom in the hall, and that would be the logical place to keep the control unit. He slid open the first door to find the cupboard stuffed tight with coats and jackets suspended from an aluminium hanging rail. Grabbing a dozen or so in both arms, he threw them onto the floor behind him, pushing the remaining items aside so that the back wall of the cupboard became visible. There it was, a small white box with a keypad and digital display panel, which was flashing the message 'activated,' as if they didn't know that already. Of course, all these systems were tamper-proof, he knew that. But there was tampering, and then there was *proper* tampering. He smiled at Maggie, took a step backwards and aimed the Glock at the middle of the unit. A gentle squeeze on the trigger and the box was blown to bits, momentarily bursting into flames as the state of the art electronics tried in vain to cope with a catastrophic re-wiring of its circuits. And then silence. Total, blissful silence. Now they were ready.

'She pointed it out to me when I was here for the garden party,' Maggie shouted. 'The door to the basement. I'm sure it was off this hall somewhere.' And then she remembered, her voice urgent. 'That one. Next to the kitchen.' It was no surprise to either that it was locked, protected by a keypad-activated combination lock. They looked at one another and exchanged a knowing smile. And then to her surprise, he handed her the pistol.

'Go on. Blow the arse off it.' He couldn't explain why, but it seemed somehow right that she should do it. 'And it probably would be a good idea if you didn't shut your eyes,' giving a faint grin as he saw her grimace. 'Just relax, and a wee squeeze will do it.'

She held the gun out in front of her, her arms rigid, squinting down the barrel to take aim, then did as he instructed. The gentlest touch on the trigger and then the deafening crack as the pistol discharged, punching a four-inch diameter hole where the lock and handle had been. He gave her a thumbs up as she thrust the pistol back into his hands, as if it was too hot to hold.

'That was brilliant,' he said, 'and I'm hoping we won't need this again. Come on.' The entrance led to a small landing with a glass-fronted elevator and to the side of that a staircase. A staircase that led down to the gymnasium and swimming pool. It took just a few seconds for them to reach the basement level, entering through a pair of satin-white doors.

But they didn't lead to a swimming pool or a gymnasium. The room looked more like the upstairs landing of an executive show-home, bathed in a beautiful natural light, warm and welcoming, the walls painted in a soothing lavender-white, the floor carpeted in a soft dusky off-grey, thick and luxuriant. Each of the two side walls had a large picture window, bordered by pretty pastel-coloured curtains held back by matching tie-backs, looking out onto a lovely sunlit garden. For a moment Jimmy was thrown, because not only were they at least three metres below ground level, but it was pitch dark outside. Until, getting closer, he saw these weren't windows but TV screens, broadcasting some weird virtual reality into this perfectly-recreated domestic paradise.

And then they saw the doors. Four of them, spaced around the room, gleaming white with delicate chrome handles, and on each of them was mounted a beautiful hand-painted enamel sign. *Kitty's Room, Jamie's Room, Lizzie's Room.*

And Ollie's Room. He leapt over and pushed at the handle but it didn't move. *Locked.* And then from behind it, he heard the sound of a child crying. *Please, please, please let him be all right. Please God.* He took Maggie's hand and squeezed it tightly. Of course it was going to be all right. He was going to make damn sure of that.

He gestured at the door. 'Right, let's get this done,' and taking two steps backward, he launched his boot at it, sending splintered wood flying in all directions.

Little Ollie Bainbridge was sitting listlessly on the edge of a bed, clutching a *Toy Story* figure and sobbing quietly to himself. For a moment he didn't react, as if unable to understand what was happening. And then, comprehension. It was his mummy, here to take him home, and he ran towards her, throwing himself into her arms. *Thank god he was all right.*

From upstairs Jimmy could hear voices, urgent barked instructions, doors being kicked open, shouts of 'clear!'

Outside, a Range Rover with blacked-out windows paused for a few seconds at the front gate then after a brief weighing up of the situation, accelerated away.

'Down here,' he shouted. 'Down here Frank. It's clear.'

He could hear his brother clumping down the stairs and then a second later he emerged, trailed by two heavily-armed officers in full assault gear.

'Oh, thanks to our Lord,' Frank said as he weighed up the scene. 'He's safe. He's safe.'

'Aye, but what about the other kids?' Jimmy said, pointing at the other doors.

'Only one way to find out,' Frank said, trying the handle of Jamie Grant's room, 'but it'll be fine, I'm sure it will.'

He nodded to one of the assault squad. 'Break it down, but go easy, eh?' then winced as the burly officer took the battering ram to the door, Frank and Jimmy following him in.

It was a perfect little boys' room, wallpapered in a navy design of spaceships and stars, furnished with a single cabin bed with pull-out desk and a soft bean-bag chair in one corner. And on the bed a little boy was sleeping soundly. Little Jamie Grant, just eighteen months old when he was taken, but now nearly four.

'Let's leave him sleeping,' Frank whispered, 'until we can get his mum and dad here.'

They had already broken into Kitty's room, gently leading the little girl by the hand and entrusting her to the care of Maggie. They were sitting on the floor, Ollie on her left, snuggling up to her, and Kitty on her right, unsure at first, and then finally tilting her head and laying it against Maggie's shoulder.

Everything was going to be alright.

***

'These kids need medical attention.' Frank barked the order to his nearest armed colleague. 'Can we get the paramedics here fast, and can one of you start making some hot chocolate.'

What they really needed fast was to be held tightly in the comforting arms of their parents. If everything went to plan,

Charles and Vivien Grant would soon be here to be reunited with their son. But Mr and Mrs Lawrence were eight hundred miles away in south-west France. He took out his phone and fired off a quick text to Inspector Marie Laurent. *Kitty Lawrence found, safe and well.* He would fill her in with the details later, and that was going to be a nice call. Afterwards, he might even invite her over to London, see the sights, take in a show, and then perhaps a little romantic dinner. It was a lovely daydream but there was no time for any of that now.

'Where is she?' he asked as his focus returned. 'Have we found the crazy bitch yet?'

'No sign,' Jimmy answered. 'I'm beginning to think she can't be at home. Nobody could have slept through that alarm.'

Maggie looked up. 'She's got a panic room. Upstairs. The door is off her en-suite.'

Frank motioned to his two colleagues. 'Right boys, come with me. And bring that great bloody thing with you.'

'Careful Frank,' Jimmy shouted after him. Because if even the maid was armed with a rapid-fire automatic, there was every chance that her boss might be too. His brother gave a dismissive wave as he disappeared up the stairwell.

The reinforced panic room door, strong as it was, proved no match for two burly police officers equipped with a fifty-kilogram battering ram. It took just three blows to burst the lock and they were in. Melody Montague, dressed only in a skimpy black negligee, stood motionless in the centre of the tiny room, a cigarette dangling between her fingers. She was not alone. Her companion, stark naked, cowered in a corner, his hands covering his crotch.

'Well well, caught a bit short sir?' Frank smirked. 'Very embarrassing.' He recognised the man from a photograph in the Fox murder file. One of the scriptwriters on Bow Road, interviewed and eliminated in the early stages of the investigation. He nodded in the direction of the door. 'Go and find yourself a towel for god's sake.'

Now he turned his attention to Melody Montague. If she knew what was coming next, it was evident from her expression that she intended to face it with defiance. At these moments he liked to get straight down to it, without messing about with any small-talk. It was a lengthy and complex charge sheet, so he had taken the trouble to put together a written copy in advance, because you didn't want any smart-arsed lawyer trying afterwards to get them off on a technicality. He took the piece of paper from his pocket, unfolded it and began to read aloud.

'Roxy Kemp, I'm arresting you for conspiracy to murder Allegra Ross, conspiracy to murder Benjamin Fox, conspiracy to murder Olivia Jane Walton, conspiracy to murder Josh Walton, three counts of child abduction and illegal imprisonment with regard to Oliver Jonathan Brooks, Jamie...'

She sneered at him. 'Spare me all that legal shit, will you? You know you can't prove any of this and if you think you can find a jury who will convict *me*...'

Frank gave a derisive snort. 'Aye, right darling. You build some weird prison in your basement and we find three wee kids locked in their bedrooms, and you say we can't prove any of it? You really think so? If you do, you're living on a different planet. And let me tell you something else. You *way* over-estimate your popularity. A second-rater like you? Lover-boy over there is already writing you out of the series. Believe me, you're history.' He gestured impatiently to one of the armed officers. 'Slap these cuffs on and make sure they're on tight. Now hold her there whilst I finish.' He glanced down at his script before continuing.

'The abduction and illegal imprisonment of Jamie Grant and the abduction and illegal imprisonment of Kitty Lawrence. You do not have to say anything...'

When he was finished, he gave a dismissive wave and Montague was led away, her face still a mask of defiance. And at the bottom of the stairs, Maggie was waiting for her. Ever since she had uncovered the terrible truth about her client, she had rehearsed over and over again what she would say to her at this moment of confrontation. But now that the moment had arrived, she could not conjure any words that came even close to expressing the anger and loathing she felt towards her. Which is why, taking the arresting officer completely by surprise, she took a step forward, steeled herself for a second then without a word of warning, smashed her fist into the actress's smirking face.

***

They had found Charles Grant at the elegant Chelsea home of his agent Edwina Fox. He had been holed up there for nearly two weeks, ever since Sharon Trent's devastating stroke. Just moments earlier, the actress had made her feelings towards him clear. Friends, that's what she had said, and they would never be anything more as far as she was concerned. And then he told her what he had done for her. *Murdered for her.* Hadn't it proved his love for her, more than any words could say? Was it any wonder that he was now going mad, after all he had been through? But now this pretty soft-spoken policewoman seemed to be telling him Jamie had been found, alive and well, and she was there to take him to his son.

They sped through the deserted city streets, WPC Green switching on the flashing blue lights and giving an occasional burst of the siren to warn any dallying vehicles of their approach. The children had been gathered in the kitchen, wrapped in blankets and sitting around the big table sipping creamy hot chocolate prepared by one of Frank's team. The paramedics had arrived together with a consultant paediatrician who had been working the nightshift at the Royal Free and had insisted on accompanying them. Still Jamie Grant and Kitty Lawrence had not uttered a single word, sitting motionless and staring at the floor. As the doctor checked their vital signs with her stethoscope, she looked at Jimmy, the sadness in her eyes confirming what they both knew. There was no physical damage, thank god, but the emotional scars would be with them for a very long time.

Ollie had not left his mother's side for a second, not that Maggie would have permitted it, but he appeared to be in good spirits as he shared some of his terrible jokes with his adopted uncle. At least the boy had only been in captivity for three days and he'd soon get over it. Jimmy placed her hand on her shoulder, causing her to look up and smile. As their eyes met he said simply, 'I think he'll be fine Maggie.' In what way he was qualified to make the statement, he could not say. He just knew it to be true, just as he knew that in one way or another, he would be bound to this little family for the rest of his life. At the other end of the table, Frank took a calming swig from his hip-flask and wished for the same thing.

***

'Mr Grant's here sir. I've left him in the car for the moment. Not sure how you wanted to play this.'

'And what about the wife?' Frank asked the young WPC. 'Has she turned up yet?'

'Up north with her family. She won't be here for a few hours.'

'All right. I hope you locked the bloody car by the way. Not that he's likely to leg it again, I don't suppose.'

She nodded. 'Yes, I did lock it but no, I don't think that's likely sir. Shall I bring him in?'

'Aye, and no cuffs,' Frank said. 'I think we can risk it, don't you?'

As he was led into the kitchen, Grant saw the child. And for a heart-breaking moment he found himself unable to recognise his son. It had been two years since he last saw him and then he was just a toddler, not long out of nappies, and now he was a proper little boy, chubby-cheeked and with a mop of auburn hair.

'Jamie?' He spoke so quietly that he was barely audible, but it was enough to make the boy look up, uncomprehending. It was clear he had no idea who this man was as he ran over to Maggie and thrust his little hand in hers.

'I'm your daddy Jamie. Your daddy.' Grant's eyes were pleading as the tears began to well up. 'Your daddy.'

'Take as much time as you need sir,' Frank said in a kindly voice. 'Why don't you take Jamie through to the sitting room so you can have some private time with him. Here, I'll take you through. There's no rush.'

It was half an hour before Frank returned to the room, this time accompanied by Jimmy and Maggie, who was still holding Ollie tightly by the hand.

'Jamie, I need to talk to your daddy for a wee while now. Will you go with this nice lady please? There's more hot chocolate in the kitchen and I think we've got some sweets too. Go on, there's a good lad.' The boy looked at his father, who gave a single nod of assent.

'Before he goes, I'd like to say something.' Grant looked at Frank enquiringly. 'If that's ok.'

'Go ahead.'

'I can never thank all of you enough,' Grant said. 'For all you've done. I never thought I would see this moment. I had given up hope, you see. Quite driven to despair. My life... it was as if I wasn't in it, but watching from outside, like a play. I know it doesn't excuse what I've done, but... well, maybe it explains it.'

Maggie smiled. 'I can't begin to imagine what it must have been like for you over the last two years. But here we are, with a happy ending.' *More or less.*

She looked at Frank as if to say, do you really need to do this? But she was a lawyer still, and she knew he must. The law was the law and it was for the courts to weigh up mitigating circumstances, such as they were, not the police.

Frank said nothing, but she had come to know him over the last year, and so she knew that what he had to do next would be done with a heavy heart.

'Jamie, come with me and Ollie please,' she said in a soft voice. 'We've got some sweets and more hot chocolate.' Reluctantly, the boy got up, not taking his eyes of his father for a second.

'Go on son,' Grant said quietly, 'I'll be through in a minute.'

He waited until they had left then stood up and said quietly, 'I'm ready.'

Frank gave a brief nod then began to speak. And this time he didn't need the help of a script.

'Charles Grant, I am arresting you for the murder of Daniel Black. You do not have to say anything. But, it may harm your defence if you do not mention when questioned something which you later rely on in court. Anything you do say may be given in evidence.'

'I won't say anything, if you don't mind,' Grant said, immediately contradicting himself. 'There is nothing I can say really. I did it you see, I did it, although I knew I shouldn't. It was just a moment of madness, that's all.'

Frank gave him a look of exasperation. 'Sir, sir, I did tell you that you do not have to say anything, did I not? And then when you agreed you wouldn't say anything, you did the exact opposite. So I'm going to assume that you didn't hear me properly the first time, which means I'm going to forget what you just told me. Now I advise you to get a lawyer before you say anything else to anyone, including me. *Please*.'

He took him by the arm and led him back through to the kitchen. 'Last chance sir. Just say goodbye to him, then we'll get him looked after until his mum arrives.'

'They're wanting to take the boys into hospital, keep them under observation for a few days,' Maggie said. 'Ollie too. I can go with him of course.'

'You'd better sneak in the back door then,' Jimmy laughed, 'or they'll cart you back off to your ward. Don't worry, I'll come with you and fight them off if they try it.'

'Aye, and Maggie, you'd probably better get these knuckles seen to at the same time,' Frank said. 'I wish I'd been there to see it.'

Actually he was glad he hadn't seen it. He already had about a week's worth of paperwork ahead of him and he had no desire to add to it.

'But what if Melody complains?' Maggie asked.

Frank smiled. 'Don't you worry about that. We warned her not to struggle when we took her down the stairs, but she didn't listen. Fell and bashed her wee nose as a result. Oh, and by the way Maggie, as a lawyer you didn't hear any of that.'

'I'm grateful Frank, although I know I shouldn't be.'

'Well that's all good then,' Jimmy said, stifling a yawn. 'So it's three o'clock in the morning and we've probably had enough for one day, don't you think? Time for bed.'

No-one was going to disagree with that.

Chapter 29

Maggie laughed as Frank threw down the menu in disgust. 'Sixty-six quid for a bottle of wine and the cheapest main on here's nearly forty quid. And chips are extra? You did say it was you who was paying, didn't you?'

She had gathered them once again for lunch at the *Ship* in Shoreditch, one of the capital's growing stock of achingly over-priced gastro-pubs. But since they were dining in way of celebration, it had seemed appropriate to push the boat out, no pun intended. Indeed, the celebratory post-investigation lunch was becoming somewhat of a tradition for the three of them, if just one previous occasion - the Alzahrani case - could be said to constitute a tradition.

'Actually Frank, Asvina's paying,' she said. 'The case has generated so much good publicity that she's now overwhelmed by work. She's very grateful to us.'

'She's not joining us then?' Jimmy asked, a hint of disappointment in his voice.

'No, I think she's already buried under a mountain of new cases. But DCI Smart's going to be here. She wants a full explanation of the case from start to finish, to fill in a few gaps as she puts it.'

Frank gave a mock grimace. 'What, you've asked my boss along? Now I'll have to be on my best behaviour.'

'How will she be able to tell the difference?' Jimmy said, shaking his head. The single-finger gesture he got in return left him in little doubt of Frank's opinion of his little joke.

'Boys boys,' Maggie laughed, 'come on, let's get on with ordering. I'm starving.'

'I'm desperate for a drink,' Frank said. As far as she could tell, Frank was always desperate for a drink. A stuffy middle-aged waiter glided over to their table and began to recite from memory a long list of that day's specials, each of which everyone forgot the second they heard it. But it seemed Frank didn't need a menu.

'Steak,' he said decisively, 'and chips. I always have steak. Medium-rare. Oh aye, and a pint of Doom Bar for starters.'

The waiter made no comment as he tapped the order into his smartphone app. 'And for you madam?'

Maggie was in a playful mood and for half a second considered it might be fun to ask him to go through the specials again. But she thought better of it, settling instead for a simple dish of chicken medallions in a lemon sauce, with vegetables of the season (nine pounds extra) and sauté potatoes (thankfully included in the price). In order to keep within a reasonable budget, and since none of them knew the least bit about wine anyway, they opted for one bottle of house red and one of house white, a choice for which the waiter struggled to conceal his disdain. She noted that Frank, the detective, had detected it.

'Don't worry pal, we won't short-change you with the tip if that's what you're worried about. Not if you get that pint here sharpish.'

'Frank Stewart, ever the diplomat,' Jimmy said after the waiter had drifted away with their order.

'What?' Frank said, looking confused. 'I didn't upset him, did I?'

Jimmy smiled and shook his head but said nothing. The gesture was wasted on his brother who now was solely focussed on the estimated delivery time of his pint. A minute later it arrived, ahead of schedule, on a tray shared by the two bottles of wine and delivered by a pretty waitress of altogether more cheerful disposition.

'Everyone having wine?' she asked.

'Is the pope a catholic?' Frank responded. The waitress smiled politely, having heard the quip a million times before.

'Red or white sir?' Evidently you weren't given the option of tasting the cheap house plonk in advance.

'Both please.'

Unfazed, she poured a generous measure into both of his glasses, before filling the glasses of the others, Jimmy opting for red, Maggie for white.

'Ah, here's Jill now,' Jimmy said, glancing across to the entrance door. Maggie shot him a suspicious look. Jill? Since when were they on first name terms? He stood up, waving to attract her attention. She smiled in acknowledgement, weaving her way through the throng of lunchtime drinkers to their table. DCI Smart had come straight from a highly-satisfactory meeting with an Assistant Commissioner, but today she was out of uniform, business-like in a dark grey pinafore dress over a crisp white blouse, which suited her pencil-thin figure.

'Hi everyone,' she said brightly, as she took her seat. 'What have I missed?'

'Two bottles of wine ma'am,' Frank said, deadpan.

She laughed. 'Just two? I thought this was supposed to be a celebration.'

'That was just for starters Jill,' Jimmy said, beaming her one of his special smiles, which Maggie did not fail to notice. 'Anyway what can I get for you? I'll nip up to the bar, it'll be quicker since Frank's already had a bust-up with our waiter.'

'A glass of prosecco please,' she said, smiling.

'Just a glass?'

'For now, but ask me later, won't you?'

'I'll make it a large one, just in case,' he said, as he disappeared off on his mission. A moment later the waiter, contrary to Jimmy's prediction, arrived at the table to take her food order. After a cursory review of the menu, she settled on the same chicken dish as Maggie, just as Jimmy returned with her drink.

'Right then,' she said after taking a delicate sip from her glass, 'let's hear everything about it, omitting no detail. I get some of it, but there's a lot I don't.'

'Yes, it's pretty convoluted I must admit,' Jimmy said, 'but we'll be speaking nice and slow for Frank's benefit.'

It was Maggie mainly who had worked it all out, and so it was only natural that she should lead the explanations.

'Well, to find the start of our story we have to go right back to the marriage of Melody to Benjamin Fox. By all accounts theirs was a whirlwind romance and in fact they married in Las Vegas - typical Melody many people might say - just six weeks after their first date. They knew each other of course from Bow Road, and I guess it developed from there.'

Jimmy nodded. 'Husband number three, I think I'm right in saying?'

'Yes that's right,' Maggie said, 'and I think she had invested all her hopes and dreams in the relationship. She was forty-seven when she married and the biological time-bomb was well and truly ticking. And believe me I know what that feels like. It happened to me and I was only in my mid-thirties.'

'Tell me about it,' Jill giggled, giving Jimmy a look that Maggie noticed and didn't like.

'So of course, they talked about children, but unknown to Melody, Benjamin Fox was sterile. That came as a massive blow to her.'

'I can imagine,' Jill said.

Maggie nodded. 'So, at first they tried to adopt but they were turned down everywhere they went.'

'Aye, I can guess,' Frank said. 'Too old and too white.'

'Probably,' Maggie agreed. 'Whatever the reason, I'm sure it was that rejection which pushed her over the edge. Because then she just lost all sense of reality.'

'Aye,' Jimmy said, 'and that's when she starts pursuing this mental plan to assemble the perfect picture-postcard family. By any means she could.'

'With the help of her brothers of course. Kidnapping was a new line for the Kemps, but when the Jamie Grant abduction netted a cool quarter of a million, they began to see the possibilities. A nice little earner *and* they get to make their mental little sister happy too.'

'Aye, so she sees these happy families in the glossy magazines,' Frank said incredulously 'and says I want one of them.'

'And they were clever,' Jimmy said. 'That's why the abductions were spread all across Europe, so that each looked just like a one-off crime. Less police attention and less resources meant less chance of them being caught.'

'Yes, that was it. And remember, these kids were very carefully targeted, so although the families lived in Europe, they were all what you might call of Anglo heritage. English speakers in other words.'

'Aye,' Frank said, slurping his beer, 'because I bet that Melody wouldn't have wanted a foreign kid.'

'God, she really is off her head,' Jill said, 'and I can't believe she built that weird palace under her house to keep her collection. It was like a little dolls' house only with real kids.'

A dolls' house but with real kids. For a moment everyone was silent as the startling image painted by Jill played out in their minds. But at that point, their food arrived and the hustle and bustle around their table provided a welcome distraction. Glasses were refilled and the conversation lightened, before Maggie continued with her explanations.

'So now we come to what is probably the most horrible part of the whole affair.'

'The abductions,' Jimmy said.

'Yes, the abductions. I'm afraid it was just so ridiculously simple. The Kemps roped in their photographer mate Eddie Taylor to take some photographs and to track the routine of the victims and then it was easy for Harry Kemp and his son Vince to do a clean snatch, with minimal risk of being caught.'

'Except in Ollie's case where it all nearly went pear-shaped,' Jimmy said. 'Poor wee Josh Clark.'

'Look, I didn't really want to ask this question,' Frank said, his voice quiet, 'but why Ollie? All the other kids had parents in the public eye.'

'I think I can answer that,' Jimmy said ruefully. 'It was that garden party at Melody's place. Do you remember I showed you the photographs? These posed family shots with her and Danny and the kids? So because it had made great business sense to return the van Duren boy, there was a vacancy. And when she saw Ollie, she decided he was the one to replace Brandon.'

'Thank god we got to him,' Jill said, giving a shudder, 'and to all of them.'

'They'll be fine,' Maggie said. 'Kids are great, they can bounce back from anything.'

If only she could be sure the reality would match the certainty with which she said it. Ollie had seen his father and his lover murdered in cold blood in his own home, but more than a year on, it seemed on the outside at least to have been forgotten. But she feared it had only been buried temporarily, to resurface when he was a little older, a dreadfulness that might blight his life forever. As for the other two kids, Kitty Lawrence was back with her family in France, and Jamie Grant was back with his mum in Chelsea. Would they be fine? She hoped against hope that they would, but for quite a while it would be in the balance.

'Aye, let's raise a glass to wee Eleanor Campbell and her big Dutch pal,' Frank said. 'Led us straight to Harry Kemp they did. She's a genius that girl.'

'Yeah, I've always been curious how you get her to do all these things for you Frank,' Jill said, smiling.

'Natural charm and charisma ma'am. You've either got it or you haven't. No, the truth is she likes being tucked away out of sight in Atlee House. She can't stand all the bureaucratic crap she has to put up with at their place in Maida Vale, and I get to take advantage of that.'

They had completed their mains and were awaiting the table to be cleared. Looking at the empty wine bottles Jimmy said, 'I think I need a wee pint, don't know about anybody else? I'll take a stroll up to the bar if you shout them out.'

Jill said, 'I know I shouldn't but I'd love a G and T. What about you Maggie, the same? I'll come and help you Jimmy.'

She didn't know why, but Maggie felt a sudden tinge of resentment towards Jill. Actually, she did know why. She was so ridiculously *thin* for a start, and that didn't help. And her and Jimmy, was something going on there? He was a colleague, an employee to be exact, and yes, he had become a friend too, but nothing more, and Jill was only going to the bar to help him with the drinks, for goodness sake. Glancing over her shoulder, she watched them, laughing, at ease in each other's company. As they made their way back, Jill's hand rested on Jimmy's elbow, gently guiding him to their table. You couldn't mistake that body language. With an effort, she pushed the scene to the back of her mind.

'There we go everyone,' Jimmy said, passing round the drinks. 'These should suitably refresh us I think.'

'Thanks Jimmy,' Maggie said. 'And cheers all. Shall I continue?'

Everyone signalled their assent, Jill saying, 'I hope you're going to come on to the murders now?'

'Yes, the murders. Well believe it or not, there was actually quite a strong connection back to that blooming pre-nuptial agreement which gave us so much trouble. We didn't think so at first, but it turned out there was.'

Frank gave her a puzzled look. 'I'm sorry, but I just don't see how.'

Maggie smiled. 'Have patience Frank and all will be revealed. But I'm afraid it's a rather long and twisted tale.'

He looked at his glass which was nearly full, giving a satisfied grin. 'Good to go Maggie. I'm going to enjoy this.'

'Me too,' Jill said.

'So as you've heard, when Benjamin and Melody found they couldn't have children, natural or adopted, she decided on her crazy abduction program, starting with Jamie Grant. We think that at first Benjamin must have been happy to go along with it, although we imagine he would have had big reservations. Anyone would.'

'Aye, do you remember that picture I found with him and a kid, in the fancy garden?' Jimmy said. 'Well that kid was Jamie Grant. So at that stage, looked like he was happy to play the doting father.'

'And *that* was the garden you recognised,' Frank said, 'after you had that wee tête-à-tête with Melody. Whatever did happen that night by the way?'

'Nothing,' Jimmy said briskly, 'nothing at all.'

'But then as she started talking of extending her little family, the full extent of Melody's delusion became clear to him and he wanted out,' Maggie said. 'By this time he had hooked up with Allegra Ross and had decided to leave his old life behind.'

Jimmy nodded. 'Aye, but then he figured out he had a wee insurance policy over Melody. He knew her little secret and guessed she would do anything to keep it hidden.'

'And he wasn't wrong there,' Frank said. 'Just not in the way he was thinking.'

'Exactly,' Maggie said. 'So we think it was the death of Kylie Ward that started it off.'

'That was definitely an accident?' Jill asked,

'We think so. Frank made a few enquiries with the officers who attended the incident and they had a description of the hit and run driver. A teenager in a stolen hot-hatch. A tragic accident, but Fox wasn't involved, we're pretty sure.'

'No, he wasn't.' Jimmy said, 'but it got him thinking. And when he found out something else, something much bigger, he realised he might have a little goldmine in his hands.'

'Explain Miss Bainbridge,' Jill said, looking puzzled.

'We can't be certain, but we reckon Benjamin must have found out about da Vinci. And he knew that if it became public, Charles Grant would be completely humiliated. So he says to Charles, there's a little difficulty with that pre-nuptial agreement you witnessed four years ago. It would be really useful if you could corroborate my version of it, because the other witness has sadly died. And if you do that, nobody need know about da Vinci. Oh and by the way, could you pay a visit to Pentonville prison and pay off the lawyer who drew the thing up.'

'And that's where we came in,' Jimmy said. 'Melody doesn't really know how to play it. She doesn't want to lose her seventy-five percent but she doesn't want Benjamin blabbing either. So she asks Asvina to sort it out, and then *she* gave us our wee mission impossible.'

'I get *some* of that, but you've still not said anything about the murders,' Jill said, shooting Maggie a smile. 'I'm getting impatient.'

Maggie laughed. 'Yes, sorry Jill, just getting to them. So we're not sure *how* exactly, but we think Melody had found out that Allegra Ross knew about the abduction of Jamie Grant. Remember we found that photograph under their bed and her diary where she talked about everything being ruined? Well it would ruin a relationship, finding out that your lover has colluded in the kidnapping of a child. That we think was the reason for the argument we saw at the awards ceremony.'

'Everybody saw it,' Jimmy said. 'Eight million people saw it. Which would have included the Kemps.'

Maggie nodded. 'And Fox and Ross were really going at it so could have easily been overheard. Whatever the case, we guess there's a Kemp family meeting where it's decided it needs to be taken care of, quietly and efficiently.'

'And the *Leonardo* message on the severed hands?' Jill asked.

'Everyone knew about that incident at the Hyde Park rally, when the White British League attacked Benjamin and Ross ,' Maggie said.

'Especially me,' Frank said ruefully, rubbing the back of his head. 'It still bloody hurts.'

'So the severed hand thing was engineered to support the narrative that these murders were carried out by the far-right. You know, to teach all these leftie liberals a lesson. We guess Fox must have told Melody about the da Vinci posts, and how Grant had originally claimed it was Venables who was behind them. So they came up with this little cryptic puzzle which was deliberately made not too difficult to solve. Leonardo leading to da Vinci, da Vinci leading to Darren Venables. And then once the false trail had been set, Terry and Harry Kemp went to work. Professional and ruthless.'

'And it worked,' Jill said, 'for a while, until you all saw through it. So come on, the Danny Black murder. Where does that fit in?'

'It was all because of Charles' doomed love for Sharon Trent,' Maggie said. 'He knew his girlfriend was going to be side-lined in the show as the Ronnie and Patty West story took centre stage, and in his warped mind, killing Danny so that the storyline died with him was the perfect way to demonstrate his love.'

'He was one mental guy,' Jimmy said, 'with that da Vinci thing and all that. Is it any wonder poor Sharon had a stroke, when he told her what he had done? *I've murdered for you and by the way I love you?* The shock must have been overwhelming.'

'Exactly,' Maggie said. 'Remember, he had been to the morgue to identify Benjamin Fox's body, and would have seen the severed hand and the message written on it. Rather clever, and he would have got away with it too if Frank hadn't seen through it.'

Frank laughed. 'Copy-cat, eh? Well I realised that Charles Grant was one of just two people outside of the media who knew the MO of the murders. You know, I do believe this is the first time in his entire career that Colin Barker has actually been right about anything.'

'Yes, and he's not stopped telling anybody who'll listen about it since,' Jill said. 'Although naturally he's not mentioning that it was you who worked it out.'

'Well, Grant's going to pay the price for it,' Maggie said. 'He's looking at twenty-five years minimum, despite everything he's been through.'

Frank was trying to suppress a smile. 'So tell me, have you two decided that you're only going to take on murderers as clients? Because if that's the strategy, maybe I wouldn't put it on your website.'

'They've not *all* been murderers,' Maggie said, with mock indignation. 'But maybe we *should* specialise.'

Jimmy grinned. 'No, I don't think so boss. Let's stick to divorces, shall we? It's much safer.'

'I don't think that McCartney lad would agree with that,' Frank said, laughing.

'Yes, what was that all about?' Jill asked.

'Quite simple,' Jimmy said, 'the Kemps found from their sources in the nick that McCartney had been having visitors. So they put two and two together, McCartney takes a beating and miraculously Melody's problem goes away. Her original document had long been destroyed, but it didn't take much for his paralegal to draw up a fake replica, and with Fox dead and McCartney now willing to vouch for its authenticity, the problem's solved.'

Jill sighed. 'It corrupts, doesn't it? Money I mean.'

'I wouldn't know ma'am,' Frank said, flashing her a sardonic smile. 'You don't pay me enough for that.'

'More than you're worth mate, more than you're worth,' Jimmy said.

'But it wasn't all about money, was it?' Maggie said quietly. 'Not for Melody. It was about love and her fanatical desire to create the family life she'd only ever experienced in magazines. She was evil I know, but in some ways I feel sorry for her. And now she will never have it.'

***

The waiter arrived with the bill, enquiring, as dictated by his management, whether they had enjoyed their lunch, not bothering to disguise that he really didn't give a stuff whether they had or they hadn't. He listened to their eulogies with indifference then said, 'Who wants this?'

Frank raised his hand and took the bill from him, theatrically unfolding it to unveil the total. With a mock grimace, he quickly pushed it across to Maggie, who glanced at it and gave a real grimace.

Out of the blue, Jill said, 'The Assistant Commissioner mentioned you by name Frank, in my meeting this morning. Said you'd done a damn good job and asked why were you wasting your time in Department 12B. We talked about my next role too and he wondered if I was going to find a place for you in my new team.'

Frank looked at her suspiciously. 'I didn't know you were moving ma'am.' The truth was he had come to like Department 12B and he liked working for Jill Smart too. He had always known of course that for her, the job was just a stepping-stone on her upward career trajectory, but still it had come as a surprise to realise that the thought of it coming to an end alarmed him so much.

'Frank, you know I didn't want to be stuck in godforsaken Atlee House for longer than necessary. I've been offered the job of heading up the Met's serious fraud team. It's a fantastic role and I'm going to take it.'

He did his best to hide his disappointment. 'Congratulations ma'am, you deserve it.'

'Thank you Frank. But the good news, for me at least, is that the AC still wants me to oversee 12B. He was kind enough to say it's made great progress under my leadership and that he didn't want to lose that. Of course I told him that most of the success was down to you, and *he* said, and this is his exact words, why don't you get your Scottish nutter to head up the Atlee house team? And I said I would ask you. So here I am, asking you. It wouldn't be a promotion, not at first at least, but well... what do you think?'

So Frank thought about it. He grimaced when he thought of the cast of casts-off and ne'er-do-wells that would be under his command. He groaned when he thought of the endless reports he would have to write and the complicated forms he would doubtless be forced to fill in and the dull meetings he would be mandated to attend. But on the other hand, he might be able to swing an upgrade to Atlee House's vending facilities as a condition of taking on the job, *and* he would ask for them to at least give the place a lick of paint. And when he'd finished thinking about all of that, the conclusion was, to his mind, a no-brainer.

Beaming her a huge smile he said, 'That ma'am, would be bloody brilliant.' Then as much to his surprise as hers, he wrapped his arms around her and kissed her full on the lips. He was even more surprised when she made no attempt to free herself from his embrace.

Furtively, Jimmy shot a downward glance. Ten minutes earlier as they stood waiting to be served at the bar, DCI Jill Smart had scribbled her phone number on the back of his left hand. Quickly, he moistened his fingertips with his tongue and began to erase it, hoping to be unobserved. But Maggie had witnessed him in the act, and suddenly, for her, everything felt right with the world.

The Aphrodite Suicides

Rob Wyllie

PROLOGUE

It wasn't hard to spot her, even amongst the dense sea of faces emerging from the office block. He'd studied her photo often enough, and not just for business either, because this bird was seriously drop-dead gorgeous. Saddled with a stupid chav name mind you, but he guessed they hadn't employed her for her brains. He watched as she strode across the concrete plaza, tall and confident and *knowing*, her sleek auburn hair flowing over her bare shoulders like a waterfall. Every now and again she gave a little flick of her head, a cascade of hair spinning around her as if in slow motion, just like these fit women in the shampoo adverts. *Knowing*. Christ, what he wouldn't give to have just one night in her bed. He could take her if he wanted, he knew he could, like he'd done in the past with a few of them, but today that wasn't on the cards. The brief from the boss was perfectly straightforward and there was a tidy little fifteen grand earner attached. Today was strictly business. Today was the day she was going to die.

He felt in his pocket for the reassuring caress of cold metal. He liked the Beretta, compact enough to be unobtrusive but deadly accurate at short range. But he wasn't going to be firing it today. The little pistol was simply his persuader if she decided to get awkward.

Now he got a little closer, slipping into the crowd about twenty metres behind her, following the snake of homeward-bound commuters up the stairs and into the entrance of the Tube station. Then through the barriers and onto the down escalator. *District Line, eastbound*. He caught up with her just as she stepped onto the platform, his firm grip on her upper arm causing her to spin round in annoyance. His face was now up close to hers, so that she could hear his whisper. *His people want to speak to you. I'm here to take you to them*.

On this occasion the operation had gone like a dream, her initial surprise quickly evaporating into surly resignation. She'd no idea why they wanted to talk to her, but she'd taken their money so didn't really have a choice in the matter. A ten-minute train ride to his office, a short meeting, and then home. In reality, it wasn't too much of a disruption to her schedule.

Except today she wasn't going on a train. Today she was going under one.

Chapter 1

As far as Maggie Bainbridge could remember, she'd never met a billionaire before. Although as her colleague Jimmy Stewart pointed out, since the recent split with his missus, Hugo Morgan was now worth only nine hundred and seventy million, which technically downgraded him to mere multi-millionaire status.

Brasenose Investment Trust occupied the top four floors of a stunning glass-fronted office block on Canary Wharf, directly opposite and almost in touching distance of the similarly ostentatious building that housed Addison Redburn, the prestigious international law firm that was Asvina Rani's employer. It was barely nine months since she, the most sought-after and consequently most highly-paid family law solicitor in the capital, had handled Morgan's headline-grabbing divorce. So why were they meeting with him so soon afterwards? Whatever the reason, they wouldn't have to wait long to find out.

A minute or so later she joined them, looking flustered as she apologised for being late. But looking as elegant and beautiful as ever, a fact that wasn't lost on the elderly uniformed commissionaire who was guarding access to the high-speed elevators. He couldn't take his eyes off her.

'Sorry guys, I just couldn't get free of my last client,' she said. 'The poor woman had just found out her husband was leaving her and as you can imagine, she's pretty distraught. But here we are now. All set.'

She gave Jimmy an admiring glance. 'Looking sharp today Mr Stewart. Nice suit.'

He smiled back at her. 'Aye, I thought I'd better make an effort. I wouldn't want to let the firm down in front of such an important client.'

The commissionaire gestured towards the first of the three lifts, eyes still fixed on Asvina.

'This way please, ladies and gents. Floor twenty-three it is. Harriet will meet you up there, get you all sorted.' He kept his finger pressed on the button that held open the doors until they were safely inside. 'Have a good morning.'

Jimmy gave him a thumbs-up as the doors began to close.

'Nice lad. Ex-forces I would say by his bearing.'

Asvina nodded. 'Yes, that wouldn't surprise me. Hugo Morgan was in the army for ten years before he started in the City. He's a big supporter of military charities and suchlike. But I guess you knew all that.'

'So what's this all about anyway?' Maggie asked. 'You didn't give much away on the phone.'

And that much was true, but she had learnt from her friend something of the background of Hugo Morgan, and was quite certain she was not going to like him. How could she like a man who, as a sort of present to himself had decided to dump his wife of twenty-two years on the day he reached his fiftieth birthday?

'I'll let Hugo give you the full details,' Asvina said, 'but let's just say there's to be a new Mrs Morgan.'

Maggie laughed despite herself. 'It's *Hugo* now is it? I hope you're not thinking of trading in your Dav.' She knew there was as much chance of Asvina swapping her lovely husband as there was of the moon going round the sun. And in any case, she earned so much she didn't need a billionaire to look after her.

A discreet ping announced their arrival on the twenty-third floor, the lift opening to an opulent reception area. Behind a curved desk sat a perfectly-groomed young receptionist, the badge on her dress identifying her as Harriet Ibbotson.

'Good morning guys,' she said, smiling a well-trained smile. 'Do you have an appointment?'

She looked and sounded like central casting's posh girl, the voice confident and assured with just a suggestion of upper-class drawl. Maggie couldn't help but admire her expensive flower-print dress, which she had teamed with a matching pink cashmere cardigan. They wouldn't have left much change from a thousand pounds in the type of stores where Miss Ibbotson evidently shopped, and she certainly wasn't paying for it out of her receptionist's salary. Rich daddy she guessed, with a hint of bitterness. It was ever thus, and it was probably mummy or daddy too who had got her this job. But maybe she was being unfair, letting her own working-class prejudices colour her opinion, because Harriet seemed perfectly nice, and efficient too.

'We're here to see Mr Morgan,' Jimmy said, smiling at her. Maggie couldn't help but notice it, the frankly *stupid* reaction whenever he smiled at a woman of any age. They went bloody gaga and she found it *very* annoying.

'He's expecting you,' Harriet said, her gaze fixed on him. 'Please, come this way.' She led them through a set of frosted double doors into a large conference room, dominated by a giant oak boardroom table. Along two walls, floor-to-ceiling glazing afforded breathtaking views across the city.

Hugo Morgan rose to greet them, wearing an amiable expression. 'Welcome to Brasenose Investment Trust. Named it after the old alma mater, I'm sure you guessed that.' He was tall and powerfully-built, with a mop of tousled greying hair, dressed casually in fawn chinos, navy jacket and open-necked white shirt. His face was smooth and tanned, with the vaguely artificial aura that was often the accompaniment to a devotion to Botox. His teeth too, perfectly aligned though they were, had that slightly unnatural dazzle that only top-end dental engineering could deliver. But with or without the work of his cosmetic surgeons, Morgan had a presence about him that Maggie recognised as more than just the effect of his wealth. He would have had this before he got rich, she was sure of that. It was a cliché, but he looked like the sort of man who knew what he wanted and how to get it.

'Take a seat guys, please. How's the family Asvina, all well I take it?'

'Yes, all fine,' she replied. 'And yours?'

He gave a rueful smile. 'Well you know what kids are like. But yes, they're doing great I think, all in all, given the circumstances. You did well for me there, I'm so grateful.'

'I don't know about that,' Asvina said. 'It was the court who gave them the choice and they chose you.'

'And these are your colleagues of course. Maggie Bainbridge, once the most hated woman in Britain, and Captain James Stewart, the Hampstead Hero himself.' He smiled. 'Done my research you see. As you'd expect.'

Maggie gave a wry nod. God, was that damn epithet going to be with her forever?

'Yes, that was me I'm afraid.' And two years on, it still hurt like crazy that it was she who had let Dena Alzahrani walk free. There wouldn't have been any need for a Hampstead Hero if the teenage terrorist had been convicted and locked away for life, like she should have been. And her beautiful niece Daisy would still be alive. It had been her fault, and that was something she was going to have to live with for ever.

'You were badly done by,' he said, 'but I guess justice was done in the end. But what a sensational outcome. Who would have thought it?'

'You served too, didn't you?' Jimmy said. 'Guards wasn't it? In Kosovo. I think we're in the same club.'

Morgan laughed. 'The old George Cross do you mean? Well, you and I both know it's simple self-preservation that drives us so-called heroes. At least it was in my case. I just wanted to get out of the damn Balkans as fast as I could and back to civilisation.'

Jimmy nodded. 'Felt the same about Afghanistan. Nice people, but you never knew who were your friends and who were your enemies. In fact sometimes they were one and the same. Totally mental country when I was there. Still is I think.'

'Yes, but we tried our best, didn't we? Couldn't have done anything more than our duty.'

Harriet had arrived with a tray of hot drinks, which she carefully set down on the table. 'Tea or coffee?' The question was directed at everyone, but Maggie noted that her eyes were fixed on Jimmy. Typical, that was.

'Just leave the tray Harriet,' Morgan said. 'I'll sort it. Tea or coffee Maggie?'

'Coffee please Mr Morgan.'

He smiled. 'Hugo, please.' So that was it then. The first time in her life she had been on first-name terms with a nearly billionaire. Correction, a cold and heartless wife-dumping nearly billionaire. It was important that she wasn't so seduced by his charm that she forgot what sort of man he really was.

'So, I guess you're interested to know why I've called you guys in?' he said. That had to be the understatement of the year. 'Asvina, maybe you can update your team?'

She nodded. 'Certainly. Getting straight to the point, Hugo has decided to remarry and has engaged Addisons to oversee the formal side of the arrangement. I'll be looking after the matter personally of course.'

Maggie smiled to herself. A new Mrs Morgan, no doubt younger and slimmer and sexier than the discarded model. Naturally there would have to be a pre-nuptial agreement given that he would be taking nearly a billion pounds' worth of assets into the marriage. But she was making the assumption that his intended, whoever she was, was no match for him financially, and she realised that need not be correct. And so the question, though a terrible old chestnut, had to be asked.

'That's wonderful Hugo. Who's the lucky lady, may I ask?'

'Her name is Lotti and it's me who is the lucky one I can assure you.'

'Miss Brückner is Swiss and works in a gallery in Knightsbridge,' Asvina said in way of explanation. 'That's how you met her Hugo, isn't it?'

He gave a fond smile. 'That's right. I was looking for some interesting modern art and I found an interesting modern girl instead. Lotti's quite an expert in the subject as it happens. She tells me she studied in Heidelberg and Amsterdam before coming to London.'

She tells me. Now Maggie began to understand why she and Jimmy were here. Asvina too had picked up on the nuance.

'This is all my doing Maggie, I take full blame. But marriage is a difficult arena for high net-worth individuals, isn't it? We all want to think it's all about love, passion and romance but you can't ignore the practical side, especially when a relationship hasn't been going very long. So my advice to Hugo, much against his instincts I should say, was that he should perform some due diligence on his intended. Obviously, a very delicate subject. But that's where you two come in.'

Maggie gave her a knowing look. So that was it. They were to dig into the background of the to-be Mrs Hugo Morgan. Looking for secrets and lies and perhaps more besides. Her friend was keen to claim it as her idea, but she doubted very much if *he* was going into the marriage with his eyes closed. No, this was without doubt a Hugo Morgan initiative.

'It goes without saying,' he said, 'that Lotti mustn't discover that she is being...' He tailed off, unable to say the word out loud. *Investigated.* Because that's what was going on here. An investigation, the act itself creating a dark secret that would hang over the marriage, suspended by a thread like that fabled sword she couldn't quite remember the name of. Because if it ever came out, ten or even twenty years down the line, then the relationship was surely finished. *'Didn't you trust me Hugo?'* she would ask, a question to which there could only be one answer.

'Of course,' Maggie said. 'That's understood. Obviously I have a few questions if you don't mind?'

He shrugged. 'Yeah sure. I'll do my best to answer them.'

'And Jimmy, chip in if you think of anything too.'

'Aye, will do.'

Maggie removed a slim notebook and pen from her bag and smiled. 'I know I should use a tablet or something but I'm afraid I like the old-fashioned methods. So, I noticed that Asvina referred to Miss Brückner as your intended. Does that mean you haven't popped the question yet, if you don't mind me putting it that way?'

'No, I haven't asked her yet,' Morgan said, 'but we have talked about it of course and I think we have an understanding. But, well, I suppose it depends on...on this exercise. And when I propose, I want to do it properly, naturally. I'm not sure, but we'll probably take the jet over to Porto Banus and then do it on my yacht.' *As you do*, Maggie thought, but she didn't say it.

'That sounds nice. And what about your children? Have you discussed your plans with them?'

He grimaced. 'Well they've met Lotti of course, and I think they like her. One of them at least. I'm not sure about Rosie. She's at a difficult age.'

'She's eighteen,' Asvina explained, 'and very sweet.'

Morgan smiled. 'Yes, she is.'

'And Lotti,' Jimmy said, furrowing his brow, 'that is, if you don't mind me asking. How old is she?'

Maggie could see Morgan tensing up. It was the question she had been dying to ask him herself, so she was grateful for Jimmy's intervention. The old good-cop bad-cop routine. It seldom failed.

'She's thirty.'

'So just twelve years older than Rosie,' Jimmy said. Christ, thought Maggie, if you're trying to get us blown off the job before we've even started, you're going the right way about it. But thirty? She had expected her to be younger, but not *that* young.

Morgan gave him a sharp look. 'I can do the maths Jimmy.'

'No no, I didn't mean to be insensitive,' Jimmy said, 'but we just need as much background as possible, I'm sure you understand that.' The tone was sympathetic and it seemed to have the desired effect, because a grin began to spread across Morgan's face.

'Yes, I know what everyone will be saying, she's much too young for me, but hell Jimmy, she's so incredibly beautiful, and we've only got one life, haven't we? And believe me if you saw her, you'd feel the same way.'

Fearing how Jimmy might respond, Maggie decided it might be smart to steer the conversation on to less contentious matters.

'So Hugo, I guess we just need to get a few basic facts from you so that we can plan our investigation.' She saw him wince at the word, but really, how else could it be described?

'As much as you know about her, parents, siblings things like that. And of course the name of the gallery where she works. Perhaps it'd be easier if I had a think about it and emailed you a list of questions.' Did it sound as if she was making it up as she was going along? Because that's what she was doing. This was the first time Bainbridge Associates had done this kind of work so she didn't exactly have a proven template to fall back on. But he seemed perfectly relaxed about her suggestion.

'Yeah sure, sounds good. Feel free to ask anything you like.'

'I'd be really interested to know more about your firm Hugo,' Jimmy said. 'I don't know anything about financial services, but it's incredible how well you've done in just, what is it, about eight years?'

'It's nice of you to say so,' Morgan said, with obvious pride. 'It's not rocket science. Brasenose just takes a different approach from its competitors, that's all. It's a simple business model, we scare the shit out of lazy and incompetent management by analysing the hell out of their businesses and exposing their failures. Force them to either perform or get out of the way. That's why they hate us so much.'

Jimmy laughed. 'Sounds simple when you say it like that, but I bet it isn't really.'

'Well it *is*, actually,' Morgan said, 'but listen, why don't you two come and see for yourselves? We're doing one of our quarterly investor updates tomorrow over at the London Hilton on Park Lane. I've heard there's going to be fireworks, it should be fun. Have a word with Harriet on the way out and she'll get you on the attendee list.'

'Nice girl,' Maggie said.

Morgan nodded. 'Yeah, she is. She's an intern, but we'll maybe give her a job at the end of it. But yeah, talk to her and hopefully I'll see you both tomorrow.'

Suddenly a thought came to her. 'I assume Lotti won't be there? Because obviously, we need to stay undercover for the time being.'

He shook his head. 'No no, she'll be at the gallery, I'm pretty sure of that,' he said, getting to his feet. 'Anyway, unless there's anything else?'

So that was it then. Their first-ever due diligence commission, and a whole different ball game from the dry financial investigations they were used to. The truth was, Maggie didn't have the first clue where to start, but somewhere in the back of her mind, a germ of an idea was forming. A crazy idea, it had to be said. Lotti Brückner, thirty years old and in the opinion of the multi-millionaire Hugo Morgan, incredibly beautiful. Jimmy Stewart, thirty-two years old and in the opinion of every woman who had ever set eyes on him, ridiculously attractive. What was it they called it again? A honey-trap, that's what it was. A perfect test of the faithfulness or otherwise of Miss Brückner.

She'd need to double-check, but she was pretty sure there was nothing preventing it in his terms and conditions of employment.

Chapter 2

They hadn't done a bad job, he had to admit it. Atlee House was still a dump and had been since the day it opened way back in nineteen sixty-three, but at least now it was a nicely-painted dump. The foyer, the first area of the building to be completed, looked and smelt fresh and clean as he dawdled his way towards the staircase. The colour was Silver Sand according to the decorator, as if Detective Inspector Frank Stewart gave a monkey's about that. He would have described it as grey, but it was quite a nice shade of grey and certainly a vast improvement on the previous nicotine-stained brown. And there was even better news to come, because later in the week the knackered old eighties vending machine was finally getting the boot, to be replaced at last by an appliance more suited to the twenty-first century. Although his mate Eleanor Campbell had told him he would need to download an app to use the bloody thing, which filled him with some trepidation. What was so difficult about stuffing a pound coin in a slot? Still, he was sure he would figure it out eventually, and as far as he knew, there would still be Mars Bars. Important, that.

He made his way up the staircase to the first floor and headed to the little meeting room in the corner of the large open-plan office. Since his appointment as acting head of the department, he had briefly considered making it his personal office, but no, that wasn't his style. He had always hated the way the brass shut themselves away in their little private enclaves and he had no desire to become like them, not after nearly twenty years of honourable insubordination. But today he needed a bit of peace and quiet to work on what he hoped would turn into his next case.

The first thing he had to do was come up with a name for it. For some reason, *Operation Dolphin* was spinning round his head and he quite liked the sound of that. There was a certain synergy with his last case, it having been called Operation Shark, and that one had turned out to be a pretty successful investigation. So maybe that was a good omen. Dolphin it would be then, unless he thought of anything better in the meantime.

It had been DC Ronnie French, one of his deadbeat colleagues in deadbeat Department 12B, who had first brought the case to his attention, although it could hardly have been described as a case at that stage. French was quite new to the department and had come with a reputation. Of course everyone in 12B had a back-story, but French's was less complicated than most. He was simply useless.

It was a few days earlier, and Frank had arranged to meet him in the same room where he now sat. The DC had been waiting for him when he got there. Fat and scruffy, French was approaching his fiftieth year and spent all of his waking hours dreaming of his impending early retirement after a long and undistinguished career in the ranks. He had greeted Frank with a perfunctory 'Morning guv,' his face carrying the same sullen expression it had carried for the past thirty years. Frank had known it wasn't personal. He was like that with everybody.

'Morning Frenchie,' he had said, casting him a mildly disapproving glance. It had often occurred to him that he might well end up looking like the DC in a few years' time if he didn't do something about it, although he recognised that dispassionate observers might already mistake them for twins.

'So what have you got for me? Something interesting, that's what you said on the phone.' It would have needed to have been something bloody earth-shattering to get the perma-bored French off his fat arse. That was why Frank had gambled it would be worth a meeting, and he wasn't to be disappointed.

'Yeah guv, quite interesting I think. A suicide that might not be a suicide. A mate of mine down the club brought it to my attention.'

And that was where it had all started. *A suicide that might not be a suicide*. Better known as a murder.

The victim was one Chardonnay Clarke, a pretty young woman of just twenty-three years of age. Correction, not just pretty, but absolutely stunning. She was the niece of a friend of Ronnie French's mate, all members of the Romford snooker club where seemingly he spent most of his leisure time. And whilst her name might have suggested otherwise, she was no stereotypical Essex girl. According to the brief background notes that DC French had thrown together for him, this was a very bright lady, with a string of A levels and a first-class Honours in Philosophy, Politics and Economics from Oxford University. Frank didn't know too much about academia, but he had read somewhere that an Oxford PPE degree was about the most sought-after and prestigious qualification you could get. Not bad for a plumber's daughter from Romford, that was for sure.

After Uni, she had gone to work for one of these international banks down at St Katherine's Dock, although as Ronnie had put it, it wasn't a *real* job, but one of these fake intern things where your rich daddy paid for your place. Except, and this was something that had particularly caught Frank's attention, Chardonnay Clarke didn't have a rich daddy.

It had occurred at around six-thirty in the evening, Tower Hill tube station still packed with returning commuters anxious to get home after a long day in the office. The eye-witness accounts were both hazy and contradictory, which didn't surprise Frank in the slightest. One was adamant that her movement had been chillingly precise and deliberate, that she had waited until the train emerged into the station before stepping off the platform to her death. Another said she had wavered uncertainly before toppling over, as if she was drunk or drugged.

In her handbag they had found her smartphone, still open on her Facebook timeline, where apparently she had been about to tell the world that life had become too painful to bear and so she had decided to end it all. *I'm sorry, I just can't go on,* that's all it said. But for some reason, she never got to press 'Post'.

The police were called of course, but there was no reason to suspect foul play. Interestingly though, or at least interesting to Frank, the post-mortem did find traces of cocaine and heroin in her blood stream. A speedball, that's what they called it on the street, a powerful cocktail of two class A drugs that was as likely to give you a heart attack as give you a thrill. But the Coroner had been unwilling to speculate whether that had contributed to her death, either in the physical or psychological sense.

According to her father, her new job had rather gone to her head and she had started moving in what he called a 'fast set.' *Over-paid bankers, wankers more like, with Ferraris and fancy penthouse pads.* That's how Terry Clarke had described them, but he had been adamant that his daughter was a good girl and certainly wasn't into drugs or anything of that nature. Frank gave a silent laugh at that. The parents were always the last to know.

And that was it, as far as the authorities were concerned. A tragedy for the family, undoubtedly, that's what the Coroner had said at the inquest, but nothing to suggest anything else, especially after the discovery of Chardonnay's virtual suicide note. So the case was closed even before it was opened.

A suicide that might not be a suicide. But what was the evidence for that, other than the father's insistence that his girl had everything to live for and so why would she do herself in? Frank hadn't known Chardonnay, but he had researched the stats, and if her death had been self-inflicted, then it was definitely an outlier. It turned out there was about six thousand suicides in a typical year in the UK and of them, more than three quarters were male. It was a bit of a sweeping statement, but generally speaking women didn't top themselves. That was especially true for young women under the age of twenty-five.

But it wasn't just the statistics that had driven Frank to dive deeper and deeper, getting him to where he was now. Firstly, he bloody hated drugs and what they did to people's lives. For him, it was personal, and as long as he could draw breath he would pursue the scumbags who made their livings from that pernicious trade.

Secondly, it was that photograph of her that French had sent him. Because Chardonnay hadn't just been pretty. She was an off-the-scale beauty, super-model stunning, and in his book, girls like that just wouldn't kill themselves. No way.

And the third thing, and this was the one which really sent him off on what he knew might well turn out to be a wild goose chase, was that he remembered an item that had caught his eye nearly nine months ago in the *Evening Standard*. About a good-looking young lad who had thrown himself in front of a tube train. He could remember at the time looking at the striking photographs of the boy and thinking exactly the same thing as he was now thinking about Chardonnay Clarke. Lads like that didn't just go out and kill themselves.

Which is why he had found himself on a government website, scanning the London suicide data for the past year, because that would tell him if his opinion, rooted in common sense, was backed up by the statistics. It was a surprise to him when he found out that the capital had the lowest rate of any region in the country, at around four per hundred thousand of population. It was less of a surprise that the highest region was Scotland, where the rate was exactly four times higher at sixteen suicides per hundred thousand. Having grown up there, he could understand why. It could be grim up in Pict country.

Searching deeper, he had found the evidence in a particular government chart that supported his hunch. In the last year, just forty-nine people under the age of twenty-five had taken their own lives in London. True, every one told a heartbreaking story, but statistically, it was insignificant. As he had suspected, Chardonnay Clarke was an outlier.

A quick call to the Coroner's office had confirmed what he had hoped. Yes, they did keep data records on each case, confidential data he as a serving police officer could request access to. Containing everything he might need except their identities of course, because this data was, what was it they called it? *Anonymised*, that was it. But that didn't matter at this stage.

He couldn't really explain what he expected to find out from the data. There was just something in the fact that most under twenty-fives didn't do this, so maybe he would discover something that stood out by looking at the few who did. He recalled that there had been a spate of recent incidents where seemingly level-headed youngsters had been encouraged to take their own lives through muddle-headed social media campaigns. Was Chardonnay's case one of them, he wondered, and were there any others like it? Maybe that other guy from a few months ago was one. He'd need to do a bit of digging to find out his name, but that shouldn't be too difficult. That was what he was looking for, patterns and connections. It might lead nowhere, but it was as good a place as any to start.

The only problem was, the data would doubtless come on a spreadsheet, and Frank didn't do spreadsheets. But that didn't matter, because his wee pal Eleanor Campbell did. If there was anything to be found, she would help him find it. And just two days after he had made the request, the spreadsheet had landed in his inbox.

This morning he found the young forensic officer at her adopted desk on the ground floor, and, as was often the case, on her phone. Eleanor's official location was at the main labs over at Maida Vale, but she preferred to be tucked away out of sight and out of mind in Atlee House, a preference that Frank liked to use to his maximum advantage. From her tone, he guessed that she was speaking to her sort-of boyfriend Lloyd, but you didn't need to be a Detective Inspector like him to figure that one out. Because Eleanor was always talking to sort-of Lloyd. A situation that he intended to take full advantage of.

He signalled her to hang up. She responded with her trademark scowl and kept talking.

'Yeah, Lloyd, look, I don't want to talk about this now...No way... look, I've told you a gazillion times before, that's never going to happen...no, I'm not doing that, like never... I've got to go...no, not tonight, not ever I said... Lloyd, no forget it...'

'Problems?' Frank knew he was on safe ground with this, because there always seemed to be problems between Eleanor and her on-off boyfriend.

'He's an idiot.'

'Seems that way,' Frank said, giving a sympathetic half-smile, 'but you know, you really shouldn't be talking to him on police time.' They both knew what that meant. She was expected to trade compliance for him looking the other way.

She heaved a sigh. 'Ok Frank, what do you want?'

He smiled back at her. 'That's my girl. So I've got a wee spreadsheet from the Coroner that I'd like you to help me with. I remembered you told me once about some sort of data matching you could do with this Excel thingy?'

'Yeah, I remember,' she said, without enthusiasm. 'So how many records does it have? Millions I expect.'

'Records?' Frank said. 'If you mean how many lines, forty-nine.'

'Forty-nine?' she replied, with visible relief. 'That's like nothing. Send it to me and I'll take a look.'

'How long do you think it will take to find any patterns?' Frank asked. 'A couple of days I suppose?'

She gave him a scornful look. 'Yeah, more like two minutes, if there's only forty-nine rows. Are you still hiding away in that corner office upstairs?'

'*Working* away, you mean. Aye, I am.'

'Whatever. So, I'll come and see you when I find something.' He noted with some satisfaction that she said *when* not *if*. He wasn't surprised, because if there was one thing he knew about Eleanor Campbell, it was that she didn't lack self-belief.

True to her word, it was barely ten minutes later when she marched into the little meeting room, her laptop under her arm.

'That was quick,' Frank said. 'Find anything?' He knew she would have, otherwise she wouldn't be here.

'Yeah, like it was simples-ville. It took me longer to walk up the stairs than find it.'

'And?'

'And there's two records that might be connected in some way to your girl. Row eight and row twenty-four. Look, I'll show you.'

She placed the laptop on the desk facing Frank and opened the lid.

'They pull together a lot of other data from the credit-checking agencies databases and other places,' Eleanor said. 'Data augmentation they call it. I don't know why, they just do.'

Frank didn't know either, but he suspected it was so the public health authorities could look for patterns too, in their case ones that might help them target their preventative education programs. Things like background and occupation, to see if certain groups were particularly susceptible to giving up on life. He seemed to remember it used to be farmers and dentists who were the worst for some reason. Maybe they still were.

'So things like the cause of death, obviously, but lots of other things like their schools and unis, who they work for, their jobs. Lots of weird stuff like that.'

'And you said you found some matches?' Frank said.
'Yeah, that's right. Twelve on the first pass. That was on method. That's what they call how they done it.'

'So twelve poor sods decided to end it all by stepping in front of trains.'

'Yeah, and like it splits the data between underground and overground for some reason. Underground is the most popular.'

Frank shook his head. 'Bloody hell Eleanor, these are real people, with families, kids, everything. I'm not sure *popular* really describes it.'

'I didn't mean anything by it,' she said, her tone defensive. 'What I mean is more of them jumped in front of a tube train than overground. Eight out of twelve.'

Frank nodded silently to himself. Every now and again the radio travel bulletins would report travel disruption on the Underground because the police were dealing with an incident. It was never spelt out, but everyone knew what it meant.

'So then I was looking for a match on the maximum number of data elements,' Eleanor said. 'I wrote a macro.'

'Sorry?' Frank said.

'A macro. I got it to like search for matches automatically. Gender, occupation, town of birth, things like that.'

He didn't even pretend to understand what she was talking about.

'Aye, well I'll have to take your word for that. But come on, tell me more.'

'Yeah, so although the data is anonymised, it was easy to work out which one was Chardonnay. From her age, town of birth and like obviously the method. You see, here she is here. Row twenty-four.'

Frank nodded. 'So then you just got your wee macro thingy to go and find other lines that were a close match, is that how it works?' Too late, he saw what he had done. *Just*. It didn't take much to offend her, he knew that from bitter experience, and then she could get difficult. Difficult, as in down tools and walk off the job difficult.

'*Just*? Like you think this stuff is easy?' Not more than one minute ago, she herself had said that it was, but Frank knew he wasn't going to get anywhere by reminding her of that.

'No no, of course not,' he said, backtracking. 'A little slip of the tongue, that was all. Of course it's not easy. I couldn't do any of this, no way.'

That seemed to satisfy her. He had found that shameless grovelling often did.

'Yeah, I know you couldn't. So anyway, I ran the macro with the maximum matches setting and that's how it found the other record.'

'Row eight. The other person.'

'Exactly. So there was matches on like four columns. *Method, University, Occupation* and some weird one called *Parental Socio-economic Group*. I've no idea what that is.'

'Right, that's very interesting,' Frank said. 'So does this mean that the other lad killed himself in the same way as Chardonnay? I guess it must do.'

'Correct,' Eleanor said. 'Fatal trauma inflicted by a railway vehicle.'

'And the Uni?'

'Yeah, same. Oxford.'

'And occupation?' Frank said. It was more a statement than a question. 'Do we know who they worked for?'

Eleanor shook her head. 'It says they were interns. I don't know what that is. And no, it doesn't give any info on who they worked for.'

'And then that last one. Socio- whatever. What does that say?'

'I've like no idea what this means either,' she answered, frowning. 'It just says *C2*.'

But Frank knew what it meant. Socio-economic classification C2, *Skilled Manual Workers*. Plumbers and brick-layers and electricians, the solid back-bone of the country. Men and women who were good with their hands. Like Chardonnay's dad Terry. And not exactly the background you expected of students at Oxford, no matter how much they tried to deny their elitism.

He thanked Eleanor for her help, smiling as he escorted her to the door, then closed it behind her. This was very interesting, no doubt about it. Two young working-class kids who had smashed through the class barriers to win places at a prestigious university. Two kids with door-opening qualifications taking the first steps of what was almost certainly destined to be glittering careers. And two young people who had decided that life was no longer worth living. Now he recognised that old familiar feeling in his gut, the one that screamed *something isn't right*.

A suicide that wasn't a suicide. Except now it seemed there might be two of them. Now he'd need to make a proper effort to find out who that other lad in the paper was.

Chapter 3

The foyer of the Park Lane Hilton was a hubbub of activity, as hundreds of investors milled around, chatting and sipping coffee, waiting for the Brasenose Investment Trust quarterly update to get going. Maggie noted that they'd had to book one of the bigger conference rooms with the capacity to seat a thousand delegates, such was the popularity of the event. Since yesterday's meeting with Hugo Morgan, she'd done some reading up on his firm, enough to discover it was the absolute darling of the small investor community. And why wouldn't it be, given that those who had been in from the start had seen the value of their shares increase ten-fold? Not a bad return in eight years and way above the FTSE gains for the period. It was no wonder that Morgan was revered as a superstar of the industry, and in just a few minutes she would get the opportunity to see him performing for his adoring fans.

Jimmy had been tasked with completing their registration formalities, which was no more difficult than giving their names to one of the girls at the reception desk and in return being issued with a smart lapel badge on which their name was printed. Jimmy being Jimmy, it was no surprise to her when she glanced over to see that he was in conversation with Harriet Ibbotson, he giving every indication of listening intently as she spoke, she gushing with ill-disguised adoration. Looking round, he caught Maggie's eye, raising an arm in greeting before strolling over.

'Nice girl that, like you thought,' he said, handing over her badge. 'Clever too. Got an Economics degree from Cambridge. Wants to make a career in financial services.'

Maggie laughed. 'Did you get her shoe size too?'

'Aye, and her phone number as well. No, only joking about that. But what was interesting, she was saying they don't actually work for their employers.'

She wasn't exactly sure what was interesting about that, but she asked him anyway.

'So?'

'So it's like an agency. She told me their name but I've forgotten already. The company just gives them their requirements and they supply the intern.'

'Fascinating,' she lied. 'But hey, look at the time. We'd better get in and grab a seat before they're all taken. Looks like a sell-out.'

They found seats towards the rear of the auditorium, at least twenty or so rows back from the front. It seemed as if proceedings were to be beamed onto the giant screen which filled the wall behind the speakers' platform, itself flanked on both sides by a towering public address system. It was like a rock concert, with Morgan cast in the role of rock god. She was just about to say as much to Jimmy when a blast of music reverberated around the room.

'Fanfare for the Common Man,' Jimmy shouted above the din. 'Our army band used to do this one all the time. Aaron Copland. Great tune.'

And entirely appropriate, Maggie thought. Investment for the common man could easily have been a Brasenose slogan. In fact, she would mention it to Hugo the next time they spoke.

Suddenly the main lights went out, the music faded and a powerful spotlight strafed the stage. In response, the audience started to clap, beating out a rhythmic swell of anticipation which she guessed was a regular feature of these events. Rock concert? It was more like some weird political rally from the nineteen thirties, or some odd evangelical cult. And then a strident thespian voice boomed out from the PA.

'Ladies and gentlemen, please welcome to the stage Mr --- Hugo---Morgan!'

As one, the audience rose to its feet, clapping and cheering wildly. Morgan raised a hand in welcome as the spotlight picked him out, staring out into the auditorium and smiling, standing quite still as he waited for the noise to subside. She thought he might bellow 'Hello London' as musical entertainers were given to do, but no, he simply mouthed a thank you and sat down behind the table, flanked by a man and a woman who Maggie assumed were executives of the firm.

'Bloody impressive eh?' Jimmy said. 'Although I was expecting fireworks, didn't he say there would be some?'

She laughed. 'I guess they'll come later. I did wonder what he meant by that.'

The room had now quietened. Morgan rose, cleared his throat and began to speak.

'Well, thank you for that and welcome to our quarter two update. It won't be any surprise to any of you that we've had a great quarter. Because we always have a great quarter, don't we...?' This drew a collective laugh from the audience and a ripple of applause. '...and yes, as Caroline here will no doubt remind me, I have a legal duty to say that the value of your investments can go up as well as down...' He took a sip of water, '...although of course ours never go down', this time stimulating a raucous cheer. Alongside him, the woman, who Maggie took to be the firm's financial director, raised her eyebrows in mock disapproval.

'So, in a few minutes, Caroline will take you through all the numbing detail of the quarter's numbers. I know all you anoraks out there love a nice PowerPoint chart, and she's got hundreds, believe me.' This time an exaggerated groan from the audience. 'But before that I'll just give you the edited highlights. First slide Harriet please.'

He swivelled to face the screen. 'So as you see, we've had another cracking quarter. The share price is up eleven percent to thirty-two pounds sixty, and the value of the fund has now exceeded three billion pounds for the first time.' He turned back towards the audience as a wave of applause swept through the room.

'Thank you, thank you. So as a result I'm delighted to announce a rise in dividend to sixteen pence per share, up from thirteen pence in quarter one.' He took another sip from glass. 'Good news, I'm sure you'll all agree. So let's look at what we've been getting up to on the investment front. Next slide please Harriet.'

He pointed at an aerial image of some sort of industrial site that now filled the screen. 'Some of you may recognise this as Greenway Mining's new cobalt mine in Cumbria. I say new, but they've been digging their bloody great hole for six years now and still not brought a gram of the stuff to the surface. Which is such a shame, because it's a hot product, in huge demand all over the world. But God, their management was crap. I say was, because as you know, we've taken steps to improve that, haven't we?' A collective nodding of heads across the audience with a few random shouts of yes!

But then, out of the blue, a man a couple of rows in front of them got to his feet and began to shout towards the stage. The few members of the audience who recognised who he was nudged their neighbours or exchanged knowing smiles. This was going to be interesting.

'What do you say to the army of small shareholders who have lost their life savings because of you? All these people up there whose retirement plans have been ruined. Do you have anything to say to them? Come on, do you?' So this was the fireworks that Morgan had been anticipating.

'Ah, Mr Gary McGinley of the Chronicle,' he said, in a condescending tone. 'Holding capitalism to account, that's what your rather pompous by-line says if I recall it correctly.' This drew a loud giggle from the crowd. 'A valuable public service no doubt.' More laughter. 'Yes, it's unfortunate that these people made such foolish investment decisions when they would have done so much better if they had trusted us with their savings. Or in fact, had just put their money on a horse at Doncaster races.' This time, loud whoops from the adoring crowd. 'But I expect even you would be forced to agree the unfortunate losses were entirely the fault of the previous management. What do you say to that Mr McGinley?'

There was something about the way he said it that just underscored what Maggie was already feeling in her gut. It was the big ego on display, like a peacock in heat. Despite the superficial charm, she had decided she didn't like this man one bit.

'So are you trying to claim that your report had nothing to do with it?' the journalist said. His tone was unmistakably combative.

Morgan scanned the audience as if to gather strength from his army of supporters.

'On the contrary Mr McGinley, it had everything to do with it. We pride ourselves on being activist investors, and when we discover incompetence and waste, we see it as our duty to expose it. Holding capitalism to account, you might say. You must approve of that, surely?'

'What I want to know is how you found out?' McGinley said. 'That information was company confidential, only known to the company's most senior executives. So how did you find out? Come on, tell us now. I'm sure we'd all like to know.'

Morgan gave him a steely look. 'Activist investors, Mr McGinley, that's our mission statement and we do what it says on the tin. Unlike some, we don't just sit on our backsides and swallow the spin that the fat over-paid management churns out. We make it our business to know what is *really* going on, even when management doesn't.' Around the room, more applause.

'You still haven't answered my question,' McGinley persisted. 'How did you find out?'

Morgan with a nod of the head signalled to one of the muscled security men who had slipped in un-noticed just as the session had got underway and were now flanking the door.

'Thank you Mr McGinley, but I think we have had enough of this unscheduled interruption. Vinny, if you wouldn't mind escorting our guest to the door.'

Vinny the security guy had reached the end of McGinley's row and was beckoning for him to join him in the passageway. 'Would you like to come this way sir, please?' he said in a voice loud enough for everyone in the room to hear. 'Don't want no fuss, does we?', his expression making it plain if there was to be a fuss then he was up for it. For the briefest moment, McGinley seemed as if he might resist, but then evidently thought better of it. He rose to his feet then in a calm voice said,

'If you think you've heard the end of this Morgan, you'd better think again. I'll get to the bottom of this, believe me. I'm not going to let it go.'

'Yes yes no doubt Mr McGinley,' Morgan said, with barely-concealed derision, 'and we'll all look forward to reading about it in your ailing rag. Now if you don't mind...' Another nod to Vinny signalled that for him, the conversation was now over.

'God what was all that about?' Maggie whispered once McGinley had been marched out. 'Was that journalist guy Mr Angry or what?'

'Already on it boss,' Jimmy said, pointing at his phone. 'Just having a wee google to see what comes up. Seems there was some massive screw-up at this Whitehaven mine. Lots of stuff online about it.'

Up on the platform, Morgan had now moved on to discussing the fund's prospects for the coming period, evidently unruffled by the interruption. It was the same super-confident tone, the same relentlessly upbeat message. And the same syrupy air of superiority that was now getting right up Maggie's nose. But as Asvina had often remarked, there was no requirement to like your clients in this line of work. As long as they settled their bills promptly at the end of the month, that was all you needed to concern yourself with.

'And I'm pleased to say you can expect more of the same in quarter two. Growth in the fund value and growth in our share price too, and yes I know Caroline, it is important to note again that the value of your investment can go down as well as up. And on that bombshell, let me hand over to my colleague Ms Short who will go through the detailed numbers. Brace yourselves folks for some weapons-grade tedium.'

He sat down to tumultuous applause, many of the audience on their feet, stomping and cheering. Maggie expected at any moment there would be demands for more, rock-concert style, but eventually the noise subsided and Caroline Short was able to begin her presentation. Morgan had been absolutely right about one thing. This was tedium on an industrial scale, not helped by Short's monotone voice and plodding just-read-the-slide presentation technique. It was all price-earnings ratios and debt indices and multiples of dividend cover and a hundred other technicalities that Maggie didn't even try to understand. But she recognised it for what it was, a carefully choreographed piece of theatre, designed to reassure rather than entertain. Naturally you wanted the charismatic investment genius at the helm, spotting value that others failed to see, picking the right companies and making the audacious calls, buying at the bottom of the cycle and selling at the top. But in the back-office you wanted solid competence and measured calm, giving investors the confidence that the dull but necessary burden of regularity compliance was being met and that as far as could be guaranteed, their money was safe. In its eight years of operation Brasenose Investment Trust had delivered an exemplary performance on that score, and Maggie had little doubt that the dull Ms Caroline Short, doubtless hand-picked by Morgan for her very dullness, would have paid a key role in that. But finally came the words that a thousand numb backsides were literally aching to hear.

'This is my last slide,' she said, giving the audience a bemused look as they applauded her announcement with an enthusiasm born of relief. She kept it mercifully short, Morgan rising to his feet to join in the polite applause that greeted the end of her pitch.

'Thank you Caroline for that tremendously illuminating session. Very interesting to all our friends here, I'm sure.'

If he was being ironic then he kept it well hidden. 'So it just leaves me all to thank you for coming today and have a safe onward journey wherever you're heading next.' He raised a hand in acknowledgement then skipped down the steps to shake hands and grab selfies with a group of investors who had congregated at the foot of the platform.

'Popular guy,' Maggie said to Jimmy, who was still buried in his phone.

'What?' he said, distractedly. 'Aye, maybe here but not in West Cumbria. Here, look at this.'

It was an article from the Financial Times, dated around six months earlier. *Greenway Shares Voided after Cut-Price Rescue.*

Maggie gave him a puzzled look. 'Sorry, I don't understand any of that. What does it mean?'

He frowned. 'I've just skimmed it, so I'm not sure I understand it myself, but according to the article there was some giant technical problem with the mine that forced the firm to go into administration. I'm not sure exactly what that involves, I think it's when a company is kind of bust but they try to keep it going. So then Brasenose came along and offered to mount a rescue, but only if the previous company was liquidated - again, I don't exactly know what that means, but in effect all the existing shareholders lose their money. That's what they mean by voided I suppose.'

Maggie nodded. 'Ok, so that was what the McGinley thing was all about?'

'Aye,' Jimmy said, 'I guess so. But I suppose Morgan was right, it wasn't his fault that the mine had problems. That had to be down to the previous guys, surely?'

'Yes, I get that. But McGinley was talking about some report or other. Does it say anything about that?'

Jimmy shook his head. 'No, it doesn't as far as I can see. But see who's coming over. Maybe you can ask him yourself.'

She looked up to see Morgan strolling up the aisle in their direction, beaming a smile and exchanging a few words with some of his investors on the way.

'Hi guys,' he said as he reached them, 'and thanks for coming. What did you think?'

Maggie assumed he was referring to his own performance rather than the journalist's interruption.

'Very impressive Hugo, very impressive.' And that wasn't a little white lie, it *had* been impressive, irrespective of what she thought about him personally. But wasn't it telling that with all his millions, he still needed that affirmation, needed to know that he had done alright? She was about to ask him about the McGinley interruption when he brought up the subject himself.

'Yes, despite that little injection of excitement from our man from the Chronicle. I must apologise for that. Most unsavoury.'

'Did you know he was going to be there?' Maggie asked. She guessed he must have, because attendance at the meeting had been by invitation only.

'Yes, yes Maggie, but we can't be seen to exclude the financial correspondents, even the ones who don't like us. I was expecting him to pull a stunt like that of course.'

'Fireworks,' Jimmy said.

He nodded. 'Exactly. Although I think it turned out to be more of a damp squib, don't you?'

'So what did he mean when he said how did you know?' Maggie said. 'I didn't understand that. What was all that about?'

He looked surprised at her question. 'I refer you to my earlier answer. We're activist investors, it's what we do. As to our exact methods, you will forgive me Maggie if I don't choose to share them with my family law advisors. But let's just say we make sure we do our research.'

Out of the corner of her eye, Maggie saw a woman approaching them. She cut a striking figure, tall and very slim, wearing skinny black jeans, stilettos and a crisp white blouse under a black leather blouson. Her hair was sleek, glossy and expensively cut, and her complexion was smooth and flawless. It was hard to say exactly how old the woman was, but she guessed late forties, maybe just fifty.

'Still talking all that crap Hugo? When you and me both know it's all just a heap of bullshit.' She smiled at Maggie. 'I wouldn't believe a word of it darling. It's all lies, every world of it.'

Morgan's head darted around the room, clearly agitated. 'Where the *hell* is she? Where's Harriet?' Failing to detect the young intern amongst the crowd, he turned to the woman. 'I don't know how the hell you got in here Felicity, but I've got nothing to say to you.'

Felicity. So that's who she was. The recently discarded ex-wife. Maggie gave Jimmy a look that said *this might be fun*.

'I'm a shareholder Hugo or had you forgotten? So I was invited. And I've got plenty to say to you, believe me.'

'Not here, for Christ sake,' he said, lowering his voice. 'We don't want to make a scene.'

'Oh no, we wouldn't want that, not if front of your *fan club*.' You could almost cut the venom with a knife as she spat the words at him. Then she turned to Maggie. 'You see, he really is a *shit*. Steer clear of him darling, that's my advice, because he really is a *shit*. Did I say that? He's a *shit*.' It was then that Maggie noticed. The slurring of the words, the eyes just a fraction out of focus, the repetition. Mrs Felicity Morgan had been drinking. And it was clear that making a scene was the reason she had come.

'You see,' she said, raising her voice, 'I *know* darling. Just like that reporter. I know how you do it, but you wouldn't want the world to know all about *that*, would you my love.'

Vinny the security guy had glided onto the scene and was looking at his boss expectantly. Directing a sneer at his ex-wife Morgan said tersely. 'Get her out of here.'

'Sure boss.' He reached over and gripped her upper arm, so tightly that she winced. 'Come on Mrs Morgan, we don't want no trouble, does we?' Pulling her arm free, she directed a withering look at her husband.

'You haven't heard the last of this Hugo. Count on it.' Then summoning as much dignity as she could muster, she swept off.

'Sorry about that,' Morgan said, forcing a smile. 'My ex-wife is finding her new situation rather hard to come to terms with. But no matter.' He seemed anxious to change the subject. 'So, you'll keep me up to date with how our little project is progressing, won't you? And now if you'll forgive me, I want to get round as many of our loyal investors as I can.' And with that he swept off, the fixed smile re-installed for the benefit of his fans.

Jimmy gave her a wry look. 'Christ, that was quite a to-do, wasn't it? First that reporter then the crazy woman.'

She laughed. 'Yeah, mental wasn't it? Massively entertaining.'

'But do you think they're right? Is there something iffy about the way our Hugo goes about his business?'

She shrugged. 'Who knows, it's not something I understand. And I don't really want to either.'

And it was true, it wasn't any of her business and certainly was of no relevance to the job in hand. Which was to find out as much as they could about Miss Lotti Brückner. *Their little project*. Morgan might be reluctant to use the 'i' word, but she wasn't. She had a plan and tomorrow she hoped to meet Miss Brückner for the first time. Yes, tomorrow the investigation would be up and running.

Chapter 4

Liz Donahue scrolled down her phone book, looking for the number. She was pretty certain she had kept it, but whether it was under 'Chronicle', 'McGinley', 'Gary' or any combination of the three, she couldn't quite remember. Like any good journalist, she had hundreds of names in her book, pretty much everyone she had ever met in the four years she'd been working on her local paper. An invaluable resource until you actually needed to find something. But after some more frantic scrolling, there it was. *'McGinley, Gary, The Chronicle.'* All three tags just for good measure.

Unfortunately, there was no mobile number but she did have an email address and that would do fine for now. This one had been the second suicide connected to the Whitehaven mine debacle. The first, bursting with local interest, had been reported by her *Westmoreland Gazette* in the outraged tones it deserved. William Tompkins, father of four and a pillar of the community, his spirit crushed after losing more than a hundred and fifty grand of his family's money in the Greenway crash, had drunk himself blind on cheap vodka before swallowing four packs of paracetamol. Four days later he had died an agonising death as his liver gave up the ghost. A tragedy, unarguably, and one that her paper was more than happy to lay at the door of Hugo Morgan.

But this one was different, quite different. Which is why Liz had spent nearly twelve hours camped outside the idyllic family home on the fringes of Wastwater. Mrs Belinda Milner had been the CEO of the company, a City darling who commentators said had only landed the job because of its desire to be seen to balance the gender gap in the leadership of publicly-listed companies. With a string of non-executive directorships too, she had been able to dedicate just three days a week to her Greenway duties, which was deemed by many to be totally inadequate. The demise of the company was not going to be the highlight of her CV, that was for sure, but unlike many of her ex-employees she wasn't to be made destitute given the million-plus per annum package she had been on, and in any case this wasn't the first failure she had presided over. No, Belinda Milner was inured to criticism, and this latest career setback would not have caused her to lose a minute's sleep. Let alone go off and kill herself.

But she *had* killed herself, changing into the sleek black designer-label swimsuit in the early hours of a cold November morning before her husband or daughter had wakened, then slipping down to the lakeside and plunging into the icy waters. Swimming out to the centre, she had let the lapping waves envelop her, filling her lungs until she could breathe no more. She left no note behind to explain, leaving her family holding a tawdry secret they were desperate to keep to themselves.

Except that Liz Donahue had already found out the truth. This was going to be a big one, perhaps the biggest story of her life. It had been bitterly cold all day, and there had been no movement in or out of the house all the time she had been there, apart from a van, which had arrived around 3pm. Two men wearing white overalls had got out and started work, without bothering to announce their presence to the occupants of the house. She had detected the sweet smell of acetate thinner as the pair expertly removed the graffiti, the task taking no more than twenty minutes from start to finish.

The slogan had been painted in foot-high letters along the side of Milner's upmarket SUV. *Justice for Greenway.* The incident had occurred too late to make that week's print edition, but she herself had covered it in the online version. There was plenty of locals seeking justice after the Greenway melt-down, but few perceptive enough to see where the real blame lay. Whoever had done this knew the truth.

At around six in the evening and just as she was about to abandon her vigil, came the breakthrough. Milner's daughter, fifteen or sixteen years old and just a week after her mother's funeral, had decided to go for a walk. Liz caught her up just as she left the driveway.

'Was your mum having an affair April?' It wasn't her proudest moment but you couldn't let your scruples get in the way of a good story. This one deserved national exposure, but McGinley wasn't going to get it unless he agreed to give her joint credit. She didn't see how he could possibly refuse.

Chapter 5

Maggie hated the bloody photograph and she hated the bloody profile. In fact she hated everything about the whole damn thing. Especially something the website called 'Your Elevator Pitch.' *A youthful and fun-loving thirty-something, into walks in the countryside, great food and great books.* That described what she would like to be, not what she actually was, but as her friend Asvina had pointed out as they were putting the whole stupid thing together one evening after one too many chardonnays, everyone used great dollops of poetic licence on these dating sites. Besides which, *Burnt-out, bad-tempered forty-something former barrister who recently tried to do herself in,* didn't quite have the same ring to it.

Anyway, thank God it was still sitting there in the 'Draft' folder, the 'Post' button mercifully un-clicked. Right now, she wasn't ready for the wild-west world of online dating, and she doubted if she ever would be. But despite that, she had no doubt that almost unnoticed, something had changed inside her. After the most horrendous two years that anyone could ever have lived through, she was now feeling cautiously positive about the future. Positive enough to think about now meeting someone to share it with. But baby steps, that was the watch-word. She had plenty of time. No need to force the pace.

Her contemplations were interrupted by a sudden jolt as the tube-train driver sharply applied the brakes. She glanced up at the indicator board. *High Street Kensington.* This was her stop. She had calculated it was no more than a five-minute walk to the gallery, but that didn't really matter, since today she was the customer and so she could turn up late if she felt like it. Choosing what to wear had been a surprising challenge, since she really only owned a few smart suits for work, all navy, and then a hotchpotch of casual wear from the high street chains. That definitely wasn't going to create the kind of impression she needed to make. And then she remembered Harriet Ibbotson and the problem was solved. The dress cost nearly seven hundred pounds and the matching tailored jacket much the same, but there was no point in false modesty. She looked amazing in it, even if she said so herself. Which left just the problem of shoes. Four hundred pounds was a ridiculous sum of money to pay, but as she remembered her dad saying rather too often, why spoil the ship for a halfpenny's worth of tar? It wasn't as if she couldn't afford it, not after finally offloading her old family home, but it just didn't seem right in a world riddled with inequality.

But then again, this being a Thursday, she and Jimmy would be as usual meeting his brother Frank in the King's Head after work, and looking amazing would be no obstacle to what she had in mind. For Maggie had finally decided she liked Frank. He didn't have the babe-magnet looks of his brother, thank God - being with someone like that would surely turn you into an insecure wreck -but he was handsome in his own way and above all he was *nice*. And kind and open and honest, everything her late and unlamented husband Phillip never had been.

However, all that would have to wait until later, because she had now reached the front door of The Polperro Gallery. Kensington Church Street was lined wall-to-wall with the places and she wondered how they all could survive with such competition. But looking at the price-tag on a couple of items in their window, perhaps it wasn't so difficult to understand. The gallery felt pleasantly cool, discreetly air-conditioned with a limed-oak floor and walls painted in a subtle off-white silk. Classy, that was the immediate impression, doubtless exactly what the owners intended. Looking around, her eye was drawn by the picture immediately to her left, an arresting landscape of stark greys and khakis which as she got closer revealed itself as a scene from the trenches of World War I. An engraved plaque attached to the bottom edge of the frame read *Ypres September 1917*.

'It's wonderful, isn't it?' The voice was deep and mellifluous, the tone warm and welcoming. 'An undiscovered Paul Nash. We were so lucky to find it, don't you think?'

'I don't know him I'm afraid,' Maggie said. 'I don't really know any artists, to tell the truth. Lowry maybe, but that's about it.'

He held out a hand. 'It's Mrs Slattery, isn't it? I was expecting you. Welcome to the Polperro Gallery. I'm Robert Trelawney. We spoke briefly on the phone.'

'Magdalene, please.'

Mrs Magdalene Slattery. That was the name she had decided on. Her own first name, obviously, it would be too difficult to keep up the pretence if she suddenly became an Emma or a Susan. And then the surname of one of her favourite teachers, old Brian Slattery, Chemistry and Biology. A good old solid Yorkshire name for a good old solid Yorkshire girl. And if probed, the story was she had reverted back to her maiden name, but kept the *Mrs*. Perfectly plausible, after the way her fictional husband was supposed to have died.

She guessed Trelawney to be perhaps a couple of years older than her, slim and of medium height, dressed in an expensive-looking light grey suit with crisp white open-necked shirt. His shoes were a highly-polished deep brown leather and like the suit, obviously expensive. Tasteful and classy, just like his gallery. Now she was really glad she had taken the trouble to tidy herself up a bit.

'So when you called, you told me you were interested mainly in twentieth century art? But I wondered, how did you find us?'

She smiled. 'Find you? I've walked past your gallery on many occasions when I've been down this way. Actually, I'm ashamed to say I've just picked a few of you guys more or less at random. In your case, it's just that I liked the name. We used to go on holiday to Cornwall when I was a child.' It sounded perfectly convincing, and after all, why would all of these galleries bother with shop fronts if not to attract window shoppers?

He grinned. 'Well, I was brought up down there, for my sins. Trelawney is Cornish, I'm sure you've worked out. '

'Polperro's a lovely place and a lovely name for a gallery too,' she said. 'And to answer your question yes, I *think* I'm interested in modern art, but I'm really quite new to all of this. It's just that my financial advisors have been nagging me to diversify my asset portfolio or some such gobbledygook. You've got far too much tied up in cash, that's what they're always saying. First off they suggested I look at wine, but really, what can you do with a seventy-year old claret?'

Trelawney laughed. 'Yes, I agree, and it might not even taste nice if one day you decide to drink it. That's the great thing about art, you get the pleasure of being able to look at it every day. Although I'm bound to caution you that there are risks associated with buying a piece or a painting purely for investment purposes. That's why I always advise my clients to buy only artworks they really love.'

Maggie furrowed her brow. 'Is that normal in this business? That sort of advice I mean?'

'More normal than you might think actually,' he said. 'There's still a few unscrupulous dealers around but eventually their bad reputation catches up with them. Most of us are pretty straight. Honest.'

She laughed. 'I believe you. But this one,' pointing to the Nash, 'would you advise me to buy it?'

'Do you like it?'

She gave a sigh. 'Well it's certainly striking, but do I like it? I'm not sure that I do.'

He smiled. 'There's your answer then. But in any case, this probably isn't a picture for a novice collector. I hope you don't mind me calling you that?'

'Not at all. If you assume I know nothing about anything you'll be pretty much right. But when you say this isn't a picture for a novice, what do you mean?'

'Provenance and history. You see, Paul Nash was a very important artist, some would say one of the most important British artists of the early twentieth century. As such, his work has been extensively studied and catalogued. So when a work like this suddenly appears more than seventy years after his death, then there are obviously question marks over its authenticity. That's why we describe it in the catalogue as *attributed* to Paul Nash.'

'So that's a sort-of buyer beware?'

He nodded. 'Exactly. I'm very confident that it is genuine, and a number of experts have concurred with me, but there is always a risk that it could be challenged in the future.'

'After someone has bought it on the assumption it's a genuine Nash?'

'That's it. But a knowledgeable collector will do their due diligence before making up their own mind on that, and of course any doubts will be reflected in the price.'

She gave him an uncertain look. 'I'm not sure if it's the done thing Robert, but am I allowed to ask the obvious question?'

He smiled. 'How much, do you mean? Of course, that's the most important question of all. I can't say for certain, but the record price for a work of his is over two hundred thousand pounds, so I wouldn't be surprised if this goes for a similar sum or even more. We will have it on display here for the next month or so and I would expect we will have no trouble in agreeing a private sale. But if not, then it'll go to auction later in the year.'

'And so would you say that is the sort of sum I should be expecting to spend on an item? Because I've really no idea at all.' And then she realised that she was enjoying her conversation with this lovely man so much that she had almost forgotten why she was here in the first place. 'I mean, is this something you personally can help me with, or are there other people in your firm who deal with this?'

If he found the question odd, he didn't show it. 'Yes, well I'm more of an all-rounder you might say,' he said in an apologetic tone, 'but by coincidence we've got a new member of the team who is very knowledgeable on twentieth century artists, and not just the usual British suspects if I can call them that. She's in today. I'll just pop upstairs and see if she's free.'

And that was how it came to be that less than sixty seconds later, Maggie was shaking hands with the woman who was to be the next Mrs Hugo Morgan.

'I'm Lotti Brückner. Pleased to meet you.'

Involuntarily, Maggie looked her up from top to bottom and it was startlingly obvious that Morgan had not overstated the beauty of this woman in any way. Tall and slim, around five-ten, with a tiny little waist and a full bosom which was displayed to maximum effect by the tight-fitting white tee-shirt, worn above a pair of tailored light grey trousers. Her dark hair was thick and lustrous, swept to one side so that it rested a few inches below her left shoulder. Smart and beautiful, an intoxicating combination which would send most men crazy with desire, that could not be denied. But what struck Maggie most was her complexion, which was ridiculously soft and peachy, like that of a child. Which drove a thought into her mind, and the more she looked at Lotti, the more certain she was. *There's no way this woman is thirty years of age.* But that was stupid of course. Women lied about their age all the time, but as she knew only too well, they generally knocked a few years off, not added them on. Why would you do that? No, she was definitely being stupid. Perhaps Lotti was simply blessed with great genes, a product of her ancestors growing up breathing all that pure mountain air. But still the thought wouldn't go away.

'Pleased to meet you too Lotti,' she said, quite truthfully. 'Robert said you might be able to help me although to be honest, I'm not quite sure what my requirements are.'

Lotti smiled. 'Well, I'm sure we can discover that with some discussions.' Her voice was soft and clear but distinctly accented.

'That would be great,' Maggie said, 'and I hope you don't mind me asking, but do I detect a German lilt?'

She shook her head. 'Nearly. Swiss actually, but I grew up in Zurich so in a German-speaking Canton. It's the biggest one in Switzerland with over a million of us, but still the Germans say we do not speak the language properly. Of course we think the same about them also.'

'Oh dear,' Maggie said. 'I do hope you're not offended.' Not that she cared too much, really. It was just another part of the subterfuge, because if, as she said, she had chosen the gallery at random, how could she know that the pretty sales lady was from Switzerland?

'Not at all,' Lotti said, smiling. 'So maybe I can get you a coffee and then we could sit down and discuss your requirements? And perhaps match them to some of the works that we have for sale here in our gallery.' She turned to her boss. 'Robert, do you wish to sit in on these discussions?'

He shook his head. 'No, I don't think that's necessary Lotti. I'm not sure how much I could add to the party. But I can certainly make the coffee.' He scuttled off, leaving the two of them alone.

'Let's go and sit over here,' Lotti said, pointing to a low glass table in the corner. 'Robert told me about your situation. It must have been rather a difficult time for you.'

It *was* rather difficult, she thought, but only in trying to remember exactly what it was she had said to him yesterday. *Widowed in unusual circumstances and now bringing up my eight-year old son on my own.* That was about the gist of it.

'There's people in far worse situations than me,' she replied. 'At least I've enough money and a lovely home. And my son of course.' All of which was true, thank goodness, making that bit of the story easy to keep up. 'But you heard how my husband died, I suppose?'

'No, Robert didn't mention that.'

'He had a lover. Twenty years younger than him and he had a heart-attack whilst he was screwing the little bitch. Served him right of course, and her too. She had to push him off her then phone for an ambulance.' She didn't have to try too hard to fake the bitterness. It wasn't so much different from what she had suffered in real life.

Lotti shuffled uncomfortably, perhaps feeling that this was a bit too close to home. Good, thought Maggie, because that was the intention. But how far should she push it? No harm in going a bit further, and anyway, she found she was actually enjoying this. Perhaps she should have been an actress instead of a bloody lawyer, she might have been quite good at that.

'It's always the same with these rich and powerful older men, isn't it? They think they can take anything they want, and sod the carnage they leave behind. My David was fifteen years older than me when we married, but then as soon as I hit forty, boom, that was it.' *David.* She'd pulled that name from thin air, and now she'd better remember it. Bound to raise suspicions if you couldn't remember the name of your own husband, whether he was dead or not. 'So when he decided he wanted a younger model, I was dumped. But look, I'm sorry. Over-sharing, I'm always doing that. You're not here to listen to my troubles.'

She wiped a tear from her eye. A *genuine* tear. God, she was getting good at this already. Better start looking out an outfit for the *BAFTAs.*

But if Lotti Brückner was affected by Maggie's performance, she wasn't showing it. 'No, I don't mind at all Magdalene,' she said, giving a little smile. 'But I've been thinking that it may be a good idea for us to start with a little tour of our gallery. We have a big display in the back room and upstairs also. If I can understand the type of paintings you find appealing, then that will help me too.'

Maggie nodded. 'Yes, that sounds perfect. Because as I said, I really have no idea where to start.' And it was true. Acting skills or not, she wouldn't have any problems in playing the part of the naive art collector, since that was exactly what she was.

Robert had returned with the coffee, laying the delicate china mugs carefully on the glass table.

'Looks like you two are all set then,' he said brightly. 'I've got to go out now, but you'll be in good hands with our Miss Brückner I'm sure. But before I go, could I have a word with you Magdalene?' He beckoned her over towards the door, smiling at Lotti, who took the hint and slipped off into the back office.

'Look, I hope you won't find this too forward or presumptuous, but I wondered...would you possibly have dinner with me tomorrow evening? There's a lovely little Italian just round the corner if that's to your taste, and the house red is really very acceptable.'

And before she really knew what she was doing, she had said yes. That was going to make the job a bit more complicated. *Magdalene Slattery, the two-timer.*

Chapter 6

Frank wasn't entirely sure why the case intrigued him so much, but it did, which was why this morning he had broken with his normal routine to head straight to Paddington Green nick. True, they had better coffee there, and the vending machine offered a wider variety of the teeth-rotting and diabetes-inducing goodies that he loved, but the principle reason for his visit was to meet up with his old mate DI Pete Burnside. He'd given him the briefest of overviews on the phone. *A couple of suicides that might not be suicides. Dig out the files and see what you can find.*

'Good to see you mate,' Pete said as Frank arrived at his desk with latte and Mars Bar in hand. 'How's tricks?'

'Oh, same old same old. Nothing much that looks as if it will turn into anything, other than the one I mentioned to you.'

Burnside laughed. 'Yeah, you must be desperate if you're having to go through the suicides file.'

'Aye, you're not wrong there mate. But the one I looked at came to me from Ronnie French. You remember him?'

'He's that fat lazy DC from your manor?'

'That's the one. You're right, he's always been an idle turd, but I have to admit he's always had a good nose for the dark side. Well anyway, it was him that sniffed this one out. This girl walked in front of a train, but there might be a drugs angle and you know how much I hate that stuff and the low-lives that peddle them.'

Burnside nodded. 'Yeah, you and me both. So, you didn't exactly give me much to go on but I went through the records on our crime system here and funnily enough, there was another case that seemed to match your one. A young bloke who decided to step off a railway platform just as a train was coming in. I remember it, it was about nine months ago and the transport muppets called us into have a look, but that's just routine.'

'Aye, that's the one I read about,' Frank said, taking a slurp of his coffee. 'Any others?'

'Give us a chance mate, we've only been at it a day. But no, I don't think so.'

'Only joking pal,' Frank said. 'So tell me about the one you did dig up.'

Burnside spun his monitor round to face Frank. 'We've been busy mate, and all for you. I hope you're bloody grateful.'

Frank gave a wry smile. 'That depends on what you've got. But it might be worth a pint, you never know. Anyway, what am I looking at?'

'We've got the post-mortem pictures. The mortuary tries to tidy them up best as they can but you don't really want to look at them for too long. But of course we've managed to get a few snaps from his social media too.'

'That's brilliant Pete, it really is,' Frank said. 'So, do we know who he is? I suppose you worked that out by now.'

'Meet Luke Brown. Twenty-four years of age, lived in Clapham, mixed-race, born and raised in Leicester, graduated from Oxford two years ago, working as an intern at some insurance company over at Canary Wharf.'

Frank stared at the screen, struggling to take in what he was seeing.

'Pete, mate, I'm no judge of this kind of thing, and I know he's a young guy and all that, but is it just me, or is our Luke a bloody good-looking boy? I mean, my brother Jimmy's irresistible to women, but this lad would give him a run for his money that's for sure. What do you think?'

Burnside gave him a contemptuous look. 'Why are you asking me, you cheeky bastard? As it happens, I did think the same, but as you say, everybody's good-looking at that age.'

'*I* wasn't,' Frank said. 'Not like that anyway. But come on mate, there's something going on here. No idea what, but something.'

'If you say so. And I kinda agree, it is a bit odd how close the two cases are. But who knows, it's probably just coincidence.' His friend smiled. 'Anyway, you know that pint you were on about? So if you make it two, then maybe I'll let you know the *really* interesting stuff we found out.'

'Two pints? Aye well, I suppose I could just about run to that. Alright, what have you got?'

'So the first thing that I thought was a bit odd was this guy had written a suicide note that turned up on social media after he did it.'

'Christ,' Frank said, 'that's exactly the same as my girl'.

'Yeah, so obviously that meant the Coroner chalked it down as a suicide.'

'Aye, took the easy way out you mean.'

'A bit harsh Frank,' Burnside said. 'There wasn't any evidence that it could have been anything else. Although the post-mortems did find evidence of some drug use, it was no more than recreational amounts. But before you say anything else, we didn't just leave it there.'

'Tell me more,' Frank said, interested.

'Well believe it or not mate, even the Met are using interns these days. It's cheap labour isn't it? Anyroads, Yvonne Sharp's the girl we've got. Sharp lady. See what I did there? Sharp by name and sharp by nature.'

Frank gave him a mock-contemptuous look. 'You make that one up yourself mate?'

Burnside ignored the jibe. 'To be honest, we were a bit stuck for something for her to do, so I gave her a morning on your case and she did really well. First of all she spoke to the insurance company that Luke Brown was assigned to. Alexia they're called. German or Dutch-owned I think, and apparently big in marine insurance. Yvonne also got the name of the intern agency that employed him. Some outfit called The Oxbridge Agency. You know, as in Oxford and Cambridge universities.'

'Yeah, got that.'

'Well I thought I'd better spell it out, you being a northern hick and all that. But anyway, here's the thing. Yvonne herself had an interview with them, just last year.

As I said, she's a clever girl. Did Law at Cambridge and that's where she came across them. Apparently they market themselves pretty heavily on their campuses. Oxford and Cambridge I mean. So as I said, she had an interview, but didn't much like the culture. She got the impression they were very elitist and upper class and she didn't think she would fit in, even if her parents could afford their fee, which they couldn't. So she came direct to us instead.'

'What, they *charge* to give these kids a crap non-job?'

Burnside nodded. 'Apparently that's quite common.'

'And yet our two were working-class kids. Remarkable, isn't it?'

'I suppose it is,' Burnside said, sounding unconvinced. 'But there was something else that our Yvonne found out. Something pretty interesting in my opinion.'

'What?'

'Just two days before he died, Luke Brown was asked to leave.'

'You mean he was sacked?'

'I suppose you could describe it that way, but I expect these kids aren't on an employment contract as such, so the firms can dispense with them anytime they want. Yvonne talked to a girl in their HR team who was pretty tight-lipped as you might imagine. What was it she said? It was an internal matter and it simply coincided with a budget review. And that was as much as she could get out of her. Said the matter was now closed as far as the firm was concerned.'

Frank pursed his lips. 'So what do you think mate? Caught thieving? Or maybe looking at some inappropriate stuff on his laptop?'

'Yeah, it could be that, I don't know. As I said, their HR lot weren't too keen to say much, but Yvonne got the impression that there was something that wasn't quite right. I suppose if you really needed to find out we could send a couple of uniforms round. Say that we're re-looking at the death of Luke, and we've got some questions.'

'Which is the truth in fact. Aye, maybe that's an option but let me think about it first. But that agency outfit. The Oxbridge Agency. Find out anything about them?'

Burnside laughed. 'Frank Stewart, you are a right bloody dinosaur aren't you? They're not a secret society as far as I can tell, so you'll probably find their address on this new thing we've got now called google.'

'Cheeky swine,' Frank said. 'I just thought maybe your wonder-kid Yvonne might have wheedled out something, that was all. But no worries, I can look into that myself, no bother.'

Burnside gave him an enquiring look. 'So have I earned my pints then?'

'Aye, and some. You've done a cracking job mate, you really have. I'm actually down the Old King's Head after work tonight if you can be arsed to make the trip into town.'

'Yeah, I'd forgot it was Thursday. That's your regular night with your brother and that very lovely boss of his, isn't it? But I'm afraid it'll have to be some other time, I've got a call with the kids tonight and I don't want to miss it.'

Frank nodded. He forgotten about Pete's horrible situation, his former wife now re-married and living in Australia with his two kids, their relationship just another casualty of the job, with its late nights and broken promises and all the stresses it brought with it. He really felt for him.

'Aye, sure mate. Some other time, eh? Well, I'll be getting back over to my gaff and I'll see you soon. Cheers Pete.'

That very lovely boss of his. Pete was right, Maggie Bainbridge *was* lovely, in every conceivable way. Lovely to look at and with the sweetest nature of any woman he had ever met, despite everything she had been through. And God, hadn't she been through some shitty times. It was cringingly old-fashioned he knew, but sometimes he just wanted to wrap his arms around her and tell her he would make everything better. But of course, he hadn't said a thing in the nearly two years he had known her. Too scared, but too scared of what? Of rejection, of dying with embarrassment, of the gentle mocking he would have to suffer from his brother? Well, whatever it was, surely now was the time to shake of his pathetic self-doubt and just bloody do it. What's the worst that could happen? So she might say no, but wasn't that what he was expecting anyway?

Perhaps the truth was he was scared that she might say yes, and then he would find himself racing down the same path that Pete Burnside had followed. Everything starting off so perfect and sunny and optimistic until the job crushed every good thing out of their lives. But bugger this pessimism, tonight he was going to grab this thing by the throat for once. Tonight, he was going to ask Maggie Bainbridge to have dinner with him. He'd seen a nice little Italian just round the corner from the Old King's Head and that looked as good a place as any. *Maggie, will you have dinner with me?* How hard could that be?

Now, as he battled through the stop-go traffic of the North Circular back to Atlee House, he could turn his attention to what he had learned in the last hour. Old Pete had done a great job for him, and that wee nugget about Luke Brown, the fact that he seemed to have been sacked for some reason, made it doubly interesting. Although, when he thought about it, it could have given him a motive to take his own life, which rather put the kibosh on his murder theory. But he would figure out where that fitted in at a later date. No, the more he thought about it, the more convinced he was right. Two near-identical deaths. Two kids from the same modest background. Two kids blessed by the fates with brains and good looks. Two kids that surely had no reason to kill themselves. What did it all mean?

But right now, there was a more pressing priority. That name, *Operation Dolphin*. It just wasn't going to cut it. It wasn't just the fact that the causes of death were the same. It wasn't even that the victims were all listed as working for that Oxbridge Agency outfit. No, it was their bloody photographs. Because Luke Brown and Chardonnay Clarke shared one characteristic that he just knew was going to turn out to be ten times more important than all the others combined. They were ridiculously, arrestingly, sensationally good-looking kids, and so the case, for that is what it undoubtedly had become, demanded a more appropriate moniker.

And then, with an uncharacteristic flash of inspiration, it came to him. Surely there was only one that would suffice. *Sorted*. Operation *Aphrodite* was now up and running.

Chapter 7

'Aphrodite? Well I suppose it's better than the usual rubbish names you come up with. Some sort of Greek goddess, wasn't she?'

They were in the Old King's Head in Shoreditch for their semi-regular Thursday meet-up, and Jimmy had just fought his way back from the crowded bar after the always-regular buying of the first round. Frank believed there was a sort of natural hierarchy in families which demanded that wee brothers always bought big brothers the first drink, and so far Jimmy had never challenged the convention.

'Aye, she was,' Frank said. 'Goddess of love and beauty and everything in between.'

Jimmy grinned as he placed the drinks on the table. 'You must have looked that up I suppose.'

'Nah,' Frank lied. 'If I was on *Mastermind*, Greek mythology would be my specialist subject.' He raised his glass and downed a generous measure. 'Ah, that's better. Cheers mate. Where's Maggie by the way?'

'She should be here in five or ten minutes,' Jimmy said, at first failing to detect the hint of anxiety in his brother's voice. 'She was just meeting Asvina for a quick coffee. Looks like something's cropped up on the case we're working on. Which is a dead interesting one, by the way. Have you ever met a billionaire Frank?'

'Not as I recall. So who're we talking about?'

'The guy's name is Hugo Morgan. He runs something called an Investment Trust. I don't really understand them to be honest but that's how he made his money. And it turns out he's an ex-army bloke like myself.'

'Never heard of him.'

'Don't you read the papers mate? The divorce of the century they called it. His ex-wife walked away with more than thirty million in cash.'

'What, actual cash?' Frank said, laughing. 'She must have needed a lot of suitcases. But aye, now that you mention it, I do remember. So that was him was it?'

'Yeah, the same guy. Reached his fiftieth and decided he wanted someone younger and sexier.'

'We could all do with some of that mate,' Frank said. But that wasn't quite true. In fact it wasn't true at all. There was only one woman that he wanted and right now he was hoping against hope that her meeting with her friend wouldn't last so long that she would decide to give the pub a miss. He stole an anxious glance towards the door and this time Jimmy did notice.

'Don't worry mate, she'll be here.'

'What're you talking about?' he said, avoiding his brother's gaze.

Jimmy gave a wry smile. 'Don't come it with me bruv, I've seen the way you look at her. What I don't understand is why don't you just get off your fat arse and ask her out?'

'Nah, couldn't do that.' Which was exactly what he intended to do later that same evening. If he could find the courage from somewhere that was.

Jimmy shrugged. 'Well, it's your loss pal. But if you take my advice, you better move fast because she's not going to be on the market for ever.'

'She's not a bloody second-hand car you know.'

'Just a figure of speech,' Jimmy said, his tone apologetic. 'You know what I mean. But talk of the devil, here she is in person.'

He leapt to his feet and waved an arm. 'Over here Maggie', bellowing to make himself heard above the background din. She spun round, giving a smile of recognition then began to squeeze her way through the throng of early-evening drinkers.

'Hi Jimmy, Hi Frank. I see you've already got me a drink, that's brilliant.'

Jimmy laughed. 'Aye, took a risk that you might just want one. Anyway, that call from Asvina. That was all a bit mysterious. What was it all about?'

'Nothing really,' she said, grimacing. 'Nothing other than she's heard on the legal jungle drums that Morgan's ex-wife might be looking to contest her settlement.'

'What, can she do that?' Jimmy asked, surprised. 'I thought these things were full and final.'

'Well, that's where it gets interesting. Because apparently that journalist guy McGinley has been in touch with her and has suggested that Morgan might not have been exactly accurate with his financial disclosures. Anyway, Asvina's looking into it, to see if there's anything she can do to nip it in the bud. Before Morgan gets to hear about it and throws his toys out of the pram.'

Jimmy nodded. 'So do you think maybe the wife's found out about his relationship with the new girlfriend and decided to try and throw a spanner in the works?'

'Yeah, Asvina thinks it's a possibility. It seems that the ex-Mrs Morgan is still off-the-scale bitter about the whole thing.'

Frank gave a look of mock disgust. 'Hey guys, I thought we're meeting up for a wee social drink. If you're going to talk shop all night, at least clue me in, eh?'

Maggie laughed. 'Yes you're right Frank. Sorry. So come on, tell us what you're working on. Although I know everything in your dodgy department is probably top secret.'

'Far from it,' he said. 'This one's a wee bit sad actually, what I'm working on. I was just saying to my brother before you came in. Look at this.'

He passed his phone over to them, pointing to the photograph. 'That's a wee girl called Chardonnay Clarke. Just twenty-three. Swipe left and the other one's Luke Brown.'

'God, they're good-looking, aren't they?' Maggie said, examining the pictures. 'Oh what it is to be young.'

'Hence Aphrodite,' Jimmy said, nodding. 'I get it now.'

'Aye, they're were both very good-looking and now they're both very dead.'

'Murdered?' Maggie said. 'How awful.'

'Aye it is awful,' Frank said. 'Except the inquests said suicide, not murder.'

'Chardonnay looks a little bit like Lotti, don't you think Jimmy?' Maggie said, screwing up her eyes. 'She's pretty enough to be a member of your Aphrodite club, that's for sure.'

'And this Lotti is?' Frank enquired.

Maggie smiled. 'Hugo Morgan's new girlfriend. I should have said, that's what we're doing. Checking her out before he proposes to her.'

Important work. That's what he was about to say, but just in the nick of time he managed to check himself. Mocking the line of work of the woman you were about to ask to dinner, however gently, probably wasn't the smartest move, even he could see that.

'Aye, well marriage is for life isn't it, so it's as well to be sure I suppose.' He said it without thinking then immediately regretted it. Out of the frying pan into the fire. It wasn't meant to be directed at Jimmy of course but that's how it came out. Why couldn't he just keep his big mouth shut? It was something he often asked himself. He looked at his brother, and knew he was thinking about Flora.

'Look I'm sorry mate, I didn't mean anything by it.' He took a crumpled twenty-pound note from his pocket. 'Same again folks?'

Jimmy gave him an encouraging smile. 'I'll go. Still on the Doom Bar?' And then he gave a wink. 'Looks busy up there mate, this might take a while.'

And now Frank knew what he meant. It was now or never. Tomorrow was Friday, the start of the weekend and for many if not most people, the best part of the week. But not for him. For him, the weekend was an interminable desert of loneliness, of cold takeaway curries and warm beer and too many whiskies and boring football on the television. But he had more than enough of that and now, as he approached his forty-third birthday, it was time to finally do something about it. Yes, it was now or never. And here he was with Maggie Bainbridge. Alone with her at last.

Chapter 8

It would have been better if they could have gone into the grounds of the house itself, but with an eight-foot wall surrounding the place, a pair of massive cast-iron gates guarding the entrance to his driveway and that damn dog, that would have to wait for another time. Besides which, the message would be just as clear to Morgan whether it was daubed on the outside wall or on the walls of the house itself. It was three o'clock in the morning, so the chances of them being observed were slight, but just to be sure they checked one more time before removing the aerosols from the back-pack. The wall was clearly illuminated by the bright LED streetlight, making it a straightforward task. A minute later it was done, the message spelt out in foot-high silver-grey letters.

Justice for Greenway

Chapter 9

She had only ever seen Miss Harriet Ibbotson in a work setting, so had no idea what that lady might wear to a first date. Something stunning, no doubt, but classy too, alluring but not too in-your-face. Not an easy look to pull off, especially for a forty-two-year-old who hadn't been on a first date for more than nine years. Maggie remembered the previous occasion as if it was yesterday. Of course she had hardly known her to-be husband at that point, but looking back, she could see his choice of restaurant, a long-since-bust and ferociously over-priced fake bistro, should have been a warning sign. The place had been briefly popular with the gossip-pages set, a place to see and be seen. The fact that it served food was purely incidental. In short, Phillip Brooks' kind of place.

So this evening she had played it safe. A little navy dress, a little shorter than she would have worn to work, but not too short. A glittery throw, but not too glittery, not Xmas-party glittery. And heels, a little higher than everyday, but not such that she would fall over with every step. She wondered what Miss Ibbotson would make of it. She was of course about twenty years younger than Maggie, and in her opinion, rather more attractive, so would probably look sensational no matter what she threw on. But putting comparisons aside, all in all she was quietly pleased with the effect.

The restaurant was exactly as Robert Trelawney had described it, dark and cosy and unprepossessing, decorated in a quaintly old-fashioned style with lit candles on every table in raffia-wrapped Chianti bottles, and crisp white linen tablecloths. There was only around a dozen tables but every place was taken, even at this early hour. He was already there, waiting in the tiny reception area.

'Hi Magdalene, I'm so glad you could make it,' he said, shooting her a smile. 'Sorry if it's a little early, but unless you're in at seven then you won't get a table. But the food is wonderful, I'm sure you'll just love it.'

She looked at him and chuckled to herself, imagining he had faced the same dilemma as her over what to wear. She didn't see him as a jeans-and T-shirt sort of a guy, and this evening he, like her, had evidently decided to play it safe. Dark navy corduroy trousers with a light-grey woollen sports jacket over a light-blue shirt, formally cut but worn without a tie. What her dad might have called smart-casual, but with a touch of class. She liked it very much.

A young waiter led them through to their table which was already provisioned, with breadsticks in paper packets, a tiny bowl of mixed olives and a bottle of sparkling mineral water. He pulled back Maggie's chair and waited deferentially until she was seated before handing each of them a leather-bound menu. This wasn't one of these places with the chalked special boards, where you had to make a special trip half way across the room then try to memorise it all before an impatient waitress came to take your order. All their dishes were on the menu, and from the faded print she guessed it hadn't changed for many years, and was probably all the better for that.

'They've got a very nice wine list here Magdalene,' Robert said, 'but I'd recommend you try the house first, because they pride themselves on always picking excellent ones. Especially the red.'

Magdalene. God, she'd better remember. Remember she wasn't Maggie Bainbridge, hopeless ex-barrister and once the Most Hated Woman in Britain, but Mrs Magdalene Slattery, rich Hampstead widow and embryonic collector of modern art. She'd better remember, because the question was bound to come up on a first date, and she'd need to be ready with the answers. *Tell me all about yourself.* She'd worked up a story, she just hoped it would be convincing.

She giggled. 'I like the sound of *first* Robert. It sounds as if we're in for a good night. Yes, the house will be great, and red's my favourite. Although I like white too. And rosé, if I'm being honest. And champagne.'

The wine arrived, and then there was small-talk whilst they perused the menu and settled on their choices, but it was easy small-talk, light and natural, not at all stilted as it so often can be.

'Are you bothering with a starter?' he asked. 'Perhaps go straight to mains?'

She wasn't really focussed on the food at all and the question took her slightly by surprise.

'What? No.. no, mains are good for me.' Now she had a moment to think about it, she was actually starving and wouldn't have minded starting with one of the delicious-looking cannelloni dishes she had seen served to an adjacent table. Out of the blue, a hint of suspicion crept into her mind. Was he having second thoughts and trying to get this over with as possible? No, surely that wasn't the case, he seemed perfectly relaxed. And then another thought struck her, causing her to give an involuntary giggle. Maybe he was careful with money. The house wine, served informally by the carafe, was nice, she couldn't deny the fact, but it was also less than half the price of the cheapest bottle on the list.

'You know, I felt awful afterwards,' Robert said, shooting her a curious look. 'After I asked you out I mean. It was just so *forward*, and believe me, that's not like me at all. I just don't know what came over me. In fact, I almost got Lotti to call you and cancel it.'

'I'm glad you didn't,' Maggie said, quite truthfully. 'Then I wouldn't have got to sample this lovely house red. I'm not a wine expert, but it does taste deliciously warm and fruity.'

'Yes, with a good nose too and a hint of blackberry, don't you think?' He held his glass up to his nose, swilled it around and sniffed, his face taking on a serious expression for a second or two. And then he laughed. 'Actually, that's all bollocks. I don't know the first thing about wine really. I either like it or I don't, simple as that.'

'Snap,' she said, amused. 'And here was me imagining you would be a real wine buff. It sort of goes with the art dealer image somehow.'

He shrugged. 'Well, yes, and some of us do collect wine that's true. But as I said before, with collectable wine, you can't tell whether you like it or not until you drink it, and then you don't have it any more. No, I'll stick to paintings, thank you very much.'

And then, as the waiter was clearing away the plates and smoothing down the tablecloths in preparation for the arrival of their mains, he asked it. *Tell me all there is to know about Mrs Magdalene Slattery.*

It wasn't difficult to sketch out a childhood story for Magdalene Hardwick. That last bit, the maiden name, she had almost forgotten about but managed somehow to pull it out of thin air. Brought up in Yorkshire of course, because there was no disguising her accent, and then onto the University of Manchester to study -what? It couldn't be law, obviously, because then there would be questions as to why she hadn't become a lawyer. *English*, that would be better. An MA in English, and then a move to London and a succession of dead-end jobs in publishing. She just hoped he didn't ask for details.

'I hadn't really done anything with my life,' she heard herself saying, 'and then I met...' Christ, had she mentioned her fictional husband's name to him before, she couldn't remember. '...*David.*' Now she remembered. It was Lotti that she had talked to about him, not Robert. And at least for this next part it wouldn't be difficult to merge the real and the fictional.

'Looking back, I don't think I ever really loved him. A terrible thing to say I know, but it was just... well, my biological clock was well and truly ticking and I wanted a baby and I thought it would be a nice comfortable life. It was all right at first, but he was much older than me, and he turned out not to be very nice.'

'But he did give you a son,' Robert said in a kindly tone, 'who I know you love very much.'

She could feel herself reddening. 'I do. Very much. Ollie's everything to me.' It was true. He was more than everything, more than could ever be put into words, and somehow she felt she was betraying her love for her son by dragging him into this silly subterfuge, but she had no choice. Magdalene Slattery's son had to be Ollie, he could never be a Jack or a Kieran or any other name.

At least with that out of the way, it would be his turn. Initially, just after he had asked her out, she had entertained a vague suspicion that he might be married. It was just something about the way he looked, she couldn't exactly put a finger on it. But if he was, he wouldn't have brought her here, to this lovely little place where he was obviously a regular. No, Robert Trelawney wasn't married.

'So Robert,' she said, toying with her glass, 'what about you? Any dark secrets to reveal?'

'Afraid not,' he said, grinning. 'Bit of a posh boy upbringing, I must confess. My family's been farming in Cornwall for centuries, own half of Bodmin Moor. But I was the third son. My oldest brother inherited the estate a couple of years ago when father died and is making rather a good fist of running the place I think. In the old days of course I would have been marked out for the church, but we're a bit more enlightened nowadays. They still packed me off to a succession of ghastly boarding schools though. The English upper classes have always liked to subcontract the bringing up of their children.'

Maggie nodded. 'But you seem relatively unscathed by the experience, if I'm any judge.'

'What? Yes, it was all I knew, and I was good at sport you see, so that made a difference with fitting in and all that. Played cricket and rugger. Too much of both probably.'

'Did you go to Uni?'

'Afraid not. Flunked my A levels big time. Father wasn't exactly pleased. He wanted me to be a doctor or a vet or something respectable like that.'

She smiled. 'So what *did* you do then?'

'Bummed around, I guess that's how you would describe it. Took a bit of a gap year that somehow seemed to last until I was about thirty. Australia, Far East, the US. It was fun whilst it lasted, but eventually you have to grow up, don't you?'

With no little envy, she contrasted that with how she had spent her twenties. The training contract at Addisons, and then the move to Drake Chambers where she slogged for years in the hope of making silk. The long hours sweating over tedious low-rent briefs whilst the toxic class snobbery and misogyny of the profession created a glass ceiling that no working class girl could ever hope to break through. That's how she portrayed it, but deep down, she knew that wasn't wholly true. The fact was, she hadn't been much of a barrister, although, briefly she had been the most famous one in the country. But one thing was certain. All work and no play had made Maggie a dull girl, she could see that now.

'So how did you get into the art world then?' she asked. 'It's quite a jump isn't it?'

'Friend of a friend of father's I'm afraid,' he said, the tone apologetic. 'I'd just got back from schlepping around India and was a bit hard up, and he was looking for someone to help him out on the sales front, so with nothing else on the cards, I thought I might as well give it a try. That was ten years ago, and I've been here ever since. Found something tolerably interesting that I also was quite good at. Learned the ropes under his tutelage and then bought the place off him a while back. That's when I renamed it the Polperro.'

So far, so interesting, but he hadn't yet mentioned anything about the subject she was most interested in. Relationships, and in particular was there an ex or even several ex Mrs Robert Trelawneys. Seemingly, he had read her mind, as his face broke into a grin.

'But I guess what you really want to know is how a guy as good-looking as me gets to forty-five years of age unmarried. I sometimes ask myself the same thing.'

She laughed. 'It must be because you're too modest. Seriously, it never entered my mind.' At least that was one advantage of pretending to be someone else. It wasn't really you who was lying.

'I know it sounds like a cliché, but I just haven't met the right woman yet.' He was right, it did sound like a cliché. All it needed was for him to add 'until now' and they would be square bang in Mills & Boon territory. But he didn't, causing her to experience a slight but perceptible *frisson* of disappointment.

'I didn't meet the right man either, but it didn't stop me marrying him. Big mistake.'

'But we mustn't look back, don't you think?' he said. 'Nothing you can do about the past.' Smiling, he raised his glass. 'Here's to bright futures. For both of us.'

'Bright futures.' That was something she never thought she would hear herself say, but somehow, it felt right. For eight years, she had lived a kind of half-life, married to a man she knew she didn't love, but clinging on out of fear. Until a teenage terrorist took the matter out of her hands. *Bright futures*. After all she had been through, it was no less than she deserved, but whether or not it involved Robert Trelawney, she could not say. *Yet*.

But then suddenly she remembered that, technically speaking, this was supposed to be work.

'I was very impressed with Lotti. She's a really lovely girl and she seems very knowledgeable.'

'Yes, she is. I was very lucky to secure her services.' He gave her a conspiratorial look. 'Especially since I don't have to pay her.'

'Excuse me?' She hated that phrase, but like so many other imported from the outposts of the English-speaking world, annoyingly she found herself saying it all the time. And she couldn't hide her surprise. 'You don't pay her?'

'Well no, not exactly.' Was it her imagination, or was he sounding embarrassed? 'She earns commission of course, on any sales. You see, I was looking for an intern.

Someone at the start of their career, looking for a foot in the door.'

Interns. She knew all about them. Nowadays, it was the only way to get a start in a legal career, treated like a slave for twelve hours a day and expected to like it.

'Isn't she a bit old to be an intern?' *Damn*, that was a mistake. How would Magdalene Slattery have any idea how old a woman she had barely met was? 'I mean, she seems so incredibly experienced from the little time that I have spent with her.'

If he noticed the slip, he didn't mention it. 'No you're right. It's her family you see. Been in the trade for generations. A friend of a friend recommended her to me. One of the skiing set. The St Moritz crowd. Her family runs a little gallery out there.'

Yes, she could imagine the type. Back at Drakes Chambers, the partners spoke of little else during the winter, of the upmarket chalet that they took for three weeks each year straddling the February half-term, of the *perfect* powder and the *simply divine* chalet-maid who cooked for them. Each year she had been invited, but the invitation was decidedly half- hearted, and she was glad because she wouldn't have wanted to spend any of her precious holiday allowance with a single one of them. And she couldn't have afforded it anyway, not unless she asked Phillip to pay, which she would never have done. Which got her wondering about Robert.

'Do you ski then?' she asked.

'Did once,' he said, 'but the old dodgy knee put paid to that. Rugger injury of course.' It sounded convincing, but there was just something in the tone that caused her to doubt it. It wouldn't be cheap to be a member of the St Moritz set. But whatever, the state of his finances wasn't really any of her business.

'But coming back to Lotti,' he continued. 'I do feel a bit guilty of course, but she was very keen to work in London to broaden her experience so the arrangement suits as both.'

'She's very beautiful, isn't she?' Maggie said, grinning. 'I guess that must have helped with her application.'

He shrugged. 'She is beautiful, but I agreed to take her on before I had even met her.'

'So you must have been pleased when you did get to meet her in the flesh so to speak.'

'Well of course. In our business although it *is* quite important to know about art of course, it's mainly about relationships, forming a bond with the client.'

And she wouldn't have any problem in that department, would she, thought Maggie. Especially bonding with billionaires with an interest in modern art.

After that, she relaxed into the evening, aided by the wine and the amiable company. It all felt so natural, stirring feelings she hadn't felt for a very long time. They decided against dessert, electing instead to share the cheese platter. And then all too soon for her, the lovely evening wound to a close. Or maybe not.

She watched as he took a credit card from his wallet and signalled the waiter to bring the bill.

'Perhaps skip coffee? We can have it at my place if you like, it's just around the corner.'

'Yes, that would be lovely,' she said, unsure of what she was agreeing to and not caring either. And at least he hadn't suggested they split the tab.

***

Personal protection was more his thing, so this wasn't his normal line of work. Not that he was too bothered about that. If that's what the boss wanted him to do, then that was fine by him, and besides, three hundred and fifty quid cash in hand was not to be sniffed at. Keep your eye on him for a couple of days, see what he's up to, that was the instruction. So that's what he did, hanging around that poxy gallery of his, watching all the comings and goings, then following him round the corner to his fancy flat in Bedford Gardens at the end of the working day. Last night, Trelawney hadn't gone out at all and so he had called it a day around nine. But this evening it was different. Tonight, he'd closed up the gallery at 6pm prompt and then walked home at pace, in fact he'd broke into a jog at one point. Big night in prospect by the look of things. And then half an hour later out he comes, all dressed up with somewhere to go. Round another couple of corners until he arrived at an Italian place. Fazolli's. For a date, with a fit-looking bird he hadn't seen before. Absolute gold-dust.

They didn't have a table for one, so they said, but he was good at persuasion and a few words in the ear of the poncey head waiter soon put that right. A quiet spot tucked up against the wall, barely illuminated. About three of four tables back from theirs, his seat facing the woman. Smart looking, forty-ish but when he got a better look at her, a bit mumsy for his tastes. It wasn't hard to sneak a couple of pictures and then he could relax a bit and enjoy his lasagne. Made sure he was done before them so he could settle down outside and wait for them to leave.

Ten minutes later he sees them leaving, all giggles and kisses. It was pretty obvious that the evening was only going to end one way, and fair play to the boy, he wouldn't have minded himself. But he followed them the couple of blocks back to his place to make sure, then hung about outside for about an hour just for insurance. In case she had second thoughts. But she didn't. Great. Tomorrow morning he'd be back outside at six-thirty prompt and snap her coming out wearing the same clothes she wore last night. As he said, absolute gold-dust. The boss was going to be pleased, no doubt about it.

Chapter 10

Frank had never been to Oxford before, as far as he could recall. He'd seen it on telly plenty of times of course, mainly down to *Morse* and its multiple successors, but never had any reason to visit until now. It made a change from the capital though and he was very much looking forward to it, especially given the news that he'd got from Ronnie French last night.

He was just about to ask Yvonne if she'd ever been to the town when he remembered, causing him to change tack.

'Did you enjoy your time at Oxford then? Quite a place to be a student I imagine, with all that history and the like.'

They were on the M40, the mid-morning traffic light on the northbound carriageway. Across the central reservation the London-bound businessmen and women weren't so lucky, a lorry breakdown in the Stokenchurch cutting causing a tailback that already stretched for six miles.

'Glad we're not going that way,' she said. 'Yeah, I enjoyed my time at uni sir. But actually I was at Cambridge, the other place. The light blues.'

He glanced at her, mystified.

'Sorry, the colour our sports teams wear. As opposed to the dark blue, which is Oxford. Before I went I thought everyone would be terribly posh and everything but they weren't all like that.' Aye, just most of them, he thought.

'So this Sophie woman we're meeting,' Frank said. 'You can just tell what she's going to be like don't you, with a name like that. *She'll* be posh, and tall and skinny too. And good looking, a bit like the Duchess of Cambridge. They always are.'

Yvonne laughed. 'Tut- tut sir, that's awful. Haven't you been on the unconscious bias course?'

'Unconscious bias? Believe me, my bias is never unconscious. But no, I haven't been on the course 'cos I don't need it. I'm never wrong on these things.'

'If you say so sir. But honestly, you should go on it. It's really good. It makes you think.'

'Aye, well we'll see who's right soon enough. Mark my words, I won't be far wrong.'

And he wasn't far wrong, because Sophie Fitzwilliam did turn out to be very much as he expected, tall and slim and very attractive and effortlessly posh. Except, unlike the Duchess, she was distinctly and unarguably black. He saw Yvonne smirk at him as Ms Fitzwilliam came to collect them from the reception area. It had been Pete Burnside's suggestion that the young intern should accompany him on the visit and he was happy enough to acquiesce. In truth, he suspected they were struggling to find anything for her to do and a wee trip up to Oxford would fill one of the days of her four-week assignment. But he was glad of the company, and she was sweet and funny and, he had decided before they had even left London, way too smart to be a copper.

They were led through to a plush meeting room, with a polished solid oak floor, the walls a light violet pastel. Dotted around the room hung a series of framed photographs, posed shots of self-assured looking youngsters that Frank assumed to be some of the agency's past clients, if that's how they should be described.

'Welcome to The Oxbridge Agency Inspector. I do hope we can be of assistance to you.' Her tone was smooth and measured but Frank couldn't help notice the wary look.

'Aye, I hope so too. By the way, this is Yvonne Sharp. She's with us for a few weeks on an internship. Trying to decide whether to be a cop or a robber. I mean lawyer.'

'Well, I know which I would choose Yvonne,' Fitzwilliam said pleasantly. 'But I think I'll let you make up your own mind on that.'

'Aye, that's probably a good idea,' Frank said. 'But anyway, I mentioned on the phone the reason we're here.'

'You did. Very sad and completely devastating for the agency as you can imagine. But I'm not sure I understand why the police have to be involved after all this time.'

After all this time. It had only been a few months since Chardonnay Clark had died. He could just about understand her desire to put it all behind her, but surely that was a bit premature. But soon she would find out that this investigation was not going away any time soon.

'Her parents are really shattered as you can imagine. Nice people. Don't you think you've let them down?'

Her expression hardened. 'I really feel for them of course, but I can assure you we bear no responsibility for what happened to either of these young people. However, be in no doubt that the welfare of our interns is and always had been our greatest concern.' It sounded exactly like the corporate speak it was.

Frank smiled. 'Aye, well that's good to hear. But anyway, let me give you a bit of background. I work for Department 12B, a wee backwater of the Met. They shove us tiddly cases that might turn into bigger cases. You know, where there are suspicions but no real evidence, stuff like that. And you've got to admit when two kids who are working for the same intern agency decide to commit suicide within a few months of one another, some people might see that as suspicious.'

Fitzwilliam shook her head. 'Of course, it was a terrible tragedy and a traumatic period for us, but we looked carefully at all our processes and procedures and it was quite clear that we were not to blame in any way. Care and concern for our people is at the heart of our HR operation, and I can assure you that if we had known that these young people were at risk in any way then naturally we would have stepped in.'

And that of course was the heart of the whole affair, because neither of these youngsters had given the slightest hint that they had been intending to take their own lives. Except for the after-the-fact virtual suicide notes, which in a blinding flash of clarity, Frank recognised for what they were. Almost certainly fake. Must be. Perhaps, or even probably, this agency had nothing to do with any of it, but he needed to know more before he could be sure.

'So maybe you can tell me how the agency works. How you select your interns, that kind of thing. And how you make your money.'

She seemed to relax, happy to be able to leave the uncomfortable subject matter behind.

'Our business thrives because there is great competition for entry-level places with the top-end organisations. I set up the business to service this demand.'

'Aye, and I see you've got some amazing customers. HBB Bank, Superfare Supermarkets, Alexia Life. Big names.'

She smiled. 'Yes, they are indeed big names, amongst the biggest. But you misunderstand our business model Inspector. These organisations are not our customers. They are our suppliers. They supply the intern opportunities that our young people crave. No, our customers are our young graduates, or to be more accurate, their parents.'

Yvonne gave him a knowing look. 'You see sir, it's all about money. All these rich mummies and daddies paying a fortune to buy their precious little darlings onto the first rung of the ladder.'

Frank raised an eyebrow. 'Is Yvonne right Miss Fitzwilliam. Is that how it works?'

She smiled. 'It's *Mrs*. And yes, that's how it works, and why should I deny it, I'm proud of our business. We simply satisfy a demand like any other.'

'And how much are we talking, money-wise?' Frank asked. 'To get on this ladder?'

Yvonne leapt in before she could answer. 'They charge about twenty-five grand sir. Now you can see why I didn't get a place.'

He grimaced. 'Bloody hell, that's steep. And how much do you pay the organisations - sorry, your suppliers - to take one of your interns?'

Fitzwilliam gave him a cold look. 'That's company confidential.'

'But not as much as twenty-five grand I assume.'

'It's a win-win for all parties,' she said smoothly. 'No-one complains about our fees. As I said, we are simply satisfying a demand that exists. If we didn't do it, someone else would.'

Which was no doubt true, he could see that. If you were the sort of parent who had paid a few hundred grand to send your kid to private schools for ten years or more, and then stumped up thousands more to get them through university, another twenty-five grand was probably neither here nor there. And as for The Oxbridge Agency, even if they had to slip their supplier organisations ten grand to take one of their interns, there was still a very tidy profit being made. Nice work if you could get it. But the thing was, the two kids who had died had been in a completely different boat. *Socio-economic class C3.* They didn't have parents who could afford twenty-five thousand quid.

'Aye, I don't doubt there's a big demand,' Frank said, 'but what about the two kids we're interested in? They weren't from well-off backgrounds, were they?'

Fitzwilliam smiled. 'No they weren't, and that's why they came in on our scholarship programme.'

Frank looked puzzled. 'So what's that all about?'

'Look, we recognise the privileged position that most of our interns are in. It's a simple fact of life and we can't change it. But what we can do is give a helping hand to talented young people from less favoured backgrounds. So each year, we fund a small handful of scholarship places, selected solely on merit. Naturally, they don't have to pay the fee and we also provide them with a nominal salary whilst they are on deployment.'

Frank raised an eyebrow. 'So that's a lot different from your normal business model. Must cost you a bit of money.'

Her reply sounded rehearsed. 'We like to give something back. It's a fundamental part of our corporate ethos. Luke Brown was the perfect case in point. A boy from a very deprived background. It was our privilege and pleasure to help him.'

'Tell me about him,' Frank said, smiling. 'And without the corporate bull if you don't mind. No offence.'

She gave him a hard look but made no reference to his barb. 'He was brought up in care from the age of eleven. His father abandoned the family and his mother had a breakdown and drunk herself to death. With nothing but absolute determination to better himself, Luke overcame all obstacles to win a place at Oxford. Of all our scholarship beneficiaries, he is possibly the one I'm proudest of. But then we are proud of everyone who has benefited from the scheme. You can find everything about it on our website, and we also have a glossy brochure I can let you have.'

'Aye that would be great,' he said.

'Actually sir, I've got it here,' Yvonne said, showing him her phone. *'All about the Oxbridge Scholarship.* Is this it Mrs Fitzwilliam?'

'Yes that's it,' she said, her tone betraying suspicion.

Frank took the phone from her. The slick website was stuffed with more corporate speak about levelling playing fields and rewarding exceptional talent and providing opportunities for everyone, regardless of background. All very dull and worthy and no doubt excellent for the agency's image. But that wasn't what caught his eye.

'Pardon me for asking, but is it a model agency you're running here?'

She gave him a sharp look. 'What do you mean?'

'Well it's just all these guys and girls. I'm no expert, but they're all bloody good-looking aren't they? What's that all about?'

She smiled. 'You may not like it Inspector, but it is one of life's truisms that attractive people generally do better in life. We all have to use the talents we are given, and one's looks are no different. And so yes, it is a factor when we decide to whom we award our scholarships. We are looking for young people who will make an immediate impression.' Was he imagining it, or did her look say *and so you'd have no chance of getting one pal?* Probably. And it almost certainly explained why they hadn't taken on Yvonne Sharp. She was a lovely girl, but there was no getting away from the fact that she was of plain appearance. Their loss, the Met's gain as far as he was concerned.

'Aye, but the thing is Miss Fitzwilliam...'

'It's Mrs..'

'Aye, sorry I forgot, but the thing is, the two young people in question, Chardonnay and Luke, they haven't ended up doing better in life, have they? Why do you think that was?'

He could see her expression harden. 'I hope you are not implying it had anything to do with the agency. Because that would be a very serious accusation.'

'I'm not accusing you or the agency of anything. But so far your agency is the only connection we have between them, so it's my job to look into it.' *Whether you like it or not, Mrs. la-di-dah Fitzwilliam.*

Out of the blue Yvonne said, 'Would it be ok if I asked a question sir? Sorry if it's one you were going to ask yourself.'

He nodded. 'No, go ahead.' He noticed Fitzwilliam glancing at her watch. 'And don't worry, we'll not be taking up much more of your time. On you go Yvonne.'

'Thank you sir. My question is, how you decide which intern goes where? So for example, how did Chardonnay end up at HBB Bank and how did Luke go to Alexia Life?'

Fitzwilliam's eyes narrowed. 'That's an interesting question. So we find out the sectors that our young people are interested in and see if we can find a match with our suppliers. I can only assume Chardonnay must have been attracted to HBB because she was interested in a career in banking or finance. Similarly with Luke Brown too. But of course, I personally am not involved in arranging assignments. We have a team who are responsible for that. Our account managers.'

'Aye, that makes sense,' Frank said. 'And once they're assigned, I presume you get some feedback on how they're doing?'

She nodded. 'Yes, of course. Our account managers will speak with the organisations once a month, to find out how they are progressing. And they speak with the interns too of course.'

'And there weren't any concerns raised about any of these two kids?' Frank asked. 'Nothing that might give any hint about what they were planning to do to themselves?'

She spat out the reply. 'No of course not.'

'But Luke Brown was sacked wasn't he? Just two days before supposedly taking his own life. What did you do when you found out about that?'

She hesitated before answering. 'Well the truth is I didn't do anything about it because it was not something that was brought to my personal attention at the time, and there was no reason why it should have been. As I said, the day to day supervision of the intern cohort is in the hands of the account management team.' The tone was confident, but there was just something in her voice that gave it away. Frank knew she was lying.

'But after he died, you would have looked into it then, surely?'

'Yes, I did ask some questions, of course. But there was no big drama as far as I could see. Occasionally these assignments don't work out, and this was just one of these occasions. I think in fact it coincided with some organisational reviews in the business and they did not have an ongoing need for him.' She fidgeted with her necklace, her discomfort plain to see. Frank smiled to himself. So his hunch had been right. There was something going on here. Time to apply the screw. By letting her stew for a week or so.

He glanced at Yvonne and winked. 'Aye well, we'll leave that for now.' Getting to his feet, he continued, 'So you've been very helpful Mrs Fitzwilliam, very helpful. There's quite a bit more we need to go through with you but that will have to wait until the next time. I'll give you a call in advance, just to let you know the stuff we'll want to see. Probably a full list of all your scholarship kids over the last five years, a list of all your supplier organisations with contact details, interview records, stuff like that.'

Fitzwilliam looked as if she was about to protest, but evidently thought better of it. 'Well, if it's really necessary Inspector?'

He smiled back at her. 'Oh aye. It really is necessary Mrs Fitzwilliam. Anyway, we'll give it a good think through and let you know. But thanks for all your help. We'll love you and leave you now.'

Twenty minutes later they were back on the M40 heading south, Yvonne still flushed with excitement after her first face-to-face interview, Frank finally relaxed after battling through the nightmare Oxford traffic.

'So how's the decision going?' Frank asked, grinning. 'Cop or robber?'

'No contest sir. Cop of course. I loved that today.'

'Good stuff. So what did you make of it all?'

'She was lying sir. No doubt about it.'

'Aye, I got that feeling too.'

She gave him a serious look. 'It was more than a feeling for me sir. You see, when I had my interview with them, they made it very plain that you didn't get any choice as to where you were assigned. You had to agree to be totally flexible and go anywhere they told you. That was something they stressed very much.'

'So all that stuff about consulting with the kids...'

'...was a lie sir. Definitely.'

So that was it, no doubts at all. Sophie Fitzwilliam was lying. Which naturally got him wondering why she would do that.

Chapter 11

They'd never really had a cross word in the year or so they had worked together. Until today, the relationship had been easy and relaxed, like a comfortable pair of old slippers. Or like she imagined a good marriage would be, although she had never experienced that herself during her eight miserable years with Phillip. Today however was different. Jimmy Stewart wasn't happy and he wasn't taking any trouble to hide his feelings, pacing around their little Fleet Street office wearing a thunderous expression.

'Absolutely no way Maggie, absolutely no way. That's not what ah signed up for and I'm no' doing it.' She just loved the way his Glasgow accent broadened when he was agitated. It made her laugh, which was probably not the ideal way to handle the somewhat delicate matter.

'I know it's a lot to ask,' she said, trying her best to be serious, 'but I couldn't think of any other way to get you in there. Unless you can come up with a better idea yourself of course.' She knew he wouldn't be able to, but there was no harm in asking.

'Well no, but I don't see why I need to be *in* there at all,' he said, his voice betraying defeat. 'Can't you handle this yourself?'

She shook her head. 'It's hard enough for me to pretend to be interested in modern art. You've no idea how many hours I've had to spend on line trying to get at least a semblance of knowledge. And we did agree that we need to find out how faithful Miss Brückner is or is likely to be, didn't we? As a key part of our investigation.'

'Aye, we did but...'

'Yes, so unless she is gay, which I think is unlikely, I don't think there's much I can do to help in that department. Not that she would be likely to fancy an old woman like me.'

'She fancies an old man like Morgan.'

'Oh yeah, like what first attracted you to the multi-millionaire Hugo Morgan?'

He gave a wry smile. 'Aye, point taken. But what about that guy you're seeing? The gallery owner. If she's so beautiful, it's odds-on he's tried it on with her in the past. Couldn't you just ask him?'

She looked at him, open-mouthed. 'You mean Robert?' She didn't expect it to come out the way it did, a hint of familiarity that suggested Robert Trelawney was already part of her life. Correction, her *fake* life. 'I don't see how I could do that without blowing my cover.'

'Well maybe *I* could. You know, get a bit matey with him, a bit of laddish banter. We could even compare notes about you. Or here's a better one. Maybe I could threaten to beat the crap out of him for making a pass at my girl. Aye, that would be better.' Too late, he realised what he'd done.

She laughed. 'Excellent, excellent, so you *will* come with me to the gallery. Now obviously you can't use your own name. We don't want anybody googling Jimmy Stewart and your bloody Hampstead Hero story popping up all over the place. James we can use, that's fine, but you need to come up with a new surname.'

'McDuff.'

'What?'

'McDuff. It just came to me. He was my old RSM. Ally McDuff. He was from Forres in the Highlands. A great lad.'

'Fine, James McDuff it is. So the back story is you've recently left the army and haven't quite worked out what to do next.'

'So far, so true.'

'We met quite by chance in a bar, resulting in fireworks. Lust at first sight, at least on my part. Now I can't keep my hands off you.'

'And yet you agreed to go out with Mr gallery guy. How's that supposed to fit in?'

'All part of the narrative. The wronged widow going a bit crazy, grabbing everything that's out there, and bugger the consequences.'

He shook his head. 'Bloody hell Maggie, you've got this all worked out haven't you?'

She laughed. 'Not all my own work I'm afraid. I nicked it from the plot of a trashy novel I've been reading. It's every older woman's fantasy, according to these books anyway. The hunky young stud insatiably satisfying her every desire, twenty-four by seven. Sheer animal passion.' To her surprise, his face began to redden. 'But it's not mine, honestly. Not my fantasy, I mean. And anyway, in the book, the heroine chooses love and money over lust, and you - I mean the young hunk -gets dumped. Sorry mate.'

Now he was laughing too. 'Well that's a relief. No, I didn't mean that the way it sounded, honestly, you're looking very lovely at the moment and it would be an honour to play your toy-boy.'

The compliment took her by surprise. 'Harriet Ibbotson, Hugo Morgan's intern. She's the one to thank. And spending eight hundred pounds on an outfit and two hundred pounds on my hair.' She was thrilled that he had noticed. It had been money well spent.

Jimmy smiled. 'Aye, but just remember, you owe me big time. Silent and broody, is that what you want?'

'Silent and shifty actually. I want your eyes all over Lotti when I'm not looking and I want her to notice. Think you can do that?'

'Suppose so,' he said, uncertainly. They decided to take a black cab, on the twin grounds that Morgan was generous with the expenses and more importantly, she didn't want to walk any further than was strictly necessary in these heels. Now she just had to remember her homework. First there was Andre Dehrain, the French painter she found on Google. He had, this apparently a well-known fact amongst art lovers, painted Big Ben and other London riverside scenes, in what she took to be an impressionistic style, although she didn't actually know what that meant. She genuinely loved some of his portrait work too, particularly one he'd done in 1923, *Portrait de*

Madame Francis Carco. An astonishingly attractive young woman, perfectly captured by the artist, her brooding sexuality bursting from the canvas. There was Paul Nash of course, and that picture she had seen in her earlier visit. Then LS Lowry, perhaps the most famous of the British artists. She knew that it was rare for any of his original works to come on the market and when they did, they fetched an eye-watering price, but that didn't matter. Hopefully their little project would be concluded before any money had to change hands. But then again, it would be Hugo Morgan's money she would be spending if it went that far, and since the purchases would be those recommended by his fiancé-to-be, he would hardly be in a position to complain.

Lotti was waiting at the door when they arrived, dressed in similar style as before in grey tailored trousers and a white tee. And, Maggie noted with envy, a pair of glittery ballet flats. Today her hair was tied up and she was wearing more make-up than before, a subtle salmon-pink foundation and heavy mascara ringing her eyes. Still very attractive, but at first glance she looked older. Maggie couldn't help wondering if that was by design. But then she looked closer at her eyes. Revealing, she was convinced, the crystal clarity and sparkle of youth. Just like Chardonnay Clarke and Luke Brown.

If she was surprised to see this woman who'd had dinner with her boss accompanied by a man, she didn't show it. 'It is very lovely to see you again,' she said. 'I am very much looking forward to it. We are able to use Robert's office today, he's at Christies with another client. There's a Matisse as the star lot and it of course has attracted much international interest. Our client hopes he will be successful but it will be very difficult I think.' Through all of this, she hadn't looked at Jimmy once. A good sign perhaps, but suddenly it opened up a possibility that Maggie hadn't previously considered. What if Miss Brückner was not actually attracted to men? It was a possibility, however unlikely, that couldn't be ruled out, and *that* was something Hugo Morgan would definitely want to know about.

She led them upstairs and along a passageway to the back of the building where Robert Trelawney had his office. Like the rest of his gallery, the room was simply but tastefully decorated, one wall lined with limed oak bookshelves holding neatly arranged volumes that Maggie took to be works of reference. There was no desk, but in one corner was a large circular table in matching limed oak, surrounded by half a dozen chairs. On top of the desk lay a number of auction catalogues, page clips inserted to bookmark particular points of interest.

'I've been doing some preparation, just to see what's on the market at the moment that might be of interest. We have two or three works ourselves that might be good for you. Please, take a seat.'

Maggie smiled as she sat down. 'That sounds great Lotti. But can I introduce you to my friend James. He's interested in twentieth century art too. Aren't you darling? So I thought I would bring him along, I hope you don't mind.'

He gave a half-smile and mumbled something inaudible in their direction. Lotti returned a polite smile but nothing more. This was something Maggie hadn't seen before, a woman who seemed totally immune to the charms of Jimmy Stewart. She was either super-professional or maybe she really was besottedly in love with Hugo Morgan to the exclusion of all others. If that truly was the case, this investigation would be over before it had even started.

'We didn't really discuss budget, did we Maggie?' Lotti was saying as she thumbed through one of the catalogues, 'but I've assumed around a hundred and fifty to two hundred thousand would be a reasonable sum to get you started. We can assemble a very nice portfolio for that. And quite by chance there are some exceptional works on the market at the moment.'

'Two hundred sounds great,' Maggie said, smiling. 'What do you think James?'

'Aye, sound,' he said. 'It's your money, although if it was me I'd buy a Ferrari.' She saw him sneak a glance at Lotti and shoot her a crooked smile. And for a split second the young girl held his gaze, a flicker of reaction in her eyes, then with a definite movement, looked away.

'Don't worry darling James,' Maggie said, squeezing his arm and kissing his cheek. 'You shall have your Ferrari.'

'Sound,' he said again.

Lotti wore the faintest smile as she waited patiently for this little love scene to conclude, before continuing. 'So the French were very prominent in the art of the period so I have a number of examples of their work. Also the later Flemish school was very popular.'

Maggie nodded. 'I came across Andre Dehrain in my googling. I like his work very much.'

'I agree, a fine artist, and popular too. Although he was a controversial figure in France. I do not know if that concerns you?'

'What do you mean?'

'You see, he was regarded as a collaborator during the war and afterwards his works were devalued as a result because many collectors shunned his paintings. Although that is not so much of an issue today. But you may also wish to consider Piet Mondrian. He was Dutch, and very much the pioneer of the abstract style in twentieth century art. His works do come on the market occasionally and are very sought after. There is also Carles Casagemas, a Catalan and a great friend of Pablo Picasso. There is a very pretty landscape of his going under the hammer in a few days' time which we may be able to secure for you. To be honest, he was not the greatest of artists but because of his friendship with Picasso and his extraordinary life story, he is prized by many collectors.'

'Extraordinary? How do you mean?'

'He fell crazily in love with a beautiful model, but then suffered terrible depression because he was unable to consummate the relationship. *Impotenz.* The German word, it is almost the same.'

Jimmy chuckled. 'Could'nae get it up eh? That's awful for a chap, so it is.' He gave Lotti a look that so clearly signalled *but that wouldn't be a problem for me.* Maggie chuckled to herself. It was nice to see him embracing the role, even although she doubted his exaggerated Glaswegian would be understood.

Lotti seemed unable to decide if he was trying to be funny or not. 'Yes, I suppose it is. For him, it was obviously important, because he then committed suicide in a crazy fashion.'

'This is fascinating,' Maggie said, truthfully, 'please, tell me more.'

Lotti nodded. 'So he invited the model, who was called Germaine Gargallo, and a few friends to dinner at the Hippodrome Cafe in Paris, where he proposed to her. When she turned him down, he drew a pistol and tried to shoot her but missed. He then turned the gun on himself and put a bullet through his head. As a result, he died of course. He was just twenty-one years of age at the time.'

'Good lord, that's awful,' Maggie said. 'Just twenty-one?'

'Yes,' Lotti said, 'and he was quite remarkably beautiful too. Picasso painted many portraits of him, including one of him lying in his coffin, which is perhaps the most famous of them. Of course, I don't think we could afford *that* work even if it ever came up for sale. Right now it is in the Musée Picasso in Paris and I doubt if they plan to sell it.'

To her surprise, Maggie found herself being absorbed into this world, transported by the infectious enthusiasm of Lotti Brückner. Which made her revise her opinion of the young woman, because although she might look as if she should still be wearing school uniform, she obviously knew what she was talking about.

'What I find interesting Lotti is how you came to learn so much about this subject,' Maggie said. 'Because I guess it's a huge field.' And then it was revealed.

'It's my family business Magdalene. My great-grandfather started a gallery almost one hundred years ago and now it is run by my mum and dad. *Gallerei Brückner*.'

'In Zurich?'

'Yes, we have a small one there, but our main gallery is in St Moritz. The town gets many rich visitors and they are often very interested in art. So it has been a very nice business for us through the years.'

'St Moritz sounds like a place,' Jimmy said. 'So how come you ended up in smelly old London?'

She smiled. 'Perhaps one day I will take over the family business, but I wanted to have more experiences in my life before then. And of course London is a very big market in the art world.' To Maggie, it all sounded so terribly plausible, which made it all the more likely that it was true. So far there was nothing about Lotti Brückner that might cause any concern to Hugo Morgan. Except, curiously, she still hadn't mentioned him at all. A fact that Jimmy had obviously noticed.

'Aye, and you'll probably meet someone, a lovely-looking girl like you. In fact I expect you've already got a boyfriend.' Once more he shot her the crooked smile, and once more, she studiously ignored it.

'Yes, there is someone,' she said, demurely. 'He's very nice. But I'm sure you're not interested in my rather dull private life. Come, let's have a look at some of the paintings I have bookmarked for you.' The message was polite but clear. *Subject closed.* Maggie decided it would be prudent to park that line of enquiry for a while. Instead she said,

'It must be lovely to come from a nice family like yours Lotti. My mum and dad divorced in 1991 and it affected me rather badly. It was a year I'll never forget. I was just twelve years old.'

She seemed uncertain how to react. 'Yes...yes, I am very lucky. I know that.'

Maggie smiled to herself before quickly changed the subject. *So it looked like her assumption might be correct after all.*

'Sorry, sorry, too much information again. Yes, let's look at what you've found for me.'

Then for the next hour she was immersed in the fascinating world of twentieth-century European art, guided by a young woman whose expertise seemed unchallengeable. Lotti had put together a shortlist of around twenty paintings, some rather affordable, some with auction estimates running well into six figures. When all of this was over, Maggie could imagine her real self buying one or two of the more modestly-priced items to decorate the walls of her little Hampstead study. She chuckled inwardly when she thought of what her Ollie's reaction would be to that. *Ugh*, his go-to word of disapproval. To him, just eight years old, the only pictures that should be stuck on a wall were of cars, the faster and more exotic the better.

At the end of the hour, they had narrowed the selection down to five or six items that which they would definitely try to acquire. Her favourite on the list was a work by Casagemas, the subject a Spanish townscape which she thought was painted rather in the style of Lowry. To her surprise, Lotti agreed with her.

'Yes, I think they do have much similarity. Neither was what you would call a great technical artist...'

'You mean they couldn't really draw,' Jimmy said.

'Perhaps you could say that,' Lotti said, smiling, 'but of course Carles Casagemas was very young and was still learning. And they were both very good at capturing the atmosphere of a scene and bringing it to life. That is a very important talent that many more technically gifted artists do not possess.'

She closed her notebook and stood up. 'So, good progress I think Magdalene? And I must ask, have you been to an art auction before?'

'Never.'

'Well I think you will find it very interesting. The little Casagemas is under the hammer at Sotheby's next Tuesday and you really must come along. The guide is only eighteen thousand pounds which I think is an amazing opportunity for you. Especially since you like the painting so much.'

Maggie nodded. 'Yes, I'll look forward to that, it's very exciting. And I must say, you have been *so* helpful, I really do feel I'm in good hands.' And it was true. Lotti Brückner had an authority about her that could not be easily faked. As far as that part of her back-story was concerned, Hugo Morgan had nothing to be worried about.

But there was something he should be *very* worried about. 1991 was a big year, the year of the traumatic fake divorce of the non-existent Magdalene Slattery's non-existent parents. And also, if Lotti Brückner was really thirty years old, the year of her birth. And yet she had said nothing. No reaction. Nil. Suspicious, because in Maggie's experience, whenever your birth year was mentioned in conversation, you just couldn't help yourself. You would smile modestly and say *that was the year I was born*. Everyone did it, as if it was a programmed reaction. Lotti hadn't. So she had *definitely* lied to Morgan about her age.

Then to her surprise, she noticed Jimmy take out a cheap ballpoint from an inner pocket of his jacket and reach across for one of the catalogues. She wasn't wearing her reading glasses, but by squinting hard she could just about make out what he had scribbled in a corner of the cover, before, with a knowing smile, he slid it across the table to Lotti.

James McDuff 07461 095712

Chapter 12

It was an incongruous setting for a meeting with a billionaire, but the fact that she could have given him an update on the Lotti investigation in a five-minute phone call was neither here nor there. He was the customer, and if he wanted a face-to-face meeting in a fast-food restaurant, then so be it. It was early for lunch, just quarter to twelve, and the place was only half-full when she arrived. Hugo Morgan was already there, seated in a quiet corner opposite a young girl in school uniform who could only be his youngest daughter Jasmine. Two tables away, Maggie recognised Vinny the security guy who had been at the Brasenose Trust quarterly update, dressed casually in an ill-fitting track suit and Chelsea FC beanie hat, clearly trying but failing to merge into the background. She shouldn't have been surprised. A rich and prominent financier needed to be very careful when he ventured out in public, especially with the events of the last couple of days. First the graffiti on the wall of his Kensington mansion, then the threatening letters in the post, the crude messages formed from words snipped from newspapers, like something from a nineteen-forties movie. *Actions have Consequences. Justice for Greenway.* As she approached him, she noticed he had one in front of him now, studying it closely as if that would yield a clue to its origin.

'Hello Hugo,' she said, glancing at the sheet as she took the seat opposite him. 'I've heard.'

He smiled. 'Yes, pathetic isn't it? I mean, Justice for Greenway, what a joke. They should have been sending all this stuff to bloody Belinda Milner. It was her that screwed these shareholders, not me.'

Maggie looked at him, momentarily dumbstruck. Bloody Belinda Milner, dismissed so callously by this man, had killed herself leaving a husband and teenage daughter. But the fact didn't seem to concern him in the least.

'Yeah, she was totally useless,' he continued. 'Anyway, this is my youngest daughter Jasmine. We call her Yazz.'

She gave Maggie a shy smile. 'Hi.'

'Hi Yazz, nice to meet you,' Maggie said. 'Gosh, is that a double cheeseburger? I haven't had one of these for ages, but you've helped me make up my mind. That's what I'm going to have too.'

'We don't do this too often,' Morgan said apologetically, 'but we've been at the dentist this morning getting measured up for a brace so we decided a little treat was called for. Although as you can see we've opted for water rather than anything teeth-rotting. And Yazz is as thin as a pencil so it won't do her any harm, will it darling?'

'No dad,' she said through a mouthful of fries.

This was a side of Hugo Morgan Maggie hadn't seen before. He was much more relaxed in the company of his youngest, shorn of the thrusting action-man demeanour that was his normal accompaniment, and the girl was perfectly delightful and clearly adored by her father. But then she remembered the discarded Felicity Morgan, shut out from these precious family moments simply for getting too old. Yes, maybe her initial impression was right after all. It was best not to get taken in by all this happy families stuff. And it was a bit strange that he was here for an update on the Lotti matter in the company of one of his kids. But then she learned Morgan's tame gorilla wasn't just there to protect his boss. He was the baby-sitter too.

'Yazz, go and sit with Vinny, will you darling?'

'Can I get a coke please?'

He smiled. 'Yes, well I'm sure if you ask him nicely he might get you one.' Obediently, she picked up her burger carton and slid off to Vinny's table.

'What a lovely girl' Maggie said. 'You must be very proud of her.'

'I am of course. She's lovely. Both of them are. I'm very lucky. Are you eating by the way? If you are I'll get Vinny to sort it.'

She tapped her phone. 'I've got the app. My son Ollie loves them. I know I shouldn't indulge him, but as you say, an occasional treat doesn't do any harm.' She gave a guilty shrug which he acknowledged with a wry smile.

'Anyway, how have you got on? With Lotti.'

'Yes, well I've made contact. Twice in fact, and undercover of course. I'm now Mrs Magdalene Slattery, a rich Hampstead widow. It's all going pretty well I think.'

He looked at her sharply. 'Especially with Robert Trelawney?'

She blushed. 'How did you know about that?'

'Lotti's told me all about her new client. About you.'

Now she was beginning to realise what she had known from the start, that accepting Robert's invite had been a mistake, adding an unnecessary complication to affairs. But it probably wasn't going to be a smart move to admit that right now.

'I thought it might help me with the investigation, find out what he knows about her. After all, he would have presumably checked her credentials before taking her on.' Said out loud, it sounded perfectly plausible. 'I do feel a little bad about deceiving him, but it's part of the job I'm afraid.'

Her explanation seemed to have convinced him. He shrugged then said, 'Yeah, I guess so. So, what about Lotti?'

Maggie smiled, happy to leave the little awkwardness behind. 'Yes, well, so far, so good I think. She certainly is very knowledgeable about her subject, I've no doubt about that. And so far she has been very discreet about her private life. She has told me she is with someone -that's you of course- but that is all she's revealed. As I say, very discreet and professional.'

She wondered if Lotti had mentioned Jimmy to her fiancé. No particular reason why she should perhaps, but given that she had told Morgan about the Trelawney date, she might be expected to mention that her new client Magdalene Slattery seemed to already have a boyfriend. That would be the type of tittle-tattle that a couple might find amusing. But he didn't bring it up.

'Well that's all very reassuring,' Morgan said. 'So what happens next?'

Maggie had anticipated the question and was able to answer it half-truthfully. 'Well Lotti has arranged for me to go to Sotheby's to look at a Casagemas...'

He gave her an amused look. 'A what...?'

'He's a Catalan artist,' she said, laughing. 'And no, I'd never heard of him either. But maybe you should look him up Hugo, because I think you may end up owning one of his paintings soon. But yes, Lotti and I are going to the auction together and it will give me the chance to get to know her better.'

The other thing that would happen next, and which in actual fact was happening at that very moment, was a deep dive into Lotti Brückner's back-story. The family history, the galleries in Switzerland, that should be relatively easy to verify, as would be her academic record. If she really was a graduate of Germany's prestigious Heidelberg University, then there would be records, and naturally the year of her graduation, if she had earned a degree at the institution, would give a pretty reliable clue to her real age. Neither she nor Jimmy spoke German, but Elsa, the super-smart Czech girl who administered their shared Fleet Street office did, and she would run through a burning ring of fire for her adored Jimmy Stewart. Maggie had left them scouring the internet for contact phone numbers and she wouldn't be the least surprised if they had progress to report when she got back. But she wasn't planning to share any of this with Hugo Morgan right now.

'Yes, so I think a couple of more meetings and I should have all the information I need. But it all looks perfectly ok at the moment.' Except for that thing about her age. They needed to get to the bottom of that and she intended to keep that doubt to herself until she had some evidence that either confirmed or demolished her suspicions.

Morgan nodded. 'Well that's great Maggie, I'm relieved. But actually, that's not the only reason I wanted to meet with you.'

She couldn't hide her surprise. 'Excuse me?'

He slid the cut-and-paste letter across the table. 'These guys. I want you to find out who's doing this. Find out who's behind it all.' Now she understood why he wanted to meet in person. This wasn't something you could do over the phone.

'Hugo, this isn't really our line of work...'

'Why not?' he said. 'You're investigators, aren't you?'

'Yes, but... isn't this a matter for the police?'

'I've tried them and they don't want to know. *No crime has been committed sir. Just some cranks sir, ignore them and they'll go away.* That's all they had to say. Bloody useless. So come on. Will you do it, or do I need to find someone else?'

She was acutely aware of what happened the last time she'd given an impulsive answer to an unexpected question. But this time she had a Plan B. So in for a penny, in for a pound. That was another of her dad's favourites. But she tried her best to sound reluctant.

'Ok Hugo, we'll take a look for you. But please understand, I'm not promising anything, and obviously if anything serious happens, you'll have to get the police involved.' That was the stock answer, but she already knew a policeman who might well be interested in Hugo Morgan and his little Justice for Greenway problem. *Plan B*. What was it he said his department did? *Cases that weren't really cases but might become cases*, something like that. The only problem was, she wasn't sure if Frank was still speaking to her. How could she have known he was going to ask her then, of all times? First he went bright red, then he clammed up, then with barely a word to either of them, he'd made some stupid excuse before rushing out of the bar. What a fool she had been, blurting it out without thinking. *I'm sorry, I've got a date with another guy.* No wonder he'd reacted the way he did, and now God knows when or even if they would get another chance.

Morgan nodded. 'Yeah understood. But I'd like to avoid that if at all possible. It's not great for business. It spooks the investors and we've got a lot of money to spend on that damn mine if we've any hope of turning it around.'

'Well obviously we'll try,' she said. 'But really Hugo, this isn't something we've done before.' That was true, and what was also true was that she didn't have the faintest clue where to start. But she realised she was already intrigued by the case, and she was pretty sure that if she and Jimmy brainstormed it for half an hour or so, some plan of action, however half-baked, would probably emerge. Somewhere to start at least, which was all they needed.

'Expenses are no object of course,' he was saying, 'because I expect you'll have to go up there and dig around a bit. Quite a nice part of the country.'

She smiled. 'Yes, I love the Lakes. We went there a lot when I was a child.'

Yazz and Vinny the security guy had appeared alongside them with her order, which they had collected from the counter. This time it was Yazz who was wearing the Chelsea beanie hat, pulled down so that it almost covered her eyes. 'Double cheeseburger with large fries and a large Diet Coke,' he announced in a comically formal tone. 'And a large regular Coke for the little lady.'

Yazz gave her father a fond smile. 'Is that all right daddy? Vinny said you wouldn't mind, not this once.'

He laughed. 'Sure darling, but you'll have to brush your teeth twice as much tonight before bed. And don't forget to give Vinny his hat back. It's his most treasured possession.'

'He's fond of her, isn't he?' Maggie said after they had gone back to their table.

'Yeah, versatile guy. He'll do anything for us. He's officially my driver, but he can handle himself, so, yeah, he comes in very useful.'

She'd witnessed his usefulness first hand at the Brasenose event when that journalist was intent in causing trouble. Officially, he might be his driver but she had little doubt where his real value to Morgan lay. The menacing hard-man, the skills honed on match days in the quiet streets around Stamford Bridge. After a few pints at the Red Lion, there would be a bit of a rumpus with the away supporters, then onto the match itself, a few more beers at the ground warming them up for the monkey chants and profanities they enjoyed hurling at their opponent's black players. Yes, a handy guy to have around when there was trouble, no doubt.

But then a thought came to her. That journalist from the Chronicle, whatever his name was. If anyone knew who was behind this Justice for Greenway stuff, it would be him. It shouldn't be too hard to track him down and she knew he would definitely agree to speak to them as soon as she mentioned she was working for Hugo Morgan. Brilliant. Now she had a plan and couldn't wait to get started.

'Hugo, if you don't mind, I'm just going to take my lunch with me and head back to the office. You've just doubled our case load so we don't have time to hang about. And Jimmy's been doing some more work on Lotti's background. I'm keen to find out how he's got on.'

He gave a broad smile as he stood up, extending a hand. 'Yeah, by all means Maggie. I'm paying you by the hour so I don't want you swanning around on lunch dates on my tab. So off you go then. Quicker you get started the better, and let me know as soon as you find out anything interesting.'

That wasn't going to take long.

***

She got back to the office to find Jimmy and Elsa half way through their own takeaway meal, his desk littered with half a tree's worth of so-called eco packaging, which caused just as much litter and landfill as the old polystyrene items. She was sitting on the edge of his desk, leaning over, quite deliberately in Maggie's opinion, so that he could get a view of her neat cleavage, on full display in the deep v-neck of her lambswool sweater, and as usual, they were sharing some private joke. *Minx*. That was the word that always came to mind when she thought of Elsa. Pretty and smart, and no more than twenty-five years old, lust for life radiating from every pore. And a lust for Jimmy Stewart too, although as far as she was aware, a lust unconsummated. He didn't speak about his private life much, although she was pretty sure he wasn't seeing anyone at the moment. What she did know was that he had been hit pretty hard when his relationship with that Swedish country singer had fallen apart. From time to time she caught him looking at her Facebook and Instagram posts. Astrid Sorensen, a real princess and bursting with raw sexuality. Nashville's new biggest thing. The woman who had ruined his marriage, leaving him wallowing in regret.

'Hi guys, I see you're having fun,' Maggie said brightly. 'You know, I was just thinking. We've not really looked at Lotti's social media, have we?'

'There isn't any,' Jimmy said. 'Not that we can find.'

Elsa nodded. 'Yes, that was first place we looked. But nothing.'

'Nothing at all?'

'She's on email and WhatsApp but that's all,' Jimmy said. 'We thought maybe it was because of Hugo.'

'We Google search and found she was on Instagram until few months ago,' Elsa said, 'but her account is deleted now so no information. So we think Hugo says no to social media. That can be only explanation.'

Maggie smiled. 'Well we can easily find out if that's true. I'll ask him. But don't worry about that right now. Have you found anything else?'

'Yeah lots,' Jimmy said. 'Elsa's a wee genius, she should have been an actress.'

She already is, thought Maggie, a wry smile crossing her lips.

'*Zu erste*,' he said. 'That means firstly in German. Elsa's been teaching me. Zu erste, we called the gallery in Zurich.'

'Yes, I call gallery and ask for Lotti. The girl says Abwarten bitte...'

'That means please wait in German,' Jimmy said, raising a hand in apology when he saw the sharp look from Maggie.

'A moment later, another voice who is Frau Brückner. Lotti's mother I think. I say I am Elsa Berger and I was at Heidelberg with Lotti. It is my thirtieth birthday and I want her to come to party but I can't find her because she is not on Facebook...'

'Which is true,' Jimmy said, 'although of course you know that.'

'And she says Heidelberg? Of course, very nice, then tells me Lotti is now working in London.'

Maggie gave a deep sigh. 'Well, that's all very...' Disappointing, that was the word she was searching for. But why should it be? They had been engaged to check out the background of Lotti Brückner, and if she turned out to be exactly who and what she said she was, then that had to be considered a success.

'...satisfactory isn't it?'

'And there's more,' Jimmy said. 'I hope you won't be too disappointed.

'What do you mean?'

He gave Elsa a nod, indicating she should continue.

'So I phone registrar office of Heidelberg University and ask for help. I am HR in big company and Miss L Brückner wants job. Can you confirm she holds degree I ask? She says it is online and I must email for one-time user-code and password. I email and user-code and password comes.'

Maggie laughed. 'I like the way you're telling the story Elsa but I'm desperate to know the ending.'

'But for you, it may not be happy ending,' Elsa said. 'Because to cut long story shorter, we found out that Fraulein L Brückner is graduate of Heidelberg University, with first class honours in Fine Arts with English Language.'

Jimmy gave Maggie a look of disappointment. 'In twenty-eleven. Making her by my calculation, thirty or thirty-one years of age.'

So that was it then. It seemed that in all regards Lotti Brückner was who she said she was. A quick update for the benefit of Hugo Morgan and that investigation could be closed down. At least she would now be able to enjoy the auction, and when she was there she would be sure to ask Lotti the secret of her youthful looks. Then that could be Mrs Magdalene Slattery's final appearance before she mysteriously vanished off the face of the earth. But would she disappear, that was the dilemma? Because after the success of their first date, the lovely dinner which led to coffee at his sleek townhouse and much more besides, Robert Trelawney had asked to see her again.

And she had said yes.

***

They knew of course where he parked the Bentley, in a so-called secure underground garage just off Strafford Street, no more than five minutes walk from his office. So-called secure, because it had only cost fifty quid to persuade the fat Greek guy they'd laughably put in charge of security to look away for as long as they needed. Morgan's Continental GT W12, to give it its full name, had been ordered with all the extras, the 21-inch diamond-cut alloys alone adding three grand to the price, the in-your-face St James Red paint-job another four. Nearly a quarter a million just for a motor-car. It was obscene, especially considering what he'd had done to all these poor bastards up in Cumbria. Now they were looking forward to see his face after what they had planned for his precious wheels. And they would get to see it too, because that was part of the deal with the fat Greek. Make sure you point a CCTV camera in that direction and don't bloody miss it when he turns up.

Naturally it needed to be done with care, because concentred sulphuric acid was nasty stuff. Firstly they donned gloves, eye-protectors and masks, checking each other to make sure they were properly protected and no flesh was exposed. Then moving slowly and deliberately, they removed the heavy one litre glass bottle from the back-pack and carefully unscrewed the top, making sure to hold it at arm's length. It was only half-full because they didn't want any spills, but that was plenty enough for what they had planned. Starting with the bonnet, they poured a generous measure onto the surface just below the windscreen, allowing gravity to spread the pool of caustic liquid forward and sideways across the gleaming paintwork. Not that it would be gleaming for very long, not once the acid got to work. Already black patches were beginning to appear, the atmosphere turning toxic as fumes rose from the blistering layer of acetate lacquer. Then on the roof, the spread made easy by the sleek fastback styling. That was twenty grand's worth of damage already, not that the money side of it would worry Hugo Morgan. That wasn't the point. It was all about the message. Actions had consequences. If he didn't know that before, he would now. And just in case there was any doubt who was responsible, they had come prepared with a neatly-printed calling card, which they slipped under a windscreen wiper.

Justice for Greenway

It was a nice touch to add the pictures of the two daughters to the card. Then he would know that this was just a little aperitif before the serious action started. When people started to die.

Chapter 13

It had been a while since Frank had been to a snooker hall, at least fifteen years by a quick calculation. That was back in Glasgow, a seedy little dump just off Ballater Street, which formed the northern boundary of the original Gorbals before the whole area was raised to the ground in the sixties. To be replaced by the disturbing fantasies of the celebrated French Modernist Le Corbusier, a nutter if ever there was one. Naturally no-one mourned the passing of the old tenement slums, but it had taken over a hundred years for the area to become an uninhabitable dump, a feat the French architect had achieved in less than twenty. At the time Frank was just beginning his career, posted to Cumberland Street nick. There, Thursday night snooker was a ritual, attended by anyone whose shift allowed it, and plenty more who turned up for a game and a couple of pints when they should have been pounding the beat. He'd been back to the area a couple of times since, and now the Corbusier experiment had been swept away, to be replaced by something more in keeping with the present aspirations of his home city. Neat low-rise social and private housing, unobtrusive commercial development interspersed with dots of green space. It looked so much better, but it was still the same low-lifes who lived there, which is why his old cop shop had been treated to a multi-million pound upgrade, the new building looking more like a mid-market hotel in its subtle pastel blue and grey paint job, with CCTV everywhere and equipped with three times the holding cell capacity of its predecessor. On the corner where Cumberland Street met Jane Place, a statue of a figure stood mounted on a four-metre high stone column, one of a handful that had been erected around the area in the forlorn hope that easy access to *object d'art* would encourage the locals to take a pride in their neighbourhood. This one, for no obvious reason, depicted and was titled *Girl with a Rucksack*. Wags speculated she was there in homage to the area's thriving drugs trade, and that the rucksack must be full of speed, the drug of choice amongst the locals.

The old snooker hall had been swept away too, but the leisure needs of the community were now met by the bingo emporium that had replaced it, the dole money disappearing into the gaudy slot machines, recently equipped with contactless technology to make it easier to take money from people who didn't have it in the first place. So much for progress.

The Romford Snooker Centre was also quite a new development, a faceless tin shed erected on a retail park on the outskirts of the Essex town. Nondescript on the outside, it was perfectly presentable if somewhat bland on the inside. There was a bar with a choice of just two beers, a fizzy bitter and a fizzy lager, and a tiny cafe that served an unappetizing range of over-priced microwaved fast food. But the snooker facilities themselves were top-notch, sixteen tables equipped with ironed-smooth baize and laid out to allow plenty of elbow room for the players.

Back in the day, Frank had been quite good at the game, and he was pleased to discover that he still had it. Ronnie French on the other hand didn't have it, and self-evidently never had, despite his protestations. Unless of course he was setting up Frank for a sting, which he doubted. Frenchie wasn't bright enough to pull a stunt like that.

'Bit rusty Frank my old son,' he was saying as Frank prepared to pot an easy black to win the match. 'Don't get the chance to play much nowadays, what with work and all that.'

Frank shot him a wry smile as he bulleted the ball into the pocket with a confident stroke. 'I'm your guv'nor Frenchie, remember? But I'll try and remember not to overwork you in future. Come on, let me buy you a pint to cheer you up.'

They wandered over to the bar and grabbed a vacant table.

'When's Terry Clarke coming?' Frank asked. 'Shall I get one in for him?'

'Should be here in a few minutes guv. He's a lager man, so yeah, get one in for him.'

That first meeting with the victim's family. You never got used to it, no matter how long you were in the job, and if you did, then you were probably in the wrong line of work. He'd done a few suicides too, and if anything they were worse. With a murder, at least there was someone to blame, somewhere to direct the bitterness and anger. With a suicide, there was the same crushing loss but the only person to blame was yourself. Surely you could have done more to prevent it happening? How could you not have known their state of mind? So in a funny way, maybe the fact that Chardonnay Clarke's death was looking less and less like a suicide might bring some comfort to the family. He hoped so at least.

Clarke appeared just as Frank was swiping his card across the contactless terminal proffered by the teenage barman. Expertly, he picked up the three pints and shuffled back to the table, setting them down without spilling a drop.

'This is Terry guv,' French said, needlessly. 'Terry Clarke. Chardonnay's dad.'

'Pleased to meet you Terry,' Frank said, extending a hand, 'and I'm really sorry for your loss. It must have been awful for you and your family. I'm Frank Stewart. I'm a DI with the Met. Same crew as your mate Frenchie here. Department 12B.'

'You're a Jock, ain't you?' Clarke said. 'We had one of them back in the old Upton Park days. Frankie McAvennie, remember him? Scored a shed load of goals. He was a bit of a lad mind you.'

Frank nodded. 'Aye, I remember him. Blonde streaks. Went to the Celtic for a spell, didn't he? On the front pages nearly as often as he was on the back.'

Clarke gave a half-smile. 'Yeah, you're right there. But a great player, and a Hammer through and through. Still comes to watch us at the new place from time to time. Gets a big welcome.'

But they both knew they weren't there to talk about the football. His voice barely audible, Clarke said,

'So is it a murder enquiry now Frank? 'Cos I know my Chardonnay would never have killed herself. Never in a thousand years.' His eyes, dull and bloodshot after weeks of grief, began to fill up.

'Look Terry, I'm sure Ronnie's told you what we do in our department. We just dig around in things where there's grounds for suspicion. And when I heard the circumstances surrounding your daughter's death, well of course we had to investigate. The way it works is if we dig up enough stuff, you know, solid evidence, then it gets handed over to the murder squad. But no, we're not there yet.' He could see Terry Clarke's shoulders droop with disappointment, but there was no point in raising false hopes.

'But he's the best Terry,' French chipped in, unexpectedly. 'Once the guv'nor gets his teeth into something, he never lets go.'

Frank gave him a surprised look. 'Well cheers for that mate, I didn't know you cared. Look Terry, we think we might have something here and I'll get to the bottom of it if I can. But I need your help, and most of all, I need you to be really honest with me about your daughter. Is that ok?'

'Sure Frank, sure.' That's what he said, but Frank wasn't convinced he meant it.

'She was a special girl, your Chardonnay, wasn't she?' Frank said. 'Brains, beauty, brilliant qualifications. You and your wife must have been... must be very proud of her.'

Clarke smiled weakly. 'Yeah, we was. She got her looks from my Sharon. She was a beauty too. Still is, though this thing has broken her. Totally broken her. Chardonnay was our only child, see?'

That was what made these encounters so impossibly difficult, because there was just nothing you could say that provided any relief for their suffering. All you had was the old platitudes, but you were expected to trot them out nonetheless. So he did.

'I know Terry, I really feel for you and Sharon.' That much at least was true. 'So, can you tell me something about this job she had at the bank?'

'HBB.'

'Aye, that's it.'

'Yeah, she was really loving it. She was always great with numbers my girl was, and they had her in the corporate finance area. Took to it like a duck to water. And she was making a packet too. Way more than I do on the tools and that's a fact.'

Frank gave him a puzzled look. 'Hang on Terry, what do you mean she was making a packet? She was just an intern, wasn't she? They don't get paid, at least not so far as I'm aware.'

'Well, I don't know all about that,' Clarke said stiffly, 'but I know what she told me. Seventy-five grand she was pulling down, without a word of a lie.'

'Are you really sure about that?' Frank said, unable to hide his surprise. 'She wouldn't be exaggerating or making it up?'

'My girl wasn't a liar,' Clarke said, the tone now combative.

'But didn't you think that was a lot of money for a young person with no experience?'

'She was special, my girl,' he replied sharply. 'They must have thought she was worth it. Look, I don't like where you're going with this.'

That was always the danger when dealing with the families. Lose their trust or piss them off and they just clammed up. Frank sensed that Terry Clarke would have to be handled with kid gloves if he was going to keep him onside. He gave an apologetic smile.

'No, sorry Terry, it's just my normal clumsy way with words. It's the Glasgow upbringing. You can take the boy out of Glasgow but you can't take... well, you know the saying I expect. Come on, let's have another beer. Frenchie, your shout I think.'

They filled the few minutes it took French to sort the drinks with more football talk. The subject was some guy called Christian Dailly, another West Ham Scot who Frank didn't remember but pretended he did.

'Class he was,' Terry was saying, 'always had time on the ball. But a bit of a nancy. Didn't like the rough and tumble.'

'Aye, that's right,' Frank said, not sure what he was agreeing with. 'Look, to get back to Chardonnay. I think Ronnie told me that she was socialising quite a lot with some folks from HBB. A fast set, that's how you described it. What can you tell me about that?'

'They was always out on the town. Bars, nightclubs, fancy restaurants and all. And I'm sure they was doing drugs too. Though she says she wasn't.' To Frank, it sounded like the bog-standard lifestyle of any reasonably well-off twenty-something, and while he wasn't going to share this observation with her father, recreational drug use had long been a fact of life amongst that age group. But as he'd often remarked, the parents were usually the last to know.

'And did you meet any of these pals Terry? What were they like?'

'She was seeing a guy. From the office.' It was dropped into the conversation as if it was the most natural thing in the world. And it was something that Ronnie French had omitted from his case briefing, probably because he didn't know.

'Posh guy, Jeremy something or other,' Terry continued. 'Me and Sharon met him the once. He was a lot older than her, but he wasn't married or nothing. It was all straight up, regular like.'

'And he was one of this fast set?'

'Yeah, there was eight or ten of them. All loaded, swanky types the lot of them. But that Jeremy was all right. Sharon liked him the one time they met.'

Frank nodded. 'And was it serious, would you say? The relationship I mean.'

Terry forced a smile. 'I don't know, you'd need to ask my Sharon about that.' He raised a hand, the index and middle fingers intertwined. 'They were like that, Chardonnay and her mum. Shared everything they did. Two peas in a pod.'

'She sounds nice, your Sharon,' Frank said truthfully. He wondered if the relationship would survive the terrible blow it had suffered, having seen plenty that had crumbled in similar circumstances. Terry Clarke was a decent guy, he'd already made up his mind about that, and now his solid marriage was all he had to cling on to.

'Yeah, she was really supporting Chardonnay when she was having her problems.'

Frank gave a double-take, not sure that he had heard him properly.

'What was that Terry? What problems?'

'We don't know what it was, honest we don't. But she was in a right state them last two or three weeks before she died. Totally depressed she was. Although she never would have done herself in, not my Chardonnay. I know she wouldn't.'

And to Frank it sounded exactly what it was. Hope, not belief.

***

Of course, this had all been so totally typical Ronnie French, the very definition of the lazy half-arsed corner-cutter, Frank could see that now. Frenchie didn't have a clue about the fancy boyfriend and he wouldn't have even bothered to ask Terry Clarke what state of mind his daughter had been in the days before her death. A mate says *my girl wouldn't have killed herself* and that was good enough for him. Tomorrow when they were back in the office, he was going to wring his bloody neck.

But maybe something could be salvaged from the mess. He would go and talk to the boyfriend anyway, and it was definitely worth paying Mrs Sophie Fitzwilliam another visit. On second thoughts, that would be a nice wee job for that fat lazy so-and-so French. Get him off his backside and send him up the M40 to see what he could make of it. Find out if someone really had been paying Chardonnay Clarke seventy-five grand per annum. And if so, why? That was a question that wanted answering and Ronnie French was just the man to ask it. As long as he hadn't forgotten by the time he got there.

Chapter 14

As Maggie had predicted, it hadn't been too difficult to arrange an audience with Gary McGinley of the *Chronicle*. Jimmy had found his email, not exactly a challenge since it was printed under his by-line at the top of his weekly column, and shot off a quick two-liner that explained they were lawyers working for Hugo Morgan and wanted to talk about the Greenway Mining affair. No more than a minute after it hit his inbox, McGinley was on the phone, ranting and raving about powerful individuals interfering with the freedom of the press, and if they thought they could now buy his silence, then they had another thing coming.

'Wait a minute,' she heard Jimmy saying, trying to stem the torrent of invective, 'we don't know anything about any injunction. That's got nothing to do with us, I can assure you. Really.'

So, a bloody press injunction. Something that Morgan had conveniently omitted to mention to them. She guessed it was something to do with the Greenway Mining report, whatever that was, and also that he hadn't used Addison Redburn, Asvina's firm to get it, otherwise she would have told them about it.

Eventually Jimmy managed to calm him down, and just two hours later they were meeting with him in their favourite Starbucks on Fleet Street, somewhat apt Maggie thought, although the national papers hadn't carried that famous address for more than twenty years now.

'We witnessed that little scene at the Park Lane Hilton,' Maggie said, as they queued to order their drinks, 'and I was looking forward to reading what it was all about. But now I'm beginning to understand why I haven't seen anything.'

He nodded. 'Yeah, money and power. Once they have it, it's so easily abused.'

'So what's this all about?' Jimmy said. 'This injunction thing.'

'Same old story,' McGinley said. 'Trying to shut up the press.'

Maggie smiled to herself. They liked to have it both ways, these journalists. All high and mighty when they printed the latest dubiously-obtained gossip about celebrities and royalty, banging on about the public having the right to know, but they weren't so happy when the establishment fought back.

They found a table in the corner where they could just about make themselves heard above the babble of the lunchtime customers.

'So what is that they - and I guess you mean Hugo Morgan - are trying to shut up?' Maggie asked.

'Dirty tricks,' McGinley replied, taking a sip from his latte. 'We were all ready to expose how Morgan goes about his work when we had this slapped on us. But our legal guys are fighting it, and it's all going to come out sooner or later, mark my words.'

Maggie smiled inwardly. The only people to benefit from these kind of cases were the lawyers, scampering back and forth to the court at seven hundred pounds an hour plus expenses. She almost wished that she hadn't given up the profession. Not that she had had any choice. After the Alzahrani case, it had given up on her.

'So can you tell us? How does he go about his work?'

McGinley gave her a dismissive look. 'What, so you can go scuttling back to him with all my secrets? You must think I was born yesterday.'

'But he must already know what you were going to print,' Jimmy said, smiling, 'otherwise he wouldn't have been able to get this injunction thing, would he? So they can hardly be secrets.'

'That's where you're wrong mate,' McGinley said. 'He thinks he knows, but he doesn't.'

Maggie was already beginning to tire of this guy's air of smug superiority.

'Well, actually Gary, you must think I was born yesterday too, because I'm a lawyer, and there's no way a judge will grant an injunction without good reason.'

McGinley leaned back in his chair, the smugness outwardly undiminished. But Maggie caught Jimmy's eye and saw that he was thinking the same thing as her. If he's so sure of himself, what's he doing here? He must want something.

'Anyway, I assume you two are here to offer some sort of a deal. Come on, let's hear it. I'm a busy man.'

Maggie gave an inward grimace. So this was why he had turned up. Maybe this was going to prove more difficult than she expected.

'Believe me Gary, what we wanted to talk to you about has got nothing to do with this injunction. I told you, we didn't know anything about it until you called us back.'

'So what do you want then?' he said, drumming his fingers impatiently on the table.

'Have you heard of Justice for Greenway?' Maggie said.

'No, what's that?' The surly expression melted, to be replaced by a mixture of surprise and interest.

'We don't really know,' Maggie said, 'but Morgan's been the target of some fairly serious vandalism and harassment carried out in their name. First someone sprayed graffiti all over the wall of his house and then they trashed his Bentley the other day. Oh, and there's these.'

She took a couple of the poison pen letters from her handbag and placed them on the table side by side.

'As you can see, these are some pretty nasty threats. That's why he's asked us to find out who's behind it. We wondered if you might have any ideas?'

He gave her a sarcastic look. 'Are you joking? He screwed nearly two thousand people when he pulled that Phoenix from the ashes stunt up in Cumbria. And then there's Belinda Milner's family. So, yeah, I've got plenty of ideas.'

'What do you mean, Belinda Milner's family?' Jimmy said.

'I thought you were supposed to be investigators. Milner, the boss lady. You know she drowned herself in the lake, just fifty yards from her back door. But what you might not know is that just before then, Morgan had sacked her and screwed her out of her three million bonus.'

'So you think her husband or someone might be involved in this?' Jimmy said. 'That's what we really could do with knowing. Or is there someone else?'

'You really don't get the newspaper business, do you mate?' McGinley said. 'This looks like a story. So if I did have any ideas, why would I tell you?'

Maggie could feel her hackles rising.

'Well I assume *you* do get the newspaper business, Gary, because you've been in it long enough. So you'll get it that if Hugo takes this Justice for Greenway thing to the Telegraph or another paper, then your little story's going to be just white noise in the background. After your publisher's spent all that money on these fancy lawyers. And they don't come cheap, you know that. I wonder what they would think about that. I don't think they would be too happy.'

That idea had just come to her out of the blue, but now that she thought about it, she rather liked it. So too, it seemed, did Jimmy.

'Aye, the Times, they'd love this too. That's a brilliant idea. In fact, I don't know why we're wasting our time with this guy. Come on Maggie, we can get a coffee back at the office.' He stood up as if to leave. 'It was nice to meet you Gary.'

McGinley's face melted into a grim expression. Maggie guessed his mind was racing through the implications of his rival getting their hands on this juicy story, and not liking the outcome one little bit.

'Well, look... maybe we can work something out here.'

Maggie smiled sweetly. 'I'm sure we can Gary.'

'Aye, no bother,' Jimmy said, 'and maybe you can start with the whole Greenway thing. What did you mean when you said it was a Phoenix from the ashes stunt?'

McGinley was silent for a moment, evidently weighing up whether he should reveal what he knew. Then finally he said,

'Morgan knew only too well that if the problems with the mine went public, the company was as good as bust and he could then pick it up for a song. The company knew that too, which is why only three insiders got to know the shit they were in.'

Maggie gave him a puzzled look. 'What shit was this?'

'You mean you don't know? That they'd spent five years and four hundred million quid digging this bloody great hole on the edge of the Lake District and then, two years behind schedule, when they finally start bringing the ore to the surface, they find that instead of naught point five percent cobalt, it's just a tenth of that?'

'Whoa, now that is *serious* shit,' Jimmy said.

'Exactly,' McGinley replied. 'That's why they tried so badly to hush it up. Piet Stellenburg's the Chief Geological Officer and it was him that did the original surveys. So at first, he's the only guy that knows naught point *naught* five is a disaster.'

'So he's in deep trouble then,' Maggie said, 'not to put too fine a point on it.'

'Yeah, too right,' McGinley said. 'So for a week or so he decides to sit on it. Tells nobody. Meanwhile Belinda Milner is all over the business media telling anyone who'll listen what a fabulous success the project has become. She was a good-looking woman, and everywhere you looked there's a picture of her with the hard hat and the hi-viz jacket holding a great lump of rock over her head. She used to run a bloody high street retail chain before she got the Greenway gig so of course she's no idea what she's got in her hand. But the City buys into the hype, the shares shoot up eighty percent, and now the local paper is running stories of ordinary miners who're now sitting on a hundred grand's worth of the B shares.'

'B shares? What are they?' Maggie said.

McGinley smiled. 'I'll come back to them later if you don't mind. Anyway, Stellenburg's getting more and more spooked and eventually decides to come clean. So he tells Belinda.'

'Who decides to continue the cover up?' Jimmy asked.

'Exactly. Slightly influenced by the mega-bonus she's looking at based on the rise of the share price. A three million quid bonanza is in touching distance, and she only has to get through a few months to the end of their financial year for it to pay out.'

'But didn't you say three people knew?' Maggie said. 'Who was the other one?'

'A guy called Mark De Bruin. Another South African. He was in charge of operations. A very experienced mining guy. Somehow Milner and Stellenburg managed to keep it to themselves for a month or so more, but eventually he smelt a rat and took a look at the lab results himself.'

'And he said nothing after he found out?' Maggie said.

'Nope. He was on a big bonus too you see.'

She shook her head. 'And nobody else knew? I mean that's impossible surely?'

McGinley shrugged. 'Well I think a few people on the ground might have sussed out that the cobalt yield was lower than expected, but nobody really grasped the significance. I talked to one of the lab technicians for example, and he said anybody who raised concerns was just told by De Bruin or Stellenburg that it was early days and they'd be ramping up the yield soon enough.'

'But then somehow Hugo Morgan found out the truth,' Jimmy said, 'and that's when it all went pear-shaped.'

Maggie gave McGinley a knowing look. 'And you think you knew who told him. Your big story. Until Morgan's lawyers shut you down.'

He shrugged. 'Yeah, for now. But we'll soon get that overturned.'

'Well in that case, you might as well tell us,' Maggie said, smiling. 'If Hugo Morgan already knows, and it's all going to come out anyway.'

But it seemed McGinley wasn't quite ready to play ball. 'You're supposed to be investigators. Figure it out for yourself. A quiz question with just three possible answers so it shouldn't be that hard.'

Maggie saw Jimmy's expression harden. Sometimes that didn't end well, but when he spoke, his voice was calm although the tone was menacing.

'Listen pal, we don't really have time to play your stupid wee games. Either tell us or just bugger off.'

McGinley held up his hands and gave a condescending smile. 'Yeah yeah, it's just us scribblers. The desire to hang on to our secrets. It's engrained in us. So let me just say you need to think about winners and losers.'

'What do you mean by that?' Maggie said, annoyed.

He shrugged. 'Three people knew. Two lost out big-time, leaving just one winner. Figure that out and maybe you'll have your answer.' Draining his cup, he got up to leave, the arrogance reinstated.

'Well, it was nice to meet you both and thanks for the tip-off on the Justice for Greenway story. That'll make a nice sidebar to my Morgan feature. But look, I feel bad about this. So here's a little tip for you. The other suicide, the guy who lost a hundred and fifty grand overnight. Maybe his family's not feeling too happy about things either. So why don't you give a girl called Liz Donahue a call. She's a reporter on some crap little paper up there and she'll know who he is no doubt. *Au Revoir.*'

***

Back in the office, Maggie was able to agree with Jimmy that all things considered, the meeting had been a success. True, Gary McGinley was an arse, but that was probably to be expected given his profession, and he was no worse than a lot of lawyers she knew. The fact was, they'd come away with some solid leads in their quest to find out who was behind Justice for Greenway and that represented progress. Winners and losers, that's what McGinley had said. Belinda Milner, the CEO-for-hire who'd lost her job, her reputation and her three-million-pound bonus. And then had taken her own life. Then there was Stellenburg, the geologist guy who had cocked up the original surveys and had slinked off back to South Africa, his reputation in tatters. As far as losers were concerned, there were none bigger than that pair,

The winner? That had to be operations boss Mark De Bruin, who, it turned out, had now been hired by Morgan to run the reborn company, on a lucrative earnings package that the Financial Times in a highly-critical article described as 'insensitive, given the losses sustained by the original shareholders.' Was he Morgan's mole, spilling the secret that let the financier make his move? It seemed possible, and they'd know soon enough, once McGinley's paper got the injunction overturned. Assuming he was right of course.

But then what of the one hundred and fifty grand guy, who had bet his family's future on the success of the mine only to lose everything as a result of Morgan's financial re-engineering, 'B' shareholders getting nothing once the banks and the revenue had grabbed their share? Miss Liz Donahue of the Westmoreland Gazette would help them with that line of enquiry.

So that was it. Progress, and lots of it, perfectly timed for when she had to report back to their client tomorrow. A couple of leads identified in the *Justice* matter, and excellent news on the Lotti front. He would surely be very satisfied with all of that, and she very much liked satisfied clients.

With that sorted, she could turn her thoughts to the other matter which had been causing her concern. What to wear for her date tonight with Robert Trelawney.

Chapter 15

It was Jimmy who had been given the job of speaking to Liz Donahue of the Westmoreland Gazette. They could have simply given her a call, but after a brief discussion of the pros and cons, they had decided instead on a face to face meeting. Actually, there wasn't too many cons. The journey from Euston up to Oxenholme took less than three hours, and the three hundred quid that would allow them to travel first-class wouldn't make much of a dent in the generous budget Hugo Morgan had agreed for the investigation. All in all, it would be quite a nice day out.

More contentious however was the debate around which of them should go. He hadn't really reflected before on the fact that whenever there was some sweet-talking of a woman to be done, Maggie automatically assumed that he would achieve a superior result to her. But the more he thought about it, the more uncomfortable it made him feel. Fair enough, he could see it made sense in the Lotti Brückner investigation, where there was an obvious need to test her faithfulness, but here, he was just talking to a bloody local newspaper reporter. It wouldn't matter what he looked like, he could even be an overweight grey-haired forty-something like his brother Frank. That made him chuckle to himself. This time, after some half-hearted resistance he had given in, but next time... the next time his bloody boss wanted him for a spot of honey-trapping, he was going to say something. Well, maybe.

The Westmoreland Times operated behind a dingy shop-front tucked away down a back street in the pretty market town of Kendal. The windows looked as if they hadn't been cleaned in decades, making it hard to tell if the photographs of Old Kendal in the window were genuine sepia or just looked that way through the layers of grime.

Pushing open the door caused a bell to sound a discreet heralding of his presence. In the tiny office, a woman sat behind an ancient desk hammering away on her computer keyboard.

'Just a mo,' she said without looking up, 'don't want to lose my train of thought. I've been buggering about with this piece all morning. It's an absolute bitch.'

A few moments later, she gave an audible sigh of relief. 'Thank God that's done.' She peered at him good-naturedly over rimless spectacles. 'You're Jimmy Stewart I'm guessing?'

She looked about forty, short and slightly rotund but pretty, with bright intelligent eyes and a pleasant ruddy complexion. Her hair, dyed a vibrant purple, was cropped short and she wore a shapeless cable-knit cardigan over a pair of denim dungarees. And a pair of men's brogues. It was important not to judge by appearances, he knew that, but there was every indication that Maggie Bainbridge's little scheme had already gone rather pear-shaped. That was all to the good as far as he was concerned.

He shot her a smile. 'Hello, that's right and you must be Liz. As I explained on the phone, we got your name from Gary McGinley of the Chronicle. I was hoping you might be able to answer some questions about Greenway Mining and a few related things.'

'And you're definitely not with the Chronicle?' Right away, he detected the suspicion in her voice. 'Because if you are, you can sod off back to London on the next train. Particularly if you're a friend of that arse McGinley.'

Jimmy laughed. 'So you think that too? Aye, I've only met him once but he's an arse right enough. So what did he do to upset you?'

'I sent him a lead for a story. A Greenway Mining story as it happens, and a bloody big one too. But he just blanked me. He got some spotty kid from his office to call me to say that what I had wasn't relevant to his line of enquiry. Not so much as a thank you either. *Arse*.'

'Aye, well as I told you I'm a private investigator, not a reporter. With Bainbridge Associates. You won't have heard of us, we're pretty small. But we're acting for Hugo

Morgan.' He gave her an ironic look. 'Who I guess you *will* have heard of.'

She nodded. 'Oh yeah Hugo Morgan, I know all about him. He's pretty famous around these parts. Not that he would dare show his face within a hundred miles of the Lakes.' She scuttled off in the direction of the small kitchen that was tucked away in the corner of the office, still talking. 'Of course, it's not really him they should be blaming but we like things nice and simple up here. Coffee or tea?'

'Coffee please. White no sugar.'

She stood hands on hips waiting for the kettle to boil. 'Yeah, in some ways Morgan is a saviour, but don't try telling that to the locals.'

'They blame him for losing their investments I suppose. I can understand that.'

She pointed to a rackety plastic chair opposite her desk. 'Take a seat Jimmy. I'll bring the drinks over.' She tip-toed across the office with the over-filled mugs, placing them down on a pair of stained beer-mats. 'Watch, it's bloody hot. Yeah, see the reality is that Morgan actually saved the mine and about eighty percent of the jobs but it was the way he went about it that pissed everybody off.'

'By somehow managing to expose the cover up, I suppose that's what you mean? By the way, did you know McGinley thinks he knows how Morgan found out about the fact the geology had all gone tits-up? The Chronicle was going to run the story a couple of days ago until Morgan took out an injunction.'

She laughed. 'You mean the De Bruin story? You know, McGinley really is an idiot if he thinks that's what happened.'

He gave her a puzzled look. 'I'm not sure I understand.'

'Mark De Bruin was one of just three people who knew the truth about that cobalt seam, and now he's sitting pretty as CEO of Morgan's new operation. So in

McGinley's simple world, it must have been him who spilled the beans.'

'Aye, winners and losers, that's what McGinley said we should look at,' Jimmy said. 'And Marc De Bruin was the big winner I guess.'

Donahue snorted. 'Except I happen to know that's complete rubbish.'

He looked surprised. 'How come?'

'Because I've done my homework, and a company connected to Brasenose Trust was taking a position in Greenway shares long before De Bruin figured out what was happening.'

'Taking a position?' Jimmy said. 'What does that mean?'

'I think it's also called short selling,' she said, 'or shorting, or buying futures, or some crap like that. Actually, I don't really know what it means. All I know is that it allows an investor to make money if the price of a share falls.' She beamed him a smile. 'It's all double-Dutch to me.'

He grinned. 'Me too. But I thought that sort of thing was illegal. Insider trading isn't it?'

'Well it would have been if Morgan had actually carried out any trading. But he didn't.'

Jimmy looked mystified. 'Sorry, I'm lost here, you'll need to help me out.'

'Well, Hugo obviously was on to something, some inside information as you say, that he knew would cause the shares to drop in value. But then when he found out just how big that something was, he quickly changed his plans. Realised he'd never pull off the short selling operation without being detected.'

Jimmy smiled. 'Aye, I get it now. So he decides to spill the beans on the fact that the ore that's being extracted is way down on cobalt content, causing the share price to crash and the banks to panic.'

'Exactly,' Donahue said, 'and when the banks decided to pull the plug, he waltzed in and picked it up from the administrators for a song. His offer was way below asset value, but since it was the only deal in town they had little option but to go along with it. The banks got about a quarter of their money back and felt themselves lucky not to have lost everything, and Morgan paid off a couple of the big institutional shareholders because he knew he would need their support going forward, but the small shareholders got nothing.'

'Those would be the 'B' shares?' Jimmy said.

'Oh, you've heard of them? Yeah, what a rip-off that was. You handed over your cash for a bit of paper that could only be redeemed by the company itself, on some never-never date in the future. But the thing was, that was the work of Belinda Milner and her fancy City advisors. Nothing to do with Morgan at all. He just spotted they weren't worth the paper they were printed on, and that's what caused the real stink up here. There was a ton of local investors, ordinary folks who'd bet all their savings on the big sure-fire deal.'

'Belinda Milner? She was the boss wasn't she? The woman who drowned herself.'

'Yeah, she was,' Donahue said, her tone non-committal. Jimmy stayed silent for a few seconds, but it was clear that the reporter wasn't planning to elaborate, so he decided to park that line of enquiry for now. Instead he said,

'Actually, I wanted to ask you about something connected to the local investors and the B shares and all that. A story I think you wrote for your wee paper. About one of the miners who lost a hundred and fifty grand I think it was. And then killed himself.'

'Not so much of the wee paper if you don't mind.' She screwed up her face in mock hurt. 'You must be talking about the Tompkins family. William Tompkins was one of the foreman at the mine and he got really taken in by the great big fairytale Belinda Milner and her mates were spinning. So not only did he invest all his savings in the project, he persuaded his extended family to do the same.

Brothers, sisters, cousins, even his mum and dad, they all chipped in to buy shares. And of course they lost the lot. Everything.'

'And so he killed himself. Another tragedy.'

She nodded. 'A terrible death too. He swallowed about a hundred paracetamol tablets.'

Jimmy wondered how that would feel like, to see your dreams of a comfortable future snatched from you by events outside your control. You were likely to be seriously pissed off, and in your anger, it would probably never occur to you that by and large you were the architect of your own misfortune. But if you had also been responsible for the same fate befalling your entire family, then that would be a wholly different kettle of fish. He could imagine the shame would be unbearable, and for William Tompkins it had been so unbearable that he had taken his own life.

But placing all your eggs in one basket was as dumb an investment strategy as he could think of, and yet hundreds of the locals had fallen into that trap, plunging their money into what they surely must have understood to be a high-risk venture. And now that it had all fallen apart, it was only natural that they would look for someone to blame, and that someone was Hugo Morgan and his avaricious investment trust. As he understood it, Morgan had been under no obligation to pay them anything, but a small gesture would have won him a ton of goodwill in the area and he wondered if he would live to rue that decision one day. *Actions have consequences.* And the people behind Justice for Greenway, whoever they were, seemed to be intent on an escalating campaign.

'I'm guessing these Tompkins aren't very happy. Do you think they might try to get revenge? Because someone's running a harassment campaign against Morgan, Justice for Greenway is what it's called. Fairly low-level stuff at the moment but there have been some more serious threats.'

'Justice for Greenway you say? Well that's interesting, because there's been a few incidents up here under that banner. A couple directed at Milner and a couple at Marc De Bruin. It does cross my mind that the Tompkins lot might be behind it, but to be honest, there's a thousand people up here who might have done it. And these Tompkins, let's just say they're not the brightest sandwiches in the picnic. But having said that, they're pretty pissed off with the whole situation, that's for sure, so perhaps it is them. I really couldn't say.'

'Maybe I should go and see one of these guys,' Jimmy said. 'They live locally I assume?'

She grinned. 'Yeah, Whitehaven. But I wouldn't go alone if I was you, not if you're planning to mention you're working for Morgan. They're pretty handy with their fists, that's what I've heard.'

'Thanks for that Liz. Forewarned is forearmed, eh?' He didn't like to tell her that he'd done plenty of door-knocking out in Helmand where the residents were often pretty handy with the improvised explosive devices and the AK-47s. Compared to that, dealing with the Tompkins would be child's play. That was the theory anyway. It remained to be seen how it worked out in practice. But the more he thought about it, the less likely it seemed that this family would be behind a sophisticated London-based harassment campaign. Nonetheless it was a line of enquiry that would need to be followed up.

'I assume you have an address? Not that it should be too hard to track him down I guess.'

She chuckled. 'I thought you were supposed to be the investigator? Yeah, of course I have it, one of the sons. And I'll give it to you if I can tag along when you go visiting. There should be another story in that.'

He laughed. 'Ok, it's a deal Liz, I'll look forward to that. Now, do you mind if I ask you about the story you were going to give to our mate Gary McGinley. The Greenway one.'

Her eyes narrowed. 'Look Jimmy, this could be the biggest thing that's ever happened to me in my career. I need to know I can trust you.'

'Of course, I get that, totally.' And in that moment, it became clear what he should do. He had only just met Liz Donahue, but already he knew she was good and honest, a quality that experience had taught him was not always in ready supply in this world. Besides which, she was immersed in the life of the community up here and if anyone could help them work out who was behind the harassment of Hugo Morgan, it was her. He gave her one of his special smiles.

'And I'd be exactly the same if I was in your position Liz, believe me. So, see what you think about this. Tell me, when's your paper planning on running your big story?'

She dropped her voice to a whisper, as if worried they would be overheard. 'In about a week I hope, but I've not even told Jonathan my editor the details yet. There's just one more fact I have to verify and then it'll be ready to go. All I've said to him is it's huge and he'll probably have to get it checked out with the owners in Swindon and then it'll probably have to go through legal.'

'Woah, it *must* be huge.'

'It is. Bigger than any story I've ever done in my life.' He saw her face flush as if overwhelmed by the anticipation of what it would mean to her.

He nodded. 'Aye, well I respect that you would want to protect it, absolutely. All I ask is if it had any bearing on the Justice for Greenway thing, then you'll tell me everything you know afterwards.' He knew it was a lot to ask given how little he was able to offer in return. But then again, they were working for Hugo Morgan. Out of the blue, the thought came to him.

'And maybe, and I'm not promising anything, we could get you an interview with the man himself. Give him the chance to put his point of view direct to the community. I'm guessing you'd welcome that opportunity?'

Her eyes widened. 'You could do that?'

He nodded. 'I think so. To be honest, he feels a bit hard done to, I mean not that I feel sorry for him or anything. But he is adamant it was the previous management who screwed up and I think he'd like to put the record straight. As he sees it of course.'

'That would be amazing, definitely.'

Jimmy suddenly had a thought. 'Just one thing though Liz. This article. It doesn't concern Morgan in any way does it? Because if it does, he might not be so willing to cooperate.'

He could tell by the way she looked at him that he had struck a nerve.

'Yeah, it concerns Morgan all right. Big time. You see, I think I know how he found out about the problem with the cobalt yield, and it wasn't because Marc De Bruin told him, no matter what McGinley might think.'

'Bloody hell,' he said, 'so come on now, are you going to tell me who it was?' He knew she wouldn't, but there was no harm in asking. She was silent for a moment, Jimmy guessing she was deciding how much she should reveal. Finally she said,

'Look, I've got an idea. Why don't we see if we can meet with Tompkins tomorrow morning, ask him what he knows? You could stay at my place tonight, it's just round the corner. Ruthie was making a big veggie lasagne and baking some bread, so I'm sure there'll be more than enough to go round.'

'Ruthie?'

'My wife. She's lovely, and she's a very good judge of people. You'll like her.'

Jimmy laughed. 'So I'll be under scrutiny, will I?'

'Put it that way if you like. But I'm sure she'll like you too, and if she does... well, maybe I'll tell you more. So what do you say Mr Detective? Deal?'

He hesitated for a moment. 'I was actually planning to head back tonight but...well, I suppose it wouldn't do any harm to talk to the Tompkins lot whilst I'm up here. Yeah, Liz, let's do it.'

She smiled warmly. 'That's great Jimmy. I'll message Ruthie and tell her to expect one more for dinner.'

'Fantastic,' he said. 'So maybe I'll just catch the bus down to the lake and have a wee wander round, and then pick up a bottle of wine or two. Oh aye, and a tooth brush and a razor.'

On the bus, he took out his phone and, suppressing a laugh, composed a careful WhatsApp to his boss.

Hi Maggie, going well up here in the lovely Lakes. Staying the night with Liz! Just popping down to Boots for some overnight supplies, if you know what I mean :-) x

***

All in all, it had been a cracking evening. As Liz had intimated, her wife Ruthie was sweet and lovely, and to his surprise, much younger than her spouse, not far off his own age in fact - and very pretty. Disconcertingly pretty in fact, so much so that he had barely been able to take his eyes off her the whole night, which had every prospect of being a bit awkward. But far from being offended, Liz had seemed amused and even flattered by his obvious attentions and it was clear too that Ruthie was deeply besotted by her wife. As the wine flowed, so did the laughter, which was the accompaniment to what he half-remembered as sparkling conversation. With him doing most of the talking. Maybe not so good.

Breakfast had been set for 8am, and he awoke to the enticing smells of bacon and sausages frying on the griddle pan, Ruthie's semi-militant veganism seemingly no obstacle to rustling up a hearty start to the day for their guest. A long hot shower went some way to blasting away his emerging hangover, and there was a distinct spring in his step as he made his way downstairs. Liz was already at the little kitchen table, munching on a slice of toast which he guessed had been made from the leftovers of the delicious home-baked ciabatta from the previous evening.

'Morning Jimmy,' she said, a wicked smile on her face. 'Sweet dreams?'

'Out like a light.'

Ruthie called over from the hob. 'Glad to hear it. Two eggs or three? And do you prefer them runny like Liz?'

'You know what, I know it's greedy but I could deal with three no bother. And yes, soft please.'

'On their way. I must say Jimmy, you were on good form last night. All these stories from your army days. Fascinating.'

He gave an embarrassed smile. 'Oh God, did I really talk that much? I'm sorry. I'll blame the wine and the great company.'

'Sounds like you were a real action man,' Liz said, laughing, 'which might come in useful when we meet the Tompkins bunch this morning.'

And so it had proved. They arrived on Wayne Tompkins' Whitehaven doorstep after a pleasant ninety-minute drive through beautiful Lakeland countryside. Outside stood a battered white van which evidently his father had used for the handyman business he started up after losing his job in the mine. *W Tompkins & Sons. Building works, gardens cleared. No job too small.* Liz had mentioned that his brother had lost his job too. No savings, no job and few prospects. Added to the death of their father, it was no surprise they felt sore about the whole thing.

Tompkins had answered the door himself, and when Liz asked him straight out if he or any of his extended family were behind the Justice for Greenway stuff, he let out a string of invective, and for a moment it looked as if things might get violent. That was, until he took another look at Jimmy, and decided that he was likely to come off second best in any altercation with the six-foot-two fourteen-stone ex-soldier. After that, he calmed down and it soon became clear that his overriding emotion regarding the Greenway affair was sadness, not anger. Although he stopped short of inviting them in.

'My family's lost all their savings because of them people. They trusted my dad and they lost everything. Bastards, all of them.'

'Who do you mean?' Jimmy asked.

'Milner, Morgan, all of them. Bloody vultures.'

'It didn't work out well for Belinda Milner though, did it?'

He shrugged. 'Well, yeah that was a tragedy for her kid and her bloke. We didn't want that to happen. But she was a right cow, and no mistake.'

'We? Who's we?'

'My family. But we didn't do nothing, honest we didn't.' That caused Liz and Jimmy to smile at one another. Guilt was written all over this guy's face.

'Someone graffiti'd her house, just a day or two before she died,' Liz said. 'Justice for Greenway in foot-high letters.'

Jimmy nodded. 'And a few days later, someone daubed the same message on Morgan's garden wall down in London. A wee bit of a coincidence, don't you think?'

'Nowt to do with us,' he said defensively, 'although I can't says that I'm not glad.'

They were disturbed by the deafening sound of a rorty car exhaust, Jimmy glancing round to catch sight of a lowered Fiesta pulling up sharply behind the Tompkins van. The elderly car had been treated to a plainly expensive paint-job, a glimmering sea of purples and vermilions reflecting the morning sun in their eyes.

'That's my brother Karl.'

'Nice wheels,' Jimmy said.

'Yeah he's into his motors,' Tompkins said, his pride obvious. 'That's his business in fact, does them up for all the lads around here. Nice little earner it is.'

I bet it is, Jimmy thought, the ownership of a crassly-customised hot hatch as much a class identifier in these parts as a tattoo. Karl Tompkins was around thirty, a couple of years younger than his brother, stocky but broad and almost as muscle-packed as Jimmy, his hair cropped short and wearing a black sleeveless top that displayed tattoo-infested biceps. So far, so stereotypical.

'What's this?' he said, ignoring them and addressing his brother.

'She's from the Gazette. He's some sort of private eye. They want to know about Justice for Greenway. I told them we didn't know nothing.'

'So who says we do?' The brother's tone was distinctly aggressive and it was instructive he had directed the comment at Liz, because Jimmy knew a bully when he saw one. But there was something else he recognised. A regimental tattoo.

'Royal Engineers eh? Served alongside a lot of you boys out in Helmand. Great bunch of lads.'

Karl seemed momentarily nonplussed. 'What? Yeah, they was. You was there too then?'

'Aye, too right,' Jimmy said. 'Bomb squad. Mental it was.' He didn't mention that he had been an officer. In his experience, squaddies either developed a lifelong respect for authority or they went completely the other way. He had only encountered Karl Tompkins for two seconds but he had no doubt which side of the fence this guy would sit on.

'Yeah these fecken' IEDs were everywhere. Took a lot of our mates they did. But you lads were fecken' brave, and make no mistake. I wouldn't have done it.'

'Just doing my job, same as everyone,' Jimmy said. 'How long were you in?'

'He was in eight years,' his brother interjected, 'Made sergeant. Bloody proud we was, the whole family. Especially my dad.'

'Then you got a job in the mine when you came out,' Liz said. 'A really good job, so it must have been gutting for you, everything that happened last year. You know, the Morgan stuff and all that.'

Karl looked at her suspiciously. 'Yeah, he's a bastard all right. Treated everyone round here like shit. But what's that got to do with you?'

'We're working for him,' Jimmy said. 'Someone calling themselves Justice for Greenway has been harassing him.

So naturally we thought it would be good to start up here, given this is where the mine is.'

'Nowt to do with us.'

'Aye that's what your brother told us,' Liz said, shooting him a sardonic smile. 'But I expect the CCTV at Oxenholme would have caught any of you Tompkins catching a London train any time over the last few weeks. I know the station manager really well, I'm sure he'd be happy to let me take a look at the footage.'

'You'd better watch what you're saying,' Wayne sneered. 'And you can look at all the pictures you like, you won't find nothing.'

And that's where they left it. Discussing the matter on the way back to Kendal, they agreed it was pretty much one hundred percent certain that one of the Tompkins brothers had been behind the harassment of Belinda Milner. As for the Morgan stuff, that seemed a bit less likely, although a former sergeant in the Engineers would certainly have the logistical and technical expertise to pull of such a campaign. So they didn't rule out that he or his brother or even someone else in the family could have driven to London with a van-load of aerosol cans. Jimmy didn't know if it was a possibility, but maybe he could persuade his brother Frank to get an APNR search done on one or two cameras on the M6, and of course Liz could talk to her mate at the station, but he didn't hold out much hope for either of these leads.

An hour into the journey, they were dawdling down the eastern edge of Thirlmere with the brooding majesty of Helvellyn rising just ahead of them, and it was impossible to talk of anything but the stark beauty of the national park. But then soon she was telling him of her difficult upbringing in Newcastle, how her family had shut her out when in her late teens she had came out, and how finding Ruthie at a time she had all but given up hope of love had saved her. And in that moment Jimmy knew he had found a friend for life, his initial warm feeling for this woman reinforced by every subsequent minute he had spent in her company. Not only that, he was pretty sure she felt the same way about him. Which meant it was probably a good time to return to the subject of her big story. The story that she hoped would make her name, the story that would reveal how Hugo Morgan found out about the problems at the mine. So he asked her if he'd passed the Ruthie test, and she said yes he had, and then he asked if she would now tell him, or at least give him a clue. And she said she would. *Pillow talk*. Pillow talk, that's all she was prepared to give away and he didn't push it. If he wanted to know more, he would have to figure it out for himself. As they approached the outskirts of Kendal, he reflected once again that Liz Donahue was one of life's good people and it was a privilege to know her.

Words that he would find himself repeating to Ruthie when he attended the funeral.

Chapter 16

Frank had decided to take the tube out to Tower Hill, the nearest station to the HBB offices which were located a couple of streets behind St Katherine's Dock. He could have got one of his deadbeat DCs to drive him, and that would have been a lot quicker and a lot more convenient, but he wanted take a look at the location of Chardonnay's death before he met with Jeremy Hart. It wasn't that he was looking for anything specific, he just wanted to take in the scene and remind himself that she had been a real living person and not just the name on the cover of the case folder. Alighting on the east-bound platform, he made his way along to the end against the flow of the handful of passengers who had disembarked, to the point where departing trains sped off into the darkness. Directly opposite was the spot where Chardonnay had been pushed to her death, the act expertly timed to coincide with a train emerging at over thirty miles an hour on the west-bound line. That evening back in October the station would have been packed with home-bound commuters, and he wondered if anyone would have noticed a beautiful young woman being forced against her will to the end of the platform. Because surely that was what must have happened. Anywhere else, the train would have been slowing and the victim might well have survived. Too much of a chance to take if you wanted a clean kill.

A few metres along the deserted platform, a Transport for London official emerged from a small glass fronted cubicle and began to approach him, a mildly suspicious expression on her face. Frank shot her a smile, fumbling in an inside pocket for his warrant card.

'Hi, I'm Detective Inspector Stewart with the Met. I just wondered, do you have any idea how long they keep your CCTV footage?'

She shrugged. 'Don't know mate. You'd need to ask security. What's this all about?'

'Nothing really, just wondered. Here, do you remember an incident a few months back, when a young woman fell in front of a train? On the other platform, just over there.'

'Nah, wasn't here mate. I was at Bank then. But we get quite a lot of them. It's nothing special.'

Nothing special. A life so easily dismissed by this ignorant woman. But Chardonnay Clarke *was* something special, someone very special indeed and he wasn't going to rest until he'd found out what happened to her.

Hart was mid to late thirties, short, overweight and balding, his unprepossessing appearance redeemed in part by an immaculate navy Italian suit and dazzling white shirt. The card he handed Frank read *Jeremy R C Hart, Chief Financial Officer.* Two middle names, when most people had to make do with one, if they were lucky. And as certain an indicator of class as an old school tie. *Posh guy, Jeremy something or other*. That was how Terry Clarke had described him and his assessment was accurate, if only to judge by his accent. He was also pretty young to be occupying such an elevated position in a big international bank, and Frank speculated how much of his career success was down to his ability as opposed to his obviously privileged upbringing. Not what you know but who you know.

HBB's office was open plan and garishly decorated in bright primary colours, looking more like a primary school than a temple of high finance. Hart led him through a maze of desks occupied almost exclusively by twenty-somethings, each with eyes glued to their laptop screens, to an area separated from the rest of the office by a floor-to-ceiling perspex screen. A label stuck to the outside read *Silent Space 1*.

'We come here when we need a bit of peace and quiet,' Hart explained. 'Which is quite a lot of the time, because it's generally pretty manic around here. Our main offices are over at Canary Wharf, this is just a bit of overspill capacity we're renting at the moment. We're still trying to work out what the takeover means for us in terms of headcount.'

'Aye, I think I read something about that. You've been bought by a German bank, haven't you?'

'Yes, that's right. CommerzialBank Stuttgart.' He didn't sound as if it was a development he much welcomed. Frank was no expert, but takeovers generally had an impact on jobs, or headcount as Hart described it, and like in war, it was the vanquished that lost out. He wondered if this guy's own position might be at risk.

The only seating provided was a pair of oblong foam blocks arranged facing one another about a metre apart. With no other option on offer, he perched himself uncomfortably on the corner of one.

'You know why I'm here Jeremy,' he said. 'Chardonnay Clarke.'

Hart stared at his shoes and gave a deep sigh. 'I know. I still haven't come to terms with what happened. I don't think I ever will.'

'You were close, I think?' Frank said, trying his best to sound empathetic.

'Close?' he said, his indignation obvious. 'I loved her. I'd never met anyone like her before. She was special. Very special.'

And way out of your league too pal, was Frank's immediate reaction, but he didn't say it. Not in so many words at least.

'I'm sorry to have to ask this question, but do you think she felt the same way about you?'

He gave Frank a dismissive look. 'Yes, I know what you're thinking, the same as everyone else did. Why would a girl like that fall for someone like me? Well, the fact is we were soul mates and we were blessed to have found each other. We thought the same way about everything. We loved the same books, the same films, the same music. Everything. It was if we had known each other for the whole of our lives. We talked about our future together. It was that serious.'

'What, do you mean marriage? But she was only what, twenty-three, twenty-four?'

'What's that got to do with it? You might find this hard to understand Inspector, but our ages were irrelevant. We were in love.'

'And yet she took her own life.' Frank left the obvious question hanging in the air, unasked. *Why?*

'I know. Something changed towards the end,' he said, his voice betraying the pain he was so plainly feeling. 'I don't know what. And I was too tied up in the Brasenose thing to notice.'

Frank felt his pulse start to rise as his *something's-not-right* instinct kicked in. Terry Clarke had been adamant. *My girl would never have done herself in.* But here was her lover with seemingly no doubts that it could have been anything other than suicide. Which meant he must have known a reason why she had been driven to commit that terrible final act. And *the Brasenose thing*. What was that all about? He had to ask.

'Brasenose? That's an Oxford college, isn't it?'

'Well yes it is, but this is actually Brasenose Investment Trust. It's a financial firm run by a guy called Hugo Morgan. I don't expect you'll have heard of him.'

But Frank had heard of him, but in what context? It was something that Maggie and Jimmy were working on, he was pretty sure of that. And then he remembered. The billionaire who had dumped his wife as a fiftieth birthday present to himself.

'Well funnily enough Jeremy I have. My brother's actually met him a couple of times I think.'

'Really?' Hart seemed mildly interested. 'Is he in finance too?'

Frank laughed. 'You wouldn't think that if you met him. No, he works around the legal profession, investigating divorces and such like. But sorry, I interrupted you. Carry on, please.'

'So, you know about the Stuttgart take-over. It was an agreed deal, but that actually can be rather complicated when the target, us in this case, is publicly quoted. Most of our stock was in the hands of just a handful of big institutions and so we had to sound out what sort of offer they might be willing to accept in the event of a take-over. As you can imagine, it's a very delicate operation.'

Frank had no idea what he was talking about so had no opinion whether it was a delicate operation or not. But he nodded along anyway.

'Aye, sure, sure, get that.'

'The last thing you want is an institution at the last minute holding out for a better offer, that could blow the whole deal apart of course. So we'd been working on it for several months, sounding out our investors and eventually settled on a price of around eight pounds fifty pence a share. That was the price that everyone was happy with. Our stockholders were getting a fair return on their investment and it was a price that Stuttgart were willing to pay. So win-win.'

Frank nodded. 'I'm sensing there's a *but*.'

Hart gave a rueful smile. 'Yeah, a big but. So, just three weeks before Stuttgart are due to go public with the offer, our registrar draws to my attention that there's been an unusual volume of trades in the preceding two or three weeks. Someone has been quietly building up a position in our stock to the extent that this entity now controls nearly eleven percent.'

'And that's this Brasenose outfit?'

'Well no, not exactly. The company behind it was called Jasmine Holdings, registered in Guernsey. We'd no idea who the owners were at that stage.'

Frank smiled. 'You'll need to forgive me, high finance isn't my thing. But I guess that spelt trouble in some way?'

He nodded. 'You could say that all right. It put the bank, and me in particular, in deep shit. With that sort of volume of trades, we were legally obliged to inform the FCA - that's the regulator - and then they started asking awkward questions about whether there had been a leak and if there was a connection between any of the bank's officers and this Jasmine outfit.'

'Aye, I think I understand how serious that would have been,' Frank said, 'because it would have been insider trading, am I right?'

'Exactly,' Hart said, 'and not a great career move for a CFO like me, to be caught up in something like that. Naturally my CEO Simon Parkside and all the Stuttgart guys are going mental, accusing everybody in this room, me included, of leaking the deal. It was horribly stressful and I didn't sleep for nearly two weeks.'

Frank gave a sympathetic smile. 'Aye, it must have been hard for everyone, I can see that. So how did it all play out?'

'Like a complete nightmare, that's how it played out, if you must know. So not long afterwards, Hugo Morgan goes public and reveals that his Brasenose Trust is the hundred percent owner of the Jasmine shell company. He named it after his youngest daughter apparently. Next he's all over the financial press slagging off the deal, a deal that somehow he knows all the details of. He was giving it his usual activist investor shtick, about how we were ripping off the small shareholders and how he intended to ride to their rescue. Anyway, the long and short of it was that unless the offer was upped to ten pounds a share, he wouldn't sell.'

Frank looked puzzled. 'Sorry, but I thought you said he only had bought eleven percent. Would that have been enough to stop the deal going through?'

Hart shook his head. 'Well in theory no, but Morgan knows that as soon as he publicly questions the value of a deal, it doesn't take long for some of the other big institutional shareholders to start questioning their judgement too. And that's exactly what happened here. Herd instincts I think they call it. Next thing you know, everybody is saying that maybe eight pounds fifty is too cheap after all.'

'But what about the Germans?' Frank said. 'Wasn't there a risk that they would just walk away?'

Hart gave a rueful smile. 'That's the genius of Morgan. He's got an amazing instinct for the true value of a company. He bet that CommerzialBank would bitch to high heavens but go through with it in the end, and that's exactly how it played out. And we were left looking like idiots for trying to sell the bank on the cheap.'

'And I'm assuming Morgan did very well out of it?'

Hart nodded. 'You could say that. He made forty million in the space of a month.'

'Nice,' Frank said, 'but did you ever find out where the leak came from?'

Hart shook his head. 'No, we didn't. The FCA compliance team interviewed loads of people in the bank and swarmed all over our emails and phone records, but they didn't get anywhere. And of course Morgan denied there ever was a leak at all. He claimed it was pure coincidence, that he had been building up a position in HBB simply because he had been researching us and decided we were poorly managed and the shares had underperformed for years.'

Frank nodded. 'Plausible I suppose? Because I think I've already worked out that's how his company operates.'

'Oh yeah,' Hart replied, his tone sarcastic, 'highly plausible. Except I happen to know it's complete bollocks. You see, I've done my research too.'

'How do you mean?' Frank said, his eyes narrowing.

'Five companies in the last three years where Brasenose Trust just happened to have taken an interest just as something big was kicking off. Two take-overs, a big contract loss, and two management screw-ups to be exact. And each time, Morgan made a killing.'

'So what are you saying? That he does this thing as a matter of course?'

Hart nodded. 'He calls it activist investment. I call it industrial espionage because that's exactly what it is. I don't know how he does it, but it's not through bloody research, believe me.'

It wasn't Frank's area of expertise, but questionable though the practice might be from a moral standpoint, he wasn't sure if it was actually illegal. Although what you did with the information you found out, well that might be a different matter. But he wasn't here to pass judgement on Hugo Morgan's business practices.

'Getting back to Chardonnay, if we can for a moment. Can I ask, how much was the bank paying her? The reason I ask is that her dad thought she was getting seventy-five grand a year, which seems a lot to me.'

Hart looked perplexed. 'Paying her? She was an intern Inspector, so we weren't paying her anything. We paid a fee to the agency, but that was it.'

'The agency? That's that Oxbridge outfit isn't it? So would they have been paying her, do you think?'

'What, are you kidding?' Hart said, suppressing a laugh. 'The internship business is just one step away from slavery. We all go along with it of course but, no, they definitely wouldn't have been paying her, no way.'

'And yet she had money, didn't she? I've heard she had a very nice flat in Clapham for instance, and what sort of rent would that command? Fifteen hundred or maybe even two grand a month? That's a lot of money for an intern. For anybody when it comes to it.'

Hart shrugged. 'I just assumed her dad was paying for it all. He's a London plumber after all. You know what they charge. And anyway, I only went there once. You see, I never... we never slept together.'

Frank looked at him sharply. Years of experience in the job had given him a well-honed instinct for the truth, or more accurately, for sniffing out untruths, and his instinct said that Jeremy Hart was telling the truth about all of this. Although it did seem a bit surprising they weren't having sex given how much in love they had supposedly been.

'Why was that sir, if you don't mind me asking?'

He smiled uncertainly. 'Chardonnay said she wasn't quite ready for that side of our relationship. I was perfectly happy with that of course.' From the waver in his voice, Frank knew that *this* was a lie. He'd been rejected and he hadn't been happy about it at all. But then who would be when you were so tantalisingly close to having a woman like Chardonnay in your bed? Perhaps Hart had misread the whole thing, and that she saw their relationship in an entirely different light. Perhaps she had decided it had run its course and was trying to pluck up the courage to tell him.

'You said that something had changed in the relationship towards the end. About the time the Brasenose thing was happening.'

A cloud of sadness seemed suddenly to envelop him. 'Yes, I don't know what it was. Something was troubling her, but she wouldn't say what it was. I speculated of course. I thought perhaps her parents were pressuring her to break it off, you know, because she was so young and with the age gap and everything.'

Frank shook his head. 'Well, I spoke to her father not that long ago and he didn't say anything about that. On the contrary, I remember exactly what he said. *That Jeremy was all right.* So it wasn't that I'm pretty sure.'

Hart gave a faint smile. 'Yes, they're nice, her parents. Good solid folks.'

'I haven't met the mum,' Frank said, 'but aye, Terry Clarke's a good bloke. And he's totally convinced that his daughter wouldn't have taken her own life, and yet I'm getting the sense that you're not so sure. Why would that be Jeremy?'

For a moment he hesitated. 'I..it was just... well as I said, she seemed troubled. There was something on her mind, but of course at the time, it never entered my mind that she would kill herself. But afterwards... there was that suicide note on Facebook...'

'Which she never actually sent,' Frank said.

'No, she didn't. Look Inspector, I don't really understand what this is all about. Are you saying her death might have been... well, suspicious?'

He shrugged. 'I don't know if it will make you feel better or not, but aye, we've uncovered certain information that raises that possibility. It's early days, but you see we found another case with some quite disturbing similarities. A lad called Luke Brown who died in exactly the same way. He was one of these interns too. Assigned to some insurance company. Arixa or Avimto or something like that.'

'Alexia maybe? Maybe that's who you mean.'

Frank nodded. 'Aye, that was it. Alexia Life. You know something about them?'

'Two years ago Alexia were facing nearly half a billion in losses over that hurricane that hit the south-west of the US. Remember it? You see, they should have re-insured it out through Lloyds but they'd decided to keep most of the risk in house so that they could book the full premium value to their accounts. It was a huge mistake on their part.'

'I won't even pretend to understand any of that Jeremy,' Frank said. 'Just give me the edited highlights if you would.'

'There's not much more to say. It was a massive cock-up, but if you're looking for a connection back to Hugo Morgan then you're barking up the wrong tree I'm afraid.

'Why do you say that Mr Hart?'

He gave a condescending smile. 'Alexia are a mutual. They're owned by their members, not by shareholders.'

***

Connections. That's what you were always on the look-out for in a case, and as Frank headed back to Atlee House, he gave a mental shrug of the shoulders. Two good-looking interns, two tube-station deaths, the Oxbridge Agency. Three connections, and in his mind, that was already too much to be just coincidence. Sure, it would have been all neat and tidy if Hugo Morgan had been involved with Alexia Life too, but he wasn't and that was something he would have to deal with. And anyway there would be something else, he just hadn't stumbled across it yet.

Now he needed to chase up the half-wit Ronnie French to see how he'd got on up in Oxford with Sophie Fitzwilliam, and then a bit more legwork, see what he could find out about that lad Luke Brown. He might do that himself or ask French to do it, and while he was at it, he could take wee Yvonne Sharp along with him.

Then it would be useful to speak to that brother of his, take him for a pint and see what they knew about Morgan. And if Maggie just happened to be there too, that would be nice. And awkward.

Chapter 17

It was an anniversary that would never ever be forgotten, but not one to celebrate. Two years on from what she now called meltdown day, the day when every ounce of sense she had ever possessed had evaporated. The day when, maybe, she had tried to end her life and that of her beloved Ollie. Except that in her waking hours, she was unable to remember a single thing about it. It was inconceivable that it had been a deliberate act, that she had planned it and executed it so coldly, and that, as Camden Social Services had asserted at the time, she had been only too aware of the likely outcome. Inconceivable, but she could never be quite certain, which is why the terrible dream came back, again and again, night after night.

Perhaps it should have been expected that last night it should have been particularly vivid, given the significance of the date, but maybe the copious quantities of red wine she had consumed during the evening might also have had something to do with. The date with Robert had been lovely, an early visit to the cinema followed by a late supper, and this time she hadn't slept with him. He had been absolutely fine about that, and in fact expressed some surprise about the turn of events on their first date. He had seen her to a cab, kissed her gently on the cheek, and expressed a wish that they could do this again.

Three quarters of an hour later she was tucked up in bed, her cheeks still rosy red, partly through excitement but mainly because of the wine. She drifted off thinking pleasant thoughts of love and marriage, soon to be ruthlessly replaced by the replaying of that horrible scene that could not be erased. She awoke at 4am, shivering with sweat and with a pounding headache, and thereafter was unable to get back to sleep. She tossed and turned for an hour or so before giving up, and at five-thirty she was in the shower, the hot jets of water helpless against her growing hangover. At least the coffee helped a bit, the extra spoonful of finest Columbian thrown into the cafetiere producing a powerful caffeine hit that went some way towards dragging her into the day.

But today was auction day and likely to be an interesting one, and so gradually she found her spirits rising. More than that, it was looking pretty conclusive that Miss Lotti Brückner was one hundred percent authentic, meaning that matter could be brought to a conclusion and she could, if she chose reveal her true identity to Robert. Although that was going to be very risky, because she would have to tell him why she had posed as Magdalene Slattery. Firstly, there was every chance that he would be angered by her deception and want nothing more to do with her. Secondly, and this was the thing that worried her the most, he was bound to tell Lotti, and that could make it very awkward indeed with Hugo. But she wasn't going to worry about any of this today.

The bidding was scheduled to start at midday with the auction room open from 9am for viewing. The Casagemas was one of the star lots, heavily promoted on the auction-house's website and having pride of place on the front page of their catalogue. They had been undecided whether or not Jimmy should come along, and he was not keen, but she had managed to persuade him it was worth having a final check on Lotti's fidelity before they wrapped up the investigation.

The viewing gallery was packed to the rafters when she arrived at around eleven, hawk-eyed auction-house staff mingling with the crowd, focussed on separating the serious bidders from the more numerous window-shoppers. Glancing around the room, she saw that Jimmy was already there, catalogue in hand, staring vacantly at a large gilt-framed painting of an undistinguished hunting scene. Alongside him stood Lotti Brückner, looking as ridiculously beautiful as on the previous occasions they had met. And still looking annoyingly young for her age.

'Morning boss,' he said as Maggie joined them. 'Sorry, I mean darling Magdalene.' He leant over and kissed her on the cheek. If Lotti had noticed his little slip-up, she didn't say anything.

'Good morning Magdalene,' she said brightly. 'I was just saying to James, I think it's going to be an exciting day. We have a very big attendance and I recognise many regular collectors. We may see some very big bids.'

'And what about our Casagemas?' Maggie said, slightly nonplussed by her colleague being addressed by his undercover name. 'Is there a lot of interest?'

Lotti nodded. 'Yes, there is. It's a pity from our point of view that they have marketed it so heavily, because that will of course push up the price. But that does not matter so much with fine works of art since it only establishes the baseline value should you choose to sell it in the future. So it will still be a good investment if we managed to secure it, I'm sure of it.'

'Good to know,' Jimmy said, stroking his chin in the manner of an expert he had seen on the *Antiques Roadshow*. 'Good to know.'

They were approached by young man wearing a nametag that identified him as *Harry Radford-James, Valuer.* He pointed up at the painting.

'Good morning ladies, sir. It's an interesting piece isn't it? Very classical in subject matter but a good example of the genre.' Correctly surmising that Maggie was the buyer, he had directed his smiling gaze at her. 'The price will be modest I think, but it would be an excellent addition to anyone's collection.'

It seemed that Lotti knew him. Giving him an affectionate look she said, 'Yes very good Harry, but we both know that this is a *very* unremarkable work. I'm afraid you will have to find some other prey.'

He seemed unperturbed by her barb. 'But art is a very personal thing, isn't it Lotti? What about you sir, do you find it pleasing? I noticed you were studying it quite intently.'

'Nah,' Jimmy said. 'It's crap.'

Harry laughed. 'Well between you and me sir, I think you may be right. But please, don't tell my boss that I said that. Anyway, I hope you have a good auction and as Lotti suggested, I'll slip off now and see if I can find another victim.' He gave a half-wave and ambled away.

'Nice lad,' Jimmy said, 'although a bit posh for me.'

Lotti smiled. 'They are here to help the lots to sell. Even the poorer ones. He was only doing his job. But come, we must move through to the sale room to get a good position. Somewhere towards the rear of the room is normally best, but seated, not standing.'

Maggie was intrigued. 'Why is that Lotti?'

'It makes it easier to see who is bidding against you. For example, if it is someone you know is very rich, or has a big interest in a particular type of work, you know you will have to bid very high to win. And so maybe you decide it is not worth it. And I prefer to be seated so that it is difficult for them to see you.'

They made their way in, finding seats just one row from the back. The room was rapidly filling up and within a few minutes it was standing room only, with hopeful bidders packed three-deep along the rear and down the sides of the room. The auction-house's staff were already on the platform, the auctioneer flanked by half a dozen colleagues who would be taking the telephone bids from keen buyers from around the world. At twelve midday precisely, things got under way.

'Good afternoon, ladies and gentlemen, and I hope you're all well and ready to raise your arm when I catch your eye.' A ripple of laughter spread through the room. He was younger than she expected and with a rich northern accent, in stark contrast to the plummy received pronunciation that seemed to be *de rigour* in his trade. A Lancastrian, she decided, speculating that he might perhaps be from Oswaldtwistle or Ramsbottom or Rawtenstall or any other of these delightfully-named former mill towns.

'Eighty-seven lots we have today, each one a gem in its genre, and many with *no reserve*.' His comic emphasis on the last two words was greeted with a loud 'Ooh' and a crescendo of applause. Maggie smiled to herself. She hadn't expected a vaudeville act at such an august gathering but it was certainly entertaining.

The first few lots were unremarkable, quickly dispatched by the auctioneer and none achieving more than two thousand pounds under the hammer. The Casagemas had been allocated lot fifteen, relatively early in the running order, but its position had been chosen quite deliberately by the auction house. The catalogue was by any standards relatively run of the mill, but at the last minute they had managed to secure a minor but attractive early work by Hockney, which had been listed towards the end of the sale. As Lotti had explained to them in perfect colloquial English, you couldn't really expect an auction to be a success if there wasn't anything to keep the bums on seats through to the end of the programme. The hope was that collectors who missed out on the star attraction - in this case the lovely landscape by Picasso's pupil - would stick around for the Hockney so as not to go home disappointed.

The screen behind the platform was now filled by the arresting abstract of a white-washed Spanish town.

'Lot fifteen, a very pretty little landscape by Carlos Casagemas. This is authenticated by the leading authority on the artist's work in Barcelona, the city of his birth. A genuine work, and one of his last before his tragic death. And of course today, we are offering this remarkable work at no reserve.'

Maggie could feel her heart start to pound as the auctioneer got the bidding under way. 'Where do we want to start with this?' he said, beaming out at the audience. 'Do I see twenty pounds?' A huge gust of laughter reverberated around the sale room. At the end of the platform, a colleague raised an arm and mouthed something in his direction.

'We're underway,' he shouted. *'Twenty* thousand pounds, on the telephone, thank you. Do I see twenty-five? Twenty-five anywhere? In the room, yes thank you sir, down there on the left. Twenty-five has it. Looking for thirty now. *Thirty* thousand pounds.'

Maggie got to her feet and peered forward, hoping to catch a glimpse of this new bidder, but he was tucked away on the right hand side of the room and obscured by a pillar. Lotti tapped her on the arm and whispered. 'Don't worry about that. We don't need to bid right now but we will watch carefully before we make our move. But forty-five thousand, that is our maximum bid, isn't it?'

Maggie nodded uncertainly. 'Yes that's what we agreed I think.'

At the other end of the platform, a second colleague gave a discreet nod.

'Thirty thousand. On the telephone. A new bidder. Do I have thirty-five? *Thirty*-five. Thank you sir. We're in the room again. Forty thousand, anyone?'

Alongside her, Lotti gave an almost imperceptible nod. The auctioneer, catching her eye, smiled.

'Forty thousand, thank you madam. Forty-five. You sir? No? Forty-five I'm asking. A sublime work with an impeccable provenance. Forty-five thousand. Do I have it?'

'I think it was the right moment,' Lotti whispered. 'It will slow down from now I think.' She pointed to the stage, where one of the assistants manning a telephone was shaking her head.

'Do I have forty-five? I will take forty-two if that helps.'

For a moment it seemed as if the bidding had stalled. The auctioneer scanned the room anxiously, then looked along the row of his colleagues, who shook their heads in unison. He glanced at the screen on front of him, his face now wearing a frown, but no internet bidder came along to offer salvation.

'Fair warning,' he said, sounding rather deflated. 'I'm selling... make no mistake...I'm selling...to you madam at the back of the room...selling at *forty* thousand once... forty thousand twice...'

Maggie squeezed Lotti's arm and gave a smile. But then suddenly there was a collective gasp from the room as the auctioneer evidently caught the eye of the bidder at the front of the room.

'*Fifty* thousand pounds. Fifty thousand. I have it here in the room. Thank you sir.'

'What do you want to do?' Lotti whispered. 'I think we are now up against a bidder who really wants this picture.'

Maggie could feel heart pounding in her chest, which she realised was stupid. Magdalene Slattery, rooky art collector, wasn't real, and anyway she was spending Hugo Morgan's money, not her own. But somehow, crazily, she had caught a dose of auction fever.

'What do you think Lotti? Perhaps it's worth more than we thought.' Without waiting for her reply, she shot up her arm and shouted 'fifty-five.'

'Fifty-five thousand! Thank you madam. At the back of the room. Do I have sixty? This lovely work by young Carlos Casagemas. Solid provenance. Sure to grace any collection. Sixty thousand I'm looking for. Do I have it anywhere?' Now the excitement in the room was palpable, as they looked forward to two motivated buyers slugging it out over a piece which had already reached more than twice its perceived market value. And it seemed the mystery bidder was not yet ready to drop out.

'I have sixty thousand pounds. Thank you for your bid sir. Madam, are you in? Can I have sixty-five?'

Maggie looked first at Jimmy, who simply shrugged, then at Lotti, who was now wearing a serious expression.

'I think we are reaching the limit of value Magdalene,' she said. 'Perhaps just one more bid but I would not advise going much further.'

'Ok,' Maggie said, raising her hand.

The auctioneer gave a nod of acknowledgment. 'Sixty-five thousand. Thank you for your bid madam. Sir, do I have seventy?' It wasn't possible for Maggie to see directly how the mystery bidder responded, but it was clear from the reaction on the platform that he had indicated a 'no'.

'I'll take sixty-seven if it helps,' the auctioneer said, smiling in the bidder's direction. 'Sixty-seven I have. Do I have sixty-eight? Madam?'

'Go straight to seventy,' Lotti whispered. 'I think that will finish them off.'

Maggie nodded. She was enjoying this, playing with Hugo Morgan's Monopoly money, and a second later she was on her feet yelling. 'Seventy!' at the top of her voice. There was a burst of laughter around the room and a beaming smile from the auctioneer.

'Thank you madam, thank *you*.' It seemed the mystery bidder had already signalled his intention to go no further, as the hammer was raised in anticipation.

'I'm selling at seventy thousand pounds... in the room...make no mistake...fair warning...once...twice...' and then with a theatrical flourish, he slammed the hammer down on the wooden lectern.

She wasn't sure if she saw him first, or it was he who spotted her. Whatever the order of events, there was no getting away from the fact that it was an awkward situation, for when the hammer had come down, Jimmy, overacting furiously, had taken her in his arms and kissed her full on the lips. Taken by surprise, she had involuntarily succumbed and returned both the embrace and the kiss, which between them lasted several long, and much to her surprise, blissful seconds. It must have been during this interlude that the mystery bidder appeared from behind the pillar. Robert Trelawney, with a strikingly attractive forty-something redhead clinging to his arm in a manner that suggested they were more than just friends. The parties made their way to the aisle to greet one another. And it was awkward, there could be no doubt of that.

'Robert...'

'Magdalene...'

'Congratulations on your purchase. An interesting auction, don't you think?' he said. 'And this is?'

Jimmy held out his hand. 'I'm Jimmy, eh...James. James McDuff. Magdalene's boyfriend I suppose.'

'Robert Trelawney.' He gave Maggie a quizzical look. For a moment she thought he was going to add something, something that might add exponentially to her discomfort, but he fell into silence. An awkward silence, due in no small part to the obvious doe-eyed devotion of this woman on his arm.

'Felicity Morgan,' she said, shooting them a beaming smile. 'But of course you'll remember me from the Hilton. I'm Robert's girlfriend I suppose.'

***

There were formalities to be attended to, and seeing the auction-house's invoice for eighty-four thousand pounds was the first time Maggie realised just how much it charged for its services. Fourteen grand commission was a tidy amount, and on top of that she, or more accurately, Hugo Morgan, would also have to find a five-figure sum to pay the Polperro Gallery's consultancy fee. She wondered what Morgan would say when he found he'd just shelled out nearly a hundred grand for a picture that had been expected to achieve no more than twenty-five. At least she could say truthfully that she had followed Lotti's advice, and of course he could easily afford it.

She tucked the receipt into her purse, then looked around to find Jimmy, spotting him standing just to one side of the doorway, chatting and laughing with Lotti. It was good to see he was taking the job seriously, especially since she appreciated how difficult it was for him. Three years since the split from his adored wife Flora, a split cause by a moment of madness or more accurately, by the ruthless machinations of the beautiful Astrid Sorenson. A woman that few men could resist, and to his shame, he had fallen for her hook, line and sinker, only to be discarded when she was finished with him, like the new toy of a spoiled child. Flirting with women evidently brought back bad memories and he wasn't anxious to go there again, but whatever he felt inside, it didn't show on the outside.

He raised a hand in greeting as Maggie came into view. As he wandered over to him, she saw him shake hands with Lotti before the beautiful young art dealer glided out of the room.

'That seemed to be going well,' Maggie said.

Jimmy laughed. 'Yeah, I hope you don't mind, but I said that I was beginning to think that you were a bit old for me and if she was ever on the market, I would be first in line.'

'Bloody cheek. So what did she say to that?'

'She let me down gently, that's the best way to put it. Said I'd definitely be somewhere on her list, but since she didn't expect to be on the market anytime soon it was all academic.'

Maggie shrugged. 'So that's it I guess. Our young Lotti gets a one-hundred percent clean bill of health. Hugo will be pleased.'

'I guess so. But changing the subject, don't you think we might have been the victims of a wee scam here? I mean, isn't it interesting that it ends up with just your Robert and our Lotti bidding against each other, and the price going up and up? And then suddenly, your Robert decides to drop out leaving you...'

She gave him an angry look. 'Look, he's not my Robert, will you stop calling him that.'

'Aye, sorry. But the thing is, you were left holding a seventy-grand painting that had an expectation of no more than twenty-five or so. Nice work if you can get it, that's what I say. And I'm assuming the Polperro is on commission, right?'

Maggie nodded. 'They get a fee from the owner. Twenty percent of the hammer price, same as Sotheby's.'

'So another fourteen grand then by my calculation. As I said, nice work.'

She was still a little bit angry with him, but the problem was the more she thought about it, the more she realised he might be right. *Had* it all been pre-arranged, a nice little scheme to relieve a gullible rich client of a substantial sum? Maybe the auction house had been in on it too, she wouldn't be the least surprised. But no, surely not, not a revered organisation like Sotheby's, and in any case, although it wasn't her area of expertise, she was pretty sure that was against the law. As for the Polperro Gallery, that was a different matter. After all, Lotti had been very insistent that they took their seats as near to the back as possible, and on the right hand side. From where, conveniently, Robert Trelawney and his *girlfriend* could not be seen.

Yes, the girlfriend. He'd kept that damn quiet, hadn't he, before and after he had enticed her into his bloody bed. Christ, she hadn't been back on the dating scene for five minutes before she had fallen for a two-timing toe-rag.

But then again, he was probably thinking the same thing about her.

Chapter 18

For once Ronnie French had come up with the goods, although Frank still couldn't work out how he'd managed to make a half-hour assignment up in Oxford last a whole bloody day. He assumed the fat slob had sloped off down to Henley or somewhere like that after the meeting, had a few beers in a nice country pub then slept it off in a lay-by on the way home. As a result, the conversation earlier that morning had been a bit terse to say the least.

'I expected you back in the office yesterday afternoon Ronnie. What is it, fifty, sixty miles? Even at the speed you drive, it should only have taken a couple of hours each way.'

'Traffic was terrible guv.' His answer was ludicrously improbable, but a few months from retirement, Ronnie clearly didn't see any point in trying harder.

'Aye sure,' Frank said, giving him a sardonic look. 'So what did you find out. Nothing I expect.'

French wheezed. 'That's a low blow guv. But that Sophie bird, I'd really love to give her one. We got on really well as it happens. Fancied me I think.'

Frank smiled to himself. Poor Frenchie, deluded as well as thick. 'Aye, I'm sure you can expect a phone call any day soon. So, come on, spill it. What did you get from our Mrs Fitzwilliam? And hurry it up, I haven't got all bloody day.'

'Well, I asked her straight out about Chardonnay Clarke, the fact that her dad thought she was on seventy-five grand or something like it. I said we knew the company wasn't paying it, so it must have been her agency that was doing it, know what I mean?'

'And?'

'Well she just laughed, said I was barking up the wrong tree. All very smooth like. But guv, I could tell by her eyes that I'd struck a nerve. Behind the mask and all that she looked worried. You can always tell when they're lying guv, can't you?'

Frank nodded. This was a new sensation for him, Ronnie French in the role of the brilliantly instinctive copper. But he played along.

'Aye you're right Ronnie, you can always tell. So what did you do then?'

He smiled. 'Yeah, so I decides to put the frighteners on her. I told her that I could easily get a warrant this very day to look at their books and then we'd all know the truth.'

'How did she react to that?'

'Well that's the thing guv. She seemed to relax when I said that. *Go ahead*, she says, *you won't find nothing*.'

Frank doubted Mrs Fitzwilliam was being quoted verbatim, but he wasn't there to give French an English lesson.

'You won't find nothing?'

'Exactly guv. It was as if this was something she was expecting. And at the moment I thinks to myself, she definitely knows something.'

'So then what did you do?'

'Then? Nothing, guv. Not with her at least. Just said we'd be in touch if we needed anything else and left it at that.'

Frank did the calculation. He'd have been in there ten, fifteen minutes at tops. He really was a lazy turd.

'Great work Ronnie,' he said, but irony was wasted on his colleague. And in any case, French wasn't finished yet.

'So anyways guv, that gets me thinking. I mean, it's obvious that *someone* was paying that Chardonnay bird a wad, so I thinks, get someone to take a look at her bank account. It's obvious, isn't it'

Now that Frenchie had said it, it was indeed obvious, but Frank didn't like to admit to himself that he hadn't thought of it first.

'Aye, it is.'

'So yeah, I thinks, that would be useful to know, wouldn't it?'

'Aye it would. But it's not that easy to get the banks to release that sort of information. Confidentiality and all that. Takes a lot of paperwork.'

French gave a smug smile. 'Yeah, it is tricky, but not if you've got a mate in the anti-terrorist squad who owes you a favour or three. Jayden Henry, he's one smart fella, but he likes a beer or two, which, well you know how it is guv. These Rasta lads aren't supposed to drink, so he needs it kept quiet like.'

Frank gave a deep sigh. Ronnie bloody French, the living embodiment of institutional racism. And he wasn't going to change no matter how many unconscious bias courses the Met sent him on.

'For your sake Ronnie, I'll pretend I didn't hear that. So this mate of yours, what did he find out?'

'Well guv, you know these security fellas have access all areas. So after I'd had a bit of lunch, I pulls into a lay-by and gives him a buzz. I just gives him Chardonnay's details, her address and the like, and then click-click-click, he's in. Turns out she's got a Nat West account out of a branch in Romford. And guess what guv? Twenty-eighth of every month, she gets lobbed over six grand. That's being going on for nearly a year.'

'Since she started with the Oxbridge Agency.'

'Exactly guv, I thought that too. Must be more than a coincidence. So anyways, obviously we've found out who's paying the dosh into her account, or at least we have a name. Rosalind Holdings Ltd. Some outfit based in Guernsey, one of these shell companies, that's what Jayden said. That's all I've got at the moment guv, but Jayden's doing a bit of digging to see if he can find out who's behind it.'

Frank didn't like to admit it, but he was impressed. Maybe he'd been underestimating French all this time. 'This is nice work Ronnie, well done. So how many favours have you used up?'

French laughed. 'That was all of them I think. But don't worry guv, another mate told me that Jayden's got a bit on the side. Someone a bit close to him, he says. Once I finds out a bit more about that, then maybe he'll owe me another one. Them black lads...'

Frank looked at him with disgust. There were still too many guys like French in the force, ignorant bigots who went about trashing its good name without a second thought.

'Ronnie, if I hear anything like that from you again, I'll personally make sure you never get to lift your pension. Understand *mate*?'

'Yeah, but Jayden's my big mate. He don't mind all that stuff. Gives it as well as takes it.'

Frank sighed. He doubted if Ronnie's big mate would share that analysis, but it was too late to do anything about the dinosaur now, after thirty years of institutional conditioning, and there was little point in trying.

But he could do something about Rosalind Holdings, that would be his next focus. He'd wait twenty-four hours or so to see what Ronnie's mate came up with, but if he drew a blank, that wasn't a concern. He could play it straight, filling in the reams of complicated paperwork which would grant them some sort of warrant that would force full disclosure of who was behind the company.

But he really hoped that Ronnie's bad lad Jayden Henry would deliver, because he bloody hated paperwork, complicated or otherwise.

Chapter 19

The commissionaire gave a double-take as they entered the atrium.

'Sorry folks, but I could have sworn I'd let the gentlemen in not half-an-hour ago. But now that I takes a proper look, you're a lot younger than he was. You don't have a brother sir, do you?'

Jimmy gave a wry nod. 'Aye I do. But he doesn't look anything like me mate, trust me.'

Maggie laughed. 'Actually he does. But surely, it couldn't have been, could it?'

But it was, a fact that became self-evident when they emerged from the lift into the reception area of Brasenose Investment Trust to find Frank leaning over the reception desk, remonstrating loudly with Harriet Ibbotson.

'Look I don't care if he's a busy man and something important's come up. I'm bloody busy too, and I had an appointment at quarter-to. So unless I'm in there pronto, I'll have you arrested for obstructing a police officer in the performance of their duties. Is that clear enough for you?'

She looked as if she was about to argue the point, then thought better of it.

'I'll go through and ask him when he will be available. Please wait here sir.'

'Aye, you do that.'

'Hello Frank,' Maggie said, smiling, 'We didn't expect you to be here too. Always nice to see you of course.'

As Harriet opened the door to Morgan's office, the sound of raised voices drifted through to the reception area. It appeared Morgan was arguing with a woman. A woman whose voice they instantly recognised. Asvina Rani.

'Look Hugo...'

'Never mind the *look Hugo*. I paid you bloody well to fix this and I expect it to stay fixed, understand?'

'We can't do anything if she's set on this course...'

'We can't do anything? That's not what I want to hear. So you need to do better than that, understand?'

A moment later they emerged from his office, she tight-lipped and unsmiling, he red-faced and clearly worked up. He surveyed the reception area, catching Frank's eye and giving an exasperated sigh.

'You must be the bloody policeman I suppose. You look like one.'

Frank smiled serenely. 'Won't take long sir. Just a few questions for you, that's all.'

Maggie had drawn Asvina to one side and was whispering to her. 'What the hell was that all about?'

'It's Felicity Morgan.'

'What about her?'

'Trouble, that's what. She's decided to contest the settlement.'

Maggie looked puzzled. 'What, can she do that? I thought that was all done and dusted.'

'It was, but she's claiming Hugo hid some material assets from the court. It's a tired old tactic, but there's not much we can do to stop it if she's got the money to pay the legal fees.'

'Which she has of course. Thirty million if I remember rightly. God, you'd think that would be enough for anybody.'

Asvina gave a wry smile. 'It's not about the money Maggie. Felicity's still consumed with hatred and she'll do anything to make him suffer. It's personal for her, believe me.'

Maggie nodded. 'That explains the scene Jimmy and I saw. I don't know if I told you, but she went off on one at one of his investment updates. She was a bit pissed and firing out all sorts of wild threats. So this is what it was all leading to? I bet Hugo isn't very happy.'

'No, he's not,' Asvina said, 'and now he's blaming me for not tying up all the loose ends, as he puts it. He seems to think I've got some sort of legal magic wand that can make it all just go away.'

'Well, at least I've got good news for him about the lovely Lotti. That might cool him down a bit.'

Asvina smiled. 'I hope so. Anyway, I think I might need your help on this Maggie. I'll give you a call later.' She gave Maggie a hug then glided over towards the lift.

The imminent departure of his divorce lawyer appeared to have calmed Morgan's mood. He smiled at Maggie and Jimmy. 'You guys ok to wait until Inspector Stewart's finished with me?'

'They're my pals,' Frank said. 'They can sit in if they want. As I said, I'll only be a few minutes.'

Jimmy gave a thumbs up. 'Fine by us. If you don't mind Hugo that is.'

He shrugged. 'Whatever. But let's get this done. I'm a busy man.'

'Aye, so I've heard,' Frank said. 'That's twice now.'

Morgan ignored the dig, leading them through to his office.

'Grab a chair,' he said, gesturing at the conference table. 'Anywhere you like.'

Jimmy had taken the seat next to Frank and for the first time, Morgan recognised the obvious likeness.

'Wait a minute. Are you two...'

'Aye, brothers,' Jimmy said. 'Just a coincidence, that's all. I'm the amateur, he's the professional, although you wouldn't know it to look at him.'

'Thanks pal,' Frank said, shooting him a wry smile. 'Anyroads Mr Morgan, I don't want to take any more of your time than necessary. The thing is, I'm investigating a couple of suspicious deaths, and it turns out one of them has a connection back to your company.'

'Well of course Inspector,' he said smoothly, 'I'll do everything I can to help you.'

'The firm in question is HBB Bank. I'm right that there's a connection there?'

'We invest in that company, that is true, but then we have positions in more than three hundred organisations across the globe.'

Frank nodded. 'Aye, but I think that one's a bit different. You didn't just have a position in that outfit, as you put it. As I understand, you were very actively involved.'

Morgan smiled. 'Naturally. It's what we do. Activist investors. But we're not involved in the day-to-day management of any of our companies. Our job is to ensure the leadership of firms we invest in is focussed on delivering value to shareholders, and when it isn't, we act. That was the case at HBB and yes, we took steps to effect change. But there's nothing unusual in that, I can assure you. As I said, it's what we do.'

'Aye, that might be the case, but you see, not everybody sees it in as straightforward terms as you do sir.'

Morgan's eyes narrowed. 'What do you mean?'

'I'm sure you're familiar with the concept of industrial espionage. At least, that's what the top financial guy at HBB was suggesting when I interviewed him. He thinks that's how you find out about all this internal stuff that's supposed to be confidential.'

He shook his head slowly and gave a sardonic laugh.

'Dear dear, not these tired old conspiracy theories again. I hate to disappoint you, but there's no magic Inspector. We just look harder at the numbers than others are prepared to do, that's all. Because believe me, it's all there in black and white if you know where to look.'

Frank smiled. 'Well I'll need to take your word for that sir. Now can I ask you, do you have any involvement with Alexia Life?'

He smiled. 'No, afraid not inspector. They're a mutual you see, *so* nineteenth century. They're run by a spectacularly useless management, but since they're owned by their policy holders, unless there's a mass revolt to kick out the moronic leadership team, I doubt much will change there. It hasn't for the last two hundred years, so I don't see why it will now.'

'I must say sir, you do seem to know a lot about them. For someone who's not involved I mean.'

Morgan shrugged. 'Business is my hobby Inspector. It's sad I know, but where other people waste their time reading trashy novels, I study the business pages. It's paid off handsomely, I think you'll agree.'

'Aye, if you say so,' Frank said. 'But coming back to the folks who died, Chardonnay Clarke at HBB and Luke Brown at Alexia. Did you know them?'

His voice took on a condescending tone. 'As I told you before, we're not involved in day-to-day management of our investments. I may have some interaction with the senior leadership, but even that is limited. I certainly wouldn't have any reason to know such junior staff.'

Frank was silent for a moment as if weighing up his next move. Maggie was studying him closely, fascinated to watch such a consummate professional at work. When she was just starting out as a lawyer, she often had to sit in on police interviews as a duty solicitor, so the situation wasn't new to her. But she'd seldom seen anything to match this, the tone of his questioning finely judged, gently probing but without risking an aggressive reaction which she knew would be counter-productive. However, to her surprise it seemed as if he was minded to draw the short interview to a close, as he nodded and said,

'No, I see now you wouldn't have known them sir. Well, it was just a loose strand of my enquiry that I had to follow up. Sorry to have troubled you.' He got to his feet and smiled at Jimmy and Maggie. 'Maybe catch up with you two in the pub later? Anyway, must dash. Got some bad guys to catch.'

***

She waited until Frank had left the room before speaking. 'He always says that, the bit about bad guys I mean. And he's very good at it, apparently. Catching them.'

Jimmy laughed. 'Aye, so he says.'

'If that's the case,' Morgan said, half-serious, 'maybe I should ask him to look at the Justice for Greenway matter. Unless of course you've got something for me.'

Maggie smiled. 'Well as it happens, we've already asked him to help. Strictly in an unofficial capacity, but then again more or less everything he does starts off as unofficial.'

Morgan looked surprised. 'I didn't know you guys worked with the police.'

'Not the police per say,' she said. 'Just Frank.'

'And has he been able to help?'

'A little. Let's just say there's been some progress on the matter, but perhaps before Jimmy updates you on what we've found out, we can share some good news about Lotti.'

Morgan's eyes lit up. 'Good news? That sounds excellent.'

'Yes, I think it is,' Maggie said, then went on to tell him about how they had spoken to her mother who confirmed that her daughter Lotti was working in London, and that they also had confirmation from the University of Heidelberg that she had graduated from that prestigious institution as she had claimed. She didn't say anything about the fact she had doubted Lotti was as old as she had told her fiancé she was. That had been disproved by the facts, and so had to be dismissed as an issue.

Finally they addressed what could have been the trickiest matter, Lotti's fidelity or otherwise. Which in the end turned out to be the most straightforward of all, Jimmy explaining how he had sought to find out whether or not she was single, and had made it crystal clear he was interested in her whatever her answer. And how she had politely but firmly made it equally clear that she was not interested because she was blissfully happy in her existing relationship.

'So I think it's safe for you to make your arrangements for the big proposal,' Maggie said, smiling. 'Porto Banus, wasn't it?'

Morgan looked as if the emotion of the moment might overcome him. His face broke into a huge beaming smile, and Maggie saw him clenching and unclenching his fists. 'Brilliant news,' he said, 'that's brilliant news.'

She shrugged. 'Glad we could help. And she really is a lovely girl, you're very lucky.' But of course it had nothing to do with luck. This was the man who had quite coldly decided he wanted a new and younger wife and had simply discarded the old one when he was finished with her. Not for the first time she found herself hoping that the same fate would befall him when he was sixty and wrinkly and Lotti had decided there was more to life than just money. That would be a cracking moment of schadenfreude.

'So these Justice for Greenway people,' Morgan said, changing the subject. 'Tell me what you've got.'

Jimmy smiled. 'Will do. Right, so it made sense to start our investigation up in Cumbria. Seemed odds-on that it would be centred around there obviously, given where the mine is. By good fortune, we found a contact on the local paper, a nice lady called Liz Donahue. Smart too. Your mate Gary whats-it gave us her name.'

Morgan grimaced. 'That arse McGinley.'

'Funnily enough, that's what Liz called him too. Anyway, it turns out there's been a couple of incidents up there as well, directed mainly at Belinda Milner. The woman who drowned herself.'

'Yes, a terrible tragedy,' Morgan said, without emotion.

Jimmy nodded. 'Aye it was, a real tragedy. Anyway, they graffiti'd her house and her car, and I heard that they also tried to poison her dog. So kinda similar to the stuff you've experienced. But to cut to the chase, Liz Donahue pointed me to a local family. The Tompkins.'

Morgan gave him a sardonic look. 'Ah yes, the investment geniuses. Bet all their savings on Milner's lame horse then started bitching when it fell at the first.'

Jimmy looked at him sharply. 'Christ Hugo, William Tompkins killed himself because of the shame of it all. That's not something to joke about.'

He shrugged. 'I don't see it as my problem. So you think it may be them behind this?'

'We went to see them. Liz and I met two of the sons, Wayne and Karl. They're pretty sore about the whole thing and I'd put money on them being behind the Milner incidents. The one's down here in London, we're not too sure of at the moment, although Karl looks a nasty piece of work so I wouldn't put it past him. And he was a sapper in the Royal Engineers, so he'd have the wherewithal, there's no doubt about that.'

'That's where Frank - DI Stewart - comes in,' Maggie said. 'If either of them was involved, we think they would have driven down in his car or in his father's old van rather than taking the train. Frank is going to pull a few favours to get a couple of the traffic cameras on the M6 checked out, see if we can spot him en route.'

It was flimsy, she knew it was, but the good news about Lotti seemed to have had a positive effect on Morgan's mood. He shrugged, 'Well ok, let's wait and see where that takes us. Is that us done then?'

He half got up, seemingly anxious to bring the meeting to a close.

'There's just one more thing Hugo, if you don't mind,' Jimmy said quickly. 'It's kinda related to the injunction you took out against the Chronicle.' The one you conveniently omitted to mention, Maggie thought.

Morgan said nothing, but his expression had hardened as Jimmy continued.

'The wee local paper up there, the Westmoreland Gazette, they had a story that they tried to syndicate out to the Chronicle. I think that's the right term. But apparently McGinley had different ideas. Something about the South African guy, Mark De Bruin. McGinley thinks he's the one who told you about the screw-up with the cobalt content.'

'McGinley's a fool as well as an arse,' Morgan said. 'I raised that injunction just as a bit of fun. Now the idiots at the Chronicle are going to spend half a million to fight it, but what they don't know is I intend to drop the action five minutes before the judge announces his verdict. God, they're going to look so stupid.'

'So that's what it's all about?' Maggie said. 'Some sort of private vendetta against Gary McGinley?'

Morgan gave a smug smile. 'Exactly right. It's sport actually. His tiny little head is full of stupid conspiracy theories, but as I've said many times, there's no magic. And this one was all in the numbers, plain as the nose on your face.'

'What do you mean?' Jimmy asked, surprised.

'Eight weeks after Greenway were supposed to have been bringing all that lovely cobalt-rich ore to the surface, the revenue line in their monthly trading updates was still showing a big fat zilch. Nothing. Oh sure, our Belinda was spouting a load of shit about tidying up some fine print in their sales contracts, but I knew that was rubbish. If that ore was yielding like they said it would, they would have recognised the revenue there and then, contract or no contract. So you see, no magic. You just need to know where to look, and we do.'

The more Maggie thought about it, the more plausible his account seemed. She hated to admit it, but it seemed a lot more credible than the frankly wild suggestions of dark industrial espionage that Jimmy had uncovered up in Cumbria. But then again, she knew that even in the short time he had known the Westmoreland Gazette reporter, he had come to trust Liz Donahue implicitly. And if Jimmy Stewart trusted this woman whom she was yet to meet, then that was good enough for her.

'Jimmy's contact seems pretty sure there was more to it than that,' Maggie said, but then, anxious not to raise Morgan's hackles added, 'but from what you said about those monthly trading things, then maybe she's wrong.'

'Aye, and I didn't really get the full story anyway,' Jimmy said, tuning into where she was coming from, 'All Liz said was something about pillow talk, and to be honest, I haven't been able to make head or tail of it. But we'll find out soon enough, because I think her paper's planning on running her story at the weekend.'

Morgan sneered. 'Pillow talk did you say? Well, I'm sure it will be great entertainment for the locals. And no doubt your reporter friend, what was her name...?'

'Liz Donahue.'

'... yes, well no doubt your Miss Donahue will enjoy her fifteen minutes of fame.'

Morgan pushed back his chair and stood up, the smooth facade fully restored. 'I think we've made some progress, and once again, thank you both for putting my mind to rest about Lotti. It's a big weight off my shoulders, it really is.'

He ushered them towards the door. 'And if you and your pet policeman dig up anything more about those Justice morons, let me know immediately.'

Afterwards when she discussed the meeting with Jimmy, she couldn't help thinking that somewhere along the line they had missed something, and she said as much to him. He also agreed there was something, a vague something he couldn't quite put his finger on, but aye, definitely something. And then out of the blue, she realised what it was. Because when she replayed Frank's interview in her mind, she was certain he hadn't said anything about Charlotte and Luke being junior staff. So how the hell did Hugo Morgan know? Now she understood why Frank had been perfectly happy for the interview to be short and sweet. Because he had noticed too.

***

They normally met on a Thursday evening, but this time they had agreed on a supplementary lunchtime date earlier the same day. The Old King's Head was packed as usual, customers being attracted by what was in City terms a good-value menu. Charging twelve to fifteen quid for a main, it served pub staples like lasagne and steak and ale pie, nothing too fancy, but it was proper food, not the pre-prepared microwaved stodge favoured by the big chain places that she knew Frank despised. You couldn't reserve a table, so timing was everything if you wanted to bag a place. Either get there before twelve-fifteen, or wait until about half past one to be in the vanguard of the second wave. They had chosen the former option, turning up at a minute past the hour and had managed to grab a little table tucked away in the corner. It was barely big enough for three, but the quiet location meant it was just about possible to conduct a normal conversation. And they had a lot to talk about.

'He's quite an operator our boy Hugo, isn't he?' Frank said, as Jimmy brought the drinks back to the table. Maggie was glad that it hadn't taken long, because sitting there alone with Frank, even for just a couple of minutes had been, as she had expected, awkward. And confusing too, because she was a forty-two-year-old woman and she ought to by now be able to make sense of her feelings. Frank was nice, more than nice, but then, casting a huge shadow over everything, there was Robert. Already that relationship had become carnal, as lovely as it was unexpected, and everything had been going swimmingly until she had discovered that Mr Robert Trelawney hadn't been exactly honest with her. Somehow omitting to mention the presence of Felicity Morgan in his life. Not exactly a lie though, it had to be said. It was not as if he was pretending to be a completely different person entirely. Not like her. *Robert, I've got something to tell you. You see, I'm not actually Mrs Magdalene Slattery.* Now *that* would be a conversation.

'Yeah he certainly is,' Jimmy said, responding to his brother's observation. 'Food should only be five minutes by the way. Pie for me again.'

'Great, I'm starving,' Maggie said, pleased to be able to focus once again on the mundane. 'So Frank, getting back to Hugo Morgan, I'm thinking you noticed that thing about the interns?'

'Aye, I spotted it. How did he know they were junior staff when I never mentioned it once?'

'Exactly. Have you any ideas what it means?'

He shrugged. 'Well it means he knew of course, but why, that's a different matter. That's why I wanted to talk to you guys, see if you can help me shed some light on it. You see, I thought it would have been connected to his Brasenose Trust business, given that Chardonnay worked at HBB Bank, and we know he was knee-deep in that, with the German takeover and everything. But Luke Brown was assigned to Alexia Life, and the financial guy at HBB said exactly the same as Morgan, that it's a mutual so doesn't have any shareholders. Meaning there was nothing for Morgan to buy into or anything like that. No connection at all as far as I can see. A dead end.'

'Could it be something personal then?' Jimmy asked. 'We know he likes them young. Maybe he was having an affair with Chardonnay.'

Maggie gave a half-smile but she wasn't convinced. 'But not with Luke surely? No, I'm certain as I can be that his relationship with Lotti is important to him. He's not faking that, I mean why else would he employ Asvina to do the due diligence? I don't like the man, but he's not a sexual predator. You can always tell, and he's not.'

'Aye, you're probably right,' Frank said, sighing. 'I've got one of my team taking a look at Luke Brown's situation. We don't really know anything about him, except that he was another one of that agency's scholarship kids. Maybe that will turn up a missing piece in the jigsaw.'

'They both died in the same way didn't they?' she said. 'The suicides that weren't suicides.'

'Aye. The Aphrodite suicides, that's what I'm calling them now. Two good-looking kids. Special kids.'

'Except they were murders, not suicides.' Maggie said. 'You're sure of that now.'

'No question, but as to why they were killed, I'm still at base camp. I've got no motive and no suspects but apart from that it's going great.'

She laughed. 'Maybe you should subcontract to us. We've wrapped up the Lotti matter already, in double-quick time, and we're making some progress on Justice for Greenway too.' She hoped he would take it as a joke. Looking at him, she wasn't sure he had.

'Aye, maybe it will come to that,' he said, unsmiling. 'But I think you had a suicide too, am I right?'

Jimmy nodded. 'Yeah, but this one's not suspicious like yours. Belinda Milner, she was the boss of the mine. One morning she just put on her costume and took a swim in the lake. Left a husband and teenage daughter.'

An elderly waitress had arrived with their food, her expression broadcasting that she would rather be anywhere on earth but here.

'Who's the pie?' she snapped, staring vacantly into space.

'Aye, that's me,' Jimmy said, standing up. 'Here, let me help you with that.' He took the plate from her and smiled.

Maggie shot Frank a knowing look. *She'll melt*, it said, *they always do.*

And she did. 'Oh, thank you sir,' she said, beaming. 'It's always so busy in this place, run off my feet I am. People don't appreciate it.'

'Aye, tough job, I can see that. He's the lasagne and she's the fish and chips. Here, pass them over, save you stretching.'

He took the plates from her and laid them on the table.

'Right guys, tuck in. Thanks miss, we'll give you a shout when we want some more drinks, ok?'

The waitress nodded her appreciation and slipped away to collect her next order. For a few minutes they concentrated on their meal until Frank, through a mouthful of lasagne said,

'So this Milner woman. Do you two have any idea why she did it? I suppose *that* must be connected to Morgan in some way. Given all the Greenway Mining crap and that.'

'It's a bit of puzzle,' Jimmy said, 'because by all accounts the collapse of Greenway on her watch wouldn't have affected her one bit, certainly not enough to make her kill herself. She was one of these smooth Establishment types you see, the type that seem to flit from failure to failure with no apparent effect on their careers.'

'Yes, plenty of them about,' Maggie said. 'That's one of the things we're trying to find out. Because there must have been something else that drove her to that awful act.'

'And I think we're going to find out pretty soon. Liz Donahue's paper's running a story in the next few days.' Jimmy nodded in Frank's direction. 'It ties up with the stuff that you heard from the HBB financial guy, industrial espionage and all that. I think her story is going to spill the beans on how Morgan found out about that problem with the cobalt content.'

'And you think there's a connection between that and Milner's death?' Frank asked.

'Got to be,' Maggie said. 'Morgan spun us some line about it all being in the numbers or in the monthly trading statements, but it sounded like bullshit to us. Or to me at least.'

'Aye, well that would be great for you,' Frank said. 'But being selfish, I don't think it helps me with my murders.'

Maggie shrugged. 'No, I guess you're right there. But maybe it reinforces what we probably already know about him. That he's not above sharp practice to get what he wants.'

But she knew it and Frank knew it and Jimmy knew it, although none of them said it. *Billionaire indulges in sharp business practices*. It didn't pass the test. The *so what* test.

Chapter 20

Frank swiped his debit card in the direction of Atlee House's new high-tech drinks dispenser and took grateful delivery of a *grande* double-shot Americano. Alongside, a sophisticated whirr from the equally hi-tech vending machine signified that a Mars Bar and a packet of cheese and onion crisps was about to join it, completing his lunch order. Scooping them up, he smiled to himself, reflecting on his earlier brief encounter with Hugo Morgan, and how excellent it was that he had caught him lying. An easy slip to make, not that he sympathised in any way, but now the connections were beginning to rack up and he loved it when that began to happen in a case. The Oxbridge Agency had supplied both Chardonnay Clarke and Luke Brown, and despite his denials, Morgan clearly knew of them both. And actually by an admittedly small margin, Luke was the more interesting of the two. Alexia Life was a mutual and therefore it was off limits as far as Brasenose's activist investor MO was concerned. So why would Morgan know of some insignificant intern in an organisation he had zero connection to?

Back at his desk, he pulled out an A4 pad from his drawer and began to doodle. He wasn't any sort of an artist, he knew that, but somehow these indecipherable sketches helped him organise his thoughts. *The connections*. Two identical murders made to look like suicides, the stand-out good looks of the victims, the Oxbridge Agency, the modest backgrounds, the billionaire Hugo Morgan. It all had to mean something, and he'd figure it out soon enough.

On a whim, he picked up his phone and called Ronnie French. It rang nearly a dozen times before he answered, Frank assuming that the fat turd was probably snoozing in a favourite lay-by somewhere off the beaten track. But he was wrong.

'*Guv?*'

'Where are you Frenchie? I need you to do something for me.'

'Me? I'm in Atlee. On the top floor with your pal Eleanor Campbell.'

'What, with Campbell?' This was a surprise to Frank, because he couldn't think what business Ronnie could possibly have with the young forensic officer.

'Yeah guv, there's been a bit of a development with my mate Jayden and your pal is helping me instead. With that Guernsey bank account. You know, Rosalind Holdings.'

'Right, stay there and I'll come and join you as soon as I've finished my lunch.'

Five minutes later, he was at her desk and pulling up a chair alongside them.

'You're keeping some dodgy company these days Miss Campbell.'

She shot him a sardonic smile. 'Yeah, like you for instance. But look at this,' she said pointing to the wide-screen laptop that seemed to cover half of her desk. 'It's running this Fraudbreaker app with sixty-four-bit decryption and eight-layer packet tracing straight out of the box. Ronnie got me it. It's like awesome.'

'I got it from Jayden,' Ronnie said in way of explanation. 'He doesn't need it at the moment due to him being sort of incapacitated. So I sort of borrowed it.'

'Along with all his passwords,' Eleanor said helpfully.

Frank grimaced. 'Christ Ronnie, I thought you said your Jayden Henry guy works for the anti-terrorist division.'

'Yeah, so? We're not doing nothing wrong, are we?'

Frank could think of a dozen things they were doing wrong, starting with theft of valuable government property, which got him pondering how Ronnie had managed to sneak it out of MI6's offices over on Albert Embankment in the first place. For the second time in a week, he wondered if he might be guilty of underestimating the corpulent slug.

'Anyway guv, what did you want me to do for you?'

Frank smiled. 'That can wait for a bit. I want to watch what's going on here first. It looks interesting.'

'You can watch, but you won't understand any of it,' Eleanor said, matter-of-factly.

'I won't,' he answered, smiling. 'That's why we pay you your pittance. But how come you got a hold of this piece of kit? Frenchie, tell us what happened to your mate Jayden.'

Ronnie shrugged. 'Our boy Jayden got caught with his trousers down. With his wife's sister. A bit of a doll so I've heard. Anyways, word got out in the community and he had the shit beaten out of him. You know what them black lads are like, all that disrespect stuff and all that.'

Frank gave him an angry look. 'Ronnie, I've told you once and I'll tell you again, if I hear any more of that bloody racist nonsense from you or anything like it, I'm going to haul you up in front of HR so fast that the skin will be scraped off your arse on the way. I won't bloody have it on my watch, you hear?'

He gave another shrug. 'Loud and clear boss.' In one ear and out the other more like, and it was too late to do anything about it now, no matter how many courses they forced the fat twat to sit through. But he meant what he said. One more strike from Frenchie and he was out.

'So you say he's incapacitated then?' Frank said, trying to calm himself.

'Yeah, and some. Stuck in the Royal Free and looks like he'll be in there for a week or two. But he gave me his pass and so I just wandered in to pick up his stuff.'

'What, you just waltzed into the headquarters of MI6, and then waltzed out again with a laptop the size of a wide-screen telly?'

French looked puzzled. 'I had a pass,' he said simply.

'God save us,' Frank muttered under his breath.

Frank noticed for the first time that Eleanor was holding something in her hand, a slim plastic device that looked a bit like an old-school iPod music player.

'What's that?' he asked.

'It's for two-factor authentication. I've told you about it before but you won't have remembered.'

'That was Jayden's too,' French said. 'You know when you're paying someone new on your banking app, or you're logging on from a different device it sends an authorisation code to your phone? Well this is a fancy gizmo that lets the spooks intercept the code. Some stonking software behind it and make no mistake.'

Frank gave him a look of astonishment. 'So you're an IT geek Frenchie? Who'd have thought it.'

French smiled. 'Not really guv. My lad's a programmer and I've picked up the lingo from him.'

'Are we like ready?' Eleanor said, not bothering to hide her impatience.

'Aye sure,' Frank said. 'Let's go.'

She hammered a few keys of the laptop, bringing up what looked like a bank statement.

'See, that's Chardonnay's and there's the six thousand you guys are interested in.' She moved her mouse so it hovered over the line in the statement. Immediately, a box popped up containing three rows of text. *Account Name, Sort Code, Account Number*.

'See, that's the account details of who paid it in. The Fraudbreaker software retrieves that from a high-security mega transaction database shared by the banks.'

'Don't tell me,' Frank said, stifling a laugh.

'What?' Eleanor said.

'It's awesome.'

'Well, like, it is,' she said, in a tone that questioned why anyone could possibly think otherwise.

Punching in a few more characters caused a dialogue box to pop up in the centre of the screen.

Welcome to Internet banking.
Enter user code and password.

'We don't need to worry about this.' A few seconds later, the device in her hand gave a gentle vibration. Immediately the lap top display changed.

Enter one-time access code.

She glanced at the device and carefully keyed in the six-digit number. 'We're in,' she said, pointing to the display, which was showing another statement, this time for Rosalind Holdings, an account held with Guernsey Bank.

'So does this work globally?' Frank said, vaguely aware that organisations and individuals often tried to hide their financial affairs behind a complex web of international accounts.

'Pretty much, according to the system docs.'

'Jayden gave us them too,' French said, with no hint of apology.

'Although not Russia or China,' Eleanor continued, 'defo not, but then, guys take their money out of these places, they don't put it in.'

'Sweet.' It was one of her favourite expressions and Frank liked to drop it into conversation just to annoy her. But this time she chose to ignore him, continuing to manipulate her mouse around her desk.

'So, this is like interesting. I've scrolled back a few months and look...' She clicked to highlight a line.

'RGBX. No idea who this is but they're paying forty thousand Euros a month into this account.' She clicked on the line and the same dialogue box as before popped up.

'Looks like a Santander account. That code's for their Spanish branches. The IBAN. So it's in Spain.'

'So this maybe explains where Rosalind gets some or all of their funding,' Frank said, surprising himself that for once he actually seemed to understand what she was talking about. 'Now you can use this mega database thing to get to RGBX's account, and then the Fraudbreaker stuff and that wee iPod gizmo gets you in. Or is it the other way around?'

Eleanor looked equally surprised. 'You're sharp this afternoon, aren't you? Yeah, like you're right, exactly. But maybe there'll be lots of layers in the web, so it might take a while to get back to the original source. And there will probably be a few false trails. Or maybe the trail will go cold. So it's not that simple.' Frank knew her well and was able to read between the lines. Stop looking over my shoulder and let me get on with my work in peace.

He gestured at French. 'Come on, Ronnie, she doesn't need an audience. Let's wander downstairs and chew the fat about the case whilst she's working on it.'

'Yeah, sure guv. Off you go and I'll catch up with you in a minute.'

Frank got up and headed towards the stairwell. Taking a glimpse back, he saw Ronnie scribble something on a piece of paper then give Eleanor a thumbs-up, which she returned with her normal disdainful look. Intrigued, he waited for him to catch up with him.

'What was all that about Frenchie?'

'What? Aw, nothing guv, just a thought I had. Eleanor's going to take a look but as I say it might be nothing.'

It seemed that he wasn't going to give anything more away, so they went back down to Frank's office where he updated Ronnie on his interesting interview with Hugo Morgan, conscious of a growing respect for his DC. Sure, Frenchie was the laziest man ever to be issued with a warrant card, but when it came to sniffing out a wrong 'un, as he might put it, it seemed his instincts were of the highest order. Frank wondered what he would make of Morgan, whether he would see through the effortlessly smooth facade, whether he would sniff out the lies that hid behind it. Because that's the job he had pencilled in for his colleague. Put the shambolic detective constable in front of Morgan and see if the billionaire, to his cost, underestimated him too.

Out of the blue, French said, 'So who do you think is behind this guv? These payments I mean.'

So Frank told him who he thought was responsible, and French, amiably disagreeing, gave him his contrary view, and then they agreed a modest wager on the outcome. Thirty-five minutes later, Eleanor Campbell appeared, laptop under her arm and a deep frown on her forehead, which Frank knew from experience meant that she had cracked it, and after a lengthy preamble describing the mountainous difficulties she had overcome, settled the bet. Forcing Frank to reach into his wallet and withdraw a crisp new ten-pound note.

***

'There's something else guv,' French said, after he'd tucked the tenner safely away in a trouser pocket. 'I asked her to look at the other one too, that Brown lad.'

Eleanor nodded. 'Fraudbreaker's got awesome search. You just like key in a name and it brings up every account they have. Luke Brown's only got one.'

'Don't tell me,' Frank said, excited. 'He was getting six grand a month too.'

'What?' Eleanor said, looking puzzled. 'Like, no way. He gets nineteen hundred a month from the Oxbridge Agency. That's like not much more than minimum wage.'

Eleanor was exaggerating of course, but this was nothing like the seventy-five grand that Chardonnay Clarke had been receiving. And then he remembered. *We also provide them with a nominal salary whilst they are on deployment.* That's what Sophie Fitzwilliam had told him, and nineteen hundred a month, or twenty-three grand a year, was certainly nominal. But there had to be something else. Because Luke Brown had been murdered in exactly the same way as Chardonnay Clarke. It was just a matter of finding it, that was all. He'd give it to Frenchie and wee Yvonne Sharp for forty-eight hours' max, and if that didn't work, he would have to dive in himself. Not a problem, that.

***

Fair play to Ronnie French, he hadn't tried to take the credit for it himself. That nudged him up a notch in Frank's estimation, although it didn't balance the fifty he'd gone down on account of him being a racist twat. But credit where credit's due, and it hadn't taken forty-eight hours, in fact it had barely taken forty-eight minutes.

'She spotted it right away guv,' he had said when he called Frank with the good news. 'On the bank statement. You see, Yvonne knows the threshold is twenty-one grand a year, so she says, why isn't this Luke paying nothing back? So we gives them a call up in Glasgow, all official like, and they confirmed it, sweet as a nut. Paid off in full it was. Nearly forty grand. Nine months ago. Lucky sod, that's what Yvonne said, to have your student loan paid off just like that.'

Aye, lucky sod, apart from the fact Luke Brown was dead. But now he had something more solid to work with and that was good. He knew Chardonnay was pulling down seventy-five grand and now he'd found out that the dead boy had his student loan paid off. Now that they more or less knew who, that just left one big question to be answered. Why?

Chapter 21

Oh what a tangled web we weave, when first we practice to deceive. Everybody knew the quotation, and everyone knew what it meant, although Maggie, with no little smugness, reflected that not everyone knew it was Sir Walter Scott and not William Shakespeare who had come up with it in the first place. *What a bloody mess you get yourself into when you pretend to be somebody else entirely.* That might be a better way of describing the situation she now found herself in, or to be more accurate, *they* found themselves in.

Felicity Morgan, the bitter ex-wife, had decided to challenge the settlement that everyone involved thought was long done and dusted, and was now asking for another seventy million on top of the thirty million she had already been awarded. On the basis that a journalist - the trouble-maker Gary McGinley -had seemingly discovered that her ex-husband had squirreled away a tidy fortune over in the Channel Islands, out of sight of the authorities. And now Asvina Rani, having failed in her technical bid to prevent the original deal being contested in court, and getting some serious grief from her client Hugo Morgan as a result, had to come up with a Plan B. Which was to find out how much the ex-wife really knew. Or rather, to get Bainbridge Associates to find out for her.

The only problem was, Maggie Bainbridge was now Magdalene Slattery and Jimmy Stewart was James McDuff. And the former Mrs Morgan had met them both, which left them with only one option if they were to win the trust of Mrs Morgan, enough to get her to share confidences. An option that Jimmy was probably not going to like. But to her surprise, he didn't object at all.

'I thought you were going to ask me to seduce her'.

Maggie laughed. 'Seduce her? How delightfully old-fashioned.'

'And I was going to say *no way*. The next Mrs Morgan, that was bad enough, but the old one, that would be a step too far. That sort of stuff's not in my employment contract you know.'

'Of course it isn't.' They both knew no such document existed, but that didn't stop him referring to it whenever she asked him to do something he didn't like. 'But you'll do it then?'

'Aye, no bother. But no seduction stuff, ok?'

'Of course not. All we want is to find out where's she coming from. See if she really has anything concrete about Hugo's finances so we can report back to Asvina.'

So he picked up his phone and called Felicity Morgan.

'Felicity? This is James McDuff, we met at that auction a couple of days ago, do you remember? What it is, I think your man's cheating with my lady.'

Two hours later, he was back in the entrance atrium of the Park Lane Hilton, just a few weeks after attending that eventful quarterly update of the Brasenose Investment Trust. Arriving ten minutes early, he found a seat tucked along a wall of the room and settled down to read that day's *Chronicle* which a previous occupant had left behind. Absorbed in a story about cuts to military budgets, he failed to notice that twenty minutes had passed and there was still no sign of Mrs Morgan. Glancing at his watch again, he was about to wander over to the reception when he caught her out the corner of his eye, dressed in the same skinny black jeans, leather blouson and stilettos as in their previous brief encounter. But unexpectedly, she wasn't alone.

Today, trailing a metre or so behind her and wearing an archetypal teenage scowl was a young woman who he assumed must be her daughter. Felicity Morgan marched up to the reception desk and, ignoring a Japanese couple who were in the middle of checking out, said loudly. 'I'm meeting someone. A Mr James McDuff.'

The young receptionist, obviously displeased by the interruption, gave her a cold look then nodded wordlessly towards where he sat.

'Thank you. Come on Rosie.'

She tottered over to him and sat down opposite.

'This is my daughter Rosie. We're booked in for lunch at one, so I haven't got long. Family time is so important, don't you think?'

Rosie Morgan was attractive, although it was difficult to tell under the layers of Goth-punk make-up. Her eyes were encircled in black mascara and her lips coated in a deep navy gloss. She wore purple Doc Martins, ripped fishnets and a skirt so short it barely covered her bottom. In a different way from her mother, she too looked amazing. But she wore a look suggesting she regarded the date as duty rather than pleasure. And then he remembered that the kids had chosen to live with their father rather than their mother. One day he would try to find out why they had made that choice, but today wasn't that day. Whatever the case, her presence was going to make the meeting a bit awkward. But he'd been on some tough missions in his time, and by comparison this would be a walk in the park. So he got straight on to it.

'Aye, I'm in a hurry too. So, I was checking my lady's phone. I always do that when she's not around. Doesn't even have a pin code, stupid bitch. That's when I saw them. Texts, loads of them. I thought you should know.'

She gave him an angry look. 'I don't believe it. Not my Robert.' *My Robert*. He'd heard *that* one before.

'Aye, that's exactly what I thought, not my Magdalene. But it's true. And I don't know about you, but I'm not going to stand for it.'

'But you're all the same you men. Use us for sex and then throw us away when you get bored. We had fantastic sex you know, the night before he dumped me. He never could have any cause for complaint in that department. I was a bloody fantastic shag all through our marriage. Anything he ever wanted, and I never had a headache, not like some women.'

Confused, Jimmy eventually cottoned on to the fact she was talking about her ex-husband. And now she was in full flow.

'He was a pig you know,' she said, taking no trouble to hide her bitterness. 'And Robert's a pig too. You're all pigs.' He was taken aback by the ferocity of this woman's anger. Her rejection had clearly opened a wound that didn't look as if it was going to heal anytime soon.

'And look at me. I'm still attractive and sexy, aren't I? James, do you find me sexy? You do, don't you?'

'Mum!' Her daughter's embarrassment was so acute you could almost taste it.

'Well, aye...,' Jimmy said, 'you're a very attractive woman Felicity.' And as mad as a box of frogs he thought, but he didn't say it.

'That's it mum, I'm going.' Rosie was on her feet, slinging her bag over her shoulder, her eyes burning with anger. 'Some other time, ok?'

'Rosie, please...' Felicity reached out a hand, trying to grab hold of the bag, but with a deft flick, her daughter swung it out of her reach, before hurrying off towards the door.

Now she was speaking so loudly that everyone in the atrium could hear her. Jimmy suspected that was her intention. 'You see, he's turned them against me. Her and Yazz. All of them. Fucking daddy is so wonderful and perfect, that's what he's got them believing. But if only they knew the truth, they would think differently, believe me.'

He gave her what he hoped was a sympathetic look. 'Kids eh? It must be awful for you, I can understand that, everything that's happened. But you know, you have to move on, there's not really any other option.'

God where had that come from? Jimmy Stewart, the relationship councillor.

'I don't want to get over it,' she said bluntly. 'I want him to suffer, the way I'm suffering. For the rest of his damn life. Fuck him. And fuck Robert Trelawney too.'

He looked up to see a smartly-suited man approaching them at speed. On his lapel, the badge read 'George

Konstantinou, General Manager.' When he spoke, he was smiling but his tone was grave.

'I'm sorry madam, but we do not like to hear foul and abusive language in the hotel. I'd be very grateful if you could think of our other guests when you are speaking. Otherwise, and with the greatest reluctance I assure you, I will have to ask you to leave.' Talk about lighting the blue touch-paper. But just as Mrs Morgan was about to say something, and probably something both foul and abusive, Jimmy jumped in. He stood up and held out a hand, screwing up his eyes to read the badge. 'Mr Konstantinou, is that right? I'm James McDuff.' He spoke slowly, his gentle Scottish lilt apologetic and mollifying. 'Sorry, we were all getting a little bit excited back then but we're good now. Look, my companion and I are booked in for lunch, so maybe you could get someone to point us in the direction of the restaurant? It's under Morgan I believe. Table for two. And it would be good if you could find a nice private spot.' When next he saw Maggie, he'd make sure she knew that he had bloody taken one for the team.

It seemed to be enough to satisfy the manager, who was smiling again, this time with evident relief. He didn't want a scene, not here in his spectacular atrium in full view of his customers, and so he was grateful for this man's intervention. 'Certainly sir, madam. I'll take you there myself. Please, come this way.'

It also seemed to have had a temporarily calming effect on Felicity Morgan, who, standing up, had taken Jimmy by the arm and was already snuggling up against him, if not quite cheek-to-cheek, then not far off it.

'This will be so lovely, and so unexpected. And now I'll be able to tell you everything about me. And you can tell me about your bitch of a girlfriend. I want to know *all* about her.'

Chapter 22

The eighteen-twelve from Euston to Glasgow Central doesn't call at Oxenholme-for-Windermere, so waiting customers are told to stand well back from the platform edge. Wise advice, because no-one would want to be blown off their feet by the shock-wave of a Pendolino roaring through the station at over a hundred miles an hour. Or fall onto the track as it approaches from the south. At nine o'clock on that dull November evening, there hadn't been many passengers around, with the last northbound stopping train, a local for Penrith and Carlisle, not due for at least another forty minutes. So as a result, witnesses to the tragic event were thin on the ground. That is to say, non-existent.

The driver hadn't seen or felt anything, hardly surprising when four hundred tonnes of solid steel runs over fifty kilos of flesh and bone at a three-figure speed, and his train was already pounding up to Beattock summit over the border in Scotland before the message was relayed through to him. It was left to the station manager, doing a final sweep of his domain in preparation for closing up for the night, to make the stomach-churning discovery. Twenty minutes later, an inspector from the British Transport Police turned up to take charge of the incident. A quick call to the ops centre in Preston established that the northbound service could be switched to the top end of the southbound platform, well away from the mangled body of Liz Donahue, allowing service to continue with minimum disruption. By two o'clock the next morning, the incident medics had all they needed and the body, or what was left of it, was carted away to the mortuary.

***

Jimmy was surprised but pleased when he glanced at his phone to see who was calling him this early. It was barely six-thirty in the morning, but already he was up and dressed, and thinking back on his bizarre lunch with

Felicity Morgan. There was a lot to report to Maggie when he got into the office. The bill for a start, thankfully taken care of by his dining companion, which had run to a ridiculous four hundred pounds, inflated by the bottle of Louis Roederer Cristal she had insisted they ordered to accompany their meal. Her husband had been a pig and now it seemed Robert Trelawney was a pig too, that had been the thrust of the dialogue, or rather monologue, because she had done all the talking. Luckily, the ordering of the champagne had allowed him briefly to steer the conversation onto money, and she confirmed what they half-knew already. She had been sought out by the journalist Gary McGinley, who asked her what she knew about Brasenose Trust's network of shady offshore companies, set up to avoid the scrutinising gaze of nosey tax authorities. When she told him she knew nothing about it, and found it hard to believe his allegations were true, he had given her his evidence. Which explained why she was now looking for another seventy million quid from her ex.

'Hi Liz,' he said breezily. 'Must be important if you're calling me at this god-forsaken hour.' But it wasn't Liz on the other end of the line.

'Jimmy, it's Ruthie. Do you remember me? Liz's wife. Liz Donahue.'

Remember her? She'd hardly been out of his thoughts in the last two weeks. But there was something in her voice that caused his heart to pound, and instinctively he knew he was about to get some terrible news.

'Of course I remember. What's happened Ruthie?'

'She's dead Jimmy. She's dead.' He could hear her muffled sobs and another female voice urging her to take a sip of her tea.

'Christ, I'm so sorry. What happened, can you tell me that?'

'An accident, a terrible accident. At the station. Last night. They don't know exactly what happened, but she

fell in front...in front of a train. The police are here now. Oh God Jimmy, I don't know what to do.'

And then suddenly it struck him. This woman whom he had met only once, had chosen to call him no more than what was it, eight or ten hours after the tragic death of her wife. Why? Why of all people, had she called him?

He spoke as softly as he dared so that she could still hear him. 'Ruthie, what do you mean, you don't know what to do?'

'She wasn't here. She wasn't here when I got back from work. And it was her turn to cook on Wednesdays and she never ever missed it. And it was cannelloni, her favourite. She wouldn't have gone out without telling me.'

His mind was racing as he ran through a list of possibilities why Liz hadn't been at home to cook her wife dinner. She could have popped out to a convenience store in search of a missing ingredient. Or maybe, perhaps more likely, something had come up at work, a big local story that needed to be followed up right away. But in that case, there would have been a message. *Had to pop out. Big story. Back in an hour or so. All my love xxx.* Or something along those lines. But according to Ruthie, she had left no message, and in any case why did she end up at Oxenholme station? It wasn't inconceivable that something so big would come up that she needed to travel to London at short notice, but surely she wouldn't have done that without letting Ruthie know. No, there was only one logical conclusion. Liz Donahue had been abducted. And then murdered by person or persons unknown. Now there was urgency in his voice.

'Ruthie, what are the police saying? Have you told them that Liz wasn't there when you got home?'

She sounded confused, which he thought was hardly surprising given what had happened. *'What? Oh yes, there's a policewoman here at the moment. Should I tell her?'*

'Yes, tell her, definitely. And ask her to get her sergeant or an inspector involved. It's important, really important.'

'Ok,' she said, uncertainty in her voice, *'but why?'*

'Listen Ruthie, is there anyone you can stay with up there? Someone you can trust one hundred percent?'

'I...I don't know. Maybe Helen at book club. Her husband's a farmer, perhaps I could go there for a few days. Or I could go back to mum and dad's in Leeds.'

Jimmy thought for a moment. 'No, I don't want to alarm you Ruthie, but it's probably better not to stay with family right now. Helen sounds like a good bet.'

'Ok Jimmy,' she said, her voice wavering, *'and Jimmy, do you think this had got anything to do with the story she was working on? That's why I called you, I thought it might.'*

'I don't know. It's possible.' It was more than possible, it was a bloody certainty, but he didn't want to say that right at that moment. 'Look, just get in touch with your friend, but please, don't tell anyone else. I'm going to get up to see you as soon as I can. I should be able to get there this afternoon. Tell me, how much do you know? I mean about Liz's big story.'

'She didn't tell me everything I don't think, but I know quite a lot.'

Suddenly, there was another voice on the end of the phone, the tone prim and abrupt. *'Sir, this is police constable Fairburn. I don't think the young woman is in any fit state to continue with this, and in any case this is now a police matter. Thank you.'* And that was it. End of conversation. The policewoman was right, of course, it was a police matter now.

But then, with a sinking feeling, he remembered that case Frank was working on. Two kids who died in the same way. Two kids who minutes before their deaths, and posted suicide notes on their Facebook timelines. He wasn't much into social media, but he did, reluctantly, follow a few friends and acquaintances. With trepidation, he touched the icon to open the app. There it was in his timeline. Just six hours ago, a posting from Liz Donahue.

I'm sorry, I just can't go on.

Maybe it *was* a police matter, but Jimmy was certain of one thing. He needed to be on the next train to Oxenholme.

Chapter 23

Ruthie had arranged that her farmer's-wife friend would meet him at the station, and he would stay with them at their remote farm near Cartmel Fell for the duration of his visit. The train was just a few minutes late into Oxenholme, and as he stepped off onto the platform, he saw a woman wave then hurry along to him wearing a wide smile. In appearance, she was exactly as he expected, around forty and quite tall and broad-shouldered, dressed in faded jeans and a navy sweatshirt, with a mass of curly reddish hair held back by a mottled headband. She was attractive but he couldn't help thinking her husband would have first and foremost saw her as good breeding stock.

'You must be Jimmy Stewart,' she said, smiling. 'At least I hope so. You certainly fit the description.'

He held out a hand. 'Guilty as charged. And you must be Helen.'

'Yes, that's me. I'm just parked outside, follow me.'

She led him down the exit stairs and along a short underpass which led out to the road down to Kendal. A battered Subaru occupied the first drop-off space.

'This is us,' she said, blipping the remote locking. 'Sorry it's a bit messy inside. Combination of kids and sheep.'

'How many do you have?' he asked, tossing his bag into the back and settling into the passenger seat.

She laughed. 'Sheep, about eight hundred, kids about five at the last count. Four girls and a boy. The girls came first and Bill insisted we kept going until we got a boy. The men are a bit old-fashioned up here in that regard.'

Keeping going wouldn't have been any hardship for Bill with a wife like you, he thought, but he didn't voice it.

'It must be quite tough, farming up here I mean.'

'I suppose it is, but we get by. We're mainly Herdwicks and they're a hardy old breed. We've also got a dairy herd on the lower pastures near the lake and they do ok. It's hard work all right, but it's all we know. And the truth is we love it, even if we're always moaning.'

Once they were clear of Kendal, the journey took about thirty minutes, the narrow road winding up from the Lyth Valley into the remote fells where every now and again they caught a distant glimpse of majestic Windermere, sparkling in the afternoon sunshine. The farm was at the end of an unsurfaced lane about a half a mile from the road, with a traditional stone-built farmhouse and a clutch of modern corrugated iron sheds arranged round the muddy farmyard. Everything looked neat and tidy and well cared for. Ruthie evidently had heard their approach, emerging from the front door with her arms wrapped tightly around her. Even from thirty yards away he could make out the dark-ringed eyes and ashen complexion. It was just forty-eight hours since she had received the terrible news and God knows how she was coping with it. Not well, if first impressions meant anything.

She forced a half-smile as he approached her. 'Hello Jimmy. Thank you so much for coming.'

'Come on, let's go back inside and have some tea,' Helen said. 'It's getting chilly.'

They sat around an old oak table in the cosy farm kitchen, heated by a cast-iron range that looked old but that Jimmy suspected was a modern reproduction.

'So how have you been Ruthie?' He knew what the answer would be but he had to ask.

She shrugged. 'Shell-shocked I suppose. I still can't believe it's real. I keep looking at my phone, expecting her to call. We must have called each other a hundred times a day normally.'

Helen brought over mugs of tea and placed them in front of them. 'I'll leave you two for a while if you don't mind,' she said soothingly. 'It'll be time to pick up the kids soon.' She gave a half-smile then slipped out of the room.

'So what are the police saying?' he asked.

'Not very much,' she said. 'They've made enquiries at the station but nobody saw anything.'

'What, even on the CCTV?'

'It wasn't working. It hadn't been for a few days but they hadn't got round to fixing it.'

That didn't surprise him, not up here, where nothing ever happened. They'd probably never had to use it in anger since it was installed, so it wouldn't have been a priority.

'I guess they know about her post?' He hoped he could have approached the subject more delicately, but it had to come out.

She stared at the floor. 'Yes. I don't believe it. She would never have killed herself. And you saw how she was, didn't you?'

Was he misreading the situation, or was there an element of doubt in her voice?

'I did, and no, I don't believe she would have. No way.'

'We'd had words you see. That morning. And we never argued, never.'

He wondered whether he should ask her what the argument was about, but decided to leave it to her to decide. Instead he said. 'But the police are still investigating, aren't they?' he said. 'Taking it seriously I mean?'

'I don't know. They sent an inspector around, but she just kept asking me if Liz had been depressed. I had to tell her about the argument, although it was nothing.'

He guessed that they would be grateful for the easy way out, no doubt about it, because it was going to look much better for the clear-up statistics if you didn't open the case in the first place. Besides, people were stepping in front of trains every day, and often their loved ones hadn't had a clue that anything was wrong. Whereas people being murdered by being pushed in front of trains, he guessed that was a whole lot rarer. Except that right now, Frank was working on two.

'Look Ruthie, my brother's a DI in the Metropolitan Police, and he's on a case right now where two young kids died... well, in exactly the same way as Liz. And those were definitely suspicious.'

And at least one of them had a connection to Hugo Morgan and his Brasenose Trust. It seemed unlikely in the extreme, but now he began to wonder.

'I'm going to get Frank to call your inspector, I think it might help. I didn't know Liz very well, but there's no way she killed herself.'

Ruthie gave him a sad look, and again he wondered whether she was having doubts. After all, they said you never really knew the person you were married to.

'Ruthie, can we talk about the story? You know, the big one that Liz was working on. How much did she tell you about it?'

'Quite a lot but not everything. Actually, I'm not sure she knew everything. She said a few times she was just waiting for a couple of things to fall into place.'

Jimmy nodded. 'Aye, I know she was very secretive about it. All she said to me was *pillow talk*. Do you have any idea what she meant by that?'

'It was to do with Belinda Milner. Liz had found out that she had been having an affair, and she thinks that's maybe how the news about the mine's problems leaked out.'

'Pillow talk? Aye, now that makes sense. And this affair, how much did she know about it? Did she know who Belinda was having an affair with?'

She shook her head. 'That was the last thing she was working on. She guessed that her husband must have found out and maybe that's why she had killed herself. She'd arranged a meeting with him and I think that's what she meant when she said she was just waiting for a few things to fall into place.'

'Do you know where they live? The Milner family I mean.'

'Yes, over near Wastwater. I know where it is, but I don't have a phone number or email or anything.'

'Of course, it's on the lake isn't it? Where she drowned. Liz told me about it.'

Ruthie nodded. 'Yes it is. Wasdale House. It's up for sale. It must be terrible for them, looking out and remembering what happened.'

He glanced at his watch. Just past three o clock. He knew vaguely where it was, over on the western side of the National Park, sitting in the shadow of mighty Scafell Pike. Quite a trek from where they were, an hour and a half's drive at least. And Ruthie was in no fit state to drive him. But if he knew one thing, it was that Belinda Milner was the reason Liz Donahue was murdered. So he had get in front of her husband, and there was no time to lose. He ran out into the yard where he found Helen loading bags of feed into the back of an all-terrain pick-up. He gestured towards the Subaru.

'I know it's a lot to ask Helen, but can I borrow your car?'

***

Wasdale House was notable enough to get itself named on the Ordinance Survey map. According to his copy, it was tucked away between the narrow road and the lakeside, on a little peninsular that jutted out just where the Nether Beck tumbled into the lake. The journey had taken nearly two hours, the distance clocking up at fifty-three miles. He knew you couldn't get anywhere fast in this neck of the woods, but even still it had been a slow and tedious drive, the unforecast rain conspiring to negate the beauty of the landscape through which he'd passed.

It was now pitch black, and he was lucky that his headlights picked out the *For Sale* sign as he rounded a narrow bend. And then a red board that had been pinned below it. *Sold*. He hoped the family hadn't already upped and gone. Finding the entrance gates open, he swung the Subaru into the driveway, crunching over the gravel and pulling up at the front of the house, alongside a gunmetal Range Rover. Promising. His entrance triggered a trio of bright security lights, and he could see that the place was stunning, constructed in a honey sandstone under a red pantile roof with decorative leaded-glass windows. He was no student of architecture, but he guessed it was late Victorian or early twentieth century, probably built by some industrialist from the North-West who had made his money in the cotton trade or in shipping. He got out the car and wandered across to the entrance. The solid oak front door, sheltered beneath an arched porch, was equipped with a sturdy brass knocker. He gave it two sharp raps then waited. Nothing. After a minute or so, he tried again, but still there was no response.

'Mr Milner?' He thrust his hands in his pockets and walked to the side of the house, where he had spotted a gate in the white picket fence, presumably leading into the garden. He released the latch and went through, closing it behind him.

'Mr Milner?'

The garden sloped away to the lakeside, about a hundred and fifty feet away, barely visible under a watery moon. It was here just a few weeks earlier where Belinda Milner had decided to end it all and as he surveyed the scene, he found himself wondering how any human being could take that ultimate step. How deep did the depth of despair have to be and what if anything could drive you to it? In the darkness, he could just about pick out the shadowy outline of a man standing by the lakeside. The man who might be able to explain it.

'Mr Milner?'

The man spun round but didn't move, as if he was unsure how to react to this unexpected visitor. And then he made up his mind.

'Who the hell are you?' he shouted, with unmasked aggression. 'Get off my property or I'll call the police.' It wasn't an unreasonable reaction but Jimmy hadn't come all this way to be disappointed.

'I'm not here to cause any trouble, Mr Milner.' As he got closer, Jimmy recognised the pain and loss etched on his face, the same pain and loss as he had seen on Ruthie only two hours earlier. 'I think you'll find we're on the same side. But it's your call, naturally. A minute, that's all I need to explain what I need from you, and if you can't help, or don't want to, then that's ok, and of course I'll leave you in peace.' He realised he'd not actually answered Milner's question and it wasn't an easy one to answer. *Just who the hell was he, and why was he here?* Nominally, he was working for Hugo Morgan, but the matter had gone way beyond that. Now he was looking for justice for Liz Donahue, and by extension, maybe for Belinda Milner too. He decided that honesty was the best policy.

'My friend Liz Donahue died under the wheels of a train two days ago. I think she was murdered and I think the reason was connected in some way to your wife. And to Greenway Mining.'

'What are you, a policeman?'

'No, I'm not the police. I'm a private investigator, but I'm working in a personal capacity. As I said, Liz was a friend and I'm anxious to find out what happened to her.'

The man held out his hand, his aggression disappearing as quickly as it had arrived. 'I'm Rod. Rod Milner.'

Jimmy shook it warmly. 'Jimmy. Jimmy Stewart. Good to meet you Rod.'

'Come inside,' Milner said. 'I could do with a drink, what about you?'

Jimmy shot him a smile. 'Sure, I don't like to see a man drink on his own.'

'I've done a lot of that in the last few weeks believe me. It's only April that's stopped me following my wife into the lake to be honest. She's my daughter. Off with her grandparents at the moment whilst I sort out the house.'

They went into the house through a back door which led to a small room that Jimmy imagined was called a boot room or something similar, then onwards to the kitchen. It had the same farmhouse feel as Helen's, but a lot grander, as if it had stepped out of the pages of an upmarket homes and gardens magazine. Which it probably had.

'Malt?' Milner asked. 'I seem to keep a bottle in every room these days. This one's hiding in the wine rack.' He slipped it out of its receptacle and placed it on the large oak kitchen table.

'Brilliant,' Jimmy said. 'Can't ever go wrong with a nice single malt can you?'

Gesturing towards the table, Milner said. 'Please, take a seat.' He took a couple of glasses from a cupboard and poured a generous measure into each. Jimmy took his and lifted it in silent toast.

'Cheers Rod. So just for some background, I work for a wee investigations firm and we were originally engaged by Hugo Morgan to find out who was behind the Justice for Greenway stuff. He was getting some harassment from them and I know Belinda was a target too.'

He nodded. 'Yes, it was quite disturbing and of course it upset Belinda a lot. They vandalised our Range Rover and there were some nasty threatening letters posted through our door. Your friend Donahue wrote all about it in that paper she worked for.'

'I'm sorry to ask,' Jimmy said, 'but do you think it contributed to Belinda... to her taking her own life?'

He dropped his head, staring at the table, saying nothing. For a moment Jimmy wondered if he had heard him, until Milner, his voice barely a whisper, said, 'It wasn't that.'

'Sorry?'

'I said it wasn't that.' Jimmy saw that his hand was shaking as he drained his glass and reached over to refill it.

'I can understand how hard this must be for you Rod. You know, I can come back another time if it's any easier.' That was the last thing he wanted to do, but he knew from his army days that when you were dealing with someone who had suffered a great trauma, you were walking on eggshells.

'I guess it must have been hard for her,' he said. 'All the problems with the mine and everything.'

Milner gave a bitter laugh. 'You think? She didn't give a shit about that actually. *Teflon Milner,* that's what the Financial Times called her. Nothing ever stuck on her.' For the first time, Jimmy wondered about the state of the Milner marriage. He wasn't faking his distress over her death, of that he was sure, but there was something else going on between them, definitely. And then out of the blue, he told him what it was.

'She was having an affair.'

Pillow talk. Now it was all beginning to make sense.

Milner threw back his whisky and for the third time reached across for the bottle. Jimmy adopted what he thought was a sympathetic look, but said nothing, content for the story to unfurl at its own speed.

'She had a string of the bloody things of course. Non-executive directorships I mean. It always made me laugh, because she knew bugger all about any of them. That never stopped her of course. You see, it helped these big companies tick the box for gender diversity on their boards. She was a very attractive woman and she always looked good in the annual report.'

Jimmy nodded. 'Aye, I understand what you're saying.'

'Of course, the job up here with Greenway should have been enough for anyone, and god knows it needed a CEO who could give it their full attention. But they needed someone with a City reputation to raise the finance so they were prepared to accept that she knew two thirds of shit-all about mining.'

Again Jimmy nodded, but said nothing.

'But she started being away almost every week, getting an afternoon train down to London and not coming back to late the following evening. At first, I thought nothing of it, until one evening we were sitting at home when she got a message alert on her phone, which was lying on the coffee table. Absent-mindedly I stretched over to pick it up but she got there before me and snatched it away. That's what made me suspicious.'

Jimmy knew what that felt like. Except it had been him who had been the cheater, and he'd regretted it every day since. But now wasn't the time to dredge all that back up again. Instead he gave what he hoped was an understanding smile.

'So I followed her one day,' Milner said. 'Pathetic really. I got on the same train, then followed her out of Euston, down Southampton Row. When I saw the route she was taking, I knew exactly where she was going of course. I saw her go into their offices, and then hung around for over two hours, just waiting. As I said, pathetic.'

'It's not pathetic,' Jimmy said. 'I'd have done exactly the same thing in your situation.'

'And then I saw them come out. They weren't holding hands or anything like that but I knew. You can tell can't you, just looking at a couple. The body language just gives it away. It made me sick to see it, even although I already knew in my gut she was cheating on me. You see, when I saw them together, I knew then this wasn't some cheap affair, it was so much more than that. I knew at that point that my marriage was over.'

Jimmy gave him a puzzled look. 'Why do you say that? What was so special about this man?'

'Special?' Milner said bitterly. 'He was half her age. That was what was so bloody special about him.'

***

And then it all came out, and with each revelation, another piece in the jigsaw fell into place. The affair had started at one of these organisations where Belinda was a non-executive director. *Alexia Life*. A place that Jimmy remembered Frank mentioning in connection with his Aphrodite investigation. The other man was young with stand-out good looks, causing his wife to quite lose her head. They'd tried to keep it a secret but someone had been watching and saw the signs. Then reported it to the trustees whom, after a cursory investigation, had asked the other man to leave. Two days later, he threw himself under the wheels of an underground train. Not long after Belinda Milner, consumed with guilt and heartache, took her last swim, following her lover to the grave.

Pillow talk. It was odds on that Milner would have shared the troubles of the Greenway Mine with her young lover, as certain as it was that *he* would have shared that secret with those that were employing him for just that purpose.

The same secret that Liz Donahue had uncovered, and that led to her death. The question was, who knew, and who cared enough to have her killed?

Chapter 24

Frank had been down the canteen grabbing a bacon roll when his brother had called with news that had caused him to pump his fists and shout *Yes* at the top of his voice. Because now that he knew all about Belinda Milner and Luke Brown, everything was falling nicely into place. The only problem was, he didn't have a shred of credible evidence. That didn't mean that there wouldn't *be* any evidence, it was just that with the death of the two interns having been officially classified as suicides, nobody had been looking very hard.

Now, he *nearly* had the ammunition to change that. Just one more wee task to complete and then he'd be able to get in front of DCI Jill Smart, and it wouldn't take more than five minutes to persuade her to open a murder enquiry. Instead of just him and Frenchie, there'd be a team of fifty or more, with boots on the ground, and profilers and forensics and analysts, the lot. Soon they'd be swarming all over the CCTV and interviewing everybody who knew them and eventually something would come out. But first, a wee trip up to Oxford.

***

It had been Frenchie's idea to go in hard, giving it the full works as he called it, with the objective of scaring the living shit out of her, and so maximising the chances of a confession if one was to be had. Frank, though harbouring reservations that centred mainly around the amount of paperwork that would be needed to authorise the operation, had decided to go along with it. Aided and abetted by the fact that Ronnie had a mate in the Thames Valley armed response squad who told him they hadn't mounted a raid for over fifteen months and accordingly were itching for some action. But what had clinched it was that the Thames Valley lads had agreed to fill out the paperwork themselves. *Result*.

The commander of the squad, an over-promoted fast-track graduate on his first live op, was nervously talking into his walkie-talkie. '*Red squad in place, red squad in place. Confirm please. Over.*'

Having evidently received satisfactory acknowledgement, he strode over to Frank, who was leaning against his car, chewing gum and appearing totally relaxed.

'So you're sure there's not going to be any shooting then Inspector?' the commander asked.

'No,' Frank said, shaking his head. 'It's not the bloody mafia, they're only a wee employment agency. That's why it said no guns on the form. We're just here because we don't want anyone trying to destroy evidence and folks always take it more seriously when we come dressed for the part.'

It was quarter to eight in the morning, and the staff of the Oxbridge Agency were now arriving in dribs and drabs for their day's work. Frank had stationed his small raiding party round a corner and out of sight, eight brawny coppers in full riot gear squeezed into the back of an unmarked white Transit. Ronnie French had been assigned to loiter in the car park at the front of the building and give the signal when Sophie Fitzwilliam arrived.

She had recognised him immediately as she swept her Range Rover into her designated parking space a few yards from the front door, giving him a puzzled look that was mixed with haughty disgust. He shot her a lewd smile then drawled a few words into his radio.

Around the corner, the commander roared his response, simultaneously banging on the side of the van, then rushed round to the back to open the doors. 'Right guys, go!' The raiding party poured out into the street and followed him through the car park at pace. Altogether more languidly, Frank spat out his chewing gum and strolled around to join them. Fitzwilliam had reached her office's reception area when the squad flooded in.

'Right, nobody move,' the commander barked. 'Spread out guys and make sure everyone knows not to touch anything. Anybody goes near a keyboard, you grab them, got it?' A few seconds later Frank wandered in, smiling.

'Morning Mrs Fitzwilliam,' he said amicably, 'Maybe we can have a wee word in your office please?' It wasn't hard to tell she was angry, her eyes burning and an almost demented expression on her face. But behind it all, Frank detected fear.

'What the hell is this?' she screamed, 'You'll pay for this, believe me you will.'

'Now now, let's just calm down shall we? Your office please.' He took her arm and with some force, led her through, glancing over his shoulder and indicating to French that he should join them.

'You remember my colleague Detective Constable French I'm guessing. He interviewed you a few days ago about Chardonnay Clarke. When you denied that your firm had any involvement in the large salary she was being paid. I'm guessing you remember that conversation, don't you?'

She wore a defiant expression, but then they all did that when they'd been found out. Now it would be interesting to see if she tried to deny it. Generally they all did that as well, a natural reaction but practical too, because maybe the police might just be bluffing, or might not have any hard evidence.

'I remember,' she said, her composure beginning to return. 'A ludicrous accusation, and I'm sure you don't have a shred of proof.'

Frank smiled to himself. That was always the dead giveaway. First deny it, then ask to see the evidence. Hedge your bets. But before he could answer, the commander stuck his head round the door.

'Place is all secure now Inspector. And we've found a bank of filing cabinets in the basement. That's all secure too.'

'Good boy,' Frank said, smiling when he saw French stifling a laugh. 'Now Mrs Fitzwilliam, I have a warrant here that allows me to take away and examine all your financial records, but I'm hoping we won't have to go to all that trouble. You see, we know all about Semaphore Trust, your subsidiary company.'

She looked at him sharply. Admit it or deny it, he could see she was weighing up which path to take. So he decided to help her with her dilemma. He took a sheet of paper from an inside pocket, unfolded it and began to read aloud.

'Semaphore Trust - a subsidiary company of the Oxbridge Agency, according to Companies House -was paying nearly thirty thousand pounds per month into a Swiss franc account held with Zurich Landesbanken. Then the money was transferred to a Santander branch in Madrid, from where it ended up with Rosalind Holdings, a company registered in Guernsey.'

'What of it,' she said, her tone defiant. 'We're not doing anything illegal. It's tax-efficient, that's all.'

Frank smiled to himself. *Got her.* 'Perhaps it is, but I do find it interesting why there was the need for such a complicated arrangement just to pay a wee girl her salary. Oh aye, and there was something else too. DC French, maybe you can update Mrs Fitzwilliam on what our fine wee colleague Eleanor Campbell discovered yesterday?'

He nodded. 'Yeah sure guv. So as well as paying six grand a month to Chardonnay Clarke, a sum of thirty-two thousand eight hundred and fifty pounds and sixteen pence was paid to the Student Loans company for the benefit of a Mr Luke Brown.'

'Really?' Frank said, feigning surprise. 'The lad who supposedly took his own life? The other lad placed by your agency Mrs Fitzwilliam. The other lad on your scholarship scheme. Interesting that.' Now his voice took on a serious tone. 'Frenchie, I think this would be a good time to read this lady her rights.'

French smiled. 'Sure guv, my pleasure. *Sophie Fitzwilliam, I am charging you with conspiracy to murder, you are not obliged...*' He shouldn't have done it, he knew that, and the CPS would throw a hissy fit if they found out, but right now he didn't give a shit about them.

'Wait, wait,' she said, her voice raised in blind panic. 'Christ inspector, I didn't know they would be killed.' *Result*.

'But you knew they *were* killed, didn't you?' Frank said. 'You knew all along they weren't suicides. Come on Sophie, you can tell me all about it. Best for everyone if you did. Especially you. Because it wouldn't be fair if you were to take the rap for something you didn't do.'

So she did tell them all about it. Of course, she continued to deny knowing anything about the murders, and chatting with Frenchie afterwards, they agreed that she was probably telling the truth as far as that aspect of the affair was concerned. But for a while she asserted that it had all been her idea, a misplaced display of loyalty that quickly crumbled when Frank pointed out that as sole conspirator she was facing at least thirty years in Holloway. So then she told them everything, including who was ultimately behind it all.

Which caused him to ask Ronnie French for his tenner back. Because he knew he'd been right all along.

Chapter 25

Maggie hadn't recognised the voice on the end of the phone, but she'd instantly recognised the name.

'Maggie, Maggie Bainbridge? The investigator? This is Rosie.'

'Rosie Morgan? Hugo's daughter?'

'That's right.' Her voice sounded nervous, uncertain. *'I think I need to see you. It's about mum and Lotti and stuff.'*

They agreed to meet at a little cafe nestled alongside the Regents canal. Arriving early, Maggie found an outside table conveniently located next to a patio heater which bathed her in a welcome curtain of warm air. She remembered Hugo telling her his daughter was studying fashion at nearby Central Saint Martin's, which explained the choice of venue, but other than her vague explanation on the phone, Maggie had no idea what she wanted to talk about. Jimmy had told her about the scene at the Park Lane Hilton of course, and she wondered if it had anything to do with that. But to Rosie, Jimmy wasn't Jimmy, he was James McDuff, cuckolded lover of rich old Magdalene Slattery, so it couldn't have been that. *Curious*.

She spotted her from a hundred metres away as she made her way down the quayside. You won't be able to miss her, Jimmy had said, and he wasn't wrong. Dressed like that, it wasn't hard to see why Miss Morgan had chosen to make her career in the fashion industry. But as it turned out, Maggie didn't need Jimmy's vivid description, because she had someone with her. Someone she instantly recognised. Maggie stood up and waved to get her attention.

'Hi, it's Rosie isn't it?' she said. 'I'm Maggie, it's lovely to meet you.'

'This is Jasmine,' she said fondly. 'My little sister. We call her Yazz.'

'We've met,' Maggie said, beaming the younger girl a smile. 'Hello again Yazz.'

Yazz gave her a shy look. 'Hi.' She was dressed in school uniform, a grey pinafore with navy blazer and brimmed felt hat, with a leather satchel slung over her shoulder. 'Rosie's taking me to the dentist,' she said in way of explanation. 'To get my braces adjusted.'

Maggie smiled. 'Yes, I had them when I was your age. They're quite annoying for a while but you soon forget about them.' But when she had gone to have hers fitted, nearly thirty years earlier, it was her mum who had taken her. She didn't have older siblings, but she was quite certain if she had, her parents wouldn't have palmed her off on one of them.

'Dad was busy today,' Rosie said, as if reading her mind. 'And I don't have any classes this afternoon. It's only down in Harley Street.' Of course, it would be. The expensive private school, the pursuit of a career in the precarious fashion industry, the up-market private dentistry. Maggie wondered if they appreciated how lucky they were.

'By the way, I love your look,' she said to Rosie, 'It's amazing.'

'Thanks. It's retro.' She didn't smile, but Maggie guessed that was because of the effect it would have on her makeup rather than any coldness in her mood.

'Yes, but it's great, really great. That fashion scene was a little before my time first time around, but not by much I'm afraid. Anyway, it's nearly lunchtime, do you want to eat?'

'I don't,' Rosie said. 'Do lunch I mean. I'll just have a water please. Sparkling.' Maggie remembered the old Kate Moss maxim and smiled. *Nothing tastes as good as thin feels.* The supermodel had long since apologised for saying it, but the suspicion was it was still close to a religious tract as far as the fashion industry was concerned.

'Can I have a cheeseburger please,' Yazz asked. 'With cola and fries. Double fries please.'

With obvious reluctance, Rosie nodded her agreement. Maggie ordered and then said, 'So Rosie, how can I help you?'

'I saw that guy yesterday. Your guy. Meeting with mum. I know who he is.'

'Ah,' Maggie said slowly. 'It's quite a long story.'

'You and that guy, you're investigating Lotti. My dad told me. I saw your pictures on your website.' So she knew. That would make this a whole lot easier. 'And don't worry, Yazz knows too. Maggie smiled. 'Well, investigating makes it sound more serious than it really is.' Especially since to all intents and purposes the investigation was over, all cut and dried and neatly tidied away. But now at least there was the opportunity to ask the sixty-four-thousand-dollar question. And one day she would google it to find out where that ancient phrase came from.

'So what do you think about it Rosie? Your dad and Lotti I mean?'

She gave her an impassive look. 'I want him to be happy.'

'And do you think Lotti will make him happy?'

Rosie shrugged. 'Suppose. She's quite nice.'

'I like her too,' Yazz said, temporarily suspending the demolishment of her lunch. 'She's quite nice and I like the way she speaks.'

'Yes, she has got a nice accent, hasn't she?' Maggie said, smiling.

'Although Rosie, isn't it a little awkward for you? I'm meaning the age difference. Lotti's only thirty and your dad is what, fifty?'

'You think?'

Maggie felt her heart skip a beat. Lowering her voice she asked, 'What do you mean?'

'Like there's no way she's thirty. Twenty more like.'

'How do you know that Rosie?'

'I don't *know*, not for defo at least. I searched her handbag one day, hoping to find something to prove it, but I didn't. But whatever, I don't care, it's like nothing to do with me, is it?'

'And have you told your dad? About your suspicions, I mean?'

She shrugged again. 'There not *suspicions*, it's not like some sort of big conspiracy is it? And anyway why should I tell him? It doesn't bother me what age she is.' Maggie could tell by the way she said it that the exact opposite was true.

'So do you think he knows?'

'Maybe. I don't care.' She took a sip of water and turned her head, staring into the distance. Maggie wasn't sure, but she thought she saw the hint of a tear begin to form.

'You said on the phone you wanted to talk about her. About Lotti.'

Rosie nodded. 'Yeah, it's mum. I think she's found out about Lotti and dad. She's seeing that guy from the gallery you see, you know, the one where Lotti works. He must have found out and told her.' *That guy from the gallery.* Robert Trelawney, the guy whom in a moment of complete madness she had slept with.

'And she's mental. I'm worried she might do something crazy.'

'Mum's not mental,' Yazz said.

'Eat your lunch,' her sister said in a kindly tone, 'and stop listening in to what the grown-ups are saying.'

'Ok.' She took a noisy slurp on her straw then returned to the fast-disappearing cheeseburger.

'What do you mean Rosie,' Maggie said, 'something crazy?'

'I don't know. Just crazy. Harm Lotti in some way. She's a complete nightmare my mum. She always has been, ever since we were little.' So now it began to make a little sense, why she and her sister had chosen to stay with her dad. Although Maggie was conscious that she would only be hearing one side of the story.

'I'm a mum too and it can be the most difficult job in the world. But have you told your dad about this?'

Suddenly Rosie looked sad in a way only a child can. 'I don't want to. It would just make everything worse than ever between them.' With what she knew about the Morgan's shattered relationship, Maggie doubted it would make the slightest difference. But that was the thing with divorces, whether bitter or amicable. The kids always wanted the parents to get back together.

'So what is it you want me to do?' Maggie asked. 'Because I'm not sure if I can help you.'

'Your guy...'

'Jimmy.'

'Yeah Jimmy. I think my mum likes him. Even though she's got Robert now. I can always tell. She's pathetic.'

Maggie laughed, immediately regretting it. 'Yes, I really don't understand it at all. It's not as if he's terribly good-looking or anything.'

She seemed unimpressed. 'Yeah whatever. But maybe he could talk to her. Something like that. I don't know. It might help, that's all.' Maggie very much doubted that, given what she knew about Mrs Morgan's feelings towards her ex-husband. But she didn't mean to disappoint this vulnerable young woman.

'We'll try,' she said. 'That's a promise.'

'Thank you. And please don't tell my dad.'

'I won't. Promise.'

Rosie gave a half-smile. 'Thank you then. Come on Yazz, we need to go, or we'll miss your appointment.'

The schoolgirl stood up, stuffing the last of the fries into her mouth.

'Ok,' she said politely. 'That was nice. Thank you Maggie.'

'Yeah, thanks Maggie,' Rosie said. 'I'll hear from you then?'

Maggie nodded. 'We'll do what we can.'

Reflecting on it as she sipped her coffee, she was still not exactly sure what the meeting had been all about.

Was Felicity Morgan really a threat to Lotti, and even if she was, could she and Jimmy really do anything about it? And just because she might have been right all along about Lotti's age, she realised that it didn't pass that crucial test that she had learned to apply to situations like this one - *the so what* test. So what if Lotti was lying about her age? Other than the fact it was a deception, it probably didn't mean anything at all. And if Hugo Morgan already knew, then it wasn't even that. Anyway her job was to find out the facts, not pass judgement. She'd let Hugo Morgan worry about what to do with it.

But then suddenly she noticed it. Hanging over the back of the vacated plastic chair was Yazz's satchel. *Bugger*. Tossing her unfinished coffee into the waste bin, she set off along the quayside in pursuit, fumbling in her bag for her Oyster card. She wasn't sure how billionaires' daughters travelled in London, but it had to be at least an each-way bet that they would be heading for the tube. Kings Cross St Pancras, the busiest station in the capital, where you could take your choice of the Northern, Victoria, District, Piccadilly, Metropolitan, Circle and Hammersmith lines. Harley Street, that's where she said she was heading. Where was that exactly? She wracked her brain and then remembered. Yes, somewhere between Marylebone Road and Oxford Street, she was pretty sure that's where it was. But which tube line would they take? The Piccadilly, or maybe the Circle or Metropolitan westbound to Great Portland Street. Either would do, but she had to decide. *Piccadilly, southbound*.

To her dismay she saw there was a queue building up behind the barriers, which was being caused by a bunch of foreign tourists trying to figure out what to do with their tickets. Ignoring a squawk of complaints, she forced herself to the front and snatched a ticket from a confused-looking elderly man, maybe Japanese or Chinese, she wasn't sure which. Shooting him a forced smile, she slotted his ticket into the machine and pushed him through the opening gates, squeezing through behind him and ignoring his profuse thank-you's. The down escalator was busy but she was able to take the left hand side like a stairway, pushing aside the few travellers who were not aware of the convention that that side should be kept clear for those in a rush. Then a one-hundred an eighty degree turn where she descended the second escalator in the same fashion. A few seconds later, she was on the platform, which was unexpectedly heaving. Businessmen, shop girls, students, tourists, school kids, tradesmen, the usual rich mix of London life, packed cheek to jowl and speaking every language under the sun. Then she vaguely remembered an item on that morning's radio travel news. *Industrial action by the RMT union meaning a reduced service on the Piccadilly and Victoria lines. Expect delays and some disruption throughout the day.* She scanned along the platform, figuring that even with the crowds, a purple-haired punk-goth wouldn't be hard to pick out, but all she could see was a sea of heads. Glancing up she saw the indicator board predicting the first arrival in one minute, the next not for another fifteen. If they were only running four trains an hour, it was odds-on the approaching one would be already jam-packed and only those brave enough to have staked a claim at the platform edge would have any chance of getting on. That made her realise she might get a better view up and down the platform if she herself was at the front. She started to push her way through, muttering perfunctory *excuse me's* under her breath.

She could feel the pattering of cool air on her face as the train approached, acting like a tightly-fitting piston in the confined tunnel. And then she was enveloped in a haze of confusion as in perfect slow-motion she saw Rosie Morgan standing at the far end of the platform. Then spinning round, watched in horror as the young woman tumbled off it in front of the arriving tube train. The girl was able to stumble to her knees before it smashed full into her, tossing her like a grotesque rag-doll against the far wall of the station, then striking her again as she fell, catapulting her already-limp body onto the platform. The echoey station was filled with a cacophony of devilish noise, the screech of steel wheel on steel rail as the driver slammed on the emergency brakes all but drowned out by the screams of the horrified onlookers. And then, as the train finally came to a stop, there was an eerie silence. A few metres back from Maggie, someone was shouting, 'I'm a doctor, let me through please,' but everybody knew it was already too late. The crowd on the platform stood motionless, stunned into inaction, not knowing quite how to react. Except for a hooded figure that Maggie just caught a glimpse of, pushing its way towards the exit. A figure who was leading Yazz Morgan by the hand.

Desperately, Maggie elbowed her way through the crowd of paralysed bystanders. 'Let me through, let me through. Yazz, Yazz!' She was screaming at the top of her voice but the sound dissipated inaudibly as the mass of humanity absorbed her cry. 'Yazz!' They were no more than twenty-five metres ahead of her and still some way from the up escalator, but new passengers were still arriving, packing the platform ever tighter. But then miraculously, a gap opened up. At the bottom of the down escalator, a young mother, clutching a tiny baby to her chest, was struggling to re-erect her push chair, causing a tail-back of irritated travellers. And blocking the entrance to the up escalator too. The hooded figure ran up to her, picked up the pushchair and threw it to one side, then pushed the young woman in the chest, causing her to fall over, still holding her baby tightly.

A shaven-headed man wearing a hi-viz vest tried to intervene. 'Oi mate, what the fuck are you doing?' but he was caught unawares by a punch that left him staggering and bleeding.

'Yazz!' Maggie had now reached them and was able to grab the schoolgirl's free arm. The girl looked round, her face wearing a dazed expression, but her other hand was still tightly in the grasp of her abductor. Who had now decided to turn his attentions to this new threat to his escape, and for the first time, Maggie was able to get a proper look at the figure. A man, definitely, squat but powerfully-built. He was wearing shades, a hat and dark scarf covering the lower half of his face which, as was no doubt his intention, would make identification impossible. And he was in no mood to give up his quarry. She saw it coming, but was in no position to avoid it, as a huge fist smashed into her face, sending her sprawling. Confused, she tried to get back on her feet but then an overwhelming nausea hit her and she collapsed onto the platform, dead to the world.

But just before the lights went out, it came to her. *There was someone else.* A face on that crowded platform that shouldn't have been there. A face she knew, but right at this moment, as she lost the fight for consciousness, could not quite place.

***

Hugo Morgan was stewing in an interview room at Paddington Green Police Station awaiting the arrival of his lawyer when a message pinged into the inbox of his phone. Had it not at that moment been lying in the small plastic tray into which he had been forced to empty the contents of his pockets, he would have been able to read the news that would shatter his gilded life forever.

Didn't we tell you actions have consequences?
Justice for Greenway

Chapter 26

'It's all kicking off ma'am,' Frank said. 'Big time. The desk sergeant's just been in to say he's got two women screaming at one another, and both of them demanding to see Hugo Morgan. One says she's his ex-wife and one says she's his fiancé. And it looks as if there's no love lost between them, if the language they're using is anything to go by.'

It was four o'clock, just three hours after the incident at Kings Cross and they were gathered in Incident Room Four at Paddington Green, which Frank had been able to commandeer for his Aphrodite Murders case, granted official status the previous day by his boss Detective Superintendent Jill Smart. In the room were Frank, Pete Burnside, Jimmy, Maggie, Jill herself and a gaggle of detective constables, tapping away on their laptops. As a DI from back-of-beyond Department 12B, he wouldn't be running the case personally, but he was pleased that it had been put in the hands of his old mate Pete, recently promoted to Chief Inspector. And in any case, it was odds on that Pete would leave most of the grunt work to him, which suited him fine. All the job satisfaction without any of the responsibility.

'You don't need to tell me it's kicking off,' Jill said, grimacing. 'I've already had an AC calling me and asking why the hell we've got Morgan in for questioning when one daughter has just been murdered and his other one's been kidnapped.'

'Aye, he's obviously got his lawyers right onto it, which is no more than I expected,' Frank said, shrugging. 'The truth is, they just overlapped ma'am. I had reasonable suspicions that he was involved in two murders himself, so it was right and proper that we brought him in. But yeah, it's bloody bad timing right enough.'

'And how are you Maggie?' Jill asked. 'Nice black eye, if you don't mind me saying so.'

'Yes, it hurts, but I'm absolutely fine,' she said, giving a rueful smile. 'I'm just so sorry I couldn't stop it happening. The abduction I mean.'

'Who's going to run that case ma'am?' Frank asked. 'I guess it can't be Pete, given that Morgan's a suspect in the Aphrodite ones. Conflict of interest I suppose.'

'No, I've given it to DCI Ahmed. In fact, Rashid's already up at Kings Cross looking at the CCTV, and I think he's going to organise a TV appeal for witnesses on the local TV news tonight.'

'Aye, he's a good bloke,' Frank said. 'And I guess one of his guys will want to speak to you Maggie in the next half hour or so. You saw it all I suppose?'

'I didn't see the push, but I saw the aftermath. It was too ghastly for words. And her little sister saw it too. God knows what's going on in her mind. I can't bear to think about it.'

'Are you sure you're ok?' Frank said in a worried tone. 'I heard you passed out. I can easily get a WPC to take you home if you like. I'm sure the interview can wait.'

She shook her head and smiled. 'No way. This is all far too important for that. And I told you, I'm absolutely fine.' Although she didn't exactly feel it. She had a crashing headache and great difficulty in seeing through her rapidly-closing eye. But despite all of that, she wasn't going anywhere.

'So Frank,' Jill said, wearing a puzzled look, 'you said you *had* reasonable suspicions that Morgan was involved in the murder of these two kids. Has something changed?'

'Aye, it has ma'am, don't you see? The murder of his daughter kind of makes me think I might need to look a bit deeper at the whole thing.'

'Because the MO was the same?' Jill said. 'Identical to your two other ones I mean.'

'Not just three,' Jimmy said. 'Four of them. Chardonnay, Luke, Rosie and Liz Donahue. Don't forget Liz.'

'And all the same MO?'

'Aye ma'am,' Frank said. 'Pretty much identical. So we've got means and opportunity, sure, But the problem is, where's the common motive? The two kids, I can see a link. Liz Donahue, we know there's a connection there, definitely. But Rosie Morgan? No way, not as far as I can see.'

They were interrupted by the desk sergeant sticking his head round the door.

'Sorry to disturb ma'am. Guv, what do you want me to do with these two woman I've got? I'm worried the older one's going to have a stroke or a heart attack or something.'

'Well, it's not exactly surprising given the news she's had, is it?' Burnside said, his irritation obvious. 'She's lost her bloody daughter for God's sake. Find a family liaison officer and put her somewhere comfortable. And get her a cup of tea.'

'Yes sir. And what should I do with the other one?'

'How should I bloody know?' he said, raising his eyes to the ceiling. 'Go and see Morgan and ask if he wants to see either of them. Or none of them. You're ok with that Frank?'

'Aye sure Pete, given the circs. And we should get a family liaison for him too I suppose. Don't want to appear heartless, do we?'

***

As Jill Smart had predicted, DCI Rashid Ahmed had rounded up the local early-evening news programmes to broadcast an appeal for the return, unharmed, of eleven-year-old Jasmine Morgan, abducted four hours earlier from Kings Cross St Pancras tube station. Given the prominence of her father, the media room at Paddington Green was packed out, attracting a full house of the dailies and national broadcast media. Maggie, Jimmy and Frank were lucky to find a spot, squeezed tight up against the back wall. Scanning the room, she noted Lotti Brückner was nowhere to be seen.

Hugo and Felicity Morgan were seated behind a desk on the low podium and holding hands, their grief evidently effecting a temporary halt in hostilities. Their eyes were blood-shot from crying and Mrs Morgan had made no attempt to re-apply her make-up, dark eyeliner tracing the path where the tears had run down her cheeks. She looked completely broken.

DCI Ahmed stared directly at the TV news camera, and although his manner was calm and commanding, he was reading from a small ring-bound notebook. 'Good evening, ladies and gentlemen and thanks for coming. As you know, there was a very serious incident earlier today at Kings Cross St Pancras tube station. Tragically Miss Rosalind Morgan lost her life and I can confirm we are treating her death as murder. At the same time, her younger sister Jasmine was abducted by a man who at this moment we have failed to identify. I appeal for eye witnesses to either incident to contact us by calling the number displayed across the bottom of your screen. Your call will of course be treated in confidence.' He paused for a moment and then flipped over a page. 'And now, I'd like to ask the Morgans to say a few words, and please, no flash photography until they've finished.'

It was Hugo Morgan who addressed the camera, his voice subdued and wavering, his message brief but poignant. 'We don't know who did this and we have no idea why. All we ask is that *please, please*, you return our lovely daughter to us unharmed.'

'Yes, *please, please*, bring her back to us. *Please.*' Felicity spoke almost inaudibly, then buried her head in her hands, motionless and numbed with pain. Immediately her ex-husband put an arm around her and gently drew a strand of hair back from her face.

'No questions please folks,' Ahmed said briskly, as the room was illuminated with the flashes from a dozen cameras now let off the leash. 'Suffice to say that we are pursuing a number of promising lines of enquiry and we will update you as and when. Finally, I should mention that the family are offering a reward for any information leading to the safe return of their daughter. Thank you for your attendance.'

The assembled press hacks waited until the Morgans had left the platform before asking the obvious question, leaving it to ITN's distinguished Home Affairs correspondent to put it into words. *How much?*

***

'Half a million?' Maggie said. 'It's a lot of money isn't it? But do you think it will have any effect?'

DCI Ahmed shrugged. 'You would think so, but this Justice for Greenway business would appear to be about exacting revenge on Hugo Morgan rather than money. So I don't know. I have my doubts, quite honestly.'

They were in a small airless interview room, the DCI accompanied by a colleague, a detective sergeant whose name Maggie hadn't quite caught and who thus far had not uttered a word. He seemed somewhat in awe of his boss, who was emanating the same aura of effortless authority that she had witnessed during the press conference. 'So tell us all about today please, if you don't mind. Take your time. And then maybe we can talk about Justice for Greenway too. Because I think you and your colleague were looking into that, am I correct?'

So she told him, about her lunch with Rosie and Yazz, how she had pursued them to the tube station. And how she had witnessed Rosie Morgan's terrible killing, and about her failed effort to prevent the abduction.

'Do you think you could identify the man if you saw him again?' Ahmed asked.

She gave him a doubtful look. 'His face was covered. His physique, maybe, but that wouldn't be good enough, would it?'

'No, probably not, but we've now got some CCTV from the scene. DS Johnston, can you show Miss Bainbridge the images please.' Johnston removed some large prints from a folder and laid them on the table facing Maggie. Dark and grainy, nonetheless they had picked out the abductor leading Yazz along the platform.

'Yes, that's him,' she said. And then she remembered. 'I thought there might be someone else.'

'What, you mean an accomplice?'

'I suppose so. I didn't really see clearly, it was just more of a feeling. Someone who I thought shouldn't be there. But I'm sorry, I can't put a face or a name to it.'

He shrugged. 'Well, these pictures will be in all the newspapers tomorrow, so maybe somebody out there might recognise him. Or your stranger. But what struck us was that she didn't seem to be struggling. Because of the shock we expect. Pity. It made it all too easy for him.'

'Yes, I'm sorry,' Maggie said. 'I could have done better too.'

'Not at all,' Ahmed said. 'You were very brave.'

He nodded at Johnson, who took out another photograph from the folder.

'Do you know who this woman is? We found this in Rosie's handbag.'

She took it from him and examined it.

'No idea, I've never seen her before.'

'And so you have no idea why Rosie would be carrying this picture?'

'No, I said I didn't know her.'

'Well if it's any help, there's a name scribbled on the back.'

'What?'

'A name. I can't quite make it out. Take a look yourself.'

She turned the photograph over and looked. The handwriting was poor, but she had no trouble in reading what it said.

Lotti Brückner.

'Miss Bainbridge?'

'Oh...yes, sorry. It's says Lotti Brückner. That's the name of Hugo Morgan's fiancé. Although he hasn't actually proposed to her yet. But Rosie told me that

Felicity had found out about Lotti and her ex-husband. She was worried she might do something crazy.'

'What did she mean by that?' Ahmed asked.

'I don't know. But that was what she said. But this isn't Lotti. As I said, I've no idea who this woman is.'

'Ok,' Johnson said. 'And there was this too.' He rummaged in his folder for a moment then extracted what looked like a glossy sales brochure.

'*The Oxbridge Agency Scholarship Scheme*. And the same question as before. Would you have any idea why she would be carrying this around with her?'

***

'Give you a tough time did he?' Frank said, laughing. 'Hard man, is our DCI Ahmed.'

Maggie had just got back to the Incident Room following her interview, and her brow was furrowed as she tried to make sense of what had just been revealed to her.

'What? No, he's nice,' she said distractedly. 'On the ball too.'

'Folks, listen up, we've got some progress on the Cumbrian connection at least,' Burnside said. 'So yesterday when I saw what Frank had turned up on the Belinda Milner suicide, I got straight onto the local force, spoke to a DCI Bragg.'

'Not Melvyn?' Frank said. 'He's a Cumbrian, isn't he?'

'Melissa actually. Smart lady by the sound of things. So anyroads, they've now decided that there's grounds for suspicion around Liz Donahue's death and they've opened up a murder enquiry with Bragg in charge. Thing is, they're only a small force and a case like this can overwhelm them but I've agreed to second a couple of DCs for a fortnight or so, just to help them out, try to accelerate things a bit.'

'Hallelujah,' Jimmy said, 'and a nice gig by the way.'

'Yeah it is,' Burnside agreed. 'And as I said, there's already some news. It seems someone remembers seeing Donahue's car being parked up outside the station on the evening in question. And it turns out she wasn't alone.'

'Got a description?' Frank asked.

He nodded. 'The guy with her was hooded and wearing shades so nothing too definite. But he was described as fairly short but powerfully-built. Like a body-builder, the witness said.'

'What, just like the guy who punched me?' Maggie said, involuntarily tracing the outline of her shiner.

'Seems that way, yeah.'

'And what, she was just strolling into the station with him, nice as you like?' Jimmy said.

'Not heard of guns bruv?' Frank said, shaking his head. 'It's odds-on he was armed. And exactly the same today up at Kings Cross, that's what I'm guessing. A pistol in your ribs and you're going to do exactly what you're told.'

And then Jimmy remembered. Those Tompkins brothers. Specifically Karl, the ex-squaddie who was built like the proverbial brick shithouse. He fitted the description perfectly.

'Karl Tompkins. He's the guy that Liz and I went to see, him and his brother. He runs a business customising cars and knocks around in a blinged-up Fiesta, and this guy looks as if he pushes some weights, believe me. They didn't exactly admit being behind Justice for Greenway, but they didn't exactly deny it either.'

'Yes, but why would they want to kill Liz?' Maggie said. 'If anything, she was on their side, wasn't she? After what she had found out about Milner?'

Jimmy frowned. 'Maybe they thought Liz was going to run a story accusing them of being behind the campaign.'

'But her story had nothing to do with that,' Maggie said.

'We know that, but they didn't. So maybe they killed her to shut her up.'

A young detective constable looked up from her laptop. 'Jimmy, that customised Fiesta. Was it anything like this?'

She swung her screen round to face them. 'This was from the CCTV on the next street to Morgan's. On the night he reported the graffiti on his wall. I remembered the car because it was so unusual.'

Jimmy peered at it over her shoulder. 'That's it, I'm pretty sure of it. I recognise the alloys and the spoiler. But wait a minute...no, this is on a 59 plate and his was definitely a 57. I remember stuff like that.'

'False plates probably,' Burnside said, turning to the young detective. 'Emma, get on to the DVLA site and do a search, see what you can dig up. He'll have cloned it, I'm pretty sure. And then check with the Northamptonshire and West Midlands boys, see if these plates have been caught on ANPR cameras on the M6 or the M1 anytime over the last month. And today or yesterday, obviously.'

'Yes sir,' she said, scribbling furiously on her pad.

'And I'll nip back to my desk and get on to Melvyn, see if she can bring this Tompkins guy in for questioning.'

'Melvyn?' Maggie said, smiling.

'DCI Bragg,' Burnside said, a hint of embarrassment in his tone. 'The guys are already calling her Melvyn, I just hope it doesn't slip out anytime she's in earshot.'

***

'So come on Frank,' Jill said after Burnside had departed, 'let's hear all about the Morgan angle and your Aphrodite case.'

Maggie watched him shuffle uncomfortably in his seat. She knew how he hated being in this situation, where to him the critical facts of a case were as clear as the light of day, but where the evidence was non-existent.

'I'm not sure you're going to like this ma'am,' he said.

'Try me.'

'Ok. Well this is a conspiracy so unbelievable and implausible that I'm afraid we're never going to get a conviction unless we get confessions by the principle actors. And I don't see how that's ever going to happen. So unless Burnside's investigation comes up with some miracle, we're stuffed. There's barely enough to question anyone, never mind getting the CPS to sanction a prosecution. It's bloody depressing, I don't mind telling you.'

'And that's the same for both of your murders,' Jill said. 'No evidence?'

'None. To be honest, I'm kind of clinging to the hope that DCI Bragg's investigation might uncover something,' he said nodding in Jimmy's direction, 'because we now believe the motive for the murder of Liz Donahue was a cover-up. To cover up the motive behind the killings of Chardonnay Clarke and Luke Brown. To stop her publishing her story.'

'Come on then,' she said for the second time, 'tell me all.'

'I suppose it was talking to Chardonnay's boyfriend or lover, whatever you want to call him, that sort of crystallized the whole thing in my mind. Hugo Morgan's always spouting this activist investor shtick to anyone who'll listen, as if he's got some magic way of predicting the future just by scrutinising accounts and trading statements and stuff like that. But this Jeremy guy, he said that was all bollocks, and that the real reason was that Morgan was actually heavily engaged in industrial espionage.'

'Which was what that journalist McGinley was saying too,' Maggie said.

'Aye, exactly. So I'm sure Morgan was involved in all sorts of subterfuge besides, but this particular one was an old classic, known since the dawn of time. Namely, a honey-trap.'

'Yeah, I get it,' Maggie said. 'The interns. That's why they were being paid these enormous sums. To do his bidding.'

'Correct,' Frank said. 'Sophie Fitzwilliam was an old university pal of his, at Brasenose college. He obviously knew that she ran this top-end agency and saw the opportunity for a bit of collaboration.'

'So she was roped in to do the recruitment I guess,' Maggie said. 'And the brief was pretty precise.'

'Aye,' Jimmy said. 'Get them beautiful and poor.'

'But it couldn't have been that easy to fill though,' Jill said. 'Are there lots of poor students at Oxford and Cambridge? I wouldn't have thought so.'

'More than you would think ma'am,' Frank said. 'Remember they've been making a big push in the last few years to get away from their privileged public school reputation. And this Oxbridge Agency is very well regarded amongst the students so they've got no shortage of applicants. You see, these days there's so many kids with degrees now that it's not easy to get a start. But they get you a foot in the door, even if it costs the parents a packet.'

'And of course they had the scholarship scheme,' Jimmy said.

'Aye, clever that,' Frank said, 'because it wouldn't have worked if poorer kids were put off applying because of the cost. Actually Pete Burnside's got a smart wee lassie on his team at the moment called Yvonne Sharp who's got direct experience of it. She applied to them but didn't get taken on. Lovely girl, and pretty in her own way.'

'But not a stand-out in the looks department I'm guessing,' Jill said.

'No ma'am, and all the better for it in my opinion. But Chardonnay Clarke was a real beauty, and that's why she got the scholarship. Except there were strings attached.'

'I can really sympathise,' Jimmy said, giving Maggie a hard look, 'being used as a sex object and all that.'

Maggie laughed. 'Says Captain James Stewart in all modesty. But when I think about it, they probably weren't overtly told to have affairs or anything like that. My guess is they were just instructed to do what they needed to do to get information out of the clients they were placed with. And then of course, being so incredibly attractive, well it was inevitable that something might happen.'

'Aye, I sort of agree,' Frank said, 'but maybe there was a bit more in the Luke Brown case. Remember, Belinda Milner was just a non-executive director there, so she wouldn't have been around at Alexia Life on a day to day basis.'

'Yes, that's easily explained,' Maggie said. 'It was Greenway Mining that Morgan was interested in, not Alexia. So Luke would have been specifically instructed to get close to Belinda.'

'But no one bargained on anyone falling in love,' Frank said. 'That's what happened with Chardonnay and Jeremy Hart. He was their top financial guy, and so he was right at the heart of HBB's takeover deal with the German bank. And it was that information that Morgan was desperate to get a hold of. The trouble was, Hart turned out be a decent guy and he was single too. Although he wasn't exactly Brad Pitt in the looks department he was kind and clever and she fell for him. And he fell for her too. So of course she was conflicted.'

'I can imagine what happened next,' Maggie said. 'She begins to get uncomfortable about what she's doing and decides that enough is enough. She tells Morgan's team that there's not going to be any more info coming their way.'

Frank nodded. 'It was worse than that I think. When she saw all the stress Jeremy was under after Morgan made his move, I believe she decided to blow the whistle on the whole thing, go public with it, and she told them that was what she was going to do.'

'Right,' Jill said, 'so Morgan decided she had to be silenced. Just to protect his damn reputation I suppose.'

'Aye, exactly ma'am. Wouldn't do if the big investment genius turns out to be a cheap con-artist, would it? But of course, he didn't do the killings himself, that goes without saying. That bit would have been subcontracted to person or persons unknown.'

'And what about the other one. Luke, wasn't it?'

'We don't know as much about that one ma'am. I think Belinda Milner was besotted with Luke, but I don't know if it was reciprocated. What we do know is that someone at Alexia found out about the affair and so Luke was quietly shovelled out the door. My guess is that Morgan then panicked and decided he'd better be shut up too, just in case he decided to blab.'

'And you say there's no evidence linking the murders back to Morgan?' Jill asked.

'I said that. Not unless Pete can catch up with the folks who shoved them in front of these trains and they're prepared to admit to being in his employ.'

'And what about that woman who runs the agency? Fitzwilliam isn't it?'

'Aye, well I'm ninety-nine percent certain that she wasn't involved in the killings, because you should have seen how she absolutely wet herself when we said she was looking at twenty-five years for conspiracy to murder. She knew that Morgan was using these kids, but that was as far as it went.'

Maggie nodded. 'If you ignore the murders, it wasn't actually a crime what they were doing. Obviously it's going to trash Morgan's reputation if it all comes out, but he'll still have his billion quid in the bank.'

'Morgan will deny knowing anything about it,' Frank said. 'I can tell you that right now.'

'So why did you bring him in?' Jill asked.

And then Maggie remembered the meeting, just two weeks ago, at the Brasenose offices.

'Because he's not infallible Jill,' she said. 'Without realising it, he let it slip he knew about Chardonnay and Luke. I guess you thought he might make another mistake. Is that right Frank?'

'Aye. Not exactly inspired detective work, is it?'

But there was something else about that meeting, and it came to her and Jimmy at the same time. He got it out first.

'It was us,' he said, looking at her in dismay. 'Do you remember, when we were bringing him up to speed on how we we're doing on the Justice for Greenway investigation?'

'I know, I know.' She felt her heart crashing as the consequences of what they had done hit her properly for the first time. *'We told him about Liz and her big story.* We told him she was going to reveal how he managed to find out about the problem with the cobalt ore.'

'Aye,' Jimmy said ruefully, 'Morgan got it from Luke. And he got it from Belinda. That's what Liz meant by pillow talk.'

Suddenly Jill Smart leapt to her feet, clenching her fists. 'Right, that's it,' she barked. 'Three murders with the same MO and Morgan's got a clear motive for all of them. I don't care what's happened to his bloody family. Bring him in.'

'Pete's job,' Frank said, smiling broadly. 'I'll go and find him right now ma'am.' He swept out of the room, slamming the door behind him.

***

Now the incident room fell into silence, a mood of quiet satisfaction pervading in anticipation of *Aphrodite* beginning to pick up pace. But for Maggie, a dense fog was beginning to clear and through the shimmering mist, she could see the road ahead. Four murders executed in an identical way, the killers placing their trust in a *modus operandi* that had proved its efficacy and reliability. And the murder of Rosie Morgan the exception that proved the rule. This time, there had been no attempt to dress the murder up as suicide. The people behind this one had a clear objective. *Justice for Greenway*, that justice being delivered by making Hugo Morgan suffer for the rest of his life. So was it with cruel deliberation they had chosen the same method as he himself had used to prevent three people tell their damning story, a chilling copy-cat killing designed to maximise his pain? But who knew about his connection to these killings? The case, if it could be called that, hadn't made the papers, so almost nobody knew that Morgan was suspected, apart from her, Jimmy and Frank. Except of course, for one other group of people. *The killers.*

That just left one big unanswered question, a question that was currently conflicting with the crazy theory that was half-forming in her head. That picture of the girl Rosie was carrying in her handbag and that brochure. Where they hell did they fit?

In her pocket, she felt the gentle vibration of her phone, set to silent. A message. From Robert Trelawney.

I hear you've had a tough day. Dinner? Pick you up at eight xx.

It was the last thing she wanted after the day she'd had, but Robert had some questions to answer, and she wanted to hear him answer them. It all depended on whether she could find a babysitter at such short notice.

Luckily she had someone in mind. Two someones in fact.

Chapter 27

It was ridiculous behaviour from a grown man of forty-two years of age, he knew it was, skulking around like some stupid love-struck teenager. Pathetic. The Protection of Freedoms Act 2012 had a lot to say about it too and he should know, he'd been on the course. Officially, they didn't call it stalking but it amounted to the same thing. *Following a person, watching or spying on them or forcing contact with the victim through any means, including social media*. He didn't do social media but he could pretty much tick off the rest of the list. No bother at all.

He had parked his car across the street from her house, about fifty metres further along so he couldn't be seen from any of her windows. This was the fourth or fifth occasion in the last month that he done it, and if that didn't qualify as stalking, he didn't know what did, but what he was trying to achieve, he wasn't entirely sure. He was pretty sure she was still seeing that gallery owner, but he had no idea how serious it was. He'd seen him just once, about three weeks ago, when he called for her in his convertible Mercedes. She'd invited him in, but it was no more than five minutes later when they emerged, and that made Frank feel a bit better, because in his nightmares, he'd imagined her showering him in kisses then ripping off his shirt and dragging him upstairs to her bedroom. But you couldn't do all of that in five minutes, thank God.

He'd already been parked up for three-quarters of an hour, inactive, but somewhere in an obscure recess of his confused mind he did have a plan. Tonight he was just going to get out of the car, walk up to her door, ring the bell, and when she opened it, he was simply going to tell her how he felt about her. How hard could that be? Hard enough to mean he hadn't been able to execute his master-plan on the previous four occasions he'd been sat there.

It was a quiet street, a few cars passing from time to time, a couple of these on-line grocery delivery vans, and the odd person out walking their dogs, wrapped up to repel the early-evening drizzle. Sleepy suburbia, where nothing much happened. He glanced in his mirror and noticed a small van making its way down the street, slowing to a crawl every few yards before setting off again. Frank assumed the driver was checking house numbers to find the one he was looking for. As it passed him, he clocked the elaborate graphics stencilled on the side. *Blooming Beautiful. Flowers for every occasion.* Fifty yards on the other side of the road it pulled up, right outside her front door. A man got out, squat and broad, wearing a dark leather bomber jacket with a beanie hat pulled down tight on his head. He made his way to the back of the vehicle, opened the double doors and emerged with a large bouquet which from a distance looked almost as tall as he was. From that bloody gallery fella no doubt. He was obviously a smooth operator, worst luck. Women loved flowers, he knew that, and of course, if he was with her, he would buy her them every week. *Some chance*.

The delivery guy scrutinised the label then, evidently satisfied, closed the doors, blipped the central locking and walked the few yards along the pavement to her gate, from where it was only three or four steps up to Maggie's front door. Frank watched as he rung the front bell and waited for her to respond. And then, with unfortunate timing, another van crept past his car, this time tall enough to obscure his view of the door. And when it was once again clear, the man was not there. A bit strange he thought, but then maybe she'd asked him to bring them through to the kitchen whilst she looked for a vase big enough to hold them. He should be back out in a couple of minutes, no worries.

But he wasn't. Five, six, seven minutes and still he hadn't emerged. Something was wrong, he was sure of that. He jumped out of the car and sprinted across the road, through the gate and then up to her door, taking the steps two at a time. He pushed the bell and waited. And listened. Nothing.

He looked in through the adjacent bay window but the room was in darkness and there was nothing to be seen. He hadn't been in Maggie's house, more's the pity, but he knew the typical layout of these upmarket Victorian terraces. Full height extensions out the back, built on top of luxury open plan kitchen-diners, with bi-folds or double doors opening into the garden. Her house was in the middle of a row of eight or so properties, with no way to get round the back except over the neighbours' fences. Awkwardly, he clambered over the low brick wall that divided her path from the nearest neighbour. No bell as far as he could see, but there was a flimsy-looking knocker. He wrapped on it firmly, four or five times, then banged the door with his fist. He waited a few seconds but there was no response. No surprise really because although it was nearly eight o'clock, it wasn't just the cops who worked stupid hours in the capital. Giving up, he jumped down the steps onto the pavement then ran the few yards to the neighbour on the other side. This time there was a bell, and he jabbed at it impatiently, muttering *come on, come on* under his breath.

The door was opened by an elderly man of South Asian appearance who gave him a curious look then asked politely, 'Good evening, can I help you?'

Frank flashed his ID. 'Sir, I'm a police Inspector, can I come in please?'

'Of course.' The man ushered him through the tiny entrance porch into his front room. 'Would you like a cup of tea?'

He shook his head. 'I need to get into your garden sir. This is an emergency. Can you show me the way please?'

The man led him through another sitting room into his kitchen, which contrary to Frank's expectations was small and had clearly seen better days. 'There it is,' he said, pointing to a green-painted panel door that looked as if it could have been there since the place was built. 'I'll get the key.'

'Quickly sir, if you don't mind,' Frank said, trying to mask his impatience.

The man walked over to a dresser, opened a drawer and began to rummage in it.

'I'm quite certain this is where I put it,' he said unconvincingly, 'or was it in the unit over there? I can't quite remember. I don't go out there all that often you see.'

Frank just managed to strangle an explicative at birth. 'Sir, I need that key. Shall I look in the other drawer?' Without waiting for an answer he yanked it open, pulling it clean off its runners, then emptied the contents onto a worktop. Which included a key.

'Ah there it is,' the man said, smiling. 'I remember putting it there now. Here, let me open the door for you. There's a bit of a knack to it I'm afraid. It can be rather stiff sometimes.'

He picked up the key and ambled over to the door, then attempted to slip the rusty key into the keyhole. After a few exploratory prods, it finally went in. Frank expected there would be more precious seconds of cocking about, but this time his fears were unfounded, as with a loud click, the lock yielded to a twist of the key.

'Right sir,' Frank barked as he swung open the door, 'I have to tell you that a serious police incident is currently ongoing and as a member of the public, I need you to stay inside for your own safety, do you understand?' He hated the cringe-worthy jargon but somehow it seemed to lend authority to the message. Fortunately in this case, the member of the public didn't need telling twice. Frank watched as he scurried indoors and closed the door. And locked it behind him.

It was a dark evening and the garden did not seem to benefit from any artificial lighting. As he had surmised, Maggie's house had been extended outwards, her wall forming the first four or five meters of their mutual boundary. As his eyes adjusted to the light, he could just about make out the fencing that bordered the unkempt garden. On the left, tidy and well maintained. On the right, the one bordering on to her garden, ramshackle and scruffy. No prices for guessing which boundary Frank's householder was responsible for.

He saw that the fourth panel along had separated from its concrete post, and was lying at an oblique angle, held precariously in place by the other fencepost. It was an eyesore, no arguing with that, but it left plenty of room for someone to squeeze through, even someone of his generous proportions.

Edging his frame into the gap, he cautiously stuck his head out, peering down the garden towards the house. As was the fashion, the kitchen extended the full width of the plot, its features illuminated by a blaze of light streaming through its windows. Although he guessed it was a relatively new addition, it had been constructed in traditional style, with a pair of glaze-panelled French doors framed on either side by decorative latticed windows above a brick base. He slipped through into the garden then tentatively crept towards the house, being careful to keep his back to the fence where the light did not directly reach. Now he was close enough to see into the kitchen. The lattice framework served to partially obscure the view but it didn't prevent him seeing all too clearly what was playing out in front of him. *Shit.*

The flower delivery guy had his back to him, but he was now close enough to make out the badge on the side of his hat. The staff-bearing lion rampant of Chelsea Football Club. In the room, facing him, were Maggie and her son Ollie, who was clinging onto his mother, his face set but betraying fear. Next to them, a young woman wearing a defiant expression, whom he vaguely recognised as the feisty girl who worked in her office, Polish or Latvian or something like that. And next to her, to his astonishment, stood his brother. Looking serious. A glint from something metallic caused Frank to involuntarily screw up his eyes, at the same time explaining the look on his brother's face. Chelsea man had a gun. *Double shit.*

Desperately, he tried to weigh up his options. Really, he should call in the specialists, trained and armed to deal with hostage situations like this. But maybe this wasn't a hostage situation and the gunman simply meant to shoot them all and be done with it. A gunman who neatly met the description of the Kings Cross abductor. And if it was he, then this was a guy who already killed once that day. *A professional.*

So that was it. *Decided.* He was on his own and the only weapon he had was the element of surprise. Doubtless, the killer would have weighed up the risks of his mission, but had he considered the chances of anything coming at him from his rear flank, such was the inaccessibility of these back gardens? Frank hoped not.

The problem was, not only did he have no clue what to do, he'd also no idea how long he had before the shooting started. Not long, was his gut feel. Calmly, he tried to put himself inside the gunman's head. This guy was a professional, so he would want to get out of the situation as quickly and cleanly as possible, but that wasn't easy when you had four victims to take care of. Shoot one and there was every chance that one of the others might make a grab for you, reasoning that there was nothing to lose, and it could go rapidly downhill from there. And then suddenly, it came to him. This was a hit that had gone belly-up. None of this had been meant to happen and now the gunman was in uncharted territory, just like he was. Frank played it through in his mind. God knows why, but it appears that Maggie is his original target. The job's straightforward, all he has to do is ring the bell, shoot her, then slip away. Mission accomplished. But to his surprise it isn't Maggie who opens the door but some unknown guy, a massive guy, and now he has to think on his feet. He jabs the gun into the guy's ribs and pushes him along the hallway, somewhere along the line bumping into Maggie, the kid and another woman whom he wasn't expecting to be there either. He ushers them at gunpoint into the kitchen which is where he is now, trying to figure out what the hell to do next.

That sounded a reasonable assessment of what had happened, but it didn't really help Frank work out what *he* should do. Somehow, the gunman had to be overpowered before he could fire his weapon, but how? That could only happen if someone in that room was prepared to act. The risk would be enormous, but perhaps he could cause a distraction that would at least give them half a chance.

But first, he had to make them aware of his presence, and that itself carried some risk. He couldn't simply knock on a window pane, obviously. Somehow he had to signal to one or more of them, catch their eye if he could, and pray that they didn't inadvertently give him away by their surprise. Right away he ruled out Maggie. From where he was, her line of sight to him was obscured by the gunman, and in any case, it would be nigh impossible for her to make any move without putting her son in danger. Jimmy would be his favoured choice, because he knew that already his brother would be working up an escape plan in his mind. He'd been in far worse situations than this during his time in the army and he wasn't going to let some second-rate football hooligan get the better of him. The problem was, he was now standing side-on to the window, his eyes seemingly focussed on Maggie and Ollie. Which only left the girl. *Elsa*, that was her name. Czech, he remembered now.

He dropped onto his stomach and began to crawl towards the kitchen. The ground was cold and muddy, the grassed area reaching right up to the doors. A couple of seconds later he was lying under the right-hand window, tight to the wall. After taking a moment to compose himself, he made his first move. As slowly as he could, he pulled himself up, edging his head above the window sill so that he could once again see into the room. *Excellent*. He had a clear sight of her, still wearing her defiant expression. Now, slowly, he raised an arm and then almost imperceptibly began a wave, his hand moving no more than two or three centimetres in either direction, and at a snail's pace. He watched her carefully for a sign that she had noticed, but there was nothing. So he tried again, moving his hand a bit further and a bit faster, his heart racing, his mind overflowing with the terrible consequences should it all go wrong.

And then he saw it. The slight change to her expression as she caught his eye. But not enough to give anything away. *Good girl*. Now it was in her hands and all he could do was wait and be ready. For what seemed an age, nothing happened. He guessed like Jimmy she was working out her options. Or maybe, out of fear, she had decided to do nothing. But then suddenly she started to scream at the top of her voice, loud enough for Frank to make out every word through the thick double-glazed panes.

'I don't want to die, I don't want to die. I want husband and baby and home. You can kill these but not me.'

'Shut the fuck up,' the gunman shouted, gesticulating with the pistol. 'Shut the fuck up bitch, or I'll blow your fucking head off.'

She took a step towards him. 'I will do anything you want. I good in bed, make all fantasies come true. Please don't kill me.' *Now*. Frank leapt up then steadying himself, smashed a foot against the gap between the doors, just below the handle, giving it everything he had. With a crack, they burst open, his momentum propelling him into the room and sending him barging into the gunman. Momentarily disorientated, he was taken out by Jimmy's huge fist slamming into his face, jerking his head back and sending him crashing to the floor onto his back, the gun spinning harmlessly across the floor.

'Nice work bruv,' Frank said, raising his hand to proffer a high-five. 'And Elsa, what a performance. Brought tears to my eyes it did.' Kneeling, he took out a pair of handcuffs and slipped them onto the prone figure.

It seemed as if the disturbing events had had no detrimental effect on Ollie, although he was careful not to let go of his mother's hand. 'Did you see that, mummy?' he said, his eyes sparkling. 'Uncle Jimmy biffed that man, and he fell over, and he dropped his gun, and then we were all safe.'

'Yes, well done Uncle Jimmy,' Maggie said, the relief tangible in her voice. 'But do you see who it is?'

'Aye, I do.'

Elsa had flung his arms around him and was nestling her head on his chest. Without thinking, he kissed her gently on the forehead, causing her to snuggle up even tighter. 'It's Morgan's security guy. I remember him from that do at the Hilton. He was the guy who chucked McGinley out, wasn't he?'

Maggie nodded. 'I met him later at that fast food place, with Morgan and Jasmine. His name's Vinny.'

'Well, we're not going to be seeing much more of Vinny when we've finished throwing the book at him,' Frank said, grinning. 'He'll be looking at twenty years just for this alone. Anyway, just give me a minute to summon reinforcements. I want this guy locked up in a nice comfy cell before he can do any more damage.'

'Just a minute,' Maggie said. She bent over the gunman and pulled open the bomber jacket. 'Yeah, here it is.' She took his phone and began to scroll. Then, under her breath, she let out an explicative, which Frank just managed to catch. *Swine*. He watched as she tapped something into it and then threw it across the room.

'Could you make us some tea Elsa please?' she asked, composing herself with a visible effort, 'and squash for Ollie.' With obvious reluctance, the girl released Jimmy from her embrace and forced a smile. 'Yeah, sure. I put kettle on now. Come Ollie, come over here and help me.'

Maggie turned to Jimmy and Frank. 'Let me show you something.' Lying on her kitchen table was a glossy sales brochure, opened at the centre spread. Looking for all the world like a school photograph, thirty or so young men and women lined up on the front steps of The Oxbridge Agency.

'DCI Ahmed let me take this away. D'you see? Last year's cohort, I think that's what you would call it.' She pointed to a figure standing in the front row.

'Recognise her?'

'Whoa,' Jimmy said. 'That's Lotti.'

'Except it isn't,' she said. 'According to the caption, this is Griselda Hauptmann, aged twenty-three years old. BA, History of Art, St Catherine's College Oxford.'

Frank was peering at Maggie through narrowed eyes. There was something in her expression which told him, even before she said another word. Something about that phone message and that brochure. *She's worked it out. Maggie Bainbridge's worked out everything.*

Chapter 28

Frank barked the instruction into his radio handset whilst, barely in control, he steered with the other hand. 'We need an armed response team mobile pronto. Forty-seven Bedford Gardens, Kensington. Over and out.' Short and sweet, as he raced the Mondeo along another rat run, siren wailing and the flashing blue lights clearing the way.

'So come on Maggie, what's this all about?' A black cab emerging from a parking space was signalling but not looking, causing him to jam on the brakes. 'These cabbies think they own the bloody roads,' he shouted, banging on the horn.

'Calm down mate,' Jimmy said, grimacing. 'Don't want you having a heart attack before we get there. It's only five minutes or so from here.'

'We can't wait for the response team,' Maggie said, urgency in her voice. 'They're going to kill Yazz, if they've not already done it. I think that would have been Vinny's next job, after he'd killed me.'

'Who's they?' Jimmy said. 'Who are they? And why did they want to kill you?'

Before she could answer, a shrill ring filled the cabin, the car's infotainment panel displaying the name of the caller. *DCI Jill Smart.*

'Crap! She must have just heard the news,' Frank said. 'This'll be the call that tells me not to do anything stupid and to wait for the armed boys to turn up.' It continued to ring as Frank swung the car into a sharp left turn, the tyres squealing in protest.

'Aren't you going to answer it?' Jimmy asked.

'Stuff that.'

He let it go through to voicemail. *'Frank, it's Jill. Please listen to what...'*

'Aye, whatever,' he said, prodding the *end call* icon. 'You can tell me later.'

'So come on Maggie,' Jimmy said, 'Why did someone want to kill you? Was it something to do with Lotti?'

'Griselda you mean. No, I don't think so, not directly. Actually I'm not a hundred percent sure about any of it, in fact I might be one hundred percent wrong. But we'll find out one way or the other in a few minutes.'

'Hang on guys, this might get a wee bit hairy.' Frank gave another blast of the siren as he hammered off Sussex Gardens and into Lancaster Terrace.

'One way street mate,' Jimmy shouted, alarmed, 'and in case you haven't noticed, you're going the wrong bloody way.'

Frank shrugged. 'No worries. Police emergency. They'll get out the way. Almost certainly.' The engine roared as he dropped a gear and floored it. 'Best get it done as quickly as we can, eh?' Jimmy glanced over at the speedometer. Touching seventy, in a thirty mile an hour limit and going the wrong way. That must be worth twelve points on the licence at least. Fortunately though the late evening traffic was light and somehow they made it on to the Bayswater Road without incident. Less than a minute later, they had arrived.

'It's that one,' Maggie said, pointing as they leapt out of the car. 'With the red door.'

'You've been here before then?' Jimmy said.

She didn't answer.

'Right,' Frank said. 'I'll ring the bell, give it a minute, and if no-one comes to the door then we break it down. Ok with that bruv?'

'They'll answer it,' Maggie said. 'They're expecting Vinny back. I texted a thumbs up from his phone. And let me lead the way, because as far as they know, I'm now dead.'

He pushed the bell and waited, each of them silent. And then the door opened and without being invited, Maggie stepped into the hallway.

'Hello Griselda.'

'But you're...you're...' The young woman stammered over her words, the shock of this unexpected development severing communication between brain and mouth.

'Dead? I'm afraid I'm very much alive.' She grabbed Griselda Hauptmann by the wrist and twisted her arm behind her back, causing her to let out a yelp of pain. And then twisted it again.

'Where is she? Where's Yazz? Tell me.'

'She's... she's in the basement.' She nodded her head in the direction of a door.

Maggie pushed the girl up against the wall. 'Frank, we need to make this one secure. She's up to her neck in it. She was there. At Kings Cross.'

'Aye, nae bother,' he said reaching for a pocket. 'I always carry a couple of pairs with me. Goes back to my old days in Glasgow. Never know when they might come in handy.' He took out the handcuffs and slapped them on one wrist.

'Ok let's go, he said, giving the girl a shove in the back, 'and don't even think about shouting a warning, or I'll break your arm, got it?'

'I didn't know,' Griselda said, looking as if she was about to cry, 'that it would go this way I mean. This isn't what I signed up for.'

'Yeah sure,' Maggie said briskly. 'Let's leave the hand-wringing for later, shall we?'

'I'm going to lock her in the car,' Frank said, 'and don't do anything until I come back, ok?'

'Sure, but maybe I should go in first anyway,' Jimmy said. 'I'm trained for this sort of thing, remember?'

'Aye, but back then you were wearing full body armour and holding an assault rifle,' Frank said. 'You can go first if you want to, but just wait for me, ok?'

'They won't be armed,' Maggie said. 'That was Vinny's department.'

Frank returned a minute later and they made their way through the doorway and down the steep steps, Jimmy leading the way, the two brothers unsure of what awaited them. But Maggie knew. She knew who would be there and she knew precisely what had been planned. She just hoped they were not already too late. Too late to save the lives of Yazz Morgan and Robert Trelawney.

But she was not expecting this. Two tall barstools had been placed in the middle of the room. Yazz and Trelawney had been blindfolded and gagged, and were each now balanced precariously on top of a stool, their hands tied behind them. Suspended from an exposed beam in the ceiling hung the nooses that had been placed around their necks. Between them stood Felicity Morgan. And contrary to expectations, she had a gun.

'Miss Bainbridge,' she snarled, looking up, 'this is an unexpected pleasure. Oh yes, I know who you really are, do you think I'm a fool?'

'It's over Felicity, come on,' Maggie said, her voice calm. 'You don't really want to kill her, do you? Your own daughter for Christ's sake. How can you do that? Look at her, she's an innocent child.' Frantically processing the situation in her mind, it wasn't long before she reached a conclusion. It wasn't looking good.

'Over? But that's where you're quite wrong,' Felicity said, her eyes blazing with menace. 'Not yet. Not until I've decided which of these two to kill first.' She gripped a leg of Trelawney's stool and began to shake it. He gave a low moan as he struggled to keep his balance.

'You see, men are such pigs, aren't they? *You* should know that Miss Bainbridge, after everything *you've* been through. Oh yes, I know all about *that*. Just like you, my husband thought he could just throw me away like yesterday's newspaper, but now he's beginning to understand that actions have consequences.'

'You're off your bloody head,' Jimmy said. 'You won't get away with it you know.'

'Ah Miss Bainbridge's trained monkey. You are a cute little thing aren't you? Well, maybe I am crazy. So what?'

'There's going to be a response team here any minute,' Frank said. 'I'd hand myself over now, if I was you, because they'll shoot first and ask questions later.'

'It'll be all over by then,' she said. 'In fact, let's get the party started, shall we?'

Now she was shrieking like a demented witch, jabbing a finger in Maggie's direction. 'Don't think I don't know about your sordid little tryst with my *darling* Robert, you little *cow*. I've been having you watched you see. Both of you. It's just a shame that Vinny wasn't able to take care of you earlier, but well, you're here now, aren't you? But first, it's *his* turn. Goodbye my darling Robert.'

Viciously, she kicked out, causing the stool to spin across the room. There was a crack as the beam took his full weight, his body plummeting towards the floor then being arrested as the noose tightened, breaking his neck. Leaving him spinning like a sack of grain.

'Christ!' Maggie yelled, involuntarily turning her head away, the shock robbing her of breath,

Instinctively, Jimmy took a step forward but was stopped in his tracks as Felicity raised the pistol and pointed at him.

'Let me help him,' he said quietly, even although he knew it was already too late. 'Please. You don't want this Felicity.'

'That's where you're wrong, this is exactly what I want,' she sneered, her eyes burning with hatred. 'Actions have consequences. Everybody has to learn that.'

Maggie turned to face her, struggling to choke back her disgust and horror. She didn't know how, but somehow she had to get her talking, to buy some time until the response team arrived. Although god knows what they would be able to do when they got here.

'You've already succeeded Felicity, you must know that. Hugo will never have another happy day in his life, you've made sure of that. He's paid a huge price for what he did to you. That's what you wanted isn't it? His reputation is in ruins and his beloved Rosie is dead. Killing Yazz won't make it any worse for him.'

'But it will make *me* feel better,' she snarled. 'He turned them against me. My own children. They had the choice and they chose to live with *him*. Have you any idea what that feels like?'

'But they loved you. Rosie told me. Both of them loved you. They loved you very much. And Yazz is just a little girl. She doesn't deserve this. She's so lovely. You know she is.'

'But she loved *him*. She loved *him* more than she loved me. It wasn't *fair*, after what he did to me. It wasn't *fair*.' For a moment Felicity was distracted, wallowing in self-pity. And Maggie saw her chance. Shooting a glance at Jimmy and Frank, she began to creep towards her, speaking softly.

'It'll be alright Felicity. It'll be alright. Let's put an end to this now, shall we? Please, give me the gun.' The other woman stared straight at her, her expression a confusion of sadness and pain. Then with an almost imperceptible shake of her head, she let the gun drop to the floor.

But then as Maggie stooped to pick it up, Morgan gave a spine-chilling scream and lunged blindly at Yazz's stool. As if in slow motion, she saw Jimmy leap forward and thrust his strong hands under the little girl's armpits, holding her aloft to support her weight just as the stool collapsed from under her. At the same time, Frank yanked Felicity's arms behind her and pushed her on to the floor, face down, his knee in her back.

'Maggie, you need to get up on the stool,' Jimmy shouted. 'Get the noose off. I don't know how long I can hold her. Quickly.'

'It'll be easier if you climb on my shoulders,' Frank said. He grabbed a handful of Morgan's hair and yanked her head up. 'And don't you *dare* make a move, got that?' He pushed her away from her, causing her face to smash into the cold flagstones of the floor.

Now he was alongside his brother and down on one knee, allowing Maggie to swing her legs around his shoulders. 'Up we go now. Hold tight.' Slowly he pushed himself up until he was fully standing, squeezing her legs tightly against his chest.

'I think I've got it,' Maggie shouted, struggling to balance as she reached out to grab hold of the noose. 'Yazz, you'll be ok darling. Let's get this thing off you, shall we?'

'Hurry up, for God's sake,' Jimmy yelled. 'This wee thing's bloody heavy.'

'It's tight. It's tight. I need to try and loosen it first.'

Frantically she pushed her fingers into the tiny gap between the looped rope and the knot that was holding it in place.

'Come on, come on,' Jimmy shouted.

'It's budging... nearly... yeah, I can feel it.' With her free hand she grabbed the knot and pulled with all the strength she could muster. And then suddenly it gave, causing her to lose her balance. But before she collapsed on top of Frank, she just managed to flip the loop over Yazz's head. 'Got it!'

Instantly, Jimmy took Yazz's full weight and gently lowered the little girl to the ground.

'Here, sit down and we'll get you untied.' Beside him, Frank and Maggie were untangling themselves. Thankfully they seemed none the worse for their fall.

'Here, let me help you Jimmy,' Maggie said. 'And Frank, take her mother out of our sight. I don't think Yazz will have anything to say to her, do you?'

'Aye, I'll do that. I'll stick her in the car and chain her to the German woman. I can see them spending plenty of time together in the future.'

***

It was all under control by the time the response team arrived. Jimmy had managed to cut down Robert Trelawney's body and had laid him on the floor, untying his hands but leaving the blindfold in place for reasons he could not explain. Maggie had taken Yazz up to the kitchen and was helping her sip from a mug of hot chocolate, holding her hand whilst offering occasional but useless words of comfort. She knew from her own experience that kids could bounce back from even the most appalling experiences, but this was different. In the last twelve hours Jasmine Morgan had witnessed the murder of her beloved sister, and now she had found out that it was her own mother who had been responsible for the killing. No-one was going to come to terms with that, not ever. With a heavy heart, she realised that Felicity Morgan, driven to madness by bitterness and jealousy, had succeeded in her warped mission. Actions have consequences and the murderer Hugo Morgan was never going to forget it.

Chapter 29

It was Friday night, and they were meeting in one of their favourite watering holes, the *Ship* over in Shoreditch. A bit of a fancy gastropub, it had gravitated to becoming their special occasion place, their patronage infrequent mainly on account of the steep prices. Maggie knew that Frank in particular found them objectionable, not because he was tight with money, because he wasn't. It was just he felt the place, or rather its regular clientele, was a bit pretentious, and he didn't like pretentious and he didn't like having to pay seven quid for a pint either.

They were six-strong, Jimmy, Frank, Elsa, Asvina Rani, Jill Smart and Maggie, gathered together for what was part-celebration, part-explanation. Because there was a lot to be explained.

Food had been ordered and they were now propping up the bar, waiting for their table to be prepared. Already the group had attracted inquisitive looks from their fellow diners. *What was it these two guys had, they were asking, to be able to pull four beautiful women like them? It must be a works do, couldn't be anything else, surely? Or maybe they had money, that would figure. Because the smaller guy wasn't exactly Brad Pitt, although to be fair the tall guy was amazingly good-looking.* Had they been able to look inside the head of one of the women, they would have been surprised to find it swimming with inadequacy. *Asvina Rani, Jill Smart, Elsa Berger.* Slim, beautiful, assured, sexy, each and every one of them. *Maggie Bainbridge.* None of the above. With an effort, she banished the negative thoughts to the back of her mind and tried to concentrate on the positive. An amazing night lay ahead, with amazing friends. What more could a girl ask for? Except, perhaps, for an amazing man to share it with. She had entertained high hopes for Robert Trelawney, but now that plan lay in ruins. But it hadn't worked out too well for him either.

'The Sunday Times Insight team are running a big story on it this weekend,' Frank said, propelling their drinks along the bar. 'They've dug up a couple more of these Oxbridge scholarship kids and apparently they're going to spill the beans on the whole operation.'

'Cheers bruv,' Jimmy said, raising his glass. 'So that's Morgan well and truly finished as far as his reputation goes, isn't it? Good, that's what I say.'

'That's right,' Asvina said. 'Although he's had our law firm talk to the paper and warned them against even the slightest insinuation that he was involved in the deaths of Chardonnay Clarke and Luke Brown.'

'So is he going to get away with it then?' Maggie asked, 'because that would be depressing and a complete denial of justice.'

Jill Smart gave a resigned look. 'We had him in a Paddington Green interview room for two days but we didn't get a thing out of him. Just sat beside his lawyer and gave us the no comment treatment. And Vinny Hadley is denying any involvement in these killings, even although it's odds-on he was responsible. So unless we turn up some other compelling evidence in the meantime, then yes, he's going to get away with it, I'm sad to say.'

'And the CPS are not that bothered,' Frank said. 'They've got our boy Vinny one hundred percent for Rosie Morgan's killing. Her mother's admitted that she paid him to do it. And of course he was caught in the act trying to kill all of you guys. So he's going down for thirty years just for those two alone.'

'But it's not right, is it?' Jimmy said angrily. 'Surely there needs to be closure for these kids' families, and for Liz Donahue too.'

'You're right,' Jill said, 'and I'm as angry about it as anyone. Rest assured the cases won't be closed until we've exhausted every angle.'

'And then they'll get quietly shelved and chucked over the wall into Frank's department,' Jimmy said, with some bitterness.

'Could do worse than that mate,' Frank said, 'And being serious, we'll happily take on these three cases if we have to. And then I'll nail that bastard if it's the last thing I do. Believe me, I bloody will.' Maggie wasn't quite sure whom this show of bravado was aimed at, but she shot a smile in his direction and was amused to see him redden.

'And what about Felicity Morgan?' Asvina asked. 'What's going to happen to her?'

'Going down for conspiracy to murder,' Frank said, 'although her lawyers are already trying to argue diminished responsibility on the grounds of her mental condition. I feel sorry for her in some ways.'

'She was completely crazy, wasn't she?' Jill said. 'And I guess her husband dumping her just pushed her over the edge.'

'I think she always was nuts, even before then,' Jimmy said. 'But aye, this was off the scale.'

'So come on,' Asvina said, 'who's going to take me through this thing from start to finish?'

Maggie smiled. 'I'll have a go, shall I? Although it's rather a long story.'

'We're in no hurry,' Frank said, downing his pint. 'But maybe wait until the food turns up. But hey, it looks like our table's ready now. Let's wander over, shall we?'

They picked up their drinks and made their way across the busy bar, Maggie watching with amusement as Elsa manoeuvred herself alongside Jimmy to make sure she was seated beside him. Which left her sitting next to Frank. Entirely fine by her.

'So, first, Felicity Morgan,' she began. 'Yes, when Hugo dumped her, she completely flipped, and her whole existence became dedicated to making him suffer. Actions have consequences, that was her mantra, and of course she had the money to make it happen.'

'So can you explain how she came to get Griselda Hauptmann involved?' Asvina asked. 'I've never really understood that.'

'Well, I think her original plan was simply to watch Hugo fall in love with another woman and then have her dump him, so he got to experience the same pain that she had. She had begun a relationship with Robert Trelawney and knew he was looking for an intern, and of course she knew of her husband's tie-up with the Oxbridge Agency. So she put Trelawney in touch with Sophie Fitzwilliam, who just happened to have the perfect candidate on her books.'

'A graduate in the History of Art,' Asvina said.

'Yes,' Maggie said, 'to Felicity, it was as if it was destined.'

'So she was paying them both for their part in this crazy scheme?' Jill asked.

'Yes. A lot. Tens of thousands of pounds, I think in Griselda's case. But the only fly in the ointment was that Griselda was too young. She was worried that Hugo would think twice about having a relationship with a woman so close in age to his daughter.'

'So Griselda became Lotti,' Jimmy said.

'Exactly. Robert knew of the Brückner family through his contacts in the art world. He'd met the real Lotti Brückner several times and as a consequence knew quite a lot about her.'

'Like her Heidelberg degree,' Elsa said. 'I spoke to University there. Lotti was real person.'

'Yes Elsa, that's right, she was. So Robert helped Griselda put together a convincing back story, and then all it needed was for Hugo to take the bait when she dangled it in front of him.'

'And he couldn't resist,' Jimmy said. 'I mean, what man could?'

'No indeed,' Maggie said, giving him a wry smile. 'Men are *so* shallow. But the problem was, Felicity in her blind anger, found that this wasn't enough for her.'

'And that's when she decided to murder her own children,' Jill said. 'God, the thought of it sends a cold chill through me, it's just too awful. Of course we do get cases like that occasionally but it's always the men taking revenge on the mother. I've never known it the other way.'

'Yes,' Maggie said. 'I think when Rosie and Jasmine decided to live with their father, that's what pushed her completely over the edge, and she decided to take the ultimate revenge.'

'So what about Justice for Greenway?' Jill asked. 'What was that all about?'

'Aye, well that was her half-arsed attempt to cover her tracks,' Frank said. 'It was Karl Tompkins who was responsible for the first couple of incidents, we're pretty sure of that. His was just the early low-level stuff, you know, the graffiti and the threatening letters. But when Felicity got to know about it, she saw the opportunity. So she stepped in, took over their identity and upped the ante. Or at least Vinny and Griselda did on her behalf. What they did to his Bentley, that really caused him some pain. Forty grand's worth of damage and Morgan got to see it all on video. And that's when we first saw the threats against the Morgan children.'

'So how did she get Vinny Hadley to switch sides and work for her?' Asvina said.

'That wasn't difficult,' Frank said. 'Hadley is a cold bastard, a professional hood who's happy to work for anyone who can afford him. He'd worked for her husband for years so she knew exactly what he was like. It was just a matter of agreeing a price, and when you have thirty million quid in the bank that wasn't going to be an obstacle.'

'And Griselda?' Asvina asked. 'Was she involved in that too?'

'Yes, she was,' Maggie said. 'She helped him with the harassment campaign, and worse than that. You see, she was there, on the platform. When Rosie was killed. I saw her. I didn't realise at the time who it was, but it came to me in the end.'

'There's no evidence at the moment to charge her other than Maggie's testimony,' Frank said. 'But we're hoping that we may be able to get a statement from wee Jasmine when she's feeling better. Because Griselda was involved in all of it, you can count on that.'

'And Robert Trelawney?' Jill said. 'What about him?'

'He didn't know Felicity's real plans, we're pretty sure of that,' Frank said, shooting Maggie a sympathetic smile. 'As we said, he was in on the Lotti cover-up, but in some ways he was as much a victim as a perpetrator.'

'And he paid a terrible price,' Jimmy said. 'I'm really sorry Maggie.'

She shrugged. 'It's Magdalene Slattery who's hurting, not me.'

Of course, it wasn't true. But as she scanned the table, she felt herself bathed in a fuzzy warmth that she knew she could never put into words. *An amazing night with amazing friends*. And a million miles from where she had been just two years earlier, despite still having no amazing man to share her life with. She looked at Elsa, bursting with life and quite certain she had already found her amazing man, although Maggie knew that she was to be disappointed, for Jimmy she had long known to be irreconcilably in love with his estranged wife. And then there was Jill Smart. An enigma. Improbably slim and elegant, attracting admiring and lustful looks wherever she went, but cool and inscrutable, revealing nothing of her true feelings to the world. And finally her dearest and truest friend, the friend who had rescued her from despair when her life had reached rock bottom. Asvina Rani, the super model beauty with the perfect life. The stellar career, her two boys, the adored husband, and so lovely in spirit that Maggie didn't bear an ounce of jealousy towards her.

And there was Jimmy. *Dear Jimmy*. Several pints into the evening, he was in sparkling form and presently speaking.

'Frank my boy,' he said, with the faintest of slurs and a wicked smile on his face. 'Frank my dear brother, there's just one think that I'm still puzzled about. Really puzzled. So tell us, how it was you just happened to be outside Maggie's house when Mr Vincent Hadley tried to kill us all?'

The table fell quite silent and five pairs of eyes stared at him.

Expectantly.

Printed in Great Britain
by Amazon